D0560871

DEPARTMENT 19
THE RISING

DEPARTMENT 19
THE RISING

WILL HILL

HarperCollins *Children's Books*

First published in hardback in Great Britain by
HarperCollins *Children's Books* 2012

HarperCollins *Children's Books* is a division of HarperCollins*Publishers* Ltd
77-85 Fulham Palace Road, Hammersmith, London W6 8JB

Follow Will Hill on Twitter:
@willhillauthor

www.department19exists.com
www.facebook.com/department19exists

Text copyright © Will Hill 2012

HB ISBN 978-0-00-735448-1
TPB ISBN 978-0-00-745540-9

Will Hill reserves the right to be identified as the author of the work.

Typeset in Berylium by Palimpsest Book Production Limited,
Falkirk, Stirlingshire
Printed and bound in England by Clays Ltd, St Ives plc

MIX
Paper from
responsible sources
FSC® C007454

FSC™ is a non-profit international organisation established to promote
the responsible management of the world's forests. Products carrying the
FSC label are independently certified to assure consumers that they come
from forests that are managed to meet the social, economic and
ecological needs of present and future generations,
and other controlled sources.

Find out more about HarperCollins and the environment at
www.harpercollins.co.uk/green

For Charlie and Nick,
the best partners in crime I could have asked for

I shall be telling this with a sigh

Somewhere ages and ages hence:

Two roads diverged in a wood, and I—

I took the one less traveled by,

And that has made all the difference.

Robert Frost

How much happier that man is who believes his native town to be the world, than he who aspires to become greater than his nature will allow.

Victor Frankenstein

MEMORANDUM

From: Office of the Director of the Joint Intelligence Committee

Subject: Revised classifications of the British governmental departments

Security: TOP SECRET

DEPARTMENT 1   Office of the Prime Minister

DEPARTMENT 2   Cabinet Office

DEPARTMENT 3   Home Office

DEPARTMENT 4   Foreign and Commonwealth Office

DEPARTMENT 5   Ministry of Defence

DEPARTMENT 6   British Army

DEPARTMENT 7   Royal Navy

DEPARTMENT 8   Her Majesty's Diplomatic Service

DEPARTMENT 9   Her Majesty's Treasury

DEPARTMENT 10   Department for Transport

DEPARTMENT 11   Attorney General's Office

DEPARTMENT 12   Ministry of Justice

DEPARTMENT 13   Military Intelligence, Section 5 (MI5)

DEPARTMENT 14   Secret Intelligence Service (SIS)

DEPARTMENT 15   Royal Air Force

DEPARTMENT 16   Northern Ireland Office

DEPARTMENT 17   Scotland Office

DEPARTMENT 18   Wales Office

DEPARTMENT 19 CLASSIFIED

DEPARTMENT 20   Territorial Police Forces

DEPARTMENT 21   Department of Health

DEPARTMENT 22   Government Communication Headquarters (GCHQ)

DEPARTMENT 23   Joint Intelligence Committee (JIC)

12 WEEKS AFTER LINDISFARNE

91 DAYS TILL
ZERO HOUR

1

ON PATROL

THE PILGRIM HOSPITAL
BOSTON, LINCOLNSHIRE

Sergeant Ted Pearson of the Lincolnshire Police stamped his cold feet on the pavement, and checked his watch again. His partner, Constable Dave Fleming, watched him, a nervous look on his face.

Half ten, thought the Sergeant, with a grimace. *I should be at home with my feet up. Sharon's making lasagne tonight, and it's never as good warmed through.*

The 999 call had been made from the hospital's reception desk at 9.50pm. Sergeant Pearson and his partner had been finishing up the paperwork on an illegal immigration case they were working on one of the farms near Louth, both men looking forward to getting the forms filed and heading home, when they had been told the call was theirs. Grumbling, they had climbed into their car and driven the short distance from the police station to the hospital, blue lights spinning above them, their siren blaring through the freezing January night.

They had reached the hospital in a little over three minutes, and were questioning the nurse who had made the call, a young Nigerian woman with wide, frightened eyes, when Sergeant Pearson's radio buzzed into life. The message it conveyed was short and to the point.

"Secure access to potential crime scene. Do not investigate, or talk to potential witnesses. Stand guard until relieved."

Pearson had sworn loudly down his receiver, but the voice on the other end, a voice he didn't recognise but which was definitely not the usual dispatcher, was already gone. So he had done as he was told: instructed Constable Fleming to cease his questioning of the nurse, and informed all staff that access to the hospital's blood bank was forbidden without direct permission from him. Then he and his partner had taken up positions outside the side entrance to the hospital, shivering in the cold, waiting to be relieved. By who, or what, they didn't know.

"What's going on, Sarge?" asked Constable Fleming, after fifteen minutes had passed. "Why are we standing out here like security guards?"

"We're doing what we were told to do," replied Sergeant Pearson.

Fleming nodded, unconvinced. He looked round at the dimly lit road; it was a narrow alley between the hospital and a red-brick factory that was falling rapidly into disrepair. On the wall opposite, in black paint that had dripped all the way to the ground, someone had sprayed two words.

HE
RISES

"What's that mean, Sarge?" asked Constable Fleming, pointing at the graffiti.

"Shut up, Dave," replied his partner, giving the words a cursory glance. "No more questions, all right?"

The young man was going to make a fine copper, Pearson had no doubt about that, but his enthusiasm, and his relentless inquisitiveness, had a tendency to give the Sergeant a headache. The uncomfortable truth was that Pearson didn't know what was going on, or why they were guarding the hospital door, or what the graffiti meant. But he was not going to admit that to Fleming, who had been on the force for less than six months. He stamped his feet again, and as he did so, he heard the rumble of an engine approaching in the distance.

Thirty seconds later a black van pulled to a halt in front of the two policemen.

The windows of the vehicle were as dark as the panels of its body, and it sat low to the ground on heavy-duty, run-flat tyres. The noise of its engine was incredibly loud, a deep roar that Pearson and Fleming felt through their boots. For almost thirty seconds, nothing happened; the van stood motionless before them, squat and strangely threatening under the fluorescent light emanating from the hospital's side entrance behind them. Then, with a loud hiss, the vehicle's rear door slid open, and three figures emerged.

Fleming stared at them as they approached, his eyes wide. Pearson, who had seen things over the course of his career that the younger man would not have believed, was more adept at hiding his emotions than his partner, and managed to keep his confusion, and rising unease, from his face.

The three figures that stopped in front of them were dressed head to toe in black: their boots, their gloves, their uniforms, belts and military-style webbing. All black. The only splash of colour was the bright purple of the flat visors that covered their faces, visors attached to sleek black helmets that looked like nothing the policemen had seen before. There was not a millimetre of exposed skin to be seen; the newcomers could easily have been robots, such was the anonymity of their appearance. On their belts, two black guns hung in holsters alongside a long cylinder with a handle and a trigger on one side. It was obviously a weapon, but it was not one that either of the policemen recognised.

The tallest of the figures stopped in front of Sergeant Pearson, the shiny material of its visor centimetres away from his face. When the figure spoke, the voice was male, but it had a flat, digital quality that Pearson knew from his time on the Met with SO15 meant the person behind the visor was speaking through several levels of filter, to avoid the possibility of voiceprint identification.

"Have you signed the Official Secrets Act?" the black figure asked, turning its visor-clad face sharply between the two policemen, who nodded, too intimidated to speak. "Good. Then you never saw us, and this never happened."

"On whose authority?" managed Pearson, his voice shaking heavily.

"The Chief of the General Staff," replied the figure, then leant forward until its visor was a millimetre from the Sergeant's nose. "And mine. Understood?"

Pearson nodded again, and the figure drew back. Then it stepped past him and strode into the hospital. The other two dark shapes followed.

"The blood bank is—" began Constable Fleming.

"We know the way," said the third of the figures in a digitally altered female voice.

Then they were gone.

The two policemen looked at one another. Sergeant Pearson was visibly shaking, and Constable Fleming reached a hand towards his partner's shoulder. The older man waved it away, but he didn't look annoyed; he looked old, and frightened.

"Who were they, Sarge?" asked Fleming, his voice unsteady.

"I don't know, Dave," replied Pearson. "And I don't want to know."

The three black-clad figures strode through the bright corridors of the hospital.

The tall one, the one who had spoken to Sergeant Pearson, led the way. Behind, shorter and slimmer than the leader, came the second of the trio, who appeared to glide across the linoleum floor. The third, shorter again, brought up the rear, its purple visor sweeping slowly left and right for any sign of trouble, or witnesses to their presence. As they passed the double doors that led to the hospital's operating theatre, the tall figure at the front motioned for them to stop, and pulled a radio from his belt. He keyed in a series of numbers and letters, then activated the handset's wireless connection to his helmet's comms network. After a pause of several seconds, he spoke.

"Operational Squad G-17 in position. Alpha reporting in."

"Beta reporting in," the second figure said, in a metallic female voice.

"Gamma reporting in," said the final squad member.

Alpha listened as a voice spoke on the other end of the line, and then replaced the radio on his belt.

"Let's go," he said, and the squad moved on into the hospital. After only a matter of seconds, Gamma spoke.

"So who made the 999 call?"

"The nurse at reception," answered Alpha. "One of the night

porters saw a man leading a young girl into the blood bank, said the man had red eyes. He told the nurse he thought it was probably a junkie."

Beta laughed. "He's probably right. But not the kind he's thinking."

The three shadowy shapes pushed open a door marked RESTRICTED, and moved on.

"Fifth call in three nights," said Gamma. "Is Seward punishing us for something?"

"It's not just us," answered Alpha. "It's everyone. Every squad is flat out."

"I know," replied Beta. "And we know why, don't we? It's because of..."

"Don't," said Gamma, quickly. "Don't talk about him. Not now, OK?"

A small noise emerged from behind Beta's helmet, a noise that could easily have been a laugh, but she let the subject drop.

"You were pretty hard on the police," said Gamma. "The old Sergeant looked terrified."

"Good," replied Alpha. "The more he pretends that tonight never happened, the safer he'll be. Now no more talk."

They had reached the hospital's blood bank, the door of which was standing open. Alpha stepped slowly into the dark room, and flicked the light switch on the wall.

Nothing happened.

He pulled a torch from his belt, and shone it up at the light fitting. The bulb was smashed, leaving a ring of jagged glass surrounding the filament. A slow sweep of the torch revealed carnage; the metal shelves of the blood bank had been ransacked. Blood and shattered plastic dotted the surfaces, and pooled and piled up on the floor.

"Don't come any closer."

The voice came from the corner of the room, and Alpha instantly swung his torch towards it. Two more shafts of white light joined its beam, as Beta and Gamma stepped into the room and followed their squad leader's example.

The beams illuminated the trembling figure of a middle-aged man, crouching in the corner of the room. At his feet lay a sports bag full of plastic sachets of blood. In his arms was a girl, no more than six years old, with an expression of pure terror on her face. The man had a razor-sharp fingernail to her throat, and was looking at the three black figures with an expression of desperate panic.

Alpha reached up, turned a dial on the side of his helmet and watched his view of the room change. The helmet contained a cryocooled infrared detector, which showed the heat variance of every object within the visor's field of vision. The cold walls and floor of the blood bank were a wash of pale greens and blues, while the little girl was darker, studded with patches of yellow and orange. The man bloomed bright red and purple like a roman candle, distorting Alpha's vision.

"I'll kill her if you come any closer," the man said, shifting nervously against the wall. He tightened his grip on the girl's throat, and she moaned.

Alpha twisted the visor's setting back to normal.

"Stay calm," he said, evenly. "Just let the girl go, and we can talk."

"There's nothing to talk about!" yelled the man, and jerked the girl off her feet. She cried out, her eyes wide with terror, and Alpha took a half-step forward.

"Let the girl go," he repeated.

"This isn't right," said Beta, in a low voice.

Alpha flicked his head towards her.

"Don't make a move without my go," he warned.

Beta snorted with laughter. "Please," she said, then pulled a short black tube from her waist, pointed it into the corner of the room and pressed a button.

A thick beam of ultraviolet light burst across the blood bank. It hit the man's arm and the girl's face dead on, and both instantly erupted into flames. Screams and the nauseating smell of burning skin filled the air, as Gamma gasped behind her visor.

The little girl wrenched herself free of the arm that had been holding her, beating furiously at her face until the flames were extinguished. She dropped to her knees, tore open one of the plastic pouches of blood, then drank hungrily, slurping the crimson liquid into her mouth.

The man watched her, a helpless look on his face, then suddenly seemed to notice that his arm was burning. He began to leap around the corner of the room, beating at the limb with his good hand. When the flames were out, he pulled a blood bag from one of the shelves, and devoured its contents. As Squad G-17 watched, the girl's face and the man's arm began to heal before their eyes, the muscle and tissue regrowing, the skin turning pink and knitting back together. When the injuries were healed, so completely that there was no evidence that they had been there at all, a process that took only a matter of seconds, the girl looked up at the man, and wailed.

"Daddy!" she cried, her mouth a wide oval of disappointment. "You said this would work! You promised!"

The man looked down at her with an expression of great sadness. "I'm sorry, love," he replied. "I thought it would." He looked over at the three dark figures, which hadn't moved. "How did you know she was turned? The poor thing sat in a bath of ice for an hour so she wouldn't look hot to those helmets of yours. Her teeth only just stopped chattering."

Beta reached up and lifted her helmet from her head. The face beneath it was a teenage girl's: beautiful, pale and narrow, framed by dark hair that brushed her neck. She wore a wide smile, and her eyes glowed red under the bright lights of the blood bank.

"I can smell her," Larissa Kinley replied.

The little girl hissed, her eyes flooding the same red as Larissa's.

"So it's true," said her father. "Department 19 has a pet traitor. How can you hunt your own people? Don't you have any shame?"

Larissa took half a step towards him, her smile fading.

"You are not my people," she said, in a voice like ice. Alpha gently laid a hand on her arm, and she stepped back, without taking her eyes from the man in the corner of the room.

Gamma removed her helmet, and shook her head. Short blonde hair flew back and forth above a pretty, heart-shaped face, from which blue eyes stared out above a mouth that was set in a firm line.

"Was it you two who hit Lincoln General last month?" asked Kate Randall.

The man nodded, his eyes still nervously fixed on Larissa.

"And Nottingham Trent the month before that?"

He shook his head.

"Are you lying to me?" Kate asked.

"Why would I lie?" the man replied. He appeared to be on the verge of tears. "You're going to stake us both anyway, so what would be the point?"

"That's right," said Larissa, a wicked smile on her face.

The little girl began to cry. The man placed his hands on her shoulders and whispered soothingly to her.

Alpha looked over at Larissa, who rolled her eyes. Then he reached up, and removed his helmet.

The boy beneath it was no more than sixteen or seventeen, but his face looked older, as though he had seen, and most likely done, things that had taken their toll. A jagged patch of pink scar tissue peeped above the collar of his uniform and climbed across the right side of his neck, stopping before it reached his jaw. His face was handsome, and possessed of a stillness more befitting an older man. His blue eyes were piercing, but he trained them tenderly on Larissa.

"Nobody is staking anyone tonight," said Jamie Carpenter. "You know the new SOP. Pass me two restrainers, Kate. Lazarus can have these two. I don't think they're dangerous."

The man began to cry along with his daughter.

"We were hungry," he said. "I'm sorry. My name is Patrick Connors, and this is my daughter, Maggie. We were just so hungry. We didn't mean to cause any trouble."

"It's all right," Jamie replied, taking the two restrainers from Kate's hands and tossing them to the man and his daughter. "Put these on, under your armpits. Pull them tight."

The restrainers were thick belts that looped over the shoulders and crossed in the middle; where they met was an explosive charge that sat over the heart of the person wearing it. Patrick and Maggie shrugged the belts over their shoulders, and tightened them as they had been told. When they were securely in place, Jamie pulled a black tube from his belt with a small dial on one side and a red trigger on the other; he twisted the dial two notches clockwise, and red lights on the explosive charges flickered into life.

24

Jamie looked at his squad.

"Larissa, you're going to lead us out of here," he said. "Sir, you're going to follow her, then Kate, then you, little one, and I'll go last. We walk straight out the way we came, we don't stop, and we don't talk to anyone. Oh – and normal eyes, please."

He grinned as Larissa and Maggie's eyes reverted to their usual colours. Larissa led them out of the blood bank, and strode along the corridor towards the exit, and the waiting van. The rest of Squad G-17 and their prisoners followed in the order that Jamie had instructed, and less than a minute later they marched past Sergeant Pearson and Constable Fleming, who averted their eyes as they passed, and slid the van's rear door shut behind them.

The inside of the vehicle was silver metal and black plastic; four seats ran along each side of the wide space, between which were fixed a series of moulded stands, with half a dozen unusual spaces in them. A wide LCD screen lay flush against the ceiling, and a series of slots in the floor lay before each seat. Jamie told the man and his daughter to take the two seats closest to the front and strap themselves in. They did so silently; when they were in position, Kate pressed a button set into the wall. A barrier of ultraviolet light appeared from a wide bulb in the floor, cutting them off from the three black-clad teenagers, and both Patrick and Maggie cried out.

"Don't worry," said Jamie. "You're perfectly safe."

He began to unclip the weapons and devices from his belt, and slide them into the slots on the stand beside one of the seats. The brand-new T-21 pneumatic launcher, the Glock 17, the Heckler & Koch MP5, the torch and the short beam gun that Larissa had used inside the blood bank – all were placed into purpose-built compartments and clicked into place. The detonator he kept in his hand, resting it on his knee as he took his seat and announced that they were ready to go. Instantly, the powerful engine of the vehicle, which was in reality less a van and more a combination of a mobile command centre and an armoured personnel carrier, surged into life, and sped them away from the hospital, leaving Sergeant Pearson and Constable Fleming shivering on the pavement.

"What do we do—"

"Nothing," interrupted Pearson, before his partner had a chance to finish his question. "We do nothing, and we say nothing, because nothing happened. Absolutely nothing. Clear?"

Fleming looked at the older man for a long moment, taking in the pale colour of his face, the lines of worry around his eyes and the firm set of his jaw.

"Crystal, sir," he replied. "Let's go home."

An hour later the black van sped through deepening forest, heading towards a place that didn't exist. Its official designation was Classified Military Installation 303-F, but it had long been referred to by the men and women who knew of its existence by a simpler, shorter name.

"Welcome to the Loop," said Jamie, as the van drew to a halt. Patrick Connors and his daughter regarded him with polite incomprehension, and said nothing.

Outside the van there was a low rumble, a metallic sound like a gate being rolled back. Then they were moving again, creeping slowly forward.

"Place your vehicle in neutral."

The voice was artificial, and it appeared to be coming from all sides at once. The driver of the van, an invisible figure to the men and women in the rear of the vehicle, did as he was ordered. A conveyor belt whirred into life beneath the van, and moved it forward, until the artificial voice spoke again.

"Please state the names and designations of all passengers."

"Carpenter, Jamie. NS303, 67-J."

"Kinley, Larissa. NS303, 77-J."

"Randall, Kate. NS303, 78-J."

There was a long pause.

"Supernatural life forms have been detected on board this vehicle," said the voice. "Please state clearance code."

"Lazarus 914-73," said Jamie, quickly.

Another pause.

"Clearance granted," announced the artificial voice. "Proceed."

The van began to roll forward again, picking up speed. Less than two minutes later it stopped, and Jamie stood up from his seat and slid the rear door open. Kate pressed a button in the wall and the ultraviolet barrier imprisoning Patrick and Maggie disappeared.

"This way," said Jamie, motioning towards the open door. The man led his daughter slowly down the steps, into a world he had heard rumours about, but could never have possibly imagined.

To the back of the van, an enormous semi-circular hangar stood open to the night sky. The huge space was mostly empty; a line of black SUVs and vans were parked along one wall, and a small number of black-clad figures moved across the tarmac floor. Standing before them, patient looks on their faces, were a man in the same black uniform that Jamie and his squad were wearing and a young Asian man in a white lab coat.

Patrick looked around, and gasped. He had a moment to take in the enormity, and the incredible strangeness, of what he was seeing: the vast curved fence beyond the runway, the labyrinth of red lasers, the ultraviolet no-man's-land, and the vast holographic canopy of trees that hung across the sky above his head. Then there was a hand on his lower back, and he was being ushered forward, towards the waiting men. His daughter grabbed for his hand, and he gripped it, firmly, as Jamie stepped round him and handed his detonator to the man in the white coat, who thanked him, then addressed the two disoriented, frightened vampires.

"Sir," he said, his voice low and gentle. "My name is Dr Yen. Please will you follow me?"

Patrick glanced at Jamie, fear blooming on his face.

"It's OK," said Jamie. "You'll be safe with him."

Patrick glanced down at Maggie, and found her looking back up at him with a determined expression on her face. She nodded, almost imperceptibly.

"We will," he replied, as steadily as he was able. "We'll follow you."

The doctor nodded, then turned and walked briskly across the hangar. After a moment's pause, the man and his daughter followed him across the cavernous room, and through a wide set of double doors.

Jamie watched them go, then smiled at Larissa and Kate. Behind them, an Operator from the Security Division climbed into the van and began unloading their equipment from the moulded stands. It would be checked, cleaned and returned to their quarters within an hour, as it always was. Jamie nodded to the Operator, before turning to the Duty Officer who had been waiting to greet them.

"Cold out here tonight," he said, watching his breath cloud in front of his face.

"Yes, sir. Bloody cold, sir."

"How's my mother?"

28

"She's fine, sir," replied the young Operator. "Asking for you."

Jamie nodded, and started to walk into the hangar. He was suddenly exhausted, and his small quarters on Level B were calling to him.

"Admiral Seward requested a debrief, sir," called the Operator, before he had got more than a couple of steps. He sounded apologetic, and Jamie sighed.

"Personally?"

"Personally, sir."

Jamie swore. "Tell him I'll be there in ten minutes," he said, then marched towards one of the doors at the rear of the hangar, Larissa and Kate following closely behind him.

The three members of Squad G-17 slumped against the walls of the lift as it descended into the lower levels of the Loop.

On Level B, Jamie said goodnight to the two girls, and almost ran to the shower block marked MEN that stood halfway down the corridor. He stood in the shower for a long time, his head under the searing water, trying to prevent the aches and pains that were the accumulation of active service as a Department 19 Operator from returning with a vengeance, as they usually did once the adrenaline of a mission had worn off.

Eventually, with great reluctance, he twisted the shower off, and dressed in a T-shirt and combat trousers. He could almost feel his narrow bunk beneath him, could perfectly visualise the moment when his head would touch the pillow and his eyes would close. He picked up his uniform, opened the door to the corridor and stopped. Larissa was standing in the doorway, her eyes red, her hair wet, her body wrapped in a green towel, a wicked smile on her face.

"Where's Kate?" asked Jamie.

"Gone to her quarters," replied Larissa. "She said to tell you she'll see you in the morning."

He opened his mouth to reply, but Larissa closed it with her own, her lips on his, and Jamie discovered that he wasn't nearly as tired as he had thought.

2

TRIANGLES HAVE SHARP EDGES

ONE HOUR LATER

Larissa Kinley flexed a muscle that the vast majority of the population didn't possess, and felt her fangs slide silently down from her gums, fitting perfectly over her incisors, the white points emerging below her upper lip. She ran her tongue across the tips of her fangs, pressing until the slightest increase in pressure would have broken the skin, her eyes never leaving her reflection in the mirror in her quarters.

She hated her fangs with every fibre of her being.

They disgusted her, filled her with a revulsion she could not fully articulate to anyone, not even Jamie. She knew he would listen to her, sympathise with her, and at least try to say all the right things. But the simple fact was that he didn't know what it felt like to be a vampire, and how it felt was impossible to explain.

She would have torn the fangs from her mouth with a pair of pliers if she didn't know full well that they would regrow the next time she fed; she would have smashed them out with the butt of her Glock pistol, filed them down to nothing with sandpaper, or simply pulled them out with her bare hands, if she had believed that anything would have rid her of them.

But she knew nothing would. Her fangs were part of her, and there was nothing she could do about them.

I'm stuck with them. I'm going to be looking at them forever.

Anger trickled through Larissa's body, and her eyes began to turn red. She leant in close to the mirror, and watched as crimson spilled slowly in from the corners, obscuring the natural dark brown. The dark red swirled and pulsed, until it filled her eyes to their edges. The black holes of her pupils expanded until she thought she would fall into them, and she took a step backwards, away from herself. A low snarl burst from her throat, and she reared back, her muscles vibrating with fury.

Larissa swung her fist into the mirror, faster than the human eye could have followed, and the polished glass exploded, sending razor-sharp slivers flying through the air. Two shards dug into the pale skin of her neck; she barely noticed them until blood began to flow, and the scent filled her nostrils. She withdrew her trembling hand from the remains of the mirror, and stared at the blood pouring out of the holes in her knuckles. She pulled the glass out of her neck, savouring the pain, and wiped the blood away. Then, with guilt and sorrow in her heart, Larissa shoved her hand into her mouth, and hungrily sucked away the running blood, her head swimming with primal pleasure and self-loathing.

The cuts healed almost immediately, and she let the hand fall to her side. Staring into the mirror, she waited until the crimson in her eyes began to recede, then let the towel she was wearing fall to the floor. Her body had been changed by the endless hours of training since she had instantly accepted Major Paul Turner's offer for her to join Department 19, grown leaner and more toned. But the thick bands of muscle that had emerged on the bodies of Kate and Jamie were nowhere to be seen; the vast majority of her strength and speed and stamina now came from somewhere else.

Larissa walked across her small quarters to the locker at the end of her bed, pulled a vest and a pair of shorts out of the drawers, dressed quickly and stepped easily into the air. She folded her legs beneath her and floated, two metres above the floor, in outright defiance of the laws of nature; there, she closed her eyes, and focused on remaining completely still.

Her powers were developing with a speed that frightened her.

The acceleration of her abilities was a result, partly, of simple ageing – but more down to the fact that she was using them every day. She could now stay in the air almost indefinitely, and fly huge distances without tiring. The truth was, she didn't even know *how* far; it had been a long time since she had attempted a flight that had turned out to be beyond her. And she was strong now too; so strong that the possibility of accidentally hurting someone she cared about was never far from her mind. She opened her eyes, slowly, and looked at the series of dents in the wall beside her door. They were the results of arguments with Jamie, of missions that had gone wrong, of petty fights with Kate, and of the days when simply being herself was too much for her.

All the punches had been pulled. The only time she had lashed out at the wall with all her strength she had smashed a hole clean through the thick concrete, setting off an alarm that woke everyone in the Loop. The following morning, she had been forced to explain herself to Admiral Seward, who had gently informed her that the combination of teenage petulance and superhuman strength was a dangerous one.

Larissa closed her eyes again, and let her mind wander. As it so often did, it made its way back to the months that had followed her turning at the hands of Grey, the oldest British vampire, a man who had committed himself publicly to peace while he fed on teenage girls in private. She had eventually confronted him in Valhalla, the vampire commune he had founded, and from which he had been expelled for what he had done to her, but his banishment had brought her little peace; it had made nothing better.

The almost two years she had spent with Alexandru Rusmanov were her deepest secret, the one thing she refused to discuss with anyone, even Jamie. He had asked her about it for the first time during the bedlam that followed the attack on Lindisfarne, when the two of them were tentatively getting to know each other, were, in essence, meeting each other properly for the first time. The persona she had presented to him during her time as a prisoner of Department 19 had not been far removed from her real self; she had played up certain aspects of her character and played down others as she fought desperately for the chance to survive the madness that was taking place around her. But it was still a persona, an act, one she dropped as soon as Marie Carpenter was rescued and she came to realise that her life was no longer in danger. Jamie had phrased his question innocuously, but there had been a tightness to his voice, a sliver of excitement, that let Larissa know how much he wanted to hear about her past.

She wanted to tell him too.

The attraction between them was tangible, and she knew with absolute certainty that their time spent as merely friends was going to be extremely brief. But more than that, she trusted him; the thought of having someone who she could tell her story to, who would not judge her for the things she had done, would not think less of her or turn their back on her, someone who might help her carry the weight that hung so heavily around her neck, was the one thing she wanted more than anything else in the world.

And for that reason, she told him not to ask her about it again. She could not face the possibility of being wrong about him, of being let down and disappointed again. Instead, she clung to the hope that he would ignore her instruction, and ask her again one day; when he did, she would be ready to tell him.

But she wasn't. Not the second time he asked her, or the third, or the fourth, and eventually he got the message and stopped persevering. Each time, she had tried to tell him, tried to will herself to open this last door to him, and to hell with what lay behind it. But she couldn't. Her panic at the thought of driving him away before they had even had the chance to become something more than friends had been replaced by an overwhelming terror at the thought of losing him now that they had. She understood now that the chance had passed, that she should have told him at the beginning, and that she was now trapped. The memories of those two terrible years ate away at her, poisoning her sleep and her dreams, and she had rejected the chance to let someone help her, someone who wanted so badly to do so.

He saw me when his dad was killed, she thought, as she floated in the cool air of her quarters. *And he knows I was sent by Alexandru to kill him the night his mother was kidnapped. He knows both those things and he's still with me. Why can't I tell him the rest?*

But she knew the answer to her own question.

Because it's worse. Oh God, it's so much worse. Because I don't know if he or Kate could ever look at me the same way again. And because they're all I've got.

In the quiet of her quarters, her hair almost brushing the ceiling as she floated, Larissa fought back the rage that suddenly spilled through her, making her muscles vibrate and her fangs burst involuntarily into her mouth. She growled, a low rumble full of imminent violence, as she tried to control herself, tried not to swoop down and add a new dent to the collection by the door.

Calm, she shouted at herself. *Be calm. Without Alexandru you wouldn't be here, would never have met Jamie, or Kate, never had the chance to make amends for what you did. Calm down, you stupid girl.*

She felt her fangs retract, and she slowly unclenched her fists. It was a source of constant amusement to Larissa, who possessed a jet black sense of humour, that she had come to fall for a boy she would never even have met had she not been the obedient servant of the monster that had tried to destroy his family. But there had been no way for her to know that as she flew with Alexandru and his followers towards the house that the unsuspecting Jamie Carpenter shared with his mother and the ghost of his father.

No way for her to know that her new life, her real life, had been about to begin.

Kate Randall closed her laptop, sat back in her chair and stared at the wall above the small desk in her quarters. She had showered and changed into a T-shirt and shorts, and her blonde hair was wet; she could feel water dripping down her neck and across her shoulders.

It was her turn to write Squad G-17's post-operation report, but she found herself unable to concentrate on it. She was tired, but that was not unusual; endless interrupted sleep patterns came with the territory of being a Department 19 Operator. What was distracting her, and preventing her from focusing on the report, was something that had become an almost constant source of annoyance to Kate.

Jamie and Larissa.

Kate had known about their relationship, or whatever they called it when they were alone, since the very beginning. The two things that annoyed her, that sometimes made her so frustrated that she wanted to scream "I KNOW!" in both their faces, was the fact that they seemed to genuinely believe she was unaware, and that they felt the need to keep it from her at all.

The former was an insult to her intelligence, and she hated being thought of as stupid almost as much as she hated being patronised. The latter was even worse; she knew, with absolute certainty, that they both believed she had a crush on Jamie.

Kate was a girl with a highly developed sense of self-awareness, and would have admitted, had anyone asked her, that there had been a tiny period of time during which she had possibly, just *possibly*, thought about Jamie in that way.

During the madness of Lindisfarne and the days that followed it, days in which the shape and course of her life had been altered forever, when she had been faced with decisions that she would spend the rest of her days second-guessing, he had been there, by her side, helping her through it. He had rescued her on Lindisfarne, as the bodies of her friends and neighbours lay discarded on the streets she had grown up in, and saved her life, all their lives, by destroying Alexandru Rusmanov. Then, when it was over, she had seen him with Frankenstein, and with his mum, and for a few short moments, she thought that she had maybe been a little bit in love with him.

Maybe.

But the feeling had passed, and passed quickly; partly because it was obvious to her from the moment they woke up at the Loop on the morning after Lindisfarne that he had fallen for Larissa, and that Larissa felt the same way about him, but also because in the cold light of day, away from the blood and the screams and the horror of the night before, the aura that had glowed around him as he stepped forward to face Alexandru was gone. She loved Jamie; in the months since her home had been attacked he had become one of the two closest friends she had ever had, and she would have done anything for him.

But she was not *in* love with him.

That was what hurt her most about the deception that he and Larissa were perpetrating; she was genuinely, unreservedly happy for them both. She had waited and waited for them to tell her, convincing herself they were looking for the right moment, until she had been forced into the bitter realisation that there wasn't going to be a right moment. They weren't waiting for anything; they had decided to keep her in the dark.

Well, to hell with that, she thought. *Tomorrow I'll tell them I know. No more of this.*

After all, it wasn't as if Kate had been without problems of her own to deal with in the aftermath of Lindisfarne; real problems, unlike the adolescent nonsense occupying her two supposedly best friends.

After they had arrived at the Loop, after the wonderful, heart-stopping moment when the news had been passed to her that her father was among the survivors who had made it to the mainland in John Tremain's fishing boat, Kate had been escorted down to the secure dormitory on Level B and crashed into a deep, dreamless sleep. She had slept until a female Operator, in the same black uniform that Jamie and his colleagues had been wearing when they arrived on Lindisfarne, shook her awake six hours later and told her that she needed to get dressed and follow her up to the Loop's Ops Room.

She had done so without complaint, still half-asleep, rubbing her eyes as they made their way into a lift and up to Level 0. The Operator had pushed open the Ops Room door, and held it wide; Kate walked through it, and looked around the large circular room.

There was only one other person in there, a strikingly handsome Latino man in his mid-forties, wearing the now familiar all-black uniform, and sitting casually on the desk at the front of the room.

"Miss Randall?" he asked. His expression was entirely neutral; there was no malice there, no threat, but no warmth either, and for a second, the strangeness of the situation she had found herself in sank into her, and she felt a sharp rush of fear as she nodded.

What if they're going to lock me up for what I saw? What if I'm never going to get out of here? What will happen to my dad?

"My name is Major Christian Gonzalez," the man said. "I'm the Interim Security Officer at this facility. Please, take a seat."

Kate did as she was told, crossing the wide room and sitting in one of the plastic chairs that were ranged round a grid of long tables. She turned it so she was facing Major Gonzalez.

"Did you sleep well? Is there anything you need?" he asked.

She shook her head.

"Good," he said. "That's good. Now, Kate – do you mind me calling you Kate?"

She shook her head again, and his lips curled at the edges.

"Thank you," he said. "So, Kate. We have a problem, you and I. We need to work out what we're going to do about it."

"What problem?" she asked, her voice low and nervous.

"That you were never supposed to see the things you've seen. The creatures that attacked your home last night, the men who rescued you; as far as the general public is concerned, none of them exist. Neither does the building you're standing in now. And that's the way we need it to stay."

Fear pulsed up Kate's spine.

They're going to lock me up. I'm never going to be allowed to go home.

Major Gonzalez saw the look on the teenage girl's face and smiled.

"We're not going to hurt you, Kate," he said, his voice kind. "We're the good guys. But we do need to protect the security of what we do, and that means you have a decision to make. A big one."

"What do you mean?" Kate managed. "What decision?"

Major Gonzalez picked a small sheaf of paper from the desk he was sitting on, and showed it to Kate.

"This is the preliminary report into the events of last night," he said. "It is based on statements from eyewitnesses, including senior members of this organisation. It describes the circumstances leading to the destruction of one of the most powerful vampires in the world at the hands of a teenage boy with nothing more than the most basic training, and the actions of the men and women that helped him. It mentions you, several times. It says that you exhibited remarkable bravery and resolve in leading Mr Carpenter and his colleagues to the monastery where Alexandru Rusmanov had made his base, and that you continued to demonstrate those qualities when confronted with a hall full of hungry vampires, led by one of the most evil creatures ever to walk the earth. It claims you destroyed one of the vampires yourself. Is that true?"

The memory of the previous night burst unbidden into Kate's mind. She remembered the screams and the crunch of weapons as the small group of men and the vampire girl fought valiantly against monsters that outnumbered them five to one, remembered the spray of blood and the tearing of flesh and bone, remembered with shuddering revulsion the vampire who had held her, and the sensation of his sharpened fingernail tracing a line across her neck. Then she remembered the primal roar that had echoed through her head as she sank her teeth into his arm and tore at it like a mad dog, the warmth of his blood coating her from head to toe after she plunged a metal stake into his heart, and the subsequent sense of overpowering elation that had shaken her to her core.

"That's true," she said, quietly. "I destroyed one of them."

Christian Gonzalez smiled at her again, and this time the smile was wide, and dizzyingly beautiful. She felt his approval wash over her, and thought she might blush.

"Well done," he said. "Very well done indeed. That you survived as long as you did on an island overrun by vampires, that you were then able to play the part you did in their defeat, is why you now have a decision to make. The first option is as follows: you can return home, with a cover story explaining your whereabouts for the last twenty-four hours, and never tell anyone about the things you saw. You'll have to sign the Official Secrets Act, you'll be monitored to make sure you comply with it, and if you don't, you will be discredited so that no one believes you, to the extent that the likely result will be a period of evaluation in a secure psychiatric hospital. But you'll be able to resume your life as it was before the events of last night, and you'll be reunited with your father."

Tears welled in the corners of Kate's eyes as she thought about her father, her brilliant, loyal dad, who must be going through hell with his daughter missing and his home recovering from a massacre.

"I should be clear," continued Major Gonzalez. "This is an offer that is made extremely rarely. Under normal circumstances, once a civilian is exposed to the existence of the supernatural, as you were last night, continuing a normal life ceases to be an option. There are obvious risks in allowing that information to be taken out into the world, and those risks are normally considered sufficient to see the civilian in question placed in classified custody. I'm not trying to scare you, or threaten you, I promise. I'm merely letting you know how this usually works."

Kate felt both scared *and* threatened, but she tried not to let it show.

"What's the second option?" she asked, her voice packed with as much bravery as she could muster.

The smile returned to Christian Gonzalez's face.

"The other option is that you stay here and help us save the world," he said. "You become an Operator in this organisation, and you help us stop what happened to Lindisfarne from happening anywhere else."

"What's the catch?"

"The catch is that the life you led until yesterday will be over. You will never be able to tell anyone who you are, who you work for, or what you do, and you will never be able to contact anyone from your former life. Including your father."

Kate felt faint.

The idea that she would never see her dad again was so abhorrent to her that she thought she was going to throw up at the mere thought of it. But what the handsome Major was offering her was a way out of the life that had been stretching inevitably out before her on Lindisfarne: she would inherit her father's boat, carry on fishing the same small stretch of water for the next forty years, maybe find a local boy to marry, have a kid or two, and live and die on the island where she had been born.

Kate knew she could never have left her father alone, could never have moved to the mainland and abandoned him to an empty house full of the memories of his family. She had come to terms with her lot a long time ago, but now this man was offering her a way to change it all, to do something that mattered, something that would be exciting, and dangerous, where there were no limits to the places she might go and the people and monsters she might meet. But even for all that, there was a price that would be too high for her to pay.

"What will you tell my dad?" she asked, carefully. "I can't let him think anything happened to me. I need him to know I'm OK."

"He'll be told that you are the primary material witness to a major terrorist incident, and that you are being voluntarily detained for questioning. In a few months' time, when all this has died down, he'll be asked to sign the Official Secrets Act and told that you have been recruited into the Security Services. He'll be extremely proud of you, I promise." This time Major Gonzalez grinned, and Kate blushed, despite herself.

"How long do I have to make the decision?" she asked.

"About an hour," replied the Major. She opened her mouth to protest, but he cut her off. "I'm sorry, I know this must seem very unfair. But I'm afraid there are time factors at work here that controlling the public story depends on. If you decide to go, we need to get you home while there is still confusion on Lindisfarne."

"And if I decide to stay?"

"Then we need to get started," he said.

In the end, she had only made Major Gonzalez wait for ten minutes before she told him she would take the second option. He congratulated her, before escorting her along a curving grey corridor to one of the Briefing Rooms where she was reacquainted with Jamie Carpenter and the vampire girl, Larissa Kinley. And even then, as she looked back on the most important day of her life, she had noticed the small glances and half-smiles that passed between the two of them.

Tomorrow, she thought again. *I'll tell them tomorrow.*

There was a knock on the door of her quarters, and she padded softly across the cold floor to answer it, smiling as she did so, knowing there was only one person who would be visiting her at this hour. Shaun Turner was standing in the corridor outside, his face breaking into a smile as she opened the door to him. Then he was pushing her backwards, his hands on her waist, his lips on hers, and a thought flashed through her head as they sank on to her narrow bunk.

At least I'm actually good at keeping secrets. Well, from one of them, at least.

Jamie stood outside the door to Admiral Henry Seward's quarters on Level A, pushing his hair back from his forehead and tucking his T-shirt into his combat trousers. When he was as presentable as he was likely to get, he knocked on the door.

"Come," called a muffled voice. Jamie pushed open the heavy door and stepped inside.

The Director of Department 19 was sitting behind his desk. Admiral Seward put the papers he had been working on atop the towering pile of his inbox, and regarded Jamie with a warm smile which the teenager returned.

They had become close in recent months, these two men; united in grief by the loss of Frankenstein, whom Seward missed almost as much as Jamie, and drawn together by the Director's terrible sense of guilt over the death of Julian Carpenter. Jamie had never blamed Henry Seward for the loss of his father; for that, there was a jet black corner in the darkest, angriest depths of his soul set aside especially for the traitor Thomas Morris, who had died before Jamie got the chance to make him pay for what he had done. But the Admiral's guilt was real, even if it was misplaced, and it had allowed Jamie the chance to get to know the man his father had really been.

They had spent many evenings in this room, the Director telling tales of Julian Carpenter, Jamie drinking them in hungrily, then passing them on to his mother, often after heavy editing for violence. It had made the Carpenters feel like a family again, had rebuilt the bonds between that had been eroded in the years after Julian had died, when neither mother nor son had known how to fill the void that had been left in the middle of their lives.

Now look at us, thought Jamie, and stifled a grin. *I hunt and destroy vampires for a living, she IS a vampire and lives in a cell hundreds of metres below the earth, yet we've never got on better.*

"Something funny, Jamie?" asked Seward.

He had clearly not stifled the grin as well as he thought, and drew himself up to attention.

"No, sir," he replied.

Seward smiled at him.

"At ease," he said. Jamie relaxed into an easy stance, his hands loosely together behind his back. "Give me your report."

"Nothing notable, sir. Father and daughter vamps robbing a blood bank."

"Were you able to capture them?"

"Yes, sir. I handed them over to Dr Yen, sir."

The Director nodded. "Well done. Lazarus needs all the warm vamps it can get its hands on."

"So I hear, sir."

"Any signs?"

"Yes, sir. On the wall outside the hospital. The same two words."

Admiral Seward swore, scribbling a quick note on a piece of paper.

"Sir," Jamie continued. "Why does the Lazarus Project need so many captive vamps? What are they doing down there?"

The Director put down the pen he had been writing his note with, and looked at the young Operator. "The Lazarus Project is classified, Jamie," he replied. "You understand what classified means, don't you?"

"Yes, sir."

"Let me remind you, just in case you've forgotten. It means that everyone who needs to know what the Lazarus Project is doing already knows what the Lazarus Project is doing. Is that clear, Operator?"

"It is, sir."

"Good. There's a Zero Hour Task Force briefing scheduled for 1100 tomorrow. Mandatory attendance."

"New information, sir?" asked Jamie, hopefully.

Admiral Seward shook his head. "Just routine, Jamie. Dismissed."

Jamie nodded, and left the Director's study. As he walked towards the lift that would finally, mercifully, deliver him to his bed, his mind drifted back to the speech Admiral Seward had given a month earlier, that had brought to light the existence of the Lazarus Project, that had birthed the Zero Hour Task Force, that had altered how every Operator in the Department went about their job.

The speech that had changed everything.

3

THE ART OF COMING CLEAN

"Do you know what this is about?" asked Larissa.

She and Jamie were walking along the main Level B corridor towards one of the lifts standing near its centre. Larissa had a towel slung round her shoulders, and was dressed in a dark green vest and a pair of shorts. Jamie guessed she had been with Terry in the Playground, the wide, sweat-soaked space in the bowels of the Loop where the veteran Blacklight instructor ruled with an iron fist, and she looked deeply unimpressed about being interrupted.

"I've no idea," replied Jamie, glancing over at her. "I got the same message as you." He had been asleep when his console had blared into life, and was almost as grumpy as Larissa.

"All right," she said. "Don't bite my head off."

"Sorry," he replied, casting her a weary smile which she returned.

The two teenagers were tired, more tired than they could ever remember having been in their lives before Department 19. You never really got used to it, not completely, although they had both become skilled at not letting it interfere with either their performance as Operators, or the tiny sliver of each day that could charitably be called their social lives. But there was something looming on the horizon that was fuelling their bad moods, something that all the T-Bones and ultraviolet light in the world couldn't stop.

In five days' time, it would be Christmas.

Even inside the Loop, surrounded by men and women utterly committed to the secret mission they had undertaken, it was impossible to avoid the festive season. The Operators who had families, who lived off-base as Jamie's father had once done, filled the officers' mess with tales of trees and decorations, of presents that had been bought or still needed buying, while the younger men and women who lived in quarters at the Loop juggled days off and swapped shifts in the hope of seeing their loved ones at some point over the holiday. For Jamie and Larissa, it was nothing more than a continual reminder of the differences between them and everyone else, even Kate.

The two teenagers were unique, in that Blacklight's Intelligence Division had taken them off the grid; they no longer existed in the outside world, on paper or in the eyes of the law. Although she didn't know it, had Larissa's mother walked into any governmental office and attempted to prove that she had ever had a daughter, it would have been impossible for her to do so; there were no longer any official records of her child having been born, or having lived, and her copy of Larissa's birth certificate would have been dismissed as a forgery.

It was the same situation for Jamie; in his case because he was now the son of a creature that did not officially exist, in Larissa's because she *was* a creature that did not officially exist. Kate still had a presence in the world; she was officially listed as missing after the Lindisfarne attack, and her father knew that she was still alive, even though he was sworn to secrecy on the subject.

Jamie and Larissa were voluntary prisoners inside Department 19, unable to live anywhere else, because they did not exist anywhere else. Jamie had asked Admiral Seward about it once, asked him what would happen if the time came that he wanted to get married and have a family, have some semblance of a normal life. Seward had told him that it might, *might*, be possible to reintroduce him into the world under an assumed identity. As far as Jamie was concerned, he had not sounded very confident about it.

Jamie would readily concede, however, that it was far harder for Larissa than for him. All that remained of his family lived in a cell in the base of the Loop, and there had been a small Christmas tree standing in Marie Carpenter's cell for over a week. Larissa's family, and in particular her little brother, were still out there, living their lives without her, making preparations for what had always been her favourite time of the year. They had talked about it several times, both of them trying hard not to make the other feel worse, but it had been clear to them both that they were united in a single wish: for Christmas to be over as soon as possible, so their lives could get back to what they had come to consider normal.

They reached the lift and pressed the button marked 0. The message that had appeared on their consoles had been sent to every single Operator, both the active and inactive lists, summoning them all to a briefing in the Ops Room. Admiral Seward had debriefed Jamie less than three hours earlier, after Squad G-17 had returned from a routine call on a housing estate south of Birmingham, and the Director had not mentioned anything about an imminent meeting. Seward had been so phenomenally busy in the weeks since Lindisfarne that Jamie was not surprised, although he was, privately, slightly hurt; he liked to believe that he had the Director's ear in a way that the vast majority of rookie Operators did not.

Jamie and Larissa emerged on to Level 0 and made their way to the Ops Room. The wide, oval room was already almost full, and they found standing room against the curved wall at the back of the sea of black-clad figures. Jamie caught Kate's eye as they made their way through the throng, and he nodded at her. She smiled back at them from her seat near the far wall, before returning her attention to the platform at the front of the room, beneath the giant wall screen that was currently lying dormant.

Admiral Seward was standing on the platform, talking in a low voice to Cal Holmwood, the Deputy Director. The expressions on the two men's faces were sombre, and Jamie felt a pang of nervousness rise into his chest. Everything had been so chaotic since Lindisfarne, as the Department attempted to adjust to the revelations that had been uncovered by the successful rescue of Jamie's mother: the unmasking of Thomas Morris as the traitor to the Department, the destruction of Alexandru Rusmanov and the tragic loss of Colonel Frankenstein, which Jamie could still barely bring himself to think about.

"Seward looks serious," said Larissa, as though she could read Jamie's mind. "What's going on?"

"I don't know," replied Jamie, softly, as Cal Holmwood stepped down from the platform and took a seat in the front row. "Looks like we're about to find out."

Admiral Seward stepped up to the lectern that stood in the middle of the platform, and gripped its edges with his hands. He looked out over the massed ranks of Operators, his expression unreadable. Then he cleared his throat, and began to speak.

"Operators of Department 19," he began. "The time has come

to put our cards on the table. Some of what I'm about to say is going to be hard for you to hear, but I believe it's necessary that you hear it. I know many of you have had questions regarding the events of October 26th, questions that many of you have brought to me in person. I'm sorry that until now I have been unable to provide you with answers. There have been investigations and inquiries under way, and the full picture has only become clear extremely recently. That picture is what I'm here to describe to you today."

Seward glanced around at his audience, and appeared to find what he was looking for on the faces of his colleagues. He nodded briefly, before carrying on.

"I'm sure the majority of you are familiar with the events that took place on Lindisfarne during the night in question; for those of you who are not, I have declassified report 6723/F, which provides a comprehensive account. What very few of you know is that despite the fact that the mission on Lindisfarne led to the destruction of Alexandru Rusmanov, to the uncovering of the treachery of Thomas Morris and to the loss of Colonel Frankenstein, the crucial event of that night took place more than two thousand miles away, at the SPC base in Polyarny."

Standing at the back of the room, Jamie bristled.

And we rescued my mother. But I guess that doesn't deserve a mention.

"On the lower levels of the SPC base," continued Seward, taking a deep breath, "there is a vault numbered 31. Until the 26th of October it contained the most highly classified artefact held by any of the supernatural Departments of the world. It contained the remains of Vlad Tepes, the man who became known as Count Dracula."

The room exploded.

Half the seated Operators leapt to their feet en masse, and the

51

air was suddenly filled with hundreds of voices, many of them shouting and yelling. Admiral Seward raised his hands in a placatory gesture, then bellowed for quiet. The noise subsided, leaving behind it an uneasy, almost hostile atmosphere. The standing Operators retook their seats, but did so slowly, the looks on their faces shot through with fear and confusion, and more than a little anger.

"I know this must come as a shock," said Seward. "The fact of the matter is that the confrontation with Count Dracula in 1892, the confrontation that led directly to the foundation of this Department, did not end with his destruction. This is a matter of open public record, since the account in Stoker's novel is accurate. Any one of you could have corroborated his account with the documents in the archive, but it appears that none of you felt inclined to do so.

"Dracula was dangerously weak after his journey across Europe, and the knives wielded by Jonathan Harker and Quincey Morris spilled the last of his blood, causing his body to collapse. They, along with John Seward, Arthur Holmwood and Abraham Van Helsing, believed him dead; they were the first men ever to challenge, let alone defeat, a vampire, and they had no reason not to. The realisation that Dracula had been rendered dormant rather than destroyed outright wasn't made until several years later, when Professor Van Helsing was able to begin his study of the supernatural and discovered that a vampire could be brought back to life by introducing a sufficient quantity of blood to the dormant remains.

"When Professor Van Helsing realised the implication of this work, he returned to Transylvania with an envoy of the Russian Tsar, to recover the remains and see them properly secured. The envoy betrayed him, however, and the remains were taken to Moscow. They remained in Russian hands ever since, until the 26th of October, when they were taken from the SPC base by Valeri Rusmanov."

Seward paused, clearly bracing himself for a second eruption, but none came. A deep shock appeared to have settled over the men and women of Department 19; what they were being told raised a prospect almost too terrifying to contemplate.

"An investigation into the theft by the Intelligence Division has returned some preliminary conclusions. Firstly, it appears that Valeri had been searching for his master's remains since the early twentieth century, since very shortly after they disappeared into Russia. Secondly, it is clear that he was able to locate and extract them using information provided to him by Thomas Morris, whose treachery appears not to have been limited to assisting Alexandru Rusmanov in settling their mutual grudge against the Carpenter family."

Jamie felt his face redden as a number of Operators turned slowly in his direction. He stared up at the lectern, refusing to meet their eyes, and silently urged Admiral Seward to carry on.

"The whereabouts of Valeri Rusmanov," said the Director, "are presently unknown. Surveillance of all Valeri's known properties and associates has yielded negative results. Interrogation of well-connected vampires has proved equally fruitless. Simply put, we have no idea where he is. In addition, we have—"

"He's going to try to bring him back, isn't he?" interrupted an Operator, whose name Jamie didn't know. "Valeri, I mean. He's going to try to bring Dracula back."

"Operator Carlisle," replied Seward, a grave expression on his face, "I am sorry to say that the Intelligence Division reports an overwhelming probability that he has already done so."

This time the eruption was punctuated by a series of what seemed to Jamie's ears to be horribly close to screams. He felt a tight ball of panic close round his heart; he had never seen such a reaction to anything from the men and women of Blacklight, men and women whom he had come to believe could not be shaken by anything, and who were certainly never scared. But the fear in the Ops Room was now palpable, thick and cloying. What the Director was announcing, in his calm, straightforward manner, was something that no one in the room had ever considered, let alone made any preparation for.

It was quite literally the worst thing he could be telling them.

"Enough!" shouted Admiral Seward. "Don't you think I know how serious this is? I'm telling you because I believe that all of you have the right to know what we are facing. Don't make me regret that decision!"

There was a gradual shuffling of feet, an embarrassed dropping of eyes and voices, and an extremely uneasy calm settled precariously over the Ops Room. Most of the Operators remained on their feet, and when Seward realised that they had no intention of sitting back down, he carried on.

"Although there is a tiny chance that Valeri has either chosen not to resurrect his master or has failed in attempting to do so, the official position of the Department from this point forward is that Dracula is once more alive on this planet. We have no way of knowing precisely how long this has been the case, but since the resurrection process requires little more than a sufficiently large quantity of fresh blood in which to immerse the remains, we are assuming that it took place within twenty-four hours of the theft of the ashes, some time on or around the 27th of October."

"Why haven't we seen him?" asked Operator Carlisle, his voice trembling. "Why hasn't he come in here and killed us all?"

"He'll be weak," Jamie heard himself say, and blinked as the entire room turned to look at him. "After the resurrection. He'll be weak."

"That's correct, Lieutenant Carpenter," said Seward, and the sea of heads swung back to face the lectern.

"Professor Van Helsing wrote at length about the recovery time of resurrected vampires, in the aftermath of the loss of the remains to the Russians. The Science Division has expanded upon this research in recent days, and has come up with some rough conclusions. There are several factors that affect the recovery time of a vampire, principally the creature's age before it was rendered dormant, and the period of time since it was reduced to ash. It's far from an exact science, but we have been able to create a workable timeline, leading towards a point that has been given the code name Zero Hour, the point at which we believe a properly tended Dracula will regain his full strength. That point, Operators, lies one hundred and twenty days from now, on the 19th of April."

"Christ," growled Jacob Scott. The grizzled Australian Colonel had not risen from his seat in the second row during any of the outbursts that had taken place around him, and even now his face wore an expression containing significantly more determination than fear. "Four months. If we don't get him in the next four months, we won't get him at all. That's the deal, right?"

Admiral Seward nodded. "That's our hypothesis, Jacob. Dracula restored to full strength presents a threat that none of our strategic simulations can accurately model. He is the first vampire who ever lived, the oldest and most powerful; we simply cannot predict what will happen if he is allowed to rise. So our strategy from this point onwards is to make sure that *doesn't* happen. We have four months to find Valeri and Dracula, and to destroy them both. After that, it may not be possible to do so. As a result, I have three further announcements to make." A series of dazed-sounding groans emerged from the black-clad ranks, but Seward ignored them.

"Firstly, I will be creating and chairing a task force with the specific remit of devising and deploying the Department's strategy where Dracula and Valeri are concerned. Those of you who are selected for this group will be notified in due course. Secondly, I'm announcing the formation of a classified sub-department of the Science Division, code-named the Lazarus Project. Access to all information relating to this sub-department will be restricted on a strictly need-to-know basis, but it relates to the third thing I want to make you aware of. Until further notice the Standard Operating Procedure will no longer be to destroy vampires: it will be to contain them wherever possible, return them to the Loop and submit them into the custody of the Lazarus Project."

There was a half-hearted outburst of objection from the dazed ranks of the Operators, but Seward had reached the end of his patience.

"Shut up!" he bellowed. "Any Operator who feels unable to implement this new procedure, or who feels unable to handle the situation that I have just outlined, should feel absolutely free to place themselves on the inactive roster. The rest of you I will expect to carry out your responsibilities to the same standards as always. If you have questions, come and see me or ask your senior commander. In the meantime, you are all dismissed."

Seward stepped down from the platform and strode out of the Ops Room, closely followed by Cal Holmwood and Paul Turner. The reeling Operators began to talk among themselves, their voices low, their eyes wide. Larissa looked at Jamie, and gave her head a tiny shake.

"Holy shit," she said, quietly.

"That's a bit of an understatement," replied Jamie.

4

GROWING PAINS

On a chaise longue the colour of blood, in Valeri Rusmanov's study overlooking the vast Landes Forest, lay the first vampire ever to walk the earth.

Three months after his resurrection, Count Dracula was finally beginning to look like himself; like the man he had briefly been, like the vampire who had lived for more than four hundred years before he had been condemned to a limbo that had lasted for more than a century. A mane of black hair spilled across the vampire's shoulders, swept back from a forehead that was high and wide. Thick, unruly black eyebrows perched above pale blue eyes which flanked a nose that was sharp and narrow, like the blade of a scalpel. A black moustache covered the entirety of his upper lip, framing a mouth that was thin and cruel. The Count was dressed in a plain black robe, and he stared at the door of the study, waiting for Valeri to return with his supper.

He was weak. Maddeningly, pitifully weak.

Each intake of fresh blood, which Valeri dutifully brought him every evening, saw a tiny fraction of his power return, but he was still little more than a shadow of his former self. For several weeks after his resurrection, he had been unable to move, his body soft and malleable, as though made of wet clay, waiting to be fired. In time it had hardened into solid flesh and dense bone, but the terrible power he had once wielded, power that could lay waste to cities and obliterate men and women with little more than a glance, was still only a memory.

In time, I will be all that I was. In time. And then this world will pay.

But for the time being, the Lord of Darkness, the Impaler, the Cruel Prince, who had been feared from sea to sea by his own people and his enemies alike, was as weak as a sickly child.

Dracula lifted his head, grunting at the effort it took, and stared out of the window of his most loyal subject's study, past the manicured grounds of the chateau to the dark expanse of the pine forest beyond. His mind throbbed with two ancient, primitive desires: for food, and for revenge on the men who had stolen a century of his life from him, the men who had reduced him to this pathetic state.

After the resurrection, as the ancient vampire began the slow, painful process of recovery, Valeri had started to carefully recount what had happened while Dracula had been lying dormant. The story of the twentieth century, in which humankind had advanced far beyond the imagination of even the most optimistic Victorian futurist, was long, confusing and, as far as Dracula was concerned, almost fatally tedious. It was not in his nature, the nature of either the man he had been or the monster he had become, to spend his time considering the achievements of others; his world view was fundamentally extremely simple.

As far as he was concerned, the rest of the world existed only for his use, and by his permission, and this new world that Valeri was describing to him would be no different.

He didn't care about the growth of the cities, about the technological developments that Valeri described to him in infuriatingly simple terms, as though teaching a lesson to an infant. Aeroplanes, cars, space travel, television, telephones, the internet – none of these innovations interested him in the slightest. He saw no reason to doubt that his place in the new world being described to him would be whatever he decided he wanted it to be, providing that one thing had remained constant over the decades that had passed without him.

"Do… they… still… bleed?" Dracula had eventually interrupted, his voice barely audible to anyone without Valeri's superhuman hearing.

"Yes, master," replied Valeri. "The humans still bleed."

"Then… I… would… hear… no… more."

The study door opened, and Valeri entered, dragging the unconscious figure of a teenage girl behind him. Her head was starred with blood and the heels of her bare feet scraped noisily across the wooden floorboards as Valeri approached his master. The scent of the blood seeping from the girl's head filled Dracula's nostrils, and his pale blue eyes coloured a terrible dark red, the colour of madness, a colour that no sane person could have looked upon for more than a second or two.

"An offering for you, master," whispered Valeri, bowing deeply.

"Thank you, Valeri," replied Count Dracula, his voice like the scratch of a pencil on a sheet of paper.

Valeri lowered the girl towards his master, then slit her throat with one of his fingernails. As the blood began to flow, Dracula clamped his mouth over the wound, sucking hungrily, like a baby at its mother's breast. Valeri held the girl in place, but turned his head away; it would not be appropriate for him to watch his master feed in such a way. Instead, he let his gaze wander around the study, a room he had not set foot in for almost fifty years until the day after his master had been reborn.

Château Dauncy had been the favourite place of his wife, Ana, her favourite place in the whole world. It had been the only thing, apart from Valeri himself, capable of soothing the madness that roared inside her. When she died, when she was taken from him, he had ordered the old building shuttered and boarded up, hoping to trap the worst of his grief inside the ancient walls. It was painful for him to be inside those walls now, far more painful than he had expected, but it was necessary; it was the one property he owned that no one else was aware of, the one place he was confident would not be under surveillance by Blacklight or one of its accursed counterparts. It was the place he could return his master to health, without interruption.

The girl's blood gushed into Dracula's mouth, and he instantly felt strength flood through him. He knew it wouldn't last, but he also knew that each passing day, each mouthful of warm, running blood, brought him closer to himself, and to his revenge.

Taking advantage of the temporary rush of power, he spoke to Valeri, his voice booming through the study, rich and deep and momentarily full of the authority that had once commanded armies, and sent thousands to their deaths.

"Where is your brother?" he asked. "Why is Valentin not here, assisting you? I would not have you shoulder this burden alone, old friend."

"Valentin is in America, master," replied Valeri, a grimace of distaste flickering across his face as he spoke his brother's name. "We do not concern ourselves with each other."

Dracula's face twisted into a snarl, and for a moment, Valeri was afraid. The resurrection of his master had been the result of a quest that had taken him more than a hundred years to complete, a quest he had remained doggedly loyal to even as Alexandru had descended into madness and Valentin had turned his back on his family, sinking happily into his life of shameful indulgence in New York. Now that the quest was over and his master had been returned to life, Valeri's position as Dracula's favourite would forever be secure; he would follow his master once more, obediently, gladly and proudly. But in the century that had passed, as Dracula lay dormant deep below the Russian snow, Valeri had forgotten what it was to be afraid. He was reminded now, and he shivered in the cool air of his study.

"Go to him," said Dracula, the snarl vanishing as quickly as it had appeared. "Tell him that his master orders him home. Tell him there is work to be done."

"Of course, master," replied Valeri. "I will leave at once."

Dracula grunted with satisfaction.

"Good," he said, and fixed his eyes upon his subject. "You have always served me with distinction, Valeri. You have never sought to question me. When this world is mine, when I have piled high the bodies of the pathetic creatures that inhabit it and set them alight, when once again my enemies stare out at nothing from the highest poles, the place at my right hand will be yours, as it was before."

"You honour me, master."

"Leave me," replied Dracula, waving a hand towards Valeri, who did as he was ordered, backing quietly out of the study and leaving the Count alone.

Dracula watched him go, then rolled back on to the chaise longue and stared at the ornate, painted ceiling above him. Already he could feel his strength ebbing away, but he refused to let it anger him. Three months had passed since he had woken in the pulsing gore of the pit beneath the Rusmanov chapel, naked and screaming, his body little more than coloured blubber, held together only by the strength of his own will. He had not known himself as he was birthed violently back into the world, had not known himself until Valeri had knelt at the edge of the pit and said a single word.

Master. When he called me master, I knew who I was.

His journey from that blood-soaked beginning had been long, and hard, but it was getting easier, with each passing day. He knew that he could be patient, for a short while at least. And he knew that he could bear whatever pain might come his way. As agonising as his recovery had been so far, it did not even bear comparison to the night his second life had begun, more than five hundred years ago.

5

REBIRTH

Vlad Tepes fled through the darkening forest, the din of the battle and the screams of his men fading behind him. He had torn his royal armour from his body and cast it aside, but he could still hear the shouts and running footsteps of his pursuers, getting closer with every minute that passed.

Five Turkish soldiers at least; maybe six, maybe more. The Prince of Wallachia knew better than anyone the horrors that would await him in the Turkish camp if he was caught, and he redoubled his efforts, the soft forest floor thudding beneath his feet.

I'll die before I let them take me, he thought. *I will bow to no one.*

The army that had advanced across his lands had outnumbered his own forces by five to one. Less than a year earlier, Stephen Bathory, the Prince of Transylvania, had helped Vlad to reclaim his throne; they had marched together into Wallachia, their forces combined, and Basarab, the foolish, cowardly old man who had succeeded Vlad's brother Radu as ruler, had fled without a fight.

But Stephen had refused to stay and help consolidate Vlad's third reign, and his departure – *betrayal, it was a betrayal* – had left him vulnerable. He had received word within months that a Turkish army was moving north, and when it had been clear that no help was forthcoming, he had ridden out to meet it on the plains beside Bucharest, accompanied by his elite Moldavian guards and a little over four thousand men.

They fought like they were forty thousand. Fought and died, as men should.

Blood ran down Vlad's arm from the sword blow that had knocked him from his horse, but he felt no pain. Instead, an ethereal calm had settled over him, bestowing upon him the clarity of a man who is running for his life. Somewhere behind him, either fleeing the battlefield or lying dead upon its blood-soaked earth, were his Generals, the brothers Rusmanov. When it had become clear that the battle was lost, that his brief third reign as the ruler of Wallachia was over, Vlad had fled, without a backward glance. He felt a momentary pang of guilt, but pushed it quickly aside.

I never promised them immortality. They followed me with their eyes open, and took their share of the spoils of victory gladly.

The sun had slipped below the horizon to the west, and darkness was gathering around Vlad as he ran. At the foot of an enormous white oak tree, he stopped and caught his breath, listening intently for the sounds of his pursuers.

The forest was silent.

Not the slightest noise could be heard, in any direction, and Vlad's savage pleasure at the thought of having lost the Turkish soldiers was replaced with a sudden uneasiness. The trunk of the oak in front of him looked ancient, gnarled and twisted beyond anything he had seen before, and he had hunted and ridden these woods a thousand times since moving his summer palace to the small town of Bucharest. Vlad looked around the small clearing in which he was standing and saw that all the trees were the same, towering structures of mangled wood, their bark splintered and grey. At the base of the enormous trunks sprouted plants that Vlad didn't recognise, sprays of black flowers and barbed, midnight-blue vines.

What is this place? I have never been here before.

This is the deep, whispered a voice, and Vlad whirled round, reaching instinctively for his sword. But the short blade was long gone, left in the gut of a Turkish soldier who had tried to prevent his escape.

Your sword will not help you here, whispered the same voice. It was light, almost jovial, and seemed to be coming from inside his head, from all sides, and from nowhere.

"Who speaks to me?" bellowed Vlad, striding into the centre of the clearing. "Show yourself!"

There was no answer.

The silence in the forest was absolute as the last of the light faded away. Vlad Tepes felt fear crawl into his stomach, as he looked around the clearing, searching for the way he had come.

There was no sign of it.

He was lost.

There were no broken branches, no flattened patches of grass, nothing to indicate that a man had passed this way within the last hundred years. Vlad stared into the darkness, trying to calm his racing heart. He was trying to decide which direction to set out in when he heard a sound, the first sound, apart from the grotesque, light-hearted voice, that he had heard since he had entered this place.

The noise was a scratching, creeping sound, and it ran up Vlad's spine like ice. It was the sound of something crawling through the ancient trees, something slow, and old, and patient. Vlad spun round, his fists clenched, searching for the source of the noise in the spaces between the trees and the dark undergrowth. Then he realised what was happening, and terror gripped at his heart.

The trees themselves were moving.

Slowly, two of the ancient white oaks curved out and down, crossing at head height to form a circular passage that led further into – *the deep, it's the deep* – the dark forest.

Come to me, whispered the voice. *Come to me.*

Vlad stared incredulously at the opening before him. This could not be real, he thought; surely his mind had broken at the loss of the battle, the deaths of his Generals and his men, and this was nothing more than the vision of a lunatic?

Do not be foolish, hissed the voice, and Vlad cried out. The lightness of tone was gone; the voice sounded like death, old and *deep* and dark. *Come to me, while I still invite you. There is nowhere else for you to go.*

Vlad looked around the clearing, and saw that the voice spoke the truth. The trees on all sides had closed together, forming an impenetrable wooden wall that surrounded him completely.

He was trapped.

Sickly sweet bile churned in his stomach, as he realised he had no choice. Forcing his legs to move, Vlad walked slowly forward, his entire body trembling, and entered the circular opening. The darkness that engulfed him was total; it was the very absence of light. He heard the trees begin to move again, closing the entrance behind him, and took a tentative step forward.

There was nothing beneath his foot.

Vlad overbalanced, his arms grabbing at nothing, then pitched forward, screaming as he did so, and fell into the deep.

*

He awoke an unknowable amount of time later.

There was grass beneath his back, and as his eyes struggled open, he saw the night sky above him. Constellations of stars spun and swirled, impossibly low, patterns of light that he had never seen before. A group of pale red stars gathered into the shape of a bull's head, then disappeared as a cluster of iridescent green lights drew the image of a vast, coiled snake across the black sky.

The images turned Vlad's stomach, and he looked away. He pushed himself up so he was sitting on the grass, fighting to remember where he was, and what had happened to him.

The grass he was sitting on was a green so dark it was almost black, even beneath the spiralling, shifting kaleidoscope of light overhead. It grew in a circle, perhaps twenty feet in diameter. Around its edge, statues of ancient grey stone stood watchfully, without the smallest of gaps between them. The carved figures were grotesque: men and women in contortions of agony, animals in the throes of violence and death, demonic creatures, horned and spiked and scaled, with expressions of lustful pleasure on their faces. Above the statues there appeared to be nothing but the inky-black sky. There was no doorway, or passage, that would explain how he had come to this awful place.

I fell. I think I fell.

Then memory exploded through Vlad's head, and he cried out as he remembered: the battle, the forest, the ancient moving trees, and the awful, unnatural voice that had spoken to him. He forced himself to his feet, and found himself looking at the only thing in the circle beside himself.

It was an altar.

A large rectangular block, crudely carved from pale grey stone and standing at the edge of the grass, beneath a pair of intertwined statues depicting such violence that Vlad, a man who had visited tortures on his enemies that had been whispered throughout the entire European continent, could not look at them. The stone was carved with letters of a language that he didn't recognise, and the top was stained dark brown with long-spilled blood.

Fury overwhelmed Vlad, and he ran forward. He beat his hands on the surface of the altar, screaming and bellowing at the alien sky above his head. This was not where he was supposed to have ended his days, alone and scared in this place of old horror; he had commanded armies, lain waste to cities and entire countries, walked with kings and emperors. He raged at the darkness that surrounded him, swearing death to whatever had brought him here, cursing his enemies, promising revenge on everyone who had ever wronged him, offering his soul for the chance to see his betrayers cold in the ground.

Nothing happened.

Above him, the stars spun, blooming into life and winking out, as though millions of years were passing in mere seconds. The statues around him stood silent and impassive, staring down at him with empty eyes. The altar remained nothing more than a lump of stone.

Vlad slumped against it, the fire gone from him as quickly as it had arrived.

Why am I here? If not for some devilment, then why? Perhaps I am mad.

You are not mad, whispered the voice he had heard in the clearing. *But you are stupid.*

Vlad looked around, but still nothing moved inside the silent circle of statues. The voice was cruel, and mocking, and he tried to think what it could mean, why it was questioning his intelligence.

His gaze landed on the brown stains atop the altar, and clarity burst through him. He dug the fingers of his right hand into the wound on his arm, tearing the flesh open. Vlad grunted in pain as blood began to run thickly down his arm, coating his hand; he lifted it high above his head, and paused.

If I am not mad, then only damnation awaits me here.

You were damned long ago, hissed the voice, and Vlad knew in his heart that it was right. He flicked his hand, and dark red droplets of his blood pattered across the surface of the altar.

Instantly, the air was full of energy; it crackled round Vlad's head, lifting his long black hair from his shoulders. He watched the hairs on the backs of his arms stand up, and felt thick, greasy power in his teeth and bones. The statues began to move, rumbling to life on their pedestals, inflicting their tortures on one another in slow, gruesome thrusts, a writhing wall of agonised, abused stone. Before him, the altar began to run with a black liquid that appeared to be bubbling up from the microscopic holes in the stone itself, a thick oil that seemed to absorb light. When the entire surface of the altar was covered, a mouth, impossibly wide, and full of teeth the size and shape of daggers, opened in the liquid, and appeared to smile at him.

"What are you?" asked Vlad, his voice trembling.

You could not hope to understand, replied the mouth. It was the same voice he had been hearing since he had run blindly into what it had referred to as the deep, but now it was smooth, almost friendly. *And it does not matter. What matters is that I know what you are.*

"What am I?"

A monster. The mouth curled into a wide, awful grin. *Capable of cruelty that impresses even one like me. A carrion bird. A parasite. A—*

"Enough," said Vlad, as forcefully as he was able.

The mouth on the altar grinned even wider.

And brave, up to a point. Often to the point of foolishness. Or danger.

"Why did you bring me here?" demanded Vlad.

You brought yourself. Your rage cried out across the deep. I merely lit the way.

"Why?" asked Vlad. "Why, for God's sake? What do you want from me?"

I want to offer you something. In return for something you haven't used for a long time.

"What are you talking about?"

Your soul, said the mouth, and bared its teeth. *I want your soul. It will amuse me for millennia. And I will pay you handsomely for it.*

Vlad stared at the slick surface of the altar. The mouth was still smiling, and he felt his stomach churn.

"What would you offer me?" he asked. "What price could be enough for what you ask?"

I can give you revenge, on everyone who has ever wronged you, or failed you. I can give you life everlasting, that you might hunt your enemies to the end of their days, without ageing, without dying. I can give you the power to lay your world in ruins. All this, I can give you.

"I sense deception," said Vlad. "Such an offer is surely too good to be true."

You are correct, replied the mouth. *There can be no light without dark, no reward without punishment. But I deceive you not. You had not asked to hear the terms.*

"I ask to hear them now."

Very well. You will never see the sun again; to look upon it will mean your end. You will not take food, or drink, as humans do; only the lifeblood of other creatures will sustain you. You will be safe from mortal hands, and mortal weapons, and you may share your new life with others, as you see fit. But when your time on this plane comes to an end, your soul will belong to me, and Hell will await you. For all eternity.

"I accept."

The words were out before he even realised he was going to say them. The abomination's offer would condemn him to a life lived in the shadows, in the presence of death, and blood, but for Vlad this would not feel unfamiliar, and the alternative was not worthy of consideration. The life he had lived was over, he knew it all too well; the Turks would hunt him to the ends of the earth, and he would stand tall in the darkness rather than run and hide in the light.

I never doubted that you would, said the voice. *But I wasn't finished.* The grin widened until it began to spill from the edges of the altar, running in thick black trails towards the dark grass.

"What do you mean?" cried Vlad. "What trickery is this?"

No trickery at all. You accepted my offer, without hearing the last of its terms.

"Tell me what you are holding back! Tell me at once!"

The mouth set into a hard, straight line, and when it spoke again, its voice was the sound of freezing blood, of pain and hopelessness.

You have nothing left to barter with. I suggest you refrain from issuing demands.

Vlad began to tremble, with rage and the terrible, creeping feeling that he had been outsmarted. Fear was again spilling into his stomach and up his spine, and he regarded the altar with horror.

"I apologise," he forced himself to say. "I humbly ask to know the final term of the covenant."

That's better, said the mouth, its smile returning. *The final term is this: the first blood you take is the sole key to your undoing. Your first victim will carry the only means of ending your second life.*

"What kind of deception is this?" cried Vlad. "You promised me everlasting life!"

I promised you nothing. I told you that I could give you everlasting life; whether you achieve it is entirely up to you. If you were incapable of dying, then how would the contract ever be fulfilled? But I have given you more than any human who went before you, and I would see you more grateful for my generosity.

"What gift is this that I receive in return for my soul, full of conditions and caveats?"

I promised no gift, replied the mouth. *I offered nothing more than the covenant that has now been agreed.*

"Then I withdraw my acceptance!"

Too late, said the mouth, grinning widely. Then it moved, bursting forward from the altar and enveloping Vlad completely in black fluid that felt as cold and wrong as the end of the world. He screamed soundlessly, over and over, but the liquid held him tight, until it was over, and it withdrew.

He fell to his knees, a desiccated thing; his eyes had tumbled in on themselves, blinding him, and his skin was as dry and leathery as parchment. He was not breathing, but he was still alive, still able to feel the indescribable pain of what had been done to him. When he felt that he could bear the agony no longer, when he thought he must die or be driven mad by the pain, the black liquid moved again, coating him for a second time.

But instead of showing mercy, and ending his torment, as Vlad prayed it would, it sank into him, disappearing into his pores, and a sensation of power beyond anything he had ever felt surged through him. His eyes spun back into place, as his skin smoothed and coloured and his heart began to beat anew, and he rose to his feet on legs that felt as strong as tree trunks, clenching fists that felt as though they could shatter mountains. A primal roar burst from his throat, and then he was falling, towards the midnight grass, through it, into blackness, back into the deep.

When he came to, he was lying on the floor of the Teleorman Forest. He opened his eyes and recognised instantly the white oaks that rose above him towards the night sky, the smell of the grass beneath his body and the cold breeze that whispered across his face. For a long, disorienting second, he wondered whether he had dreamt what had occurred, whether his mind, ravaged by exhaustion and the horror of his army's defeat, had rebelled against him, conjuring impossible terrors from the depths of his nightmares. But then he got slowly to his feet, felt power bubbling beneath his skin, and remembered the deal he had made with the terrible grinning mouth.

It seems you kept your word, devil. And I will do everything in my power not to keep mine.

He grinned in the darkness, and felt something shift in his mouth; new teeth slid down from inside his gums, fitting perfectly over his incisors. The tips of these new teeth were razor-sharp, and they cut through his lower lip as though it was tissue paper. Blood spilled into his mouth and he fell to his knees in the throes of an ecstasy beyond anything he had ever imagined, pleasure so overwhelming that he had no option but to close his eyes and wait for it to pass.

When it eventually did, he rose again, and looked at the patch of forest where he had awoken. In a wide circle around him, partially hidden by overgrown bushes and wild undergrowth, were pieces of stone that looked as though they had once been the bases of statues, and a small mound of rocks that might once have been part of something large and rectangular. But the stones were buried in the earth, covered in moss and dirt, and looked as though they had been undisturbed for hundreds, maybe even thousands, of years.

This is the place I went to. But it's old now. Where I went it was new.

He left the stone ruins behind, and began to walk in the direction of the distant battlefield. The occasional scream still floated through the night air, and in the distance he could see a dull orange glow emanating from the fires he knew the Turks would have built to burn the bodies of the dead. Although he did not know what he was going to do when he reached the site of the battle, he knew he no longer feared the invaders and their weapons, and he was determined that he would discover the fates of his Generals, the three brothers whose loyalty he had rewarded by leaving them behind. As the forest began to thin around him, he heard voices in the darkness, and headed silently towards them.

In a clearing, gathered round a roaring fire, was an encampment of villagers from the plains beyond the forest, who had fled their homes as the Turkish armies approached. There were perhaps fifteen families: men, women and children, warming themselves near the heat of the fire, nursing infants, boiling water in metal cauldrons, holding spitted meat over flames. A number of the women were singing an old working song, and it was their voices that Vlad had heard, the ancient melody carrying sweetly on the cold air. He circled the encampment, slipping silently through the trees, looking for an opportunity. He was hungry, and the smell of the roasting meat was invading his nostrils and making him salivate.

"Stand where you are, sir."

Vlad turned slowly in the direction of the voice, and found himself face to face with a middle-aged man, standing in the shadow of one of the towering oaks. The man was dressed in the sturdy clothing of a farmer, and was holding a bow and arrow at his shoulder, the metal tip of the bolt aiming steadily at Vlad's chest. He raised his hands in placation, and took a small step towards the farmer, who backed away immediately.

"No closer," he said. "And speak, so I would know if you are friend or foe."

"I'm neither," replied Vlad, a smile creeping across his face. "I'm something else."

The man lowered his bow by a couple of degrees.

"You are not Turkish," he said. "Are you Wallachian? Answer."

"I was," replied Vlad. Then the hunger hit him like a bolt of lightning, and he folded to his knees, his head wrenched back in agony.

The hunger roared through Vlad Tepes like a hurricane, opening a huge abyss in his chest and stomach, a clutching pit of emptiness. He grabbed at his breast, tearing at his own skin with his fingernails, trying to pull himself open, trying to find a way to fill the gaping hole that had appeared at the centre of his being. His head thundered with agony, as though drills were being applied to his temples, and his limbs were suddenly as heavy as lead.

The farmer threw aside his bow, and ran to the stricken man. He knelt down and pulled at the stranger's shoulders; the head came up easily, inches from his own. The farmer looked at the vision of horror before him, the glowing red eyes that stood out in the middle of the twisted face, the gleaming white fangs that extended below the upper lip, and drew in breath to scream. Then the stranger plunged his teeth into his neck, and the scream died in his throat.

Vlad lunged on instinct alone; the pain of the hunger had driven rational thought from his head. His new fangs slid through the farmer's skin, piercing the jugular vein, sending blood gushing into his mouth and down his throat. And instantly, the pain and the hunger were gone, replaced by a feeling that was almost godlike. He swallowed the blood that sprayed from the man's torn throat, until he was sated, and withdrew his fangs.

The two figures fell to the cold ground.

Vlad's chest was thumping up and down, alive with power; the farmer's was barely moving, as blood seeped steadily out of the ragged hole in his neck. The former Prince of Wallachia leapt to his feet, and found himself floating several inches above the ground. He spun slowly in the air, then laughed, a terrible cackle that echoed between the silent trees and floated across the fire at the centre of the encampment, drawing frowns from the men gathered round it. Several of their wives crossed themselves, and the infants among the group began to cry.

The laughter faded as Vlad resumed his course back towards the battlefield, floating slowly and effortlessly between the trees and over the undergrowth, spinning and swooping in the air, like a child who had been given a marvellous new toy. Where he had been, there was nothing but a patch of spilled blood, and the dark shape of the farmer on the ground, his body cooling as his life ebbed away.

6

CARPENTER AND SON

Jamie walked along the corridor of the Loop's detention level, feeling as conflicted as he always did when he was about to see his mother.

Hers was the only occupied cell; the others had been emptied three weeks earlier, their inhabitants placed in restraining belts and taken into the depths of the Blacklight base to be handed over to the Lazarus Project. The ultraviolet barriers that filled the open front walls of the cells shimmered in the quiet air, the vampires they had contained long gone.

Marie Carpenter was in the last cell on the left, the same cell that Larissa had occupied for the three chaotic days after Jamie's mother had been kidnapped by Alexandru Rusmanov, until her heroics on Lindisfarne had seen her released from custody and offered the chance to join the Department.

Jamie made his way down the corridor, aware that his mother's superhuman senses would have alerted her to his presence as soon as he stepped through the airlock door and into the containment block, equally aware that she would pretend to be surprised to see him. His mother hated nothing more than drawing attention to the fact that she had been turned into a vampire. He reached the last strip of concrete wall before his mother's cell, stopped and took a deep breath. Then he stepped out in front of the ultraviolet barrier.

Jamie's first instinct, as always, was to laugh; his mother's cell was like something out of a home interiors catalogue.

Because she had voluntarily gone into Blacklight custody, and because she was the mother of an Operator, she had been allowed to request items that were not available to any other vampire that had been brought on to the block, and she had made the most of it. In the middle of her cell was the oval rug that had lain in the living room of their old house in Brenchley, and sitting on top of it was the coffee table which Jamie's father had rested his feet on every evening after he got home from work. The chest of drawers from Marie's old bedroom stood against one wall, topped with a cluster of photos of her son and her late husband. The battered leather sofa that had dominated their old living room filled most of the rear wall of the cell, and her bed was covered in the lilac sheets and duvet cover that she had slept in for as long as Jamie could remember.

His mother had politely, but very determinedly, imported her old life into this concrete cube deep below the earth. The Christmas tree that had sat on the coffee table, its multicoloured lights twinkling beneath the fluorescent strips in the ceiling, was gone, much to Jamie's relief.

"Hey, Mum," he said, stepping into the cell. "How's it going?"

Marie Carpenter was sitting on the sofa, her nose buried in a paperback book. She looked up, the predictable frown of fake surprise creasing her features, then broke into a huge smile and leapt to her feet. She stepped forward to meet him, and mother and son hugged in the middle of the square room.

"Hello, love," she said, squeezing him tightly. "Are you all right? Have you been out today?"

Despite the uniform he wore and the things he had done, Jamie was still a teenage boy, and never more so than in the presence of his mother. He blushed immediately at the enthusiasm of her embrace, while at the same time a broad grin emerged on his face. This was why he had walked voluntarily into the darkest depths of horror, why he had stood in the middle of an ancient building full of the dead and faced down the most dangerous monster in the world; so that he might be able to hug his mother again, and feel the love that radiated out of her when she was with him, a love that he had only realised he needed when it was taken away.

"I'm all right, Mum," he replied. "Yourself?"

Marie gave him a final squeeze before releasing her grip, and stepping back to look at her son. She cast her eyes quickly up and down him, taking in the black uniform with a look of immense pride on her face, before she reached the pink patch of scar tissue on his neck, and a grimace flickered across her face.

"I'm fine," she replied. Her gaze lingered on his neck for a moment, as it always did, before she forced her eyes away and broke into a smile. "How's Kate?"

Jamie's own smile faded.

His relationship with his mother had improved immeasurably since they had returned from Lindisfarne. The truth about Julian Carpenter, about the man he had really been and the circumstances surrounding his death, had liberated them; the dark mess of grief and betrayal that had crippled them both in the aftermath of his death, that Jamie had been unable to stop himself from taking out on his mother, had cleared, leaving them free to rebuild. They both still missed him, in their different ways, and Jamie had come to terms with the fact that he probably always would. But the grief now seemed manageable. What had been a yawning, unfillable chasm was now merely a hole, deep, and slippery at the edges, but that he could now avoid falling into, most of the time at least. Sadly, it was no longer the only one; there was now a hole of almost equal size with Frankenstein's name above it.

It had been slow going at first, the thaw between Jamie and Marie. There were new complications, not least of which was the condition that required Marie to spend her days and nights in the depths of the Loop behind an ultraviolet wall. There was much to say, and over the first couple of weeks, as both of them adjusted to their new lives, it was all eventually said.

Jamie apologised for how he had behaved since his dad had died, cutting off his mother's attempts to tell him he didn't need to, plunging ahead until it was all out of him. Marie had listened, tears running down her face, until he was done, then offered an apology of her own, for failing to cope with the death of her husband, for failing to realise that her son still needed her. By the time she was finished, they were both in tears, tears that turned out to be as cathartic as they were painful. There was only one remaining aspect of their rebuilt relationship that caused Jamie to worry.

Marie Carpenter absolutely adored Kate.

And hated Larissa.

He understood why; it was Kate who had put her arm round Marie after the hunger had hit her in the aftermath of Lindisfarne, Kate who had escorted her on to the rescue helicopter, talking to her in the gentle, friendly way that came so naturally to her. Larissa, on the other hand, was a vampire, and as far as Marie was concerned, vampires were all monsters, despite Jamie's protestations to the contrary.

He knew he was wasting his time; Marie had been kidnapped and tormented by the very worst the vampire world had to offer, and was appalled by the change that had been inflicted on her. But he tried anyway, because he knew that eventually the time would come when he would want to tell his mother about what was happening between him and Larissa, and he didn't want her first reaction to be revulsion.

"She's fine, Mum," he said. "She said to say hello."

Larissa is fine too. More than fine, actually.

"She's a good girl," said Marie, firmly. "I knew it from the moment I met her."

Jamie didn't say anything. Instead, he wandered across the cell, and looked at the photos his mother had arranged on top of the chest of drawers. A small picture in a silver frame caught his eye, and he leant in for a closer look.

His mum, heavily pregnant with him, was leaning back on the bonnet of the dark blue BMW he remembered from when he was very young, a wide smile on her face. The sun was shining from outside the frame, illuminating a bright green row of trees beyond the car, casting the dark silhouette of his dad across the bottom of the photo. The shadow's hand was raised to its face, holding the camera that had recorded the moment.

She looks so happy, Jamie thought, then straightened up and turned back to his mum, as he realised she had said something he hadn't heard.

"What was that, Mum?" he asked, and she rolled her eyes.

"I was saying that Henry came down to see me today," she said. "Did he tell you?"

"Henry?" replied Jamie. "Who's Henry?"

"Henry Seward," answered Marie, the look on her face suggesting that it should have been obvious.

"*Admiral* Seward?" asked Jamie, incredulous. "My commanding officer? Is that who you mean?"

"Of course that's who I mean, Jamie," replied Marie. A look of concern had emerged on her face. "Is something wrong?"

No, nothing wrong. Definitely nothing weird about my boss hanging out with my mum in her cell. Not at all.

"I suppose not," said Jamie. "What did he want?"

"He didn't want anything. He just came down to say hello. He normally pops down about once a week."

"Once a week? Like, *every* week?"

"I've upset you," said Marie, a look of slight panic on her face. The possibility of her son stopping coming to see her was never far from her mind, and was the thing she was most afraid of. "Can we talk about something else?"

Jamie was still attempting to stretch his head round the concept of his mother and Admiral Seward socialising, but he let it go when he heard the nervousness in his mother's voice. He took a deep breath.

"Of course we can, Mum," he said. "What do you want to talk about?"

Marie smiled a broad smile of relief, and floated over on to her bed, apparently so relieved she had avoided a fight with her son that she didn't even realise she was using her vampire abilities in front of him.

"Tell me where you went this evening," she said, settling down on the lilac bedding. "I worry about you, out there with all those monsters. Tell me what you were doing."

Jamie crossed to the rear of the cell, flopped down on to the battered sofa and began to tell his mother about his day.

7

VALENTIN RECEIVES
A VISITOR

CENTRAL PARK WEST AND WEST EIGHTY-FIFTH STREET
NEW YORK, USA

Valentin Rusmanov stood at the floor-to-ceiling window of his study, on the top floor of the Upper West Side mansion he had lived in since its completion in 1895. His ownership of the grand, stately building was, like most aspects of his life, a closely guarded secret.

Throughout the twentieth century, his long existence had required him to take certain steps to avoid attention, including the formation of a number of shell companies to administer his assets. His name appeared nowhere on any document relating to the building and, from the outside, it seemed little different to the other grand apartment buildings that faced Central Park from the west.

It was most similar in design to the Dakota, thirteen blocks to the south, but whereas that famous landmark had been originally designed as sixty-five individual residences, Valentin's building was a single, almost obscenely spacious residence, arranged over seven vast floors, the majority of which were filled with the accumulated spoils of more than four centuries of wealth and influence. The seventh floor contained the suite of rooms in which Valentin slept, to which entrance was expressly forbidden without invitation. The study he was now standing in occupied the north-east corner of the seventh floor, from which the view of the park was nothing short of spectacular.

Valentin looked down at the wide-open space, an oasis of dark corners and shadows amid the blinding lights of Manhattan. The last of the joggers were making their way to the exits, leaving behind them the teenage couples, junkies, muggers and homeless men and women that made up the park's nocturnal population. He watched them, observing their small lives from high above without objection or condemnation. He had never felt disgust, or anger, when he looked at ordinary humans; he had always left such sentiments to his brothers, and to his former master.

Valentin's nose twitched, and a second later his face curdled into a grimace of disgust. He turned away from the window, flew swiftly across his study and landed gracefully in the blue leather armchair that sat behind his wide, dark wood desk. He leant back in the chair, staring expectantly at the door on the other side of the room. A moment later there was a polite knock, and the door slid open just wide enough for Valentin's butler, a skeletal figure in exquisite evening wear, to slip through the gap and into the study.

Lamberton had entered service in the vampire's house in 1901 and immediately demonstrated both impeccable professional ability, and an admirable willingness to ignore the horrors that routinely took place beneath his master's roof; he had served Valentin for forty years as a human, and almost seventy more as a vampire.

His turning had been Lamberton's idea; although Valentin had promised the butler that no harm would come to him while in his employ, a promise the ancient vampire had kept with great dedication, Lamberton had eventually been forced to confront his master with the problem of his advancing years.

After discussing the matter over half a case of 1921 Château Latour, Valentin had reluctantly agreed that no other solution seemed acceptable and, after checking for a final time whether the butler was sure, had bitten Lamberton's throat with the tenderness of a lover, allowing the barest minimum of blood to escape. He had then flown out into the New York night and found a young nurse from Oklahoma who was about to ship out to the battlefields of Europe. He had brought her home and given her to Lamberton, when the turn was complete and the hunger gripped him for the first time. Once the girl was spent, the butler thanked his master, and returned immediately to his duties, duties he had continued to discharge admirably ever since.

Lamberton was now standing silently by the study door, waiting to be acknowledged before he spoke. When Valentin nodded in his direction, he spoke five words that his master had hoped never to hear.

"Your brother is here, sir."

Valentin swore in Wallachian, his eyes flashing momentarily red. Then he regarded Lamberton, and sighed deeply.

"Show him in," he said.

The door was flung wide, and Valeri Rusmanov strode into the study, as Lamberton exited silently. The oldest of the three Rusmanov brothers was wearing simple clothing: a black tunic, heavy woollen trousers and leather boots, and his grey greatcoat. He stopped halfway across the room, and looked around, taking in the opulence of his surroundings with obvious distaste.

Ridiculous old fool, thought Valentin, from behind his desk. *He thinks he's still a general, commanding troops on a battlefield. Pathetic.*

Valentin opened a beautifully carved wooden box and withdrew a red cigarette from the velvet-lined interior. The cigarette contained Turkish tobacco laced liberally with Bliss, the heady mixture of heroin and blood to which he had become mildly addicted over the last three decades. He applied the flame from a wooden match to the tip of the cigarette, then leant back in his chair as Valeri, who had still not spoken since entering the study, paused in front of a shelf containing a glass tank in which three basketballs were floating in a clear solution.

"What do you call this?" asked Valeri, his tone gruff and unfriendly.

"*I* don't call it anything," replied Valentin, forcing himself to remain polite. "The artist called it *Three Ball 50/50 Tank*. It's Jeff Koons."

"And this is art, is it?"

"I would say so."

Valeri turned away from the shelf, waving a hand dismissively at its contents. He crossed the study in three long strides and stood before Valentin's desk, his nose wrinkling at the smell of the smoke from the cigarette in his brother's hand.

"Is that Bliss?" he asked, spitting out the last word.

"Why, yes it is," replied Valentin, opening the box again. "Would you care for one?"

Valeri stared coldly at him.

"Do you have no shame whatsoever?" he asked.

Valentin smiled, drew deeply on his cigarette and exhaled. The smoke floated up into the air in a thick cloud, enveloping Valeri's head as it dispersed.

"Apparently not," he said, lightly.

The two brothers faced each other for a long moment, until eventually Valeri spoke again.

"Our brother is dead," he said. There was no emotion in his voice.

"I know," replied Valentin. "He has been dead for more than three months."

"You don't seem upset by the news."

"Are you?"

Valeri drew himself up, and glared at his brother.

"Alexandru and I differed on a great number of matters," he said, slowly. "But he was still blood, still *our* blood. And now he's gone."

"That's right, he's gone. But we're still here. Isn't life marvellous?"

Valeri grunted, a deep, throaty sound that Valentin thought might be what passed for his brother laughing.

"You call this living?" Valeri asked. "Surrounded by lackeys and boot-lickers, in this castle of decadence?"

"Yes," replied Valentin, and for the first time he failed to keep the steel from his tone. "I do. I also remember the size of your domestic staff in Wallachia, Valeri. There were times when I believe it numbered in the hundreds."

Valeri stiffened.

"I was a different man in those days," he replied.

You were actually a man, thought Valentin. *That was certainly different.*

Valentin got up from behind his desk and walked back to the window that overlooked the park. He motioned for Valeri to join him, and after a long pause, with a look of great reluctance on his lined face, the elder Rusmanov did so. Valeri stood beside his younger brother, and looked out at the towering lights of Manhattan.

"Have you ever been to New York before?" asked Valentin.

"Never," replied Valeri, grimacing. "Until fifteen minutes ago I had never set foot in this sordid place, and I would have preferred for that to remain the case."

"Of course you would. Yours are the dark open spaces, the wilderness of our youth. You are a creature of tradition, Valeri. I don't criticise you for it; I'm merely stating the facts. But mine? Mine are the bright lights, the crowded streets, the noise and the bustle and the life of the city. An American writer once wrote that, 'One belongs to New York instantly, one belongs to it as much in five minutes as in five years.' Well, I've been here for more than a century."

"Why are you telling me this, Valentin?"

The younger vampire sighed, and regarded his brother with a pitying look.

"You always were so literal. Never mind. I assume you have come with word from your master?"

"Our master," said Valeri, his voice like ice.

"Of course. Our master. I apologise."

But Valentin didn't look sorry, not in the slightest. A half-smile played across his lips, causing anger to surge through his older brother. Valeri pushed it down as far as he was able, and focused on the order he had been given.

"He calls you home, Valentin. Your life belongs to him, as it always has, and he calls you home."

Valentin bared his teeth.

"My life is my own," he hissed. "Do you hear me?"

Red spilled into the corners of Valeri's eyes. He took his hands from where they had been crossed behind his back, and let them dangle loosely at his sides.

"I disagree," he said. "As I am confident our master will too."

The two brothers stared at each other, violence pregnant in the still air of the study. Then Valeri smiled broadly, raising his hands in mock placation.

"Enough, brother," he said. "I have no time for posturing, or children's games. I must leave, with or without you. Will you refuse the call of our master, to whom you owe this gilded cage you call a life? Or will you honour him, as you swore you always would, and do your duty now he has returned to us?"

Valentin looked at his brother, and favoured him with a smile of his own.

"Of course I will," he replied. "I will need two days to set my affairs in order, then I'll return home like the dutiful lapdog."

"Your affairs are trivia," replied Valeri. "You are to accompany me tonight."

"In which case, I would remind you of two things," said Valentin, his smile still in place. "Firstly, that you are a guest in my home. And secondly, that I have not been afraid of you for more than five hundred years now."

Valeri took half a step forward, a dangerous look on his face.

"Is that a fact, brother?" he asked, his voice little more than a whisper.

"It is," replied Valentin. "A fact that leaves you with two options. You can allow me to conclude my *trivia* as I see fit, after which I will return home, as I promised. Or you can try to remove me from this house by force, which will result in one of us explaining to your master why we have destroyed the other. So what's it going to be, *brother*?"

90 DAYS TILL
ZERO HOUR

8

THE BIG LEAGUES

Jamie swung his legs out from under his bedding and sat on the edge of his mattress, rubbing his eyes with the heels of his palms.

He had headed straight to his quarters after leaving the detention level, his mind full of relief and his heart heavy with guilt. He always felt bad after seeing his mother; the sight of her in her cell was painful, and filled him with feelings of impotence. But his visits were the only things that she looked forward to, and he would not dream of denying her them. When Alexandru had taken her, he had feared, in his darkest moments, that he was never going to see her again, never going to get the chance to make it up to her, to make amends for being such a bad son. He was not going to fall back into his old pattern of complacency, of taking her for granted, even if the sight of her in her cell made his heart ache and his skin tingle with helpless anger.

She needs me. That's all that matters. And I'm not going to let her down.

The electric clock on his bedside table read 8:55. Jamie hauled himself to his feet and raised his arms above his head, feeling the muscles creak and tremble as they stretched. He shook his head, trying to clear it, but thoughts of his mother refused to leave him.

He grabbed his towel, walked to the shower block at the centre of Level B and climbed into one of the stalls, hoping that the relentless drumming of the water would empty his mind, giving him a few minutes of peace.

Dried and dressed, Jamie sat down at his desk and attempted to review the minutes of the first Zero Hour Task Force meeting. He read the dry, colourless text of the report from start to finish, but realised he was looking at the shapes of the letters rather than taking any sense from the words, and pushed the folder aside. He looked at his watch, and saw that it was time to make his way to the Ops Room.

The prospect filled him with little excitement; the pride he had felt when Admiral Seward summoned him to his office and told him that he was being appointed to the Department's most highly classified Task Force had been short-lived. The Director had immediately made it clear to him that he was only being involved because of his first-hand experience with Alexandru Rusmanov, and that he would be largely expected to speak when he was spoken to. Seward had also warned him that his presence on the Task Force was likely to be unpopular with the more experienced Operators, and this had proven to be an understatement.

Jamie was the second person to arrive for the meeting.

Major Paul Turner glanced up at him as he stepped through the door, then returned his attention to a sheaf of papers splayed across the table before him. Jamie considered saying hello, then decided against it. The Security Officer, who had succeeded the late Thomas Morris in the post, had been among the small group of Operators who had arrived on Lindisfarne after Jamie had destroyed Alexandru Rusmanov. Although they had been too late to help, to prevent the loss of Frankenstein or the turning of his mother, Jamie would always be grateful that they had tried. The reason he held his tongue was very simple: Paul Turner scared the hell out of him.

There never seemed to be anything behind the Major's eyes, no emotion, or empathy. Since Lindisfarne, Jamie had been astonished to learn that Turner was married to Caroline Seward, a union that made him Admiral Seward's brother-in-law. They had a son called Shaun, who was himself a Blacklight Operator, and this Jamie found almost impossible to believe; Turner appeared to him more like a robot than a loving husband and a father.

I can't picture him having dinner with his wife and asking her about her day, or taking his son aside and giving him advice, he thought. *I just can't see it.*

Jamie took the seat opposite Turner, and silently waited for the rest of the Zero Hour Task Force to arrive. Less than a minute later the door to the Ops Room opened, and Operators began to file in and sit down.

Henry Seward took the seat at the head of the table, the Director of Department 19 nodding briefly in Jamie's direction as he did so, then leaning over and engaging in conversation with Paul Turner at a volume too low for Jamie to hear.

Two Operators that Jamie had met for the first time at the previous meeting, men in their early thirties who represented the Science and Intelligence Divisions of Blacklight, walked through the door, deep in conversation, and sat down across from him. Neither so much as glanced in his direction; both had made it abundantly clear that they opposed his presence on the Task Force, and had clearly not changed their minds since the first meeting. Jamie was trying to make sure that the anger he could feel bubbling up in his chest didn't show on his face, when the door opened again, and Jack Williams walked in.

Jamie smiled gratefully at the sight of his friend, who strode across the room and flopped down in the seat beside him.

"All right?" whispered Jack.

"All right," replied Jamie. "How's it going?"

"It's going," smiled Jack. "Yourself?"

"Fine," replied Jamie, feeling his mood lift.

Jack Williams was a descendant of the founders of Blacklight, just like Jamie, and although he was eight years older and had been an Operator for almost four years, he had become one of Jamie's closest friends in the Department. He was widely regarded as the finest young Operator in the Department and a man destined for great things, a viewpoint reinforced by his membership of the Zero Hour Task Force, but he also had an uncanny ability to make Jamie laugh, to make him feel like there could still be light in the middle of all the darkness that surrounded them.

Jack's father was Robert Williams, a veteran Operator who had served Blacklight since the 1970s, and the grandson-in-law of Quincey Harker, the greatest legend of the Department, whose tenure as Director had transformed the organisation into the hi-tech, highly classified unit it was today. Jack's younger brother Patrick was also an Operator, but where Jack was loud and confident, the life of the party and the biggest personality in any room, Patrick was quiet and appeared to be almost pathologically shy.

Jamie had spent a lot of time with the two brothers in the officers' mess, and the differences between them were like night and day. What was even more striking, though, was the fierce love that so clearly existed between them, the loyalty that was utterly beyond question, to which Jamie, an only child, responded with deep admiration, and more than a little jealousy.

Jamie was about to tell Jack that he still appeared to be the

96

unpopular kid in the room when the door opened for the final time, and the last two members of the Zero Hour Task Force arrived.

Colonel Cal Holmwood, Blacklight's Deputy Director and one of its most senior and decorated Operators, was the man who had piloted the *Mina II*, the supersonic Department 19 jet, to Lindisfarne on the night that Frankenstein had been lost, dragged over the steep cliffs by a werewolf whose intention had been to kill Jamie. He had flown survivors back to the Loop after that terrible night was over, and now entered the Ops Room deep in conversation with the man who fascinated Jamie more than any other in the entire Department.

Professor Richard Talbot, the director of the Lazarus Project, was remarkably tall and thin, like a giant stick insect wrapped in a spotless white lab coat. He was in his sixties, his face lined and weathered, his bald head perfectly round, flanked by two strips of grey hair that rested above his ears. The Professor was smiling gently at whatever Cal Holmwood was saying to him; then, as they made their way to opposite sides of the long table, he locked eyes with Jamie, smiling broadly at him. Jamie smiled back, involuntarily; the Professor made him feel something close to star-struck, even though they had only spoken to each other once, as the first meeting of the Zero Hour Task Force had come to its conclusion.

The Lazarus Project was an enigma, even within an organisation as secretive as Department 19.

It had only been officially mentioned once, during Admiral Seward's speech about Dracula; its purpose was unknown, and its laboratories, located on Level F of the Loop, were off-limits to all but the tiny number of senior Operators who possessed the necessary clearance. The Project's staff were rarely seen; their quarters were inside the security perimeter, and they made only occasional appearances in the dining hall or the mess. Nobody even knew how many of them there were. Doctors, scientists, administrative staff: all were hidden away behind an Iron Curtain of secrecy.

So when Professor Talbot had strolled into the inaugural Zero Hour meeting and introduced himself to the rest of the group, there had been a sudden sense of excitement in the room. Talbot was a mystery, whose work was classified far beyond Top Secret, yet the man himself was utterly disarming, friendly and charming to a fault. After the meeting ended, he had fallen into stride beside Jamie as they walked to the lift at the end of the Level 0 corridor.

"Mr Carpenter," he said, his voice deep and warm. "I read the Lindisfarne report. I'm very sorry."

Jamie looked up at him, completely thrown by the fact that this man was talking to him, this man who answered only to Admiral Seward himself.

"Thanks," he managed. "It was a bad night."

Understatement of the bloody year.

"I can't imagine," Talbot replied. "But you should take heart from what you did. The destruction of Alexandru will save hundreds of lives. I'm sure that doesn't feel like any consolation at the moment, but hopefully in time you'll be able to understand that you did something remarkable. And if there's anything I can do to help, please do let me know."

"I will," Jamie replied, his voice thick with confusion. "Thank you."

Talbot smiled, then accelerated away down the corridor, leaving Jamie standing as still as a statue, his face wearing the look of someone who is not completely sure that what has just happened to them was actually real.

*

Since that one brief conversation, Jamie had been fascinated by Professor Talbot; so much so that Larissa, the only person to whom he had described the conversation, had started to use a different word.

Obsessed, thought Jamie. *She says I'm obsessed with him.*

He could understand why she might think so. In the week that had passed since the first Zero Hour meeting, Jamie had asked almost every Operator he had spoken to what they knew about Professor Talbot and the Lazarus Project. The answers he had received had ranged from incredulous demands that he not ask such questions, to wild theories about what was taking place in the Project's sealed laboratories on Level F.

"They're cloning Operators," one earnest civilian contractor had insisted. "They're going to bring back Van Helsing, and Quincey Harker, and all the others. They're going to declare war on the vamps."

Jamie had scoffed, but continued to ask the question, undeterred. Some Operators claimed that it was a weapons project, devising new ways of destroying vampires, while one member of the Science Division swore blind that the Lazarus Project was building a microwave emitter tuned to an electromagnetic frequency that only existed inside the brains of vampires. When it was complete, the scientist promised, all that would be required was the push of a single button, and every vampire in the world would be destroyed, instantly. Jamie asked tens of men, and women, and got tens of different replies, leading him to the only conclusion that could be rationally drawn.

Nobody has a clue what they're doing down there. Not a clue.

"Zero Hour Task Force convened, January 19th," said Admiral Seward. His personal secretary, a small, plump man named Marlow, had positioned himself a deferential distance behind the Director and now began to take minutes, his chubby fingers flying silently across the keys of a portable console. "Second meeting. All members present."

The Director looked at the seven men gathered round the table. "Gentlemen," he continued. "Operational data since the last meeting is as follows. Vampire activity remains heightened, but stable, as do sightings and incidents involving the public that require our involvement. Patrol logs indicate that incidents of the graffiti that was discussed last week continue to occur, in increasing numbers."

Seward nodded to Marlow, who punched a series of keys on his console. The huge high-definition screen that covered the entire wall behind the Director powered up. A series of photographs filled the frame; the same two words, in tens of different colours and handwritings, printed and sprayed on walls and roads and bridges.

HE
RISES

Jamie felt a chill run through him as he looked at the photos. The two words represented the Department's greatest fear, the moment the Task Force had been created to prevent.

Zero Hour.

The vampires knew what was coming, just as surely as Blacklight did; the graffiti was proof of that. But more than that, it seemed to be directly addressed to them, left at the scenes of crimes that only they would be called to.

It seemed to be a challenge.

No, that's not it, thought Jamie. *They're not challenging us. They're mocking us. They don't think we can stop Dracula from rising. And they might well be right.*

"What are our vamp contacts saying?" asked Cal Holmwood.

"Nothing," replied Paul Turner. "Less than that in fact. Most of them have disappeared, and the ones that haven't won't talk. They know what's coming."

"We should stake them all," said the Operator from the Intelligence Division. "What use are they if they won't talk?"

"Absolutely none, Mr Brennan," agreed Turner. "But still more than they would be dead. Circumstances change."

"I don't get it," pressed Brennan. "If Dracula rises, if it's as bad as everyone thinks, they're going to lose everything too. Why don't they help us stop it?"

"Because they don't think we can," replied Turner, evenly. "Stop it, I mean. And whatever may happen if Dracula rises, the one thing they can be sure of is that helping us is not going to make them popular."

Operator Brennan stared at Turner with a look that suggested he had more he wanted to say, but he held his tongue.

"Fine," said Admiral Seward. "Paul, keep at them, but I don't think you'll have much luck, as you said. I spoke to the SPC this morning and they assured me they're doing all they can, so let's—"

"All they can?" said Jamie, without thinking. "Apart from not losing the remains in the first place, you mean?"

Seven pairs of eyes swung in his direction, and Jamie swallowed hard.

"Sorry," he said. "It's just frustrating. Nobody knew they had them, so there was nothing we could do to make sure they were safe."

"I knew the SPC had the remains," said Seward, coolly. "As did the other Directors. What would you have had us do?"

Jamie looked at the Director for a long moment, then dropped his eyes. "I don't know, sir," he said. "I'm sorry, sir."

Seward's face softened. "I don't like it any more than you, Lieutenant Carpenter. Clearly, there are lessons to be learnt from what has happened, for all of us. But we have to play the hand we've been dealt, to the best of our abilities. So, on that note, and because I'd like to keep this meeting as short as humanly possible, if there is nothing—"

"I don't like it either," interrupted Operator Brennan, scowling at Jamie. "I don't like any part of this. And I still don't see why some kid who isn't even old enough to wear the uniform gets a say in this just because his surname is Carpenter."

Jamie felt his face flush with anger. He opened his mouth to reply, saw Seward do the same and was surprised when someone beat them both to it.

"Mr Brennan," said Professor Talbot. "Have you ever seen a Priority Level 1 vampire?"

"What does that have to—"

"This young man," continued Talbot, glancing at Jamie, "has not only seen one, but faced it down and destroyed it. Compared to every vampire *you* have ever seen, Operator Brennan, Alexandru Rusmanov might as well have been a different species; a natural disaster made flesh, like a hurricane, and Mr Carpenter destroyed him. He is the only living soul to have destroyed a Priority 1. *That's* why he's here. Because what Alexandru was to normal vampires, so Dracula will be to Alexandru if he is allowed to rise, and I for one will want Mr Carpenter on our side if that happens. Is that clear enough for you?"

Jamie looked at Professor Talbot, stunned. He had not expected his defence to come from the most unknown quantity in the Department.

Sometimes I forget about Alexandru. He had my mum, so for me it was simple. I forget how big a deal it is to everyone else.

"There you have it," said Admiral Seward. "Couldn't have said it better myself. Anyone else have any more questions they want to ask, or speeches they'd like to make? No? Well, thank heaven for small mercies."

He stood up from the table, and the rest of the group followed his lead.

"I would remind you, one more time," said the Director. "Everything that has been said here is only for the ears of the men in this room. Any violation of this very simple instruction will be considered a court-martial offence. I ask you all not to force me to make good on that promise. Dismissed."

9

NO STONE UNTURNED

STAVELEY, NORTH DERBYSHIRE

Matt Browning shoved his chair back from his desk and rubbed his eyes with the heels of his palms. He had been in front of his computer for more than thirty of the last forty-eight hours, and his eyes were killing him.

He walked out of his bedroom, stuck his head into his little sister's room, waited until he heard the gentle rise and fall of her breathing, then made his way downstairs to the kitchen. As he passed the door to the front room, he heard his father swear at the television, berating an offside decision he had clearly not agreed with. At the table in the small dining room that was attached by French doors to the back of the living room, he could hear his mother on the phone to her sister, talking with quiet animation about a minor celebrity who had left her equally minor celebrity fiancé at the altar. It was evidently quite the scandal.

In the kitchen, Matt poured himself a glass of water and leant against one of the counters. He doubted that anyone in the world knew as much about vampires as he had learnt in the two months since he had been returned home.

*

Matt knew, as he sat in the back of the car with the blacked-out windows that was taking him home, that the first few moments of his return were going to be crucial. If he was going to be believed, if his parents were going to accept, as the doctor at the base had, that he could remember nothing of what had happened to him, then he was going to have to play his hand perfectly.

The doctor was so pleased with his recovery from the coma that his apparent amnesia had been almost an afterthought. Tests were carried out, a great number of them, but Matt realised quickly that the doctor had been convinced that he would emerge from his coma with significant brain damage, and that lent him the courage to lie with conviction. He picked a point four days before the incident in his parents' garden, and stuck resolutely to his claim that he could remember nothing since then. He feigned frustration, and concern for the state of his memory; he summoned tears of apparent confusion and fear, while the doctor had held his hand and told him it was all going to be all right.

There was one brief, terrifying moment when the nurse suggested a polygraph test to assess whether there might be recoverable memories, to check whether, in effect, Matt was lying without meaning to. But the doctor rounded angrily on her, and told her that the boy had been through enough. The nurse, chastened, apologised for the suggestion, and Matt breathed a little easier.

He stood on the doorstep of his parents' small house for several minutes, the letter he had been told to give them in his hand, as he prepared himself to give his performance. Then he rang the doorbell, and waited until his father answered. In the end, very little was required of him; he had barely begun a stuttering, rambling apology when his father interrupted it by wrapping him into a crushing bear hug and dragging him inside the house.

Greg Browning carried him into the kitchen, set him down, then flopped into one of the battered plastic chairs. His eyes were bulging and he was clutching at his chest, and for one terrible moment Matt was sure his father was having a heart attack. Then a great sob burst from Greg Browning's mouth, and the tension in his body evaporated as he began to cry. He grabbed for the phone, tears pouring down his cheeks, his gaze fixed on Matt as he found the handset and dialled a number with trembling fingers; it was as though he feared that if he averted his eyes for even a second, his son might disappear again. Then a voice answered the phone, and Greg's face had crumpled into a blubbery mess of tears and snot as he told his wife that their son had come home.

Matt's mother arrived the following morning, on the first train west. Matt assumed, although he didn't say anything out loud, that she and his father had been fighting, and his mum had gone to visit Matt's aunt in Sheffield. She carried his sister through the front door, yelling Matt's name until she saw him, and fell silent. The look on her face was indescribable, to Matt at least; the sight of it had brought instant tears to his eyes. Then his mum started to cry as well. She put his sister carefully down on the sofa, then wrapped her arms round him so tightly that he wondered whether she was ever planning to let him go.

That evening, the three of them sat in their front room, and had the only conversation they would ever have about the night he had been lost. Sticking to his story was easy; his parents were so overcome with relief that he had been returned to them that they never even entertained the thought that he might know more than he was saying. When they were finished talking, Matt's dad silently handed him the letter he had brought home with him.

106

"You should see this," he said.

Matt took it from his father, unfolded it and read it.

Mr and Mrs Browning,

The incident in which your son sustained injury remains a matter of the highest national security. You are hereby instructed not to discuss the incident with any other party; doing so will be considered an act of treason, and appropriate action will be taken. Acceptance of this letter constitutes acceptance of this instruction.

Your son has received all appropriate medical care, and his recuperation is progressing well. If he develops further medical problems, you should inform medical personnel that he suffered a myocardial infarction due to sudden rapid blood loss. You should not discuss with anyone the circumstances surrounding his injury.

Matt handed the letter back to his father, and told them he was going to bed. And the very next morning, his parents began the long process of trying to forget that any of it had ever happened.

He didn't even blame them, not really; the girl, the helicopter and the men in the black uniforms holding guns did not fit into the small lives his parents had carved out for themselves in their quiet corner of the world. He supposed they had known, in some abstract way, that there were things out there beyond the end of their suburban street that were wild, and dangerous, that might defy explanation, but they had been perfectly happy for such things to stay where they were. Football, and reality TV, and lager, and celebrity magazines – these were things they could understand, could hold on to and relate to. Not girls who healed before their eyes, then tore their son's throat out on their back lawn, before soldiers told them it had never happened, the implicit threat obvious to all.

The darkness the world contained had been thrust upon them; they had not looked for it. And now that the darkness had receded, now that their son had been returned to them and they had been able to largely rebuild the lives they had been living before, they were gradually allowing themselves to believe it had never happened at all. He understood their position, and didn't judge it. It was fine for them.

It was not fine for him.

Matt's brain swooped and swirled round new ideas, gravitating hungrily towards anything he didn't know; it was an all-consuming thirst for knowledge, for all knowledge, from how his mother's Dyson worked to what would happen if you were able to stand on the event horizon of a black hole. In his mind, there was no distinction between the two; knowledge was knowledge, every bit of it as valuable and satisfying as the next.

To call him intelligent would be insufficient; Matt Browning was possessed of an intellect so powerful it would technically be classified as genius. He was as skilled at hiding this intelligence from his family as he was from the bullies at school, who he knew would target him even more viciously if he revealed how much cleverer he was than all of them. He yearned for a time, which he fervently believed would one day come, when he would no longer need to hide who he was, when his intellect would be admired rather than reviled.

Without his parents' knowledge, he had submitted an application to Cambridge the previous autumn, and received an unconditional offer to attend after a phone interview he had also kept secret. He was due to begin his studies in less than a year, and it had become the only thing that mattered to him, the only thing that kept him getting out of bed every morning. Until the girl landed in their

108

garden, and he woke up in a hospital bed, with his throat bandaged and his head full of vampires.

He was now consumed by a burning need to understand what had happened to him. It felt like his entire view of the universe had suddenly been revealed to be a peephole in a hotel room door, a door that had suddenly been flung open in front of him, making him realise how tiny his understanding had been, how small his world really was.

From an encyclopaedia page he learnt about the origins of vampire mythology, learnt the cultural and social theories that had been applied to the idea of such a creature in the centuries since Bram Stoker had crystallised the legends and folk tales of eastern Europe. He read scientific theories, proto-feminist theories, theories of vampires as a metaphor for AIDS, deconstructionist theories, Freudian and Jungian theories, and an American professor's theory that vampires represented the nascent anti-Semitism in the western world.

He read *Dracula*, marvelling at its epistolary structure even as the story thrilled him; he held his breath as Van Helsing staked poor doomed Lucy Westenra, as Renfield's madness offered clues to the Count's whereabouts. He felt his heartrate surge as the heroes chased Dracula into the Transylvanian mountains, felt triumph as the evil monster was stabbed through his undead heart, and a terrible sense of loss as Quincey Morris made the ultimate sacrifice for the sake of his friends.

He read what felt like hundreds of adolescent vampire websites, where teenage girls called themselves Raven and Bloodwynd and wrote excruciatingly lustful prose about pale, mysterious, uniformly beautiful boys who could make them live forever with a single kiss from their wine-red lips.

He read blogs by people who genuinely believed they were vampires, people who claimed to drink blood and eat no food, who claimed to be able to influence people and animals to do their bidding, and even on occasion claimed the ability to turn into a bat or a wolf. These had piqued his interest for a short while, until it became clear that in almost every case the author was either desperately lonely or mentally ill, in some cases obviously quite severely.

He read dozens of websites created by people who believed vampires were real, believed it with such longing and such desperate hope that he found their sites almost painful to read. He scoured page after page of alleged sightings, of shadows in graveyards and alleyways, of people who appeared to be casting no reflection in a shop window at night, of neat pairs of circular puncture wounds, of strange men and women with pale skin who appeared to float above the ground.

He read, and read, and read, and he found nothing that in any way resembled what had happened in his garden, or the place he had spent a month of his life.

Matt finished his water and placed the glass on the draining board. He was physically exhausted but, as usual, his brain would not stop whirring. He was sure that somewhere out there was what he was looking for, something that would reinforce what he had been through; he just had to find it. He would get some sleep, and start again in the morning.

He walked back up the stairs and into his bedroom. His computer monitor glowed in the dark, and he was about to reach over and turn it off when he saw an instant messenger box in the bottom right corner of the screen. He clicked on it, watched it expand into the middle of the monitor and read the contents.

Matt's heart leapt in his chest. He quickly clicked REPLY, but whoever had sent the message was no longer online. He clicked the link in the subject line, and his browser filled the screen, loading a white page with four lines of text and a grey box with a SUBMIT button next to it. He read the text, trembling slightly with excitement.

ATTENTION: If you have arrived at this page in error, please click BACK on your browser immediately. If you have been directed to this page, do NOT submit your password. Leave this page immediately, enter the URL into an IP masking service and then enter your password.

Matt could hardly contain himself.

This was the most promising lead he had found in almost two solid months of searching, a page that told you to hide your whereabouts before entering it, that insisted you leave if you had not been invited.

Why would they want us to hide our IP addresses, unless they've got information they don't want anyone to be able to trace?

Matt closed the window, then opened a new one and typed in the URL of a site that allowed you to browse the internet under a fake IP address; he had used it in the past to watch TV shows that were restricted to the US, and within a minute he was safely behind a dummy IP that would make him appear to be a user from Charlotte, North Carolina. He pasted the link from the message into the browser and hit ENTER. The same white page with the warnings and the empty white box appeared; this time he entered the string of letters and numbers that had been sent to him, clicked SUBMIT and waited. The page loaded, and Matt audibly gasped in the darkness of his bedroom.

The site that opened up in front of his eyes had no title, had wasted no time on fancy designs or technology, but its purpose was immediately obvious; it was a site devoted to the belief that vampires were real, and at large in Britain. At the top of the page was a greeting, and a warning.

Welcome. If you are here, it is where you are meant to be.

We recommend that you vary the IP masking service you use, and delete your browser's history and cache each time you visit us. It is no exaggeration to say that they are watching – it is up to you to minimise how brightly you appear on their radar. Click here to learn more about Echelon, and how you can work around it.

Matt was about to click on the link, when he noticed the headline in the site's main panel, and a chill ran through his body. Below the greeting was a menu, simple black text on a white background, like the rest of the page.

HISTORY   SIGHTINGS   COVER-UPS   THE MEN IN
BLACK   ETYMOLOGY   PROTECTION

Beneath the menu were a headline, a short article and the top few centimetres of a photograph.

112

MEN IN BLACK CAPTURED ON FILM?

Is this the first real photographic evidence of the existence of the men in black? It was sent to us by an anonymous source, on the same date we received a number of reports of vampire activity in north-west London. Note the purple visors, and the unmarked uniforms and vehicle.

Matt scrolled quickly down to look at the entire photo. What he saw made him feel like crying.

The photo was blurry; it looked like it had been taken with a long lens by someone in a hurry, someone who didn't want to be seen with a camera in their hand. It showed a nondescript suburban street at night, the rows of houses almost identical to one another, the cars parked in front of them Japanese and German, the gardens neatly tended. It had been raining when the photo was taken; water was running along the kerbs and rushing into a drain opening.

In the middle of the frame was a black van, parked in front of a driveway and directly under a streetlight, its rear doors open. Matt squinted at the photo and saw that the article's author was correct; he could not see a licence plate above the vehicle's rear bumper. Beside the open doors were three figures, and it was the sight of two of them that had sent a great wave of relief pouring through him.

They're real. It was real. It all really happened.

Two of the figures were dressed all in black, a matt material that didn't reflect the amber glow of the streetlight. They were wearing black shapes on their heads, and both had an unmistakable blob of purple where their faces should have been.

Visors. Purple visors.

The two black shapes were pushing the third, a scrawny figure wearing jeans and a white T-shirt, into the open doors of the van.

113

The third figure didn't seem to be struggling; Matt looked closer, then drew in a sharp breath. The black figure nearest the camera had something in its right hand, a dark oblong that was pressed between the shoulder blades of the person being loaded into the van. He scrolled down, but there were no more pictures. Matt let go of his mouse, sat back in his chair and put his hands over his face.

It had really happened. People knew.

The photo on his computer monitor was blurry evidence that he hadn't lost his mind, that it hadn't all been some vivid coma dream. No matter what his parents were allowing themselves to believe, he knew now that he was right.

It was real. Which meant the boy who had spoken to him after he woke from his coma was real. And now he had found the first step on the path to a wider world.

Matt clicked on **SIGHTINGS**, and began to read. The experiences, page after page of them, bore such similarity to his own that he almost began to feel annoyed that so many other people had grasped at the edges of this strange world; it seemed to render his own experience less unique. He chastised himself for such petulance, and read on.

The details of the accounts were different, as were the locations; they came from as far afield as Dover and Aberdeen, and almost every part of the British Isles in between. There were reports from several European countries, of similar figures operating in Romania, France, Germany and Hungary. But in all cases the key points remained constant: figures dressed all in black, their faces covered by purple visors, unmarked black vans, helicopters where no helicopter should ever be seen. And they all ended in the same way, with a warning to tell no one what they had seen. Matt shivered at the memory of the last thing the men in black had said to his father, as his own blood pumped out across his chest.

This never happened. Do you understand?

He understood all right. But he no longer cared. Because it *had* happened, and he was damned if he was going to pretend otherwise. He scrolled back up to the greeting at the top of the page and clicked the link in the final sentence. A new page opened, a short paragraph followed by an incredibly long list of words.

THE ECHELON MONITORING SYSTEM
The British government, along with every other government in the world, monitors electronic communication between its citizens. This is NOT speculation, or paranoia; this is standard military and security service procedure. Emails and mobile phone calls are run through powerful computers and scanned for words that feature on a flagged list, a list that is updated on a daily basis as new threats emerge. Below is the most recent list of Echelon flagged words that we have. Be aware that just because you do not see a word on this list does not mean it has not been flagged. For safety, only communicate sensitive information in person or via landline telephones. And be aware that even those methods are far from secure if the government decides to take an interest in you. Keep your ears open.

Matt scanned the list quickly. Most of the words on it were what he would have expected, overtly provocative phrases like bomb, plot, cell, jihad, terror, martyr, suicide, Afghanistan, Al Qaeda. But interspersed among the obvious words were several that seemed out of place, unless you had seen the things that Matt had seen: purple, black, visor, uniform, teeth, flying, bite, throat, blood...

Vampire.

The word was there, in black and white. Matt said it out loud, letting it roll off his tongue, as he had in the quiet of the infirmary when the doctor had left him alone.

"Vampire. Vampire."

A grin spread across his face; the tiredness that had been threatening to overwhelm him only five minutes earlier was gone. He felt energised, like he had put his finger against a live wire. His skin was prickly, and his brain was fizzing with new questions and ideas.

One idea in particular.

He settled into his chair to read the rest of the site, knowing deep down that he had already decided what he was going to do.

10

SLEEPLESS NIGHT

Greta Schuler tiptoed down the staircase of her family's farmhouse, taking care to avoid the third-to-last step, the one that always creaked. Her sleep had been fitful, full of bad dreams, and for an unsteady, wavering moment she had been unsure whether the noise she had heard had been real or imagined. But then it had come again, a deep rumble from the direction of the north field, and she sat upright in her bed, drawing the covers round her.

It was cold in her bedroom; she could see her breath in the air. She waited for the noise to come again, and when it didn't, she climbed out of bed, crossed the cold wood of her bedroom floor in her bare feet, pulled on her boots and her thick woollen coat and set out to investigate. For a second or two, she considered waking her parents, but decided against it; days on the farm were long and tiring, and they needed their rest. And besides, Greta was almost twelve years old, and a country girl; she had run off countless stray dogs and foxes, and even the occasional wolf.

At the foot of the stairs she eased her father's shotgun out of

117

the umbrella stand that stood beside the heavy front door, took the battered black torch down from the shelf on the wall, then gripped the brass door handle and slowly, centimetre by centimetre, pulled it towards her. The door creaked once, ominously loudly, then settled, and slid open. A blast of cold air whistled through the gap between the door and its frame and Greta shivered, her skin breaking out in gooseflesh. She pulled her coat tighter round herself, and slipped out into the night.

On the doorstep she broke open her father's gun and checked that it was loaded. She saw the bronze discs and red tubes of the cartridges lying in place, snapped the gun shut and looked around the wide farmyard that lay before the house. Snow covered every centimetre of the ground, shining silver beneath the light of the full moon that hung in the night sky above her head, light that illuminated a long streak of something dark. It ran across the yard, from the thick woods bordering the gravel track that led to the main road, to the wooden gate of the north field that stood beside the farmhouse. Greta stared at it, feeling fear crawl momentarily into her stomach before she pushed it away, then flicked on the torch and stepped forward.

She gasped as the beam fell across the streak. In the yellow light of the torch, it glistened a dark, shiny red. She could see steam rising from it, tendrils of pale mist spiralling up into the night sky, and she knew immediately what she was looking at.

Blood. A lot of blood. Freshly spilled too.

Fear rose through her, and this time she was unable to make it retreat. But she did not go back inside to wake her parents, even though she knew she should. She was her father's daughter, stubborn and fiercely independent; she would not ask for help unless it was absolutely necessary, and she would rather die than admit there was anything that frightened her. So she stepped away from the door, her boots crunching the thick snow beneath her feet, and headed towards the north field.

As she approached it, the torch beam wavering unsteadily before her, she saw that the heavy wooden gate was standing open; the snow at its base was swirled into drifts and ridges, and smeared thickly with blood. The smell of the steaming liquid hit her nose as she leant in to look at the gatepost, and she retched. The heavy chain that was slung round the post every night by the last farmhand to leave was lying in the snow, its links bent and twisted open. As Greta shone the torch into the field, her heart beating rapidly beneath her narrow chest, she forced herself not to think about how much strength it would have taken to bend steel as though it was cardboard.

Her torch beam picked out a large shape on the far side of the field. She stepped through the gate, taking care not to stand in the cooling red liquid, and headed towards it. She was halfway across the field before her torch cast enough light for her to realise what she was looking at.

The cattle that grazed the north field were huddled together in its furthest corner, packed tightly together like sardines. Greta, who had been around livestock since she was old enough to stand, had never seen anything like it before. The animals were shifting constantly in the cold night air, taking half-steps backwards and forwards, their heads up, their eyes wide discs of white. As she approached, the herd let out a long, deep rumble of noise, and she stopped.

They're warning me not to come any closer. Something has scared them half to death.

Greta turned away from the frightened cattle and followed her own footsteps back to the gate. She looked along the long smear of blood, to where it disappeared into the pitch-black of the woods.

She was shaking now, partly from the cold, partly from fear, and she followed the trail of gore with short, hesitant steps. When she was three metres away from the treeline, her bravery failed her, and she stood, rooted to the spot, staring into the woods.

Then a growl, so deep and low that Greta felt it vibrate through the bones in her legs, sounded from somewhere in front of her, and her breath froze in her lungs. The shotgun fell softly to the snow at her feet, as she heard something move through the trees. Then two yellow eyes appeared in the darkness, floating high above her head, at least two metres from the ground. Slowly, they moved towards her, and a shape emerged from between the trees.

Standing in front of Greta was the biggest wolf she had ever seen.

It squatted in the darkness, its enormous head peering down at her, its mouth and snout soaked with crimson, its thick neck attached to a body the size of her father's Land Rover. Its fur was greyish-green, and its flanks and back were horribly misshapen; ridges of bone rose and fell beneath the creature's skin, its legs were crooked and bent, and a vast patchwork of scar tissue criss-crossed the animal's hide, jagged white lines shining out from the fur in the light of the full moon. Behind the wolf's bloodstained head something glistened, and Greta saw two angular shapes emerging from the skin, shining in the night air.

Metal, she thought, her mind reeling. *It's got metal sticking out of its neck.*

The growl came again, accompanied by a blast of warm air and the coppery scent of blood. She gagged, staring helplessly up at the wolf, which was regarding her with a look that was fearsome, but also appeared curiously sad; the corners of its wide yellow eyes were turned down, its lips drawn back against its razor-sharp teeth in what looked like a grimace of pain.

You can't outrun it. You can't fight it. Your only chance is to make it realise you're not a threat.

Greta took a deep breath, and looked into the wolf's eyes.

"Hello," she said, her voice trembling. "My name's Greta."

The wolf recoiled instantly, as though it had been stung by a hornet. It took half a step backwards, then threw back its head and let loose a deafening howl, an ear-splitting cry of misery and pain. Behind Greta, the light in her parents' bedroom came on, and the sound of heavy boots on wooden stairs echoed across the farmyard. But Greta neither saw nor heard; she was staring, transfixed, at the monstrous creature in front of her. As the howl died away, the wolf opened its mouth again, and made a sound that Greta recognised. Her eyes widened, and she took an involuntary step towards the wolf, her arms rising before her in placation.

The roar of a shotgun thundered through the night air, and the snow at the wolf's feet exploded. Greta shrieked as the wolf bolted into the woods, so quickly that she could have believed it had never been there at all. Then she saw the thick streak of blood where it had been standing, and realisation flooded through her. She heard shouted voices and running footsteps behind her, before her eyes rolled in her head and she crumpled towards the ground. Arriving at a flat sprint, Peter Schuler threw his shotgun aside, slid across the snow, shoved his hands under her back as she fell and wrapped his daughter in his arms.

In the kitchen at the rear of the farmhouse, Greta's father sat at the battered wooden table that dominated the room. He was sipping a mug of thick black coffee that his wife had made him once she had finished putting their daughter back to bed. She was now watching him silently, leaning against the stove beneath the window, her expression unreadable.

Standing around the kitchen, equally silent, were three of the Schuler farmhands, whom Peter had roused from sleep when he returned to the house. They had come uncomplainingly, and were leaning against the walls, sipping coffees of their own, shotguns broken over their forearms, watching their employer struggling to control his temper.

Peter Schuler was full of a fury beyond anything he had ever known.

He was trying to rationalise the events of the night. Peter had spent his entire life on the farm he now owned, had worked it for his father until Hans Schuler had succumbed to the cancer that had eaten him away before his son's eyes, had married his wife and raised his daughter there. As a result, he believed he understood animals, both domestic and wild, as well as anyone, and better than most. And he knew that was all the wolf was; a wild animal that had wandered into the Schulers' territory, incapable of malice, or viciousness. But it had been standing over his daughter, his maddening, arrogant, beautiful daughter, standing over her with its teeth bared, its shadow swallowing her, and he had never wanted to kill another living thing as much as he did right now.

The wolf had scared Greta terribly. He had been carrying her back to the house, shouting for his wife to bring blankets as he did so, when she had suddenly stiffened in his arms, then screamed so loudly that he almost dropped her. When the scream had died away, she began to sob against his shoulder, her small body trembling. She was still shaking as his wife tucked her blankets tightly back round her, mumbling nonsense about the wolf being made of metal, insisting that it had spoken to her, that it had said "Help me" as she stood beneath its blood-soaked muzzle, waiting for it to tear her throat out.

"What do you want to do, boss?" It was Franck who asked, the farm's head wrangler, a soft-spoken bear of a man. He was looking steadily at Greta's father, waiting to be told what to do.

"Get your coats," Peter replied, and a minute later the four men were marching across the farmyard, their guns slung over their shoulders.

Peter led them to the spot at the edge of the woods where the wolf had loomed over Greta, then took a deep breath and followed the trail of blood into the trees. Lars and Sebastian, brothers who had worked the Schuler farm since they were fourteen, walked steadily behind him, with Franck bringing up the rear.

The snow crunched beneath their heavy boots as they tracked the wolf through the forest. The animal was not hard to follow; it had left a trail of paw prints the size of dinner plates, and a long corridor of flattened bushes and broken branches that stood out in the yellow light of the men's torches. Eventually, the forest widened into a clearing, and the men's eyes widened as they entered it. The small, circular gap in the trees looked like the inside of an abattoir.

In the middle, strewn across the snowy forest floor, were the last identifiable remains of one of Peter Schuler's cattle. A horn lay in a puddle of blood and offal, a hoof and a thick piece of the animal's hide thrown to one side. Blood covered the ground, studded with steaming chunks of meat, through which the wolf had tracked its giant paws. The four men standing at the edge of the trees were hard country men, but the violence that had taken place in the clearing shook them to their cores.

"Shoot on sight," said Peter Schuler, softly. The men swung their shotguns from their shoulders, racked them with trembling hands, then followed the enormous footprints deeper into the darkness of the forest.

An hour later, with dawn creeping above the horizon to the east, four shivering men emerged from the trees at the edge of the road that led south to Bremen. The tracks had continued in a straight line, until they finally stopped a metre in front of where the men were standing. They disappeared in a wide circle of disturbed snow that looked as though a group of men had been wrestling in it. The snow, and the frozen earth beneath it, had been churned and tossed and thrown in every direction. On the other side of the circle a new set of tracks led away from the circle, parallel to the road. The men stepped carefully round the disturbance, and looked down at the new trail.

"My God," whispered Lars, and crossed himself.

Stretching away before them was a series of enormous human footprints.

"I don't understand," said Sebastian. "I don't—"

"Quiet," hissed Peter. "The Langers' farm is just over that rise. Let's move."

The four men marched quickly alongside the footprints. After five minutes or so, the grey roof of the farmhouse where Kurt Langer, Peter Schuler's oldest friend, lived with his family appeared above the top of the slope they were climbing, and Peter accelerated, urging his men to keep up with him.

I hope we're not too late. Please don't let us be too late.

They hurried over the rise, and Peter's heart sank. Even from thirty metres away he could see the footprints leading through the front gate on to the Langers' property, towards the farmhouse where the family would normally now be waking up. He shouted for his men to follow him, and took off running down the slope, skidding and sliding as his boots fought for purchase through the thick snow. He grabbed the gatepost, steadied himself and then paused, examining the ground.

There were two sets of footprints, running parallel to each other, in opposite directions. One led into the Langers' yard, and the second, the heavy treads of winter boots, led back towards the road.

Too late, too late, too late.

Peter shoved the gate wide and lurched into the yard, heading towards the front door of the house, his shotgun at his shoulder. He was about to yell for the Langers, horribly sure that he would receive no reply, when he stopped again.

To his left, running between a low branch of the oak tree that stood at the edge of the farmyard and a brass hook inserted into the wall of the house, was a thick nylon washing line. Fluttering from it in the bright morning air were a number of heavy garments: plaid shirts, long johns, thermal socks and undershirts. But half the line was empty, and beneath it, scattered on the snowy ground, were a handful of wooden pegs. The first row of footprints ran beneath the line, then to the back step of the house. The second started there, a row of boot prints leading back towards the road.

A hand fell on Peter Schuler's shoulder, and he jumped. But it was only Franck, his big, gentle face staring at Peter's, his gun lowered at his side.

"You need to see this, boss," said the head wrangler, jerking a thumb towards the road.

The four men gathered at the edge of the tarmac, looking down at their feet. The last of the prints were etched neatly into the snow, alongside the tracks of a set of heavy-duty winter tyres.

A truck. Four-wheel drive. Probably a pick-up, like the one in the barn at home.

The tracks formed a shallow semi-circle where the driver had brought his vehicle to a halt at the side of the road, before accelerating back on to the highway. There were no more footprints, in any direction.

"I'll ring Karl," said Lars. "He can bring the truck up here. We can follow it."

Peter shook his head. "No," he replied. "It's gone. Whatever it was, it's gone. Ring Karl, and tell him to come and pick us up. I'll call Kurt later and tell him what happened. Let's go home."

An hour to the south, a battered red pick-up truck chugged steadily along the motorway. The driver, a round, red-faced man in a heavy woollen jacket and an ancient deerstalker hat, watched the road ahead of him, a short cigar clamped between his teeth. On the passenger seat beside him sat a plastic flask of coffee laced with cherry brandy, from which he was taking regular sips.

Behind him, in the truck's flatbed, shivering beneath the pile of animal hides that the driver was taking south to market, his sleeping face a mask of contorted misery and confusion, lay Frankenstein's monster.

11

THE BARE BONES

Jamie was about to open the door to his quarters when he felt the console on his belt beep three times, signalling a message that had been unread for more than thirty minutes.

His mind was reeling with everything he had just seen, everything he had just been told, and he was struggling to understand the implications of it.

I can't believe I got to see that, he thought. *I can't believe Talbot let me. It's amazing.*

Jamie had turned off the beeper during the Zero Hour Task Force meeting, left it off during the unbelievable, mind-bending twenty minutes that followed it, twenty minutes that he knew he could never tell anyone about, not even Larissa, and had only just switched it back on. He pulled it free of its loop, swearing loudly in the empty corridor, and read the short line of text that had appeared on the screen.

G-17/OP_EXT_L2/LIVE_BRIEFING/BR2/1130

The Department 19 shorthand had become second nature.

The first set of letters and numbers was the designation of his squad, G-17, and the second told him that they had been given an external operation with a Level 2 priority. The third was self-explanatory, that there would be a live briefing rather than data supplied to them once they were already on the move, the fourth was the location of the briefing, in this case Briefing Room 2, and the final set of numbers were the time that the briefing would begin. Jamie checked his watch, and saw that it was 11:28. He swore, then ran back down the corridor towards the silver doors of the Level B lift.

On Level 0 he piled out of the lift and ran along the corridor that served as the level's central thoroughfare. On one side, accessible by the heavy yellow and black striped doors that stood at regular intervals, was the huge hangar that served as the embarkation point for all Blacklight operations. On the opposite side of the corridor, filling the other half of the huge circular level, were the suites of offices and rooms that comprised the Department's Communications and Surveillance Divisions.

The Ops Room, where Jamie had just been, sat in the middle of the corridor, and therefore at the centre of Level 0. Beyond it, along a series of semi-circular corridors, like the layers of an onion, stood offices, server farms and inventories, accessible by security-coded doors set into the long wall.

Jamie pressed his ID against the sensor beside one of the doors marked BRIEFING ROOMS, pulled it open and raced down the corridor. He skidded to a halt outside the door to Briefing Room 2 and walked through it, as calmly as he was able.

The room was a curved box, much like a classroom. At one end, to the right as Jamie entered, beneath a high-definition screen that filled most of the wall, stood a lectern, from where the briefings were given. Jamie looked immediately in its direction, and felt his heart sink.

Standing behind the lectern was Major Paul Turner.

Great, thought Jamie. *That's just great. He knows I was in the Zero Hour meeting, and he knows I can't say so in front of the rest of them.* Then a smile threatened to rise on his face. *He doesn't know where I went afterwards, though.*

"Good of you to join us, Mr Carpenter," said Turner, staring at him. "I hope we haven't interrupted whatever you were doing. I've no doubt it was extremely important."

You've no idea, thought Jamie. *No idea at all.*

There was a giggle from his left, and he felt his face flush with heat. He turned to see who had laughed; it had not been Kate or Larissa, and they were the only other people he was expecting to see in the room. But he immediately saw that he had assumed wrongly; five faces were staring at him, not two.

Sitting at one desk were Kate and Larissa, the former regarding him with a stern look, the latter with a mischievous little smile. Two desks away, a distance that was clearly deliberate, sat three more Operators, two of whom Jamie recognised immediately; the third was a girl in her early twenties whom he had heard a lot about, but had never met. She was smiling widely at him; it had clearly been her who had laughed.

The three Operators made up Operational Squad F-7, commanded by Lieutenant Jack Williams. Jamie's friend smiled at him from across the room, and Jamie returned it with an uncertain one of his own.

What the hell are you three doing here? he wondered.

Sitting beside Jack, Shaun Turner's face regarded Jamie with wide grey eyes that were as expressionless as his father's. He was tall, taller than Jamie or Jack, and broad, the naturally powerful figure of a rugby player. He sat easily in his chair, waiting for Jamie to say something.

The girl, who Jamie knew from Jack's fervent, fluttery descriptions was called Angela Darcy, was still smiling at him, and as he looked at her, actually *looked* at her, he was struck by how remarkably attractive she was. Her blonde hair was darker than Kate's, almost a golden colour, and her face was sharp and angular, drawn in straight lines by a hugely talented artist. He knew from Jack that she had been an SIS agent, recruited out of Oxford in her first year, and had served with distinction in some of the most unstable and dangerous backwaters of the globe. She apparently spoke at least six languages, and was an expert in the art of wetwork – assassinations and state-sanctioned murders carried out at such close range that it was impossible to avoid being covered with the blood of the target.

Jamie was pretty sure that Jack was at least a little bit in love with her; he was absolutely sure that he was scared of her. But her smile was wide, and friendly, and Jamie was glad it was her laughter that had made him blush; he was sure that her smile would have had the same effect, and would have been a lot more difficult to explain to Larissa.

Behind him, someone cleared their throat, and he realised he hadn't answered Major Turner. He looked back to the front of the room, and saw the former SAS officer staring at him with an unnervingly patient expression.

"I'm sorry, sir," he lied. "Something came up on the lower levels. It won't happen again, sir."

"I find that difficult to believe," replied Turner. "But I suppose I'll have to take your word for it. Sit down, Carpenter."

Jamie walked sheepishly over to the table where Larissa and Kate were sitting, pulled a chair out and flopped into it between them. As Paul Turner set the pages of his briefing on the lectern, Jamie cast a glance at Angela, who favoured him with a sympathetic smile. He smiled back, then returned his attention to the front of the room, his blood boiling at the unfairness of it all.

"Operators," said Major Turner. "This is OPERATION: PROMISED LAND, a two-squad reconnaissance and elimination mission. It's relatively straightforward, but please try and concentrate. I'd rather not have to keep stopping to answer stupid questions. Clear? Good."

Turner pressed a button on the portable console in his hand, and the wall screen above his head burst into life. It showed a satellite image of a large container ship; the tiny swells of white water at her aft showed the Operators that the ship was in motion.

"This," continued Turner, "is the *Aristeia*. She's a Panamax-class freighter, two hundred and twenty-eight metres long, thirty-two metres wide, able to carry three thousand standard freight containers. She's Greek-built, flying the Bahamian flag."

"If she can carry three thousand containers," said Angela, "why does it look like she's carrying about fifty?"

Turner favoured her with what passed for a smile, and tapped his console. The image magnified until the ship filled the screen.

"You're correct," he said. "She's carrying sixty-eight containers on a deck built for forty-four times that many. She departed from Shanghai eighteen days ago; those containers would need to be filled with diamonds to cover the cost of the fuel it's taken to get her where she is now."

"Where's that?" asked Larissa.

"About eighty miles off the north-east coast," replied Turner. "Her heading puts her destination as the entrance to the River Tyne, where she'll arrive in roughly seven hours."

"What does this have to do with us?" asked Shaun Turner.

"There has been only a single radio contact with the *Aristeia* since she left port," replied Major Turner. "When she passed through the Suez Canal. Before and since, nothing. She spent the last week making her way through the Mediterranean, and all attempts to contact her, by the Italians, the Spanish and the Portuguese, have failed."

"Pirates?" asked Kate.

Angela snorted, and Larissa fired a stare full of razor blades in her direction.

"No," replied Major Turner. "Or at least, we don't think so. There's never been an instance of a pirated vessel being taken voluntarily through the Med, or through the Canal. If she'd been boarded, we'd expect the pirates to have taken her to the coast of Somalia, where they could moor her and make their demands. This ship had to go *through* Somali waters to get to Suez."

"Terrorists?" suggested Jack Williams. "Could it be carrying a bomb?"

"Satellite spectro-analysis says not. Also, why would you use a ship like this to make an attack? They'd know we could sink her in the middle of the ocean. Cargo freighters are not renowned for their manoeuvrability."

"So what is it then?" asked Jamie, sharply. He was getting bored with playing guessing games.

Paul Turner gave him a look full of warning, then continued.

"The Surveillance Division monitored the attempts to contact her, and when she entered UK waters, we put a satellite over her. Here's the infrared."

The image on the screen blurred out, then sharpened into a bright rainbow of colours. The frigid water surrounding the ship was a blue so dark it was almost black, the hull and deck of the

Aristeia a pale shade of aquamarine. A thick bloom of red glowed at the rear of the ship, where the huge diesel engines were producing the power that pushed the enormous freighter through the water. The rectangular containers on the ship's cargo deck glowed a pale orange, and were studded with small blobs of yellow which, the watching Operators realised, were moving around inside the boxes.

"Jesus," said Jack Williams. "There must be two hundred people in those containers."

"Two hundred and twenty-seven," confirmed Major Turner. "Look at the bridge."

The huge crescent-shaped bridge, which towered almost four storeys above the surface of the deck, was pale yellow. The heat was emanating from seven points of light that were almost white, such was the heat they were giving out.

"Vamps," said Shaun Turner, matter-of-factly. "Seven vamps, and two hundred humans. What the hell is this ship?"

"It's not a ship," said Angela. "It's a prison. A floating prison."

"What do you mean?" asked Larissa, frowning. "What are they being imprisoned for?"

"So they can be delivered to whoever paid for them," said Angela. "I've seen it before, but never on this scale. It's like the snakehead gangs bringing workers out of the Far East. They get them as far as the Med, then use trucks the rest of the way. Someone is waiting for this ship in the north, I can guarantee you. Someone waiting for the cargo they ordered."

Larissa looked at Paul Turner, who nodded.

"Operator Darcy is correct," he said. "Our understanding is that the men and women on this ship are to be delivered into vampire hands as soon as the ship docks. What is planned for them after

133

that, we don't know. But given that the oldest vampire in the world, who is currently unaccounted for, is most likely in a condition that requires a regular supply of blood, we thought it might be worth looking into. Don't you agree?"

"You think those people are being shipped to wherever Valeri and Dracula are hiding?" asked Kate.

"We think it's possible."

"What do you want us to do?" asked Jamie, his voice firm.

Larissa looked over at him, saw the set of his jaw, the calm in his blue eyes, and felt her stomach flip. She was incredibly proud of him, and as attracted to him in that moment as she had ever been. A low growl emerged from her throat, barely audible to anyone except Jamie, who was sitting beside her. He turned to her, and a flicker of red spilled into the corners of her eyes, so quickly that only he could have possibly seen it. He grinned; he knew very well what it meant.

Maybe we won't have to leave right away, he thought, hopefully. *Maybe we'll get to wait until after dark.*

The thought of the long hours of remaining daylight, and what they might contain, widened his grin. He dragged his gaze away from Larissa, and tried to focus once more on Paul Turner's briefing.

"You leave immediately," said the Major, and Jamie's heart sank. "We surveyed the area, and the only place anyone could illegally dock a ship that size is the old Swan Hunter shipyard at Wallsend. We're having the surrounding yards closed as we speak, and the coastguard has been given orders to allow the ship to enter the river. I want you to take up surveillance positions before nightfall, then intercept the ship when it docks. The first priority is to find out where these people were being taken, and why. The second is the captives themselves. The new SOP does not apply on this operation. Is that understood?"

We don't have to capture the vamps, realised Jamie, and felt a savage wave of pleasure flood through him. *We can destroy them.*

"Yes, sir," he answered, and a second later Jack Williams said the same.

"Good," said Major Turner. "Now. There are more than two hundred men and women on that ship, all of whom are going to be weak, and probably terrified. So you're going to need to manage the situation; if they panic, which they probably will, if they start running across your lines of fire, make them get down. The collateral loss limit for this mission is nine. Is that clear?"

"It's not clear to me," said Jamie, although he had a horrible idea that it was.

I hope I'm wrong, he thought. *I really do.*

"It means we don't want to see more than nine civilians die on this Operation. That's the acceptable level of loss."

"My squad doesn't deal in acceptable losses," said Jack Williams, his voice low and steady.

"Mine neither," said Jamie, instantly.

"Really?" asked Major Turner, his expression glacial. "Because I do. And so does Admiral Seward. And for this mission, yours is nine. Understood?"

"I don't think—"

"Shut up!" shouted Major Turner, and the room immediately fell silent. He glared round at each of the six men and women in turn. "This is a Level 2 mission that Intelligence suggests may be directly related to this Department's highest priority. You don't like talking about collateral losses, fine, but you will bear them in mind when you're out in the field. Because they can be the difference between

135

a medal and six months on the inactive roster, especially on a mission like this, a mission that I expect you to be able to accomplish, even with only two squads."

"Why are you sending two squads?" asked Shaun Turner, mildly. "We normally work alone. Sir."

The young Operator's words dripped with insolence, but his father favoured him with a look full of such icy threat that he quickly dropped his gaze. Unseen by anyone else in the room, Kate's cheeks flushed momentarily as she watched Shaun buckle under his father's stare.

"If it was possible to do so," said Major Turner, "we'd be sending four squads on this operation. If I had three at my disposal, I'd be sending three. But I don't; I have two. You two. So that's why you're both going. Because we're down to the bare bones here."

"Seven vamps, though?" said Jack Williams. "It doesn't need six of us to handle seven of them."

"I don't care if it's one newly-turned vampire in the middle of an open field, Lieutenant Williams. You have your orders, you have your briefing, the surveillance data has been transferred to your consoles and your transport, and I am deeply bored of talking to all of you. Dismissed."

For a moment, no one moved, then Turner walked swiftly round the podium and took two long strides into the middle of the room.

"I said, dismissed," he said, and this time they all moved, quickly.

Six and a half hours later Operational Squads F-7 and G-17 huddled together in the shadow of a grey factory building on the banks of the River Tyne.

The towering cranes that had once been such a feature of the skyline of this part of the world were gone, dismantled and sold to an Indian shipyard two years earlier. The huge yard, where thousands of men had laboured to build the legendary RMS *Mauretania* in the first years of the twentieth century, where their grandsons had built the Royal Navy's flagship, HMS *Ark Royal*, seven decades later, was silent. The floating dock, with its four wide berths, sat open to the lapping water of the Tyne; it was already becoming overgrown, and was slowly filling up with discarded bottles and cans, left by the teenagers who prowled its wide-open space after dark.

The factories that had once manufactured engine parts and hull panels were empty, their heavy machines sold to shipyards around the world that were still enjoying better times. They were coated in graffiti, and beginning to rust at their corners. The roads that ran between them, which had once hummed with the accumulated sound of thousands of men's voices when the evening whistle blew, were covered in a spider's web of cracks and holes; tangles of weeds emerged from these gaps, as though the earth was already beginning to reclaim land that had once been home to the very best of human ingenuity and innovation.

A thick fog was rolling down the Tyne from the North Sea; as Jamie looked out across the desolate, creaking yard, he could not see the far bank of the river. The grey tendrils were drifting up to the edges of the concrete dock below them, but were not, as yet, cresting them and moving on to the land.

"This is going to be no fun at all if that fog breaks over the dock," he said. "Seven vamps may as well be seventy if we can't see them."

Jack Williams nodded. The six Operators had finished their reconnaissance of the old shipyard, and concluded it was sufficiently isolated for their purposes. It was far from secure, however; there was a main thoroughfare, Hadrian Road, less than two hundred metres to the north, and the fences that surrounded the yard were in significant disrepair. There was no time to plug the holes and tighten the net round the yard; instead, the plan was to never allow the vampires to get more than a few metres from their ship.

"I'll take Kate and Larissa down there," Jamie continued, pointing to a series of rusting metal containers that stood at the edge of the concrete dock, fifteen metres from the river's edge. "Jack, why don't you take your squad over there, behind that wall? That way they'll have to come between us, and we can ambush them from both sides. OK?"

He turned away, ready to jog towards the position he had just described, when Larissa grabbed his arm, and he turned back. The three members of Squad F-7 were not moving, and Jack Williams was staring at him with a look of enormous apology on his open, friendly face.

"What's the problem?" asked Jamie.

"I take my orders from Jack," said Shaun Turner, a belligerent look on his face. "Not from you. Nothing personal."

Temper flared in Jamie's chest.

It bloody well sounds like it's something personal, he thought. *Does he just naturally hate me, like his dad does?*

"Really?" asked Kate, her voice fierce. "You really think now is the time for this petty crap?"

Shaun's face flushed, but he didn't look away.

"Jack outranks Jamie," said Angela, who had the decency to sound embarrassed as she spoke. "In terms of experience. We think he should take point."

Larissa snarled, and her eyes flickered red. "This is complete bull—"

"Angela's right," interrupted Jamie. "Tell us what you want us to do, Jack."

Larissa looked at him, her face pained on his behalf, but he shot her a tiny smile, pleading with her not to make a big deal out of what was happening. She returned it, and his heart swelled with fierce affection for the vampire girl.

Jack Williams gave him a brief glance, full of gratitude. "Positions as Jamie described," he said. "Remember that we need at least one vamp alive for questioning. At *least* one. The new SOP doesn't apply, which I'm sure we're all very happy about, but let's not get carried away. Dead vampires aren't going to tell us where Dracula is. Let's move."

The six dark figures were crouched, ready to scuttle-run to their posts, when the air around them changed; it seemed thicker, as though something huge was altering the pressure. At the same moment, the six Operators realised they could hear something too: a steady *thud-thud-thud*, and the low rush of breaking water. They looked up the river, into the thick, swirling fog, as the vast, curved prow of the *Aristeia* burst into view, blinding them with its running lights, its enormous control tower looming far above them. The huge ship was slowing rapidly, slicing through the river parallel to the long concrete dock.

"Move! Now!" hissed Jack, and the six Operators scattered, hunkering low to the ground as they sprinted to the positions that Jamie had suggested. Then Larissa's head was up, turned to the north, her supernatural hearing picking something up in the dark, sodden night air.

"What is it?" asked Jamie. He was standing with his back to the corner of the container nearest the dock, peering out at the incoming ship. Its size was boggling his mind; the deck was a football-field long, the hull a daunting, vertical wall of steel, the control tower the size of a large office building. It approached with eerie quiet;

he could hear no voices, no sounds of any activity on the decks, or below them, just the steady thud of the engines.

"Trucks," replied Larissa, then turned to look at him. "Three trucks inside the gate, heading this way."

"Any idea what's inside them?" asked Jamie.

Larissa nodded.

"Vampires," she replied. "Lots and lots of vampires."

12

INSIDE THE VOID

Frankenstein was jolted awake as the truck shuddered to a halt. He opened his eyes, and looked over at Andreas, the skinny, speed-addicted kid who had given him a lift out of Dortmund as the sun set on the previous day.

"This is as far as I go," said Andreas. He twitched constantly, gnawing at his fingernails until they bled, but he had shared a flask of soup and some black bread with Frankenstein when they had stopped for petrol, and for that, as well as the lift, the monster was grateful.

"That's fine," said Frankenstein. "Thanks for bringing me this far."

He unwrapped a grey-green hand from the moth-eaten blanket the kind lady at the homeless shelter had given him, and extended it towards Andreas, who shook it. Then he wrapped the blanket tightly round himself, grabbed the plastic bag that contained everything he owned and stepped out into the freezing night.

*

Frankenstein had woken up four weeks earlier, in the bowels of a fishing boat, without the slightest idea of who he was. When the ship's captain, a weathered, salt-encrusted old man called Jens, had asked him his name, he had not been able to answer. Subsequent questions – where he lived, his family and friends, and how he had come to be floating adrift in the North Sea with the little finger of his left hand missing and a wound to his neck that should have killed him – were met with the same response: a panicked look of utter confusion. He had lain on the floor of the cabin, as he was too tall to fit into any of the bunks, and tried to remember something, anything, a place he had been, a conversation he had had, a person he had met, but there was a yawning void in the centre of his mind where his memory should have been.

He was weak from the hypothermia that had nearly killed him, that *would* have killed him had the crew of the *Furchtlos* not found him tangled in their nets as they drew in the first catch of their trip. The net, studded with orange buoys at regular intervals, had kept him afloat, and was the reason he had not drowned. His Department 19 uniform, made of heat-regulating material that acted in the same way as a wetsuit, was the reason he had not succumbed to the punishing cold of the water; without it the fishermen would have hauled in a corpse with their catch.

By talking with the crew as they ate their vast meals of meat and potatoes, he discovered that he spoke German, English, French and Russian, although he had no memory of having been to the countries where he was told these languages had come from. He talked for a long time with Hans, the boat's first mate, a veteran of more than forty years' fishing, and as he listened to the old man's stories, of places he had been and women he had known, of the adventures of the man's youth, occasionally Frankenstein had felt something tighten in his mind, as though he had almost been able to feel the edge of something solid, before it slipped away through his fingers.

The crew had sent him on his way when they reached port, with a jumper and a pair of overalls that were far too small for his giant frame. But he appreciated the men's kindness, and their lack of suspicion; he was half-expecting to see the police and the coastguard waiting for him when the ship steamed into Cuxhaven harbour. But the only people on the dock to greet the boat were the crew's wives and girlfriends, relieved to see their men home safely once more. The crew, who were fishermen born and raised, and had seen a lifetime of strange things at sea, had clearly decided that the huge grey-green man, whom they had hauled from the water as though he was nothing more than a grossly swollen cod, was none of their business.

Frankenstein had walked off the dock with no idea where he was, beyond the rudimentary picture of European geography that Hans had described to him, and no idea where he might go to begin the process of attempting to piece together who he was.

He was completely lost.

As night fell, and the cold wind drew in around him, carrying heavy flakes of snow with it, he had found a group of homeless men and women beneath a bridge on the outskirts of Cuxhaven. They had not welcomed him, nor offered to share their small amount of food, but they had not driven him away either, and had eventually allowed him to huddle round their brazier, and keep the worst of the cold from his bones. The following day he had headed south, away from the sea; he reached the tiny farming hamlet of Gudendorf as night fell, and the full moon rose above him, sickly yellow and swollen in the clear sky.

Suddenly a bolt of agony had burst through his body, driving him to his knees. It felt as though his skin was on fire, as though his bones had been replaced by molten metal, and he screamed up at the moon, as his body began to break. With sickening, agonising crunches, his bones snapped and reset in new shapes. Blood boiled in his veins as thick grey hair sprouted from his skin before his eyes, which had turned a deep, gleaming yellow. His face stretched and lengthened, his teeth bursting from his gums and sharpening into razors, as he fell on to all fours, no longer able to scream; what came from his gaping mouth was a deafening, high-pitched howl.

As the moon shimmered above him and the transformation neared completion, he began to run, shambling forward on four unsteady, newborn legs, then faster and faster, as the last vestiges of his rational self succumbed to the animal that roared in his blood, until he was racing through the dense, snowy forest, towards a distant light and a plume of grey chimney smoke, towards the thick smell of animal fear that drifted through the frozen trees.

The following morning, for the second time in barely a week, Frankenstein had woken up in a strange place, with no memory of how he had arrived there, or what he had done; compounding the strangeness this time was the fact that he was naked, and lying beside a main road.

Mercifully, the road was deserted, as dawn was barely scratching the sky in the east. But even as he looked around in an attempt to get his bearings, the cold of the German winter bit at his naked skin, and he knew he needed to find shelter, quickly. The patch of ground where he had woken up was a circle of damp green grass, the snow thawed away, as though he had been emitting tremendous heat while he slept. He was coated in something sticky, and when he rubbed his hands across his face, they came away streaked with red.

Frankenstein reeled, but then the wind blew hard across him again, and he tried to put the red substance from his mind and concentrate on staying alive. He began to stagger alongside the road, his breath clouding in front of him, towards a gentle slope in the terrain, above which smoke was rising in lazy loops.

Beyond the rise lay a farmhouse, facing away from the road and out over frozen fields and the forest beyond. Frankenstein tried to open the small gate, but his fingers were so cold that they refused to grip; he half-climbed, half-fell over it, his body screaming in pain as he landed in the hard, freezing snow. He staggered towards the house, prepared to risk the likely wrath of whoever it belonged to, knowing that he had to get out of the cold, had to or else he would surely die, when he saw a long washing line strung between the house and a tree that rose from the middle of the garden's small lawn. He made for it, his feet numb and his grey-green skin now a virulent shade of purple, and hauled clothes down from the line, scattering the pegs on the ground.

Once he was dressed, Frankenstein thumbed a lift in the back of a pick-up truck, burying himself deep beneath a pile of sheepskins, which had carried him as far south as Dortmund. He had spent nearly two weeks in a homeless shelter on Kleppingstraße, only being forced to leave when a kind, nervous woman named Magda had started to take a little *too* much of a friendly interest in him.

Frankenstein still didn't know who he was, but he knew that nothing good would have come from encouraging her affection. And so he had left, in the middle of the night, and resumed his journey, following the cargo routes through Germany, looking for something, anything, that might unlock his memory.

Frankenstein watched as Andreas slowly wheeled his truck round, and headed out on to the northbound lane of the road. Behind him were row after row of articulated lorries; huge rigs, eighteen and twenty-two wheeled, their trailers towering above him in the darkness of the parking area. When Andreas's pick-up had been absorbed into the stream of red lights on the motorway, he made his way through the labyrinth of vehicles towards the diner that lay beyond the filling station.

Jeremy's was a no-frills kind of place; a simple, greasy, one-storey building, in which Jeremy and his wife Marta sold heaped platefuls of cheap, starchy food to the endless stream of lorry drivers making their way south, to Paris, to Bordeaux, to Spain and Portugal beyond. Most were wired on coffee or amphetamines, and wanted nothing more than something hot to line their stomachs; it was these low expectations that Jeremy and Marta were experts in accommodating.

Frankenstein was not interested in the food, or even the temporary respite from the cold that sitting in one of the café's linoleum booths would provide. He was only interested in finding a way of continuing his journey, of continuing south. He had no money to offer any of the drivers, and no goods to barter: no drugs, or alcohol, or pornography. There was always a chance that he might find a driver who craved human companionship, who was quietly going crazy at the isolation of being on the road, of the disembodied voices that floated into his cab via CB radio. But it was unlikely; the men who lived this nomadic life did so largely because they wanted as little to do with other human beings as possible.

"Are you a thief?"

The voice was soft, and lilted sweetly on the night air. It seemed to contain no accusation, only curiosity. Frankenstein turned to see the owner of it standing in the shadows between two of the enormous lorries.

It was a little girl, a tiny thing of no more than eight. She was wearing jeans, a T-shirt, thick, sensible work boots and was holding a small model of a truck in her hand; she was every inch a driver's daughter. She was frowning at him, staring up at his huge frame, her forehead furrowed.

"I'm not a thief," Frankenstein replied, lowering his voice. "Are you?"

The little girl smiled, involuntarily, at such a naughty idea, then remembered herself, and frowned again.

"Of course I'm not," she said, firmly. "This is my daddy's lorry." She reached out and touched the wheel of the truck she was standing beside; it was taller than her.

"Where is your daddy?" asked Frankenstein. "You shouldn't be out here on your own. It's cold."

The little girl pointed to Jeremy's transport café.

"Daddy's playing cards," she said. "The clock said he had to stop driving, but he's not tired."

"Does he know you're out here on your own?"

"No," she replied, proudly. "I sneaked out. No one saw me."

"You shouldn't do that. It's dangerous."

"Why?" she asked. "Aren't I safe with you?"

Frankenstein looked down at the tiny figure beside the wheel.

"You're safe," he said. "But we should still get you back to your daddy. Come on."

He held out a huge, mottled hand, and the little girl skipped forward and took it. She smiled up at him as he began to lead her towards the café.

"What's your name?" she asked, as he stopped at the edge of the parking area, checking that nothing was about to pull up to the fuel pumps.

"Klaus," he said, leading her forward across the brightly lit forecourt.

"That's a nice name."

"Thank you."

"My daddy's name is Michael."

"What about yours? What's your name?"

"My name is Lene. Lene Neumann."

"That's a pretty name," said Frankenstein.

"You're nice," replied Lene, smiling up at the monster that was holding her hand. "I like you. Are you going south? I bet my daddy will give you a lift with us."

Frankenstein was about to reply when an almighty crash rang out above the noise of the idling engines. He looked at the truck stop, and saw a commotion in the small diner, before the screen door slammed open, banging with a noise like a gunshot against its metal frame.

A man was silhouetted against the fluorescent lighting of the transport café. He was short, and heavy-set, with a baseball cap perched on the top of his round head.

"Lene!" the man bellowed. "Lene! Where are you, sweetheart? Lene!"

The man leapt down from the doorway, and ran across the forecourt in their direction. He would see them as soon as he reached the shade of the fuel station's canopy. Behind him, a cluster of men and women followed him out of the diner, all calling Lene's name.

"That's my daddy!" exclaimed Lene. "He's looking for me! I bet we can go when he finds us!"

A sinking feeling settled into Frankenstein's chest, and as he looked down at the little girl's hand wrapped tightly in his own, everything seemed to slow down. He saw the rotund figure of Lene's dad pass under the canopy and out of the blinding spotlights that illuminated the entrance and exit ramps. The man's face was ghostly pale, his eyes wide, his mouth a trembling O of panic. The men who were following him across the forecourt were all drivers, some of them carrying wrenches and crowbars. Frankenstein looked again at his hand, and Lene's hand, and realised what was going to happen, realised it was too late to do anything about it.

"Daddy!" cried Lene, and the group of running men bore to their left, adjusting their course towards the sound of the little girl's voice, like a flock of birds in flight. Lene's father skidded to a halt in front of them, and took in the scene he found before him.

"Lene," he said, gasping for breath. "Are you all right? Did he hurt you?"

"Don't be silly, Daddy," his daughter smiled. "This is my friend, Klaus."

The rest of the men drew up behind Lene's father, weapons in their hands and looks of anger on their faces.

"He's your friend?" asked Michael Neumann. "That's nice, sweetheart. But you come over here next to me now, all right? Come on."

Frankenstein let go of Lene's hand; she ran happily over to her father, and hugged his leg. Her father stroked her hair, his gaze never leaving Frankenstein, his eyes like burning coals.

"You shouldn't sneak off like that," he said, his voice low and soothing. "How many times have I told you? It scares me when I don't know where you are. You don't want to scare me, do you?"

Lene looked up at her father, an expression of terrible worry on her small face.

"I'm sorry, Daddy," she said. "I won't do it again, I promise."

"It's all right," he replied, still staring at Frankenstein. "I want you to go with Angela and wait inside, OK? Daddy will be there in a minute, and then we can go. All right?"

Lene nodded. A teenage girl wearing a white waitress uniform stepped forward, looking at the monster with obvious disgust, and took Lene's hand. The little girl waved at Frankenstein as she was led away. He raised his hand to wave back.

When the door of the diner clanged shut a second time, the group of lorry drivers stepped slowly towards Frankenstein, who found himself backing away down the narrow space between two rigs.

"What were you doing with my little girl, mister?" asked Michael Neumann, his voice trembling with anger. "What the hell do you think you were doing?"

Frankenstein knew that nothing he could say would change what was about to happen, but he tried anyway.

"I was bringing her back to you," he said, trying to keep his voice level. "She was hiding from you, and I told her it wasn't safe. I was bringing her back."

"He's lying, Michael," said one of the other drivers, a huge man in a leather jacket that was creaking at the seams. "I'd bet my last cent on it. He knows he's caught."

"I'm telling the truth," said Frankenstein. "She told me you were playing cards and she sneaked out. She saw me next to your truck and asked me if I was a thief. I'm not lying."

"What were you going to do to my daughter?" asked Lene's father, his voice little more than a whisper. "What were you going to do if we hadn't stopped you?"

You didn't stop me, thought Frankenstein, anger spilling through him. *If I was the kind of person you think I am, I'd be twenty miles down the road with your daughter and you'd never see her again. Because you were playing cards instead of watching her. Because you—*

The thought was driven from his mind as a crowbar crashed down on the back of his neck, sending him to his knees. One of the drivers had crept round the back of the rig that Frankenstein had been retreating along; now he stood over the fallen giant with the bar in his hand, bellowing.

"He's down, boys!" the man roared. "Let's show him what we do to his kind!"

The men surged forward, their weapons raised, Michael Neumann in the lead. Rage exploded through Frankenstein; he erupted to his feet, his enormous frame jet black in the shadows between the trucks, and grabbed one of the drivers by the neck. The man's roar died as his throat was constricted by the monster's huge hand, and then he was jerked off his feet and into the air, as Frankenstein threw him against the side of one of the trailers with all his might. The man crashed into the thin metal, leaving a huge dent, then slid to the ground, blood spraying from his head.

The rest of the men skidded to a halt, their eyes wide. This was not how it was meant to go; they were supposed to teach the stranger a lesson, and leave him on the ground while they went back inside and finished their game.

"Come on!" shouted Michael, his voice faltering. He ran forward, a torque wrench raised, but then the enormous shadow of Frankenstein engulfed him, and he stopped. He stared up into the terrifying face of the monster, and his courage deserted him, along with the men who had accompanied him; they fled back towards the café, shouting for someone to call the police as they did so.

Frankenstein reached out and took the wrench from the man's hand. Lene's father offered no resistance; he was transfixed by the sight of the giant man standing over him.

Frankenstein lowered his head until it was level with the man's. Breath rushed out of his mouth and nostrils in huge white clouds, and blood trickled over his shoulder from where the crowbar had split the skin of his neck.

"Next time," he said, his voice like ice, "pay more attention to your daughter than to your cards. Do you hear me?"

Michael Neumann nodded, shaking.

"Good," said Frankenstein, and dropped the wrench. It clattered to the ground at Michael's feet, beside the unconscious shape of the man who had been thrown against the trailer. Michael turned and ran, without looking back.

Frankenstein prowled the edge of the parking area, looking for a way out.

His heart was pounding, his stomach churning at the memory of the sound the man had made when he crashed into the side of the truck, and at the ease with which he had inflicted the violence. He had just attacked, on instinct, without thinking.

It had felt so normal.

Once their fear subsides, they will call the authorities, he thought. *And it won't matter that they attacked an innocent man; when they see me, it won't matter at all.*

He reached the end of one of the long lines of trucks, and suddenly found himself bathed in light. The last rig on the stand, an enormous thirty-wheeler, was covered in hundreds of bulbs of different colours, like a vast Christmas tree laid upon fifteen pairs of wheels. Frankenstein looked up at the cab, and something opened up in his mind.

Above the wide windscreen was a dot matrix display, like the ones that displayed the destinations on the fronts of buses. This one displayed only a single word.

PARIS

A nauseating tangle of memories burst through the monster's head, images and voices, feelings and places he couldn't identify. But he understood that the word was familiar, the first thing he had found that was.

Movement in the cab caught his eye, and he ducked low beside the truck's wide radiator as the driver settled himself behind his steering wheel. A moment later Frankenstein's whole body vibrated as the huge diesel engine roared into life.

Now. You need to move now.

Still crouching, he ran around to the side of the rig. There was no time to break into the trailer; the truck would be moving before he could even get the locks open. He ran past the huge tyres of the cab until he reached the trailer's frame. Beneath the container, lying on steel cross members, were three large storage pods, most likely for spare parts and tools. The space between them was a coffin-shaped gap, below the trailer's container and a metre and a half above the tarmac of the road.

With no time left, Frankenstein dived into the gap, landing hard on the cross members, which were arranged in an X shape. He hauled himself into the space, and found that the bars were close enough together to support his weight. He wedged himself hard against the round edge of one of the storage pods and braced his legs against a second. Diesel fumes filled his nostrils as the driver put the truck into gear and resumed his journey south, to Paris.

13

HUDDLED MASSES YEARNING TO BREATHE FREE

"Incoming," said Jamie. He spoke into the microphone built into the side of his helmet, which linked him to the other five Operators on the Operational frequency. "Heads up, Jack."

"How do you know?" asked Jack, his voice sounding directly in Jamie's ear.

"Larissa," replied Jamie. It was all that needed to be said; the vampire girl's senses were hundreds of times more sensitive than those of a normal human, and she had heard the trucks entering the shipyard long before the rest of the squad would have been able to.

Jack swore. "How long?" he asked.

"Less than a minute," answered Larissa. "Three trucks, I don't know how many vampires. At least ten."

"Ready One," said Jack. "Nobody moves until I give the go, clear?"

Squad G-17 immediately lowered their visors, pulling their T-Bones from their holsters. Ready One was the code for imminent contact with the supernatural; it meant that the use of force was authorised.

Four heavy thuds sounded from the edge of the dock, and Jamie craned round the corner of the container to see what had made them. Thick ropes were lying on the ground, thrown from the deck of the towering freighter. He looked up at the high steel wall, and saw a flash of movement through the fog, a dark shape disappearing into the gloom. Then the rumble of engines began to shake the ground beneath their feet, and three black trucks appeared from the north.

They drove in single file, approaching slowly along the crumbling central road of the shipyard. The Operators, concealed in the deep shadows cast by the containers and the high concrete wall, watched them as they passed. Their paint was peeling, and the trucks were coated in dirt and dust. But the engines purred as they made their way towards the ship, and Jamie saw that the tyres were new, the walls black, the manufacturer's logos still bright white. He could not see anyone inside the vehicles; the windows were smeared with grime, and the cabs were high above his low vantage point, making the angle impossible.

He watched the trucks pull to a halt in a line near the edge of the dock, then waited, his breath held tight in his lungs, as the door of the first cab creaked open, and a figure emerged.

The fog drifted lazily round its feet as it made its way to the back of the truck, and began to unlock the rear doors. Behind Jamie, somewhere back towards the main road, something clattered; an animal most likely, skittering across the concrete. The figure's head instantly flashed round, and Jamie saw the glowing red coals of its eyes.

For a long moment all was still, then the vampire, a man who looked to be in his late thirties so far as Jamie could tell in the gathering darkness, turned back to his task. Seconds later the lock

156

was undone and cast aside, and doors were pulled open, exposing a square of jet black emptiness. Then movement filled the space, as a crowd of vampires piled out of the truck and on to the dock.

They gathered at the back of the vehicle, laughing and shouting, shoving each other with playful familiarity as the vampires who had driven the other two trucks joined them. Several lit cigarettes, and then they got down to business; eight of them went to the ropes, tied them on to huge metal mooring hooks, and began to pull the freighter tight alongside the dock, a display of casually superhuman strength. From somewhere on the hull there came a shout of greeting, which was returned by the vampires as they hauled at the thick lines.

Two of the vampires went to the other trucks and opened their rear doors, so all three vehicles sat open to the night. The first vampire who had emerged oversaw the activity, a cigarette clamped between his teeth; those without specific jobs milled around at the edge of the river, waiting for the ship to be pulled into position.

"I count fourteen," whispered Jack Williams.

"Me too," replied Jamie. "Plus seven on the boat. Twenty-one of them."

"Hold positions," said Jack. "Let's see what they're up to."

From somewhere up on the high deck there came the sound of a metal door creaking open. Seconds later the seven vampires that they had seen as blobs of bright white heat on the infrared satellite image appeared at the railing at the edge of the deck, and began to shout greetings and insults at the vampires waiting below, their eyes glowing red as they traded friendly barbs and jibes with their welcoming party. This continued for a couple of minutes until the vampire who had opened up the first truck, who was clearly in charge of things, lit another cigarette and told them all to shut up. With a few snarls and hisses, the vampires did as they were told.

"Let's get this done!" the foreman shouted. "There'll be time enough for jokes later. Open up the containers; let's have a look at what you brought us."

The vampires on the ship disappeared from the railing and got to work, assisted by a number of the greeting party who flew up on to the deck to lend a hand. Another vampire flew easily up on to the freighter, and hauled down a long folding gangway, which met the concrete surface of the dock with an almighty clang of metal and settled beside the row of trucks.

As the doors to the containers screeched open, terrible sounds began to fill the air. There were cries of fear and misery, screams of pain and terror, and a relentless chorus of sobbing, pleading human voices, many of them speaking languages which were alien to the ears of the listening Operators. Then, through the mist, a small figure appeared at the top of the gangway, silhouetted against the grey canvas of the thickening fog. It took a nervous, shaky step on to the metal walkway, then another, and another. Then it passed through the beam of one of the freighter's huge running lights, and Kate gasped.

Bathed in the bright white beam stood an Asian girl who could have been no more than five or six years old. Her tiny face was pale, her eyes narrowed against the light. She wore a dress printed with a pattern of flowers that had once been white, but was now the deep grey of dust and dirt. In her small hand she clutched a filthy doll that was missing one of its arms and both of its legs. She took a hesitant step forward on bare, filthy feet, then another, then stumbled backwards, grabbing desperately for the gangway's metal rail. She sat down hard on the metal panel, looked around with awful confusion on her small face and began to cry.

A second silhouette appeared at the top of the gangway, running down towards the girl. In the light, the shape became a tiny Asian woman, as pale and filthy as the girl, who dropped to her knees beside the sobbing child and began to shush her gently.

On the concrete dock, one of the vampires began to laugh, and suddenly Jamie was full of an anger so intense he had only ever felt anything like it once before in his life, when he saw the terrified face of his mother standing beside Alexandru Rusmanov in the monastery on Lindisfarne.

"Let's get them," he growled.

"Negative," replied Jack Williams, instantly. "Not until everyone clears the ship."

Jamie gritted his teeth, and forced himself not to reply. Larissa's hand rested momentarily on his arm, a show of support invisible to everyone else, and he felt his rage subside, just a fraction. He refocused his attention on the freighter, where a steady stream of men and women, emaciated, filthy, with looks of blank terror on their faces, were now making their way down the gangway.

The woman and the little girl had reached the bottom, where they stepped nervously off on to the concrete of the dock. Immediately, one of the vampires grabbed for the girl, who cried out with fear, pressing herself against the woman. There was more laughter, and more boiling, acidic anger spilled into the pit of Jamie's stomach.

"Let them be," said the vampire foreman. "Makes no difference if they want to stay together. They're all going to the same place. Start loading them up."

The vampire who had grabbed for the girl hissed, but did as he was told. He reached out, and grabbed the woman by her shoulder, sinking his nails into her flesh as he did so. The woman gritted her teeth, but did not cry out; instead, she fixed the vampire with a long look of utter contempt.

Good for you, thought Jamie. *Just keep it together for a few more minutes.*

The men and women, a dirty, shambling mass of damaged humanity, reached the bottom of the gangway, and began to spill out across the dock. The vampires moved beside them, funnelling the ragged group towards the waiting trucks; the prisoners, weakened and disoriented by their time in the containers, went unprotestingly.

"This is stupid," breathed Kate. "It's much easier with them still on the boat. Down here they're just going to get in the way."

"Hold your positions," insisted Jack.

"She's right," said Angela. "We need to go now."

"Angela, I'm warning—"

"Warn me later," interrupted Angela, and moved.

Angela Darcy slid silently out from behind the wall that was sheltering Squad F-7 from view and brought her T-Bone to her shoulder as though it was the most natural thing in the world. There was a fluidity to the way she moved that was almost feline, and Jamie watched her from the other side of the dock with a feeling that made him almost guilty.

She sighted the vampire who had laughed at the little girl, who was now ordering the woman holding her to climb into the back of the nearest truck. The woman was refusing, shaking her head left and right, spitting torrents of what Jamie thought might be Mandarin. The vampire stared back at her with a lazy smile on his face, the face of someone who is eager to commit violence, and knows his chance is about to arrive.

Angela squeezed the T-Bone's trigger, and then a loud bang and a rush of escaping gas sounded through the quiet evening air. The smiling vampire was beginning to turn his head towards the source of the noise when the T-Bone's metal stake smashed into his chest, punching a hole the size of a grapefruit clean through him. His eyes widened, before he exploded in a steaming gout of blood, splashing the back of the truck and the woman and the girl standing beside it.

The freshly spilled blood hit the noses of the other vampires instantly, and their eyes darkened red. The Chinese woman, her face coated with blood, was staring at the space where the vampire had been standing, her eyes wide. The little girl pulled a strand of something red and wet from her hair, held it up before her face and started to scream. In an instant, the rest of the vampires appeared around her, snarling and hissing. The ones who had been unloading the containers on the freighter's deck swooped down from the air and landed softly beside their colleagues. The foreman muscled his way through the crowd and grabbed the woman by her arm.

"What did you do?" he demanded. "What did you—"

His question was cut off as the stake from Jamie's T-Bone tore through his throat, spraying his blood across the rest of the vampires, who recoiled, howling with alarm. Jamie hadn't missed; the foreman's heart was blocked by the throng of vampires. But he was confident that the rest of them would be a lot easier to deal with if their leader was unable to speak.

"Goddamnit, you two," snarled Jack Williams. "We are go, repeat, we are go."

The Operators broke cover and advanced from both sides towards the vampires, who immediately panicked. The foreman, who had sunk to his knees as blood gushed from his throat, was waving his hands and gurgling incomprehensibly, but the rest of the vampires ignored him. Instead, they hurled themselves at the approaching figures.

Kate dropped immediately to one knee, pulled her MP5 submachine gun from her belt and strafed the onrushing vampires at knee height, exactly as she had been trained to do. Bullets ripped through their legs, tearing flesh and shattering bone, and three of them crashed to the ground, screaming in pain.

Three more leapt into the air, where Larissa met them, her eyes red as lava, her teeth bared in a savage grin. She tore into them three metres above the ground, sending sprays of blood arcing high into the night sky, then landed as gracefully as a cat. The three vampires tumbled to the ground behind her, their blood pumping out across the concrete.

Across the dock, Shaun Turner drew his ultraviolet torch from his belt and raked its beam across the vampires who were streaming towards his squad. As the purple light touched their bare skin, five of the vampires burst into flames and immediately abandoned their attack, racing instead towards the cold water of the river.

They didn't make it.

Angela detached herself from her squad and sprinted after them, firing her MP5 from her shoulder as she ran. Bullets thudded into the backs and legs of the burning vampires, and they crumpled to the ground, screaming and writhing in pain. They tried to crawl towards the water's edge, but Angela kept firing, her shots calm and precise, and the vampires eventually slumped to a halt, their bodies billowing with purple fire and the revolting smell of cooking meat.

Shaun Turner watched her for a split second, a huge grin on his face, then he and Jack Williams threw themselves at the four vampires who were still coming. They attacked with deadly precision, and teamwork that bordered on instinct; the vampires, who wore looks of desperation on their faces, desperation born of the realisation that they were outmatched, fought with a panic bordering on mania. They leapt and clawed and bit and spat as Jack and Shaun slid through them like knives through butter; the flashing claws and snapping jaws touched nothing but thin air.

Shaun pulled the metal stake from his belt, ducked neatly beneath the flailing swing of one of the vampires, a man in a Sunderland football shirt who looked to be about thirty, with a shaved head and arms covered in blotchy blue tattoos, then drove the stake upwards with vicious accuracy. The metal point crunched through the vampire's breastbone, soaking Shaun's arm with pumping blood, until it pierced the wildly beating heart and the vampire burst like a balloon, his insides splashing across Shaun's visor and helmet.

He wiped them clear, in time to see Jack Williams sling his arm round another of the vampires, and drive his stake through the creature's back. It exploded into putrid liquid, and Jack staggered backwards as the thing he had been holding tightly in his grip ceased to exist.

Behind him, a vampire snarled with anticipation, and reached for Jack's shoulders, its fangs gleaming in the reflected light from the ship. Shaun, whose brain was capable of an icy precision that was at least the equal of his father's, didn't hesitate; he drew the Glock 17 from his belt and fired from the hip, like a gunslinger in an old Western. The bullets tore away the vampire's head above his eyebrows, and the vampire went down to the cold concrete, his eyes rolling, his hands grabbing reflexively at nothing as his brain lay in pieces on the dock. Jack regained his balance, spun round and buried his stake in the chest of the twitching vampire, then leapt clear as it exploded.

Shaun watched his squad leader with a look of great pride on his face; he and Jack had been through so many fights together, so many battles in dark corners of the world, and there was no one Shaun would rather have at his side. Then he felt the movement of air at his back, and realised that something was behind him.

He lunged forward, away from it, turning as he did so, and saw the contorted, hate-filled face of a vampire barely an arm's length away from him. It was a man in his fifties, wearing a dark blue suit and tie, and Shaun had time to crazily think how much he looked like the housemaster he had so hated during his time at boarding school. The vampire was reaching for him, its hand centimetres from his chest, its eyes blazing red, its fangs huge and sharp as razors. Shaun started to swing the Glock up from his side, knowing it was going to be too late to stop the vampire reaching him.

"Down!"

It was Angela's voice, cool and calm through his earpiece. As he heard the word, he also heard a loud bang he knew as well as any sound on earth. He threw his legs out from beneath him, and let himself fall to the concrete of the dock.

Confusion passed briefly across the face of the vampire, as he looked at what appeared to be a bizarre act of surrender. Then the stake from Angela's T-Bone blew clean through his chest, directly above where Shaun Turner was lying, and the vampire exploded in an expanding column of blood, the majority of which came crashing down on Shaun. The T-Bone's stake whirred back into its barrel, as Angela appeared above him. She pushed her visor up, and gave him a mischievous smile.

"Naughty boy," she said, reaching down and hauling him to his feet. "Keep an eye on your six, Shaun. You can't always rely on me to bail you out."

"Piss off," he said, mildly, then smiled at his teammate.

Jack Williams arrived beside them, his eyes wide with the thrill of the fight.

"I staked the ones you torched," he said. "Let's help Jamie's team."

Angela looked across the dock, towards Squad G-17.

"I think they're doing fine," she said, the smile widening on her face.

Kate ran forward, drawing the stake from her belt as she did so. Jamie ran with her, his MP5 in one hand, his stake in the other. They reached the trio of wailing vampires that Kate had blown the legs out from under, and staked them without a second glance. Then they were moving again, in the direction of Larissa.

Three more vampires fell out of the sky, blood pouring from wounds that looked like the work of a wild animal, and Kate skidded to a halt.

"Go on!" she shouted. "I'll clear up!"

Jamie nodded, sprinting after Larissa, who had dropped back to the ground and taken cover behind the nearest truck. Behind him, he heard three gargled screams and three thuds of changing air pressure, as Kate staked what was left of the vampires who had met Larissa in the air. A second later she was at their side, panting, her uniform splashed with blood.

"How many left?" asked Jamie.

Larissa lifted her visor back and sniffed the air. Her eyes were blazing red, the colour of boiling blood, and her fangs were gleaming white triangles beneath her upper lip.

"Five," she answered. "The one you T-Boned is still alive, but only just. The other four are between the trucks. The scents are too close together – I can't separate them."

Don't worry, thought Jamie. *Four frightened vampires. Easy.*

A noise began to swell from the direction of the freighter, and Jamie peered round the corner of the truck. The woman who had been the second to leave the ship was standing at the bottom of the gangway, surrounded by a small group of emaciated men and women; she was still holding the little girl with one arm, but with the second she was waving frantically up at the deck of the freighter. As Jamie watched, an elderly woman nervously poked her head above the railing at the top of the gangway, then slowly started down it. Behind her, a crowd of men and women followed, the metal creaking beneath them as they made their way towards dry land.

Movement blurred in the corner of Jamie's eye, and he pulled back round the corner next to Kate and Larissa.

"At least one is on the other side of this truck," he whispered, his voice inaudible to anyone but them, the noise cancelled by the dampening contours of his helmet. "Kate, work your way round the other end. Larissa, go over the top. We'll corner him."

The two girls nodded. Kate moved away silently down the length of the truck, as Larissa floated easily up into the air. Jamie took a deep breath, and stepped round the corner. The vampire who was standing between the two trucks looked almost pitifully frightened; he was twitching and turning in circles, nostrils flared, trying to look in every direction at once. Then Kate appeared beyond him, and the vampire saw her. He hissed, a low, terrified noise, and turned to run, only to find Jamie barring his escape route. He screeched, a look of pure dread on his middle-aged face, and turned his head to the sky, to the one way he might escape the fate that had befallen his colleagues.

"Hi," said Larissa, sweetly. She was sitting on the edge of the truck's roof, staring down at the vampire with her red eyes glowing.

166

The vampire let out a howl of despair, and ran towards Kate. Then the stakes from two T-Bones pulped his chest, and he exploded in a shower of blood. Larissa floated down, then suddenly accelerated past Jamie, a low snarl of pleasure emanating from her throat. One of the three remaining vampires, his instinct for self-preservation overwhelmed by the torrent of fresh blood that had been spilled on the other side of the truck, was careering round the corner, a look of primal hunger on his face.

Larissa shot past him like a bullet, without even slowing, and tore his head from his shoulders without so much as a grunt of effort. The headless body took a couple of faltering steps, then fell face down in front of Jamie, who staked it, a grimace of disgust on his face. The head burst in Larissa's hand like a water balloon, and she let out a yelp of annoyance.

"Give me a chance to drop the head next time," she said. "I nearly made it through this mission without getting any blood on me." She laughed, and Jamie felt his stomach flip.

Sometimes the awesome power that coursed through his girlfriend – *is that what she is now? My girlfriend?* – scared him more than he would ever have admitted to her, and made her take pleasure in things that even he, as battle-scarred as he was, found appalling. He knew it wasn't really her, it was the vampire side of her; surrounded by blood, in a fight for her life, it took her over completely. But when it was over, she would be Larissa again, he knew.

Or at least, he hoped he knew.

Behind him, he heard the snarl of a vampire, but he didn't even hurry to turn around. He trusted Kate completely; by the time he was facing her, the vampire was already staggering back against the side of the truck, a gaping hole in its chest. Kate turned her back as it burst, splashing blood and viscera against the backplate of her body armour.

Three down. One to go.

Squad G-17 regrouped at the front of the second truck, and walked slowly towards the third. They were careful, but not overly so; a single vampire was no match for them, and they knew it. As if on cue, the final vampire burst out from where he had been cowering as his friends died around him, took a single look at the three approaching figures, turned tail and ran for his life.

He made it ten metres before he collided with the mass of men and women emerging from the freighter's gangway.

The first blow was struck by a tall Asian man with a metal fire extinguisher in his hand, crushing the vampire's skull almost flat on one side. Blood pistoned into the air, and the vampire fell to the floor, his mouth working uselessly as he tried to form words, perhaps trying to beg them not to do it, to plead for mercy.

There was no mercy.

When it was over, the prisoners slumped to the ground, their heads in their hands, their arms wrapped round loved ones. Almost all of them were weeping, their narrow chests heaving up and down. The woman holding the little girl did not sit down, however; she had taken no part in the destruction of the vampire, but nor had she made any attempt to stop it. She looked at the six dark figures, their purple visors hiding their faces from view, and said two halting, uncertain words.

"Thank. You."

"You're welcome," replied Jack Williams, and pointed at the ground. "Stay here. Help coming. Stay here."

The woman nodded, then lowered herself to the ground, keeping the little girl carefully cradled against her.

168

Jack led the combined team away, and gathered them into a circle.

"Good work," he said, raising his visor. "Damn good work today. That was as clean as I've ever seen it done, and we got the leader alive. Great work, truly." He smiled around at the five Operators, who raised their own visors and grinned back at him, grinned at the pleasure of a job done well as the adrenaline began to leave their systems. "Alert the Northumbrian Police; tell them they've got two hundred refugees on the banks of the Tyne. Then let's take our survivor home and find out what he knows," Jack continued. "Shaun, radio the chopper."

Shaun Turner nodded, and pulled the radio from his belt. As they made their way back towards the truck, he coded in and told their pilot that they were ready for extraction. A deep noise instantly rumbled through the night as the helicopter that had brought them north lumbered into the air less than a quarter of a mile away, on the other side of Hadrian Road.

At the rear of the truck they found the vampire foreman.

He was slumped on his knees, his head lowered against his chest, in the middle of an enormous pool of blood. He was pale, and his skin was flickering as his veins pushed what blood remained in his body desperately round his system, trying to keep it operational. He was breathing, incredibly slowly, as they approached him.

"He's on the brink," said Larissa. "He'll be dormant by the time we get him back to the Loop. He's lost too much blood."

"Then they can revive him in the lab," said Jack. "Makes transporting him easier."

Shaun Turner stepped forward, and hunkered down in front of the vampire.

"Where were you taking all those people?" he asked.

There was the tiniest movement in the vampire's shoulders, suggesting he understood he was being spoken to, but no response. Shaun reached out to lift the injured vampire's head up, and Kate was suddenly overcome with panic. She stepped forward, saying Shaun's name, as his gloved fingers touched the vampire's chin. He paused as she arrived at his side, shooting a look of annoyance in her direction as she reached out to pull his hand away. Then the vampire's head reared up, his eyes glowing a dull red, and he lunged forward with the last of his strength, like a dying dog.

His mouth closed on Kate's arm.

The fangs slid into her flesh, and she watched with what was almost amazed detachment as the vampire shook his head, once, and tore a ragged chunk of flesh out of her arm. He spat it out on the concrete, and collapsed backwards, his eyes rolling back in his head.

14

SHOULD AULD ACQUAINTANCE
BE FORGOT

Frankenstein sat on a bench outside Notre Dame de Paris, watching the worshippers file out of evening mass. It was Christmas Eve, and the ancient cathedral had been nearly full to capacity.

He had taken to coming here at the same time every evening, as the last of the sunlight played across the ancient ramparts and gargoyles far above his head. There were usually crowds of tourists gazing up at the huge stone building, cameras slung round their necks and guidebooks in their hands as teenage kids glided around and between them on skateboards and bikes, but the plaza had been largely deserted while the service was taking place. The cold and the festive season had seen most of the tourists leave the city, and most Parisians stay inside.

Those whose faith had compelled them out into the freezing night had flocked into the comparative warmth of the cathedral as the bells rang for the Christmas mass at six o'clock. Frankenstein had stood among them on several occasions as the grand organ boomed and wailed, as the choir harmonised, as the incense smoked and fumed, and the bishop conducted his service from before the ancient altar.

Today, he had chosen to stay outside.

He found watching the faces of the men and women who departed from the cathedral after the mass as illuminating as the service itself; the blank disinterest of those for whom the ritual was nothing more than a chore, a habit they weren't quite able to break, against the beatific rapture of the faithful, full to the brim with God's blessings and trembling at the almighty power of their Lord.

The depths of their feelings fascinated him. Because he, after almost three weeks in the city whose name had sparked his only flash of recognition since beginning his shallow, empty second life, felt nothing.

He felt nothing at all.

Frankenstein had arrived in Paris with his entire body a ball of flaming agony. After a day and a half pressed tightly into the bowels of the truck, he had managed to hobble away unseen when the driver brought his rig to a halt outside the Marché d'Intérêt National, the vast food market in the southern suburb of Rungis. Frankenstein had asked a man working in a mobile café for directions to the centre of the city, and began walking north. As he made his way towards the middle of Paris, a creeping sense of disappointment had settled on him.

He recognised absolutely nothing.

Not a single building, or landmark, not a street sign or the name of a restaurant; nothing triggered a rush of memory like the one

172

he had experienced at the transport café in Germany. He saw nothing that made him feel like he had ever been to this place before.

He reached the river, the wide, winding expanse of water at the heart of the city, and felt nothing. He was waiting for an epiphany, for the locks in his head to grind into action and release, spilling his memory back into his possession.

But it never came.

For almost three weeks now, he had wandered the Parisian streets. He was as confused and disoriented as ever, more so perhaps, having been given what had felt like the first clue to unlocking his identity, only to be denied further progress. The stares of the tourists and the people going about their lives made him uncomfortable, and he began to spend his days in the dark corners of the museums and churches that littered the city, hidden away from prying eyes.

At night, he walked the streets of Pigalle and the Marais, keeping to the shadows. He watched the laughing groups of men and women as they spilled from the bars and cafés, the drug dealers and the sex workers, as they conducted their transactions in the narrow alleyways and dark street corners.

Frankenstein had no idea what he was going to do with the new life he had been given, and was aware of a growing sense, deep in his bones, that he did not want to continue with it at all. Several times he had stood on one of the bridges, staring down at the dark, freezing water of the Seine, wondering how it would feel to pitch himself over the railing; a moment of panic perhaps, a second or two of falling, then icy oblivion, washing down his throat and filling his lungs.

He would not steal, and he was too proud to beg, so he subsisted on the thin soup ladled out by the bright-eyed, enthusiastic young men and women who brought their vans to the arches beside the

Gare du Nord every night. He queued patiently, alongside the drunks and the addicts and the mentally ill, waiting for his turn, while all the while a small voice in the back of his mind told him not to waste his time.

You're prolonging your own misery, it whispered. *Nothing more.*

Frankenstein got up from the bench and walked north, ignoring the stares of the tourists and the pointing fingers of their children. He crossed the Seine on Rue de la Cité, and cut right then left on to Rue Vieille du Temple. He was walking quickly, his head down, his moth-eaten, second-hand coat drawn tightly round him, when a voice shouted loudly from the other side of the street, shouted a name that split his head wide open.

"Henry Victor?"

Just as it had in the parking area of the transport café, something gave way in Frankenstein's mind, and a torrent of indecipherable information poured out, overwhelming him. He staggered, as his mind filled with the lost sights and sounds of his life; they were jumbled, non-sequential to the point of abstraction, but he felt, for a moment, as though he might weep. They were fractions of something bigger, something *whole*, and they filled him with hope that who he was, the man he had been, might not be lost forever.

Then they were gone, as suddenly as they had arrived, and a man was standing in front of him, a wide smile on his face.

"Henry Victor!" he exclaimed. "It is you!"

The man was tall, although Frankenstein still towered over him. He was dressed in an elegantly cut navy blue suit, and a cream shirt that was open at the neck. His face was narrow, his blond hair combed into a neat side parting, and he was looking at the monster with an expression of utter incredulity.

174

"Do I know you?" asked Frankenstein, slowly.

The man frowned, and took a half-step backwards.

"You are Henry Victor, are you not?" he asked. "It's me, Latour. I know it has been almost a century since we last saw each other, but I didn't think I was quite so forgettable."

Frankenstein looked at the man. He was clearly no older than forty, and probably several years younger than that.

"Almost a century?" he asked. "How can that be?"

Latour narrowed his eyes, and for an instant, Frankenstein was sure he saw red flicker in their corners. Then it was gone, and geniality returned to the stranger's face.

"You don't remember me, do you?" he asked.

"It's no business of yours, but I remember nothing beyond the last ten weeks," replied Frankenstein, allowing a rumble of anger into his voice. "Regardless, it is impossible that either of us could have been alive a century ago. It is ludicrous to even suggest it."

"My God," said Latour, his voice low. "Are you serious? You remember nothing?"

Frankenstein didn't answer; he simply stepped round Latour and continued to make his way up Rue Vieille du Temple, without a backward glance. But Latour immediately appeared in front of him again, and he stopped.

"I'm getting tired of—"

"Please, let me speak," interrupted Latour. His eyes were wide, and he was looking at Frankenstein with something close to pity. "You must be so confused. And, to be honest with you, it looks as though you find yourself somewhat down on your luck. Is that fair?"

Frankenstein glanced down at his battered clothing.

"And if it is?" he replied. "What do you propose to do about it?"

"*I know you,*" said Latour, and suddenly there was passion in his voice. "If you tell me that you don't remember, then I believe you. But it is the truth, whether you find it ridiculous or not. So perhaps I can be of service. Perhaps I can help you to remember."

"How would you do that?" asked Frankenstein. His voice remained gruff, but a sliver of hope had opened in his heart.

If this man knew me before, perhaps he really can help.

"I think dinner would be a good place to start," replied Latour, and smiled. "You look as though you're starving. I have a table in a restaurant five minutes' walk from here. We can share a meal, and talk, and maybe something will come back to you. If it doesn't, then we part as friends. It's Christmas, after all, and no one should be on their own. How does that sound?"

Latour was right about one thing: Frankenstein was starving. Latour watched as his companion devoured a thick slab of foie gras and a chateaubriand that had been intended for two, washing it down with a bottle of Château Batailley. But he was wrong about the other: nothing he said prompted any reaction from the monster, whose memories appeared completely inaccessible.

This is a piece of astonishing good fortune, he thought, as he watched the huge man eat. *Remarkable even.*

He told Frankenstein of the time they had spent together in the distant summer of 1923; the places they had been, the men and women in whose circles they had moved. The names would have been impressive, to even a casual listener, but to the monster they were meaningless.

Frankenstein listened politely as Latour explained, with frustration creeping into his voice, that the two of them had walked and eaten and drunk with the finest minds of the generation, that they had

176

been present at parties and gatherings that society columnists would have killed for an invitation to. He listened, and then he apologised for his inability to remember the famous artists and writers who appeared to still have Latour under their spell, even now.

When both men had eaten their fill, they strolled north, into the heart of the Marais. Their conversation remained pleasant, and amicable, but it was clear to them both that it was fruitless. Frankenstein remembered nothing more than he had when they sat down together, and remained extremely sceptical about Latour's claims of the time they had spent in each other's company.

He believed that the man had known him, had become convinced of that; the detail in his stories had been too compelling, too closely woven to be entirely fabricated. But the year that Latour kept returning to, 1923 – that was simply impossible for Frankenstein to accept. He had eventually asked his companion outright how such a thing could be possible, but Latour had refused to answer.

"Some things you must find out for yourself," was all he would say.

They passed across Place de la République and headed north-west on Boulevard de Magenta, discussing trivialities: the weather, the architecture of the city, the hordes of wandering tourists. For all his doubts, Frankenstein was in no hurry to take leave of his companion, as he had nowhere else to be.

As the two men crossed the entrance to a dimly lit alleyway, a female voice issued from the darkness.

"Both of you for sixty," it said, the words slurring slightly as they echoed from the shadows.

Latour stopped, and regarded Frankenstein with a look that chilled him; a look of naked hunger. Suddenly Frankenstein wanted to be away from this man; he didn't know why, but the feeling was clear and strong. He was formulating an excuse when Latour grabbed his arm and hauled him into the alleyway.

The source of the voice was a girl, barely out of her teens. She was leaning in the shadows, her exposed arms and legs bony and pale. She was smoking a cigarette and staring coolly at the two men as they approached her. She opened her mouth to say something more, but never got the chance.

As Frankenstein watched, Latour's eyes changed. Dark red, almost black in the flickering light of the street lamp on the main street, spilled into them, and they began to glow with unnatural fire, sending a wave of terror hurtling through Frankenstein, freezing him to the spot where he stood. Then Latour moved with inhuman speed, and lifted the girl into the air by her throat.

Before Frankenstein had time to react, Latour hauled her pale throat to his mouth, and sank his teeth into it. The girl tried to scream, as blood began to gush out of her neck, but Latour held her tight, and it emerged as little more than a gurgle. A revolting slurping sound issued from the man as he drank the warm blood from her veins, and after less than a minute, her head slumped sideways, her eyes closed.

Frankenstein stood, paralysed by absolute fear. When Latour turned, a dreadful smile on his blood-smeared face, his eyes the glowing colour of Hell, and held the girl out towards him, he thought for a nauseating second that he was going to faint.

"Drink," said Latour. "It's been too long, old friend. Drink. Maybe the man you were will remember the taste."

Frankenstein stared at the glistening wound, at the thick streams of blood that were running down the girl's chest, and lurched back, his hands raised in horrified protest. He collided with the wall of the alleyway and lost his balance, sliding to the wet ground, his eyes fixed on the girl's bleeding neck.

"No?" said Latour. "A shame. Clearly, your tastes have changed somewhat in the last ninety years."

He dropped the girl to the ground as though she was nothing, then slid liquidly across the alleyway and flopped down next to Frankenstein, who was so overwhelmed with revulsion that he scrambled away, crawling across the ground like a baby.

Latour reached over, grabbed the collar of his coat and hauled him back.

"Where do you think you're going?" he asked, conversationally, pulling a cigarette from a silver tin in his jacket pocket and lighting it. His face was coated in the girl's blood, with red light glowing from his eyes and a wicked smile twisting his lips. "I know you have nowhere to go. I know there is no one to miss you. But most importantly, I am the only person in this city who knows who you really are. I'm the only friend you have."

He smiled at Frankenstein, then leapt back to his feet and crossed the alleyway. He lifted the barely breathing girl from the ground, and placed his hands round her throat.

"D-don't," managed Frankenstein. His voice came out as a rasp. "Please don't. Let her live."

Latour cocked his head, and looked at the monster.

"Why?" he asked. "That would be far more unkind."

Then he strangled the girl, as Frankenstein squeezed his eyes shut, and waited for it to be over.

Seconds later, seconds that seemed like hours, he felt hands on his shoulders, and opened his eyes a fraction. Latour, his eyes returned to normal, the majority of the blood gone from his face, was crouching in front of him, regarding him with a kind expression.

"Come," he said, nodding his head in the direction of Boulevard de Magenta. "You will stay with me. My apartment is only a short walk from here."

Frankenstein shook his head, slowly. His mind was reeling with the sheer unnatural cruelty of what Latour had done. His stomach was churning, and a hopelessness, a self-loathing more powerful than anything he had ever felt, was washing over him, threatening to drown him.

Crack.

Latour slapped his face, hard.

"Don't make me repeat myself," he said. The kindness was once more gone from his face, replaced by a look of vicious amusement. "Come now, while you can do so under your own steam."

He gripped the lapels of Frankenstein's coat, then pulled him to his feet. He linked arms with the monster, as though they were nothing more than two old friends out for a stroll on the town, and led him out on to the street. Then he began to walk north, with Frankenstein following mechanically at his side, lost inside his own ravaged mind, trapped in a nightmare from which there seemed to be no waking.

15

ALL FALL DOWN

For a moment, nobody moved. Kate stared at the blood pumping out of the hole in her arm, as Shaun Turner looked on with an expression of total incomprehension. Jamie felt like his legs had been turned to lead, as though he couldn't move them, physically couldn't move them. In the end, it was Larissa who reacted first.

Her eyes flooded involuntarily red at the sight and smell of the running blood, but the look on her face was pure concern. She shoved Jamie and Jack out of the way and slid to Kate's side, ignoring Shaun completely.

Her movement broke the spell that had been momentarily holding them fast; Jamie started to shout, asking Kate over and over if she was all right. Jack got on the radio and ordered the helicopter to make an emergency medical pick-up. Angela stared at Kate, her face unreadable, the face of someone who has seen horrors that no one should have to see. Larissa clamped her hand over the wound, squeezing it tightly with her superhuman strength, and Kate cried out in pain. Shaun Turner pulled the stake from his belt, turning towards the comatose vampire.

"No!" yelled Jack Williams, as he realised, too late, what his squad member was going to do. But Shaun gave no indication that he had even heard his squad leader's voice; he dropped to his knees and hammered his metal stake into the motionless vampire's chest. The foreman exploded with a dull thud, a pathetic spray of blood that flickered briefly in the cold night air. Then Shaun was moving again, this time to Kate's side, demanding that Larissa let him see the damage.

"Get back," growled Larissa, and Shaun recoiled.

"It's OK," said Kate, in a low voice, but Larissa ignored her.

"Jamie," she said, her eyes blazing. "Call the Loop and tell them to have a transfusion ready when we land."

"I'll do that," said Jack Williams, then took a step backwards as Larissa snarled at him, her fangs bared and gleaming in the light from the truck.

"I don't want *you* to do it. I want Jamie to do it," she growled. "Your squad has done enough already. We'll take care of her from here."

"Take it easy," said Angela. "Shaun didn't—"

"It's OK," interrupted Turner. "She's right. I shouldn't have... it was stupid."

"We agree on that at least," said Larissa, her voice vibrating with anger. She looked over at Jamie, who was watching her with wide eyes. "Jamie," she snapped. "Get on the radio. Why am I having to ask you again?"

Jamie's face flushed with heat, and he fumbled the radio from his belt. He entered his passcode, acutely aware of the look of enjoyment on Angela's face as she watched, then tuned into the Operational frequency.

"NS-303, 67-J reporting a medical emergency. Over."

The radio crackled as his message was passed through layers of encryption and voice recognition in the Loop's Communications Division.

"What is the nature of the emergency? Over."

"Vampire bite to the left forearm of Operator Kate Randall. Over."

"Significant blood loss? Over."

Jamie glanced over at Kate. Her arm was still bleeding, but the pressure Larissa was exerting had slowed it to a steady trickle. Kate's face was pale, but her jaw was set with determination; as he watched, Larissa leant in and whispered something, and Kate smiled, weakly.

"Negative," he replied. "Infection is the primary risk. Over."

"What's your ETA? Over."

Jamie was about to answer when the squat black helicopter roared into view above the deserted shipyard. He heard screams from the men and women who had been captive on the freighter, and saw Larissa lift Kate into her arms as though she weighed nothing, ready for the chopper's arrival.

"Approximately thirty-five minutes. Over."

"Understood. A trauma team and transfusion unit are being scrambled. Over."

"Out."

Jamie clipped the radio back on to his belt, and ran to his friends. The noise from the helicopter was deafening, its engines screaming as it prepared to touch down.

"How's she doing?" he yelled, over the howl of the rotors.

"She didn't lose much blood," shouted Larissa. "She'll be all right as long as we get her transfused."

The helicopter hit the ground, hard, the tyres of its wheels screeching. The side door slid open and the co-pilot appeared, framed against the glowing green light of the helicopter's interior. He reached out his hands towards Kate, but Larissa ignored him and floated quickly up into the chopper, with her friend in her arms.

183

"Come on!" shouted Jack, waving his squad towards the door.

Shaun and Angela climbed nimbly into the belly of the chopper, and then Jack was shouting at Jamie. He ran forward and leapt up into the vehicle, his boots thudding on to the metal floor. He turned back to pull Jack Williams aboard, then the pilot fired the helicopter's huge engines and they were airborne before Jamie slid the door shut.

The helicopter raced south, skimming low over the countryside, its rotors sending a bone-jarring cacophony of noise through the insulated cabin as the pilot pushed the huge aircraft as hard as she would go.

Kate had refused to lie down on one of the benches that spanned the width of the chopper's cabin, despite pleas from Larissa and Shaun Turner for her to do so. She was sitting upright beside Larissa, who was eyeing the four male Operators with the same expression that a wolf gives when someone comes too near to one of her cubs.

Kate's face was pale; she was holding her free hand over the wound on her arm, which Larissa had wrapped with a field dressing as soon as they were all safely aboard, and staring directly ahead, looking at no one. Jamie appeared to be doing the same; he had his head back against the rest behind his seat, and seemed to be looking at the opposite wall. But he was really looking at Shaun Turner.

Every few seconds, Turner glanced at Kate. It was almost nothing, little more than a flicker of his eyeballs, but it was there, and it was as regular as clockwork. Jamie watched, turning over what had happened in his mind.

As far as I knew, they'd never met until today. But when he knelt down in front of the vampire, she called him Shaun. And there was worry in her voice. Then after she was bitten, he staked the vampire, even though it was our only lead, even though information was our first priority. Like he wanted to punish it for what it had done. And then he tried to push Larissa out of the way, to get to Kate.

It wasn't a 'eureka' moment; no light bulbs burst into life above his head, no explosion of realisation hit him between the eyes. He was just suddenly aware of something that now seemed obvious.

There's something going on between them. Between Shaun and Kate.

Jamie was surprised to find that the first emotion he felt was jealousy.

He didn't fancy Kate, and in truth he never had. There had been something desperate between them on Lindisfarne, as the darkness closed in on them from all sides, but it hadn't been real. It had been the fear of death, followed by the euphoria of survival, the primal joy of being alive. And Jamie knew full well, looking back, that by the time they had landed on the island, he was already falling for Larissa; had been ever since the first time he had gone to see her in her cell, deep in the lower levels of the Loop.

He had believed, however, without arrogance or vanity, that Kate's feelings for him were somewhat more complicated than his for her. So had Larissa; it was why they had kept their slowly blossoming relationship a secret. Not because they were seeking to exclude Kate, or because they didn't trust her to keep their secret – relationships between Operators were strictly against regulations – but because they didn't want to hurt her. If they were right, and she saw Jamie as potentially more than just a friend and a colleague, then revealing their relationship to her would have been insensitive at best, and cruel at worst. Their plan had been to give her time to move on, then gently break the news.

But if he was seeing things clearly, and he was sure that he was, then all their care and concern had been for nothing. Because now it appeared that Kate's feelings for him were truly nothing more than fraternal.

Her feelings for Shaun Turner, however, were clearly another matter.

Jamie thought about all the time they had spent worrying about Kate's feelings, all the tiptoeing around, all the lies and half-lies and secrets. It had all been for absolutely nothing, he realised, and his jealousy was suddenly replaced by a deep anger. It made him feel ashamed, as he looked at the blood leaking from the hole in her arm, but it was there, nonetheless; anger at the fact that she hadn't told him and Larissa about whatever was going on with Shaun, even though he knew it was appallingly hypocritical of him to do so, and a tiny ball of anger, shot through with disappointment and rejection, that she had not been interested in him after all, that there was someone else she wanted more.

To hell with you then, he thought, viciously. *We don't need you, and we definitely don't need him. Larissa and I will be fine on our own.*

Kate looked over at him, and gave him a small smile. Her teeth were gritted against the pain, but it was as if she was trying to tell him silently that she was all right.

Jamie watched, and the anger went out of him so quickly it was as if it had never been there at all. He realised instantly that he *did* need her, that *they* needed her. She was the ice to Larissa's fire, the one who thought everything through, who could control her emotions and do what was best, with neither the impulsiveness that fuelled Larissa nor the lightning temper that Jamie knew was his own greatest weakness. Without her, they would be incomplete; he knew it, and he knew that Larissa would know it too. The three of them were tied together, had been ever since the morning after they had returned from Lindisfarne.

After reading the letter that Frankenstein had left for him, Jamie had fallen into the deepest sleep of his life; he had eventually awoken ten hours later, and even then only because Admiral Seward had sent for him.

The Director of Department 19 had debriefed him in his office, where he had jumped instantly at the offer to make his temporary position at Blacklight permanent, pride flooding through him when Seward announced that he was the youngest descendant ever to take up an active commission. He immediately asked about Kate and Larissa, and felt his heart sink when Seward told him that they had decisions of their own to make, and that he might not see them again. But as it turned out, the three of them had been reunited less than an hour later, in one of the Briefing Rooms on Level 0 of the Loop.

They had made small talk in the beginning; they barely knew each other at all, not really, and the bonds that had been temporarily forged between them had been in response to a threat that no longer existed. Nervously at first, then with increasing passion, Jamie told them about his mother, and Kate explained that her dad had been confirmed as one of the survivors of the massacre on Lindisfarne. Larissa had asked Admiral Seward for a favour, and he had compiled for her a report on her younger brother Liam, who was apparently living with their mother, and doing well at school.

They exchanged pieces of trivia about their lives, talked around the terrible events of the previous night and confirmed that they had all accepted the invitation to join Department 19. Somewhere in the midst of it all, they became friends.

From that point on, they had been inseparable.

They had gone through accelerated Operator training together, encouraging each other as they neared the finish line and the course hardened and sharpened. They stood side by side as they received their commissions from Admiral Seward, smiling happily as the Director told them they were going to be formed into an Operational Squad together, even though it was not customary to do so with three inexperienced Operators.

Jamie had been embarrassed to discover that he had been commissioned as a Lieutenant, rather than as an Operator like the two girls, and that he was technically their immediate superior, but neither Kate nor Larissa had appeared anything other than delighted for him. He had loved them both for that, and had gone out of his way to ensure that beyond his being the first call sign that was announced when they entered or left the Loop, there would be no differences between them, no hierarchy to be adhered to. They had gone out together, night after night, to every corner of the country, responding to intercepted Echelon messages, or information supplied by the Intelligence Division; they had fought and survived, time and again, and they had done it together.

They all knew that Jamie, as a Lieutenant, was sometimes privy to information that he was unable to share with his two friends; it was an unspoken thing, made bearable by the fact that it was obvious to both Kate and Larissa that Jamie hated the situation even more than they did. That Kate would keep something like her and Shaun from him hurt Jamie deeply, mainly because he could now clearly imagine how Kate would have felt if she had ever found out about him and Larissa.

At least she doesn't know about that. That's something.

Part of him, the childish, vicious part that he was always

disappointed by, wanted to tell Kate right now, while she was at her lowest point, when it would hurt her the most. But he fought back the urge. He was still staring at the wall above Shaun Turner's head, wondering how things had become so complicated, when the pilot announced that they were beginning their descent to the Loop.

The helicopter's wheels screeched down on to the tarmac, and Shaun Turner hauled the door open while it was still slowing to a halt. Then he was reaching for Kate, the look in his eyes daring Larissa to try to stop him a second time. The vampire girl's eyes flared red, but she relaxed her grip on Kate's arm, and let Shaun help her down from the chopper's open door. Kate winced as she moved, a fresh trickle of blood running from beneath the dressing on her arm. Then she was surrounded by men in white coats, who lifted her gently on to a stretcher and ran her into the hangar and out of view.

Jamie and the rest of the combined Operational Squad stepped down from the helicopter and stood beside Shaun Turner, watching the doctors disappear.

"She'll be all right," said Larissa, floating a couple of centimetres above the tarmac of the runway. "We got her back here in time."

"I know," said Shaun Turner, quietly. "I just—"

"She wasn't talking to you," Jamie growled, and saw Jack Williams recoil out of the corner of his eye. "She was talking to me. Kate's a member of my squad. She's nothing to do with you."

Jamie was absolutely sure that wasn't the case, but he wasn't trying for the truth; he was trying to provoke Shaun Turner, and the look in the Operator's eyes told him he had succeeded.

"Maybe you don't know everything," replied Turner, his eyes narrow, his voice like ice. "Did you ever think of that?"

"Maybe I know more than you think," replied Jamie. "I know that you destroyed our only way of finding out where that boatload of prisoners was being taken, which means we lost what might have been our only lead to find Dracula, for no reason. I know that you disobeyed your squad leader's direct order to make sure we got one of the vamps alive, again for no reason. I know that much for certain."

"Yeah?" asked Turner, his voice rising in volume. He turned to face Jamie, who took half a step forward; there was no way he was going to let Turner intimidate him. "That's what you know?"

"That's why I said it," replied Jamie.

The two Operators stared at each other. They were not quite nose to nose, but the space between them was pregnant with the possibility of violence. Behind him, Jamie heard a low growl emerge from Larissa's throat, as she readied herself for whatever was about to happen. Standing off to one side, Jack Williams watched in horror; he hadn't the slightest idea of how he should respond to what was taking place before him, between a member of his squad and one of his closest friends. In the end, Jamie spared him the decision.

He casually turned away from Shaun Turner, as though the Security Officer's son was no longer worthy of his attention, and found Larissa staring at him with her beautiful brown eyes, all traces of red gone from them. He gave her a smile, which she returned; a tight, narrow smile that had little humour in it, but a smile nonetheless. Jamie walked over to her, leaving Shaun fuming on the tarmac, and leant in close.

"Go inside," he said, softly. "I'll be in soon. I'm going to give everyone a few minutes to cool off. OK?"

She nodded, and walked calmly towards the hangar. He stood on the shadowy runway, and watched her go.

*

Jamie made his way into the hangar ten minutes later.

Far from having cleared, his head was spinning with everything the people around him wanted him to be. A friend, a leader, a boyfriend, a confidant, a senior member of Blacklight; it all seemed so irreconcilable, as though someone had deliberately constructed a scenario that would pull him in every direction at once.

As he walked into the hangar, the Duty Operator told him that Jack had taken his squad to the Ops Room for debriefing by the Security Officer, and that Jamie and Larissa were ordered to attend.

A debriefing by Shaun's dad. Great. No prizes for guessing whose side he's going to be on.

Jamie nodded at the Operator, and walked through the double doors and into Level 0's main corridor. He strode quickly past the Ops Room and pressed the button beside one of the lift doors set into the wall. When the doors slid silently open, he stepped inside the car and hit the button marked C.

The lift slowed, then stopped. Jamie strode along the corridor until he reached the large double doors marked INFIRMARY, pushed them open and stepped inside.

Kate was lying in the first bed on the left.

Her eyes were closed, and two thick tubes had been inserted into her, one in each arm. Blood was running steadily out of one and disappearing inside a cylindrical metal cabinet; it was pouring, equally steadily, down the other and into her body, from a series of bags that had been hung on a drip stand beside the bed. She was connected to a large trolley full of steadily beeping machines, and Jamie felt cold fingers grab at his spine as he remembered the first time he had seen Matt Browning in this very same room.

The teenager had been hurt, much more seriously so than Kate, and the Blacklight doctors had induced a coma to try and prevent any damage to his brain. It had left him looking like a plastic doll; his skin had been so smooth and pale that he didn't look real. It had been one of the most unsettling things Jamie had ever seen, made worse by the fact that Matt was the same age as him, and had almost died merely by the dubious virtue of being in exactly the wrong place at exactly the wrong time.

For a second, Kate had looked like Matt did.

But as he approached her bed, he saw that the similarities were superficial; the machines were the same, the rhythmic beeping was the same, but Kate still looked like herself. Her face was a little paler than usual, but it still had colour in it, and her brow was furrowed in what looked like a frown, even though she was asleep.

"Can I help you?"

The voice came from behind him, and Jamie turned towards it. A doctor was standing at the foot of the bed, holding a clipboard in his hand.

"Is she going to be all right?" asked Jamie. "I'm her squad leader."

And her friend.

"She's going to be fine," replied the doctor. "We were able to begin transfusion before the turn even started. She's going to need to rest here for twelve hours, then you can have her back, good as new."

"Thank you," said Jamie. "That's good to hear."

The doctor nodded, before walking away down the infirmary. Jamie pulled a chair up to the side of Kate's bed, and lowered himself into it. Kate stirred, her shoulders rolling as she shifted position.

"Can you hear me?" Jamie asked, softly. "Kate?"

A smile spread across her face, but her eyes remained closed.

"Shaun?" she whispered. "Is that you?"

Jamie recoiled. He lurched up from the chair, and stumbled towards the door. Behind him, he heard Kate say Shaun's name again, a mild tone of concern in her voice, but he didn't look back. He shoved his way through the doors and almost collided with one of the Loop's administrative staff, a young man in a dark grey suit and tie.

"Watch where the hell you're going," Jamie snarled, feeling savage satisfaction as the man took a step backwards, his eyes flickering nervously across Jamie's uniform and body armour.

"Lieutenant Carpenter?" the man asked, his voice trembling.

Jamie saw the fear on the man's face, and shame flooded through him.

Why are you taking it out on him, you bully? It's not his fault.

"I'm sorry," he said. "I'm Lieutenant Carpenter. What can I do for you?"

"Major Turner sent me to find you, sir," the man in the suit replied, his voice a little steadier. "You are ordered to the Ops Room for debriefing, sir."

Jamie swore, then thanked the man, who backed away with a look of relief on his face. Jamie watched him go, then made his way back to the lift. He stood in the metal box as it ascended, trying to empty his head of everything, trying to find a neutral space before he faced Paul Turner's inevitable wrath.

Jamie opened the Ops Room door, and instantly felt relief; Admiral Seward was standing at the lectern, with Paul Turner a respectful distance to the side. He knew the Security Officer would be eager to draw Jamie's attention to the fact that he was late, for the second time today, but he also knew that he wouldn't do it with the Director in the room. It would be disrespectful, and Paul Turner was nothing if not a believer in the chain of command.

He glanced around the room, and saw Larissa sitting with the members of Squad F-7. She looked at him as she entered, her expression tight with worry, presumably about Kate. Angela's was more transparent; she regarded him with a wide, friendly smile, a direct counterpoint to the look of distaste that appeared on Shaun Turner's face. Jack Williams gave him a grin, as he took the seat next to Larissa.

"Lieutenant Carpenter," said Admiral Seward, and Jamie felt all the eyes in the room turn to him.

"Yes, sir," he replied.

"How's Operator Randall?" asked Seward. "I presume you were checking on her?"

Thank you, sir.

"Yes, sir," Jamie replied. "She's going to be fine, sir. The transfusion is almost complete, and they're predicting twelve hours for a full recovery."

He heard the small sound he had been expecting escape from Larissa's throat. He knew it would be a mixture of two emotions: relief that Kate was going to be fine, and sorrow that Jamie had gone to the infirmary without her.

"That's good news," said Seward. "Very good news. As is the fact that all two hundred and twenty-seven of the ship's prisoners are now recuperating in hospital in Newcastle, with none of their injuries classed as life-threatening. Sadly, that's where the good news ends. The first priority of this mission was to ascertain exactly where the prisoners were going to be taken. Who feels like giving me the coordinates?" The Director peered at the five Operators. "Anyone? No? Am I to assume that you've all come down with a crippling

194

case of shyness, or that you COMPLETELY FAILED IN YOUR PRIMARY OBJECTIVE?"

"Sir, we—" began Jack Williams.

"Quiet!" roared Seward. "Operators, these are perilous times. We are ninety days from Zero Hour. If those prisoners were intended to aid Dracula's recuperation then I'd rather he had drained each and every one of them if it meant we knew where he and Valeri were. Do I make myself clear?" The Operators nodded as one. "Terrific," continued Seward, the fury suddenly gone from his voice and replaced by a deep weariness. "I've asked PBS6 in Beijing to investigate this from their end, but I'm not going to be holding my breath. In the meantime, I'm standing both of your squads down for eighteen hours. Unless the Loop is attacked or the vampires declare war on all of humanity, you can consider yourself off-duty till then. Dismissed."

Five sets of chair legs screeched across the floor of the Ops Room as the Operators hauled themselves to their feet. Major Turner shot Jamie a look that made it very clear they weren't done, but Jamie ignored him; he wanted to get away from everyone apart from Larissa, wanted to take her to his quarters, tell her about Kate and Shaun, and try to find a way to fix what appeared to be collapsing beneath them all.

They walked down the corridor, and piled into the lift when it arrived. Jack and Angela were heading to the mess for a drink before they turned in, and Shaun Turner was going to his quarters on Level D, so Jamie and Larissa were first to exit the lift.

"I have to tell you something," Jamie said, as soon as they were alone in the Level B corridor. "You're not going to believe it. It's about Kate and Shaun Turner. I saw—"

"Where were you this morning, Jamie?" interrupted Larissa, her eyes narrow.

"What?" asked Jamie, frowning. "I'm trying to tell you something here."

"I don't want to talk about Kate right now. I want to know why you were late to the briefing this morning."

Jamie paused. "I can't tell you," he said, slowly. "It's classified."

"And aren't you just super pleased about that?" said Larissa, her smile curling into a snarl. "Isn't the descendant of the founders just so happy that he gets to know things that we mere mortals don't, gets to run off to the infirmary to check one of his squad without taking the other one with him. What a hero you are."

"What the hell's going on here?" asked Jamie, his temper rising. "Why are you so angry?"

"I'm not, Jamie," she sighed. "It's just a relief for me to know what your priorities are. The Department. Then Kate. And then is it me? Or am I further down the list?"

Jamie stared at her, incredulous. The attack had come from seemingly nowhere, and his head was spinning. He opened his mouth to answer her, but Larissa turned away from him and flew quickly along the long corridor.

16

ALWAYS AND FOREVER

TELEORMAN FOREST, NEAR BUCHAREST, WALLACHIA
13TH DECEMBER 1476

The creature that had, until recently, been Vlad Tepes stood silently in the dark forest and watched the bodies of his army burn.

The roaring pyre of Wallachian soldiers rose in the middle of the battlefield, some distance from where he was standing, but Vlad found that he could see every detail, as though his eyes had been replaced with those of an eagle. The metal of the soldiers' armour was glowing white-hot as the flames rose around the bodies, and he could hear the crackle of roasting skin with ears that were now unnaturally sharp.

He felt grief for his fallen men, but no guilt; they had died in the heat and fury of battle, died for their Prince and for their country, and there was no more honourable way to depart this earth. The guilt he *was* feeling, in the furthest corner of his heart, was reserved for three men, who had deserved better than to be abandoned by their master when it became clear the battle could no longer be won.

Three men only.

The three men he had returned to the battlefield to look for.

Although he tried, straining his new hearing until his head began to thud with pain, he could not hear them. The air of the battlefield still rang with the screams and moans of dying men; occasionally a high-pitched shriek would pierce the cool night air as a Turkish soldier put an injured man out of his misery with the blade of his scimitar. Yet in the distance, how far away he could not accurately estimate, were Wallachian voices, full of fear but alive, and he knew that these were the fleeing remnants of his army.

Vlad listened closely, searching the tumult of noise for any suggestion that the Turks had sent men after them, but heard nothing. Three parties of the enemy were still scouring the woods for Vlad himself, or his body at least, and the bulk of the victorious army were either celebrating or helping to move their caravan of tents and carts down on the field itself, where it could be pitched within sight of the fires. The survivors, it appeared, were being allowed to flee. Vlad raised himself slowly into the air, and set off towards them.

The first vampire floated through the warm, still air at the edge of the woods, marvelling at the sensation. It was not weightlessness; his body still had mass, and he could move his limbs as normal. It was as though the air around him had somehow thickened, as though his body's relationship with it had changed; he could push against it, like he could the solid ground that usually lay beneath his feet. Vlad flexed his new muscles, or altered muscles, or whatever he now possessed instead, and accelerated in the direction of the distant voices. He had floated no more than five or six feet when a hand wrapped itself tightly round his ankle and hauled him to the ground.

Vlad sprawled on to the cool grass. Anger, hot and wide, burst

198

through him; he turned to see who had dared to touch his person, pushing himself up on to his knees as he did so.

Lying in the deep shadows at the edge of the forest was a Wallachian soldier. His face was pale, flecked heavily with drying blood, but his eyes were clear and staring. They regarded Vlad without fear; they appeared to be full of a dreadful resignation. With one hand, the soldier was gripping his Prince's ankle; with the other, he was holding his intestines inside his body. A vast, gaping slit had been sliced across his belly, and glistening purple ropes bulged round the man's hand, pulsing and shifting. Vlad's expression did not change as he observed the man's injuries; he had ordered horrors inflicted upon men and women that were a thousand times worse than disembowelment. But he felt pride, as he looked down at the soldier.

Such courage, he thought. *His insides are escaping, but still he lives.*

The soldier whispered something that even Vlad's newly powerful ears could not detect. He lowered his face down beside the man's, and encouraged him to repeat his words. The soldier took a deep, rattling breath, and Vlad moved even closer.

"*Devil*," whispered the soldier, and spat a thick wad of congealing blood into Vlad's face. The vampire recoiled, despite himself. A crimson pillar of outrage burst through his chest, and he grabbed for the man's sword, which was lying on the ground beside him. He raised it above his shoulder, turned back to the soldier and found blank eyes staring up at him.

The soldier was dead, a final expression of satisfaction etched on his face for all eternity. Vlad stared down at the man, then slowly wiped the blood from his face with the back of his hand. He hesitated for a second, staring at the dark smear on his skin, then raised his hand to his mouth and licked it clean. He threw back his head as a momentary wave of shuddering ecstasy flooded through him, then lifted himself back into the night air and resumed his course.

Four and a half miles to the west, a ragtag column of Wallachian soldiers made their slow, halting escape from the battlefield.

They numbered perhaps two hundred; all that remained of the army that had begun the battle four thousand strong. The majority were injured; men held bleeding arms tightly against their armour, dragged themselves forward on damaged legs, pressed dressings against running wounds. The small number who had survived the battle unscathed helped their fellow soldiers, hauling them onwards, towards a destination that was unknown. At the head of the groaning, staggering crowd, three men walked slowly side by side.

Valeri, the eldest of the Rusmanov brothers, walked in the middle. His General's armour was dented and nicked, but he had sustained no injuries beyond a dislocated shoulder when his horse had been hacked from beneath him. He had killed the Turk that brought him down, then ordered the nearest Wallachian to pull the shoulder back into place. It had crunched into its socket with an audible pop, causing Valeri to grit his teeth momentarily. Then he had thrown himself back into the battle, without giving it another thought.

To Valeri's left walked a nightmare. Alexandru Rusmanov strode easily along the dusty road, a wide smile on his face. He was covered in blood from head to toe, crimson spilled from the veins of innumerable Turkish soldiers; his armour gleamed red, his face ran with gore. His eyes were wide and shining, flickering with the madness lurking beneath the thin layer of humanity that Alexandru wore like an ill-fitting coat. The battle had found him in his element, free of even the mild veneer of civilised behaviour that was expected of him during peacetime. In battle, quarter was not expected, nor mercy either, and he was able to give himself over entirely to the animal that squatted inside him.

Alexandru had appeared to onlookers as nothing less than a blur of death; Turks had fallen to the ground in droves around him, hacked and slashed and sliced to bloody ribbons. There had never been the slightest concern that he might sustain injury; such a thing had never happened at any point in his violent, chaotic life, and it had not happened here either. Now he walked calmly beside his brother, his mind racing with blood and violence.

On the other side of Valeri, his expression unreadable, walked the youngest of the three Generals of the Wallachian Army. Valentin Rusmanov had also escaped injury, but his demeanour was nonetheless sombre. He did not share Alexandru's visceral love of violence, or Valeri's belief that the deaths of thousands of their soldiers constituted, at worst, an inconvenience.

No. The annihilation of their army had filled Valentin with disgust, and sorrow; he had left the bodies of men he considered friends behind as they fled, men who had fought bravely in the face of insurmountable odds. The battle could never have been won, and should never have been fought; it had been obvious to Valentin, and even to Valeri, although the older Rusmanov would never have admitted it, long before the first sword was swung in anger. It came down, as battles almost always did, to simple numbers, and those numbers had favoured the Turks by a wide margin. Occasionally, the numbers could be upset, by brilliant leadership or favourable geography, but this had not been one of those occasions; the rout had been fast, and merciless.

Valentin walked with his eyes fixed on the middle distance. To anyone watching it would have appeared that he was staring at nothing, but that was not the case. Beneath his outer calm he was, as always, assessing everything around him, searching for potential threats; beyond the dusty curves of the narrow road, within the thick rows of trees that ran on either side, and from the muttering crowd that was trudging along behind him and his brothers. His sharp ears could hear an increasing number of whispered voices beginning, inevitably, to question the circumstances that had seen them brought this low. Valentin knew that it would only be a matter of time before their search for answers led to the questioning of their officers, and, in particular, of their absent Prince.

It came even sooner than Valentin was expecting.

"Why has he abandoned us?" shouted a voice from within the crowd of soldiers, followed by a clatter of metal as a sword was thrown down in the road. The mass of men began to shift and draw back, revealing the man who had called out. His armour was filthy with blood and dust, and crimson was running steadily from his left arm, dripping from his fingers and pattering to the ground. His eyes blazed with anger as he stared at the brothers Rusmanov, who had turned towards the source of the commotion.

"Why are we creeping away like rats in the night?" asked the man. "When our brothers lie dying behind us, and our Prince has fled? The same Prince who promised us victory."

Alexandru Rusmanov took a step towards the man, a look of anticipation on his blood-streaked face, but Valeri raised a hand, and he held his ground. Valeri stepped forward instead, eyeing the soldier as though he was a particularly interesting species of insect.

"What is this you say?" he asked, softly. "What manner of treason?"

"Is it treason to speak the truth?" demanded the soldier, who Valeri believed was named Florin. "Prince Vlad left us behind to die in his name. How could he do so? How could he turn his back on us in such a manner?'"

Valeri forced himself to remain calm. "If Prince Vlad left the field of battle," he said, as evenly as he was able, "his reasons will have been sound. It is not for the likes of you to speculate about them."

"The likes of me?" cried Florin. "What are the likes of me? Good enough to die at the end of a Turkish scimitar, but not good enough to ask where my Prince was when we were down to our last? Not good enough to—"

The rest of the soldier's sentence would go forever unheard.

Valeri stepped forward, drawing his sword as he did so, and plunged the blade into Florin's throat.

The man's eyes bulged, so widely that Valeri wondered for a split second whether they were about to tumble from their sockets. Florin made an awful gurgling noise, and slowly raised his hands to the blade, gripping it with what strength he had left. Valeri noted the man's resilience admiringly, then pushed the blade forward again, sending the soldier's severed fingers tumbling to the dusty earth. He felt the blade connect with the man's spine, and gave a final heavy shove. The spinal cord broke with a dry crunch, and the tip of Valeri's sword burst through the skin at the back of Florin's neck. His eyes rolled back, and his body went limp. Valeri's sword was suddenly the only thing holding the man up, and he withdrew it. The soldier crumpled to the floor, blood gushing out of the gaping hole in his throat.

"For heaven's sake, brother," said Valentin, mildly.

Valeri shook the blade clear of Florin's blood, but did not place it back in its sheath. Instead, he held it out towards the remaining survivors.

"Anybody else?" he bellowed. "Is there anybody else here who would speak against their Prince?" He stepped forward and levelled his sword at the nearest soldier, who took half a step backwards. "You?" asked Valeri, then swung his blade towards the next man in line. "You?" The soldier shook his head violently, his eyes wide and terrified. "Good," said Valeri, and finally sheathed his weapon. "Then let that be the last of such talk. You are soldiers, regardless of whether the battle is over or not, and you will remember your places or I will make you. Is that clear?"

"I believe they understand, General," said a voice from behind Valeri. The Rusmanov brothers and the frightened, angry mass of soldiers turned as one towards it, and let out a loud communal gasp.

Standing calmly in the middle of the road was Vlad Tepes.

The former Prince of Wallachia's royal armour was gone; he was standing in the cool night air in his chain mail, his billowing tunic and his leather trousers and boots. He wore a thin smile on his narrow face, and his eyes flickered with what almost appeared to be red in their very corners. He stood easily on the flattened dirt of the road, looking at his men.

Valeri was the first to react, dropping sharply to one knee and bowing his head. "My lord," he said, his eyes fixed on the ground. Alexandru and Valentin quickly followed their brother's lead, with the ragged group of soldiers close behind.

"Rise, my faithful subjects," said Vlad, walking forward. "Rise and attend to me one last time."

The crowd of men hauled themselves back to their feet and looked at their Prince. Valeri's face furrowed with concern as he considered his master's words.

One last time?

Vlad walked between the Rusmanov brothers, favouring them with brief nods of his head as he passed, then stopped in front of the remains of his army. The three Generals turned and stood silently behind their Prince.

"My loyal soldiers," said Vlad, casting his gaze across them. "I could have asked no more from you than you gave on the field of battle. The day may have been lost, but our honour remains unbroken, and for that you should be proud."

"Thank you, Your Highness," said one of the soldiers, dipping his head deferentially, and a murmur of assent rose from the crowd.

"I cannot tell you what the future holds for Wallachia, or for myself," Vlad continued. "But I can tell you the future of each man standing before me; the answer is that it will hold whatever you can make of it. I hereby release each of you from your oaths of service, and I wish you all the best of fortune. A chapter closed today, men, and a new one began, and from this point forward, our paths must diverge. So go, and live well. You are all dismissed."

Not a single soldier moved. Shock stood out on every face; mouths hung open in gaping expressions of surprise. Vlad stared at them for a long moment, then his eyes suddenly clouded a terrible red, and his mouth twisted open in a snarl.

"You are dismissed!" he roared. "Do you not hear me? Go now, before I regret my generosity!"

The paralysis among the soldiers broke, and they scattered, screams and shouted prayers rising from them as they did so. A small number turned and ran back in the direction they had come, towards the orange glow on the horizon that marked the location of the battlefield, but the majority simply fled into the dark woods on either side of the road, melting quickly into the darkness between the ancient trees. Vlad watched them go, able to do so for far longer than any of the fleeing men would have believed was possible, then turned to face his Generals, his eyes returned to normal, the thin smile back in place.

"My lord," said Valeri, his face the deep purple of outrage. "I must—"

"You must do nothing, Valeri," interrupted Vlad. "None of us must again do anything beyond what we wish to do. My friends, this day I have been favoured by a great gift, a gift that it is my intention to share equally among us. Set camp, and I will explain all."

"You wish to make camp here, my lord?" asked Valentin. "In the middle of the road?"

"Do not worry, Valentin," replied Vlad, his smile widening. "Nothing will approach without my knowledge, I assure you."

"Very well," said Valentin. "We will see to the tents." The three brothers began to walk towards the packs abandoned by the fleeing soldiers, in which lay the materials for making camp.

"You stay, Valeri," said Prince Vlad. "I would speak to you for a moment."

"Of course, my lord," said Valeri. He could not keep the pleasure out of his voice. His status as the Prince's favourite was a position he had always guarded with great jealousy.

While Valentin and Alexandru got to work, hiding their scowls from their lord, Prince Vlad led Valeri away, over the brow of a low hill. Soon, they were far enough away that the others would not hear them, beside a small grove of trees.

"I used to rise with the dawn," Vlad mused, considering the sky to the east, which grew pale. "I considered each new day a gift. Now the coming light seems to me a curse."

"Why so, my lord?" asked Valeri, in a low voice.

206

"It matters not," replied Vlad.

"My lord, this is far from the end, for either of us," said Valeri, fiercely. "Today was a frustration, nothing more. In time, we will restore your rightful position, I swear it."

Vlad stared blankly at his faithful servant for a long moment, then laughed.

"You speak of the battle," he said. "Of the throne of Wallachia. Of course you do. You do not yet see how little they matter."

Valeri's brow furrowed. "How little they matter, my lord?"

"Yes, Valeri. How little anything matters. How unimportant everything has become. But I will show you. I will show you how the world has changed. Approach me."

"As you wish, my lord," replied Valeri, and walked towards his master. "What is it…"

But before he could finish the question, his master was upon him. Vlad's eyes blazed a terrible unnatural red, and his lips were peeled back in an expression that looked close to lustful. His hand closed round Valeri's throat and he pressed his oldest servant to the cold ground. Even as his master's fingers sank into the flesh at his throat, even as he looked up into the swirling red of Vlad's eyes, Valeri's first instinct was still not to resist; he stared with bulging eyes, until his master spoke to him in a low voice.

"Do you trust me, Valeri?" hissed Vlad. "You swore that you would follow me until death. Will you follow me beyond it?"

Valeri took a shallow breath between the bands of pressure caused by his master's fingers. His answer required no thought whatsoever, even through his pain and confusion.

"I will… follow you… to the ends of the earth… my lord."

Vlad smiled, an expression robbed of all levity by the roiling crimson of his eyes. "Then give me your arm," he said.

Valeri raised his trembling left arm before him. Vlad gripped it with his free hand, and Valeri watched, uncomprehending, as his master opened his mouth to reveal two pointed white fangs emerging from beneath his upper lip. Then the mouth closed over his arm, and Valeri felt pain, for the briefest second, as they punctured his skin. A thin trickle of blood ran round his arm as Vlad closed his eyes. Valeri felt an awful moment of suction, and then it passed. His master threw back his head for a long moment, then looked back down at his servant, his eyes returned to their usual pale blue.

"It is done," Vlad breathed. "Dress your arm, then go to your brothers. Tell them I would see them."

Valeri sat up, and looked at his arm. Two small round holes stood out on his flesh, neat and barely bleeding. He pressed his other hand over it, then regarded his master with confusion in his eyes.

"My lord," he said, in a trembling voice. "I apologise. I don't understand."

"It doesn't matter," replied Vlad. "I do. Go to Alexandru and Valentin, and remember what you said. To the ends of the earth, my most loyal friend. To the ends of the earth."

89 DAYS TILL
ZERO HOUR

17

FAMILY TIES

Kate Randall woke up with no idea of where she was.

Before she even opened her eyes, she knew she was somewhere unfamiliar; the bed beneath her body was different, as was the feel of the covers against her skin and the smell of the air around her.

She opened her eyes and stared at the ceiling above her. For a moment, she resisted raising her head and solving the mystery; the ceiling above her was white and featureless, and there was no discernible sound. She knew she was probably in the Loop, or somewhere similar, because the ceiling had a featureless, utilitarian quality to it, and the absence of noise led her to conclude she was somewhere safe, somewhere secure. Then the events in the shipyard, temporarily lost in the fog of just-waking and the after-effects of sedatives, crawled into her mind, and she realised she was in the infirmary.

Kate had only been in the wide, white room once before, the day after she accepted her commission into Blacklight. Jamie had wanted her to see the teenage boy who had been down here – *Matt, his name was Matt* – but they had found the door to the room in which he was lying guarded by Operators from the Security Division. They would not explain why they were there, or why Jamie and

Kate were not allowed to see him, and they had been forced to leave, disappointed. They had later heard along with everyone else in the Loop that the boy had woken up from his coma with no memory. As a result, he had been placed under the strictest quarantine, to prevent him learning anything about where he was, or what had happened to him; it was a precaution that might mean he was able to return home and pick up his life where it had left off.

"How are you feeling?" asked a familiar voice.

She turned her head to one side, and saw Larissa sitting in the chair beside her bed, a worried look on her face. Kate gave her a smile that she hoped was encouraging, and pushed herself up against her pillows.

"Not bad," she replied, hearing the croak in her voice. She reached for the glass of water standing on the bedside table, drank half of it and felt instantly better. "Not too bad at all, considering."

"That's good," said Larissa, and smiled. "You're completely clear of infection. The transfusion was a complete success."

Kate nodded. She didn't know how to respond; delight at having avoided being turned into a vampire, although perfectly reasonable, seemed unkind given that she was talking to one, a vampire who also happened to be her best friend.

"You're allowed to be relieved about that," said Larissa, as though reading her mind. "I won't be offended."

Kate grinned. Then Larissa reached out, curled her fingers round her hand and squeezed it tight.

"I have to tell you something," said Larissa, her voice suddenly low. "I know this isn't the best time, but I should have told you ages ago, and I didn't, and now I just have to or I'm going to burst."

Finally, thought Kate. *Finally, it comes out.*

"It's OK," she said, trying to keep her voice as neutral as possible. "You can tell me, whatever it is."

"It's about Jamie," Larissa said, her face pale, her throat working as though she was physically struggling to get the words out. "About Jamie and me."

"What about you and Jamie?"

"We've been seeing each other," said Larissa, and an expression of misery and shame burst across her face. "For the last two months."

Kate felt sadistic pleasure spill through her.

At last, she thought. *Now I get to tell you exactly what I think about this; about all the lies, and all the secrets.*

"I know," she began. "I've known since the very beginning. How stupid do you—" Then she stopped, and stared in horror at her friend.

Larissa was crying.

The vampire girl's head was lowered, and her chest was heaving up and down. As Kate watched, tears began to run down her cheeks and patter softly to the floor.

The anger she had been holding deep within herself for months was instantly gone. She no longer had any desire to tell Larissa off; all she cared about, she realised, was that her best friend was crying, and needed her.

"Hey," said Kate. "It's OK. Don't cry, it's OK, honestly it is."

Larissa lifted her head, and glowing red eyes stared straight into Kate.

"It's *not* OK," she said, fiercely. "None of it's OK. It's all going bad."

Kate looked at her, but said nothing; it was obvious that there was more Larissa wanted to get off her chest.

"It's not fair for me to want to talk to you about this," she continued. "I know it isn't, not after we kept such a big secret from you. Or thought we had at least. But I've got no one else to talk to, and you're my best friend, and I just…"

She broke off, turning her face to the ceiling, staring at the flat white plaster above her. Her tears reflected the burning crimson of her eyes; they looked like little drops of fire as they rolled down her cheeks.

"You can talk to me," said Kate, gently. "You can tell me anything. You know that."

Larissa returned her gaze to her friend, and forced a tiny smile.

"I feel like I'm losing him," she said, eventually. "To this place, to this awful uniform." She pulled at the black material covering her legs, and snarled at the very feel of it against her skin. "To the way people like that nasty slut Angela Darcy look at him because of what his surname is and what he did to Alexandru, to a bunch of old men who died a century ago. I can't compete with that; I can't compete with something that everyone in this building tells him is his destiny."

"Have you talked to him?" asked Kate. "Does he know you feel like this?"

"Of course not," said Larissa. "He'd tell me he's just doing his job, trying to be the best Operator he can be. And maybe that's all it is. Maybe this is all just in my head. But I don't think so. If I asked him to choose between me and this place, I don't think he'd even hesitate."

"He's not doing it maliciously," said Kate, carefully. "You have to believe that. He's never belonged anywhere in his life. Here he has his mum, and you, and me, and people respect him. Admire him even. You have to see what that must be like for him."

"I do," sighed Larissa, and her eyes momentarily reverted to their usual beautiful dark brown. "But he's starting to enjoy it, Kate; he likes being at the middle of everything, likes being a descendant of the founders. And that's not him. The old him, I mean."

Kate resisted the urge to ask Larissa what she expected; she had only known Jamie for three months, both of them had. The intensity of their experience often made it feel longer, sometimes made it feel like a lifetime, but it wasn't. It was hardly any time at all.

"Then you have to talk to him," Kate said, firmly. "You don't have to make it a fight. But you have to make him see that how he's behaving is hurting you."

"I know," said Larissa, wiping her eyes with the back of her hand. "You're right. Oh God, I'm sorry, Kate, this is so bloody *teenage* of me."

"It's OK," smiled Kate. "You don't have to be superhuman all the time. It's all right."

"There's something else," said Larissa. "I think he knows about you and Shaun. He hinted at it last night, before we got into a fight. I think he saw something in the chopper on the way back."

"Did you tell him he was right?" asked Kate.

"No," said Larissa, but her face twisted into a momentary grimace. The heavy weight of all the secrets and lies was beginning to take its toll on them all. "You asked me not to tell him, so I haven't. But I think he knows."

Kate sighed. "I suppose he was always going to find out eventually," she said. "I would have liked to have been the one to tell him, but what's done is done. I'll talk to him next time I see him, try to make him understand. But you need to go and talk to him now, before this turns into something serious. Right?"

Larissa nodded, but there was no conviction in her face. She looked miserable, and completely exhausted.

"I'll go and find him," she said. "Fingers crossed for me, OK?"

She forced half a smile, and Kate returned it with a fierce grin, full of love.

"Always," she replied.

Jamie Carpenter closed the door to his quarters, turned right down the corridor and saw Larissa making her way down the corridor towards him.

He felt his heart sink instantly; she was moving quickly, floating a few centimetres above the ground, which was never a good sign. Larissa kept her vampire abilities as hidden as possible when she was inside the Loop; there were still plenty of Operators who thought it was a betrayal of everything Blacklight stood for to let a vampire wear the uniform, no matter what she had done to help them on Lindisfarne. Flying along the corridor like she was meant one of two things: she was either nervous, or she was angry. And Jamie had a feeling that whichever it was, it was unlikely to be good for him.

Larissa floated to a halt in front of him.

"I'm sorry for how I behaved," she said. "But I think we need to talk. Don't you?"

Jamie nodded, then unlocked his door and held it open. She floated inside, and sat on the edge of his narrow bed. Jamie closed the door, and turned towards her; she was sitting in a weirdly formal way, her back straight, her knees together, her hands at her sides.

She looks like she's here for an interview, he thought, feeling a flutter of panic in his chest. *Jesus, this might be worse than I thought.*

"Everything all right?" he asked, forcing lightness into his voice.

Larissa didn't reply. The expression on her face was blank, and for some reason this worried Jamie more than anything else. The

216

vampire girl had many qualities, but being hard to read was not one of them; she wore her emotions on her sleeve, and on her face. It was normally obvious what she was thinking, or feeling; it was something Jamie relied on enormously.

"OK," he said, and walked across his quarters. He pulled his chair out from beneath his desk, spun it to face her and sat down. "I'm going to take that as a 'no' then."

Then Larissa told him something that punched every molecule of air from his lungs.

"I told Kate about us," she said. Her tone was neutral, almost pleasant, but it froze him to his chair.

"What?" Jamie managed. "You did what?"

"I told Kate about me and you," she replied. "I didn't want to lie to her any more. We should have told her the truth from the start."

Be calm be calm be calm be calm.

"You didn't want to lie to her any more?" asked Jamie, each syllable as heavy as the beating of a drum. "So you thought the best thing to do was to tell her we've been lying to her? For two months? Without even telling me you were going to do it? That's what you thought was the right thing to do?"

He was shouting now, as the enormity of what she had done began to register; he could hear his voice rising with each word.

Kate will never forgive me for this. Never. Larissa will get a free pass because she's the one who told, but me? Not a chance.

"Yes," Larissa replied. "I couldn't do it any more. It was wrong, Jamie, you know it was wrong."

For a brief moment, when she said his name, Larissa's face softened, and if Jamie had been watching, he would have seen the desperation and misery on her pale, beautiful face. But he wasn't;

rage, now rampaging unchecked through his mind, blinded him to what was really in front of him.

"Of course it was wrong!" he yelled. "Just like it was wrong of you to let me think you could help me find my mother! She could have died while we wasted time on your stupid wild goose chase, but did I ever hold it against you? No, I didn't. I forgave you, and we moved on. And this is how you repay me, by going behind my back and sabotaging my friendship with Kate? For what?"

Sitting on the bed, her expression unchanging, Larissa felt like Jamie had stabbed her in the heart.

His words cut her more deeply than he could imagine. What Jamie said was true; she had led them into the wilds of northern Scotland, claiming to be able to uncover the location of Alexandru Rusmanov, and therefore the location of Marie Carpenter. Jamie had been desperate to believe her, and she had used that, used the way he looked at her, to get what she wanted, which was revenge on the man who had condemned her to life as a vampire.

It had been a cruel, heartless thing to do, but it had been her only option; Jamie still didn't understand how scared she had been in her cell on the detention level, how desperate. She had been sure she was about to be destroyed every time she heard footsteps echo down the long corridor, sure that an Operator in a black uniform was going to appear with a T-Bone in his hands and execute her where she stood.

"I'm sorry," she managed, her voice little more than a whisper.

This had all gone so badly wrong.

She had wanted to come clean about Kate and move on to her and Jamie; she had never meant to make him this angry, never thought that telling what she had done would push him to a place where he would bring up Marie. Now she was defenceless; there was no way for her to atone for what she had done, and they both knew it.

The pain in Larissa's voice pulled Jamie back from the brink, from the point where his temper would overwhelm him completely and he might easily say things that could never be taken back. He took a deep breath, and looked at Larissa.

"Kate's keeping secrets too," he said. "It wasn't just us. There's something going on between her and Shaun Turner, I'd swear to it."

Larissa looked at him, her eyes wide, and Jamie realised what she was going to say a millisecond before she said it.

Oh no.

"I know," said Larissa.

The fight flooded out of Jamie, and he slumped in his chair.

"What do you mean, you know?" he asked, although he already knew the answer.

"She told me," Larissa replied. "About a month ago. Not long after it started."

Lies, thought Jamie. *So many lies. So many secrets. I don't know which way to turn any more.*

"Did she tell you not to tell me?" he asked.

Larissa nodded.

"And that was fine with you?" he said. "You were happy to just go along with that?"

"I wasn't happy," she spat, and her eyes suddenly blazed red. "I wasn't happy at that any more than I was when we decided to lie to her. I'm not happy about any of this."

"But you did it," said Jamie. "Whether you were happy about it or not, you still did it."

"You're right," she replied. "I did it. Just like I lied to her for months so you could be sure that you wouldn't upset poor, fragile little Kate. It doesn't matter how that made me feel, that you were happy to keep whatever the hell this thing between you and me is a secret. It doesn't matter that it made me feel like you were ashamed of me. As long as Kate was happy and your conscience was clear, then who gave a damn about me, right?"

Jamie opened his mouth, but no words came out. He wanted to tell her she was wrong, that she was being unfair, to him and to Kate, but he couldn't do it.

Because he knew, deep down, she was right.

He was about to say that to her, about to apologise for everything, when the consoles on both their belts buzzed into life.

He swore, and grabbed the device from its loop. Larissa made no move towards hers; instead, she stared at him, incredulity on her face. Jamie hit ACCEPT on his console, and a message glowed on the narrow screen.

G-17/OP_EXT_L2/LIVE_BRIEFING/HA/IM

Briefing in the hangar immediately. Brilliant. Great timing.

Jamie stood up out of his chair, and waited for Larissa to do the same. She didn't move; she merely stared up at him, her face so pale it was almost translucent.

"Let's go," he said.

"Are you serious?" she asked, her voice so small it almost broke his heart.

"We can finish this later," he said. "I know you said we need to talk and I agree with you, more than ever now. I don't like this any more than you. But we've got a job to do. So we have to go."

She stood up from his bed, slowly, and looked at him, her eyes full of sadness and loss. Then she walked across the room, opened the door and disappeared along the corridor without another word. Jamie stood still for a long moment, trying to process what he was feeling, and was surprised at the conclusion he reached; the feeling, even though he knew it couldn't be true, that he was never going to see her again.

18

KEEP YOUR FRIENDS CLOSE

"To the ends of the earth," said Dracula. "That's what you once told me. To the ends of the earth. Yet when my blood was spilled by the American and his friends, you were nowhere to be seen, and I lay below the ground for more than a century before you revived me. I would hear your explanation for these crimes, Valeri, and I would hear it now."

Valeri hesitated. The subject of his master's defeat at the hands of Van Helsing and his friends was not taboo, but Valeri sought to avoid it where possible, for a simple reason.

He had never forgiven himself for failing his master.

When Dracula's throat had been laid open to the cold Transylvanian air, Valeri had been in Moscow with Ana. Relations between Dracula and himself had been sour for many months, ever since Vlad had informed the three Rusmanov brothers that he intended to leave eastern Europe for London, where he hoped his boredom might be alleviated and where he believed he might, after centuries alone, consider taking a third wife.

Valeri, who believed in tradition, in the old darkness of the forests and savage emptiness of the plains, thought it obscene. He considered it a profound betrayal of Sofia, his master's beautiful, fiercely loyal first wife, of whom Valeri had been extremely fond. Sofia had thrown herself from the highest peak of Poenari Castle in 1458, believing the Turks were approaching; she had chosen to die rather than be enslaved by them.

When his master had remarried in 1461, it had been an act of naked politics; Ilona Szilágyi was the cousin of King Matthias of Hungary, who at the time was holding Vlad prisoner in the city of Buda. But this idea of embarking upon a life of modernity in London, of seeking a third marriage based on companionship rather than expediency, had struck Valeri as almost blasphemous. He had moderated his response when his master had explained his intentions, although he had made it clear that he did not approve.

Dracula, in an unusual display of self-restraint, had dismissed his oldest friend without reprimand, and the following morning Valeri and his wife had set out for Moscow, where they would summer with a small group of aristocratic acolytes who regarded Valeri as something close to godlike. He had still been there, enjoying the myriad pleasures of the Moscow night, when word had reached him of the death of his master.

Valeri had immediately made plans to return, and sent word to his brothers. Valentin was indulging himself, as always, somewhere in southern France, but promised to depart immediately. Alexandru, as was often the case, had been impossible to find; the darkest, deepest corners of the world were the natural home of the middle Rusmanov brother, and that was doubtless where he was, immersing himself in the very worst of humanity as his master's life ebbed away on the Borgo Pass.

Valeri and Valentin had stood beneath Castle Dracula, staring out across the Transylvanian mountains, and drunk a toast to the memory of their fallen lord. The details of his death were inconclusive;

the gypsies who had been with him at the last knew little beyond the nationalities of the men who had killed him: an American, whom they were eager to repeatedly point out they had killed while trying to defend Dracula's coffin, and four Englishmen.

The motive for the murder, beyond the mere fact that their master had been a vampire, was unknown. In the shadow of the towering stone building, the two brothers had sworn to continue upholding the rule that Dracula had made clear to them on the day of their turning: that they would create no new vampires, that their gift was to be kept between the three brothers and their wives. They parted on good terms, pledging to remain in contact with one another.

They saw each other only three times in the following century.

For this, and for many other things, Valeri felt guilt. His failure to search for and acquire his master's remains, if for no other reason than to have given them a burial befitting a Prince of Wallachia, was a misjudgement that would haunt him always.

The epidemic of vampirism that had swept first through Europe and then the world in the early years of the twentieth century, as the direct result of their failure to live up to the one thing their master had expected of them, was another; he knew the time was coming when Dracula would hold him and his brothers to account for what they had done, and in many ways, he relished the prospect. He would admit his failings, and he would take the punishment that was due to him; he would not beg for mercy, or lie to his master.

"Valeri?" said Dracula. "I asked you for an explanation. Since that seems to be beyond you, why don't we try a simpler question instead? Do the men who killed me still live?"

The ancient vampire was staring out of the window of Valeri's study, across the swaying canopy of the pine forest. The distant rustling of the trees in the cold night air sounded as loud to the two vampires as a round of applause.

"No, master," replied Valeri. "They died. Many years ago."

"That disappoints me," replied Dracula, his dark red lips curling into a snarl.

For a long moment, there was silence in the study. Valeri waited patiently, as his master sank into the deep darkness of his memory.

Although he had not been destroyed, Vlad had been dead for more than a century. The collapse of his body had been the same, to all intents and purposes, as the death of a mortal human. His systems had ceased to function, his consciousness had disappeared; the only difference between what had been done to him and what befell every human being in the end was the vampire virus that lurked in the cells of his remains, ready to rebuild him if provided with enough blood.

As a result, the years had passed instantaneously; when his sense of self returned, after Valeri had resurrected him in the pit beneath his family's chapel, when his memory had returned to him in a moment of exquisite pain, the last thing he remembered was the feel of Jonathan Harker's kukri knife sliding through his throat like butter, and the last thing he remembered seeing was blood, his own precious blood, spraying out on to the frozen Transylvanian ground.

He had no idea what had happened to him since, nor of how much time had passed. When his powers of speech returned, nursed back to health by Valeri's attentive and regular provision of blood, he had asked his most loyal servant. Valeri's answer, given in a voice that trembled with nerves, had stunned him.

More than one hundred and twenty years beneath the ground.

It was inconceivable, beyond his comprehension. He had felt his body begin to fail him as a rage as intense as any he had ever known flooded through him, and he had forced himself to be calm, before he began to collapse back into dust.

He had delayed the question he wanted the answer to more than any other, delayed it until he was stronger, until he was something closer to what he had been. He had tolerated Valeri's long-winded, turgid descriptions of the developments and innovations that had taken place while he had been gone for as long as he was able, biding his time. Today, more than three months after his rebirth, he had summoned his oldest friend, and asked him to explain himself.

Valeri swallowed hard. "Master, you must understand; there was no way for me to know that you could be revived. That didn't become apparent until many years later, and by then it was too late."

"Explain."

"Master, the men who pursued you in 1891 returned to London after committing their crimes, and took up their lives where they had left them. But when there began to occur an outbreak of newly-turned vampires the following year—"

"Do not," interrupted Dracula, his voice like ice, "make the mistake of thinking that we have finished discussing that subject."

Valeri felt a cold shard of fear embed itself in his spine.

"I understand, master," he continued, trying not to show his unease. "As I was saying, when new vampires began to appear in European cities, the four men whom you encountered in London were tasked by the British Prime Minister to form an organisation dedicated to the eradication of our kind. They called it the Department of Supernatural Protection, master, although it is now known as Department 19."

"Jonathan Harker," said Dracula, his face twisting with hatred.

"John Seward. Albert Holmwood. And Abraham Van Helsing, the most detestable of them all. I remember them all so clearly."

"And Quincey Morris, master," said Valeri. "The American who died at the hands of your servants."

"Morris," snarled Dracula. He remembered the look on the Texan's square, handsome face as he plunged his bowie knife into Vlad's heart, a terrible, awful expression of triumph.

"They remained four men for several years, master," continued Valeri. "Some time in the late 1890s Van Helsing's valet, a man named Carpenter, was permitted to join them, and they became five. They destroyed many of our kind, my lord, but they were unable to stem the flow of the newly turned, even with the resources that Holmwood made available to them from the estate of his father. Until after the First World War, when things changed."

"A world war," said Dracula, the hunger in his voice plain to hear. "I would have liked to have seen such a thing."

"It was wonderful, master," breathed Valeri. "It was unlike anything before or since. More than fifteen million humans died in less than five years. The whole world bled, my lord."

Dracula gave a low growl of pleasure, and Valeri continued.

"Quincey Harker, the son of the man with whom you once had dealings, was brought into the Department when he returned to Britain in 1919. He immediately set about evolving them into an organisation run on military lines, and expanded the Department aggressively. They began to attack us in a systematic way, master, rather than merely reacting to our presence in their cities. For a time, there was widespread fear among our kind."

"Fear?" sneered Dracula. "Over a handful of mortal men? What vampires were these, to be so easily frightened?"

"Newly-turned, master. Their powers were barely under their

control, and they had no understanding of their strengths or their weaknesses. Hundreds were destroyed, not just by the men of Blacklight. By this time, there were equivalent organisations in a number of other countries."

"Working together?" asked Dracula.

"Not in the beginning, master. But Harker's son reached out to them, and tentative alliances were formed, most notably with the Russians. They also began to expand, my lord, rapidly. We had no equivalent, no hierarchy or means of communication. We were routed, master. By the beginning of the Second World War, our numbers had been reduced to mere hundreds; mercifully, we were able to rise again, under the cover of the bombs. Since then, we have increased steadily, master."

Dracula narrowed his eyes, peering at Valeri. "How is it that you possess so much information regarding these organisations?" he asked.

"My lord, I flatter myself that I know more about them than they do themselves," said Valeri, forcefully. "If nothing else, I know far more than they could ever imagine I know. Department 19, the American NS9, the Russian SPC, the German FTB and the Chinese PBS6, Brazil, India, South Africa and the rest."

"There are so many?" asked Dracula, incredulous.

"Yes, master; the whole planet has been carved up in such a way that every square foot is under the jurisdiction of one of the Departments."

Dracula was silent; he appeared to be deep in contemplation. After a long moment, he instructed Valeri to continue.

"The first Department 19 man I ever captured provided me with the history I have just relayed to you, master. But after a certain amount of persuasion he was able to unwittingly deliver information to me that was of much greater significance; it was he who informed me that there might be a chance to resurrect you, my lord. He had been given access to the journals of Van Helsing, in which the Professor described the results of experiments he had conducted on men and women of our kind; cruel, immoral experiments, master, little more than torture under the pretence of science.

"One of these so-called experiments had involved the regeneration of a vampire who had been burned to no more than ashes, but who was revived with a sufficiently large quantity of blood.

"Upon receiving this information, I immediately returned to our homeland to search for your remains, master. But they were gone, as was the body of Quincey Morris; this was why I knew they had been removed, rather than lost to the elements. I instructed my spy to discover their whereabouts, but he was unable to do so. As were all the men who came after him, in all the Departments of the world; the whereabouts of the remains was the most closely guarded secret on earth. Until Thomas Morris, that is."

"Was he a spy?" asked Dracula. "Was he loyal to you?"

Valeri smiled. "No, master, he belonged to my late brother; he was nothing to do with my quest to resurrect you, at least not initially. His job was to deliver to Alexandru the whereabouts of the family of the man who killed Ilyana, the descendant of Van Helsing's valet Carpenter. But Morris was the first descendant that any of us had ever managed to reach, and his position within Blacklight was at the highest level. So Alexandru asked him to search for information I had been hunting for more than eighty years. He delivered it within twenty-four hours."

"Delivered what?" asked Dracula. There was a note of excitement in his voice, and he craned his weak frame in Valeri's direction. "What was he able to find?"

"A section of Van Helsing's journal," Valeri replied. "Kept separate from the main archive, in which he described his journey to recover your remains from where they had been buried on the Borgo Pass. The journey, the recovery and his betrayal at the hands of an envoy to the Russian Tsar, a man named Bukharin, who transported the remains to Moscow. The journal marks the last time they are mentioned in any context, anywhere in the world, as far as I have been able to discover, but it proved more than sufficient. Once I knew the Russians were the keepers of the remains, there was only one place they could be hiding them. The place from where I took them, master, the night before you were reborn."

Valeri beamed with pride at the memory of the attack he had led into the SPC base at Polyarny, but if he was looking for approval, or gratitude from his master, he was to be disappointed. Dracula's attention was elsewhere; he had returned his gaze to the window, and was deep in thought. Eventually, he opened his mouth to speak, but the sudden ringing of Valeri's mobile phone interrupted him. Valeri pulled it free, saw the name on the screen, laughed and looked over at his master. Dracula nodded his permission, and Valeri answered the phone.

He opened his mouth, but the voice on the other end of the line spoke first, and Valeri froze; his open mouth widened, and his eyes flooded a red so intense it seemed as though the eyeballs themselves must surely burst into flames. He listened, for almost a minute, then slowly lowered the phone from his ear. There was a moment of silence, before Valeri let out a deafening roar of anger that shook the foundations of the house, and hurled the phone against the wall, where it exploded into a thousand tiny fragments of metal and plastic.

"Speak to me, Valeri," commanded Dracula. "What news, that would anger you so?"

230

Valeri turned to face his master, his face twisted with hate, his eyes blazing in their sockets.

"Master," he said, his voice so full of fury that the word was barely more than a grunt. "I have to tell you something that is going to be difficult for you to hear."

19

AT THE CROSSROADS
AT MIDNIGHT

NINETY MINUTES EARLIER

"What did the briefing say?" asked Jamie Carpenter.

Operational Squad G-17 sat in the back of one of the Department's vans as it rolled across the grounds of the Loop, towards the wide gate that led out into the world beyond.

"Didn't you read it?" asked Kate.

Jamie gave her a long, slow look, and eventually she rolled her eyes. "999 call from the Twilight Care Home, Nottingham," she said. "The duty nurse made it. Said someone was breaking in through the second-floor windows, mentioned red eyes and screeching."

"What about the place itself?"

"Caters for the elderly and the infirm, has a hospice wing and a mental health wing. Most recent records show eighty-four residents and staff rotas suggest a night shift of eight."

"Security?" asked Larissa.

"None," replied Kate, shaking her head. "Nurses. That's all."

"Let's get there quickly then," said Jamie, leaning back in his seat. The two girls exchanged the briefest of glances, and Squad G-17 exited the Loop without saying another word to each other.

The silence was thick with recrimination and tension, like a tidal rip beneath the surface of the ocean, capable of pulling your legs out from under you without warning; it hung in the back of the van, silent and heavy, until the squad reached their destination, and Jamie Carpenter ordered them to check their kit and weapons.

"Checked them before we left," replied Kate. She had been discharged from the infirmary when the operation had appeared on her console, and had met Jamie and Larissa in the hangar. It had been immediately obvious that Larissa's conversation with Jamie had not gone to plan; the atmosphere between them was arctic, and both of them appeared to be at least as angry with her as they were with each other.

"Check them again," said Jamie.

Kate shot him a glance that was almost pitying, then loudly hauled her weapons from their pouches on her belt, checked them cursorily and slammed them back into place. Jamie watched her, anger simmering inside him, threatening to bubble up to the surface, and turned his attention to Larissa.

"You too," he said.

She stared at him for a long moment that contained a clear question.

Are you really going to make me do this?

He stared back, his face unmoving, and she realised that he was.

"Aren't you going to check yours, *sir*?" she said, as she pulled the weapons from her belt and checked them quickly. "Wouldn't want anything to happen to you in there, would we?"

Jamie didn't look at her, but he knew she had him. He quickly ran through his own weapons checks and, satisfied that his squad was ready, physically at least, stepped to the rear of the van.

"Come on," he said, throwing open the double doors. "Let's get this done."

The two girls waited for a moment before following him. It was a barely noticeable pause, but it was there and its meaning was clear.

We'll come when we're ready. Not when you tell us to.

Jamie bit his tongue, and watched as they disembarked from the van. His head was spinning; the secrets had piled up so quickly, and resentment had followed close behind.

Larissa had lied to him, about almost everything, about the very person that she was, since the first time he had spoken to her in her cell at the Loop. But had he ever made her feel bad about it, had he ever punished or judged her for the things she had told him, even though they had put his mother's life in danger? No, he had told her it was all OK, told her that none of it mattered.

And Kate? Kate was being a total hypocrite if she was angry at him for keeping her in the dark about his relationship with Larissa, when all he'd ever done was try to protect her feelings, try not to make her feel like she was the odd one out. And all the while she had been secretly seeing Shaun Turner, which she had seen fit to tell Larissa about, but keep from him.

Jesus, what a mess.

Jamie slammed the van door closed and pulled his visor down over his face, glad that no one would be able to see his face for a while; he didn't trust it not to betray how angry he was.

Larissa and Kate did the same. They were standing in an alley that had been closed off at both ends by blue and white emergency tape. Two policemen were making their way towards them, nervous looks on their faces, and Jamie had time to glance up at the source of the intercepted 999 call. Rising above them was a large angular building, constructed from thousands of red bricks and topped by a dull lead roof. Windows stood in long rows, smeared on the inside with white residue, the result of half-hearted attempts to clean them. In front of Jamie stood a large wooden gate, big enough for cars and vans to pass through it. Beside the gate, bolted to the brick wall, was a tarnished brass plate on which had been stamped five words.

TWILIGHT CARE HOME
DELIVERY ENTRANCE

The two policemen arrived, glancing nervously at the purple visors hiding the Operators' faces. They were both young, not much older than the black-clad figures they were staring at, although there was no way they could have known that.

"Er…" said the shorter of the two, a man with hair so blond it was almost white. "Do you…" He trailed off, visibly unsettled by sight of the strange trio standing in front of him.

"What's the security status, Constable?" asked Kate, her voice distorted by her helmet's audio filters. The policeman took half a step backwards, then looked at his partner, a taller man with a closely shaved head and a helpless look on his face.

"We secured the perimeter," replied the second policeman. "No one has been in since we were instructed to hold our position."

"Thank you," said Kate. "Stay back, and let us do our job, please."

He nodded, and stepped back, followed by his partner; the two men watched as Jamie pushed open the wooden gate. It protested loudly, its metal runners screeching across the tarmac, and then the three Operators stepped through it, and out of sight.

*

They found themselves in a small courtyard, surrounded on three sides by the towering walls of the care home. Two large canvas trolleys filled with sheets and pillowcases stood abandoned by the large back door to the building, beside a pallet of tinned fruit. They made their way quickly across the yard, up three concrete steps and inside.

They emerged into a large industrial kitchen. The floor was coated with a sheen of grease, as were most of the work surfaces. Two gas rings were still lit on one of the stoves, beneath a large metal pot. Jamie crossed the room, twisted off the gas, then peered into the cauldron. A thick brown stew, its ingredients unrecognisable, had boiled itself almost dry, burnt to the sides of the pan in thick, crusty brown ridges, like the rows of a ploughed field. The smell, of cheap meat and old vegetables, hit the back of Jamie's throat, and he stepped back.

"Clear," said Kate.

Jamie looked around. She was standing with Larissa by the double doors at the end of the kitchen, waiting for him; the angle of her head and the set of her hips suggested she was not feeling particularly patient.

"Clear," he confirmed, and went to join them.

They quickly checked the rooms on the ground floor, and found them empty. The whole floor was offices and supply cupboards; nothing moved in any of the rooms, or in the long corridors that connected them. The Operators' boots thudded across the linoleum floor, and the doors creaked and groaned as they were opened and closed; apart from that, the building was silent.

Jamie led the squad up the staircase, which switched back on itself after a small landing halfway up. On the wall of the landing, in green letters a metre high, two familiar words had been spray-painted.

HE
RISES

Jamie squared up to the wall, and clicked the button on his belt that operated his helmet's camera.

"I've logged it," he said, and started up the stairs again. "We're not here for graffiti. Let's get on with it."

After a second or two, Kate and Larissa followed him. As they pushed through the doors that led to the first residential floor, a low snarl emerged from Larissa's throat.

Jamie stopped instantly. "What is it?" he asked.

"Blood," she replied, her voice thick with hunger. "A lot of blood."

"Ready One," said Jamie, and the three Operators drew their T-Bones from their belts. "Contain where possible, as per the SOP. Destroy only if necessary."

"Understood," said Kate.

"Understood," echoed Larissa. The anger and petty mischief were gone from both their voices; they were ready to do their jobs.

Jamie led them through the door. A long central corridor extended away to their left and right, with doors set into it on both sides. In front of them was a wide reception desk and nurses' station, and behind the desk was a dead woman.

She wore a look of terror on her frozen features, and her white tunic was soaked red with the blood that had poured from the hole in her neck. She was slumped in a plastic chair, her limbs at unnatural angles, dumped there once her killer was finished with her.

Kate unclipped the ultraviolet beam gun from her belt, flicked it on and ran the purple light across the woman's face.

Nothing happened.

"She's dead," Kate said, quietly.

"Confirmed," replied Jamie. "Let's keep moving."

The squad made its way down the right-hand corridor, checking every door. The rooms that lay behind them were little more than prison cells, wire-framed beds topped with thin, heavily stained mattresses, uncomfortable-looking plastic chairs and tables, a metal sink and a metal toilet, hidden behind a ragged curtain that was evidently supposed to provide privacy. The windows were high up on the whitewashed walls, near the ceilings, and were barred from the outside. On the tables of some of the rooms stood birthday cards, and crayon drawings, and letters from relatives and friends.

"I would *not* want my grandma to end up here," said Kate, as they examined the last room of the corridor. "What kind of place is this to put people? It's awful."

"I don't know," said Jamie, in a low voice. "Maybe if you can't afford somewhere better, this is where they send you. When you can't look after yourself any more."

"Nonsense," whispered Larissa, fiercely. "This is where you put people to forget about them. No one would ever choose to be here. Their families put them here when they became a burden."

"Christ," whispered Kate. "How could you do that to someone you loved?"

Her question went unanswered.

The final room contained more of the same green graffiti, written large on one of the bare walls, and a wide arc of crimson blood, sprayed at high velocity across the narrow bed and worn pillow. The occupant of the room was nowhere to be seen.

"Double back," said Jamie, leading them out into the corridor and back to the nurses' station. "Same again."

Down the second corridor they found more bodies.

They were sprawled on uncomfortable-looking beds, slumped on the cold concrete floor, hurled unceremoniously on to the chairs and desks. They were all elderly; the youngest maybe seventy, the oldest a tiny wizened man with bright, fierce eyes, who could have been anything from eighty to a hundred and fifty. They wore the same thin nightdresses and pyjamas; some had reading glasses around their necks; some had small portable radios beside their beds that were still quietly broadcasting Radio 4.

Terrible violence had been done to them all; blood coated the barren rooms, ghoulishly bright under unforgiving fluorescent lights that cast harsh illumination on broken bones and severed limbs, rent flesh and spilled innards. A single mercy had been visited upon the residents of the Twilight Care Home, on these men and women who were parents and grandparents, who had been so obviously taken by surprise by the carnage that had engulfed them, and could not have hoped to understand the evil that had descended upon them.

One tiny mercy.

"They're all dead," said Kate, finishing her sweep with the beam gun. "None of them have been turned."

Her voice was low, and thick with emotion. There was a level of desensitisation that came with being a Blacklight Operator, where horror and bloodshed were daily occurrences. But it was impossible to completely cut yourself off from the reality of things, from the human tragedies you witnessed.

"There's nothing we can do for them then," said Larissa.

"Agreed," said Jamie. "Let's continue our sweep."

The squad moved back to the staircase, and climbed higher into the building. On the second floor they found more of the same;

bodies in their rooms, drained of blood and life, nurses and orderlies strewn on the floor of the corridors, left where they had fallen as they tried to run.

"Six or seven vamps," said Jamie, as they climbed the stairs again, passing more green graffiti, the same two words over and over, seeming to mock them. "It would have taken at least that many to do this."

"First Wallsend, now this," said Larissa. "It's not good."

"No kidding," said Kate. "Nothing about this is good."

But as the three Operators climbed the stairs to the top floor of the Twilight Care Home, they had no idea just how right she was.

Beyond the double doors, the nurses' station stood empty. Blood was pooled on the desk, and dripped steadily to the floor. Where it had come from was not immediately apparent; there was no body in sight.

The layout of the third floor was different to the two below; one wing contained the same corridor of bedrooms, but the other wing was a single large room, where the residents socialised and ate their meals. The squad turned away from the double doors that led that way, and moved down the corridor, checking the bedrooms one by one.

The first two rooms were empty.

The third was not.

Unseen by her squad mates, Larissa's eyes flooded red before the door was even fully open; her fangs burst into place as a low growl rose from her throat. Then she was moving, shoving the door out of Jamie's hands and disappearing into the room. There was a second snarl, then a crash as something in the room was sent flying. By

240

the time Jamie and Kate followed her, less than half a second later, she was holding an elderly vampire up against the wall, her fingernails digging into his throat.

The vampire was wearing a pair of threadbare pyjamas, and although his eyes had reddened involuntarily, he was looking down at Larissa with complete bewilderment on his face. His arms hung at his sides, tear tracks lined his weathered face, and he looked pleadingly at Jamie and Kate as they ran into the room.

"Help me!" he pleaded. "Please help me!"

"Larissa!" shouted Jamie. "Put him down!"

Larissa reached up with her free hand and pushed the purple visor away from her face. Jamie recoiled; her eyes were blazing red, her mouth twisted into a grimace of fury. She stared at him for a long moment, then threw the old vampire on to his narrow bed, where he curled into a ball and began to whisper to himself.

Jamie strode forward, anger clouding his judgement, and grabbed Larissa's hands.

"Contain!" he yelled. "Not destroy! You told me you understood that!"

Larissa jerked her hands from his grip, with such force that he stumbled backwards. Kate caught him before he fell; he felt himself redden with embarrassment and was thankful, not for the first time, for the visor that hid his face.

"What does it matter?" Larissa growled. "It's a vampire. We destroy vampires. That's what we do, right? They're all the same, they're all monsters, so that's what we do."

She whirled away and smashed her fist into the wall, which exploded in a cloud of dust and powdered plaster. She rounded on Jamie, her chest heaving as she fought to control the anger that had risen through her without warning.

The sight of the old man, forgotten and left to rot in this horrible place, had broken something loose inside her, something she usually managed to keep buried; the awful prospect that even if she and Jamie and Kate kept getting lucky, kept surviving, then the end result was that she would have to watch them get old and die, leaving her alone. She felt the weight of the curse that had been inflicted on her by Grey, the casual way he had torn the chance of a normal life away from her, and she was suddenly furious, more furious than she could ever remember being.

"Aren't we?" she screamed at Jamie. "We're all monsters! We all deserve to be destroyed! That's what your mother thinks, and I know that's what you think, so why won't you admit it, you *coward!*"

Very slowly, Jamie reached up and removed his helmet. His face was pale, his eyes wide. He dropped the helmet to the floor, and stepped towards her. She backed away, hissing loudly, but he kept moving, until her back was against the wall, and she had nowhere to go. He reached out and took her hands again, and this time she let him, the red fire in her eyes blazing uncontrollably.

Then he wrapped his arms round her and, after a moment's resistance, she let herself be drawn against him.

Kate stood by the doorway, and watched them. She wanted to be angry, to be jealous, but she wasn't. She watched them with envy, wishing Shaun was there, so she too had someone who could make the darkness recede, if only for a moment. And she realised in that moment how thoughtlessly the three of them had treated each other, and resolved that it would not continue.

The vampire on the bed was watching too, a look of fear on his elderly face. Kate crossed the room, and knelt beside him.

"What's your name?" she asked, pushing back her visor.

"Ted," he whispered. "Ted Ellison."

"What happened to you, Ted?"

"I... I don't know. I was asleep, and then there were screams, and shouting, and then someone came in here, and then... I don't know, I'm sorry, I don't know."

He began to cry again, and she shushed him, gently. Jamie and Larissa joined her beside the bed, and she quietly asked Jamie for a restraining belt. He unclipped it and handed it down to her.

"Ted," she said, softly. "We're not going to hurt you. We're going to get you out of here, and we're going to take you somewhere safe. But I need you to put this on for me, OK?"

Ted looked at the belt in her hand; a flicker of fear crossed his face, but he slowly sat up nonetheless. She helped him lift his arms and slide the harness over his shoulders, then clipped it in place over his heart. She pulled a cylindrical detonator from her belt and twisted it a single click to the right. Red lights appeared on the two devices, then she replaced the detonator in its loop.

"I need you to stay here, Ted," she said. "We'll be back for you as soon as we check whether everyone else is OK. We're not going to leave you here. I promise."

Ted nodded his head, and then smiled, a crooked grin that lit up his aged features.

"What is it?" Kate asked, smiling back.

"You remind me of my granddaughter," said Ted. "She's always telling me what to do as well."

"You just wait here for us to come back, and hopefully you'll get to see her again soon. All right?"

Ted nodded again, and Kate stood up.

Squad G-17 looked at each other; there were things to be said, but all three knew it was not the time to say them. Instead, Jamie lowered his visor into place, and the two girls did likewise.

"Let's see who else is still here," he said.

Squad G-17 moved quickly along the remainder of the corridor, checking the rooms on both sides.

They found evidence of struggle, they found spilled blood, and in one room they found the tattered remains of an elderly man who had been literally pulled apart. Kate gagged at the sight, at the thick smell of blood in the small room, and Jamie pulled her quickly back into the corridor and closed the door. He held her shoulder for a long moment, then told her there was nothing she could do. After a second, she nodded, and they moved on, until the three Operators were standing outside the last room at the end of the corridor.

Jamie eased the door open, and heard a series of gasps from the darkness. He felt for the light switch, found it, flicked it on and stepped into the room, with Larissa and Kate behind him. The bed had been turned on its side and set on the floor at an angle to the walls, creating a triangular space behind it, which had been covered by the stripped mattress. It looked like the kind of fort children would make when playing, the kind you could pretend was a Rebel Alliance base or the secret lair of a Bond villain. They stepped forward, and Larissa pulled the mattress aside.

Beneath it, piled together in a cowering mass of pale skin and nightclothes, were twelve of the residents of the Twilight Care Home. Twelve pairs of eyes stared up at the three black-clad figures, wide with fright and damp with tears. For a long moment, no one moved, or said a word. Then Jamie gripped the bed, and pulled it aside.

An old woman, her body pressed tightly against a man who

Jamie guessed was her husband, cried out, and grabbed pitifully for the bed frame, as if the flimsy grid of metal and springs was all that was protecting them from the fate that had befallen so many of their fellow residents. Her husband shushed her, stroking her hair with a gnarled, arthritic hand, staring defiantly at the blank purple visage of the figure that had crouched down in front of them.

"Get it over with," he spat.

Jamie recoiled, then suddenly realised how frightening his appearance must be to these terrified survivors. He quickly pushed the visor away from his face, and looked down at the huddled men and women.

"Thank God," whispered an elderly lady, gripping a silver cross tightly in her hand. "Oh, thank God."

"You're safe," said Jamie, in as comforting a voice as he could manage. His throat was tight at the thought of the ordeal these men and women had been through. "They're gone, you're safe. I promise."

Several of the survivors began to cry, and he heard a gasp of sorrow through the earpiece in his helmet. He glanced round, saw that Larissa and Kate had also lifted their visors, and that Kate was holding a hand over her mouth.

"Is anyone hurt?" he asked, returning his attention to the cowering men and women. "Does anyone need a doctor?"

The survivors looked at each other, and shook their heads, one by one.

"Good," said Jamie. "That's good. Can you all walk?"

"We can walk," said the man who had spoken. "We can all walk fine."

"OK," said Jamie. "I need you to walk down to the ground floor, and out of the building through the main door. There are police outside, who'll take care of you. But I need you to go now. All right?"

The men and women murmured their agreement. Jamie took one woman's hand, and gently lifted her to her feet. She stared at him, her face a mixture of confusion and naked relief. Larissa and Kate leant forward and began to do the same, and quickly the room was full as the survivors were helped to their feet.

Jamie took hold of the shoulder of the man who had spoken.

"I need you to lead them out," he said. "Can you do that? I need you to be honest with me."

"I can do that," he replied, staring into Jamie's eyes.

"Good. Do it now, please."

The man held his gaze for a moment longer, then nodded sharply, and walked steadily towards the door. The rest of the survivors followed him; a moment later, they were gone.

Squad G-17 stared at each other. Jamie gave both girls a fierce smile of pride, and led them out of the room, towards the communal hall at the other end of the corridor, steeling himself as he did so for what they might find behind its large double doors.

The huge room was empty.

Jamie pushed the doors open with the barrel of his T-Bone, and the squad slipped into the hall with their weapons at their shoulders, ready for the worst their imaginations could conjure.

But it was empty.

Small circles of plastic chairs were still gathered round metal tables, on which chess sets and draughts boards still stood, and tea sets and piles of small plates remained unbroken. The long table to their right, where meals were served to the residents, was upright. A small television sat in the corner of the room in front of a semi-circle of moth-eaten sofas, playing BBC News 24 at a volume that was barely audible. Punishing fluorescent lights still blazed overhead, giving the room the sickly feeling of a vast operating theatre.

They spread out, searching every square inch for blood or signs of violence, but found none. They regrouped in the middle of the huge room, and raised their visors.

"Whoever did this is gone," said Jamie. "I think they took some of the residents with them, but they're gone. There's nothing for us to do here."

"Agreed," said Kate. "We should get out of here."

Larissa opened her mouth to concur, then her eyes suddenly exploded with a red darker than Jamie had ever seen before, a red that was almost black. She fell to her knees, her fangs involuntarily sliding into view, her nostrils flaring, her head twisted back and her gaze fixed on the ceiling.

"What's wrong?" shouted Jamie, dropping to his knees beside her, and grabbing her shoulders. "Larissa, what is it?"

"We're... dead," she gasped, her throat convulsing. "He's... coming."

"Dracula?" asked Kate, her voice tight with terror.

"No... it's—"

Then the ceiling above them exploded, and the three Operators were sent crashing to the ground by a torrent of tumbling lead and flying plaster.

Larissa was the first to her feet, before the thick cloud of dust began to clear. The paralysis that had gripped her was broken, and a guttural growl emerged from her throat as she hauled Jamie and Kate to their feet.

"Stay behind me," she said, softly. She was staring into the swirling dust at the far end of the room. "Both of you stay behind me."

"What's going on?" asked Kate. "What is it, Larissa?"

"Be quiet," Larissa hissed. Her head was twitching to the left and right, like an animal searching for a scent on the air. She had thrown her helmet aside, and Jamie and Kate did the same; the visual filters were useless in the dense dust. Jamie put a placatory hand on her shoulder, and manoeuvred them both in behind Larissa.

"There," whispered Larissa, raising a single finger.

In the direction she was pointing, two dark shapes could be seen through the thinning cloud.

"Identify yourself!" shouted Jamie, pointing his T-Bone at the taller of the two figures. "Identify yourself right now!"

A laugh floated through the dust, a high laugh full of genuine amusement. Then the last of the dust settled, and Squad G-17 saw what had caused the wide hole in the ceiling above them, through which a handful of stars could be seen.

"Oh God," whispered Kate.

Standing before them, less than four metres away, was Valentin Rusmanov.

His pale, elegant face was instantly recognisable; the face of one of the three most wanted vampires in the world, one of the three Generals turned by Dracula himself more than four hundred years ago, a face that was now smiling warmly at the three black-clad figures standing before him.

"I flatter myself that the looks on your faces mean you recognise me," he said, his voice soft and smooth. "However, a gentleman always introduces himself. I am Valentin Rusmanov, and this is my associate, Lamberton."

248

He extended a thin arm, clad in the sleeve of an immaculate navy blue suit, and the second figure stepped forward. It was a vampire in his fifties, clad in an equally beautifully tailored tuxedo. He dipped his head in a perfunctory bow, then stepped back a respectful distance behind his master, next to an utterly incongruous pile of elegant, dark leather luggage.

"You, of course, are Jamie Carpenter," said Valentin, and red flickered momentarily in the corners of his eyes. "I don't know your companions, however. Perhaps you would be good enough to introduce us?"

"Certainly," said Jamie, staring at the ancient vampire, his heart racing in his chest, his mind screaming at him to stall for time. "These are Department 19 Operators Larissa Kinley and Kate Randall."

"A pleasure to meet you both," said Valentin, smiling widely. "And a genuine, long-awaited delight to meet you, Mr Carpenter. You look very much like your grandfather, did you know that?"

Jamie frowned, disarmed by Valentin's friendly tone. "My grandfather?" he asked.

"John Carpenter," replied Valentin. "He was only a few years older than you are now when I met him for the first time. He was a somewhat unexpected guest in my home in New York, not much less than a century ago. He was extremely brave, which I'm told is something you and he have in common. Or have I been misinformed?"

"Why don't we find out?" growled Larissa. "Or are you just going to bore everyone to death?"

Valentin stared at her for a long moment, then burst out laughing.

"Oh, my child," he said. "I'm not here to fight with you. If I wanted you dead, surely you realise that you already would be?"

"Then what do you want?" asked Jamie, stepping forward. "Why are you here? Why did you do this to these people?"

A momentary look of confusion passed across the ancient vampire's face, before realisation dawned on him.

"You think I attacked this place?" he asked. "My dear Mr Carpenter, you must think so little of me. No, the vampires who did this departed more than twenty minutes since. I can take you to them, if you wish to destroy them?"

"Why would you do that?" asked Jamie. "They're your own kind. They're the same as you."

Valentin's face clouded with anger. "There is no one the same as me," he hissed. "No one." Then his smile returned. "I just thought you might be interested. That is what you do, after all, is it not? Destroy vampires?"

"That's what we do," said Kate, firmly.

"Indeed. And I'm sure you all do it wonderfully well. But I'm afraid you are no match, no match whatsoever, for what is coming. Which is why I'm here, enjoying this pleasant conversation with you all."

"We know what's coming," spat Jamie. "We know about Dracula. Why aren't you at his side where you belong?"

"Because I choose not to be," replied Valentin, smoothly. "I choose instead to be here with you three fine young people."

"Why? What do you want from us?"

"I want to help you, obviously."

"Stop talking in riddles!" shouted Jamie. "Tell me what you want!"

Valentin's smile disappeared. "Mr Carpenter, I have no intention of spending the foreseeable future fighting a war that will likely result in the deaths of the majority of the people on this planet.

I enjoy my life, and to be entirely honest with you, I enjoy people. They are so admirably determined."

"And?" asked Jamie. "Where do we come in?"

"I'm offering you a deal," replied Valentin. "I'm offering to help you defeat Dracula, and my dear brother. Once they are destroyed, you will give me complete immunity from the attentions of your organisation, and all its equivalents, in perpetuity. I want to be free to continue to live my life, for as long as it lasts."

"Never," growled Larissa. "We will never give you a licence to murder innocent people."

Valentin smiled at her. "Believe me, little girl, the tiny number of souls that I require to fulfil my appetites pales into insignificance compared to the thousands and millions who will die if Dracula is allowed to regain his full strength."

"I don't care," said Kate, and the strength in her voice almost broke Jamie's heart. "That's not what we do. Ever."

"Really?" asked Valentin, his voice as slippery as a snake. "I see something in your friend's eyes that tells me he thinks differently. Don't you, Mr Carpenter?"

Jamie's stomach squirmed, as he realised that the ancient vampire was right.

He *was* thinking about it, thinking how if what Valentin was saying was true, then the youngest of the three brothers' power could help to even the odds. He was thinking about what would happen if he arrived at the Loop with the world's third oldest vampire beside him, promising to help them defeat his master. But he was mostly thinking about Dracula; he had seen Alexandru Rusmanov up close, felt the elemental power of the ancient monster, like a terrible force of nature, and his stomach was churning at the thought of a vampire who was allegedly so many times worse.

"Jamie?" said Larissa, grabbing his shoulder and spinning him to face her. "Tell me you aren't considering this? Please?"

Jamie looked over her shoulder, to where Kate was staring at him with an expression of disgust, then back to his girlfriend's pale, crimson-glowing face.

"What if he's telling the truth?" he replied. "If we don't find Dracula and Valeri before Zero Hour, then we're going to need all the help we can get. He could be useful."

"You're right, Mr Carpenter," said Valentin, from behind him. "I could be."

"We can't trust him, Jamie," said Larissa, her voice full of pleading. "We could never, ever trust him. Not for a second."

"I know that," said Jamie. "Of course I know that. But I destroyed his brother, and he's standing here talking to us. Maybe he means what he says."

Behind Jamie, Valentin's eyes flared momentarily red at the mention of the destruction of Alexandru. "Listen to him, girl," the ancient vampire suggested. "He is your superior, is he not? I trust the youngest Seward made him so for a reason."

Valentin, who had more than four centuries of experience at reading people and situations, had chosen his words carefully, and they had exactly the effect he had intended. The mention of Jamie's rank hit Kate and Larissa hard, and their faces betrayed them; Kate's mouth curled down at the edges, as though she had tasted something extremely sour, and the red light in Larissa's eyes dimmed as she released her grip on Jamie's shoulder. Jamie saw it all, and felt his heart harden.

To hell with you then, he thought. *It's not my fault. I didn't ask for any of this.*

"I believe him," he said. Kate and Larissa opened their mouths to protest, but Jamie never gave them the chance.

252

"Enough!" he yelled, his voice astonishingly loud in the empty room. Surprise burst on both of the girls' faces, their eyes wide, their mouths perfect circles. Jamie had never spoken to either of them in such a way, and neither of them had been prepared for it. He saw his chance, and pressed his advantage.

"I'm the leader of this squad!" he shouted. "Not either of you! Me! If you have objections, you can make them back at the Loop. If you want to file a complaint against me, I'll take you to Seward's office myself. But for right now, just SHUT THE HELL UP AND LET ME DO MY JOB!"

He stared at them, his breath coming in harsh bursts, like a panting dog. Adrenaline was coursing through him, and he was hoping that one or other of them would challenge him.

But neither girl said a thing. Larissa and Kate just stared at him, expressions of painful disappointment on their faces. He returned their stares for a long moment, then turned back to the end of the room.

"Valentin Rusmanov," he said, and the ancient vampire inclined his head. "I'm placing you under arrest, for transportation to the Department 19 central facility. The decision to accept or refuse your offer is not mine to make, and I give no guarantee as to what that decision will be. Is that clear?"

"Perfectly," replied Valentin, a beaming smile rising on to his handsome face. "I am confident that I can convince Mr Seward of the merits of a truce between us."

"Good. I doubt our usual restraining harnesses will have much effect on you, but I'm going to ask you both to wear them anyway, as a show of good faith, if nothing else. Is that going to be a problem?"

"Not at all, Mr Carpenter," said Valentin. "It will be our pleasure."

*

253

Jamie led his squad and his prisoners back into the corridor, and down the stairs to the second floor. The adrenaline was wearing off, and he was starting to feel sick about the way he had spoken to his friends. But it was too late to do anything about it now; he would just have to hope that the journey back to the Loop would give them enough time to begin to understand why he had done what he had.

"Kate," he said, as they reached the doorway to the second floor. "Please can you go and collect Ted from his room?" There was a note of pleading in his voice, which he hated, but if Kate heard it, she gave no indication. She didn't even look at him as she pushed through the door and disappeared down the corridor. She returned less than a minute later, leading Ted by the hand. The old man was looking at her with an expression that was close to love.

He didn't think she was going to come back for him, realised Jamie, looking at them. *He told her he believed her because he knew she needed to go. He didn't think she meant it.*

They made their way down the stairs, a ragtag collection of humans and vampires. Larissa, Valentin and Lamberton floated above the linoleum-covered stairs, the two ancient vampires wrapped in the black crosses of their restraining belts. Jamie, who had the cylindrical detonator in his hand, Kate and Ted, who could have flown but didn't yet know how, took them slowly, one at a time. Valentin and his servant were talking in low voices, as were Kate and Ted. Larissa was staring straight ahead, her eyes fixed anywhere other than on Jamie, who descended alone.

In the cold air of the delivery yard, Ted began to shiver, and Kate wrapped her arms more tightly round him. Valentin watched her, a look of fascination on his face. Jamie led them out through the gate, to where their van was idling on the tarmac, waiting for their return. As they walked towards it, Jamie heard raised voices at the end of the alley, and turned in their direction.

"Helmets,'" he said, instantly.

The three Operators slid their sleek black helmets back on to their heads and watched as a policeman bustled down the road towards them, the two officers who had spoken to them trailing behind him. He was a large man, and his stomach swung heavily from side to side as he approached in a fast walk that was almost a run. He started to shout when he was still several metres away from Jamie.

"Stop right there!" he demanded. "Stop, I tell you!"

He reached the strange collection of figures that were standing beside the van, and as he caught his breath, he looked at them, his eyes wide.

"I don't know who the hell you think you are," he spluttered. "Or who the hell you spooks are working for. But I'll be damned if you're going to come into my town and—"

He got no further.

Jamie lunged forward, grabbed the man by the throat and slammed him hard into the wall. The two other policemen recoiled, as Jamie squeezed his fingers deep into the fat of the man's neck.

"Question me again," he snarled, "and I will make the rest of your life a misery. Do you understand me?"

The policeman gurgled something incomprehensible; his eyes were full of terror as he stared at the blank purple visor in front of him.

"Do you understand?" Jamie repeated, anger coursing through his veins like liquid fire. "Nod if you understand. Nod right now if you—"

Then suddenly his feet were no longer on the ground, and his grip on the policeman's neck slipped. He was hauled into the air, where he dangled impotently; he could not see who was holding him, and he bellowed to be let down, to be let down immediately. For a moment, nothing happened, then he was gently lowered back to the tarmac of the alleyway.

He spun round as soon as his feet touched the ground, and was shocked to find himself staring into Larissa's pale, beautiful face. She had never used her supernatural strength on him, not even on the first day they had met, in the park near the canal in Nottingham, the night his mother had been taken from him. But she had used it now, and she was looking at him with an expression of such concern on her face that he almost had to turn away from it.

"Jamie," she said, softly. "This isn't you. Why are you acting like this?"

He stared at her, his face burning with anger and embarrassment, then shoved her aside and strode towards the van. He slid open the doors, climbed up into the vehicle and ordered everyone else to do the same.

Larissa cast an expression of despair at him, but stepped into the air and floated slowly towards the van. Kate led Ted in the same direction, as Lamberton slid smoothly into the air. He was the second one inside the vehicle, landing gracefully in one of the moulded seats and looking expectantly at Jamie.

But Jamie didn't return his gaze; he was watching Valentin Rusmanov.

The ancient vampire was staring at the brick wall beside the wooden gate they had emerged from, where two familiar green words had been painted. As Jamie watched, Valentin took a deep breath. Then his eyes flashed red, so quickly that Jamie barely saw them change, and he spat on the graffiti.

Less than a second later he turned to Jamie, his eyes already back to normal.

"Shall we go?" he enquired politely, and floated up into the van.

20

MASTER AND COMMANDER

Valeri Rusmanov stood rooted to the spot and watched with rising panic as his master destroyed his study.

Dracula's rage – a churning, elemental fury that burned so brightly it had once called something dark and terrible out of a dimension other than our own, that had condemned thousands of men and women to agonising, indecent death – boiled out of his pores like a cloud of hungry fire. He had asked only a single question after Valeri had passed on the news he had received from his informant inside Blacklight, news that he was still struggling to come to terms with himself; the unthinkable revelation that his younger brother Valentin had betrayed them, had voluntarily sided with Department 19 against them.

"Is your man sure?" Dracula had asked.

Valeri, his heart gripped with fear at the likely outcome of his reply, had nonetheless told his master the truth.

"Yes, my lord," he had replied. "He says his information is one hundred per cent reliable. Valentin has gone to them."

There had been a moment of silence, in which Valeri had felt the air thicken and begin to shimmer. Then Dracula had leapt up from the sofa on which he had been convalescing for almost three months, and let loose a bellowing howl of outrage that had blown out every window in the study, sending the glass tinkling on to the lawn outside in a jagged, glittering rain.

He had launched himself across the room, tearing at the walls as he went, gouging long claw-tracks in the old wood, and wrenched the huge oil-painted portrait of the three Rusmanov brothers down from its place on the wall above the fireplace. He had torn it to shreds, his hands little more than a blur, then hurled the pieces through the wall that stood between the study and the chateau's grounds. The slivers of frame and ancient canvas had been thrown with such force that they had exploded through the wood, leaving a spray of tiny holes that let the cold night air in; it looked as though someone had loaded a shotgun with buckshot and fired it.

Now he was rampaging through Valeri's bookcases, a dark blur, barely identifiable as human. Books and parchments, documents and maps – all were obliterated by his frenzied, tearing hands and nails, exploding into the air and falling slowly to the floor like drifting snow. As Valeri watched, completely dumbfounded by the news about Valentin, but filling rapidly with concern at the sight of his master exerting himself so terribly, the door to the study flew open and Benoît, the elegant French vampire who had served as Valeri's valet for more than a decade, thundered into the room.

"My lord!" he shouted, over the noise of the carnage. "What on earth is happening in here? I was worried that you were being attacked."

Valeri raised his hand towards the butler, and Benoît fell instantly silent. The two vampires stared into the snarling hurricane that was Dracula; as the shelves that had held his now decimated library were smashed to splinters, a fine rain of blood began to fall to the floor beneath Dracula's blurred feet.

My lord, thought Valeri. *This fury is unsustainable.*

"Master!" he bellowed. The screeching, howling tornado spun to a halt, and Dracula stared at him, his eyes like jet black fire, steaming and burning in their sockets.

"You dare call for me?" he snarled, and took a step towards Valeri. "Like you would a dog? As I call for you? Your manners have deteriorated in my absence, Valeri. Perhaps a lesson is—"

Dracula stopped in the middle of his sentence, a strange look crossing his face. The ancient monster's chest was hammering up and down, his face covered in sweat, and his arms and shoulders were visibly trembling with fury. Then he staggered backwards, and Valeri had time to notice a drip of blood fall from one of his master's ears, before a thick gout of dark red blood exploded from Dracula's nose, and his body began to fall apart.

Blood burst from his hairline, running in rivers down his face, as though a crown of thorns had been forced atop his head. Crimson liquid jetted from beneath his fingernails, and as his eyes lost their fire, they began to bleed too, dark red tears bubbling in the corners and cascading down his cheeks. Valeri watched, horrified, as a patch of skin on his master's neck dissolved, so quickly and smoothly it was as though it had never been there at all, displaying the tendons, muscles and the pale knot of his spine through the widening hole. Then he moved, praying it was not already too late.

In a single stride he crossed the room and, without wasting even a second to give his faithful servant the apology he deserved, tore Benoît's head clean from his shoulders with one smooth jerk of his arms. The head came free with an audible pop as the spine separated; the butler's face was a mask of utter surprise.

Valeri hurled the decapitated head aside, and grabbed the headless torso of his companion. Blood was gushing from the open neck like water from a fire hose, splashing against the study's high ceiling; Valeri shoved his hand into the gaping wound, feeling the warm blood soak his entire arm, and hauled together the erupting ends of the carotid artery and the jugular vein, holding them tightly closed in his superhuman grip. He lifted Benoît's body effortlessly in his other hand, and flew to his reeling master.

Dracula was staring up at Valeri with a look of dying outrage on his face; one of his eyes had fallen in, and his face and neck were a sickening patchwork of missing sections of skin, dissolving muscle and disintegrating bone. Blood was coursing out of the bottom of Dracula's tunic, and was pooling in huge quantities round his feet. His mouth was trying to work; Valeri could see the muscles moving clearly, but could not make out the words his master was trying to form. He ignored them; whatever Dracula was trying to say was not important now.

Valeri grabbed his master's jaw, feeling with terrible panic and revulsion the way the flesh gave beneath his fingers, as though it was tissue paper. Dracula's one remaining eye managed to look affronted at this invasion, but he had not the strength left to attempt to resist. Valeri pulled his master's mouth open, realising with calm horror that he could see the study wall through the widening holes in the back of Dracula's head, then shoved Benoît's neck towards his master's mouth, and released his grip on the throbbing, pulsing wounds.

Blood sprayed into Dracula's mouth in a roaring crimson torrent. The effect was instantaneous; Dracula's missing eye bubbled back into place, and both burst into flaming red. Valeri felt the flesh beneath his fingers begin to solidify, like cooling wax, and then his master's hand flew up from his side, and pushed him away across the study. He skidded to a halt and watched as Dracula buried his face in the gushing flow of blood, and drank and drank.

Minutes passed.

Valeri stood silently, waiting to do his master's bidding, as he had been all his adult life. Dracula sucked and bit and chewed at the stump where Benoît's head had been; the butler's neck and hands were quickly turning blue as blood left the cooling body in huge gulps.

Eventually, Dracula stood up, and let the servant's body fall to the ground.

Valeri's master's face was appalling; it was coated thickly in blood, which dripped heavily on to the study floor. Dracula threw back his head and took a deep breath, then released it as a guttural groan of pleasure; he looked more like his old self than at any time since his resurrection. The air around him seemed to vibrate with power, as though he was at the centre of a strong electric field, and his arms and shoulders rippled with new muscle. He slowly lowered his head, and regarded Valeri with a wide smile. Then he seemed to remember the headless body lying at his feet, and gave it a curious look.

The butler's head was lying where Valeri had thrown it, in the far corner of the study; it had landed upright, and appeared to be watching the events with a look of genuine hurt on its pale face.

Dracula glanced at it, at the body it had been attached to, then raised one of his feet, and stamped it through Benoît's chest, crunching through the butler's breastbone and squishing his heart to mush. With a series of low thuds, the body burst; there was so little blood left in it that it did little more than fold in on itself, before disintegrating beneath Dracula's foot. The red in the ancient vampire's eyes flared briefly with pleasure, before he turned his attention to Valeri, who had not moved.

"I cost you your servant," said Dracula. "I apologise."

"Do not trouble yourself, master," replied Valeri, his voice thick with worry. "Servants come and go, as they always have."

Dracula glanced around the study, and appeared to notice for the first time the damage he had inflicted upon it.

"Did I do this?" he asked, softly. He did not appear to be directing the question to Valeri, who remained silent. "I do not remember."

The world's first vampire walked slowly across the study, his head lowered with confusion. He sat down heavily on the edge of the chaise longue, and looked at Valeri.

"This group that your brother has allied himself with," said Dracula. "They are the descendants of the men who pursued me?"

"Among others, master. They have become significantly more numerous than that, across the years, as I told you."

Dracula nodded. "You know where they reside?" he asked.

"Yes, master," replied Valeri. "I have the location of their headquarters."

"And you have never seen fit to deal with them? You have never simply wiped them from the map?"

Valeri hesitated. "Master, Blacklight is both well-manned and well-armed. They monitor the skies around their base for a hundred miles in every direction, and the ground for ten. A frontal assault has never seemed strategically wise."

Dracula laughed, a short snort of derision.

"You always were a coward, Valeri," he said. "You never had any real stomach for battle, unlike your brothers. There was a reason I always placed you in charge of our defences; you never possessed the audacity necessary for a decisive attack."

"I'm sorry I disappointed you, master," replied Valeri, his jaw set firm.

The hurt in Valeri's voice was audible, and Dracula's face softened as he registered it.

"I'm sorry, my old friend," he said, his voice low. "You never did, and I would not have you think otherwise. The battles we won, we won together. Always remember that."

"I do, master," said Valeri, proudly.

"Do you have the stomach for another?" asked Dracula. "Will you take a company of our kind, go to this Blacklight and do what needs to be done?"

"I will, master."

"Bring me their commander, alive. I would speak with the man who presumes to hunt us. Leave no one else drawing breath. No one."

"What of the other descendants of your enemies, my lord?"

"They are nothing to me," said Dracula. "The men I would take revenge on are all dead. Kill them all, and let us close this unhappy chapter of our history."

"I understand, master."

Dracula nodded, then narrowed his eyes.

"I'm ordering you to kill your brother, Valeri," he said. "Does this not perturb you?"

Valeri smiled at his master, a thin look of pure wickedness.

"Not in the slightest, master."

21

HEROES' RETURN

The atmosphere in the back of the van should have been triumphant; instead, it was as cold and treacherous as the surface of a glacier.

Kate and Larissa were sitting next to each other, their arms folded and their eyes fixed on the wall opposite them. Between their gazes sat Jamie, deliberately looking anywhere other than at either of the two girls. Separated from Squad G-17 by an ultraviolet screen that had been generated more for reasons of protocol than any faith in its effectiveness sat Valentin Rusmanov, his butler Lamberton and Ted Ellison.

The servant appeared to be asleep, his head resting against the wall, his eyes closed, his hands folded neatly in his lap. Ted unquestionably *was* asleep; the old man's chin had descended towards his chest as soon as they pulled away from the Twilight Care Home. Valentin, on the other hand, was wide awake. He was sprawling lazily in his chair, his left foot resting on his right knee, and was watching the three Operators intently.

They're so young, he marvelled. *They're just children. But the boy, Jamie, whom the two girls are so angry with, destroyed Alexandru. How is that possible?*

*

Valentin was hosting a party at his mansion in New York when word reached him of the death of his brother.

He was sitting on a sofa in one of the rooms on the second floor, sipping a glass of bourbon that was almost as old as the building and smoking Bliss through a clear crystal pipe, watching the show that was being played out in front of him. There were a number of people, men and women, vampires and humans, begging for his attention, but he ignored them all; in the middle of the floor, a small company of actors were acting out the death of Julius Caesar, with the part of the Roman Emperor being played by a human man in his fifties.

When the scene reached its climax and the vampires thrust their daggers into the man's flesh, spilling his blood across the wooden floor, Valentin began to applaud. The vampires bowed, before one of them knelt beside the dying man, and gently bit his neck. Within minutes, the newly-turned vampire was back on his feet, his eyes glowing red with pride as he accepted the congratulations of his audience, revelling in his rebirth.

Around the room, flesh intertwined with flesh, and the air was thick with grunts and muffled screams. The scent of blood filled Valentin's nostrils, and he savoured it. He had thrown his annual Theatrical Revue for more than a century, yet it was still one of his very favourite nights on the social calendar he maintained; the willingness of mortal men and women to offer up their bodies for the chance of immortality, or just to quench the darkness inside themselves, never ceased to delight him.

He turned his attention to a woman who was standing against the wall, a look of nervous excitement on her face. She remained within a pace of the door, as though she was not sure whether she had the courage to enter the room and give herself over to what was happening within it, needed to know she was within easy reach of escape if her nerve failed her. The woman was tall and slender, with long curls of strikingly red hair, and Valentin was deciding whether to go and introduce himself or have her brought before him when Lamberton appeared silently at his side, and whispered that he bore bad news.

Valentin nodded, and followed the servant out of the room. They walked along the corridor towards the stairs that led to Valentin's private suite of rooms on the building's uppermost floor, Lamberton following a respectful distance behind his master. They reached the seventh floor, and Lamberton stepped smoothly in front of his master. He opened the study door, stepped inside the room and held it wide.

Valentin nodded, then made his way to his wide desk as Lamberton turned on the collection of antique lamps that illuminated the study. With the room acceptably lit, he appeared before Valentin's desk just as his master settled into his chair. His timing was, as always, impeccable.

"Bad news, you said?" asked Valentin, pouring himself a drink from the crystal decanter on his desk. He could have told Lamberton to do it, but they were long past such petty demonstrations of authority.

"Yes, sir," replied Lamberton. "I'm afraid so."

"Out with it then," said Valentin. "I doubt it's going to get any better the longer I have to wait to hear it."

"It's your brother, sir," said Lamberton, his voice tinged with exactly the appropriate amount of sensitivity. "Alexandru. I'm afraid he is dead, sir."

Valentin's hand froze halfway to his lips. Then he raised the glass the rest of the way and drained it.

"Is that so?" he said. "Your source is reliable?"

"It is, sir," replied Lamberton. "I sought confirmation before I disturbed you and, regrettably, was able to secure it from a number of trusted acquaintances. I'm very sorry, sir."

Valentin nodded. "Thank you," he said. "Do you know how it happened?"

"The details are still somewhat unclear, sir. It appears that he was destroyed by Julian Carpenter's son, in retaliation for the abduction of his mother. That is all that is currently known, sir."

"One of the Carpenters," said Valentin. "I confess to being unsurprised. I warned him that his obsession with avenging Ilyana was dangerous, warned him several times. I have never understood why our kind seeks to provoke the likes of Blacklight; they may be mere insects, but even insects can sting you."

"Exactly as you say, sir," replied Lamberton.

Valentin nodded, then reached for a second glass and poured a measure of bourbon into both. "Toast my fallen brother with me, Lamberton," he said, holding one of the glasses out to his servant. "I suppose he deserves that much."

Lamberton stepped silently forward and accepted the glass.

"Thank you, sir," he said, then raised himself straight, as if standing to attention, and lifted his glass into the air. "To Alexandru Rusmanov, who lived life exactly as he pleased."

Valentin laughed. "Perfect," he said. "To my brother. Noroc."

"Noroc," repeated Lamberton, and the two vampires drained their glasses.

Sitting in the back of the van, with the laughable ultraviolet wall separating him from the three young members of Department 19, Valentin found himself full of an emotion he had not been expecting.

For all their differences, Alexandru had still been Valentin's brother; the blood that coursed in their veins had been the same. This was why he had sought out Jamie Carpenter, why he had decided to make his offer to him rather than to Henry Seward, who was widely known to be the current Director of Blacklight; because he had needed to see the boy who had destroyed his brother face to face. Now, sitting merely metres away from him, what he felt as he looked at Jamie was not anger, or grief, or the desire for revenge; what he felt was nothing short of admiration.

The bravery it must have taken for this boy to stand face to face with my brother and not falter, I simply can't imagine. I would have thought twice about it, had the situation ever arisen.

It was not merely that Alexandru had been old, or powerful, although he had been both in enormous measure; it was the rampaging flame of madness that burned at the heart of the middle Rusmanov brother which had always made Valentin uneasy.

As a man, it had been there, buried deep beneath a mostly convincing veil of humanity, appearing rarely and always apparently at random. As a vampire, it had been given free rein, and it had consumed Alexandru from within, until it was all that remained. His sadism, his unpredictability, his absolute lack of interest in the preservation of any life, including his own, had made him less a vampire than a force of nature; he moved through the world like a hurricane, dispensing death and pain and misery wherever he touched down, leaving nothing but devastation behind him.

Valentin, who considered such indiscriminate carnage to be both reckless and vulgar, had ceased to have anything to do with him several decades earlier. They had last spoken in the aftermath of Ilyana's death in Hungary, when grief had temporarily overwhelmed madness, and the man Alexandru had once been had resurfaced, if only for a few short days, days in which the middle Rusmanov brother had spoken exclusively of his desire for revenge on Julian Carpenter and his family.

It had been painful for Valentin to turn his back on Alexandru. He had done the same to Valeri many years earlier, without even a second thought; he had hated his oldest brother since they were children, and four centuries had not changed his feelings. He and

Alexandru, on the other hand, had once been as close as it was possible for two brothers to be.

Since Valentin had been old enough to be allowed to play without the supervision of the gaggle of nannies their mother had employed to protect her fragile nerves from the vexations of her sons, they had been inseparable. Alexandru had never resented the presence of his little brother, even when the older boys in the village remarked on it with derision; he had allowed Valentin to follow him around like a nervous puppy, without complaint or resentment.

On one occasion the son of a local farmer had pushed Valentin over in the village square, sending him home in tears. Alexandru had patiently waited until his little brother spoke the culprit's name, then quietly slipped out of the house, returning several hours later unable to lift his right arm above his shoulder. An hour later the farmer had arrived at their house, demanding compensation; Valentin, listening in secret from the top of the stairs, heard the man explain to their father that Alexandru had taken a branch from a white oak tree and beaten his son so badly with it that the boy would never walk again.

Valentin's father listened carefully, expressed sympathy and handed the farmer a bag of coins. As soon as the man departed, he called for Alexandru, who appeared immediately, ready to accept whatever punishment was about to befall him. Instead, his father gave his middle son a glass of schnapps, poured one for himself, then toasted him and told him he was proud of him. Valentin, crouching in the darkness overhead, had been overcome with a love for his brother that was so powerful he had thought his chest might explode.

The last embers of that love had still flickered in Valentin's chest when he made the decision to remove Alexandru from his life. He assuaged his guilt with the conviction that the man he had once loved so fiercely had, in truth, been gone for many years; that the destructive, impulsive creature who now answered to his brother's name was not his brother, not in any sense beyond the physical.

There had been attempts by Alexandru to make contact in the years that followed; each one had been met with polite refusal from Lamberton, and eventually Valentin knew his brother had ceased to try. The thought made him feel something close to grief, even though he doubted their estrangement had been a cause of significant distress to Alexandru, a creature who lived from appetite to appetite, on instinct and desire.

The growing admiration for Jamie that Valentin now felt confirmed to him what he had long suspected; that the feelings he had had for his brother, feelings that had once burned so fiercely that he would have killed for Alexandru, gladly and without hesitation, had been extinguished.

"Why are you staring at me?" asked Jamie. His tone was curious rather than aggressive, but it carried a subtle undercurrent of threat.

Valentin awoke from his memories, and smiled at the teenager.

"You destroyed my brother," he said, in a friendly voice, and his smile widened as he saw Jamie take a sharp intake of breath. "I was just wondering how such a thing came to pass. Gossip is a remarkably prized commodity in the world I inhabit, but the details have never reached my ears. I was wondering whether you would tell me how you did it."

Jamie appeared to consider this for a moment, as an almost infinitesimal glance of worry passed between Kate and Larissa, then began to talk.

He told Valentin the truth; that he and his friends had fought Alexandru's acolytes for as long as possible, but that they had been defeated, leaving him standing alone in front of Valentin's brother. He told him that he had known there was no way he could hope to actually harm Alexandru with any of his weapons, but that he had also realised that Alexandru knew that too.

He explained that he had emptied his MP5 into the base of the huge cross behind the chair in which Alexandru was sitting, and then fired his T-Bone into its heart, under the pretence of having aimed for Alexandru and missed. And finally, he told Valentin how he had used the winch mechanism of his T-Bone to pull the cross down on top of Alexandru, tearing him to pieces, before he stabbed his stake into the ancient vampire's beating heart.

Valentin listened to Jamie's story with slowly widening eyes. When the teenager finished, he brought his hands together in a single silent clap, and smiled widely at Jamie.

"You are your grandfather's grandson, Mr Carpenter," he said. "He would have been proud to have thought up such an idea, and he was the kind of man who once faced me in my own home while wrapped in explosives, threatening to destroy us both if I did not permit him to leave unharmed with his friend."

"My granddad did that?" asked Jamie, incredulous. "Why?"

"It was a long time ago," replied Valentin. "He had been sent by your organisation to destroy a vampire who happened to be a guest at a New Year's Eve ball I was hosting. When we discovered his presence, and that of his monstrous friend, we unmasked them, and were considering what to do with them when your grandfather revealed the ace contained in his sleeve."

Jamie's blood turned cold in his veins.

"Monstrous friend," he said. "Who do you mean by that?"

"I'm sure you know," said Valentin.

"Frankenstein," Jamie said, softly. "He was with my grandfather, wasn't he?"

Valentin nodded. "I may be wrong," he said. "But I believe that night marked the beginning of their friendship. I don't believe they were acquainted before then."

"What year was this?" asked Jamie.

"1928," replied Valentin.

More than eighty years ago, thought Jamie. *More than eight decades of protecting my family, right up until I got him killed.*

The van slowed to a halt, and Jamie heard the rumble of the gates opening in front of them. As the vehicle pulled slowly into the authorisation tunnel, his mind was full of Frankenstein, full of regret that he could never undo the chain of events that had led to the monster's death, a chain of events that had been set in motion because he, Jamie, had been stupid enough to believe the words of Thomas Morris over the words of a man who had dedicated his life to the protection of the Carpenter family.

Valentin sat quietly, watching the pain etched on the teenager's face. He didn't know why the mention of the monster was causing the boy such anguish, but he resolved to find out.

This is a business arrangement, he thought, smiling inwardly. *But that doesn't mean it can't be fun too.*

"Place your vehicle in neutral."

The artificial voice boomed through the van, waking Lamberton, who opened his eyes and regarded the three Operators with mild disinterest. Ted slept on, a small puddle of drool gathering on his nightshirt. Then the conveyor belt beneath them rolled the van forward, and the artificial voice spoke again.

"Please state the names and designations of all passengers."

"Carpenter, Jamie. NS303, 67-J."

"Kinley, Larissa. NS303, 77-J."

"Randall, Kate. NS303, 78-J."

There was a long pause.

"Supernatural life forms have been detected on board this vehicle," said the voice. "Please state clearance code."

"Supernatural life forms present on authority of Carpenter, Jamie, NS303, 67-J, requesting a full containment team and the presence of the Director and the Security Officer upon arrival."

There was a long silence, and then Admiral Seward's voice sounded through the speakers that surrounded the van.

"Jamie?" he said, sounding annoyed. "What's going on? Why didn't you code in with the Lazarus authorisation? What've you got in there?"

"Trust me, sir," replied Jamie, and grinned widely at Valentin. "You'd never believe me if I told you. But I really, really recommend that you meet us in the hangar, sir. I promise you don't want to miss this."

The van was still for several minutes, time that Jamie knew the Director would be using to scramble a meeting party to the hangar. Eventually, the conveyor belt slid them forward, and Jamie heard the interior doors grind into motion as their engine roared back into life.

"We're approaching the hangar," said their driver, his voice metallic through the intercom that linked the cab and the body of the vehicle. "You might want to be ready with some answers, sir."

"Show time," said Valentin, and straightened his navy blue tie.

The van stopped. Larissa reached for the door handle, then looked at Jamie, her eyes full of remorse.

"Last chance not to do this," she said.

Jamie looked back at her. "Just open the door," he said.

She held his gaze for a final moment, then her eyes flared red as she turned the handle and shoved the door clean off its hinges. It crashed to the concrete floor of the hangar, a doctor who was standing near the back of the van leaping out of its way. Jamie peered out of the opening, and felt his heart stop in his chest.

Staring silently back at him was the entire active Operational roster of Department 19.

More than a hundred men and women stood in a wide semi-circle, interspersed with members of the technical and medical staffs, their white coats standing out amid the sea of black. Many of the Operators had their T-Bones drawn, some resting them across their chests, some allowing them to dangle at their sides. At the front of the vast, silent mass stood Henry Seward, with Paul Turner and Cal Holmwood flanking him. Either side of them stood a squad of Operators with their visors down and their T-Bones at their shoulders, aiming them into the van. Behind them, an Operator stood holding a rack of restraining harnesses.

Jamie forced himself to breathe, then reached down and flicked the switch that killed the ultraviolet barrier. In silence, Larissa, then Kate, and then finally Jamie, stepped down from the van's mangled doors, and faced the Director.

"Well," said Seward. "What's this all about, Lieutenant Carpenter? What have you got in there, Bigfoot?"

Jamie opened his mouth to answer, but Valentin moved before he could form the first syllable. In less than the time it would have taken any of the watching Operators to blink, he was out of his seat and standing in the open door frame of the van, as though he had teleported across the short distance.

"Valentin Rusmanov," he said, a wide smile on his face. "What a pleasure it is to meet you all."

For a moment, nothing happened.

Admiral Seward's jaw fell open as the rush of a hundred sharply taken breaths sounded through the hangar. Even Paul Turner raised an eyebrow, an expression of enormous surprise by his usually unreadable standards. Then suddenly, as if a switch had been flicked, everyone moved.

Jamie saw an Operator near the front of the crowd raise his T-Bone to his shoulder and pull the trigger. "No!" he yelled, but was too late.

The projectile exploded out of the weapon's barrel, and hurtled towards the centre of Valentin's chest. The ancient vampire turned his head. His eyes burst into a terrible, nightmarish crimson black, then his hand flashed out and plucked the metal stake from the air, as casually as if he had caught a ball that had been thrown to him. His eyes faded back to normal, and he smiled as he examined the metal projectile in his hand.

"Hardly the polite way to greet a guest," he said, then turned and threw the stake out of the hangar, into the darkness beyond the runway. The metal cable that attached it to the weapon hissed as it unwound, then reached the end of its length and pulled taut. There was a shout of pain from within the crowd as the Operator who had fired was jerked off his feet and slammed to the concrete floor, his weapon flying out of his hands and away into the gloom.

"He's here voluntarily!" shouted Jamie. "Hold your fire."

Discontent rumbled through the crowd; T-Bones twitched in the cold evening air as gloved fingers rested on their triggers, but the Operators complied, at least for the time being.

Valentin floated down from the van, the smile on his face still broad, his heels clicking the concrete as he walked briskly over to Admiral Seward. "You are Henry Seward, are you not?" he asked.

276

"I am," the Director replied, his eyes staring directly into the vampire's.

"How lovely to meet you," said Valentin. "Director Seward, my associate and I formally request asylum among the fine men and women of Department 19. I have information I believe you will find useful, and I offer my service in the coming fight against my brother and his master."

"Valentin Rusmanov," replied Seward, "I accept your request for asylum, pending an assessment of the value of the intelligence you claim to be able to provide. You will be remanded into Blacklight custody, while that assessment is carried out. Is that clear to you?"

Valentin grinned. "It certainly is, my dear Director. And I am ready to begin whenever you are; if you would be so good as to show Lamberton to our rooms and provide me with a pot of coffee, I'll happily tell you anything you want to know."

Jamie stood in Admiral Seward's office, waiting for the Director to finish his call to the Prime Minister.

The Loop was buzzing with the news of Valentin's arrival; Jamie and his squad had been deluged with questions as they tried to make their way through the hangar, and Jamie had been regarded with a level of awe that seemed to border on suspicion.

There had only ever been four Priority Level 1 vampires; Dracula himself and the three Rusmanov brothers. Jamie had now destroyed one and had a second make a point of surrendering to him personally. He knew that even as he stood, waiting patiently to be debriefed by the Director, his name was once again being whispered through the levels of the Loop, and he knew that not all of what was being said would be complimentary.

As Valentin and his servant walked casually out of the hangar, surrounded by three squads of Operators looking for the slightest suspicious movement and watched incredulously by almost a hundred men, Admiral Seward had appeared at Jamie's side and told him he expected to be debriefed in his office in ten minutes. Jamie had asked whether the Director was requesting the presence of the whole of Squad G-17, and was told that only he need attend.

Admiral Seward hung up his phone, then regarded Jamie with a smile of mild incomprehension.

"It's always you, isn't it?" he said. "Why don't these things happen to anyone else? Why is it always you?"

"Just lucky, sir," replied Jamie.

"You don't believe that any more than I do," said Seward. "Tell me the truth; why do you think Valentin Rusmanov chose you, out of all the Operators from all the Departments in the world, to surrender to?"

"Honestly, sir," said Jamie. "I don't know. When I saw him, I thought he was there to kill me for what I did to Alexandru. But then he mentioned something about my grandfather; he told me they met a long time ago. I think him coming to me had something to do with that, sir."

"That makes a certain amount of sense," said Seward. "John, your grandfather, was officially retired by the time I joined the Department in '81, but he was still around so much you would never have known it. He used to talk about Valentin with a sort of grudging respect; I always thought it was a worthy adversary sort of thing, but maybe there was more to it."

"Maybe, sir," said Jamie. "My granddad certainly seems to have left an impression on him."

"You'd have liked John," said Seward, nostalgia creeping into his voice. "Everybody did. It's a shame you never got to meet him; he'd have been incredibly proud of you."

A lump leapt into Jamie's throat.

"Thank you, sir," he replied. "I'd like to think that's true." He tried to force the lump back down, and struck out for safer ground where his dead ancestors weren't waiting around every corner to pull at his heartstrings.

"Who's going to lead the interrogation of Valentin, sir?" he asked.

"Major Turner," replied Seward.

"Good news," said Jamie. "Sir, I really need to get some sleep. May I be dismissed?"

"By all means," replied Seward. "I'd advise you to get as much as you can. The interrogation is scheduled to begin at 0800 tomorrow, and attendance is mandatory for all Zero Hour Task Force members. Please try not to be late."

Jamie's face fell. "Sir, how long do you think the interrogation is going to last?" he asked.

Seward laughed. "You mean, how long will it take for Valentin Rusmanov to tell us everything he knows that we don't?" he replied. "I'd clear your schedule. Indefinitely."

Jamie walked along the corridor outside the Director's quarters, his head pounding.

The exhilaration of bringing Valentin Rusmanov to the Loop was wearing off, leaving in its place a sticky, bitter-tasting feeling of unease. He had spoken to Kate and Larissa in a way he had never done before, and he had no idea where his words had left them, whether what seemed to be broken between them could be repaired.

Suddenly he was overcome with an overwhelming wave of grief that he couldn't talk to Frankenstein about what was happening; the monster's advice was often not the easiest to hear, but his motives had proved to be beyond question.

He was the one person who had always been on Jamie's side.

Then the nervous, earnest image of his mother appeared in his head, and guilt quickly displaced grief.

I forget, he thought. *Sometimes I forget she's down there.*

He walked quickly to the lift at the end of the corridor, and pressed the button that would take him down to Level H, the detention level. Despite everything he was, everything the people around him wanted him to be, he was still a teenage boy who sometimes, just sometimes, really needed his mother.

22

TINFOIL HATS

STAVELEY, NORTH DERBYSHIRE
TWO HOURS EARLIER

Matt Browning was almost at the front door when his father called his name from the living room. He cursed silently, dropped his backpack by the umbrella stand and went to see what his dad wanted.

His mother had taken his sister to visit Matt's grandparents in Grantham for the weekend, leaving the men of the family alone. The debate had lasted almost a week, as Lynne Browning tried to convince herself it was all right for her to let her son out of her sight for a whole forty-eight hours. She had eventually caught a taxi to the train station the previous evening, casting glances back at the house as the car pulled away, despite Matt and Greg's endless reassurances that they could look after each other for a single weekend.

"All right, Dad," he said, as casually as he was able to manage.

It had taken him most of the day to work himself up to what he was about to do, and he knew himself well enough to know that if he was delayed too long by his father, he might conceivably lose his nerve.

"How's it going?" asked Greg, brightly. "Everything all right?"

Matt's father was sitting in his armchair in front of the TV, peering round at his son. On the previous occasions that his wife had gone away for the weekend, the area surrounding the chair would by this point have already become a mountain of empty lager cans and crumpled takeaway trays, but the floor was scrupulously clear. It was one of many small things that changed since Matt had come home.

"I'm fine, Dad," replied Matt, forcing a smile. "You OK?"

Greg nodded. "You heading out?" he asked.

"Going to Jeff's," replied Matt. "We've got a project. Is that all right?"

"Of course," replied Greg. "Of course it is." There was a pregnant pause, which Matt resisted the urge to fill. It seemed as though his dad wanted to say something else, but after a few seconds, he simply smiled at his son. "Have a good time," he said. "Don't stay out too late, OK?"

"I won't, Dad," replied Matt. "I promise."

His father nodded, then turned back to the TV.

Matt gratefully backed out of the living room and into the hall. He slung the backpack over his shoulder for the second time, took a quick glance around the house he had lived in his whole life, then opened the front door and stepped outside.

The backpack contained nothing that would have been any use to Jeff, who Matt knew was playing football in the park at the end of their road, or that would have helped with a school project. Inside his bag were two sandwiches he had bought on his way home from school, a bottle of water and a wooden stake he had carved in the school woodwork shop during his lunch hour.

He had felt faintly ridiculous carving it, and had kept a close eye on the doors to the technology block; he had no desire to try and explain what he was making to anyone. He doubted that it would be of any real use if he encountered a vampire; he had always gone to great lengths to avoid even the remote possibility of a fight with anyone, let alone a creature like the girl who had landed in his garden. But it made him feel slightly better to have it in his backpack.

Matt closed the gate to the small front garden behind him, turned to his right and started walking. Behind him, he could hear shouts and whistles from the park at the end of the road, the soundtrack of a dozen ramshackle games of football, of teenage boys and girls furtively smoking and drinking cheap cider and wine. He had never had much interest in that world, filled as it was with pitfalls and dishonesty and insincerity, and since waking up in the infirmary, he had turned his back on it entirely.

He had barely spoken to anyone at school, a stance that had gone unnoticed for the first day or so, before boys who had no normal desire to talk to him began taking fraudulent offence at his distant demeanour, and began to demand he speak. They had realised he didn't want to, so now there was sport in making him do so.

He walked quickly through the fading light of the evening. He passed the small high street, ignored a couple of half-hearted shouted insults from some of the sixth-formers who were congregated round the Chinese takeaway, swigging heartily from brown plastic bottles of cider. At the end of the road, he swung left through a narrow alley between a furniture shop and an empty lot, his heartrate rising momentarily as he remembered the time that Mark Morris had chased him through the alley with a pot of UVA glue, promising Matt that he was going to glue his eyes shut if he caught him. He hadn't, but the memory still made Matt's stomach churn.

At the end of the main road, fifteen minutes' walk away, was another park, and it was this expanse of green, far enough away from his house and the prying eyes of the small number of people who might recognise him, that was his destination. He adjusted the backpack, and walked quickly towards it.

Next to the metal gates that led into the park was a public phone box. Matt stepped into it, placed his bag on the ground and lifted the receiver from its cradle. He took a deep breath.

You know it's real. You were there. You know.

He reached out with a hand that trembled slightly in the evening air and dialled 999. A female voice answered instantly.

"999 emergency, which service do you require?"

"None of them," he answered, his voice steady.

"Pardon me?" asked the voice.

"I need something else."

"Please state your emergency or I will report this as a nuisance call."

Matt fished a piece of paper out of his pocket, and held it up in front of his face. On it were written six words.

"My name is Matt Browning," he said. "I just saw two vampires attacking a girl in Centenary Park, Staveley, North Derbyshire."

"Sir, I don't have time—"

"I saw their fangs clearly. I saw blood on the girl's neck. Then two men showed up and followed the vampires. They were wearing black uniforms. With purple visors."

"Sir, I have reported this call. Please clear the line immediately, or there will be serious consequences."

"Absolutely," said Matt. "Thank you."

He hung up the phone, slung his bag back over his shoulder and stepped out of the phone box. The gates to the park were still open; he walked steadily through them, then made his way to a small children's playground not far from the entrance. He sat down on a swing, and began to wait.

One hundred miles to the north, inside the Department 19 Northern Outpost at RAF Fylingdales, a light began to flash on the wide radio desk, and a console standing beside it began to beep.

The Duty Operator, a young man named Fitzwilliam, hit a button on the control panel, and a printer whirred into life. The sheet of paper that emerged from the tray was headed ECHELON INTERCEPT, and contained a transcript of the call that Matt had made, only ninety seconds earlier. Fitzwilliam read it, entered it into the electronic logbook on his computer screen and keyed a six-digit code into a panel on the radio desk.

In the Loop's Surveillance Division, the message emerged from a bank of printers next to a real-time satellite map of the UK, on which a new red dot had now appeared. An Operator passed the printout to the Divisional Duty Officer, who immediately picked up the telephone on his desk, and told the person on the other end of the line that they had a Condition 6.

Somewhere else, the transcript of the phone call appeared on the screen of a laptop, the letters glowing green in the darkened room. A hand pressed a series of keys, opening a live VOIP connection.

"There may be a problem," said a voice.

Twenty minutes later Matt was swinging his legs gently beneath him, lost in thought, when a voice called his name. He started, almost overbalanced, then gripped the chains of the swing in his hands and looked towards the source of the sound, a surge of excitement bursting through him.

It worked. It really worked.

Then he caught sight of the two men approaching him, and his excitement was swiftly replaced by a cold ripple of fear.

The men were walking towards him with smiles on their faces, their arms dangling loosely at their sides, but neither was wearing the black uniform that Matt had seen on the soldiers who came into his house, the military overalls and body armour that he had been expecting. Nor was either wearing a helmet with a purple visor. The two men, who were now only fifteen metres away from him, were wearing dark suits, and the smiles on their faces were too wide, like the grins of sharks.

Matt leapt down from the swing; he could feel adrenaline pouring into his bloodstream, could feel the muscles in his legs tensing, telling him to run, but he forced himself to stand his ground. Then one of the men drew back his lips and grinned at Matt with a mouthful of teeth that looked like carving knives, and he turned and sprinted across the playground.

He ran hard, his arms and legs pumping, his eyes locked on the copse of trees that stood beyond the low fence that enclosed the children's area. He didn't look back, not even when he heard two strange rushes of air, like the noise a foot pump makes if it is not connected to anything; he just ran. Then the air fluttered around him, and the two men dropped casually out of the sky in front of him. They made no sound as they landed, their feet sliding gently to the ground. Matt skidded to a halt, no more than two metres away from them.

"Where do you think you're going?"

It was the one with the mouth full of knives who spoke, his grin now so wide it looked as though it was about to tear his face in half.

"Little boys who cry wolf need to be punished," he continued, and this drew a dull, rasping laugh from his partner.

Matt stared at them, rooted to the ground by fear, the adrenaline in his system already used up and gone.

"I've got an idea," said the second man, the one who had laughed. "Let's see if he can still make phone calls without a tongue."

From behind him, there came a screech of tyres, but Matt's brain barely registered it. He was going to die, or worse. Vampires were real; he had been right, and it was going to be his undoing.

Then a voice bellowed for him to get down, and he threw himself to the concrete. Two loud explosions of air burst in the silent park, then two somethings whistled above his head, whining through the air. Two horrible crunching noises sounded, awfully near him. A pair of dull thuds shook the ground beneath him, and something foul and wet pattered down on his hands and the back of his neck, like a thick rain.

Matt lifted his head. The two vampires were gone; where they had been were wide splashes of crimson, studded with lumps of steaming flesh. His gorge rose in his throat, and he gagged, clamping a hand across his mouth and looking away.

"Matt Browning?"

He rolled over on to his back, looked up and saw his reflection in a curved piece of purple plastic. There were two figures standing over him, dressed in black uniforms, their faces covered by visored helmets. Both were carrying a weapon Matt had never seen before, a long wide tube with a handle and a trigger set into the underside. One of the figures, he guessed it was the one who had said his name, was extending a hand down towards him. Then a wave of nausea hit him, and his vision turned grey at the edges.

"Oh good," he said, dreamily. "You came. I knew you would."

Then he fell back on to the concrete in a dead faint.

88 DAYS TILL ZERO HOUR

23

THE INTERROGATION OF VALENTIN RUSMANOV

Jamie walked on to Level H ten minutes before the interrogation was due to begin, but still found himself the last to arrive. The rest of the Zero Hour Task Force were already gathered outside the Security Office as he emerged from the double airlock and cast a glance down the corridor, to the last cell on the left where his mother now lived.

Admiral Seward glanced round as Jamie approached, and nodded.

"Good morning," he said, formally.

"Morning, sir," replied Jamie, then quickly greeted the rest of the Task Force. Jack Williams gave him one of his usual grins, Cal Holmwood and Professor Talbot threw genial nods in his direction; Marlow, Brennan and the Communications Operator whose name Jamie had now learnt was Jarvis, gave no indication that they were even aware of his presence. Paul Turner, whose job it would be to interrogate the ancient vampire, surprised Jamie by giving him a brief nod of acknowledgement before he addressed the group.

"Shall we get started?" Turner asked. "I see no reason to wait any longer."

"Lead the way, Paul," replied Seward.

Turner did as he was ordered, turning on his heels and striding away down the cellblock, with the rest of the Zero Hour Task Force following behind him. He drew to a halt at a cell halfway down the corridor on the right-hand side; the rest of the group lined up alongside him and looked through the shimmering ultraviolet wall.

It was empty.

"What the hell?" said Cal Holmwood, turning to look at Admiral Seward.

The Director's face drained of all colour. He scrambled the radio from his belt, keyed in a nine-digit code and held it to his ear.

"Code seven," he said into the mouthpiece. "Unauthorised supernatural presence in the facility. Scramble all—"

"That's really not necessary," said a smooth voice. "I'm right here."

Seward froze, then muttered "Stand by" into the radio. The voice had come from the next cell down the block, and the eight men stepped slowly round the dividing wall.

Valentin Rusmanov was sitting in a chair in the middle of the cell with a towel around his shoulders, and shaving foam covering one side of his face. Lamberton, the old vampire's butler, glanced briefly up at the black-clad figures as they appeared on the other side of the ultraviolet barrier, then returned to his task. With three smooth strokes of a beautiful, pearl-handled straight razor, he finished Valentin's morning shave, and retreated to the sink at the rear of the cell to wash the blade. Valentin stood up, using the towel to dry his face. When he turned back to face the line of Operators, his expression was warm and friendly.

"Oh, don't be annoyed, for heaven's sake," he said, seeing the looks of outrage on the faces before him. "This barrier may be all well and good for a vampire who was turned the day before yesterday, but when you've been around as long as I have, it's little more than decoration."

There was a blur of movement, too fast for the eye to follow, and Valentin was standing outside the cell, in the corridor beside them. He extended a hand towards Operator Brennan, who instinctively took a step backwards.

"Valentin Rusmanov," said the old vampire. "Lovely to meet you."

Brennan, suddenly incredibly aware that the rest of the group were watching him, struggled for composure, found it and stepped forward.

"Brennan," he said, shaking the vampire's hand cautiously. "Operator Brennan."

"Operator?" asked Valentin, rolling the word around his mouth as though it was some delicious morsel. "That's marvellous. What's your Christian name, Operator Brennan?"

"No names," said Admiral Seward, sharply, before Brennan had a chance to answer. "Mr Rusmanov," he continued, turning square to face the vampire. "I'm sure you'll forgive me if I'd rather my men don't give you their personal details. And while your ability to pass through our barrier unharmed is certainly very impressive, I'm going to ask you to step back into Mr Lamberton's cell, at least for the time being. Providing you have no objections?"

Valentin looked at the Director for a long moment, then smiled.

"Of course not, Mr Seward," he said. "No objections whatsoever."

The old vampire blurred a second time, and was back inside the cell. He flopped lazily into the chair, facing the men on the other side of the redundant wall of light.

"Are we to talk like this?" asked Valentin. "You on your side, me on mine? Hardly civilised."

"We're not here to talk, Mr Rusmanov," said Paul Turner, stepping forward. "We're here to ask questions, that we expect you to answer. If you'd rather I asked you them from inside the cell, that's fine with me. I am not afraid of you."

"Then by all means, join me," replied Valentin. "Although do me the courtesy of your rank and your surname at least. I don't think I will be able to use those small pieces of information for nefarious means."

"My name is Major Paul Turner," he replied, stepping through the barrier and ignoring the grimace of anger on Admiral Seward's face. He walked across the cell, to where Lamberton was already holding out the second plastic chair for him to take. He lifted it from the vampire's hands, and set it down a short distance away from Valentin, who turned his own chair to face the Security Officer.

"I'm sure it will not surprise you," Turner continued, "to know that this interview is being recorded. I hope you will also realise I'm telling you this only for reasons of civility. It's not required that I do so."

"Noted," replied Valentin. "And appreciated."

The Security Officer nodded, then looked over at his Director.

"Proceed, Major Turner," said Admiral Seward.

"Valentin Rusmanov," said Turner, "would you mind repeating the verbal offer you made to Lieutenant Carpenter last night?"

"Not at all," said Valentin, stretching his long legs out before him and crossing them at the ankles. "I offered young Mr Carpenter my assistance in defeating my brother, Valeri, and the newly resurrected Count Dracula. In exchange, I requested indefinite immunity from persecution by this organisation, and all others like it."

"And you stand by that offer today?"

"I do."

"Before we address the specifics of your proposal," said Paul Turner, "I have two questions; firstly, why would you do this, and secondly, why would you possibly expect us to be able to trust you?"

After Valeri left the study on the top floor of the old building on West Eighty-Fifth Street, Valentin continued to stare out of the window for a long time.

A news helicopter hovered over the north end of Central Park, its spotlight roving among the thick tangles of trees that ringed the reservoir; in the distance, tiny pairs of flashing lights gleamed above the runways of Newark and La Guardia, a constant stream of arrivals and departures. Valentin noticed none of it; his mind was adrift in the past.

He was remembering the time before the death of Dracula, remembering what it was like to be subordinate, to live at the beck and call of another. He was remembering how it felt to be the youngest, to stand in the shadows cast by his brothers, especially by Valeri, hated, stupid, arrogant Valeri, who never strayed more than a few yards from his master, like a bloodhound panting at his owner's side. He was remembering how it had felt, and thinking about everything he would be forced to give up if he returned home, when he made a decision that felt immediately right.

"Never again," he whispered. "Never again."

He turned from the window, summoned Lamberton and told him to cancel the evening's festivities. Lamberton raised an eyebrow; the Feast of the Souls, the annual black-tie dinner party where the food was a living menu gathered from every continent, was one of his master's favourite social events. But he immediately did as he was told, and left Valentin in peace.

The following morning Valentin called for his loyal aide again, and told him he was dismissing him from his service.

"I see," said Lamberton, his face a sombre mask of utter professionalism. "Might I ask what aspect of my performance has been unsatisfactory, sir? I would be most grateful to know, so I can attempt to improve it."

"You know full well that your performance has never been anything less than exemplary, Lamberton," replied Valentin.

"I appreciate that, sir," he replied. "In which case, I must confess I find myself at something of a loss as to the reasons for my dismissal. Sir."

Valentin looked at his old friend with enormous warmth in his eyes.

"I've made a decision, Lamberton," he said, slowly. "A decision that will put me in great peril, peril that I cannot ask you to share. I am not going to return to my brother and his master; I am, in fact, planning to do the exact opposite. I will shortly depart for England, where I intend to offer my services to Blacklight, to help them destroy Valeri and Dracula both."

Silence descended on the study, as Lamberton considered the implications of his master's words. Eventually, he spoke.

"In which case," he said, "I refuse your dismissal."

"Pardon me?"

"I have never cared for your brother Valeri, sir," said Lamberton, his eyes flashing momentarily. "I have always considered him a pompous fool, a boot-licker who has spent the last century trying to revive his master because he is incapable of living a life in which there is no one to tell him what to do. Alexandru, if nothing else, was his own man; I shed no tears over his death, but he was, to me, the equal of a thousand Valeris."

Passion was rising in the servant's voice. "I have no wish to spend the rest of my life trailing at the heel of anyone," he continued. "Not Valeri, and not his master either. It has been my honour to serve you this past century and more, and I swore to myself long ago that I would never serve another. I have long fulfilled my own small ambitions, and I am proud of my life, here at your side. I do not wish to see Dracula destroy *everything we have built, nor see him tear this world apart for no better reasons than arrogance and hubris. Both he and Valeri are relics of a long-dead world who I would gladly see put out of their misery."*

Valentin's eyes widened as Lamberton spoke. He had never, in more than a hundred years, heard the servant speak in such a way; a feeling of great pride swelled within his chest, and he broke into a wide smile of admiration.

"Very well," he said. "Your position remains as it was. Please, begin making the arrangements for our departure."

"Very good, sir," said Lamberton, the tiniest flicker of a smile curling the corners of his mouth. Then he floated backwards out of the study, closing the door gently behind him.

"I would have thought my reasons would be obvious, even to you," replied Valentin, smiling. "I have no desire to see Dracula rise to power again. As to why you should believe that my motives are genuine, I offer you this: you are all still alive."

"What do you mean by that?" asked Turner, his eyes narrowing.

"Exactly what I said, my dear Major. Standing before me are the Director of Blacklight, the Security Officer of this facility, and members of the Holmwood and Carpenter families. If I had come here with some devious plan to hurt the Department from the inside, then surely all I would need to do was step through your little barrier and tear the heads from your shoulders. But I haven't. If you don't find that compelling evidence of my honesty, then I'm afraid I don't know what else to say."

"Let's say I choose to believe you," said Turner. "Explain to me exactly what you are proposing."

Valentin rolled his eyes, and glanced at Lamberton, who was watching the exchange with professional disinterest. "You cannot

297

defeat Dracula if he is allowed to regain his full strength," he said. "It will be impossible. You would have little chance of destroying my brother, even with all your men and all their little stake guns, and comparing Dracula to Valeri is like comparing a Rottweiler to a poodle. Without me, he will rise, and you will all die."

"And with you? How exactly will you help us defeat him?"

"I offer no guarantee that I can," said Valentin, simply. "In all likelihood, my assistance will merely delay the inevitable. But I promise you this: with me on your side, you have a chance. A tiny one, in all likelihood, but a chance, nonetheless. Without me, you don't."

Valentin looked directly at Jamie as he spoke, and he flinched under the vampire's immortal gaze. He looked down the line of men at Admiral Seward, who was staring silently at Valentin; he looked extremely pale under the fluorescent lights of the cellblock.

He knows what Valentin is saying is true, realised Jamie, and felt a chill race up his spine. *We can't stop Dracula on our own.*

"For what you are suggesting," continued Major Turner, "which is essentially nothing more than a promise to *try* and help us defeat your former master, you are expecting to be allowed to murder innocent men and women, with impunity, for the rest of your life. Have I got that right?"

"You have," replied Valentin, a cruel smile creeping across his face. "But I'm afraid that's not all."

"What else would you like?" snarled Turner, his composure momentarily deserting him. "The keys to the Loop? A virgin girl sent to your house every day?"

"Sarcasm is the lowest form of wit," replied Valentin, coldly. "And no, since you ask, I require nothing so crass. I want the opportunity to engage in conversation with Mr Carpenter, alone. That's all."

298

Jamie felt the eyes of every member of the Zero Hour Task Force turn slowly towards him, and felt heat rise in his face.

"With me?" he asked. "Why would you want to talk to me?"

"You destroyed my brother, Mr Carpenter," said Valentin, "and I knew your grandfather. I think we have a great deal to talk about, don't you?"

Jamie flicked a glance at Admiral Seward, then looked back into the cell.

"Maybe we do," he said. "Maybe we don't. But I'm happy to find out, if that's what this is going to take."

"Excellent," said Valentin. He jumped up from the chair and approached the barrier, until he was less than a metre away from Jamie. He tilted his head to one side, as if examining the teenager.

"You look like him, you know?" Valentin said. "Your grandfather. You look very much like him."

"Step back from the barrier," warned Major Turner.

"I've only ever seen a portrait," said Jamie. He could feel himself sinking into Valentin's wide grey eyes. "He died before I was born."

"You could be his double," said Valentin. The air between them was thick with tension, as though the UV barrier was giving off a field of static electricity.

"Mr Rusmanov, step back from the barrier," said Turner, his voice as cold as ice. "I'm not going to ask you again."

Valentin blinked, and then stepped back, breaking the spell.

"My apologies," he said, smoothly. "Please, by all means, continue with your questions."

24

THE FOURTH MUSKETEER

Almost three hours later the men of the Zero Hour Task Force made their way down the corridor of the detention level.

The interrogation was progressing well; in fact, it was progressing far beyond even their most optimistic projections. So far, Valentin Rusmanov had been true to his word; he had told them everything they wanted to know. He had not restricted his disclosures to Valeri and Dracula either; he had encouraged them to enquire about all aspects of vampire life, and when a question had been posed to which he did not know the answer, he had simply given the briefest of glances to Lamberton, who had immediately supplied it.

The information was flowing at such a rate – everything from known vampire habitats and congregations, to sources of black-market blood, to how much awareness the vampire community had of the supernatural Departments and the tactics they used to evade their attention – that Seward had called the first session of the interview to an end and ordered a resumption the following morning. He intended to spend the rest of the day formulating a structured approach for extracting the enormous amount of valuable intelligence that Valentin Rusmanov was carrying in his head.

As the lift made its way up through the Loop, the Operators

filed out one by one. On Level B, Jamie made for the door; his plan was to gather his thoughts for a few minutes in his quarters, then go and find Larissa. But as he stepped forward, he felt a hand fall across his shoulder, and he turned back. Admiral Seward was looking at him with a strange expression.

"I need to see you in my quarters, Lieutenant Carpenter," the Director said.

"Now, sir?" asked Jamie.

"Now."

"Yes, sir," he replied, and watched the grey metal doors of the lift slide shut.

Admiral Seward held the door to his quarters open, waited for Jamie to step through it, then followed him inside and closed the door. Jamie stood patiently as the Director removed his jacket and settled himself behind his desk.

"I got a reply from Beijing," said Seward. "In less than forty-eight hours, remarkably. Damn nearly a record for PBS6."

"What did they say, sir?"

"They're investigating the circumstances of the Chinese citizens who arrived in Britain on the *Aristeia*, and they'll keep us up to date on their findings. Standard stuff."

"Can we offer to send a team out to help them?"

"We certainly can," answered Seward. "And I probably will. But I can tell you now what their reply will be; they'll thank us for our kind offer and tell us they'll be sure to inform us if they need our assistance."

"But they won't."

"No," said Seward. "They won't."

There was a long moment of silence that was not entirely

301

comfortable; the obvious concern on the Director's face made that impossible.

"You do realise," said Seward, eventually, "that Valentin's reason for being here may well be to take revenge against you, for what you did to Alexandru?"

Jamie recoiled. "I don't understand, sir," he replied. "If he wanted to kill me, why didn't he do it in the Twilight Home? Why go through all this?"

"I don't know, Jamie," said Seward, rubbing his eyes. The Director looked old, and worn down. "It may be part of a plan that we can't see the shape of yet; it may just be for his own amusement. I may be completely wrong, and his reasons for wanting to be alone with you might be exactly what he says they are. But you need to know the possibilities, Jamie, because I'm not going to order you to speak to him. I'm leaving that decision up to you."

"Why, sir?"

"Because all the information in the world is not worth putting an Operator of this Department alone in a room with a Priority Level 1 vampire against their will," replied Seward. "Much of what we do here lies within the grey areas of morality; that is our burden, one we all share, and it weighs heavier on some than on others. But we do not throw our people to the wolves, Jamie; we do not put lives at risk on the whims of monsters. And we are not about to start now, on my watch."

"Is he going to stop answering questions if I don't talk to him?" asked Jamie.

"He says so," replied Seward. "He wants to talk to you tomorrow, before we continue. I say again, Jamie, I will not order you to do this. But if you think you can handle it, I won't stop you either. It's up to you."

Jamie thought about the lives that Valentin Rusmanov's information could save, remembered the feeling of standing before Alexandru, the sensation of total helplessness, and tried to imagine the power that Valentin said Dracula possessed.

"I'll do it, sir," he said. "Tomorrow morning, like he wants."

"We'll be watching you every second," Seward replied. "But we won't be able to have anyone in the cellblock with you; Valentin specified that it be just you and him, and he'll detect anyone else from a mile away."

"It doesn't matter anyway, sir," said Jamie, a small smile on his face.

"Why not?"

"Because if Valentin decides to kill me, we could put the entire Department in the cellblock and it wouldn't be enough to stop him. Sir."

The two men considered the awful truth of Jamie's words; they were standing in the centre of the most highly classified, technologically advanced and heavily armed military facility in the country, but sitting casually in a worthless cell several hundred metres below them was a creature they were powerless to control if it decided to do harm.

It felt like standing on quicksand.

The intercom on Admiral Seward's desk buzzed into life, startling both men. Jamie smiled, a sheepish, nervous grin that the Director returned before he pressed the button on the intercom.

Marlow's voice appeared instantly.

"Sir, we have a situation on Level B that requires your attention."

"What kind of situation?" asked Seward.

"A civilian boy was brought in last night, sir, after making an emergency call he admits was designed specifically to attract our attention. Squad B-9 picked him up in Derbyshire, destroying two vamps that were about to kill him. He spent the night in the secure dorm, sir."

"So what?" asked Seward, impatiently. "Quarantine him, explain what will happen to him and his family if he talks, give him twenty-four hours in isolation to think it over, then send him home. Why are you involving me in this?"

"Two reasons, sir," said Marlow, his voice like that of a parent trying to explain something simple to a child. "First, how did the vamps know where he was? They can't be monitoring the entire 999 system for anything supernatural, sir, it's too vast; that's why we have Echelon, to filter through it all."

"I know exactly why we have Echelon," snapped Seward. "Get to the point, Marlow."

"Yes, sir. They were there before our squad was, which means they knew about the call at least as soon as we did. How did they know that?"

"My God," said Jamie, softly. An image of Thomas Morris's smiling face burst into his mind. "The vamps have access to Echelon."

"How could they?" asked Seward, his voice sounding far more confident than he felt. "There are only two monitoring stations: GCHQ and…"

"Here," said Jamie. "The leak's here in the Loop, sir. It has to be. GCHQ doesn't scan for the supernatural."

"Christ," said Seward, then addressed the intercom. "Marlow, are you still there?"

"Yes, sir," his aide replied. "What do you want me to do, sir?"

"Kill it," Seward said. "No mention of this goes beyond the people who already know. I have Lieutenant Carpenter with me; who is with you?"

"Major Turner, sir."

304

"OK. This goes no further. Don't touch the logs or the database; I don't want anyone in Comms to know we're looking into this. I want recommendations from Major Turner on how to proceed by 1900 hours, is that clear?"

"It is, sir," said Marlow.

"Good," replied Seward. "What was the other thing?"

"Sir?"

"You said there were two things that required my attention. What's the second one?"

"Sorry, sir. The civilian they picked up last night is the same boy who was injured on the night Lieutenant Carpenter arrived at the Loop, sir."

Jamie's eyes widened. "Matt?" he asked, incredulous. "They brought Matt back in?"

"That's right, Matt Browning," said Marlow.

"So what?" asked Seward. "The Security Division has protocols for every possible civilian eventuality, Marlow. I really fail to see why you're telling me this."

"I'm sorry, sir. I'm telling you because when we asked him why he made the emergency call, he confessed that he was trying to engineer a way back to the Loop. It appears that the amnesia he was diagnosed with after he woke from his coma was fake, sir."

"And?"

"We asked him why he wanted to get back here so badly, and he said that Lieutenant Carpenter told him to. Sir."

Seward froze, then slowly craned his neck upwards.

"Stand by," he said into the intercom, and then fixed Jamie with a look that could have been carved out of a mountainside, an expression of indescribable disappointment. "Jamie," he continued, his voice low and full of menace. "Is there something you want to tell me?"

Jamie took a deep breath. "Sir, I don't *want* to tell you—"

"Tell me what you did!" bellowed Seward.

The teenager swallowed hard, and began to talk.

Jamie waited in the corridor beyond the infirmary, leaning against the wall, attempting to look casual. His head was lowered, and he had an open folder in his hands that he appeared to be leafing through, but his attention was surreptitiously fixed on the double doors of the infirmary, forty metres down the corridor.

He had been denied permission to see Matt Browning ever since the boy had awoken from his coma. The operating theatre at the rear of the infirmary had been cordoned off, and the boy had been placed in complete isolation; only his doctor and the nurse who had treated him were allowed entry, and they were forbidden from discussing anything other than strictly medical matters with the teenager.

Jamie understood the protocol that had been put in place; the boy was lying in the middle of the most secret government installation in the country, and the only way it would ever be possible for him to be returned home was to prevent him from seeing or hearing anything that would make him a security risk. It was the right thing to do, but Jamie didn't care; he felt a remarkable bond with the boy, with whom he had never spoken.

Matt's life had changed forever on the same day as his, and in the dark nights that followed, as Jamie had fought to keep himself going as horror descended around him, he had sought solace in the unconscious teenager, making regular visits to his bedside. He had told Matt what he was going through, grateful to have the ear of someone who was incapable of lying to him, or trying to manipulate him.

It was more than that, though; Jamie had been at the Loop for less than an hour when Matt had arrived, barely breathing, after Larissa had torn his throat out in his small suburban garden. Larissa hadn't meant to do it, claimed to not even remember having done it, and Jamie believed her; it was merely one of the long list of things that filled the vampire girl with guilt, and was why she had refused to help him when he explained his plan to her.

But whether she had intended to or not, she had almost killed Matt, and the sight of the pale, critically injured boy in the hangar on the night that Jamie had arrived had served as a warning more real than any of the hundreds he had received during his training. Matt had been the barely-living proof that what Jamie had found himself a part of wasn't a game, or an adventure; it was life and death.

Since Matt had woken up, Jamie had repeatedly petitioned Admiral Seward for permission to visit him, until the Director had threatened to place him on the inactive list. Jamie hadn't asked again, but nor had he given up; he had begun to observe the patterns of the security that had been placed around Matt, and after a week or two, had identified a window of opportunity.

Every evening, there was a hole, sometimes as long as six minutes, often no longer than three, where Matt was unattended; it happened during the shift changeover at 8pm, when the doctor in charge of the infirmary went to his office to send his update report to Admiral Seward. His office was at the far end of the corridor, near the lift, and he was always gone for at least ten minutes.

The problem was the Operator who was on guard outside the door; only once in the time that Jamie had been watching had the sitting officer been physically relieved; the vast majority of the time he left with the doctor on the stroke of eight, before his replacement had arrived. This was by any measure unacceptable, and Jamie's response to the discovery should have been to alert Major Turner, the Department's Security Officer. Instead, he kept it to himself, and waited to put his plan into action.

Now that moment had arrived.

Jamie checked his watch, and saw that it was thirty seconds until 8pm. He lowered the visor on his helmet, not far enough to look suspicious, but enough to obscure his features to anyone who took more than a passing look at him, and waited. Then he heard the rush of air as the infirmary doors opened, and two voices echoed along the corridor, decreasing in volume as they walked briskly away from where Jamie was standing.

Regular as clockwork, he thought to himself, and grinned.

He raised his head a fraction, and saw the doctor disappear into his office. The Operator was standing with his back to Jamie, waiting for the lift. This was the crucial moment; if the lift opened and the relieving Operator stepped out of it, then he was screwed. He felt his heart begin to beat a little bit faster as he heard the lift slow to a halt.

The doors slid open to reveal an empty metal box. The Operator stepped inside, then turned to face down the corridor; Jamie felt a sudden burst of panic as the man's eyes seemed to momentarily meet his own. But the expression on the Operator's face didn't change; the lift doors closed, leaving Jamie alone in the corridor.

He immediately set off towards the infirmary, his footsteps loud on the concrete floor. He reached the double doors, took a deep breath, then pushed them open and stepped quickly inside. The beds that lined the walls to the left and right were all empty; establishing that fact had been the first thing Jamie had done, via a conversation with one of the nurses in the dining hall. At the rear of the room, the door marked THEATRE was closed, the chair positioned at the side of it standing empty.

Not for long, he thought. Hurry.

Jamie crossed the wide room, gripped the handle of the theatre door and pushed it open. Matt Browning looked up from the bed he was lying on, the expression on his face one of awful boredom, but then his eyes flew wide as he saw the dark figure entering his room.

"Who are—" he began, but Jamie cut him off.

"Keep your voice down," he whispered. "I'm not supposed to be in here. If they catch me, it's going to be really bad for us both."

"Who—"

"My name's Jamie. Jamie Carpenter."

"What do you want?"

Jamie paused. He was suddenly unsure why it had seemed so important that he see this boy again. "I don't want anything," he said, eventually. "What do you want?"

"I want to go home," said Matt, instantly.

"I can imagine," said Jamie. "Have they told you what happened to you?"

"Sort of. They said I had an accident. But I can't remember."

"I heard. How far back?"

Matt's shoulders tensed, ever so slightly. It was barely noticeable, but Jamie saw it.

"I remember working at my desk," said Matt. "It must have been late afternoon, early evening. Then I woke up here. Everything in between is gone."

Jamie stared at the boy for a long moment, then leant down towards him. "I don't believe you," he whispered, then smiled.

Matt's eyes widened. "What do you mean?" he asked, his voice trembling.

"I mean, I don't believe you," repeated Jamie. "I think you're either a brilliant liar or a natural actor. Because I think you remember exactly what happened to you. And when you do what I do for a living, you rarely believe what anyone tells you."

"So you kill vampires?" asked Matt, his face and shoulders relaxing, and his mouth curling fractionally upwards at the edges.

Jamie recoiled, then grinned. "I knew it," he said. "I knew you knew. What made you lie?"

"I didn't know what they would do to me if they knew," replied Matt.

"Smart," said Jamie. "They're releasing you tomorrow, did they tell you that?"

"No," said Matt. "They don't really tell me very much."

"It's the protocol," said Jamie, his voice still lowered. "They can't let you see anything that would make you a security risk if they let you go. If you want to see your parents again, stick to what you've been doing."

"You came here to tell me that?" asked Matt, his brow furrowing. "I was doing that anyway. Why are you here?"

"I came to visit you when you were in a coma," said Jamie. "The night I arrived here was the same night you got hurt. I... don't know. I just wanted to meet you."

"Can I ask you something?" asked Matt. His voice rose as he spoke, and Jamie shushed him again.

"Go for it," he whispered.

"Where the hell am I? You're wearing the same uniform the men who came into our house were wearing, and the girl who landed in my garden was a vampire, it's obvious now. She should have been dead, but she wasn't. And then she..."

"Don't think about that," said Jamie, quickly. "Her name is Larissa, by the way; the girl who hurt you. She didn't mean to do it."

"You know her?" asked Matt, his eyes widening.

"Yeah," replied Jamie. "I do. It's... complicated. But that doesn't answer your question."

He took a deep breath, as he prepared to break the most fundamental rule that Blacklight operated by. "This place is called the Loop. It's a military base, completely classified. It's the home of a branch of the government called Department 19, the department that polices the supernatural. I'm what they call an Operator; it's like a soldier, but a top-secret version. There are hundreds of us here, hundreds more abroad; basically, you're lying in the middle of the biggest secret in the world."

Matt stared at the ceiling for a long moment, and Jamie feared, for a moment, that he had overwhelmed the teenager, given him too much too quickly. Then he said something that Jamie wasn't expecting.

"That sounds amazing," he said. "How do I join?"

"Join?" spluttered Jamie.

"Yeah, join. How do I get to be like you?"

"It's not that simple," said Jamie. "Most of the Operators are recruited from the military, or the police. I was just lucky; I'm allowed in because I'm a descendant of one of the founders."

"The what?"

"No time," said Jamie, checking his watch. He had been inside the infirmary for more than two minutes already. "If this is what you want, then there's only one bit of advice I can give you: find your way back here."

"How do I do that?" asked Matt, his eyes full of excitement.

"I don't know," replied Jamie. "You seem like a smart guy, figure it out. You can't let them know you know; you have to let them take you home tomorrow. I don't know what they'll do if they find out you've been lying to them. And I can't say anything to help you, it wouldn't do either of us any good for them to know I've been in here. So once you're out, find your way back. It's the only thing I can think of."

Jamie backed away towards the door.

"Wait," said Matt, his voice rising again. This time Jamie didn't quiet him, he just stopped with the door handle in his grip.

"What?" he asked. "I really have to go."

"Why are you doing this?" asked Matt. "Why are you trying to help me?"

"I don't know," said Jamie, and then grinned, a broad smile that was beautiful to look at. "I just have a feeling about you. I don't know why. Good luck."

With that, Jamie threw open the door and ran across the infirmary at a dead sprint. His watch read 20:02:41; over two and a half minutes had *passed. He mentally cursed himself for being so careless, but even as he did so, realised that he didn't regret it; finding a way to see Matt, to tell him what he had told him, was the right thing to have done, he was absolutely sure of that.*

There was a moment's silence, then the Director of Department 19 exploded.

"Despite all the times I explained to you why you couldn't!" shouted Seward, his eyes blazing with anger. "And all the times you told me you understood. You stood where you're standing now and you lied to me, Jamie. I could have you court-martialled for this."

"I know, sir," said Jamie, his eyes never leaving the Director's. "I really am sorry, sir."

Seward held his gaze for a long, fiery moment, then rubbed his eyes with his hands. Suddenly the Director no longer looked angry; he looked simply exhausted.

"Do you realise how many regulations you just confessed to breaking?" asked Seward.

"I'm guessing quite a few, sir."

"That's right," said Seward. "Quite a few. A lot in fact."

The Director leant back in his chair, and regarded Jamie with a look of obvious disappointment.

"What am I supposed to do about this, Jamie?" he asked. "If you were me, what would you do?"

"I don't know, sir," replied Jamie, his stomach churning; it was only now occurring to him that his Blacklight career was hanging by a thread. "I suppose I'd do what I thought was for the best, sir."

Seward looked up at him, and the slightest hint of a smile curled the corners of the Director's mouth. He leant forward and spoke into the intercom again.

"Marlow?"

"Yes, sir?"

"Bring Mr Browning up to my quarters immediately. Ask Major Turner to accompany you. Try not to let anyone else see him."

"Yes, sir," replied Marlow. "On our way, sir."

Seward got up from behind his desk, then walked over to the arm-chairs that stood before the wide fireplace that dominated the Director's study. He flopped heavily down into one, and motioned for Jamie to take the other. As he did so, Seward lifted a cigar from the box on the coffee table, and lit it with a long wooden match. Once the cigar was under way, he leant back in his chair and looked at Jamie.

"How does this end, Jamie?" he asked, breathing out a cloud of thick blue smoke. "What good can come of bringing this poor boy back here?"

"Let him help us, sir," Jamie replied, instantly. "He's smart, sir, and there's no doubt that he's brave. I can look after him, put him in my squad, show him—"

"Out of the question," said Seward, firmly. "I bent the rules once for you, Jamie. I'm not going to do it again just so you can have a friend your own age. If he stays, he doesn't set foot outside this base until he completes his training. Is that clear?"

"Yes, sir," replied Jamie. He was disappointed to hear the Director refuse to allow Matt to join his squad, but he was elated that Seward appeared to be at least considering the possibility of a role within Blacklight for Matt.

"This won't make up for it, Jamie," said Seward, suddenly. "What you're trying to do. It won't bring him back."

"I don't understand, sir," said Jamie, confusion on his face.

"Frankenstein," said Seward. "Matt isn't going to be able to replace Frankenstein. It's not going to make losing him any easier."

Jamie felt as though the armchair beneath him was collapsing.

Is that what I'm doing? he asked himself. *Trying to use that poor kid to make up for what happened?*

"I don't think that's what I'm doing, sir," said Jamie, his voice unsteady. "If I am, I didn't know it."

"I'm sure you didn't," replied Seward, regarding the teenager with a smile that was very close to paternal. "You're many things, Jamie, but cruel isn't one of them. I'm sure you were doing what you thought was for the best."

Silence descended over the two men, so different in age and experience, so similar in temperament and love for the job that had been entrusted to them. For a long time, Jamie watched the smoke from Seward's cigar coil into the air, before he spoke again.

"What was he like, sir?" he asked.

"What was who like?" replied Seward, although he knew the answer.

"Frankenstein, sir," answered Jamie. "When he was young, I mean. Before I knew him. What was he like?"

Seward considered for a moment exactly how much to tell the teenager; his own memories of Frankenstein were complex, as full of pain and fear as they were of triumph and companionship.

"He was a man," he replied, slowly. "As full of flaws as any other, perhaps more than most. But more than that, he was my friend."

25

THE ILLUMINATED CITY, PART I

PARIS, FRANCE
23RD AUGUST 1923

Frankenstein leant back in his chair, the tightly woven wicker groaning appreciably beneath him as he did so, drank deeply from his glass of wine and surveyed his companions for the evening, arranged around one of Café de Flore's round, glass-topped tables on the wide pavement of Boulevard Saint-Germain. He had found himself between conversations, and was content for the moment to merely observe, and listen.

To his left, Jean Hugo, Ernest Hemingway and Gertrude Stein were engaged in a heated debate about the merits and principles of literary patronage. Frankenstein knew without paying attention to the details that the cause of the disagreement was the presence for dinner at Stein's apartment two nights earlier of a young French writer whom Hemingway thoroughly disliked, and had been actively offended at being forced to share a table with.

Stein was making the not unreasonable argument that she would invite whoever she damn well pleased into her own home, and that Hemingway was more than welcome to decline any future invitations if he felt so strongly about the issue. Hemingway, the bluff, belligerent American, was slowly colouring a dark shade of purple, and rhythmically clenching and unclenching his fists, a sure sign that his perennially loose grip on his temper was in danger of failing him completely.

Hugo could clearly see it too, and was attempting to play the role of peacemaker; he was suggesting compromise after compromise, to little response from either party. Stein was sitting calmly to his left, a sweet, eminently reasonable expression on her face, while to his right, Hemingway openly stewed, and fought to control himself. Frankenstein watched them for several minutes, then turned his attention to the trio to his right.

Jean-Luc Latour, the only member of the company whom Frankenstein genuinely considered a friend, was discussing art with Pablo Picasso and Jean Cocteau, gesturing enthusiastically with both of his pale, slender hands as he held forth on the excitement that the recently-named New Objectivity movement was causing throughout the salons and cafés of Paris. He had, he was informing his companions, been greatly impressed with the recent work by André Derain, and was keen to hear Picasso's views on the matter.

Picasso was, for the moment at least, keeping his own counsel, while Cocteau was agreeing in declamatory terms, praising what he called the "return to order" that had flooded through European art in the aftermath of the Great War. It was, he was claiming, the bedfellow of German New Objectivity, and marked the first steps of a fractured continent back towards the sublime.

Frankenstein, who enjoyed both art and literature, but thought the endless debate that surrounded the two cultural pillars, the use of one's abilities to criticise the work of others rather than creating work of one's own, to be the worst type of intellectual indulgence, was beginning to become bored.

The evening had passed agreeably enough, with a hearty northern European supper in Brasserie Lipp, followed by several fine bottles of Lynch-Bages in the warm air of the Parisian night. But his patience had been gradually eroded by the endless, circular conversations regarding every tiny aspect of modern culture, fuelled as they were by the egos of the men and woman sitting around him, all of whom wanted, first and foremost, to talk about themselves. He was thus relieved when Latour stood up from his chair and announced, to the expected chorus of jeers and heckles, that he and Frankenstein had to leave.

"Again?" bellowed Picasso. "Why must every evening end with the two of you sneaking away into the night? This is how lovers behave, not friends. Are you in love with one another?"

Latour swept his arms wide in placation, and smiled.

"I would not dispute that I love this man," he said, casting a glance at the monster. "But to say that we are lovers is untrue. We merely have another engagement to attend, one to which, most regrettably, it is impossible for you to accompany us."

"Nonsense," snorted Hemingway, his red face brimming with anger. "What place in all of Paris is open to the likes of you and not to us? I demand you reveal it."

"I would love nothing more, Ernest," replied Latour, his tone smooth and conciliatory. "Believe me when I say so. But the rules that govern our destination are not mine to interpret, much less break. So we must say farewell."

"Let them go," said Stein, waving a hand dismissively. "They were beginning to bore me anyway."

"And me," said Cocteau, loyally, but when Frankenstein shot him a stern look, he immediately dropped his eyes to the table.

"Then it is for the best that we depart," said Latour, his expression remaining warm and friendly. "I apologise if our company has not been to your tastes this evening. We will endeavour to make it up to you. Tomorrow, perhaps?"

There was a grumbling murmur of assent. Everyone gathered round the table knew that the following evening would pass in much the same way as this one had, complete with similar conversations and the same awkward, well-rehearsed ending. The pattern had been repeating itself for more than two months now, right down to the chorus of boos that followed Frankenstein and Latour as they left the café and walked out into the Parisian night.

Their route took them north on Rue de la Cité and across Île de la Cité, before the towering gothic façade of Notre Dame cathedral and the throngs of late-night worshippers and tourists, then east on Rue de Rivoli, heading towards the open splendour of Place des Vosges, the residential square that had been inaugurated in 1612 to celebrate the wedding of Louis XIII.

"I don't know why you put up with their insinuations night after night," rumbled Frankenstein, as the two men strolled, the waters of the Seine lapping against its stone banks to their right. "It takes all my strength not to break a bottle over Picasso's damn head. I wonder how bold he and Hemingway would feel then."

"Your passion is perhaps your greatest quality, my friend," replied Latour, smiling. "My self-control is mine. What good would come of splitting that great bald dome open, beyond the momentary satisfaction of the act itself? We would be shunned by all of Parisian society, and though I'm sure that feels like no loss at all to you now, I believe you would feel differently if it came to pass."

"Perhaps," grunted Frankenstein.

"Indeed. So let them make their comments, and their innuendoes.

It represents nothing more than petty jealousy, and it does us credit to rise above such juvenile concerns. Agreed?"

"Your words are pretty, Latour," said Frankenstein, the beginnings of a smile creeping on to his wide, rectangular face. "As always."

"One tries," said Latour.

The two men reached the corner of Rue de Sévigné, and turned north once more. Their destination lay halfway between Rue des Francs Bourgeois and Rue Saint-Gilles, behind the old, elegant façades of the Marais.

Standing back from the pale stone pavement, behind an intricate wrought-iron gate, was a theatre that had not presented a production to the public for more than fifty years. The building was immaculate in every way; the rose beds that flanked the path beyond the gate bloomed beautifully, their scents intoxicating in the still night air, the wide flagstones scrubbed clean and devoid of even the tiniest of weeds.

The only features that might have prompted a passer-by to give the building a second glance were its windows, or rather its lack of them. The spaces where they had once been were obvious, four large square recesses in the walls, two either side of the grand carved wood door. But where glass had once let in the light and noise of nocturnal Paris, the spaces were now filled with stone, as pale and featureless as the walls that surrounded them.

Latour drew a key from his pocket and entered it into the gate. There was a whisper of noise as the key turned in the oiled lock, before the gate slid silently open. Frankenstein followed him through, closing the gate behind them, and joined Latour in front of the door, upon which the Frenchman had already knocked three times in quick succession.

After a moment's pause, the door was opened. Anyone who had been standing beyond the gate and watching this strange procedure take place would have heard a brief burst of music and a mingled chorus of voices, some of which were raised in what they would no doubt have convinced themselves were screams of laughter, before the door thudded back into place, and the theatre was silent once more.

Inside the ancient building an elderly vampire, resplendent in immaculate evening wear, stepped from around a wooden lectern and approached the two newcomers with a deferential smile on his face.

"Welcome back to La Fraternité de la Nuit, gentlemen," he said, in perfect English. "May I take your coats?"

They were standing in a small lobby, the walls and ceiling lined with thick crimson velvet, the floors varnished wood. At the rear of the lobby stood a second door, through which the riotous piano of the cancan could be heard. Then a second sound emerged from behind the door, rising above the music; a shrill scream, so full of terror and despair that Frankenstein grimaced, even as he handed his long overcoat to the maître d'. Latour, who had already shed his coat, grinned widely at the sound, his fangs bursting into view as unnatural red spilled into the corners of his eyes. He clapped Frankenstein on the back.

"I believe it is going to be a good night," he said, as he strode towards the door.

The inner door closed gently behind the two men, and Frankenstein took a familiar deep breath, giving his stomach time to settle.

The smell of blood, thick and metallic, hung heavily in the wide arc of the theatre. It rose like a cloud from the pools of crimson liquid that had collected on the low stage, where grotesque acts were committed each and every night to the baying approval of the vampire audience. It drifted through the air from the great arcs that had sprayed against the once white walls of the building, from severed veins and ruptured arteries. Blood permeated every inch of the theatre, ages old and freshly spilled, dried brown and glistening scarlet.

An attendant greeted Frankenstein and Latour as soon as they entered, telling them that they would, as always, be welcome in Lord Dante's private chamber. Latour thanked the vampire absently; he was looking around the room, his ears full of screams, his eyes molten red as he watched the horrors that were unfolding around him. His face wore an expression of such naked lust that Frankenstein turned away, even though it forced him to witness what was taking place.

The theatre was small, no more than sixty seats arrayed in a semi-circle before the stage. Perhaps two-thirds of the seats were occupied, by vampires of all races, ages and nationalities. An atmosphere of terrible bonhomie rose from them, with good reason; the Fraternité was a safe place, where they could indulge their darkest desires at their leisure, without fear of interruption. The seats of the theatre rippled with frantic movement, as the vampires who occupied them tortured, abused, bled and murdered the lost innocents of Paris.

Each night, from whence Frankenstein didn't allow himself to ponder, a new collection of human victims was released among the vampires. Most were young, although all ages could be found, depending on a particular member of the Fraternité's tastes, and were evenly split between males and females. They were ushered on to the stage as night fell, then abandoned to the hissing, roaring audience of monsters.

Frankenstein had only seen this with his own eyes once; since then, he had insisted to Latour that they not arrive until well afterwards. The utter terror, the hysterical, disbelieving horror on the faces of the men and women, and the snarling, clawing and biting of the vampires as they fought and squabbled over their favourites, had been too much, even for him.

By this time, well past midnight, most of the humans were already dead, ravaged and empty and abandoned in the aisles of the theatre, their last moments spent in agonies they couldn't possibly have understood.

Frankenstein followed Latour round the rear of the theatre, to a door standing almost invisibly in the wall. A vampire attendant, as elegantly dressed as the others, nodded respectfully to them, and held the door open. They passed through it, into the inner sanctum of La Fraternité de la Nuit.

Into the realm of Lord Dante, the vampire king of Paris.

26

FULL DISCLOSURE

"I think Frankenstein is part of what Valentin wants to talk to me about," said Jamie. "He seems to have had something to do with my grandfather."

"I can tell you now that he did," replied Admiral Seward. "It was your grandfather who brought Frankenstein into the Department, in 1929. He came back from a mission in New York and Victor was with him; apparently, he told Quincey Harker that he was here to help, and simply refused to take no for an answer. He was with us from that moment onwards."

Until I let him die, thought Jamie. *You won't say it, but we both know that's what you mean. Until I failed him.*

There was a knock on the door of Admiral Seward's quarters, and the Director shouted for whoever it was to enter. The door swung open, revealing the pale, frightened face of Matt Browning, flanked by the black-clad figures of Marlow and Paul Turner. The teenager took a hesitant step into the room, his eyes flicking nervously left and right; then he saw Jamie sitting in the armchair before the fireplace, and relief burst across his face.

"Jamie!" he cried. "Oh, thank God."

He ran across the study and hurtled into Jamie before the teenage

323

Operator was fully out of his chair. Matt wrapped his arms round him as Jamie fought to keep his balance, telling the boy as he did so that it was all right, he was safe, nothing was going to happen to him. He prised Matt's arms from around his torso, and turned him gently to face Henry Seward, who was watching the scene in front of him with obvious, but apparently kind, bemusement.

"Matt?" Jamie said, and the boy nodded. He had noticed the seated figure now, the grey-blue tendrils of smoke rising above him. "This is Admiral Henry Seward," Jamie continued. "The Director of Department 19. Sir, this is Matt Browning."

Seward hauled himself wearily to his feet, and extended a hand. Matt shook it, nervously.

"How are you, son?" asked Seward. "That was quite a stunt you pulled last night."

"I'm not going home," said Matt, instantly, and Seward laughed.

"What do you mean?" the Director asked.

"I mean, I'm not going back," said Matt, firmly. "Not again. You're going to have to kill me this time if you won't let me stay. I want to help."

"That's a laudable attitude," said Seward. "But it's not that simple. This is a highly classified branch of the British government, Mr Browning. You do not simply walk up, knock on the door and ask to join the club. Do you understand?"

"Yes, sir," replied Matt. "I understand that you're keeping the biggest secret in the world inside this base, and I understand that I'm never going to be able to forget the things I saw. This is the only place I want to be."

"You want to help, yes?" said Seward. "You want to do what Mr Carpenter here does, what the men who visited your house last year do?"

"That's right, sir," replied Matt.

"It takes months of training to become an Operator in this Department, Matt. Months of painful, tiring, gruelling training, for the privilege of spending your life in the darkness fighting monsters. Is that really what you want?"

"Yes, sir," Matt replied, but there was a moment's hesitation before he did so, which Jamie knew everyone in the room had seen.

"I don't believe you," said Seward, gently. "I believe you want to help us, I believe you want to be part of what we do here. But I've seen two generations of Operators come through this base, and I flatter myself I can tell the ones who are going to make it from a distance. And you, Mr Browning, are not one of them. That's not an insult, I promise you; it's just a fact."

Matt's shoulders slumped, and tears began to brim in the corners of his eyes.

They're going to send me home again, he thought. *Or worse.*

"I'll take him back to the secure dorm, sir," said Marlow. "We can start working on a cover story to send him home with."

Matt looked helplessly at Jamie, who felt his heart go out to him. He racked his brains for a way to help, to stop this before it was all over and Matt was gone, again.

"Admiral," he said, suddenly. "Maybe there's something else we could consider?"

Jamie saw Marlow roll his eyes, and ignored him. The Director turned to face him, and he continued.

"He doesn't have to be an Operator to help us," he said. "You saw the files Intelligence put together when he was here last year; extremely intelligent, with particular aptitude for maths and science."

"How do you know that?" whispered Matt, a horrified look on his face. Jamie shot him a look of apology, but pressed ahead.

"Why don't we ask Professor Talbot if he needs more help in the lab, sir? Or an assistant – anything?" He could hear the desperation creeping into his voice, but he couldn't help it. If this didn't work, he couldn't think of anything else he could do. Matt would be going home again, or worse; imprisoned in the Loop for the rest of his life, or – *no, they wouldn't do that. We're soldiers, not murderers.*

I hope.

"I'll think about it," replied Seward, and Jamie breathed an audible sigh of relief.

"Sir, this is most—" began Marlow, but Seward waved a hand at him.

"I know exactly what this is, Marlow," he said. "I said I'll think about it, and I intend to. Jamie, take Mr Browning below, get the boy some food, then return him to the secure dormitory. Major Turner, you stay with me, please. Dismissed, everyone."

Marlow rolled his eyes again, before striding out of the Director's quarters. Jamie followed, gently pulling a confused-looking Matt behind him.

Seward watched them go, waited until the door was closed, then told Paul Turner to sit down. The Major nodded, settled into the second armchair and faced his brother-in-law.

"What am I doing, Paul?" Seward asked. "With these kids, I mean. What would my ancestors think of me if they could see this?"

"They'd think you were doing your job, Henry," replied Turner, immediately. "Carpenter may be an insufferable little brat, but he's the most naturally gifted Operator I've seen in fifteen years, and an absolute born leader. He's proven himself to be one of our very finest assets, regardless of how old he was when he was commissioned. And did you read the file on Browning? IQ of 196, top 0.1 per cent of the world's population. The boy's an official, documented genius, Henry; he knows about us, he wants to help, despite what happened to him, and he was brave enough to risk everything to try. So what are you supposed to do? Lock him up for the rest of his life, and let all that intelligence, all that courage go to waste? I think your ancestors would have made exactly the same decisions you have, sir."

Seward closed his eyes for a moment, then opened them and regarded Turner with a look of immense affection.

"Thank you, Paul," he said.

"It's the truth, sir," replied Turner. "You know I wouldn't say it if it wasn't."

"I know," said Seward.

Turner waited for his Director to continue, to address the matter that he knew he had been asked to stay behind to deal with, but there was only silence. Henry Seward suddenly looked old to Turner, who had known him for more than ten years, had seen him when he was a fiery, ambitious young Operator, every bit as impulsive and pig-headed as Jamie Carpenter was now.

The past weighed heavily on him, Turner knew; his wife, Caroline, whom Paul had married after a courtship that had lasted less than six months, worried endlessly about her older brother. Blacklight's history was arguably both its greatest asset, and its most profound weakness; every decision that Seward made was second-guessed by long-dead men, legends whose example he spent every minute trying to live up to.

"Henry?" he asked, gently. "Is there anything else?"

Seward's eyes focused, and he forced a narrow smile.

"There's a leak in the Communications Division, Paul," he said. "I need you to find it, quickly and quietly; I want the person responsible in this office within forty-eight hours. Understood?"

"Absolutely, sir," replied Turner. "I'll start immediately."

"I know you will," said Seward. "Thank you. Dismissed."

Turner nodded, then stood up and walked across the study to the door. As he pulled it open, he took one last glance into the room; Admiral Seward was staring at the wall opposite his armchair, surrounded by the ghosts of the past.

Jamie and Matt stood in one of the lifts as it descended towards Level G, where the dining hall was located. An Operator had joined them on Level C, taken a long look at Matt in his T-shirt and jeans, opened his mouth, then clearly decided that he just didn't want to know and closed it again.

The two boys were trying hard not to laugh, the natural response of teenagers everywhere who are placed in a situation where they know they are supposed to behave. The lift doors opened on Level G, and the Operator strode off down the corridor without a backward glance. Jamie and Matt waited for a few seconds, and then followed him.

Matt walked alongside Jamie, stealing glances at the black uniform his – *friend? Can I call him my friend? We've only met twice* – was wearing, at the array of weapons and gadgets that hung from the belt around Jamie's waist. Jamie noticed Matt looking, but said nothing. He remembered how utterly bewildering his arrival at the Loop had been, even though the circumstances had been somewhat different, and he knew how many questions must be jostling for position inside the teenager's brain. Eventually, the first of them wrestled its way to the front.

"So how does it work?" Matt blurted out. "What you do. Are you like the police, just out there looking for vampires?"

Jamie laughed, saw a look of embarrassment bloom on Matt's

face and moved quickly to reassure him. "Not really," he said. "You have to understand what vampires are like. They don't advertise themselves, or at least the vast majority of them don't. They live in towns and villages, in houses and flats, just like everyone else. You can't just go out there and look for them."

"Oh," said Matt. "Sorry. That was stupid of me."

"Not at all," said Jamie. "Think about it this way: how many vampires have you seen in your life?"

"One," replied Matt. "The girl in our garden."

"Larissa," Jamie reminded him. "Right. Which makes you one of the tiny percentage of people who know they exist at all. But there are thousands of them out there, in every country in the world, in every town and city. You don't see them because most of them don't want to be seen, and they're very good at hiding. And because in most cases, if you do see one, it's the last thing you ever do."

A chill raced up Matt's spine.

"We have sixty-five Operational Squads here at Blacklight," said Jamie. "Three Operators per squad. About half of them are on active duty at any one time, the rest are either on rotation here in the Loop, or overseas, or on leave. The system you used to get back here is called Echelon, a monitoring system that scans all electronic communication for certain key words – phone calls, emails, internet posts, everything. When something happens like the 999 call you made, the system flags it, and one of the active squads is immediately sent out in response. So in that way we're not unlike the police; we respond to emergencies that appear to involve the supernatural."

Jamie checked to see whether he was losing Matt's attention, but saw only excitement and curiosity in the teenager's eyes.

"Also, here in the base, we have an Intelligence Division," he continued. "They investigate patterns of vampire activity, maintain surveillance on Priority Level vampires, and work to infiltrate the vampire community. Like the SIS investigating a terrorist cell, understand?"

Matt nodded.

"Right. From their work come the strategic operations, missions designed to actively disrupt the vampire world: destroying safe houses, interrupting the black-market supply of blood, that kind of thing. There are less of them than the emergency ops, but they're almost more important, in the long run. They're how we take the fight to them, rather than just responding to what they do."

"Got it," said Matt. "So you're like the police and MI5 rolled into one. For vampires."

"Pretty much," laughed Jamie, and was heartened to see Matt smile, shyly. "That's pretty much it exactly."

"It's crazy," said Matt. "Doesn't it feel crazy?"

"The weird thing is, it doesn't," said Jamie, honestly. "It feels completely normal to me now. I just get up every day and go to work."

The two teenagers reached the door to the dining hall. The large, bustling room always reminded Jamie of the first time he had eaten there, during a break in the training he had begun the day after his mother had been abducted. He had been battered and bruised, bleeding and more tired than he would have ever thought it was possible to be, but Terry, the instructor, had told him something that had given him the resolve to keep going.

What your dad did, I don't blame you for. I'll judge you on your actions, not his.

With those words, Terry had been the first member of Blacklight apart from Frankenstein, who had reasons of his own to be loyal to Jamie, to show any faith in him.

330

At the time – before Lindisfarne, before the revelations Thomas Morris had unleashed before he died – Julian Carpenter had been believed to be the greatest traitor in Blacklight's long, blood-soaked history. His father's actions had hung round Jamie's neck like a millstone, tainting almost everyone in the Loop's opinion of him. But not Terry's; the instructor had made it clear that he didn't give a damn what Jamie's father had done or, as was eventually revealed, hadn't done. It was something Jamie had never let Terry forget, much to the gruff, battle-hardened instructor's embarrassment.

Operators milled around the dining hall, chatting casually to one another, or to the doctors, scientists, engineers and administrators who kept the Loop functioning. Jamie led Matt to the back of the queue, where they each took a plastic tray and shuffled their way along the counter. Matt's eyes widened as he approached the seemingly endless trays of food, and he realised it had been a long time since he had last eaten. His stomach growled, loudly, and the female Operator in front of him cast him a look of surprise.

"Sorry," he said.

"Sounds like you need to eat something quick," said Jamie, grinning. "It's not going to help our case with Admiral Seward if he hears you fainted in the dining hall."

"I suppose not," said Matt, an embarrassed smile on his face. Then he turned towards the long metal counters and began piling his plate high with food from what seemed to be every tray within reach. Jamie watched, helping himself to a large plate of pasta, then carried it over to an empty table near the corner of the room. Matt followed behind him, already picking at his plate with his fingers, and they sat down to eat.

"So," said Matt, around a huge mouthful of mashed potatoes. "How did you end up here? I mean, I remember what you told me that night in the infirmary, about descendants of the founders, but it didn't make a lot of sense, to be totally honest with you."

Jamie considered the sheer enormity of Matt's question; the chain of events that had brought him into Department 19 had begun more than a hundred years ago, when his great-grandfather had been employed as the valet to Abraham Van Helsing. Even the more immediate reasons, which involved his father and a vampire he had killed in Budapest almost a decade earlier, were still tortuously complicated.

"That story's going to have to wait a bit," Jamie replied. "Let's save it for when we've got more time, OK?"

A lot more time.

Matt nodded, then attacked his plate anew. Over Matt's shoulder Jamie saw Larissa and Kate enter the dining hall, and waved them over. A look passed between them that Jamie didn't like in the slightest, but when they had filled their trays, they picked them up and headed in his direction.

At least they're still acknowledging my existence, thought Jamie. *That's something, I suppose.*

He finished his food, pushed the plate aside and watched the two girls pick their way through the tables and chairs. They stopped behind Matt, who was still demolishing his plate, completely oblivious to their presence, and looked down at the teenager in the civilian clothes with curiosity on their faces.

"Who's your friend?" asked Larissa.

Matt spluttered, almost choked on a mouthful of food, swallowed, then turned round to see who had spoken. He saw Larissa smiling down at him, and all colour drained from his face. Larissa watched it happen, frowned and then her eyes widened with terrible recognition.

332

"What—" she began, but then Matt was moving, leaping up out of his seat, sending it crashing to the floor with a clatter that drew the attention of everyone in the room, and running to Jamie's side, putting the table between himself and Larissa.

"Oh Christ," breathed Jamie.

He leapt to his feet, and grabbed Matt's shoulders. The boy was physically shaking, his body trembling in Jamie's grasp, his eyes wide with terror.

"Matt!" he shouted, not caring that the rest of the Operators in the dining room had now fallen silent as they watched him and his friends. "Matt, it's OK! Calm down, OK?"

"What the hell is going on?" demanded Kate. "Who's he?"

"That's him," said Larissa, distantly. "The boy from the garden. The one I hurt."

"What?" snapped Kate. "I thought they sent him home weeks ago? What's he doing here?"

"He risked his life to come back here because he wants to help us," said Jamie, rounding on her. "I'd call that pretty admirable, wouldn't you?"

Kate looked at him for a moment, then dropped her eyes. Jamie turned back to Matt. The boy was still staring at Larissa, his eyes wide; Jamie stepped in front of him, and shook his shoulders hard.

"Matt!" said Jamie. "Larissa is on our side, OK? She defected from the vampires, and they almost killed her because she did. She's one of the good guys, OK? Matt?"

Slowly, Matt's eyes began to focus, and his shoulders, which had felt like iron bars when Jamie grabbed them, began to relax. Then Matt blinked, and looked at Jamie.

"I'm sorry," he said. He sounded as though he was on the verge of tears. "I'm sorry, Jamie. It was just a shock. I'm sorry, OK?"

"Stop apologising," said Jamie, and grinned at Matt. "You're fine, everyone's fine. But you've got to try and relax, because I want you to meet my friends. All right?"

Matt nodded. Jamie stepped aside and the four teenagers faced each other across the table. Around them, the other Operators returned to their food, satisfied that there was going to be no more excitement.

"Matt, this is Kate," said Jamie. "Kate lived on Lindisfarne when... well, it's another long story."

Kate smiled. "It's a pretty good one, though," she said, then laughed as Matt extended his hand towards her, in a peculiarly formal manner. "It's nice to meet you, Matt," she said, taking the offered hand and shaking it gently.

"You too," said Matt, and a shy smile crept across his face.

"And you've already met Larissa," said Jamie. It was a risky joke, but he knew that if this was going to work, he had to defuse the tension between his new friend and his girlfriend, and do it quickly.

Larissa smiled guiltily, then frowned, as though she wasn't sure how to respond. But mercifully, Matt broke into a broad grin, and extended his hand towards her, which she gratefully took.

"It's nice to see you again," said Matt, and Jamie laughed. Larissa still looked slightly unsteady, but she smiled.

"You too," she said. "I guess there's probably a conversation we need to have at some point, but for what it's worth, I'm so sorry for what I did to you. I don't expect you to forgive me, but I really didn't mean to do it."

"It's OK," replied Matt, his hand fluttering instinctively to the scar that ran across his throat. "No harm done."

There was a chilly moment of silence before Jamie, who had no intention of letting his good work be undone, pulled his chair loudly across the floor and flopped down into it. The noise and the movement broke the spell, and the other three followed suit. There was another, warmer, silence, until Kate asked Matt how come he was back here, in the Loop, and Larissa asked Jamie how his day had been, and then all four of them were talking, as though they were old friends, the stress and heartache of the previous day seemingly put aside, at least momentarily.

This is right, thought Jamie. *The four of us, like this. I don't know why, it just feels right.*

Then a powerful sense of guilt washed through him, as he realised something he should have realised far, far earlier; that it wasn't Larissa or Kate that had changed the dynamic between the three of them.

It was him. *He* had done it.

Well, no more, he thought. *I'm putting an end to all of it. Today.*

27

THE ILLUMINATED CITY, PART II

PARIS, FRANCE
23RD AUGUST 1923

The private dining room of Lord Dante, the vampire king of Paris, was the colour of blood.

The walls were thickly lined with crimson velvet, the floor covered in a dark red carpet of such thickness that a visitor's shoes would sink up to the laces. The domed ceiling was painted red and decorated with patterns in similar hues, whirls and spirals that hurt the eyes. The grand circular dining table that dominated the square room was covered in a scarlet cloth; the armchairs that surrounded it were upholstered in crimson leather. The only elements of the room that did not follow this gruesome colour scheme were Lord Dante himself, and the small number of companions he had chosen to share his evening with.

Dante was dressed, as always, in evening wear. The black of his tuxedo was so deep that it appeared to absorb light, creating the illusion of a vacuum, of an absence that the eye could not discern.

The starched white shirt was flawless, as was the black bow tie that perched beneath its winged collars. The vampire king's cape, an affectation that he proclaimed allowed him to feel closer to days long gone, to the youth he had spent in centuries now consigned to the history books, was the shiny black of oil on the outside, the thick, dark red of arterial blood on the inside.

The vampire king looked no older than twenty-five, but had been turned by Valeri Rusmanov himself more than three hundred years earlier, as he so delighted in telling the endless gaggles of vampires who flocked adoringly to his table. It made him, to his understanding, the fourth oldest vampire in the world, the oldest who was not a Rusmanov, and significantly older and more powerful than any other vampire in Paris, or indeed the whole of France. His belief in his superiority over younger vampires was unshakeable, and he would not tolerate any suggestion to the contrary.

Less than two weeks earlier Frankenstein had watched, his eyes wide, his mind twisted by opium, as Dante tortured a vampire for the crime of merely suggesting that perhaps there should be more to a vampire than merely the time elapsed since they had been turned.

The vampire king's response had been to push his hand into the treasonous vampire's head, through his lying mouth, so deeply that his fingers could be seen moving beneath the man's scalp. He had demanded that the vampire take back his comment, even though he was fully aware that such a retraction was impossible while his fingers danced inside the stricken man. Eventually, tiring of the sport, he had torn the head from the shoulders, cast it aside with the same disdain that a child discards a toy they have become bored with, and pierced the insubordinate man's heart with a silver fork. The explosion of blood soaked Dante and his guests, but the vampire king appeared not to notice, and his fellow diners pretended to do the same, for fear of similar treatment if they objected.

Lord Dante looked up as Frankenstein and Latour entered the room, and smiled widely in their direction.

"Gentlemen!" he cried. "You honour me with your presence! Join me at my table, do!"

The vampire king was sitting at the rear of the room, his armchair facing the door. There was no head to the round table, but Dante's position made it somehow feel as though he was sitting at it anyway. Three of the seven remaining seats were occupied, although the chairs directly to Dante's left and right had been left respectfully empty.

A middle-aged woman in a painfully narrow corset, her face powdered bright white, her long limbs slender and delicate, sat opposite the vampire king. To her left sat a nervous-looking vampire in a drab suit. The regularity with which he glanced at the woman, and the henpecked expression on his face, marked him out immediately as her husband.

Sitting alone on the other side of the table, equidistant between Dante and the white-faced woman, was a vampire of indeterminate age, his long hair hiding his face as he slumped in his seat, wrapped in a thick black overcoat. In the corner of the room lay the body of a young girl, her clothes soaked with the blood that had spilled from the wide tear in her throat. She was slumped over, as though drunk, or asleep, but she was neither.

Latour bowed theatrically towards Lord Dante, his eyes closed, a beatific look on his face. Frankenstein dipped his head briefly, his eyes never leaving those of the vampire king. They took the two seats either side of Dante, provoking a look of profound jealousy from the woman at the opposite end of the table.

"Do not be envious," said Dante, noticing. "All seats at my table are of equal worth. The distance between us, dear Agathe, does not correspond to the depth of my feelings for you."

"Of course, Your Majesty," whispered Agathe, the woman with the white face, but her eyes burned red, and she stared at Frankenstein and Latour with open loathing.

"Jacques!" cried Dante, throwing his arms in the air. A door, set subtly into the wall of the dining room, opened immediately, and a vampire waiter appeared beside the vampire king's chair.

"Yes, Your Majesty?" asked the servant, and Dante favoured him with a broad smile.

"A libation, Jacques, for my guests," he said.

The waiter bowed, then disappeared through the door. A moment later he returned, holding an ornate crystal bottle, full of a dark red liquid.

"Less than an hour out of the vein," said Dante, nodding in the direction of the slumped, lifeless girl. "As sweet a drop as you will ever have tasted."

There was a murmur of approval from the table, as the waiter poured blood into the delicate crystal glasses that stood in front of each of the guests. When the glasses were full, Dante raised his towards his guests, who lifted theirs in kind.

"Long life," he said, solemnly. "Lived to its fullest."

The diners repeated the toast, then drank deeply from their glasses. Frankenstein winced at first, as he always did; the blood had thickened since it had been collected, and was unpleasantly lukewarm. But he persevered; the metallic taste of the blood, and the sense of uncompromising, self-loathing decadence that accompanied it, soon overcame his initial distaste.

The table descended into conversation, and Frankenstein again

339

found himself stranded between two streams of chatter. The woman with the white face was talking to Lord Dante and Latour, leaning so far towards the vampire king that she was in danger of overbalancing in her chair. Latour was unable to complete a sentence; the woman interrupted him every single time, her eyes fixed on Dante, desperate for his attention, and his approval.

Latour, for his part, appeared amused by her naked hunger, and allowed himself to be overridden. The woman's husband was attempting to engage the long-haired vampire, who was refusing to offer more to the fledgling conversation than a series of brief, deep grunts. As a result, it was Frankenstein who first heard the commotion in the theatre's auditorium.

The sounds coming through the door were muffled by the thick wood, but were nonetheless unmistakable; the grunts and growls of excited vampires, the thunder of running feet and then, clear above the racket, a solitary female scream. The sound, high and full of abject terror, drew the attention of the diners, who turned their gazes to the door.

"Who disturbs our evening?" asked Lord Dante, his voice full of affront. "Jacques! To me!"

The door slid open again and the vampire waiter instantly appeared, as though he had been standing on the other side of the door, waiting in case he was needed.

Probably exactly what he has been doing, thought Frankenstein. *Pathetic, subservient creature.*

"Go and learn the nature of this commotion," ordered Dante. "They all know full well that I expect revelry kept to a minimum when I am entertaining guests."

Jacques bowed deeply, crossed the dining room and disappeared through the door.

340

"Intolerable," muttered Dante, shaking his head. "A king should be able to dine in peace, should he not? I ask so little of them, and they treat me thus. Perhaps I need to remind them of their places in the order of things."

"Quite right, my lord," said the woman, enthusiastically. "You should destroy them all."

"Perhaps I should," replied Dante, fixing his dark red eyes on her. "Perhaps I will start with you, if you don't curb your impertinent tongue. How would that be?"

The woman shrank back in her chair, a look of fear on her brilliant white features.

"Your Majesty," she spluttered. "I must apologise. I-I meant no disres—"

"Hush your pleading," said Dante. He was no longer looking at the woman; his attention was firmly fixed on the door. The noise in the auditorium had ceased, and the vampire king and his guests waited for the waiter to return.

The door slammed open and Jacques backed into the room, hissing and snarling, his red eyes blazing. Held tightly in one of his arms was a blonde girl, no older than twenty-five, her eyes blank with fear. She was struggling in his grip, half-heartedly grabbing and slapping at the arm, but the waiter paid no attention to her in the slightest. Jacques kicked the door violently shut, a low growl dying in his throat as he turned to face the vampire king. The red disappeared from his eyes, and he smoothed himself down with his free hand. The savagery that had been emanating from him as he backed into the room was gone; the servile, neatly groomed waiter had returned.

"My apologies, Your Majesty," he said, smoothly. "I would not have had you see me like that."

"There is no need to apologise," replied Lord Dante, although he was not looking at his servant. He was staring with open desire at the girl who had been dragged into the room. "It is not healthy for men such as us to hide our natures at all times. The beast that dwells within us requires release, does it not?"

"As you say, Your Majesty," replied Jacques, bowing once more, his grip on the girl remaining tight.

"Who is this girl that you have brought to join us?"

"A gift, Your Highness," said Jacques. "Girard believed she might be to your tastes, and brought her here, as a token of his loyalty and his love for you. Babineaux objected, and tried to take her for himself. The dispute was in full swing when I entered."

"Did you resolve it?" asked Dante.

"I did, Your Majesty."

"Satisfactorily?"

"Not from Babineaux's perspective, Your Majesty," replied the butler. "He will make no further attempts to deny the king of Paris what is rightfully his. Or further attempts at anything else, my lord."

"Excellent," said Dante, a cruel smile on his face. "Let me inspect this gift, Jacques. And be sure to send Girard to me before the night ends, so I might make him aware of my gratitude."

"Of course, Your Majesty," replied Jacques, and held the girl out towards his master. Her head was slumped, her chin resting on her chest. She appeared to be barely conscious. Jacques shook her by the shoulders, and when she failed to respond, reached a gnarled hand around and slapped her pale cheek.

The sound was like a rifle shot in the small dining room, and the girl's eyes instantly flared open, rolling around in their sockets before settling on the lustful face of Lord Dante. When she faced him, her eyes widened even further, but Frankenstein, who was

342

watching intently, didn't believe it was from fear. He felt his muscles tighten involuntarily; to his old eyes, the expression looked like something else.

It looked like recognition.

"Pierre?" said the girl, her voice little more than a whisper. "Oh, thank God. Please don't let them hurt me, Pierre. Please."

The smile on Lord Dante's face didn't so much as flicker, but something in his eyes changed. Frankenstein, who had turned his attention to his host, saw it happen, and realised with a rush of savage pleasure that it was fear.

The vampire king was afraid.

Why, though? he wondered. *Why does this girl frighten him?*

"Leave us, Jacques," said Dante, his smile rigid.

The waiter released the girl, who didn't move; she was staring at the vampire king with a look of salvation on her face, her hands clasped between her breasts. Jacques bowed, and backed out of the dining room, leaving Dante alone with his guests, and the gift that had been given to him.

The atmosphere in the room had suddenly become charged, to the obvious bafflement of the vampire king's guests. Latour, who was looking at the girl with outrage written all over his face, was the first to speak.

"Wench," he hissed. "You dare speak to Lord Dante in such a familiar manner? You are addressing a being to whom you are less than nothing, who has lived for four centuries and more. You will bow your head before you speak to him again, and you will refer to him as Your Majesty. If you do not, I will tear the tongue from your head."

The girl looked at him, tears brimming in the corners of her eyes.

"B-but," she replied, her voice quavering, "I... I know him. He lived in Saint-Denis, when I, when I was growing up. His name is Pierre Depuis. Or it w-was. He disappeared when I was just a little girl, more than t-twenty years ago. Everyone thought... everyone thought he was dead."

"Kill her, Latour," said Dante, his face colouring a red so deep it was almost purple. "I would hear no more of her ravings."

Latour leapt from his chair, his eyes colouring red. The white-faced woman did likewise, and grabbed the girl by her shoulders, causing her to shriek with fear.

"Wait!" boomed Frankenstein. He had not taken his eyes from Dante's face, nor had he moved in his seat. The volume of his voice and obvious severity in the tone made both Latour and the woman hesitate.

"You contradict me, monster?" hissed Lord Dante. "In this place, you would do so? You would dare?"

Frankenstein looked evenly at his host. "Do you know what she is talking about, Dante?" he asked.

"Of course not," blustered the vampire king. "She has clearly mistaken me for some peasant boy."

Frankenstein glanced at the girl, who was openly trembling.

"She seems quite sure," he said. "Why do you suppose that might be?"

"I have no idea," replied Lord Dante. "Are you asking me to attempt to understand the thinking of this girl? I cannot begin to perceive the primitive way her mind works. Now kill her, Latour, while the mood of the evening might still be salvaged."

Latour looked at Dante, then back at Frankenstein. His face wore a look of confusion, and a conflict of loyalty was evident in his eyes.

"W-why would you want to hurt me, Pierre?" asked the girl, tears now flowing down her face. "What d-did I ever d-do to you?"

Lord Dante leapt to his feet, so quickly that it was impossible to see the movement. His eyes burst crimson, and he swept the glasses, bottles, china plates and silver cutlery from the table, where they crashed against one of the red walls.

"Enough!" he screamed, his voice high and furious. "That is more than enough! I am Dante Valeriano, the vampire king of Paris, and I have never heard of this man you are mistaking me for. Now kill her, Latour – I command you to kill her!"

Latour didn't move.

He was staring at Frankenstein, a pleading look on his face. The monster realised that everyone around the table was looking at him, that the authority in the room was shifting away from the vampire king. Dante followed the gazes of his guests, and realised it too.

"You doubt me, Frankenstein?" he asked, his voice full of menace. "After all the time we have spent in each other's company, you doubt me?"

The monster ignored him, and stared around at his guests.

"Tell me," he said, his voice like rumbling boulders. "How long have any of you ladies and gentlemen actually known our illustrious host?"

The cowed man, the husband of the white-faced woman, wiped his brow with a handkerchief, and looked at Frankenstein.

"Well, sir," he said, nervously. "Of course we have only had the pleasure of Lord Dante's presence among us these last ten years or so. It is common knowledge that before that he was in seclusion, avoiding the Tartars who had been sent to bring his head to Moscow."

He smiled, like a schoolboy who is relieved to have been asked a question to which he knows the answer. Frankenstein thanked him, then turned a gaze of utter contempt towards Dante, who visibly recoiled.

"You mongrel," growled the vampire king. "You dare doubt that I am who—"

"I dare," interrupted Frankenstein, pushing his chair backwards and rising to his full, towering height. "I doubt you, *my lord*. I have seen better fakers and far better liars than you this past century, and *I doubt you*. I call you Pierre Depuis, of Saint-Denis. I call you a fraud."

"Kill him!" shrieked Dante. "Kill them both, and bring me their lying tongues on—"

Thunk.

Dante's eyes widened. He looked at Frankenstein, then followed his gaze down to the monster's outstretched arm. The pale grey-green hand at the end of it was gripping the handle of the heavy *kukri* knife the monster always wore on his belt. The thick, heavy silver blade was buried up to the hilt in the vampire king's chest, pinning him solid to the wall behind him. Frankenstein had moved so quickly that nobody had realised what was happening until it was already done.

Dante reached out a trembling hand towards the monster, then watched with uncomprehending horror as it began to dissolve before his eyes, falling apart into wet chunks of scarlet flesh that pattered on to the table. Then, just as quickly, it began to regrow, new muscle knitting, new skin bursting into place. As it did so, his neck began to slide apart, then stopped, and repaired as his arm had done. A thick gout of blood exploded from the vampire king's chest, then was stilled. Dante's face began to melt into blood, then solidified, then melted, then solidified, as he stared down at the blade that had crunched through the centre of his heart.

For a moment, the dining room was utterly still. Then the white-faced woman shrieked, and the vampire guests leapt back from their chairs, their eyes flooding red, their fangs bursting into view. Latour stood, frozen to the spot, staring at the stricken vampire king.

Frankenstein didn't wait.

He leapt over the table towards the long-haired man, his vast size driving the vampire back against the wall. Without looking, he reached out, grabbed the white face of the woman and smashed her head against the wall. She went to the floor, blood spraying from the holes her fangs had punched in her own lips. Frankenstein kicked out to his right, connecting solidly with the woman's partner and sending him sprawling. Before either had a chance to get back to their feet, he pulled a short dagger from inside his waistcoat and plunged it into the long-haired vampire's chest.

The vampire exploded, soaking Frankenstein from head to toe in steaming gore. He turned away, appearing not to notice. The side door to the dining room crashed open, and Jacques stepped through it, his eyes blazing, drawn by the pungent scent of fresh blood. He stopped dead in his tracks, staring at his master; it gave Frankenstein all the time he needed. He thrust the dagger into the waiter's back, and was moving again as the servant exploded, showering his gaping master with blood.

He advanced on the white-faced woman, who was hauling herself to her feet. She raised her hands to protect herself as Frankenstein, a giant blood-soaked nightmare, bore down on her. The dagger went clean through her left palm, pushing the hand backwards as it thudded into her chest, cleaving her heart in two. She burst like a balloon, but Frankenstein was already moving again, and the blood splashed across his broad back. The woman's husband was backing away, an apologetic look on his face, his hands out in placation.

"Please," he said. "Please don't. I'll leave, I'll—"

What he was offering to do, Frankenstein would never know. The dagger flashed out for a fourth time, and a millisecond later a final eruption of blood soaked the dining room. The four vampires had been destroyed in less than ten seconds, and their destroyer whirled to face the head of the table, where Dante was still gasping incredulously at the injury that had been done to him, where both the girl and Latour were staring at him with frozen horror.

"We must go, Latour," said Frankenstein. "Right now."

Latour glanced at Lord Dante. The fraudulent vampire king was staring in horror, as his body threatened to dissolve then healed, over and over again.

"What have you done to him?" whispered Latour. "What dark magic is this?"

"I don't know," replied Frankenstein. "Nor do I care. Take hold of the girl, and let us leave, while we are able to do so."

Latour's gaze flicked between the girl, Dante and Frankenstein. His face was a mask of torment.

"Last chance, my friend," said Frankenstein. "Are you coming or not?"

Latour said nothing, but a look of terrible shame passed across his face.

It was all Frankenstein needed to see. He stepped forward quickly and grabbed the blonde girl. She cried out as his mottled fingers closed round her forearm, but when he hauled her towards the door, she went willingly. He paused for a moment, placing his ear to the door, then pushed it open. He cast a final look back into the blood-soaked room, and saw Dante staring at him, a wide-eyed expression of utter outrage on his face. Then he was gone, pulling the girl behind him.

*

The following morning, Frankenstein stood outside an elegant stone building on Rue Scribe, and took a deep breath.

He had dragged the unprotesting girl, whose name he eventually discovered was Daphne, through the theatre of La Fraternité de la Nuit, without attracting so much as a glance from the assembled vampires; the destruction of Babineaux had thinned the crowd, and those that remained were focused on the stage, where two female vampires were deflowering an adolescent boy.

Frankenstein had pushed through the foyer, abandoning his overcoat, and out into the Paris night. Only once they were clear of the theatre, and had attained some measure of safety, did Daphne begin to cry. Tears spilled from her eyes, and her legs gave way beneath her; she would have fallen had Frankenstein not caught her by the waist. He had taken her to a small hotel on Rue Saint-Claude, and coaxed her gently on to the bed. She had lain awake for a long time, staring at him, but thankfully she had been unwilling, or unable, to ask any questions.

He had no answers for her.

Eventually, she slept. Frankenstein stared out of the hotel room's window, and as he watched the sun rising to the east, he made a decision.

For as long as he could remember, he had considered himself worthless. The circumstances of his birth, the recycled nature of his very body, had made it an easy conclusion to reach, and what he had done to Victor Frankenstein, the man whom he had eventually come to recognise as his father in every way apart from the biological, whose name he had ultimately taken in a belated attempt to honour the dead man, had confirmed it.

He had intended to die in the Arctic, had believed he deserved to, was looking forward to welcoming the end. But a Norwegian explorer vessel had denied him even that most fundamental of rights, the right to end one's own life. He had been suffering from advanced hypothermia when they found him, and had been unable to articulate that he did not want, or deserve, their assistance. Instead, they had nursed him back to health, and several months later, his recuperation complete, he had arrived in Paris.

The pleasures of the night came easily to him because he believed, deep inside his tortured soul, that he was less than human, and therefore that human morals and human decency need not apply to him. He had done terrible things in the decade he had spent in the French capital, under the cover of darkness, and the long shadow of war. In Latour he had found someone similarly unburdened by guilt, or by conscience, and they had indulged the very worst of themselves, together. And when the doubts came, as they occasionally did in the dead of the night, as he was washing blood from his hands or shivering through an opiate haze, he pushed them away. He would not listen; doubts were for the good, for the human.

He did not deserve them.

But something had happened in the Fraternité's dining room; he had felt something change within himself. He did not know if it was the brazen, pathetic nature of Dante's deception, or the revulsion he felt towards the pathetic, cloying sycophants the fraudulent king surrounded himself with, but when Daphne had been brought into the room, he had felt something more clearly and powerfully than anything he could remember.

He had felt guilt.

Guilt that he was a part of the dark underbelly of Paris in which girls like this were tortured and murdered, guilt that he was standing of his own free will in a club where torture and evisceration were viewed as entertainment, night after night, victim after victim. Guilt that he had let weakness and self-pity determine the path his life had taken, when he could have used the curiosities of his condition, his incredible strength and stamina, his immortality, for the good of others, rather than in the service of his own worst desires. And guilt over the things he had done, with his own two hands, things he now resolved to never speak of again, providing he survived the next night.

He knew Dante's men would come looking for him as soon as the sun set, but felt no fear. Saving one girl did not begin to atone for the hundreds he had failed to save, for the ones he himself had helped on their way to the next life, for the harm he had done and the pleasure he had taken in it. But if it was the last thing he did, if it turned out to be the final deed of his long life, he believed he could be content.

But as he stared towards the east, he realised that he was lying to himself.

He *wasn't* content for this to be his end; moreover, he would not permit it to be. He was suddenly full of a fire he had not felt in many decades, as if his soul had been pulled from his body and held up to the sun, cleansing it and filling him with a righteousness he would not have believed he was capable of.

He would atone for the evil he had done.

Even if it took him until the end of eternity.

28

THINK BUT THIS AND
ALL IS MENDED

When everyone had finished eating, in Matt's case so much that he was leaning back in his chair, holding his stomach with both hands and letting out the occasional groan, Jamie spoke to the two girls sitting opposite him.

"Can you meet me in my quarters in fifteen minutes?" he asked. "There are some things I need to say, to both of you."

The girls glanced at each other, and despite the realisation that had flooded through him only moments earlier, that he was the source of the problems that had grown up around and between them, the gesture still annoyed him.

Ignore it. Just let it go. It's not their fault, it's yours.

"I can," said Kate, and looked over at Larissa, who nodded.

"Me too," said the vampire. "I'll see you both there."

With that, she was up and away from the table, her tray in her hands, heading for the exit. Kate waited a few extra seconds, then stood up, said goodbye to Matt and disappeared in the same direction, leaving the two boys alone.

"Oh wow," said Matt, distantly. "I'm so, so full. I haven't eaten that much in years."

"Feeling better?" asked Jamie, smiling.

"Not at this precise moment, to be fair," grinned Matt. "But generally speaking, a lot better, thanks."

"You feel like you can walk?" Jamie asked. "I need to show you how to get back to the dormitory before I take care of something."

"No problem," replied Matt, and then groaned as he levered himself to his feet. He stood unsteadily for a moment, then smiled at Jamie. "Let's go," he said. "I don't think it would be wise for you to keep those two waiting."

"You've no idea," replied Jamie with a smile.

The two boys walked out of the dining hall and along the long central corridor of Level G. As they walked, Jamie began to explain to Matt the rough layout of the Loop, the spherical base that was the heart of Department 19. The vast majority of the facility was beneath the ground; only the huge hangar, the Ops and Briefing Rooms, and the Communications and Surveillance Divisions were located in the wide metal bubble that rose from the grass and tarmac.

"Think of it like a ball," said Jamie. "There's a reinforced concrete wall that runs all the way through the base, from top to bottom; in there are the main corridors, the lift shafts, the seismic dampeners, the steel struts, everything you would expect. So really, it's like two semi-circular bases separated by long, straight corridors along the middle of each level, like this one. So at the top, one whole side to the west of the central corridor is the hangar, then the other side is offices. The same shape applies all the way down; Operator quarters, dormitories, labs, gyms, shops, everything you need to run a facility this size, arranged either side of the central corridors. Right down to the bottom."

"What's down there?" asked Matt, fascinated. "At the very bottom, I mean."

"The power plant, water purification, seismic monitoring equipment," replied Jamie. "Or so I'm told at least; I've never been down there."

"Is it restricted?" asked Matt.

"Not that I know of," replied Jamie, noting the curious expression on the teenager's face. "Why d'you ask?"

"I just think it would be fascinating," said Matt, eagerly. "I can't believe you haven't explored every inch of this place."

Jamie laughed. "I see the Ops Room, the Briefing Rooms, the officers' mess, the dining hall, the hangar and, when I'm lucky, my quarters. I don't really have time for much else."

"I guess not," said Matt. His face fell for a moment, then brightened once more. "Do you think Mr Seward would let me have a look down there? If he decides to let me stay, that is."

"Admiral Seward," corrected Jamie, gently. "Or Director Seward. And I don't see why not. Although I reckon we should just concentrate on persuading him to let you stay for now, OK?"

"Absolutely," enthused Matt. "No problem."

"Cool," said Jamie, stepping in front of the lift and pressing the CALL button. "I'll take you through all the levels and the rest of the base when we've got more time, I promise, but for now, let's get you back to the dormitory."

The lift arrived and the two boys stepped inside. Jamie hit the button for Level B, and the lift car rose quickly through the levels. The doors slid open and the two boys stepped out. Matt fidgeted nervously, a look of mild anxiety on his face.

"Here we are," said Jamie, pointing to his left. "Last corridor at the end, then the second door. Got it?"

"Aren't you coming with me?"

"My quarters are this way," he replied, pointing in the other direction.

Matt nodded, and Jamie gave him a wide grin.

"You'll be fine," he said. "There'll be an Operator outside the dormitory door to let you in. There's nothing you need to be doing right now, so just try and get some rest. I'll come and get you as soon as I hear anything."

Jamie was very familiar with the secure dormitory where Matt had been placed; it was the same room that Frankenstein had taken him to when he first arrived at the Loop, months earlier.

"All right," said Matt. "Thanks, Jamie. And good luck with Kate and Larissa."

"Cheers," he replied, and laughed. "I think I'm going to need it."

Jamie made his way along Level B towards his quarters, trying to work out in his head what he was going to say to Kate and Larissa. As he approached his room, he saw the two girls standing outside the door, leaning against the wall.

Not a good sign, he thought.

Both the girls knew the code to open his door, had let themselves in hundreds of times. But this was not one of those times; they were waiting silently for him to arrive, eyeing him steadily as he approached them.

"All right?" he asked, his voice full of forced levity.

Neither girl replied. Larissa raised her eyebrows a fraction, in what he hoped might be a gesture of encouragement, but Kate remained impassive.

"OK," he said, and held his ID against the panel beside the door. It unlocked with a heavy thud, and he pushed it open. He held it wide, and the two girls stepped silently inside the room. Jamie took a deep breath and followed them, closing the door behind him.

For a long, painfully awkward moment, the three of them stood in the small room, unsure of how to proceed; the dimensions of the room forced them into a proximity that was clearly uncomfortable for all.

Jamie hesitated, then pulled the chair out from beneath his desk and turned it into the room. He waited to see if there would be a response, and when one failed to materialise, he sat down in the chair. The two girls remained standing for a few remarkably uncomfortable seconds, then sat down on the edge of his narrow bed, facing him. Their faces wore expressions of expectation.

Just do this, he told himself. *Get on with it already.*

"I've been an idiot," said Jamie, and was heartened to see the sudden widening in both girls' eyes. "I've been stupid, and unfair, and I let you both down. There are lots of things I want to say, but the most important one is simply this: I'm really, really sorry. Kate, it was my idea that Larissa and me should lie to you about us, and Larissa, I know I've been putting the Department first, that I've been pulling away from you. I'm really, really sorry."

"Jamie," said Kate, gently. "It's not all your fault. I kept secrets too."

"About you and Shaun," said Jamie. "I know. But you wouldn't have felt you had to if Larissa and I hadn't kept you in the dark about what was happening between us. And like I said, that was my idea."

"Hey," protested Larissa. "I went along with it. It's my fault too."

356

"That's right," said Jamie. "You went along with it, because I told you it was the best thing to do. I know you never agreed with me, I know how much you hated lying to Kate; you only did it because you trusted me, and I was wrong. We should have been honest from the start, like we told each other we would be."

The two girls looked at each other, and something passed between them: a moment of unexpected peace, in which Jamie hoped lay the shoots of recovery.

"We understand, Jamie," said Larissa, softly. "Both of us understand what it's been like for you since Lindisfarne, how much your life has changed. We get it, we really do, and neither of us has ever wanted to make it any harder for you than it already is. We see how happy being here makes you, how you get to feel like you belong to something for the first time, how you can be proud of your name and what it stands for. That was never the problem; the problem was it started to feel like you were turning your back on us, like we were losing you, losing each other, over nothing. Does that make any sense at all?"

Jamie felt a deep pang of shame stab at his heart; what Larissa was describing was the exact realisation that it had taken him months to come to.

"It does," he said, softly. "I see it now."

"It's all right," said Larissa. "Really it is. We're just glad you realised it eventually." Then she smiled at him, *really* smiled at him, for what felt like the first time in ages, and Jamie realised he had been a fool. There was no prestige, no pride to be gained from keeping things from his friends, from hoarding exclusivity as though it was something real, something that mattered.

No more secrets, he thought. *No more lies.*

Jamie leant forward and smiled at the two girls.

"Can you keep a secret?" he asked.

"That depends," said Kate, curiosity rising instantly on her face, "on how big it is."

"It's pretty big," said Jamie, and started to talk.

87 DAYS TILL
ZERO HOUR

29

IN CONVERSATION WITH A MONSTER

The following morning, Jamie Carpenter leapt out of bed more easily than he had in months.

His mind was usually heavy when he awoke, weighed down by tiredness and worry; this morning, it was as light as a feather. The conversation with Larissa and Kate had done him enormous good, as had unburdening his last remaining secret to them, a secret he had told nobody else and only one other person in the entire Loop had known about. It was as though someone had crawled in through his ear in the night and scrubbed his brain clean. Even the meeting he had agreed to have with Valentin Rusmanov, which was due to begin in less than half an hour, could not dampen his spirits.

Jamie towelled himself dry, smiling as he remembered the looks on the girls' faces as he told them his secret, pulled on his black uniform and set out for the lift. He walked quickly, partly because his good mood was filling him with energy, and partly because he didn't want to keep Admiral Seward waiting.

The Director's faith in him, the almost paternal attitude he had begun to adopt, was something that Jamie had come to greatly appreciate and, in the absence of his own father, begun to rely on.

Admiral Seward was not affectionate towards him, not even close, but he treated him with the same respect he treated anyone else, without making his age a factor, either positively or negatively. For Jamie, who had spent two years angry at a father he had believed had betrayed not only his family but also his country, and who had been without a constant male role model even after his father's memory had been rehabilitated, it was exactly what he needed; someone who believed that he could be trusted, who could look after himself, and others.

He reached the lift at the end of the long corridor and pressed the CALL button. He was thinking about the kiss Larissa had given him as the two girls left his quarters the previous night, the first time they had ever kissed in front of Kate, who had giggled of course, but then averted her eyes with a wide smile on her face. The kiss had been filled with the same fire as their very first, fire that seemed to burn everything else away, everything but the two of them, that roared and spun and made him feel like they were the only two people in the world. This kiss had not been quite the same, as first kisses are unique, and impossible to recreate.

It was close, though, thought Jamie. *Pretty damn close.*

The lift doors slid open and Jamie stepped into the car, nodding to an Operator he knew slightly, one of the many almost-familiar faces that populated the Loop. It was not a place in which it was easy to get to know people; Operators spent the vast majority of their time with their squad mates, on missions in far-flung corners of the country, and beyond. When they were actually off duty, most fled for the warmth of their beds.

Some frequented the officers' mess for drinks, or a cigar, or a game of cards, but it was largely the older generation of Blacklight that inhabited the dark, wood-panelled room. They had been Operators before the title existed, before the explosion of vampire numbers in the 1980s and 1990s brought with it triple shifts and endless days without sleep. Most of them were now on the inactive list, and were content to while away their remaining years until retirement swapping stories and toasting fallen friends in the warmth of the mess. Much of the time, Jamie envied them.

The lift drew to a halt on Level A, and Jamie walked quickly down the corridor. He nodded to the Operator stationed outside Admiral Seward's quarters, knocked on the door and waited. After a couple of seconds, it swung slowly open. Jamie stepped inside to see the Director in his usual position, seated at his desk behind a mountain of paperwork.

"Lieutenant Carpenter," said Seward, glancing up from a report he was making notes in the margin of. "At ease."

Jamie waited for the Director to finish what he was doing, his hands crossed loosely behind his back. Seward traced the final paragraph of the report with the tip of his pen, swore loudly, crossed out the entire paragraph, and then shoved the paper aside and looked up at Jamie.

"Feels like half the Operators in the Department are trying to win creative writing prizes," he said. "What happened to facts? Just the simple facts of the matter, in plain language?"

"I don't know, sir," replied Jamie. "Writing reports is pretty dull, sir. Maybe people are trying to make it more fun."

"It's paperwork, Jamie," snapped Admiral Seward. "It's bloody red tape. It isn't supposed to be fun."

"Yes, sir."

"Good," said Seward, and smiled at Jamie. "Glad we've got that sorted."

"Me too, sir," replied Jamie, a smile of his own threatening to emerge.

"How are you feeling about this morning, Jamie?" asked Seward. "Ready for your meeting with Valentin?" There was a slight hitch in the Director's voice, which Jamie realised was concern.

He doesn't want me to do it, thought Jamie. *He doesn't think it's safe. He doesn't want me to go down there on my own.*

"I'm fine, sir," he replied, feeling a slow warmth in his chest. "It's got to be done."

Seward looked at him for a long moment, then nodded. "I suppose it does," he said. "It feels completely wrong to be sending you in there on your own, but I can't think of any other solution."

"Nor can I, sir."

There was a moment's silence, in which many things went unsaid between the boy and the middle-aged man, and then Seward grabbed for a sheet of paper on his desk, and they returned to business.

"I spoke to Professor Talbot," said Admiral Seward. "Last night. I asked him about your new friend, Mr Browning."

"What did he say, sir?" asked Jamie, excitedly. If Matt was allowed to stay at the Loop in any sort of capacity, it would be a huge victory.

"He laughed," replied Seward, and Jamie's face fell. "Or at least," continued the Director, "he did until I showed him Mr Browning's file. Then he stopped. The first thing he actually said was, 'The only member of my team with a higher IQ than this boy is me.'"

"That's great," said Jamie. "Isn't it?"

"Professor Talbot certainly seems to think so," replied Admiral Seward. "He's agreed to take Matt into the Lazarus Project, on a trial basis. The security risk is minimal, because as I'm sure you know, whether this works out or not, Mr Browning isn't going home again. We can't take that chance. So we might as well see if he can make himself useful."

The implication of the Director's words hung in the air; Jamie wanted, *needed* to believe that Admiral Seward was referring to incarceration.

The alternative was too horrible to consider.

He was suddenly overcome with a sickly wave of guilt as he realised that, compared to his three friends, he was actually remarkably lucky; he still had his mother, even if she now lived in a cell two hundred metres below ground. Kate, Larissa, and now Matt, had lost everyone important to them.

"He'll be brilliant, sir," said Jamie. "Talbot's lucky to have him."

"Let's hope he proves you right," said Admiral Seward. "I've sent his temporary commission and his release forms down to the dormitory for him to sign; Talbot wants him to start work immediately. I put him on Level B, in the quarters next to yours; I assume you have no objection to that?"

"No, sir," said Jamie, gratefully. "Thank you, sir."

"All right then," replied the Director, nodding sharply. "Once you've jumped through Valentin's hoops, perhaps you could show Matt to his room? I imagine he'll still be asleep."

"Definitely, sir," said Jamie.

"Good," said Seward. "In which case, you're due in containment in a few minutes. We'll be watching you from the Ops Room; just keep calm, and try and give him whatever it is he wants. You'll do fine, Jamie; I have faith in you. Dismissed."

Jamie headed back to the lift with Admiral Seward's words ringing in his ears.

I have faith in you.

The Director had said the five words casually, without drawing attention to them; it was as though he believed they shouldn't even need saying.

I have faith in you.

Jamie chewed them over as he waited for the lift to arrive. The only person who had ever said anything similar to him was Larissa, as they stood in the darkness of the Lindisfarne woods with an innocent man's body at their feet; she had told him that she wouldn't let him give up. The words had heartened him, filled him with the strength to keep going, and Admiral Seward's words had done the same; he stepped into the lift as its doors slid open, and pressed the button that would take him down to Valentin Rusmanov.

On Level H, he found Paul Turner waiting for him. The Security Officer nodded curtly at him as he approached.

"You know I can't come in there with you," he said. It was a statement, rather than a question. "We've moved your mother to a temporary location. Valentin's butler too. It's just going to be the two of you. Are you ready for this?"

"I am," said Jamie, and realised that he was.

"OK then," said Turner, with the tiniest approximation of a smile. "You'll do fine."

The Security Officer stood aside. Jamie walked into the gleaming double airlock door that controlled access to the cellblock. He stood in the narrow space as the door behind him closed, shut his eyes as the rushing gas of the spectroscope billowed around him, then walked calmly out of the second door. As he walked down the long, wide corridor, he was incredibly aware of his heart beating in his chest; he tried to control it, tried to force it to slow down, aware that it would sound like the thumping of a bass drum to Valentin as he approached.

Jamie stepped out in front of the wide ultraviolet wall, and looked into the cell. Valentin Rusmanov was waiting for him in the same chair he had sat in the previous morning, a wide, welcoming smile on his face. The vampire's shirt collar was open, as was the jacket of his grey suit.

"Mr Carpenter," he exclaimed. "A very good morning to you. I had begun to suspect you weren't coming."

Jamie looked at his watch to see that it was seven minutes past eight.

"I'm sorry," he said. "I had a meeting that overran."

"No doubt you were being briefed thoroughly on the dangers of being alone with me," smiled Valentin. "By Admiral Seward, I would guess? He seems rather fond of you."

"I'm here now," said Jamie, determined not to let the vampire dictate the conversation. "Alone, as you requested. May I come in?"

Valentin nodded at the empty chair in which Paul Turner had sat.

"Please," he replied. "*Mi casa es su casa.* Make yourself at home."

Jamie took an involuntary deep breath, which he hoped Valentin didn't notice, then stepped through the ultraviolet wall. He felt his skin tingle momentarily, then walked steadily across the room and sat down in the chair.

Less than two metres away, smiling gently, sat one of the most powerful beings in the world.

"So," said Valentin, crossing one leg over the other. "What shall we talk about?"

"You wanted this meeting," said Jamie. "Why don't you tell me why?"

The vampire's grin widened, and Jamie thought he saw the tiniest flash of red in the corner of its eyes; it had been so fleeting that he couldn't be sure, but he felt a chill run up his spine nonetheless.

"There is so much for us to discuss, Jamie – may I call you Jamie? Or do you prefer Mr Carpenter?"

"Jamie is fine."

"Lovely," said Valentin. "Jamie it is then. The first thing I would like to ask you about is exactly how you were able to kill my brother. Does that seem like a fair place to start the conversation?"

Jamie's stomach revolted as a thick wave of unease crashed through him. This, he knew, was the topic that was most likely to place him in danger; unlike the other members of the Zero Hour Task Force, he didn't believe that Valentin meant him any harm, at least not consciously. But the subject of Alexandru, more specifically of Alexandru's death, seemed to Jamie the likeliest trigger, if there was to be one.

"I told you," he replied. "In the van. Two days ago."

"Details, Jamie," exclaimed Valentin, sitting suddenly forward in his chair and smiling at the teenager. "The devil is in the detail. Tell me again, without tailoring the story to your audience."

Jamie hesitated.

Tell the truth, he thought. *He'll know if you're lying.*

"I pulled a seven-metre-tall cross down on the back of his head," said Jamie. "It weighed about two tons, they told me afterwards. It smashed his body to pieces, and I put a stake through his heart. That's it."

"What did he do when it hit him?" asked Valentin, softly. "Did he scream? Did he try to get out of the way? My brother was very fast, if nothing else."

"He didn't see it coming," said Jamie. "It was behind him, and he was watching me. He thought I'd aimed at him and missed, so he was smiling at me. But I hadn't; I'd aimed for the cross."

"Go on," said Valentin, his voice low and hungry. "Tell me."

"At the last second, just before it hit him, the shadow of the cross fell across him, and he frowned. I can remember it really clearly; it was just a normal frown, like when you see something unusual. He didn't even try to move, and a second later it landed on him."

Valentin leant back in his chair, and raised his eyebrows, a clear sign for Jamie to continue.

"It broke him," said Jamie, simply. "There was blood everywhere. I couldn't believe he could still be alive, but he was. I went and knelt down next to him, while the rest of my team attacked his followers, and he was staring at me. He only had one eye, but it was looking right at me, and he was trying to speak."

"What was he trying to say?" asked Valentin. "Could you understand him?"

"He told me I was too late," replied Jamie. "Then he said 'He Rises', and told me that everyone I loved was going to die. And that's when I staked him."

Valentin looked at him, and Jamie saw open admiration on his face.

Perhaps I'm not going to die down here, he thought.

"How did you know it would work?" asked the vampire. "The cross, I mean. How did you know my brother wouldn't simply move out of the way?"

"I didn't," said Jamie, honestly. "But I knew I couldn't fight him, and I knew that he knew it too. So I thought that if it looked like I had failed, then he'd be too pleased with himself to notice what I'd really done."

"That's a very large wager. You quite literally gambled your life on it."

"Not really," replied Jamie, shrugging his shoulders. "I was dead either way, or worse, and so were my mother and my friends. I had nothing to lose by then."

Valentin leant back in his chair, and drew a beautiful silver cigarette holder from inside his suit jacket. He plucked a dark red cigarette from beneath a band of white silk, placed it in his mouth and lit it. Pungent, aromatic tobacco smoke wafted into the air, laced with a metallic undercurrent that Jamie recognised instantly.

"That's Bliss, isn't it?" he said.

Valentin nodded, cocking his head to one side.

"You're familiar with it?" the vampire asked.

"I am," said Jamie, his hand instinctively touching the patch of scar tissue on his neck, the result of a chemical burn he had received in the laboratory where the majority of the British supply of the vampire drug was produced.

"Have you ever tried it?" asked Valentin, offering the case towards Jamie. "I'm told it is quite agreeable to humans."

"No thank you," said Jamie, politely. "I'm fine."

Valentin nodded, then took a deep drag on the cigarette. His eyes glowed involuntarily red, and he threw back his head, the muscles on his neck standing out. When the rush of the heroin and the human blood had passed, he slowly returned his gaze to Jamie, the red light dwindling in his eyes as he did so.

"My brother was a monster," he said, slowly. "I have come to believe that he always was, since we were children, and probably since birth. He felt nothing for anyone other than himself, with the possible exception of Ilyana, his wife. The world is a better place without him in it; he was cruel, and pitiless, and arrogant. It pleases me that the last of those ended up as the reason for his downfall."

Jamie didn't reply; he had no idea what to say to such an admission.

"I thank you for being honest," continued Valentin. "I would have known if you weren't of course, but I'm sure it made you nervous to tell me about murdering a member of my family."

He grinned, and Jamie fought the urge to grin right back.

Don't do anything to provoke him. Don't trust anything he says. View everything as a potential trap.

"It wasn't top of my list of potential topics," he replied.

Valentin's grin widened even further, until it looked as though his face was going to split in half. "And what was?" he asked. "What would you like to talk about?"

"My grandfather," said Jamie. "I know almost nothing about him. It's crazy to me that you knew him; he died before I was born."

"Didn't your father ever speak of him?"

"Not really," said Jamie. "He told me he flew in the war, and that was about it. Dad never really talked much about him, or any of his family. I only realised why once I was here."

"And the monster?" asked Valentin. "He was closer to your grandfather than anyone. He told you nothing?"

"He told me that my grandfather saved him," replied Jamie, feeling a twinge of pain in his chest as he thought about Frankenstein. "He told me that he was the reason he swore to protect my family, because of something that happened in New York a long time ago. He promised he was going to tell me everything, but he never got the chance."

"You miss him, don't you?" asked Valentin, softly. "The monster. I can hear it in your voice."

Jamie nodded. "I do," he said. "I miss him, and I feel guilty every day. He wouldn't be dead if I had trusted him."

"How so?"

"I let Thomas Morris manipulate me," replied Jamie, feeling his face heat up with shame. "He told me that Frankenstein was there the night my father died, that he was one of the men sent to bring him in. I asked him if it was true, and he admitted it. So I told him to stay away from me, and I went to Lindisfarne with Morris. Right into the trap he'd set for me."

"But the monster followed you regardless?"

"He had suspected Tom Morris," said Jamie. "He followed us, and he arrived in time to help. But when we thought it was all over, a werewolf that was loyal to Alexandru attacked me, and Frankenstein stepped in between us. They went over the cliffs together."

"That doesn't sound like it was your fault," said Valentin. "Not to me at least."

"If I had trusted him, he would have been with us on Lindisfarne. Morris wouldn't have been able to do what he did."

"Why not? My brother was more powerful than a hundred Frankensteins combined. Do you really think his being there would have made any difference?"

"I don't know," said Jamie, miserably.

"You said he died after the battle with my brother was over," continued Valentin. "Defending you from a werewolf. How can you say that things wouldn't have transpired exactly the same way, whether he had arrived on Lindisfarne with you and Mr Morris or an hour after you, as he did?"

Jamie looked at Valentin, searching the old vampire's face for amusement or enjoyment, looking for any sign that he was being toyed with. He saw nothing; the vampire's face was open, full of what appeared to be honesty.

"I don't know," he said. "I just know that it feels like my fault. It feels like he's dead because of me."

"It sounds to me," said Valentin, "that the reason he is dead is because he chose to put your life ahead of his own. You didn't ask him to, nor did anyone else; he made that choice for himself. Who are you to take responsibility for it?"

Jamie's throat worked, but no sound came out. His mind was reeling; he had become so accustomed to the weight of his guilt that even the suggestion that he had been carrying it unnecessarily was almost impossible for him to comprehend.

"It was his life, Jamie," said Valentin. "He lived it as he chose, and it sounds like he ended it as he chose, a luxury not granted to many. I would be willing to wager that he wouldn't want you to blame yourself for what he did. I'm sure that wherever he is now, he's quite content."

30

THERE IS NO STATUTE OF LIMITATIONS FOR REVENGE

Frankenstein lay on a sumptuously soft four-poster bed, staring at the gilded golden frame above him.

He had been lying perfectly still for more than an hour; he was trying to wake up, to force the slippery dissolution that marks the collapse of a dream and the return of the real world. He was hoping, futilely, to be returned to a world where his memory was restored, where Latour's insinuations would not haunt his every waking moment, where he would be a free man instead of a prisoner.

He had no idea how many days it had been since the vampire had brought him home. More than one but less than ten was the best estimate he could make; the time ran like syrup, sticky and nauseating. He had been fed and watered, and wanted for nothing except the freedom to leave the grand apartment, with its high ceilings and towering windows, its salon and study and vast, elegant bedrooms.

He had apparently been here before, had spent many voluntary nights in the bed on which he was now lying; Latour had expressed utter delight when he finally accepted that Frankenstein was genuinely unable to remember any aspect of his life, no matter how small or insignificant, and had taken sadistic pleasure in filling in as many of the gaps as he was able.

For long hours, Latour had held forth with tales of horror and violence in which he and Frankenstein had been the starring participants; numbed by his captor's stories, unable and simply unwilling to believe that he could have been capable of perpetrating a single one of the acts of savagery being described, Frankenstein had begged Latour for mercy. The vampire had immediately begun to beat him, chastising him with every blow for his weakness, exhorting him to wake up from his daze, to once again be the man that Latour had once considered his friend.

By day Latour slept, but Frankenstein remained a prisoner. The vampire's house was staffed by an army of servants, many of them human and perfectly capable of operating during the hours of daylight. They were unfailingly polite and attentive, but all were armed with heavy black pistols, and they never entered his room alone. There were always at least two of them, one of whom would approach the bed and enquire as to any needs Frankenstein may have, while the other would remain close to the door, ready to act if the prisoner showed any sign of attempting an escape. He hadn't, and nor did he have any plans to do so, for one simple reason.

He was absolutely terrified for his life.

Frankenstein didn't recognise the man that Latour kept assuring him he used to be, a creature of violence and temper, of awful appetites and disregard for the innocence of others, but he wished that man was here now; it did not sound as though he would have lain passively on his bed, waiting for whatever lay in store for him.

A key turned in the lock, and the bedroom door opened. Latour stepped into the room, his narrow frame covered in an elegant tuxedo. The black was the colour of midnight, the white of the collars and the narrow vertical stripe of the exposed shirt were the colour of the full moon. He smiled at Frankenstein, then flew across the room at such speed that the prisoner's teetering mind could only perceive it as teleportation; one moment Latour was standing in the open doorway, the next he was beside the bed.

"It's time," said the vampire. "We're going to see an old friend, and I'd prefer we not be late. You can understand that, can't you?"

Frankenstein nodded weakly.

"Splendid," said Latour, beaming down at him. "In which case, we'll take a cocktail downstairs in fifteen minutes, before we set out for the Marais. That is ample time, I hope?"

"Time for what?" whispered Frankenstein.

"For you to dress of course," said Latour, favouring the monster with the kind of look usually reserved for the simple-minded. He extended one of his long, slender arms, and indicated in the direction of the door. A servant was standing in the empty space, holding a huge leather suit carrier carefully in his hands.

Frankenstein stared, uncomprehending.

"I took the liberty of having you measured while you slept," said Latour. "An uncivilised way to do things, I appreciate, and I do apologise. However, time was short, and one simply cannot be dressed as you are to attend the theatre, can one?"

Frankenstein looked down at what he was wearing, the same heavy woollen jumper and hard-wearing trousers Magda had given him in Dortmund, a lifetime ago.

376

"I don't know," he said.

"Luckily, I do," replied the vampire. "I'll leave Lionel here to help you. Fifteen minutes, please; don't make me come back up here."

Then Latour was gone, leaving him alone with the servant, who regarded him with professional neutrality and eyes that momentarily flashed a clear warning red.

"Whenever you're ready, sir," said the servant, and unzipped the leather case.

Ten minutes later Frankenstein made his way awkwardly to the bottom of the grand staircase that spiralled up through the centre of Latour's apartment.

The tuxedo he was wearing fitted him perfectly, but he still felt incredibly uncomfortable; he plucked at the sleeves and shook his feet, trying to make the hems of the trousers settle atop his mirror-gleaming shoes. A piece of classical music was floating through the open door of the large salon at the end of the eastern corridor, and he made his way towards it.

Latour was lying on a chaise longue in the centre of the room, his eyes closed and a smile on his pale face; one hand held a dark red cigarette that Frankenstein had come to learn was liberally laced with a drug of some kind, a drug that was distilled at least in part from human blood, while the other floated back and forth in the air in time with the music that was emanating from a sleek black stereo system in the corner of the room.

"Chopin's *Nocturnes, Op. 27*," said Latour, without opening his eyes. He had heard his prisoner's clumsy, uneven footsteps since the monster had stepped on to the first stair, three floors above. "It was your favourite, once upon a time. But I assume you don't remember that?"

377

"You know I don't," replied Frankenstein. "I remember nothing else, so why would a piece of music be any different?"

"Music has the capacity to lift the soul," said Latour, swinging his long legs gracefully down to the floor and regarding Frankenstein. "Even a soul as dark and broken as yours. But indeed, I am not surprised; as always, what I feel for you is pity."

To hell with your pity, thought Frankenstein.

Latour strolled over to a long wooden bar beneath the wide pair of windows that dominated the room. The sun was long set, and the neon lights of nocturnal Paris glowed through the glass. The vampire poured two glasses full of a clear liquid from a silver cocktail shaker, picked them up and floated back across the room. He handed one to Frankenstein, and raised the other.

"To experience," he said, softly. "To all the accumulation of a life, both good and bad."

Frankenstein raised his glass, held it for a moment, then lifted it to his lips and took a sip. The liquid was sharp, and bitter, and felt hot as it rolled across his tongue.

"What is this?" he asked, fighting the urge to cough.

"It's a martini," replied Latour. "You used to love them. I thought it might… oh, never mind."

There was silence in the salon for a long moment. Frankenstein was watching Latour closely, and had seen the momentary grimace pass across the vampire's face when he had asked what the drink was. Part of it was embarrassment, he knew; the vampire was an epicure, a devotee of the very finest things that life had to offer, and the question had made him uncomfortable. It was an unpleasant reminder that he lived in a world in which there were people who did not know what a martini was, despite his strenuous efforts to avoid crossing their paths.

378

But it was more than that; it was disappointment, and sadness too, and Frankenstein realised something profound. Latour's repeated efforts to jar his memory back to life by providing him with familiar objects and sensations from the past were not just a source of entertainment for the vampire; they were genuine attempts by Latour to bring back his friend, a man that, Frankenstein suddenly saw with enormous clarity, the vampire deeply missed.

"It's good," said Frankenstein, motioning towards the beautiful, delicate glass in his huge grey-green hand, then drained the rest of the drink. "I can see why I used to like them."

Latour nodded, then checked his watch and almost sadly announced that there was sufficient time for a second drink, and then they would need to depart.

"Where are we going?" asked Frankenstein, as Latour refilled their glasses. "You mentioned a theatre?"

"Of a sort," replied Latour. "The place we're going is the place we met, and where I flatter myself we spent many contented evenings together. It goes by the name of La Fraternité de la Nuit, and it is the home of—"

"The Brotherhood of the Night," said Frankenstein, softly. The words had appeared in his head from nowhere, translated from the French without his having needed to consider the process. It was a strange feeling, a reminder of the vast realms of knowledge that were locked away inside his mind.

"Exactly," said Latour, narrowing his eyes. "Clearly, not everything has been lost to you."

"It would seem not," replied Frankenstein. "When I saw the word Paris, I knew it was familiar, and it led me here. I understood the words you said, so I said them. My most fervent hope is that more information will be returned to me, in time."

Latour said nothing; he merely drained his second martini in one long swallow, and set the glass on the varnished wooden surface of the bar. Frankenstein followed suit, his hand trembling ever so slightly.

"It's time," said Latour. The warmth that had momentarily infused the vampire's voice was gone; what was left was cold, and sharp. "Are you ready?"

Frankenstein raised himself up to his full height. He towered over his former friend, his head nearly brushing the lowest crystals of the chandelier that hung in the centre of the high ceiling.

"Let's go," he said.

Forty minutes later Lionel brought Latour's black Rolls Royce smoothly to a halt on Rue de Sévigné and stepped out of the long, angular car. A second later he appeared beside the passenger door, and pulled it open; the door swung from a hinge at the rear, rather than at the front, as Lionel stepped respectfully out of view, and held it open for his master.

Fear welled up inside Frankenstein as he stared at the open door.

"What are we doing here, Latour?" he asked. "Tell me that much, please? I know I can't stop whatever it is that is about to happen, so just tell me. Please?"

Latour's face creased for the briefest of moments, and a tiny flame of hope bloomed in Frankenstein's chest. But then the vampire's eyes flared red, and it was extinguished.

"Get out," he said. "You'll see soon enough."

Frankenstein swallowed hard, then did as he was told. He clambered out through the door and on to the immaculate pale stone pavement outside, casting a desperate look down the quiet street in the vain hope that there might be someone in sight who could help him. Then Latour was ushering him towards an ornate black gate, beyond which stood a beautiful pale stone building which Frankenstein couldn't help but notice had no windows. The vampire produced a key and unlocked the gate, then led Frankenstein up to an imposing wooden door, upon which he knocked three times.

Frankenstein waited silently; fatalism had settled over him, bringing with it an eerie sense of calm. He was under no illusions that what was waiting behind the door was going to be anything other than awful; Latour had not held him against his will to deliver him somewhere pleasant. But he realised that he was no longer scared, and that was a blessing to be appreciated, if only a small one.

The door swung silently open, and Latour looked pointedly at Frankenstein. He took a deep breath and stepped through the door, hearing Latour close it firmly behind them. He found himself standing in a small lobby; to his left was a lectern, behind which was standing an elderly man in immaculate evening wear. The man was staring at Frankenstein with an expression of utter shock on his lined face.

"Staring is generally considered rude," said Latour, removing his coat and holding it out towards the lectern.

The old man blinked, and his equilibrium returned. He dragged his gaze away from Frankenstein, then stepped smoothly out from behind the lectern.

"Welcome back to La Fraternité de la Nuit, gentlemen," he said, his voice like oil. He took Latour's coat, waited for the monster to shrug his over his misshapen shoulders and then addressed Frankenstein specifically. "It is a particular pleasure to see you again, sir. It has been far too long; your presence has been greatly missed."

"Thank you," said Frankenstein, warily. He had seen the flicker of red in the corners of the man's eyes as he spoke, and it had disconcerted him.

What place is this? Where have I been brought?

"Enough chatter," said Latour, shooting the elderly man a look of obvious warning. "We have business with Lord Dante; I presume he is in attendance?"

"Of course, sir," replied the old vampire. "His dining room is open to you both, as it always has been."

"Fine," replied Latour. He strode across the lobby to the small door at its rear, and waited. Frankenstein slowly followed him, like a man going to the gallows, and, lowering his huge head below the frame, walked through the door as Latour opened it.

He emerged into a small theatre, and was instantly struck by two contrasting sensations; the first was a churning nausea, as the smell of spilled blood hit his nostrils, and his eyes absorbed the horror of what was playing out before him. On the small stage, in front of the sixty or so seats that were arrayed before it, a vampire man was dancing with the dead body of a woman. Her neck and shoulders were studded with bloody circular holes, her mouth was huge and empty, her eyes wide and staring.

But the second sensation he felt, as he stood unsteadily in this old place of violence and misery, was, if anything, even worse; he felt an immediate comfort, a deep, reassuring feeling that he had been here before, a tangible moment of feeling something other than empty.

It felt like coming home.

What kind of man was I that I would ever have come to a place like this? thought Frankenstein, wretchedly. *This is a place for the worst the world has to offer, the things that live in the shadows, in the darkest corners of the night.*

382

The monsters.

"I've been here before," he said, slowly.

"Of course you have," said Latour. "I told you as much."

"I know you did," replied Frankenstein. "But even if you hadn't, I would have known. I can feel it."

"Do you remember the things you did here?" asked Latour. "The things that we did together? Do you remember Lord Dante?"

Frankenstein searched his shattered mind for answers, but found none. He shook his head with frustration.

"Not to worry," said Latour, a smile of unbridled pleasure on his face. "I'm quite certain he remembers you. Come with me."

Latour led him behind the seats, round the sloping left-hand wall of the theatre, to a wooden door. The vampire knocked on it once, and then pushed it open. He nodded towards Frankenstein, who walked forward, to the place he had always been destined to return.

31

ECHOES OF THE PAST

Jamie Carpenter got up from his chair and walked slowly around the cell, his mind whirring. Valentin Rusmanov watched him, a gentle smile on his ancient face.

I don't believe him, thought Jamie. *I can't. It was my fault that Frankenstein died. I've always known it was.*

But the vampire's words wouldn't leave him, no matter how hard he tried to convince himself that they were untrue. And in the very back of his mind, the sly, wheedling voice that usually told him the things he didn't want to hear was whispering to him.

Maybe you just wanted to believe that. Maybe it was easier to think it was your fault than to believe he sacrificed himself for you.

That made no sense to Jamie; why would he have carried around such a heavy weight of guilt voluntarily? But as the voice kept whispering and Valentin's words churned over and over, he was forced to admit to himself that he *had* used the belief that he was to blame for Frankenstein's death as fuel to keep him going, to keep him moving forward; it was the indignant fire at the heart of his desire to prove himself to everyone, the thing that kept him searching, kept him trying to atone.

That doesn't have to change, whispered the voice. *He died so that you could live. You can still honour him, honour his sacrifice, and show everyone that he didn't make the wrong decision. But maybe you need to put down the guilt, before it becomes too heavy.*

"Jamie?" asked Valentin. "Are you all right?"

He stopped pacing, and turned to face the vampire.

"Why did you say all that?" he asked.

"All what?"

"About it not being my fault about Frankenstein. What were you trying to do?"

"I wasn't trying to do anything," said Valentin. "I was merely giving you my honest opinion."

Jamie stared at him for a long moment, then walked back to his chair. He lowered himself into it, his eyes never leaving Valentin's face.

"I told you I wanted to talk about my grandfather," said Jamie. "Not about Frankenstein. I don't want to talk about him any more."

"Usually, I would agree without reservation," replied Valentin. "The mere thought of him, of his discoloured, uneven skin, his second-hand blood, turns my stomach. But I'm afraid he and your grandfather are inextricably linked. So I may not be able to avoid mentioning him altogether. Is that going to be all right? I really don't want to upset you again."

A wicked smile curled at the corners of Valentin's mouth, and a red-hot pillar of anger surged through Jamie.

Calm. Be calm. Don't let him get to you. Don't give him what he wants. Calm.

"That's fine," he replied, as neutrally as he was able.

"Marvellous," said Valentin, the smile still in place. "It's difficult to know where to start, to be completely honest with you. There isn't really a vampire society out there, at least not in the way that

385

I think some of your colleagues believe there is. There are vampires who live together in groups that I suppose one could charitably refer to as social, there are vampires who operate as family units, as husbands and wives and children, and there are individual vampires who enjoy each other's company, just as humans do. The latter is the situation that I have spent my life in; I live alone, in New York, discounting my dear Lamberton of course, but I regularly socialise with the same men and women of my kind. In some cases I have been doing so for almost a century."

"All right," said Jamie. "I get it. Why are you telling me this?"

Valentin sighed, clearly disappointed.

"I'm telling you because the consensus in Blacklight, and the other Departments like it, seems to be that there is some kind of unified organisation of vampires out there in the night, with leaders and goals and strategies, working towards the downfall of humanity. Which, I'm afraid to tell you, is ridiculous. Most of the vampires out there live their lives as they alone see fit, often taking great pains to avoid others like them. There are two things you need to understand: firstly, that the vast majority of vampires don't know nearly as much as you think they do about you and your friends, and your compatriots around the world. Secondly, that everything I've just described will change, for the markedly worse, if Dracula is allowed to rise to his full strength."

A shiver ran up Jamie's spine at the mention of the first vampire, but he was determined not to allow Valentin to dictate the conversation.

"I understand," he said. "And I want to talk about Dracula. But you said you were going to tell me about my grandfather, and yet you seem to be talking about everything apart from him."

"The point, my impatient little friend," said Valentin, "is that even though word does not travel as widely and quickly through the vampire ranks as your superiors would like to believe, there are those of us who tend to be more aware of what is going on in the world than others. I have always been such a vampire; I have made it a priority to be aware of any developments that have the potential to impact on the life I lead. The formation of your little group, after Dracula's defeat, was such a development.

"My brother Valeri encountered Quincey Harker and his friends in Rome after the end of the First World War, and barely escaped with his life. So I began to take an interest in what was happening in London, from the perspective of self-preservation; as a result, when your grandfather appeared in my home threatening to blow it sky-high unless I allowed him to murder one of my guests, his name was already familiar to me."

Jamie felt a surge of pride rush through his chest, pride in the bravery of a man he'd never met. He tried to imagine what it must have been like for his grandfather, standing in the middle of a room full of vampires, the only thing stopping them from tearing him to pieces the whim of the creature that was sitting two metres away from him.

"Why did you let him go?" asked Jamie. "You could have killed him before he had time to trigger the explosives. I've seen how fast you are."

"You might be right," replied Valentin. His voice was soft, and his eyes were slightly glazed, as though his mind was no longer in the cell with Jamie, but in a ballroom many miles and years away.

"But I couldn't know that for certain. His thumb was on the trigger of the detonator; even if I had killed him, he might have pressed it involuntarily. I had no more wish to be blown to pieces then than I do now, to say nothing of the damage that would have been done to my home. And even in the 1920s, an explosion of that size on Central Park West would have drawn questions that would have been tedious to answer. But more than any of that, what I told him was the truth; I admired his conviction, his apparently genuine willingness to die to accomplish his mission, if that was what it took."

"So you let him go," said Jamie. "And he took Frankenstein with him?"

Valentin nodded. "He wouldn't go without the monster, so I let him take him. A friend of mine was very disappointed; she had plans for him. But yes, I let them both go."

"When did you see him next?"

The vampire didn't answer immediately; a small smile crept on to his face, as he cast back through memory.

"We met for the second time in 1938," he said, eventually. "In Berlin."

John Carpenter was sitting outside a café on Potsdamer Platz when one of the three most dangerous vampires in the world lowered himself into the seat opposite him.

He had just finished a hearty supper of schnitzel and potatoes and an equally hearty bottle of Riesling, and was enjoying an aromatic Turkish cigarette, letting the perfumed smoke billow fragrantly around his head before floating away on the warm evening breeze. The London newspapers were reporting that Germany was heading back into a state of deprivation, that wages were tumbling and unemployment was rising once more, that the economic recovery the National Socialists trumpeted endlessly via their propaganda ministry was little more than a sham.

Carpenter had seen and heard a number of disquieting things in his three days in the German capital – the absence of a political opposition, the whispered rumours of camps in the east where dissidents and undesirables were allegedly being shipped on trains that ran at night, the aggressive, almost comically blustering anger of Chancellor Hitler as he held forth on the many, many enemies he perceived Germany to be facing – but deprivation had not been one of them. The capital was awash with luxury, with food, cars, fine clothes and equally fine wine, although he had heard that the same could not be said away from Berlin.

The previous evening an earnest socialist poet had told him that as near as Potsdam, the city twenty-five miles to the south for which the square he was sitting in was named, the citizens were quite literally starving. The farms are failing, *she had said,* and what is produced is brought to Berlin. The rest of the country is being left to die.

The National Socialists were far from John Carpenter's idea of how a political party should conduct itself, let alone one in a western European state as culturally advanced as Germany; he found Hitler somewhat ridiculous, a rabble-rouser of moderate intellect, and he thought even less of the Chancellor's chief lieutenants, Himmler and Goebbels, whom he thought the sort of men who should have been kept in positions where their obvious personal shortcomings could cause no harm.

But he had met Field Marshal Göring and Admiral Dönitz on several occasions, and found them to be men of substance, while Prime Minister Chamberlain himself had returned from Germany earlier in the year with the clear message that Hitler was no threat to Britain. John had met the Prime Minister too, on more than a few occasions, and was inclined to believe his assessment of the situation.

Carpenter had been sent by Quincey Harker, the Blacklight Director, to brief Obergruppenführer Heydrich, the head of the SD, the internal security service of the SS, on the supernatural situation in Europe. The request had come from Hitler himself, whom Harker had briefed in 1934, as Heydrich was about to be placed in charge of all the German security apparatus under a new organisation called the Reich Main Security Office.

Carpenter had delivered the briefing in the new Department's headquarters on Prince-Albrecht-Straße, then taken tea and black bread with the charming, strikingly blond officer in his rooms on the third floor.

They had talked amiably for half an hour or so, in which time Heydrich had quizzed Carpenter about his experiences in Blacklight, and asked his advice on the establishment of an equivalent German organisation. Carpenter had been glad to offer the advice; it was one of the objectives that Harker had set for him before he left London. Then they had parted ways, and Carpenter had strolled down through central Berlin to the café where he was now sitting, no longer alone.

"Good evening, Mr Carpenter," said Valentin. "Please don't be alarmed. I'm not here to fight."

Carpenter had instinctively grabbed for the stake that hung from his belt, hidden behind a leather pistol holster, and the vampire had seen him do so. He slowly drew his hand back, and replaced it in his lap.

They sat in silence for several minutes, as Valentin ordered coffee and waited for it to arrive. When the waiter placed it in front of him and departed, the vampire took a sip, sighed with pleasure, then smiled broadly at John Carpenter.

"I told you our paths would cross again," he said. "This is mere coincidence, but I am always happy to be proven correct. How are you?"

"I'm well," replied Carpenter, cautiously. He felt as though he was drunk; the situation he found himself in was almost too surreal for his mind to process. "How about you?"

"Oh, perfectly fine," said Valentin. "A little bored, waiting for this all to get under way, but apart from that, I can't complain."

"All what to get under way?" asked Carpenter.

"Why, the war, obviously," said Valentin, studying Carpenter carefully for any sign of mockery. "Surely you feel it too?"

"There won't be any war," said Carpenter. "Hitler has promised that the return of the Sudetenland is the limit of his territorial ambition."

"And you believe him?" asked Valentin, smiling widely. "Oh my. You do, don't you?"

"Do you have any reason why I shouldn't?"

"John, men who seek to acquire power as desperately as Hitler are never satisfied. They never wake up one morning and say 'I have achieved everything I set out to do, I am now replete.' They are always looking for whatever is next; the next target, the next quarrel, the next victory. Hitler is an angry, violent little man, desperate to leave his mark on this world, and your plucky little island will take arms against him soon enough. I can assure you of that."

"What's your interest in this matter, Valentin?" asked Carpenter.

"Entertainment, Mr Carpenter," replied Valentin, with a smile. "I consider myself a student of the human condition, and nowhere does that condition more clearly reveal itself than during war. You can see the very best and very worst of humanity, at the same time, in the same place. I find it fascinating. And, of course, I was a General once, so I have the remnants of professional curiosity."

"You were a General?" asked Carpenter. He didn't want to engage the creature sitting opposite him, but nor did he want to provoke it. "Of which army?"

"The Wallachian armies of Prince Vlad Tepes," replied Valentin. "A long time ago."

"The armies of Count Dracula?"

"As he later came to call himself, yes. My brothers and I were his loyal subjects. We waged war across eastern Europe, for more than two decades."

"With success?"

"Sometimes," replied Valentin, his eyes haunted by memory. "Other times, less so. Such is the nature of war; it is a shifting continuum. All any player can do is try to remain upright for as long as possible, then try to minimise the fall when it comes. Which it always does, eventually."

The man and the vampire sat in what both were oddly aware had become a reasonably agreeable silence for several minutes, drinking their coffee and watching the men and women laughing and strolling and carousing through Potsdamer Platz. Eventually, Valentin spoke again.

"I have a proposal for you, Mr Carpenter. Would you hear it?"

"I would," replied Carpenter, lighting another cigarette. There was an awkward moment of pause, and then he extended his silver case towards Valentin, who took a cigarette with a nod of his head.

"Thank you," said the vampire. "Turkish, I believe?"

Carpenter nodded, sliding his book of matches across the table. Valentin struck one, and raised the flame to the end of his cigarette. He drew deeply, then exhaled smoke into the air.

"You and I are not natural enemies, Mr Carpenter," said the vampire. "I am not what your Department was founded to destroy."

"You are a vampire, are you not?" asked Carpenter.

"I am," replied Valentin. "But I flatter myself that I am somewhat different from the rest, from the savage creatures you and your comrades hunt down and destroy like rabid dogs. My life is carried out with discretion, without any cause for alarming the general public. I am invisible, as are my crimes, as you would no doubt choose to view them."

"You still take innocent lives," said Carpenter. "Whether you do so in the privacy of your home or on the streets of London is irrelevant to me."

"Really?" asked Valentin, narrowing his eyes as he looked at John Carpenter. "I'm not so sure that it is. But it doesn't matter, in truth. What

I hope remains relevant to you is the fact that I spared your life, and that of the monster who accompanied you to my home."

"I remain grateful," said Carpenter, choosing his words carefully. "I know that events that evening could have played out differently, had you wanted them to."

"I'm grateful for your gratitude," said Valentin, his eyes once more wide and friendly. "It is the sign of a true gentleman, the willingness to admit such a sentiment, and it is fine to see. But admitting your debt is one thing; repaying it is quite another."

"What do you have in mind?" asked Carpenter.

"A simple truce," said Valentin. "An agreement between two gentlemen that neither will pursue the other, that we will permit each other to live out our lives as we see fit."

"I do not speak for Blacklight," said Carpenter. "Such a truce is not for me to agree to."

"If I wished to negotiate with Blacklight, I would pay a visit to Quincey Harker," said Valentin. "This would be an agreement between you and me, sealed with a shake of the hand. You would agree not to pursue me, and to not overtly assist Blacklight in doing so. I, in turn, would agree to leave you in peace. I would not seek the revenge that so many of my friends have urged me to."

"You're asking me to let you murder with impunity?"

"I am," agreed Valentin. "But think of what I'm offering you in return; the burial of a grudge that you must have known would one day make itself apparent to you again. I don't wish to lower the tone of our conversation, but you must also be aware that if I chose to do so, I could kill you before you had time to even reach again for that little splinter of wood on your thigh. And I'm asking so little in return, merely that you not shed too many tears over the deaths of a handful of people that you have never met, and never would have met."

Carpenter looked at Valentin, fear rising in his chest. He knew the vampire was right; he was hopelessly outmatched if their conversation turned physical. And there was something extremely tempting about the offer that was being presented to him: safe passage, in essence, from one of the three most dangerous vampires in the world. But the cost was huge; the acceptance, however tacit, of murder.

"Why would you make this offer?" he asked, slowly. "Why would you not just kill me now, and render the need for a truce between us redundant?"

"Mr Carpenter, the world is far more interesting with you in it," replied Valentin. "I am neither of my brothers; I have no wish to spend my life at war, under constant threat of attack. I am a man of peace, as hard as that may be for you to believe. I think my offer would be mutually beneficial, and is somewhat generous. Do you not agree?"

John was silent for a moment, as he considered what the vampire was saying. On the one hand, a truce with one of the most dangerous vampires in the world was a betrayal of everything Blacklight stood for. On the other, the chance to guarantee his safety from Valentin, for the rest of his life, was extremely tempting. And there was a third thing to consider: the very real possibility that refusing Valentin's offer could very well be the last thing he ever did.

"My family," he said, carefully. "Extend your truce to cover my family, and we have a deal."

"Of course I include your wife in my offer," replied Valentin, looking hurt. "I think the former Miss Westenra has suffered more than enough at the hands of my kind, don't you?"

"She has," said Carpenter. "But I'm not just referring to her. I mean everyone who bears the name Carpenter, for as long as you live. I mean my children, and their children."

Valentin paused, his head tilted slightly to one side as he looked at John. Then he smiled, and nodded his head.

"Done," he replied, and extended a pale, delicate hand across the table. John reached out slowly, and shook it, once.

"Done," Carpenter agreed.

"In which case, let us speak of less gloomy matters," said Valentin, leaning back in his chair. "I hear that Jonathan Harker's son is doing quite wonderful things in his role as head of your little group. I'd love to hear the latest news."

Jamie stared at Valentin for a long moment after the vampire finished speaking. There remained no hint of mischief on his handsome, ancient face, no telltale signs in his eyes or the curve of his mouth that he was toying with Jamie.

"I don't believe you," he said, slowly. "My grandfather would never have made a deal with you."

"On what basis can you make that statement?" asked Valentin. "By your own admission, you never met the man, or knew anything of him."

"Exactly," replied Jamie, fiercely. "You know I never met him, so you can tell me whatever you want and think I'll have to believe it."

"What would be the point of that, Jamie?"

"I don't know," spat Jamie. "To hurt me, and my family. To get a little bit of revenge for the fact that my granddad beat you in 1928."

Valentin's eyes flared red.

"Why do you think that what I'm telling you is negative?" asked the vampire. "Your grandfather made a deal with me, just as you and your colleagues have done. Why does what he did make you so upset?"

"Because they're different," said Jamie. "We made a deal with you to try and protect the world from a monster. He made a deal that only helped himself."

"And your father," said Valentin, softly. "And your mother. And you. You're right, the deals are different. My deal with you will hopefully protect millions of men and women that neither you nor I will ever meet. Your grandfather's deal made sure that the people he loved, the people he cared most about, were a little bit safer as they went about their lives. Are you going to sit there and tell me what he did was wrong? Honestly?"

"It's cowardly," said Jamie, his face red with anger. "It's weak."

Valentin looked at him with an expression of disappointment. "To put aside your own morals to protect the people you love is far from weak, Jamie. If anything, it is the exact opposite. He took the choice he made to the grave, carried the burden of it with him his entire life, and never told a soul, never begged for forgiveness or absolution. He did what he did, and he carried on. You cannot afford to continue to look at the world in such absolutes, such black and white. There is no good and evil, no heroes and villains. There are only people, with all their flaws; the sooner you understand that, the less the world can hurt you."

"The sooner I can be a monster like you?" asked Jamie. "Never."

Valentin sighed, his eyes returning to their usual dazzling pale green.

"Jamie, your grandfather was a good man, who saved hundreds of lives, who made the world a better place by having lived in it. But was he perfect? Was he some paragon of virtue? Of course he wasn't. Neither is Admiral Seward, or Major Turner, neither was the monster that you miss so much. Neither was your father."

"Don't. Talk. About. My. Dad," hissed Jamie, his voice as cold as ice.

"I wouldn't presume to," replied Valentin. "I never met the man. But without knowing him, I can still promise you, with one hundred per cent certainty, that he wasn't perfect. Because no one is. That's what I'm trying to make you understand."

Jamie's head was spinning as he tried to stay calm, to think through what he was being told rationally. Then something the vampire had said came back to him, and he gasped.

"You still honour the deal, don't you?" he asked, his voice low. "I was never in any danger from you, was I?"

Valentin shook his head. "No, Jamie," he said. "You were not. But only I knew that, and I didn't want to tell you until it was necessary to do so."

"Why not?" asked Jamie. "This could have been so much easier if you had."

"If I had what?" asked Valentin, smiling. "Told Seward and the others about a seventy-year-old deal with a man who died several decades ago? Why would they have believed me?"

"Why should I then?"

"Because it's the truth. And because you killed my brother, yet you're sitting in front of me breathing in and out. Surely that is sufficient?"

"You told me you didn't like Alexandru," said Jamie, slowly.

"And I told you the truth," said Valentin. "But in matters of family, especially in families as old as mine, honour outweighs personal feelings. Or is supposed to."

Jamie considered this for a long moment, then sighed deeply. "I can't believe he never told anyone," he said. "My granddad. I can't believe he kept your deal a secret."

"It's not that remarkable, Jamie," said Valentin, smiling gently. "Haven't you ever done anything you didn't tell anyone?"

Jamie flinched, noticeably, but Valentine didn't react, outwardly at least. Although Jamie wouldn't have noticed if the vampire had; his mind was suddenly elsewhere, drifting back to the conclusion of the first Zero Hour Task Force meeting, and the event he had finally told Larissa and Kate about.

32

THE DEPTHS OF KNOWLEDGE

THREE DAYS EARLIER

Jamie was first out of the Ops Room as the second Zero Hour Task Force meeting drew to a close.

He waited in the corridor while the members of the group filed out. He wanted to thank Professor Talbot for standing up for him when Brennan asked what justified Jamie's presence on the Task Force, and reminding him that Jamie had taken down a Priority 1 vampire. He'd been surprised, and grateful.

Professor Talbot emerged, and gave Jamie a quizzical look.

"Can I help you?" he asked.

"I just wanted to thank you," Jamie replied. "For what you said. To Brennan."

"There's no need," said Talbot, but he smiled. "I merely told the truth. You killed Alexandru. I doubt anyone else in that room could have done the same."

"Nevertheless. Thank you."

Professor Talbot nodded. "Walk with me," he said, and set off down the corridor.

Jamie fell eagerly into step with him.

"It must be very difficult, being you," continued Talbot. He didn't look at Jamie as he spoke, but his tone was kind. "The son of a traitor. Then the son of a hero, all over again. The boy who destroyed Alexandru, but who lost Colonel Frankenstein. It must be a heavy burden for you to carry."

You have no idea how heavy, thought Jamie. *No idea at all.*

"It's difficult sometimes," he said, feeling embarrassed at the crack in his voice. "When I got here, everyone hated me for what they thought my dad had done. But I was trying to save my mum, and I didn't really care about anything else. Then when we got back from Lindisfarne, everyone applauded, like I was some kind of hero, because of what I did to Alexandru. But then they realised that Frankenstein was gone, and everyone knew that if I had listened to him instead of Thomas Morris, things probably would have turned out differently. I couldn't tell them that what happened to Frankenstein made me feel worse than any of them, that I blame myself more than they can possibly blame me. But I can't wave a wand and bring him back. He's gone."

"And your father?"

Jamie felt the familiar pang of pain in his chest that gripped him whenever he thought, *really* thought, about his dad.

"It was easier to hate him," he said, eventually. "When I thought he had abandoned us, when I thought he was a criminal and a traitor, I didn't want him back. I missed him, but I didn't want him back. Does that make sense?"

Talbot nodded.

"Now I know the truth, that he died because he was trying to protect me and my mum, that Thomas Morris framed him and he never did the things they said he did. That he was a hero. And

400

knowing that…" He paused, and looked up at Talbot. "Knowing that was like losing him all over again," he finished.

There was a long moment of silence, broken eventually by the Professor.

"Are you finished feeling sorry for yourself?" asked Talbot, and Jamie recoiled.

"What…" he managed, but the Director of the Lazarus Project rolled over him.

"You've had it hard, Jamie. I don't dispute that, and I feel for you, and for your family. But self-pity is nothing more than self-indulgence, and it's something you should have grown out of by now." Talbot looked at Jamie; his face bore no malice, and there was no anger in his voice, but Jamie still felt as though he had been punched in the stomach.

"What you do every day," continued the Professor, "saves lives. It saves souls from damnation. It's important, and you do it well. It should be enough for you, to know that you make a difference every time you put that uniform on and go out there, helping people that can't ever thank you. You should be too old to care so much about what other people think."

Jamie was reeling. The Professor's casual demeanour as he lectured him had caught him completely off guard.

Why the hell is he saying this to me? Who the hell does he think he is?

"I'm telling you this for your own good," said Talbot, as though he could read the teenager's mind. "I believe in you, and I want you to believe in yourself. And if you won't, then I'll keep at you until you do. Because someone has to."

They walked on in silence, Jamie churning with grief and a sensation that was new, and alien; he found himself feeling a swell of affection for the man walking beside him.

His mother loved him, he knew that, and he loved her back with all his heart. But since she had been turned, since she had discovered the truth about Department 19, about her late husband and the life her son had thrown himself so completely into, what she mainly did was worry about him. She was so grateful every day when he returned home safely, when she heard his footsteps echo along the corridor of the detention level as he made his way down to visit her, that parental discipline was the furthest thing from her mind.

And although she was safe in the cells, she was isolated from him, from the world he was a part of; he told her everything he could, but there was still a wall between them, beyond the ultraviolet barrier that separated them physically.

He had confided in Larissa, and she had told him it was part of growing up, part of becoming a complete person in his own right, separate from the parents that had raised him. She had warned him it could be a painful process, for him and his mother, and Jamie believed he was starting to understand what she had meant.

All of this merged into the affection he was now feeling for Professor Talbot; he was proud of the things he had done, he was thankful that the men and women of Blacklight treated him as an equal, as an adult, but there were times when he yearned to feel like a kid again, like the boy he had been not that long ago. Talbot's words had reminded him of what that felt like, and he was grateful for it.

Despite all that, he was still seventeen, and it was not in his nature to receive a lecture without at least attempting to answer back.

"What's the Lazarus Project?" he blurted out. He prepared himself for a reprimand, but instead, Professor Talbot smiled at him.

"Come and see for yourself," he replied.

Jamie stared. "Are you serious?" he asked.

"Always," replied the Professor.

When they reached the lift at the end of the grey corridor, Talbot pressed the F button on the control panel, and the lift began to descend. They waited in silence until the lift slowed to a halt, and the doors slid open. Talbot stepped through them, Jamie following.

He was as excited as he could ever remember being.

Since its announcement in Admiral Seward's speech, the Lazarus Project had remained a mystery; no one knew what went on behind the heavy white doors in the depths of the base.

But now Jamie Carpenter was going to find out.

Larissa and Kate are going to puke when they find out I've been down here, he thought, a mischievous smile on his face. *Although I'm probably not going to be able to tell them.*

He followed Professor Talbot along the main corridor of Level F, a long grey hallway indistinguishable from every other in the Loop. When his companion stopped outside a large white door, Jamie felt a burst of excitement in his chest, like a child on Christmas morning. He couldn't wait for Talbot to open the entrance; it was all he could do to stop himself hopping from one foot to the other in anticipation.

Talbot keyed a long series of numbers and letters into the panel beside the door, then lowered his face to a black lens and let a green laser slide across his eyeball. With a series of heavy thuds, the locks that separated the Lazarus Project from the rest of Blacklight disengaged, and the door slid open with a loud hiss and a rush of air. Jamie was suddenly wary, and he grabbed the Professor's arm as the old man was about to push the huge white door.

"Wait," Jamie said. "Aren't you going to get in trouble for letting me in here?"

Talbot laughed. "My dear boy," he replied. "Admiral Seward may be in charge of every other level of this facility, but down here, what I say goes. You have nothing to worry about."

With that, he pushed the door open, and Jamie got his first look inside the Lazarus Project.

The room beyond the door was long and wide.

It was bright white: the floors were white tiles, the walls and ceiling were painted a flat matt-white, the desks and surfaces were a gleaming metallic white, the coats worn by the doctors and scientists were white. It was a wide rectangle, with a high ceiling. Along one wall stood a row of silver cabinets; they hummed in the quiet, studious atmosphere of the room, rows of lights blinking in erratic patterns on their black displays.

A grid of desks had been positioned in the room, four sets of eight. Some of these were occupied, by men and women who barely glanced up from their screens as Talbot and Jamie entered. The wall to Jamie's left was half-filled with shelves, upon which stood an enormous number of grey box files, labelled with long combinations of letters and numbers, and half with long benches covered in an amazing array of laboratory equipment. Jamie saw all this with his peripheral vision; his attention was dragged instantly to the centre of the room, and what stood there.

On the floor, a wide circular lens had been placed; its mirror was attached to the ceiling directly above it. Between them, spinning slowly, was a three-dimensional hologram of a double helix: thousands of tiny spheres, the majority red but a significant minority blue, linked by transparent white bars. As he watched, a single sphere on the arm of the double helix closest to him suddenly enlarged, and spun out of the pattern. Unintelligible lines of code appeared next to it, then the sphere changed colour, from red to blue, and shrank back into its place on the strand.

A woman in a white coat, who looked barely older than Jamie, got up from one of the desks, walked over to the hologram and peered at the sphere that had just changed colour. Apparently satisfied, she returned to her seat.

Beyond the hologram, set into the middle of the rear wall, was a thick airlock door. Biohazard signs flanked it, and red letters were printed on to the wall above it.

STERILE ENVIRONMENT
NO UNAUTHORISED ACCESS BEYOND THIS POINT
ALL STAFF MUST COMPLETE DECONTAMINATION
BEFORE ENTERING

Jamie's mouth hung open as he looked at the hologram and the men and women working on it. He collected himself, and turned to Talbot, who was watching him with an obvious look of pride on his lined face.

"What are you doing down here?" Jamie asked, his eyes wide, his voice shot through with wonder.

"I'm sorry," replied Talbot, "I thought that would have been obvious. We're trying to find a cure."

33

IN THE COURT OF
THE VAMPIRE KING

The room Frankenstein entered was so dark that, for a moment, he couldn't tell whether it was occupied. Then he heard a deep, rattling gasp, and a quavering voice issued forth from the gloom.

"Can it be?" asked the voice. "After all these years, does it really stand before me?"

There was motion in the darkness, and then a pair of lamps bloomed into life; what Frankenstein saw before him threatened to eradicate what was left of his damaged mind and send him teetering towards the edge of madness.

A round dining table stood in the middle of the small room, set for eight. The plates were chipped and dusty, the glasses flecked with dirt. Seven of the chairs that stood haphazardly around the table were empty; the eighth, facing the door, was occupied. The chair was old, and had once obviously been ornate, almost a throne;

the carving on the arms and the sides was still clearly fine work, even through the layers of dirt and brown, flaking blood that coated it. In it, squatting like a spider in its hole, was an ancient, wizened vampire.

The creature's skin was the grey of funeral ash, its face lined so deeply that all Frankenstein could see of its eyes was the red glow emerging from beneath the drooping, hooded skin of its brow. Its mouth was open in surprise, exposing rows of dark brown teeth, and a tongue the colour of rotten meat. The head was topped by long streams of vividly white hair, emerging from the grey, liver-spotted scalp like tendrils of smoke. The vampire was wearing a tuxedo, but the garments had been tailored for a larger man; they hung as heavily and shapelessly from its limbs as lumps of dead skin, giving the ancient monster the appearance of moulting, of decay being held at bay by the flimsiest of barriers.

From its sunken chest, something angular protruded, raising the dirty white fabric of its shirt away from the skin in a pyramid. Frankenstein's eyes were drawn to this anomaly; he had taken a quick glance round the room as the lamps flickered into life, and he believed that unless he focused on something, on one tangible thing, he would collapse, or worse.

Piled haphazardly around the chair the monster was sitting in were the remains of more men and women than Frankenstein could even allow his reeling mind to estimate.

Gleaming white bones, picked clean of all their flesh, shone in nauseating lumps from a mass of dead, rotting meat. Long strands of hair, of every colour, tracked through the carnage like veins, light reflecting on their shiny strands. There were arms, and legs, and hands; some of the skin was black with age and decay, some the vivid, mottled white of the newly dead.

The smell was beyond imagination, a scent of blood and filth so thick it felt as though you could have bitten into it. Faces stared out of the vile mess; skulls with a papery-thin covering of skin, green-black bubbles of what were left of the features of men and women who had long since died in this room, the bright-white faces of the most recently murdered, their expressions of pleading and outrage still visible, even without eyes that had fallen in or been plucked out.

As Frankenstein stared at the vampire's chest, his eyes caught the slightest movement at the side of the chair, and although he didn't want to, he was unable to stop himself from looking. The monster's ancient grey fingers were absently stroking the long blonde hair of a disembodied head that had clearly been placed within his reach. The dead girl stared out across the room, mercifully bereft of signs of torture or violation; she wore a perfect expression of surprise, and Frankenstein was able to hope, with all his heart, that it was because her suffering had been brief.

"My Lord Dante," said Latour, softly. He had bowed his head as he followed Frankenstein into the room, and it was still lowered as he spoke. "After almost ninety years, I have brought the monster back to you. I have brought you revenge, Your Majesty."

"Latour," said Lord Dante, his voice like nails on a blackboard. "My favourite. Still you honour me where others have forsaken me. You shall be rewarded for this work, rewarded with anything you desire. Name it, and it shall be yours."

"My lord," said Latour. "My reward comes from seeing justice served, finally. But if Your Majesty insists, then there is a small prize I have coveted."

The vampire king laughed, an awful rattling sound, like a last breath.

"I know what you speak of," he replied.

Lord Dante reached out a trembling hand, picked up a small golden bell that stood on the table and rang it sharply. Almost instantly, a door that Frankenstein had not noticed slid open, and a butler appeared. The man was dressed immaculately, and as he approached his master, Frankenstein saw his nose wrinkle momentarily with disgust.

"Your Majesty," said the butler, bowing his head. "How may I be of assistance?"

"Bring Sophie here," said Lord Dante, a revolting smile twisting its way through the wrinkles of his face. "She belongs to Latour now."

Behind him, Frankenstein heard a low, guttural growl of excitement emerge from Latour's throat, and his stomach churned.

"At once, Your Majesty," said the butler, backing smoothly away from the table and disappearing through the door. Lord Dante watched him leave, then turned his attention back to Frankenstein.

"I never believed I would see you again, monster," he said, his voice little more than a whisper. "I had come to accept that I would never have my vengeance. Yet here you are, standing before me; how amusing the way the world works. What do you have to say for yourself?"

"I have nothing to say," said Frankenstein, as firmly as he was able. "I don't know what bad blood exists between you and I, and I have no memory of us ever having met. So I have nothing to say to you."

Lord Dante slowly turned his neck, the creaking of the sinews and bones audible in the small room, and looked incredulously at Latour.

"What madness has befallen your friend, Latour?" he asked. "Does he speak the truth?"

"He does, Your Majesty," replied Latour. "His mind is gone, for reasons I have not been able to ascertain. He remembers nothing, beyond the last few months."

The vampire king tapped his chest, slowly, his fingers drumming against the angular bulge in his shirt.

"And this?" Lord Dante asked. "He does not remember this? He has forgotten what he did to me?"

"Yes, Your Majesty," replied Latour. "There is nothing left of the man that he used to be. I have tried to coax that man back to life, so that your vengeance might be all the sweeter, but it appears there is nothing to be done."

Frankenstein listened to the two vampires talk about him as though he wasn't there, and wondered at their words. It was clear that the monster in the chair, the creature that Latour referred to as Lord Dante, had been waiting many years to make him answer for some long-past crime, although he had no idea what that crime might have been. But it appeared that whatever he had done had caused the ancient vampire considerable distress, and he felt a savage surge of satisfaction at the thought.

"You remember nothing," said Lord Dante. "That is your claim, monster?"

"Don't call me that," growled Frankenstein.

"I apologise, Mr Frankenstein," said Lord Dante, a smile emerging on his face. "But that is your position? That your memories are lost to you?"

"It is not a position," replied Frankenstein, his voice low. "It is simple fact."

"You do not remember the many nights you spent in this room, in my company?"

"No. I do not."

"You do not remember the meals we shared, the happy hours we idled away?" Lord Dante's voice was rising, the tremble in it becoming more pronounced.

"No."

"The tortures we revelled in, the blood we drank, the lives we brought to their end?"

"No!" bellowed Frankenstein, his voice booming through the small room, deafeningly loud. "I do not remember, and I'm glad that I don't!"

"What about this?" roared Lord Dante, rising from his chair and tearing open his shirt. "Do you remember this, you foul, disloyal monster?"

Frankenstein stared at the narrow, mottled grey chest of the vampire king of Paris, and felt his eyes widen involuntarily. Emerging from the sagging flesh, directly over the ancient monster's heart, was a wide, thin piece of metal, extending perhaps two centimetres beyond the surface of the vampire's skin. Where the metal penetrated the flesh, there was a thick ridge of scar tissue, a crust of pale pink amid the expanse of fading grey.

"No," said Frankenstein, distantly. He could not take his eyes from the unnatural sight before him. "I don't remember that."

The fire in Lord Dante's eyes subsided, and he looked at Frankenstein with an expression that was strangely close to pity.

"I *do* remember," he said. "For almost ninety years, I have been unable to forget what you did to me, for even a single minute. You put this blade in my chest over a common, lying little whore, and left me here for dead. You, whom I considered my friend. Can you imagine how that felt?"

Frankenstein said nothing; he was sure the vampire was not interested in a reply.

"Of course you can't," continued Lord Dante, after barely a pause. "You can't imagine what it was like to have your heart almost cleaved in two by someone you would have trusted with your life. You can't imagine what it's like to feel your body begin to collapse, only to hold together at the final moment as your heart heals round the blade, condemning you to a life of mortal proportions."

"I can't imagine," said Frankenstein, simply. "I don't know what you're talking about."

A thick, vicious growl emerged from Lord Dante's throat, and the old monster took half a step towards Frankenstein, who suddenly realised how much effort the vampire king was expending on trying to keep his fury under control.

"This blade, your filthy peasant's knife, has been in my body for almost a century," Lord Dante snarled. "The flesh of my heart grew back round it before I expired, saving me from destruction, but removing it would have been the end of me. Worse than that, crueller even than that, is the fact that the blade stops my heart from properly regenerating my cells, no matter how much blood I take."

Frankenstein stared at the vampire king, then looked helplessly at Latour; he understood that he stood accused of having stabbed a blade into the monster's chest, but the rest of the vampire king's words were meaningless.

"His Majesty is ageing," said Latour, softly. "The blade you placed in his heart has robbed him of his immortality."

Frankenstein looked back at Lord Dante, his frail body heaving up and down as he fought to control himself. His red eyes stared at Frankenstein, who fought the overwhelming urge to smile.

It almost doesn't matter if I never know the rest, he thought. *Knowing this will be enough. This is one good thing I can be sure I did.*

The door at the side of the room slid open, and the butler re-emerged, dragging behind him a dark-haired girl who could not possibly have been more than fifteen. She was clutching a beautiful porcelain doll, and wearing a summer dress the colour of daffodils; her eyes were wide with fear as the butler hauled her into the room and pushed her towards Latour. The girl bumped her hip on the edge of the table, cried out and almost fell, but Latour moved invisibly quickly across the room and caught her.

"Shush," he said. "Shush, child. You're safe. I've got you."

The girl looked hopefully up into Latour's pale, handsome face, then burst into tears and buried herself in his chest. Frankenstein watched crimson rise in his old friend's eyes as the girl pressed herself against him, and saw an awful expression of lust creep across his mouth.

The butler silently placed a large, ornate bottle on the table. Frankenstein was not watching as Lord Dante lifted it in his shaking hands and drained it of the dark red liquid it contained; his eyes were fixed with utter revulsion on Latour. If he had been watching, he would have seen the vampire king wipe his mouth with the back of one shaky hand, then throw his head back as his body begin to change.

Power, old and familiar, flooded through Lord Dante. He required as much blood as any other vampire on earth just to keep his degrading body in one piece, such was the unhealable nature of the injury Frankenstein had inflicted on him. But no amount of blood appeared to delay the passage of time; he was more than one hundred and twenty years old, and his body was failing him.

But the litres of blood he had just drunk would return to him an approximation of the power he had once had, even though it would be short-lived, and carry with it the most excruciating pain the following day. It would, he knew, take all his remaining strength to hold his body together. But right now, he could not have cared less; he had waited for this day for almost a century, and nothing would deny him his vengeance.

The vampire king of Paris felt the loose, old man's skin that coated his bones begin to pull tight as the blood flowed through him; his eyes rose forth from their sunken depths, and again blazed the unholy red that had once struck fear into every nocturnal creature in northern France. He felt his muscles grow, filling the suit that had once fitted him like an exquisitely tailored glove, and felt strength flood into them. His throat worked soundlessly as he rode the crest of the wave of ecstasy that was rolling through his body, firing his nerves with starbursts of electricity so exquisite it was all he could do not to fall to the surface of the table and weep.

Eventually, it passed; his vision cleared, his heart slowed back to its usual irregular staccato and Lord Dante looked around the dining room with new eyes. His butler had disappeared through the servants' door, Latour was kneeling beside his new pet, whispering reassurances that he had absolutely no intention of honouring, while the monster, the hated, cursed monster, watched his old friend with disgust curdling his face. The vampire king stretched his arms above his head until he heard his muscles creak, then stepped silently around the table and approached his nemesis.

The first Frankenstein knew of Lord Dante's proximity was when the vampire king's hand encircled his throat. He would have screamed, but the ancient vampire's grip was like a vice, constricting his windpipe and leaving him unable to draw breath. Lord Dante lifted him up and back, slamming him into the wall with an impact that shook the entire room, and terror galvanised Frankenstein's body, and he swung his arms at the smiling, suddenly youthful face of the vampire king.

The blows landed solidly, hammering roundhouse swings that would have levelled most creatures on earth, but Lord Dante didn't so much as flinch; if anything, his smile widened. Frankenstein grabbed at the hand that was holding him, trying to prise open the fingers as his lungs screamed for air, as his vision began to grey at the edges.

As the room grew dark, he tore his gaze away from Lord Dante and threw a desperate, pleading look in the direction of Latour. His old friend wore a sour expression, the look of a man who has belatedly discovered that something has proven to be much less fun than he had expected, but he made no move to help, even as Frankenstein began to suffocate.

Constellations of white and grey spots whirled across his vision, and he felt his chest begin to contract as the last of the oxygen in his lungs was absorbed, leaving him empty. There was an enormous pressure in his head, as though it was about to burst, but he felt strangely calm; there was no panic, no fear, just an unexpectedly easy acceptance of the fate that was about to befall him. He felt sadness at never having regained the memories of his life, but he also felt a gentle wave of relief; it was awful to live in the dark, and he would be glad to be released from it.

Then, at the last second before he slipped into unconsciousness, the pressure eased. But far from providing relief, it brought with it a screaming wave of agony as his body fought for air. It felt as though every part of him was on fire. He slumped down the wall and rolled lamely on to his back, his chest heaving, his mouth hauling in burning lungfuls of oxygen.

His vision began to clear, and he stared up from the floor into the face of Lord Dante. The vampire king was looking down at him, his chest heaving as he tried to calm himself, the expression on his face something close to lust.

"Not so fast," breathed the ancient vampire. "You don't get away so easily, not after all these years."

Lord Dante looked over at Latour, and gestured towards the prone, gasping monster. "Pick him up," he said. "I want to introduce him to the rest of our guests."

Latour hesitated for a moment, long enough for Lord Dante's eyes to flare in their sockets, an unequivocal gesture of warning. Latour nodded, then stepped forward and scooped Frankenstein up with one hand by the back of his neck, like a cat picking up one of her kittens. Frankenstein dangled limply as the vampire lifted him into the air and carried him towards the door. His chest rose and fell steadily; his chin slumped against it, his eyes barely open. The monster had realised that he was no longer going to die, and it had broken the last of his spirit.

Just let it be over quickly, he thought, distantly. *That's all I ask. Whatever is in store for me, let it be quick.*

Latour shoved open the door that led back into the theatre, and held it open for the vampire king. Lord Dante strode through it, his eyes blazing red, his face a mask of triumph.

"Brothers and sisters!" he bellowed, and the theatre fell silent. The audience turned their heads to look in his direction and the vampire on the stage let the dead girl fall to the floor. The look on the majority of the vampires' faces was one of surprise; it was rare for any of them to see Lord Dante, much less hear him address them.

In the decades since Frankenstein had buried his *kukri* knife in the vampire king's chest, he had become a peripheral figure in his own club, seldom seen except by the tiny handful of vampires he still considered his favourites. Latour was one of them, and he had often been forced to answer anxious questions from other members about Lord Dante's health, to rebuff desperate entreaties that they be allowed to enter the private dining room and offer him their supplication.

The vampire king had withdrawn into his small room, where he had feasted on men and women supplied by his butler, and in time he had become little more than a legend; a monster hiding in the shadows where none were allowed to venture, a dark presence behind the scenes who, if the members of the Fraternité were honest, made them feel uncomfortable.

Attendance had steadily declined over the years, a sign that all was no longer right in the old building. It remained the safest place for vampires in all of Paris, a place where every appetite, no matter how obscene, could be indulged, yet fewer and fewer vampires chose to take advantage of its debauched freedoms. The presence of Lord Dante, so diminished from the godlike creature he had once appeared, caused them a discomfort that was almost physical, like an itch that they could not reach to scratch. As a result, fewer than fifteen vampires were inside the Fraternité to hear Lord Dante's voice boom across the theatre, to see him stride down its aisle as Latour carried Frankenstein easily towards the stage.

"My God," someone whispered, as the small procession passed.

The look on Lord Dante's face was one of pure, unbridled joy; it looked as though he had been brought back to life. His dinner jacket billowed behind him as he reached the front of the stage, and floated effortlessly up on to it. Latour followed him at a respectful distance, carrying his prisoner, and floated up beside the vampire king as he turned to address the meagre crowd.

"Friends," he boomed. "You find yourselves witness to a truly auspicious event, an event that will stand alongside any in the great history of this Fraternité."

He paused, beaming out at his confused audience. There was whispering, and one or two fingers pointing in the direction of Frankenstein, but most of the vampires were staring at Lord Dante, scarcely able to believe that he had left the dining room that had become his self-imposed cell, let alone that he was standing before them and addressing them, his face filled with a fire that even the longest-serving members of the Fraternité had not seen for many decades.

"Nearly ninety years ago," continued the vampire king, "a great wrong was done to me. An act of betrayal so cowardly, so unjustified, that it left me questioning the wisdom of continuing to provide this sanctuary for the creatures of the night, among many other things. I have withdrawn from you, my brothers and sisters; it cannot have escaped your notice, and I apologise for it. The perpetrator, who I am at last able to bring before you, was something base and rotten, a foul thing that should never have been given life; a mistake that I am finally, after long years, in a position to correct."

In the centre of the stage stood a thick wooden post that had been used for every conceivable horror in the long years since Lord Dante had erected it, when the Fraternité was founded. It was to this post that the vampire king now instructed Latour to tie Frankenstein securely.

As Latour bent to his work, leaning the limp monster against the wood and gathering thick coils of rope from where they lay strewn on the stage, Lord Dante continued to speak.

"Some of you have been members of this Fraternité long enough to recognise the creature beside me," he said, his eyes burning coals. "This is the creature that did this to me, whom I have waited almost a century to take my revenge upon." As he spoke, he unbuttoned his shirt and held it open, displaying the thin slice of metal that protruded from his chest. "And now, my friends, that time is at hand."

Lord Dante turned away from his audience, and regarded the helpless monster. Frankenstein's arms were tightly bound behind the post, looped and tied at the wrists, without so much as a millimetre of give. His feet had been set at a more forgiving angle, but were equally secure; the only part of his body that he could move more than a centimetre or two was his head, which he raised slowly as he heard Lord Dante's approaching footsteps. He forced his eyes open, and saw the ancient vampire looking at him with an expression that seemed almost regretful. Then the vampire king's face twisted into a wide, teetering grin of madness, and Frankenstein saw the vampire's right shoulder move as he cocked his fist.

He never saw the punch itself.

It pistoned into his stomach, driving every molecule of air from his lungs; he heard a sound explode involuntarily from his mouth, like a huge balloon bursting, and felt his eyes bulge in their sockets as his body attempted to process the agony that was blooming in his midsection. He opened his mouth to scream, but found he could not; his body was in spasm, paralysed by the need to drag fresh oxygen into his shocked lungs.

He stared helplessly into the face of Lord Dante, his chest tightening and constricting as his lungs deflated, and realised, strangely calmly, that he couldn't breathe. Panic burst through him, and he twisted and turned against his bindings, his oxygen-starved muscles weakening by the second, his mind racing with terror at the thought of dying like this, like an animal, for the amusement of a handful of monsters. As he thrashed and struggled, increasingly weakly, Lord Dante leant his terrible smiling face in close to his own.

"It's an awful feeling, isn't it?" said the vampire king, softly. "Helplessness. It physically hurts."

Frankenstein stared, incapable of responding. His vision was starting to grey at the edges, and he felt an enormous pressure building in the centre of his chest. He was waiting for darkness to envelop him when Lord Dante sighed, then shoved one of his pale, delicate hands into his mouth.

He felt the cold fingers invade the back of his throat, and then his gag reflex triggered, even as his body teetered on the brink of shutting down. There was nothing in his stomach, so all that burst up and around the vampire's fingers were strings of watery bile. Lord Dante withdrew his hand, a look of utter disgust creasing his face; he flicked his hand down towards the stage, splattering the liquid on to the wooden boards.

Frankenstein felt his whole body tremble, as his gag reflex broke his paralysis; he sucked in a single quavering, tremulous breath, and air that felt like razor blades scoured his throat and lungs. He slumped against the wooden pole, his eyes rolling back in his head, his huge, lumpen chest heaving, and knew nothing more.

Breathing heavily, Lord Dante turned back to his audience, who were staring at him with rapt attention, cruel excitement on their faces.

"Send word," he breathed. "To every member of the Fraternité de la Nuit, wherever they may be. Tell them that Lord Dante is risen, and that he summons them here two nights from now. Tell them he has something planned that not a single one of them will want to miss."

34

HOW TO STEAL FIRE FROM THE GODS

"A cure?" asked Jamie. "What do you mean a cure?"

"A cure for vampirism," answered Professor Talbot. "What else?"

"Is that even possible?"

"We certainly think so."

"But how?"

"Using a self-replicating, DNA-authoring, genetically engineered virus."

"What?"

Talbot smiled again, more openly this time, and led Jamie towards the huge hologram double helix. They stopped in front of it, and Jamie watched the impossibly complex design rotate slowly as the Professor began to talk.

"OK," said Talbot. "Tell me how the condition that we refer to as vampirism is transferred."

"By biting," answered Jamie. "If a vampire bites you, and you don't die, you turn."

"That's right. But can you tell me what makes you turn?"

Jamie shook his head.

"Exactly," continued Talbot. "Nor would I expect you to; there are only a handful of people in the world who really understand the process. But in the simplest terms, this is what happens when a vampire bites you. Their fangs are coated with a fluid, a unique type of plasma that is passed into your bloodstream in the act of biting. This fluid contains a virus, unlike any other that occurs in the natural world. For one thing, it's remarkably aggressive; it replicates itself millions of times over, spreading through your blood until it infects every cell in your body. You understand what a cell is, yes?"

"I'm not stupid," replied Jamie, casting a hard look in the Professor's direction. Talbot smiled, and continued.

"This aggressiveness is why there is such a small window in which the process can be stopped. But it is possible; the virus is aggressive, and fast-acting, but short-lived. If blood is transfused into the victim faster than the virus is able to multiply, it burns out within a few hours, and the turn doesn't take place. But if that doesn't happen, or happens too slowly, the virus will multiply, and multiply, and multiply, until it reaches saturation. And then the turn begins in earnest."

Talbot gestured in the direction of the hologram.

"This is a strand of human DNA," he said. "Roughly twenty-three thousand genes arranged around twenty-three pairs of chromosomes. These genes contain the blueprint for building, and then maintaining, the systems that make up a human being. How they do this is too complicated for me to explain to you now, so just understand that a combination of genes accounts for why you look the way you do, why you are as tall as you are, why your eyes are blue rather than green. This information is coded into every single cell in your body, ready to be passed on to your children, and your grandchildren. Are you with me so far?"

"I understand," said Jamie, his eyes fixed on the spinning hologram.

"Good," said Talbot. "The virus that is passed on to the victim during a vampire attack is not what gives them their superhuman abilities. The virus is merely the agent of that process. Once it has achieved saturation, the virus begins to alter parts of the victim's DNA, essentially overwriting the existing code. This new code, which is rapidly copied to every cell in the victim's body, is what causes the turn. It's what makes vampires."

"Hang on," said Jamie, his brow furrowing. "If you change my DNA, does that mean I change too? Like, physically? I thought it would just mean I passed the new code on to my kids?"

Talbot stared at Jamie, admiration on his face.

"Bravo," he said. "There are men and women a lot older than you who fail to understand that. You're absolutely right; under normal circumstances, changing an organism's DNA would not result in physical changes to the organism in question. There are specific instances in which it is possible; there is a gene therapy treatment for cystic fibrosis sufferers that involves them inhaling a genetically engineered aerosol that essentially fixes some of the broken cells in their lungs, but that is a very specific case, dealing with only a tiny, tiny number of cells. Ordinarily, a change to the DNA would do nothing."

"That's why the vampire virus is different, isn't it?" said Jamie. "Because it changes people, right away."

"Exactly," replied Talbot. "The new DNA code that the virus writes into the victim's cells has a kind of trigger within it, an update button, if you like. Once the code is copied across all the cells, the new DNA acts upon the body, changing it physically, giving the victim their strength and speed, and their compulsion to feed. It is absolutely unique. And the process is irreversible. For now at least."

"And that's what you're trying to undo?" asked Jamie. "The changes that are made to the DNA?"

"That's right."

"How? How would you even attempt something like that?"

Talbot waved his arm towards the bank of silver cabinets that stood along one of the walls of the Lazarus Project.

"Those machines are gene sequencers," he replied. "Powered by the largest supercomputer array in the world. We're mapping the altered DNA, isolating the new code that the vampire virus writes into each cell. Once that process is complete, the plan is to engineer a counter virus that will go through an infected system, delete the new code and return the victim's DNA back to its original state."

"Why can't we do that now?" asked Jamie.

"As I already told you, there are approximately twenty-three thousand genes in a strand of human DNA. That in itself might not sound like many, but you can take my word that it is. And there is a far bigger obstacle in the way: the DNA of every single person on earth is unique. Deleting the vampire viral code from the DNA is not the difficult bit – the difficult bit is restoring the code that the virus has deleted. There is no all-purpose code we can write in once the vampire code is gone; the code that would have been overwritten in your cells is completely different to the code that would have been overwritten in mine."

"So how can you make it work?"

"The virus we're designing is like a tiny biological supercomputer. It analyses each cell as it replicates through the body, deletes the vampire code it has been programmed to recognise and then, using incredibly sophisticated chemical analysis of the proteins in the

424

surrounding cells, rewrites the empty sections of the code. Once it has done that for every cell in a system, it uses the same trigger as the vampire virus, an amino acid that we've been able to isolate and map, and the victim's system is returned to normal, all traces of vampirism gone from their body."

"That sounds impossible."

"Conventional wisdom would tell you that it is. But we've made developments and breakthroughs in this lab that are generations beyond the genetic work being done out in the world, in even the most highly resourced research facilities. What you see around you, Jamie, is the most ambitious, most complicated and most expensive science project ever conducted. And it's what we believe will eventually bring an end to the curse of vampirism."

"How long?" asked Jamie, his voice trembling. "How long until you can make this work?"

How long until I can tell my mum and Larissa that they're going to be all right?

"I don't know," said Talbot. Jamie opened his mouth to voice his dismay, but Talbot raised a hand and cut him off. "I understand your agitation, really I do. And I can tell you, honestly, that the progress we've made is staggering. But I also have to tell you, with equal honesty, that it could be years before we have a workable vaccine."

"Years?" said Jamie, his heart sinking in his chest.

"It could be less," said Talbot, forcing a smile that was clearly meant to be encouraging. "It could be a year, or even a matter of months. But we aren't going to be able to cure your mother tomorrow, much as I'd like to."

"But we will be able to cure her?" Jamie could hear the desperate pleading in his voice as he asked the question. "One day? That's what you're saying, right?"

Talbot looked at him solemnly.

"Perhaps I was wrong to bring you down here," he said, softly. "I didn't mean to get your hopes up. I'm sorry."

"You weren't wrong," said Jamie. "Really you weren't. It's better knowing that someone is working on a cure, even if it might take a while. I'm not a child; I didn't expect you to be able to cure her tomorrow. But if you're saying there's a chance you might be able to cure her in the future, then that's something I'm grateful to know."

"Well," said Talbot, a smile on his face, "in that case, I'm glad."

He walked away from the hologram, and Jamie followed him across the wide room. The Lazarus Project staff, the majority of whom had stopped what they were doing to watch the conversation between Jamie and Talbot, returned their attention to their work, although several of them nodded and smiled at Jamie as he passed their desks. Talbot led Jamie round the DNA hologram and towards the row of gene sequencers, passing by the heavy airlock door at the back of the room.

Jamie slowed as they passed it. There was a rectangular window set at eye level in the thick white metal but, frustratingly, he could see nothing through the small block of glass. Talbot noticed that the teenager had dropped back, and turned to him.

"Everything OK?" he asked.

Jamie blushed slightly. "Yeah," he replied. "Sorry. I was just wondering…"

"What's behind the door?"

"Right."

"It's OK," said Talbot. "That's where we keep the research subjects."

"You mean the vampires we've been catching for you?"

"That's right. They need to be isolated from any viruses or

bacteria the staff or Operators might be carrying, and they need to be contained. They're still vampires."

"My squad brought two in yesterday," said Jamie, a flicker of pride on his face.

"Of course," said Talbot. "Mr Connors and his daughter. Very useful from a genetic perspective, two members of the same family."

"Are they doing OK?" asked Jamie. "They were really scared when we caught them."

"They're fine," replied the Professor. "We treat all our subjects extremely well."

"Can I see them?"

"I'm afraid not," replied Talbot. "The sterilisation procedure to access the clean room takes almost forty minutes to complete, and I can't spare any of my staff to take you through it. I'm sorry."

Jamie stared at the airlock door, and realised he wanted to go through it incredibly badly. It was partly the fact that he had been told he was not allowed to, but it was also the idea that behind the heavy white door lay the key to finding the cure that Talbot had described to him, a key that he was, at least in part, helping to provide.

But he could wait.

He had no intention of pushing his luck with Professor Talbot, who had already demonstrated enormous trust by allowing him even this far into the Lazarus Project. He resumed his course towards the gene sequencers, and after a momentary pause, Talbot joined him.

"So how long have you been working on this?" he asked, as Talbot began to check the readings on the front of the machines. "How long have you all been down here?"

"I've been working on a variation of this project for most of my adult life," replied Talbot. He took a small console from his pocket, and entered a series of numbers into a spreadsheet. "I was recruited into Department 19 a year ago, and we accelerated our efforts after Dracula's remains were lost. But my work was already well under way before then; I worked with Francis Collins on the Human Genome Project in Maryland, then on viral engineering at the Strangeways lab in Cambridge, and then I got the opportunity to continue my work down here."

"Opportunity?" asked Jamie, grinning. He knew full well that it would have been made clear to the Professor that refusing the offer was not a realistic option.

"I suppose it was really more of an instruction," replied Talbot, smiling back. "But not one I was reluctant to follow, especially once the scale of the project was made clear to me: complete authority to recruit staff, a computer array more powerful than any in the world, a basically limitless budget and the challenge to do something that would save thousands of lives. Who could have turned that down?"

"Obviously not you," said Jamie.

"Obviously."

They moved down the line of gene sequencers, Talbot taking readings from each one in turn.

"So who are all these people?" Jamie asked, nodding towards the men and women hunched over their desks.

"Geneticists," replied Talbot, without looking round. "Virologists. Doctors. All hired from the best research institutes around the world. They're the finest minds in their fields."

Jamie stared at the Lazarus Project staff; there was a focused intensity in the room, a feeling of communal genius bent to a single purpose. Each of the men and women in the white coats appeared to be simultaneously in a world of their own and part of a greater organism, like super-intelligent bees in a hive. He knew he could never, ever, in a thousand years, understand the work they were doing, but the thought did not make him feel inadequate. Instead, all he felt was admiration.

Talbot straightened up, regarding Jamie with a warm smile.

"Is there anything else I can show you?" he asked. "Anything else you want to know? If not, I should probably be getting back to work."

Jamie was about to say no, when a thought suddenly leapt into his mind, and he blushed a deep, dark red.

"What is it?" asked Talbot.

Oh God. Can I? I haven't turned, so it must be safe. But still.

"If a human being," he said, cautiously, "were to, er, kiss a vampire? That would be risky, right?"

Talbot gave him a long look, then broke into a laugh.

"Speaking hypothetically," he replied. "I assume we are speaking hypothetically, Mr Carpenter?"

"Of course," said Jamie, his face burning.

"Of course. Well, in that hypothetical situation, the human would be quite safe as long as the vampire in question kept his or her fangs withdrawn. The virus that causes the turn doesn't exist anywhere else, so the risk of infection would be negligible."

"Right," said Jamie. "That's good to know."

"Hmm," said Talbot. "I'm sure it is." He grinned broadly at Jamie, then placed a hand on his back and led him towards the door. "If you have any other questions," he continued, "or if you just want someone to talk to, you know your way down here. OK?"

"I understand," said Jamie. "Thank you. Really."

"You're welcome," replied Talbot. He opened the door, and Jamie stepped through it and back into the corridor of Level F. As Talbot swung the door closed, Jamie saw a flicker of something else pass across the Professor's face, as though he wanted to say something else, but was either unable to do so, or decided against it. Then the door thudded into place, shutting Jamie out.

35

HOPE IS A DANGEROUS THING

"I have secrets," said Jamie, slowly. "But I have no intention of sharing them with you."

"I wouldn't dream of asking you to," said Valentin. "But I can see on your face that there is something you want to say. What is it?"

Jamie was impressed, despite himself; the old vampire's powers of observation were remarkable. "There is something," he admitted. "Last year, when we were searching for my mother, we visited a place called Valhalla. Have you heard of it?"

Valentin nodded. "The commune in the north," he said. "Vampires holding hands and singing songs and denying what they are."

"OK," said Jamie. "It was founded by a man called Grey, who is supposed to be the oldest British vampire. It was him who turned Larissa; she was one of a lot of teenage girls he attacked over the years, all while he was preaching peace and love. He was cast out of Valhalla when his followers found out what he'd done, but before he went, he told me something, something he thought was why we were there in the first place. Something about Dracula."

Valentin said nothing, but he narrowed his eyes slightly as he waited for Jamie to continue.

"He told me that there was only one way to destroy Dracula for good, and that it had to do with the blood of his first victim, the first person he ever turned. Frankenstein knew the legend, and asked him why he was bothering to tell us because even if it was true, everyone knew that Valeri was the first human being Dracula ever turned, and he would never allow himself to be used to destroy his master. But Grey told us that he had once been at a party thrown by you, where you had told him that the accepted story might not be the true story. Do you remember that?"

A smile crept across Valentin's face.

"I do," he said. "We were on the roof of my home in Manhattan, waiting for the sun to come up. I don't believe he was calling himself Grey at the time, although I can't remember what name he *was* using. I liked him; he was a regular fixture in New York that summer."

"So you did tell him that there was more to the story than people think?" asked Jamie. "He was telling the truth?"

"He was," said Valentin. "I told him that my brother is not quite so important to the legend of Dracula as most people believe, and certainly not as important as Valeri would like to think. But if you're going to ask me for more details, I should warn you now that I don't know them."

Jamie's heart sank. "What do you mean, you don't know them?" he asked.

"I mean, I don't know them. I don't know for sure that I'm right; perhaps Valeri *is* the key to my former master's immortality. But over the years, more years than you can possibly imagine, things were said, or not said, and I came to the conclusion that there was more to the story of Dracula's transformation than we knew. Put simply, I don't believe my brother was the first victim."

"Did Dracula ever say that?" asked Jamie. "Did you ever ask him directly?"

Valentin laughed.

"I never asked him anything directly, Jamie," he replied. "He was our master, our Prince, our second father. He demanded nothing less than utter obedience, utter subservience, and that was what we gave him. He told us the story of his rebirth only once, and what he said was that after he was turned in the forest outside Budapest, he came straight back to the battlefield to find us. When he did so, he turned Valeri, then Alexandru, and then finally myself. He made no mention of any others."

"So why do you think—"

"Instinct, Mr Carpenter," interrupted Valentin. "Centuries of watching the way men and women lie, and cheat, and conceal. Glances, looks, body language. None of it matters now; I have told you the conclusion I have come to, as the vampire who now calls himself Grey told you. You can choose to believe me, or not."

Jamie absorbed what the vampire was saying; it seemed so loose, so tenuous, but he did not think the ancient monster would have mentioned it at all if he didn't believe in the truth of what he was saying. Jamie was sure that being wrong ranked highly on Valentin's list of least favourite experiences.

"So you don't think the key to stopping Dracula lies with Valeri?" he asked. "You think it's out there somewhere?"

"That's what I believe," replied Valentin. "But I would urge you not to get your hopes up too quickly, Jamie. If I am right, and there was a vampire turned by Dracula before my brothers and me, then he or she would now be more than five hundred years old, if they are even still alive. There's every chance that they have been destroyed, and the chance to stop my former master is long gone."

"You don't believe that, though, do you?" asked Jamie. "If you did, you wouldn't be here. If there was no chance to stop Dracula, I mean."

"Think that if you wish, Mr Carpenter," replied Valentin, smoothly. "But I have already told you why I'm here: because I have no wish to watch Dracula tear this world, of which I am very fond, to pieces."

Jamie hesitated, then asked the one question he really didn't want to hear the answer to.

"What will it be like?" he asked. "If Dracula is allowed to rise. Tell me the truth."

"It will be terrible," said Valentin, simply. "When he was still a man, I helped him wage a campaign of terror across eastern Europe, for no other reason than his own lust for power, and the insults he believed he had received at the hands of the Turks. The things that were done beneath his banner, I cannot even describe to you; things that make my stomach churn at the memory of them, almost five hundred years later. His appetites for power, and for revenge, are beyond any I have seen in any other living creature. And for a while, after he was turned, they were sated.

"We lived like kings in the shadows, in the dark places, safe in the knowledge that we were invulnerable to harm, or so we thought. Until Vlad began to become restless, and sought companionship. Valeri was disgusted when he announced his plan to move to London; he would never say it, but it was clear. He thought it a rejection of everything we had fought for, bled for. But Dracula was unmoved by my brother's disapproval, and we went our separate ways. Until he was killed by the men who founded this very organisation, on the plains beneath his castle."

"But he wasn't killed, was he?" said Jamie, in a low voice. "That's the whole problem."

"Indeed. However, at the time, we had no way of knowing that was the case. It wasn't until many years later, until the experiments carried out by Van Helsing himself, that we realised there was a chance our master could be revived. And by then it was too late; the remains were gone, and it took Valeri almost a century to recover them."

"But you said that Dracula was sated, before he died," said Jamie. "You said he was on the verge of moving into society, of leaving behind his old ways. Why are you so sure he will want to terrorise the world now?"

"I once saw my former master murder every single inhabitant of a small town in what is now northern Romania," said Valentin. "And not just murder them. For three days, our army visited every torture you can imagine on these poor people, and plenty that I hope you can't. We killed, and tortured; we made the streets run with blood. We forced parents to kill their children, brothers to rape their sisters, husbands to blind and maim their wives. When it was over, we burned the bodies and the buildings, and we salted the ground, so nothing could ever grow there again. And do you know why we did it?"

Jamie shook his head.

"Because as we rode through the town, the mayor's wife did not bow deeply enough as Prince Vlad passed her," said Valentin. His face looked haunted, the face of a man who knows he can never make peace with the things he has done, and has decided not to try. "For that one tiny unintentional insult, more than a hundred men, women and children died in agony. So I ask you this: can you even begin to imagine what Dracula will do as revenge for having lain dormant beneath the ground for more than a century?"

Jamie stepped through the second door of the double airlock, his hair still fluttering from the rush of the gas that had billowed around him, and was not at all surprised to see Major Turner waiting for him. The Security Officer was leaning against the wall; he did not appear to have moved at all while Jamie had been inside the cellblock.

"You made it then," said Turner, the ghost of a smile on his narrow, empty face. "Well done."

"Thanks," said Jamie, slightly unsteadily. The horror of the tale Valentin had told him had shaken him; its implications for the wider world if Dracula was allowed to regain his full strength were almost beyond comprehension.

"The Director wants a full report," said Turner. "Immediately."

Jamie nodded. He walked slowly past the Security Officer, who reached out a hand and gripped his shoulder, surprisingly gently. Jamie stopped, and turned to face him.

"You did well," said Turner. "I was listening. You should be proud."

"I don't feel proud," said Jamie.

The two men looked at one another for a long moment, then Turner nodded, and removed his hand. Jamie turned away, and walked slowly to the lift at the end of the corridor.

He got out on Level A, and made his way slowly towards Admiral Seward's quarters. The euphoria he had felt during the early part of his conversation with Valentin, as he heard about his grandfather's exploits in New York, as he began to allow for the possibility that he was not to blame for Frankenstein's death, had been replaced by a crushing weariness and a sense of terrible foreboding. Valentin's description of the things he had done on the orders of Dracula, the details of the first vampire's sadism and thirst for revenge, had filled him with horror; he had first thought about his mother, happily busying herself in her cell, then about Larissa, and Kate, and Matt. What would become of them if Dracula was allowed to rise?

He wondered, not for the first time, if he was putting them in danger by merely being their friend; he was certain that Dracula would be taking a special interest in him once he discovered that it was he who had destroyed Alexandru.

I'm putting them in harm's way, he thought, as he trudged along the corridor. *They'd be safer without me around.*

He attempted to push such gloomy thoughts from his mind as he approached Admiral Seward's quarters. The guard Operator nodded at him as he passed, and then Jamie knocked on the heavy door. It unlocked almost instantly, and the Director of Department 19 called for him to enter.

By the time Jamie was standing in front of Admiral Seward's desk, the exact same spot where he had been standing only an hour or so earlier, where he felt like he had spent an awfully large amount of time since he had arrived at the Loop, the Director's face was a mask of even professionalism. But as the door had been swinging open, Jamie had seen, for just a split second, a look of open relief on the Admiral's face.

"Lieutenant Carpenter," said Seward. "Good to see you made it. How was it?"

"It was… interesting, sir," replied Jamie, carefully.

"I've seen a transcript of the conversation," said Seward. "Do you believe what he told you about Dracula? About how to destroy him?"

"I'm not sure, sir," replied Jamie. "I think he believes it. But I don't know. Like he said, sir, even if he's right, it would have taken place so long ago that I don't see how there would be anything we could do about it."

"Nonetheless," said Seward, "you were sitting there with him, looking at him as he spoke. Do you think there is anything to his claim?"

Jamie considered for a moment, remembering the look on Valentin's face as he explained his theory, a look that was almost smug, full of delight in his own superior knowledge.

"Yes, sir," he said, eventually. "I think there might be."

"Then I'll have it investigated," said Seward, making a note on one of the many pieces of paper that cluttered the surface of his desk. "I'm sure I don't need to remind you that—"

"Everything Valentin told me is Zero Hour classified," said Jamie. "I understand, sir."

Admiral Seward nodded. There was a look of slight discomfort on his face, as though he was about to do something he didn't really want to.

"I also have to investigate his claims about your grandfather, Jamie," he said, softly. "You understand, don't you?"

"Yes, sir," replied Jamie. "I knew you would. And I need to know if what Valentin said was true."

"You'll be the first to know," promised the Director. "And whatever happens, I won't let anyone sully John's memory. He was one of the best we ever had; nothing is going to change that."

"Thank you, sir."

The two men sat in silence for a long moment that wasn't exactly uncomfortable, but was thick with the secrets of the past. After a moment, Jamie sought out safer ground.

"Do you want to hear my initial report, sir?"

"No need, Jamie," replied Seward. "I have the transcript, like I said."

Jamie frowned.

"Sir, Major Turner told me that—"

"I know what Major Turner told you," interrupted the Director. "He told you what I ordered him to tell you. There's something I need to share with you, but I don't want to get your hopes up unnecessarily."

Jamie felt a tingle of excitement run up his spine.

"Hopes up about what, sir?"

Seward reached out and plucked a folder from the top of a teetering pile of identical folders. He held it in the air for a moment, as though debating the wisdom of handing it to the teenager. Then he sighed, and extended his arm; Jamie took the folder eagerly from his fingers, opened it and looked down at the cover sheet.

MEMORANDUM
From: Marcus Jones MD, County Coroner (Northumbria)
To: Sergeant Richard Threlfall, Northumbria Police

Jamie raised his eyes to Admiral Seward, a look of confusion on his face.

"Just read it," said the Director.

Jamie nodded, and turned his attention to the second document in the folder.

Dick,

One for the curiosity files I suspect, but thought I should let you know anyway.

Last night I carried out the autopsy on the body that was found in the cave at Bamburgh (shock horror! – wrongful death. The neck was broken intentionally, and the trachea and larynx are crushed almost flat, from where the assailant gripped the throat – full report attached). As I was stitching him shut, something odd happened.

My initial estimate is that the body had been in the cave for several months, and it was in an extreme state of decay; but all of a sudden thick black hair started to emerge from the remaining skin, as coarse as animal fur. I'm not making this up, I promise you! I was the only one in the office, and this morning when I took my assistant in to verify the phenomenon, it was gone. I really have no explanation for it; perhaps some kind of anomalous follicular stimulation, or some genetic twist I've never seen before.

Anyway, I doubt it's of any particular importance, but I thought I'd let you know in case it's any use to you in terms of identification.

See you on Sunday – tee time is at 745. Love to Judy.

Marcus

Jamie read the short letter twice, then looked up at Admiral Seward.

"Where did this come from?" he asked.

"It was intercepted by the Northern Outpost," replied Admiral Seward. "It's three and a half weeks old. It got sent down here as a matter of course, and the Intelligence Division pulled it out."

"Why?" asked Jamie. He was confused; he could not see

what the Director clearly wanted him to see in the short, affable letter.

"Three and a half weeks ago was the last full moon," said Seward, softly. "And Bamburgh is about five miles north of Lindisfarne."

Realisation bloomed in Jamie's mind, as huge and bright as the sun.

"My God," he whispered. "It's the werewolf, isn't it? The one that went over the cliff with Frankenstein."

"We believe so," said Admiral Seward. "I've sent a team to collect the body. They're due back within the hour. We should be able to confirm it as a lycanthrope once we have it in the labs."

"It was alive when it went over the cliff," said Jamie, his voice trembling. "It howled all the way down to the water. I heard it, sir."

"I know," replied Seward. "I read your report, and those of the other survivors."

"So it died after it fell," said Jamie, working it slowly through in his mind, trying not to jump to the conclusion that was screaming in the front of his brain. "Its neck was broken by human hands. Hands big enough and strong enough to crush its throat."

"So it would appear."

"That means Frankenstein survived the fall," said Jamie, slowly. "He was still alive when he hit the water, and still strong enough to kill the werewolf."

"That seems likely."

A surge of emotion burst through Jamie, so strong it turned his legs to water and he felt for a second as though he was going to collapse to the floor of the Director's quarters. He felt tears well in the corners of his eyes.

"He could still be alive," whispered Jamie. "That's what you're telling me, isn't it, sir? Frankenstein could still be alive."

Seward stared at Jamie for a long moment, then slowly nodded his head.

36

VISION QUEST, PART I

HOPI RESERVATION, NORTH-EASTERN ARIZONA, USA FOUR DAYS EARLIER

The man who was calling himself Robert Smith stopped for a moment, swaying in the heat of the pounding desert sun. Dizziness had suddenly come over him, but the feeling passed as quickly as it had arrived. He took a long, slow drink from the water bottle on his belt, wiped his brow and continued up the steep slope of the mesa.

The brown dirt slid beneath his feet as he climbed, rattling away behind him with a soft sound like running water. Tall grasses sprouted from the dry ground in tight clumps, their leaves brown and cracked like ancient skin, and he picked his way cautiously between them, assessing the placement of each foot, allowing his body weight to settle before moving again. Slowly, carefully, he made his way up the last of the slope, and crested the ridge.

Before him, standing silently at the edge of the flat top of the mesa, was one of the oldest inhabited settlements on earth, a Hopi village almost a thousand years old.

Old Oraibi. This is where I'll find answers.

*

Smith had paid a pilot instructor in Salt Lake City to fly him into Polacca Airport, a barren strip of asphalt in the middle of the Hopi reservation, flanked by a single row of trailers. From there he had hiked up on to Route 264 and begun walking west, hoisting a thumb at every passing car and truck. After an hour or so, he got lucky; a college student, heading home for the weekend from the University of Arizona in Tucson, pulled his battered, dusty pick-up truck over to the side of the road and shoved open the passenger door. Smith ran up and climbed in, thanking the student as he settled into the worn seat.

"No problem," replied the kid. "What's your name, friend?"

"Smith. Robert Smith."

"Good to meet you, man. I'm John. John Chua."

"What does that mean?" asked Smith.

"What, John?" replied the kid, smiling at his passenger.

Smith laughed. "Chua. What does Chua mean?"

"It means snake," answered the kid, and without warning, a chill surged up Smith's spine. It was fleeting, less than a second, but John Chua saw it, and frowned momentarily.

"So where are you heading?" he asked. His voice had lost a touch of its warmth, and Smith realised that the kid was starting to regret picking him up.

"Not far," he replied. "Old Oraibi."

A tiny wave of relief flickered across John Chua's face.

"Cool," he said. "I'm going to Kykotsmovi. Oraibi's only a couple of miles further on, on third mesa. Should only take you half an hour to hike up there."

Smith settled into his seat, and watched the barren rock and sand of the desert as it flew past his window.

"That sounds good," he said.

*

John Chua had been telling him the truth. It had only taken him thirty minutes to hike across the dusty, green-brown plain that lay between Kykotsmovi village and the bottom of the slope that led up on to third mesa. But it had taken him another forty to circle around to the south-west, and pick his way up the treacherous surface to the point where he now stood, atop the mesa's ridge. He had not wanted to follow the highway up to the main entrance of the village; it felt exposed, and obvious. Part of it was experience, and part of it was overcaution, but the upshot was simple: Smith did not want to be seen before he chose to be.

Slowly, he made his way to the back of the row of buildings standing before him. The village was arranged in uneven rows. To the north, closest to the road, stood modern houses of concrete and sheet metal in varying states of disrepair. Pick-up trucks stood outside one or two, beside propane tanks and overflowing trash cans. He could hear the scurrying of rats and smell the caustic, bitter scent of crystal meth on the warm air. The place was thick with deprivation, and desperation.

The village had once been a series of stepped plateaus, the entrances to the houses raised two and a half metres above the surface of the mesa, with the carved wooden ladders that provided access leaning against the stone walls. Most of the original settlement was gone, beaten and battered by the passage of the centuries, but to the south, towards the edge of the mesa, beyond the sign telling tourists to go no further, stood what was left. Smith could see the broken spire of one of the oldest churches in America looming from beyond the rise to the south, and slowly headed towards it.

He didn't know why, not exactly; the vision that had compelled him to come to this ancient place had not dealt in specifics. Smith crept along the crumbling stone wall, past the sign, over the rise at the edge of the mesa, and then stopped dead.

A man was standing in the dust, staring directly at him.

He was old, his face lined and weathered, his skin the colour and consistency of leather, dried and tanned by the relentless desert sun. He was clad in traditional Hopi dress: a multicoloured breechclout that hung just above his knees and deerskin moccasins to protect his feet. His hair was bound into a Hömsoma, a tight figure-of-eight bun, and he wore a cloth band around his forehead. He was staring at Smith, a gentle smile on his face.

Smith stepped away from the wall, clearing his range of movement; his arms swung loosely at his sides, and he rolled forward on to the balls of his feet, ready for any eventuality. Then he regarded the man with a neutral expression, and asked him who he was.

For a long moment, the old man did not reply, then his smile widened, displaying a broken mountain range of chipped and yellowing teeth, and he spoke.

"I am Tocho. You are welcome here, traveller."

Smith took a step towards the ancient Hopi man.

"Thank you," he replied, carefully. "I am Robert Smith."

The old man laughed. "That is not your name."

Smith felt a tremor of panic rumble through him. He was floundering, taken aback by the presence of this ancient figure, who had caught him completely off guard, who seemed unsurprised to see him and who somehow knew that the name he had given was false.

How does he know that? Who the hell is this man?

"That's right," Smith replied, refusing to back down. "That's not my real name."

The old man regarded him closely. "A man who is lying to himself will find no truth here," he said.

"I'm not lying to myself," replied Smith. "I'm lying to you."

The Hopi elder laughed again, a short sound, like a bark, that echoed through the stone and dust of the settlement.

"That is fair," he replied, and walked towards Smith, his moccasin-clad feet silent on the parched ground of the mesa.

Smith did not retreat, but he shifted his weight away from the approaching man, ready to run if it became necessary to do so. But as Tocho approached, his dark eyes sparkling in their deep, lidded sockets, his lined face breaking into a wide smile, Smith realised that he had nothing to fear from the man, who extended a hand as he came to a halt before him. Smith took it, cautiously, and then felt his arm almost wrenched from his shoulder as the old man pumped it vigorously up and down, his grip like a vice. When he released Smith's hand, he clapped him hard on the back, and turned him towards the western edge of third mesa.

"Come," said Tocho. "What you are looking for is this way."

The two men walked quickly through the remnants of Old Oraibi. As they passed the crumbling church on their right, Tocho asked Smith why he had come.

He considered telling the old man the truth – that a raving, clawing lunatic on the Lower East Side of New York, his body covered in occult tattoos and self-inflicted scars, had spoken to him in his father's voice and told him to – but decided against it, even though there was something about the old man that made him want to trust him.

"I can't tell you that," Smith replied. "I'm sorry."

Tocho nodded, then, as they cleared the last of the fallen stone walls and moved towards the ridge that marked the edge of the mesa's flat top, spoke again.

"Why are you hiding your name?" he asked. "A man's name has power. To deny it is to sacrifice that power."

"I can't tell you why," replied Smith. "It wouldn't be safe."

"No harm will come to you here," replied Tocho.

"It's not my safety I'm thinking about."

The words hung in the air, barbed and unsettling. Tocho stopped, and stared closely at Smith, who forced himself to remain still under the ancient man's steely gaze. Then abruptly, Tocho began to walk forward again, and Smith fell in beside him.

"I do not believe that you are an evil man," said Tocho, softly. "Although I believe that you have done evil things. Am I right?"

"You are," replied Smith. "You see a lot. You weren't surprised to see me today, were you?"

Tocho smiled. "I was given warning of your arrival."

This time it was Smith who stopped. He reached out and grabbed the old man's arm, and turned him so they were face to face.

"By who?" he asked. "If there are people watching me, then I need to know. Now."

Tocho glanced down at the hand gripping his arm, and Smith removed it. He had gripped the old man's flesh so tightly that four fingermarks stood out, bright white on the dark skin, but the old man had not even grimaced.

"Spider Grandmother told me you were coming," he said, eventually. "She told me I was to help you, that you were a traveller in need of direction."

"Spider Grandmother?" asked Smith. "Who the hell is she?"

"She is the messenger," replied Tocho. "The link between my people and Tawa, the Creator, who made the first world out of

448

Tokpella, the Endless Space. She speaks to us, and we listen. She bids us, and we do as we are told. Do you understand?"

"No," replied Smith, and smiled. "Not in the slightest."

Tocho returned his smile. "It doesn't matter. I do."

The old man stepped forward again, and Smith followed him. As they approached the edge of the mesa top, Smith saw a plume of smoke rising into the sky. Then, as they crested the ridge and looked down the steep desert landscape, he saw where they were headed.

Dug into a small plateau on the steep ridge was a sweat lodge.

The hut was small, and had been sunk at least half a metre into the dry ground. It was low and roughly rectangular in shape, made of animal hides tied tightly across a wooden frame. Beside it, a fire had been built in a circular depression, and placed in the middle of the flames were a number of flat, round stones. Heat was shimmering from them, distorting the idling column of smoke into a twisting, pulsing thing that appeared to be alive.

"Follow me," said Tocho, starting down the slope. Despite his obvious old age, the Hopi elder moved quickly down the side of the mesa, as sure-footed as a mountain goat, and Smith struggled to keep up with him. The ground moved beneath his feet, his arms wheeling at shoulder-height as he fought to keep his balance. He managed not to fall, though, and skidded to a halt beside Tocho, who was staring into the fire.

"Jesus," Smith said, out of breath. "That was crazy. I nearly broke my neck."

Tocho looked at him. "But you didn't," he replied. "Go inside and sit down. I'll follow you in a moment."

The old man turned his gaze to the fire and the arrangement of stones that lay in the middle of it, so Smith did as he was told.

He pulled open the loose flap of hide that passed for the lodge's door, stooped down and climbed inside.

The heat was incredible.

Desert sun had beaten down on the lodge since dawn, twelve hours earlier, and sweat immediately burst from Smith's pores, soaking his shirt and running freely down his forehead. He wiped his face with the back of his hand, looking around the small hut. A pit had been dug in the middle of the structure, and there were two flat areas, one either side of the pit. Smith clambered across the central depression, then sat down on the hard, burning ground. There wasn't enough room for him to do anything other than sit upright, so he crossed his legs beneath him, and waited for Tocho to appear.

He didn't wait long. After less than a minute, the door twitched open and the old man appeared, clutching a large bottle of water in one hand and a leather harness in the other. As soon as the flap fluttered shut behind him, Tocho lowered the leather harness into the pit in the middle of the hut, and shook it open. The flat stones, which had been cooking in the fire until they were close to white-hot, fell to the earth and the temperature inside the lodge exploded, a wall of scalding, expanding heat flooding the structure, so hot and overpowering that Smith's first instinct was that he had to get out, that he must get out, that he would die in here if he didn't. Tocho saw the panic in the stranger's eyes, and spoke to him, his voice low and soft.

"Let it pass," he said. "Let the heat fill you and move on. Let it pass."

The air was so hot that it burned Smith's nose and mouth as he inhaled, so he held his breath.

"Small breaths," urged Tocho. "Focus. Small breaths."

Smith's eyes were watering in the heat, his head pounding, but he did as he was told. He took a tiny breath in through his nose, and let it out of his mouth. Then he took another, and another, and as the first blast of heat began to subside, he opened his lungs and filled them again. The sweat still poured across him, his head still swam, but he realised he could bear it.

"I'm OK," he gasped. "I'm OK."

Tocho nodded, then handed him the bottle of water, taking care not to reach over the pit of stones. Smith took it, his hand slick and trembling, and wrenched the cap off. He raised it towards his mouth, and a bitter scent stung his nostrils. He paused.

"Mescaline?" he asked. "I thought this was a purification ritual?"

Tocho grinned at him. "I don't believe you're looking for purity."

Smith considered for a moment, then tipped the bottle and took a long swallow. The water diluted the bitter taste of the peyote extract, but it still crawled across his tongue like desert sand, leaving him with a feeling of nausea as he focused again on his breathing, and settled into the heat.

"Are you ready?" asked Tocho. Smith nodded, and the ancient Hopi took a small flask from his breechclout and tipped the contents on to the stones. Sandalwood oil fizzed and sizzled on them, the air thickening with renewed heat and pungent, sickly incense.

"Close your eyes," said Tocho. "And breathe."

Smith did as he was told.

The heat surrounded him, thickening the air until it felt like he was breathing hot water, but he focused – *in, out, in, out, in, out* – and felt his throat open. The panic, which had risen through him again when the sandalwood oil had hit the stones, subsided. His head felt fuzzy, from the heat or the mescaline, he couldn't tell which. He kept his eyes closed, even as sweat ran into them in sharp, salty rivers. He fumbled blindly for the water bottle, found it, took a long, bitter swallow, then placed his hands on the ground at his sides, gritting his teeth as his palms met the burning desert.

His head felt heavy, so he allowed it to slump forward against his chest, as pale streams of colours began to slide across the backs of his eyelids, brightening and intensifying and erupting into spirals and loops and whirls. He stared at the lights, unable to open his eyes, and felt saliva slide from his mouth, which had fallen open. It sizzled when it touched the bare skin where his shirt was open, a loud boiling sound that Smith understood, somewhere in the back of his mind, couldn't be real.

The temperature began to drop, slowly at first, then faster and faster. Colours danced and spun behind his eyes, then receded to the corners where he could no longer follow them. Cautiously, he allowed his eyelids to part, then opened them wide.

Tocho and the sweat lodge had almost disappeared.

There remained a faint, translucent image of the old Hopi man, his arms and legs folded, his gaze fixed firmly on Smith, and the wooden frame of the hut was still just barely visible. But around and through them, Smith could see the great expanse of the mesa and the desert beyond it.

As he watched, the shadows cast by the shrubs and cacti moved steadily, and he looked up. The sun was moving rapidly across the sky, heading for the horizon before him. It sank towards the earth, the mesa darkening as it did so, and then it was gone, taking the last of the day with it.

The smouldering fire to Smith's right cast a pale red glow on the area around him, and as he looked, he saw that the sweat lodge, and the man who had brought him to it, were now completely gone. He was sitting cross-legged, alone on the hard desert floor. He shivered, as the last of the sun's residual heat faded away, and attempted to stand up.

He couldn't move. His legs felt as though they were made of concrete, and he could not uncross them, let alone stand on them. As he tried, he pitched forward at the waist, and mercifully, his arms responded to his urgent command: he was able to put them out and steady himself. But the sensation didn't frighten him, nor did the rustling noise that began to emanate from the scrubland in front of where he sat; his instincts, which were so finely honed that they remained active even as his conscious mind drifted away, told him he was in no danger in this place.

The rustling got louder and louder, and Smith waited for the source of the noise to show itself; he was curious, rather than afraid, to see what it was. Slowly, the scrub parted and the thick, angular head of a reticulated python emerged. Its forked tongue darted in and out of its mouth as it slowly slid across the desert floor, its huge weight sending small rivers of sand cascading down the slope.

Smith watched as the snake slid its entire body into the clearing in which he sat, and gasped. The python was four metres long, at least, as thick as his waist at its midpoint. Its skin gleamed in the glow of the fire, the beautiful, incredibly complex patterns appearing to move independently as the huge muscles flexed beneath the surface, pushing the snake forward.

As it neared Smith, the snake's tail began to coil, followed by the body itself; the huge snake spun upwards, resting on a tapering series of coils, until its head was level with his own, its black eyes staring into him.

Smith stared at the animal, transfixed. Then, as he felt himself teeter towards the brink of being lost in its expanding black eyes, it began to change. The smooth lines of the snake bulged and twisted, and the heavy, angular head drew back on itself, stretching and widening. In less than ten seconds, the transformation was complete, and Smith felt a grin spill across his face, the unashamed, childlike grin of someone who has just seen something wonderful.

Where the snake had been there now sat a handsome, middle-aged black man, stretching his arms out above his head and twisting his neck from side to side. Smith heard a series of clicks, before the man lowered his limbs and regarded him with a smile.

"Metamorphosis is a bitch," he said. "Even here. I spend the first five minutes worrying that I didn't do it right, like if I take my shoes off, I'm going to find I got snakeskin toes. You know what I'm saying?"

Smith shook his head, and the man smiled at him.

"You don't, do you?" he said. "You don't belong here at all. Who opened the path for you?"

"One of the Hopi," replied Smith. "I'm in Arizona. Or I was."

"You still are," confirmed the man. "Your body doesn't move. Your mind, on the other hand..."

"So I'm dreaming?"

"In a way. This is the inner reality, the space between. It's not really a physical place. More metaphysical, if you follow me?"

"And you live here?" asked Smith, his head spinning.

The man grinned. "I live in New Orleans," he replied.

Smith took a closer look at the man, who was sitting with his legs crossed easily beneath him, his face open and friendly. Over the left breast pocket of his denim shirt was a sticker, the kind that employees of electronics shops wear.

HI!

My name is

Papa Lafayette

How can

I help you?

"Papa Lafayette," he said, softly.

"That's me," replied the man. "What can I do for you, now that you found me?"

"Found you?" asked Smith. "I didn't know I was even looking for you."

"But you were, whether you know it or you don't. So what's going on? I don't have all night."

Smith paused, and gathered his thoughts. His mind was slipping around him, drifting and sweeping in a mescaline haze, but he forced himself to concentrate.

"I'm looking for answers," he said.

"To which questions?"

"Questions about vampires."

Papa Lafayette grimaced. "I'm no expert on the supernatural," he said. "I doubt I have the answers you're looking for."

"Then what are you doing here?" Smith asked. "Why are we talking to each other? A madman told me to come to Oraibi, so I did. Tocho, the old man, was expecting me, and he told me that this was the next step, and I believed him, and here I am. With you. So why do you think that is, if you're telling me you can't help me with what I need to know?"

"I don't know," replied Papa Lafayette, his expression back to its usual easy half-smile. "Genuinely, I don't. Vampires are creatures of the earth, of blood, and death. I deal in the spiritual."

"So I ask you again. Why are we here?"

Papa Lafayette sighed. "I felt a compulsion to enter the inner world tonight," he said softly. "As powerful as I've ever felt. *This*, this conversation, is not what I was expecting to find. But..."

"But what?"

"But I believe in fate, and destiny. I believe that everything is connected, and I believe that something felt it was important that you and I meet here, in this place, at this time. So ask your questions. I will answer them if I can, I promise you that."

Smith stared at the man sitting opposite him, and saw nothing but honesty on the open, handsome face. He took a deep breath.

"I've been following a legend," he said. "The legend of a vampire that was cured, supposedly the *only* vampire that has ever been cured. They call him Adam. Apparently, he was an American, apparently, he lived in the second half of the twentieth century and apparently, once he was cured, he disappeared. I've been following the story for over a year, and that's all I know. That's all *anyone* knows. I don't know whether he's alive, or dead, or whether he even existed at all. But I need to find out."

Papa Lafayette looked at him, and Smith saw a flicker of admiration in the stranger's eyes. "I know you do," he said. "I can see the need shining out of you, from every cell in your being. I'm not going to ask you why you need to find this creature, but I believe that you do. And it seems like there's something out here in the inner that wants to help you along."

"What do you mean?" asked Smith. "Help me how?"

Papa Lafayette smiled. "Take a look behind you."

Smith turned his head, slowly. He didn't fear the man sitting before him, even though he had watched him transform from a snake, but it went against all his instincts to voluntarily turn his back on anyone. Behind him lay the dark rising expanse of the mesa; he could see smoke drifting into the night sky from somewhere beyond the upper ridge, and could hear distant snatches of music as they floated on the soft wind.

He stared for a long moment, and was about to turn back, to ask Papa Lafayette what he was supposed to be seeing, when the air before him shimmered, and then slowly parted, as though a window was being opened in the fabric of reality.

Through the widening hole Smith could see more desert, but it was immediately apparent that it was somewhere else; the sand was fine and yellow and the sun was beating down on it, turning it a glaring, blinding white. As he watched, the window expanded, and he saw first a strip of grey tarmac, shimmering and pulsing in the heat, and then the scuffed, battered metal pole of a road sign at its edge. As the blurry, shifting edges of the window moved outwards, he saw the sign itself, plain white text against a green background.

CALIENTE 12
CALIFORNIA HIGHWAY DEPARTMENT

Smith was reading the short message for a third time, committing it to memory, when a tall, slender man, wearing a dusty checked shirt, blue jeans and a battered cowboy hat, strolled casually up to the signpost, and leant against it. Then he stared directly at Smith, smiled, reached up and tipped the front of his hat to him. Smith stared, incredulous; he had the overwhelming urge to say hello to this vision, but his tongue would not form the word. Then, as suddenly as it had appeared, the shimmering window began to contract, and less than a second later it was gone.

Smith immediately turned back, his mind racing with questions for Papa Lafayette, but the handsome, genial man was also gone. There was a scuffed patch of sand where he had been sitting, but apart from that, there was no sign of him, nothing to suggest that he had been there at all.

37

FROM PILLAR TO POST

If anyone had asked, Jamie Carpenter would have been unable to describe exactly what he was feeling as he stood in front of Admiral Seward's desk. The slow, almost reluctant nod of the Director's head had turned the world around him to nothing and the ground beneath his feet to quicksand. He felt as though his body was about to dissolve and drift away, such was the ferocity of the hope that had ignited in his chest; it threatened to engulf him and everything around him.

"It's no more than a possibility," said Admiral Seward, his voice thick and distant, as though it was coming from underwater. "A remote one at that. But I didn't feel right, keeping it from you."

Jamie fought for equilibrium, like a swimmer who has found himself too far out and realises that unless he kicks for shore now, he might not be able to make it back.

Focus, he told himself. *Focus, for God's sake. You can't help him if you're catatonic.*

"We have to find him," he heard himself say. "We have to start looking now."

"We are," replied Seward. "I've scrambled a Field Investigation Team to depart for Bamburgh this afternoon. If there's anything to find, they'll find it."

"I want to go with them, sir," said Jamie, firmly.

"Out of the question," said Seward, instantly. Jamie opened his mouth to protest, but the Director didn't give him the chance. "The interrogation of Valentin Rusmanov is still ongoing, Jamie, and the presence of all Zero Hour Task Force members remains mandatory. No exceptions."

"Sir, this is far more important," protested Jamie.

"It is to *you*, Jamie," replied Seward. "For personal reasons, which I assure you I do understand, and sympathise with. But from my perspective, there is nothing more important right now than the work of the Zero Hour Task Force, of which you are a member, whether you like it or not. I'm devoting every appropriate resource to investigate the possibility that Colonel Frankenstein is still alive, but I'm afraid that does not include letting you tag along. I'm sorry, Jamie."

Anger surged through Jamie's body, and he fought his hardest to keep it at bay, to stop it erupting in Admiral Seward's direction. Because the equation was simple: the one man in the world who had never failed him, never betrayed him or let him down, who had readily offered up his life in exchange for Jamie's, might be out there somewhere, and he wasn't being allowed to help bring him home.

Admiral Seward saw colour rising in the teenager's face, and moved to extinguish it. "I told you because I believed you could handle it, Jamie," he said. "Don't make me regret that decision. There is more at stake here than even you understand."

With a Herculean effort, Jamie forced himself towards calm.

"I can handle it, sir," he said, slowly. "But I think I could be useful to the Field Team, sir."

"You're useful right here," replied Seward. "You have a rapport with Valentin that no one else has. Right now, and for as long as we continue to question him, I need you here."

"Will you let me see the reports from the Field Team?" asked Jamie.

"I will," replied Seward. "And I would let you go with them if it was any other time than now. I hope you understand that."

"I do, sir," replied Jamie, honestly. "I just hope they find something in Northumberland."

"So do I, son," replied Admiral Seward. "So do I."

Jamie walked down the corridor, away from the Director's quarters, his mind racing.

If he's alive, then where has he been for the last months? If he survived the fall, if he made it back to land, why hasn't he come home? Or contacted anyone?

His mind kept drifting towards the likeliest answer to its own questions, that even though it appeared the fall over the cliffs had not been the end of Frankenstein, it was overwhelmingly likely he had not made it to safety, that he had died in the cold waters of the North Sea. Jamie pushed such thoughts firmly away; he would not entertain such a conclusion, not when he had just been given the tiniest shred of hope to cling to.

If he's alive, they'll find him. That's what Admiral Seward said, and I believe him. I have to believe him.

Jamie was sufficiently engrossed in his own thoughts that when the lift doors slid open, he stepped forward without thinking, and almost walked straight into Shaun Turner, who skipped out of the way of the impending collision. The movement brought Jamie back from his daze, and he looked at the Operator he now knew was Kate's boyfriend, and blushed.

461

"Sorry," he said. "I was miles away."

"It's all right," Shaun replied. "Don't worry about it."

There was a moment of silence that, if not exactly comfortable, was not uncomfortable either, in which Jamie saw the chance to build some bridges, for Kate's sake if not for his own.

"How's it going?" he asked.

"Busy," said Shaun. "We went out three times last night. I'm shattered, to be honest with you."

"Anything interesting?"

"Routine 999 intercepts," said Shaun. "A home invasion in North London, a really messed-up ritual thing in a cemetery in Winchester and two vamps living under a railway arch in Stevenage. Nothing out of the ordinary, apart from the 'he rises' graffiti. Found it at all three places."

"It was in the home where Valentin found us yesterday too," said Jamie. "There's more of it every time we go out."

"The vamps know what's happening," said Shaun. "It's why they've been so brazen these last few months; they know that Dracula is rising."

"Until we stop him," said Jamie, and Shaun smiled.

The two men looked at each other, and both felt the tiniest shoots of a potential friendship between them. Although neither of them knew it, they had both been ordered by Kate to be nice to the other, for her sake, but what they were feeling now was the camaraderie of shared experience, and shared purpose.

"So I've been meaning to come and speak to you," said Shaun. "About Wallsend, and what happened to Kate. I'm sorry for how I behaved."

"It's cool," said Jamie, quickly. "You were just being loyal to Jack, and then you were scared for Kate. I get why now."

Shaun paused. "She told you?"

"I worked it out," said Jamie. "That night. I asked her, and she told me."

"She told Larissa," said Shaun. "I know that much. I didn't know you knew, to be honest, but it's probably for the best."

"I think it's great," said Jamie. "She seems really happy."

Shaun grinned, a wide smile that lit up his handsome features.

"That's good," he said. "I'm crazy about her, between you and me. I think she's amazing."

"I do too," said Jamie. "I'm pleased for you both. And the thing in Wallsend, just forget about it, OK? It was messed up sending two squads without a clear chain of command. And you and Angela were right, Jack was the senior Operator. It's all forgotten, honestly."

"Cool," said Shaun, the smile still wide on his face.

"OK. See you later then?"

"All right," said Shaun. He stepped out of the lift, and Jamie moved round him and into it. The two men nodded at each other as the doors shut, separating them. Jamie found himself smiling as he pressed the button that would take him down to Level B, where Matt would be waiting for him.

That's my good deed for today, he thought. *Kate should be pleased.*

He was still smiling when he opened the door to the quarters next to his, took one look and then burst out laughing.

Matt was sitting cross-legged in the middle of his mattress, surrounded on all sides by towering mountains of box files and lever-arch folders. The trolley that had been used to transport the vast reams of information up to him from the Lazarus Project labs stood off to one side. Matt had one of the box files open in front of him and was absorbed in a thick sheaf of documents; he had not moved when Jamie opened the door, but his pale, earnest face shot up when he heard his friend begin to laugh.

"Hey, Jamie," he said, then frowned. "What's so funny?"

"Nothing," replied Jamie, walking across the room towards him. "Just glad to see they're letting you settle in before they throw you in at the deep end."

Matt grinned at him, and put the documents back in the file.

"The stuff they're working on is unbelievable," he said, excitedly. "I'm trying to catch up as quickly as I can, there's a whole new biological system I have to understand before I can even think about being any use to them. Look at this." He scrabbled through the avalanche of paper, and held out a series of photocopies for Jamie to look at. He took them and leafed quickly through them; they were copies of small handwritten pages, full of diagrams and formulas.

"Cool," said Jamie. "What is it?"

"It's Abraham Van Helsing's journal," said Matt, his voice full of wonder. "I mean, not the original, obviously, but that's his actual handwriting. Professor Talbot wanted me to start at the beginning, you know, so I could get a sense of how the study of vampires has progressed. A lot of his theories turned out to be flawed, or just wrong in some cases, but the work he did was still remarkable. It's the foundation of everything anyone knows about vampires."

"He was an amazing man," said Jamie.

"Yeah. I just can't get my head round the fact that he was *real*."

"He really was," said Jamie, pride filling his chest. "My great-grandfather worked for him."

"Are you serious?" asked Matt. "That's incredible."

"I know," said Jamie. "It's why my family are part of this place. He was Van Helsing's valet when the Department was founded in 1892, and he was the first person the founders allowed to join them, a couple of years later."

"That's crazy," said Matt, softly.

"I know," said Jamie, smiling at his friend. "What's this stuff?" he asked, pointing to heaps of what looked like academic papers.

"Professor Talbot's research on the DNA differences between humans and vampires," Matt replied. "The work he's doing is completely fascinating."

Jamie stared at the papers. There were hundreds and hundreds of sheets, not counting the multiple volumes of Van Helsing's journals. "And you're seriously expected to read all this stuff?" he asked, awed.

"Oh," said Matt. "I've already read them."

38

VISION QUEST, PART II

CALIENTE, CALIFORNIA, USA
YESTERDAY

The man who was calling himself Robert Smith pressed the brake pedal of the jeep, bringing the vehicle to a halt at the side of the highway, churning up a thick cloud of orange dust as it did so. Smith waited for the dust to clear, then looked up at the road sign standing in front of his jeep.

CALIENTE 12
CALIFORNIA HIGHWAY DEPARTMENT

The green sign looked exactly as it had during his vision in the sweat lodge: the chipped paint around the edges, the dents and scratches where stones had been thrown against it by passing cars, and the shallow indentations made by small-calibre bullets, presumably fired from cars as they roared along this desolate desert highway.

I found it, he thought. *It's real, and I found it.*

Smith was coated in dust, his skin as rough as sandpaper where sand had glued itself to the sweat of his body. He had not showered for two days, had barely even slowed the jeep's progress west. He had taken food when he stopped to fill its tank with petrol, and slept, for three fitful hours, when the lines on the highway had started to blur before his exhausted eyes, sometime around dawn of the second day.

Just after the sign lay the entrance to a dirt road, rutted by the repeated passage of wide, heavy-treaded tyres. It headed straight into the desert. Smith shaded his eyes with his hand and followed the track through the sand until it disappeared, apparently at the horizon. The desert shimmered with rising heat as he put the jeep into drive, and turned on to the road.

The jeep's suspension howled in protest as the little vehicle bounced and rolled along the track. Smith kept it slow; he did not want to break an axle or puncture a tyre out here in the middle of nowhere; he had not carried a mobile phone for over a year, knowing that it could be used to locate him even if it was turned off in his pocket, and he guessed he was at least a two-hour walk from Caliente, two hours across uneven, unfamiliar terrain beneath the relentless desert sun.

After ten minutes, the road dipped and turned, following the contours of a wide valley with the long-dry bed of a river snaking along its shallow floor. On one side, built on a small plateau, was a small cabin – a square building with wooden walls and a stone chimney, from which a gentle, winding column of white smoke was drifting up into the morning sky, and a white roof that cast a thick band of shadow around the walls of the cabin.

Leaning casually against one of the wooden walls, as if he had been waiting for the vehicle to appear over the crest of the valley side, was a man in dusty jeans and a red and white checked shirt.

He had an easy smile on his face, and as Smith nosed the jeep down the slope towards him, he checked his watch theatrically, then grinned at the approaching vehicle.

Smith rolled the jeep to a halt, and stepped cautiously out of the car. There was nothing overtly suspicious about the man; yet Smith's instincts had kept him alive thus far, and he listened to them even when he could see nothing wrong.

"Hello," said the man, pushing himself away from the wall and extending a hand. "I'm Andy. I knew you were coming. It's good to see you."

Smith paused momentarily, but then stepped forward. He had trusted whatever force was guiding him so far, and he knew he had to do so again. So he shook the man's hand, and told him his name, and accepted when he was invited into the cabin.

Andy's home was small and neat; a main room that doubled as a living room and a kitchen, with a wood-burning stove, a sink, a sofa and a chest of drawers, the top of which was crowded with photos in frames that looked old. Andy – *if that is his name, you don't know that for certain, not yet* – filled a coffee pot from the sink and placed it on the stove. As he did so, Smith asked him how he knew.

"I'm sorry?" asked Andy.

"You knew I was coming," said Smith. "How did you know that? *I* didn't know I was coming until eighteen hours ago."

Andy grinned at Smith, as he took two mugs down from a shelf and placed them on the chipped coffee table that sat in front of the sofa. "The spirits told me," he replied.

"Figures," said Smith.

"Spirits said you were a searcher. Told me I should help you."

"I'm looking for information."

"Guessed that much. About anything in particular?"

"Vampires. One vampire in particular."

"Don't know much about vampires," said Andy. "Know enough to avoid them, but that's about it."

"This one is special. He was cured. Does that ring any bells?"

"Can't say that it does."

The coffee pot on the stove began to whistle, and Smith felt his temper begin to boil too. His patience was at an end, exhausted by everything that had happened to him in the last year or so, by the cryptic leads he had received from the strange men and women he had met along the way, by his journey west to this scorched, barren landscape that now appeared to hold no more answers than anywhere else. He was about to open his mouth and take it all out on the man called Andy, when he saw something that made him pause.

In the middle of the collection of photos on top of the chest of drawers was a dull silver frame. There was nothing ornate about it: just four strips of metal arranged into a rectangle. Inside the frame was a black and white photo of Andy and a pretty blonde woman. As Smith quickly surveyed the photos, he saw that almost all of them were of the couple: in front of landmarks, outside theatres and restaurants, wrapped in coats and scarves with snow falling around them.

The photo that had caught his eye was different, however. It was a souvenir photo, the kind that was sold in booths at county fairs and showgrounds. This one depicted Andy, who looked no more than ten years younger than he did now, and the blonde woman at the New York World's Fair. They were smiling at the camera, Andy's arm around the woman's waist, with the looming steel globe of the

Unisphere behind them. Smith leant in and read the date that had been stamped at the bottom of the photo.

September 19th 1964

Smith turned and stared at Andy, who was pouring coffee into the mugs on the table, and realisation flooded through him.

"Let's drink those outside," he suggested. "What do you say?"

Andy nodded. "Sure thing," he replied. "There's a bench out back."

He opened the door and led Smith round the side of the cabin to where a rough wooden bench, that looked as though it had been nailed together from whatever Andy had been able to find strewn across the desert floor, stood in the shadow cast by the overhanging roof. The two men sat, looking down the canyon at the riverbed. A lizard darted out from underneath a rock and scuttled down the slope, away from the intrusion.

Smith watched as Andy settled on to the bench and stretched his legs out. His feet extended beyond the wide band of shade cast by the oversized roof, and the sun gleamed on a narrow band of skin between the man's worn leather shoes and the frayed hems of his jeans.

"Adam," Smith said, staring at the strip of skin.

Andy frowned, then followed his guest's gaze down to his ankle. When he saw what Smith was looking at, he laughed, briefly. "Knew you'd figure it out eventually," he said, his voice warm and friendly. "At your service, Mr Smith. So what can I do for you?"

"Tell me what happened to you," replied Smith, instantly. "That's all I need to know, and then I'll leave you in peace."

470

"You know that's not why you're here, don't you?" asked Adam. "That that's not what you've been searching for?"

"It's the *only* thing I've been searching for. The only thing that matters. Please. Just tell me."

"OK," said Adam. "I'll tell you."

"I was turned in 1961," Adam began. "When I was twenty. I was working in New Mexico, on a cattle ranch near Alamogordo. I was raised in Bakersfield, until my grandmother died, and my grandfather went south looking for work. I was fifteen when he sent me to the ranch, to work for a friend of his from the Marines.

"The guy who turned me was a drifter named Barratt, who was working his way south towards the border; he came on for a few weeks as a night watchman, and we got friendly. He used to talk about the places he'd been, the things he'd done, horrors he'd seen. I thought he was talking about war; this was the time when the first men were rotating home out of Vietnam, after it had started to go bad. And the country was still full of broken World War Two veterans, men who'd left parts of themselves overseas, and found there was nothing for them when they got home. But that wasn't what he was talking about."

Adam pulled a leather pouch from his jeans pocket, and quickly rolled a cigarette, his fingers moving with well-practised ease. He put the cigarette in his mouth and lit it with a silver Zippo lighter, breathed smoke into the hot, dry desert air and continued.

"The night Barratt turned me, we got drunk on whisky. We were in a barn at the edge of the ranch, and when he leant for my neck, I thought he was trying to make a move on me, and I tried to push him away. But he was suddenly strong, so strong that I couldn't move him an inch. I started to get scared, and then I saw his eyes, and the next thing I remember is waking up the next morning, lying in the straw."

He looked at Smith, the pain of the memory etched on his face.

"He meant it as a kindness, I'm sure of that. A lot of what he talked about was not letting your life drift away to nothing, that you only had one chance to do something extraordinary, and I'm sure he thought he was giving me that chance. But he never asked me if I wanted it, he just assumed, and when the hunger hit me ten minutes later, he was gone, and I had no idea what was happening.

"I remembered just about enough of the things he'd said the night before, things I thought were just stories, like campfire spook tales, that I pulled out the throat of one of the horses, and drank her dry. I ran out of the barn, and as soon as the sun touched my skin, I burst into flames. It was the worst pain I'd ever felt, at least up until then. I made it back into the barn, and rolled out the fire. The last of the horse's blood repaired me most of the way, and I hid there until nightfall. Then I ran."

Adam carefully crushed the remains of the cigarette beneath the heel of his shoe, and stared out across the canyon.

"I ended up in New York, working on the docks," he continued. "I kept myself to myself; night shift was quiet, the docks were crawling with rats that I could feed on and my workmates left me alone. Then one night a man came ashore from a freighter out of Indonesia, a man that didn't look like he had any business on a cargo ship; he was wearing a suit as elegant as any you'd see on Fifth Avenue, but he had no luggage. He took one look at me and knew exactly what I was, because we were the same.

"I was scared, but a bit of me was relieved, to tell you the truth; I really didn't know if there was anyone else in the whole world apart from Barratt that was like me. And I was lonely, and I guess that made me weak. He took me to his brother's apartment on Central Park West, gave me some clothes and a bath, then scolded me for living the way I was, for wasting the gift I had been given."

Adam paused, and favoured Smith with a look of incredulity. "That's what he called it. A *gift*. Although when I look back, knowing what I know now, I'm not surprised; he was a monster, barely human at all. Over the years I heard stories of the things he had done, the cruelties and the tortures, and I thanked God that I only saw him that one time."

"What was his name?" asked Smith, although he was sure he already knew the answer.

"Alexandru," replied Adam, and shivered momentarily in the heat of the desert. "Alexandru Rusmanov."

"The middle brother," said Smith, in a low voice. "You were lucky to cross his path and escape with your life. Not many were so fortunate."

"So I came to realise," replied Adam. "It's been almost fifty years, and the memory of him still scares me."

"It needn't," replied Smith, with vicious satisfaction in his voice. "He's dead."

"Dead?" replied Adam, his eyes wide. "Are you sure?"

"I'm sure. He was destroyed in England, three months ago. Destroyed completely."

"Thank God for that then. One less monster walks the earth."

"Agreed."

Adam shook his head, as if to clear it, and continued.

"His brother was throwing a party the night Alexandru found me, and he insisted that I accompany him, that I allow him to show me how a vampire should live. He took me downstairs and opened the doors to the ballroom and..."

Pain clouded Adam's face as memory overwhelmed him.

"It was a massacre," he said, flatly. "An orgy of violence. There were at least a hundred vampires in the room, and God knows how many men and women. They were running, trying to hide, screaming for mercy, and the vampires were laughing at them. They were *laughing* as they tortured and violated and murdered them.

"There was blood everywhere, and so many screams I couldn't think, and I looked at Alexandru, who was still standing next to me, and he looked back at me with those red eyes, eyes that were almost black, and I saw what madness looked like, true end-of-the-world, implacable, relentless madness, and I was about to scream as well, but then Alexandru disappeared into the crowd, and I was on my own.

"I ran for the doors, but they were bolted from the outside, and even my vampire strength wasn't enough to force them. There was a band playing, I remember it so clearly, playing on a small stage at the back of the room as horror after horror was visited upon innocent men and women, some of them little more than children. Then a hand grabbed my arm, and I screamed."

Adam quickly rolled another cigarette, lit it and inhaled hungrily.

"It was a girl. A beautiful, terrified girl, about my age, looking at me with huge red eyes. I took a step away from her, but she held on to my arm, and her face twisted and she looked like she was going to cry. 'I'm so scared,' she said. 'Can you help me get out of here? Please?'

"I told her there was no way out, and then she did start to cry, the tears glowing bright red as they rolled away from the light in her eyes. I tried to calm her down, I told her I would stay with her, that I wouldn't let anything happen to her, and she looked at me with this terrible hope in her eyes, like she wanted to believe me, but didn't know whether she dared to do so.

"I led her to the corner of the ballroom, away from the worst of it, and I wrapped my arms round her, hiding her as best I could, even if I couldn't shield her from the screams and the sounds of violence. We stayed like that all through the night, until there was an hour or so until dawn, and the doors were unlocked. Only vampires walked out of the room; everyone else was dead.

"I led her out, avoiding the gazes of the other monsters, and for a terrible second, I saw Alexandru looking at me through the crowd as I left his brother's house. I lowered my head, and forced myself not to run, and then we were outside, on West Eighty-Fifth Street, and I picked the girl up and ran with her into the park and never looked back."

Adam stubbed out the cigarette. Smith watched him do so, saw that the man's fingers were trembling as he pressed the smouldering end against the wood of the bench.

"We hid in a storm drain on the north side of the park, and waited for the sun to go down. In those few hours, we learnt everything there was to know about each other, and we realised that we loved each other, instantly, and completely.

"She was twenty, from a little town in the Midwest. She'd been at summer camp in the Catskills that summer, when something had taken her in the woods and turned her. She survived the hunger, although she never told me how – it was the one thing she would never talk about – but her family thought she was dead, and she was too scared to go home and show them what had happened to her. Her father was a Methodist preacher, and she thought he would believe she was possessed by the devil.

"So she drifted east, and got picked up by an old vampire in Boston, who took her in as his pet. She told me the things he made her do – what she did to survive that first hunger was the only secret she ever kept from me – and for years I swore that I would hunt him down and kill him. But she didn't want me to, so I never did. And he had brought her down to New York for the party, so in some way I suppose, I ought to be grateful to him; I never would have met her if he hadn't.

"We waited until the sun went down, and we started running west. She didn't know whether the old vampire would try to find her, and I didn't think Alexandru would give a damn about me, but we couldn't be sure. We zigzagged all over the Midwest, up and down the Pacific coast, until eventually we settled in San Francisco."

Adam paused, and looked at Smith, his face hot and tears gathering in the corners of his eyes. "Her name was Emily," he said. "And we spent the next twenty years together."

Smith sat alone on the bench, staring out over the canyon. Adam had excused himself for a moment, and gone inside the cabin. The effort of telling his story had visibly taken its toll on the man, and Smith had a feeling there was worse to come.

Part of me doesn't want to know. I don't want to know why Emily isn't here with him. I don't want to know how he was cured. I just want to leave him in peace, with his memories, with all he has left. But I have to know. I've come too far to back out now.

"I'm sorry," said Adam, rounding the corner of the cabin and retaking his seat beside Smith. "I've never told anyone this story, not willingly at least, and it's hard. Harder than I thought it would be."

"I'm sorry to put you through it," replied Smith. "Believe me, I wouldn't unless I was sure it was important."

"I believe you," said Adam, and forced a smile. "And I think you're right, although I don't know why. So where was I? San Francisco, right?"

476

Smith nodded, and Adam continued.

"We lived as man and wife for twenty years, in the Mission. Boring night jobs, boring lives really, but we had each other, and we were happy. We fed on blood we bought from a Halal butcher in the Castro, kept ourselves to ourselves, and lived, like any other couple. But over the years, and then the decades, Emily started to change.

"It was little things at first, like it always is: bad moods, arguments, fights. Nothing I thought meant anything. But she wasn't happy, and I didn't realise she wasn't until it was too late to save her. I thought we had our condition under control; we never used our strength or our speed, we drank only the necessary amount of blood to keep us alive and we lived in every other way like ordinary humans.

"But we weren't ageing. We never met our neighbours, never socialised in the same places too often, so there was no chance of detection, which I thought was all that mattered. But it wasn't. I thought immortality was the only good thing to come out of what had been done to us, because it meant I could spend forever with her. She didn't feel the same way."

"Why not?" asked Smith.

"She thought it made everything meaningless. That everything, experience, intimacy, even love, was insubstantial, that nothing that had no end could ever mean anything. I tried to convince her otherwise, tried to convince her that our lives had meaning because we loved each other, and for a while she seemed to be placated. But she wasn't; she was just a much better actress than I had given her credit for. One evening I woke up, and she was gone. There was a note in the kitchen, telling me she loved me, and that she was sorry. And I never saw her again."

Adam lowered his head, and tears fell steadily on to the dry desert earth, creating tiny dark craters in the orange sand. Smith watched, his heart breaking for the man sitting beside him. After several minutes, he spoke.

"I'm sorry," he said. "I truly am."

Adam raised his head, and forced the kind of smile that is only available to those unlucky people to whom the worst thing that could possibly happen to them has already happened and who are faced with having to somehow find a way to carry on, to simply keep breathing in and out; a smile of utter tragedy and bewilderment, without a flicker of happiness in it.

"Thanks," he replied, his voice little more than a whisper. "I appreciate it. It was the worst moment of my life, even after all the ones that followed it. But it still doesn't justify what I did next."

39

BACK FROM THE DEAD

Jamie left Matt arranging the piles of files and folders on his shelves, and opened the door to his own quarters next door.

Matt had been thrilled to have been given a room of his own, and even more so because it was the one next to Jamie's. He had no possessions to speak of, merely the small rucksack he had been carrying when he had been rescued in the park near his home. He had only a single change of clothes, which he had dutifully hung in the narrow wardrobe at the foot of his bed, and a small framed photograph of him and his parents and sister, which he placed carefully on his small bedside table. Then he had set about making sense of the great mass of papers he had been sent by Professor Talbot, and Jamie had told him that he would be back in half an hour, ready to show him round the rest of the Loop.

Inside his room, Jamie flopped down on to his bed and closed his eyes, just for a moment. It had been, even by the standards of life inside Department 19, an exhausting day, and it was barely noon.

His conversation with Valentin had been a rollercoaster: unsettling, occasionally terrifying, but ultimately thrilling. His conversation afterwards, with Admiral Seward, had been nothing of the sort; the revelation that there was even the slightest possibility that Frankenstein was still alive had destabilised him so completely that he could now understand why it was obvious that the Director had wrestled with the decision of whether to tell him, or leave him in the dark.

But his time with Matt had made him feel better, as talking to the boy when he was comatose in the infirmary had done, six months earlier. There was something about him that put Jamie's mind at ease, and he thought he had figured out what it was: Matt was one of those people whose outlook was so positive, so enthusiastic, that it made Jamie feel churlish and spoilt for failing to see the same wonder in everything that Matt saw. He was not naive, or annoying in his positivity; it just radiated out of his pores, infecting those around him.

Jamie had read his file while he was being held in seclusion in the infirmary, had seen the history of bullying that had started when Matt was no more than six or seven, and his heart had gone out to the teenager.

He knew bullying, knew it very well; knew what it was like to feel worthless and alienated from everyone around you, to want so desperately to fit in even though you understand that it's not a choice you get to make, because some part of the very person you are is what the bullies hate, and there's nothing you can do about it.

But Jamie had only been on the receiving end for a couple of years, in the aftermath of his father's death, when the official story was that Julian Carpenter had been a traitor to his country. Matt had been bullied since almost the first day he walked through the gates of a school, and Jamie knew, just from the information in the file, exactly why. Matt was prodigiously clever, had no interest in sport, loved books, and hated rudeness and impoliteness. He might as well have walked into school with a target on his back.

A fierce thread of anger ran up Jamie's spine as he thought about the tormenting his new friend must have endured. He could picture it all too clearly; he had seen it done to the quiet, intelligent kids at every school he had been to, was ashamed to admit that he had participated on occasion himself when he was younger, although with little appetite. It had been a self-preservation thing, the horrible choice that so many schoolchildren face, of whether to help make someone else unhappy or risk drawing the wrath of the bullies on to themselves by refusing to do so.

No one will mess with him again, he thought. *Not here. And not anywhere else, if I'm around. I dare anyone to try.*

Jamie pulled his console out of his pocket, and quickly typed a message to Kate and Larissa, telling them he had been ordered to show Matt round the base, and asking if they wanted to come with him. Two quick return beeps told him that they did, so he closed his eyes again while he waited for them to arrive, and was fast asleep in less than thirty seconds.

He was roused from a deep, dreamless void by a distant thudding sound that grew louder and louder as he drifted awake. Cursing, Jamie hauled himself off his bed, crossed the room and opened the door. Standing in the corridor outside were Kate and Larissa.

"What took you so long?" asked Larissa. "We were starting to worry."

"I fell asleep," replied Jamie, groggily. "Hold on while I grab Matt."

He walked out into the corridor and knocked on the door to Matt's new quarters. He smiled as he heard a frenzy of movement, before the door burst open and Matt's excited face peered out at him.

"Hey," said Jamie. "How's the sorting going?"

"I got bored," smiled Matt. "So I haven't really done it. Are you going to show me round now?"

"That's the plan," said Jamie. "Come on."

Matt nodded enthusiastically, then stepped out into the corridor, pulling the door shut behind him. He followed Jamie the tiny distance along the corridor and through the open door, to where Kate and Larissa were waiting for them.

"Hello," Matt said, shyly, as the two girls looked up at him. "Nice to see you again."

Kate and Larissa smiled at each other.

"You too," said Kate. "You settling in OK?"

"Definitely," said Matt. "I've got about a thousand things to read for Professor Talbot, and then Dr Yen is going to brief me on the progress of—"

He stopped, and a horrified look emerged on his face. He looked over at Jamie, his eyes wide.

"It's OK," said Jamie, gently. "They know about the Lazarus Project."

Matt let out a huge sigh. "Oh, that's good," he said, breathlessly. "I'm sorry, I just get so excited."

"It's great that you do," said Larissa. "You might want to be a bit more careful, outside of the people in this room, though."

Matt nodded.

"All right," said Jamie. "Let's get started then. Matt, is there anything you particularly want to see first?"

Matt looked at Jamie, a mischievous smile emerging on his open face.

"Did I hear someone say you had a plane?" he asked.

*

Jamie woke the next morning feeling deeply conflicted.

The prospect of spending several hours on the cellblock again, as Major Turner picked up the interrogation of Valentin Rusmanov, was not the most appealing, especially when his mind was dominated by the Field Investigation Team, who were somewhere out there looking for any clues that Frankenstein was still alive. But his own conversation with the youngest Rusmanov brother had gone better than he or, he suspected, anyone else had expected, and he felt that he had proved himself again, to Admiral Seward and the others.

He showered quickly, and returned to find a message from Admiral Seward beeping on his portable console, a message telling him to attend a briefing in the Ops Room. This had become such a regular occurrence since he had been placed on the Zero Hour Task Force that it no longer even qualified as surprising, or disconcerting. He simply got dressed, then headed towards the lift that would take him up through the Loop.

Jamie walked into the Ops Room expecting to see at least some of the Zero Hour Operators gathered in the large oval space, but was surprised to find only two men waiting for him. Admiral Seward and Major Turner were huddled round one of the grey desks; both looked up at him as he entered, and he fought the immediate urge to check his watch. He knew that, for once, he wasn't late.

"Lieutenant Carpenter," said Seward, nodding in his direction. "Over here, please."

"Sir," replied Jamie, and walked over to join the two men.

They were gathered round a schematic drawing, a complicated-looking maze of lines and blocks that meant nothing to Jamie.

"Tell Mr Carpenter what you just told me, Paul," said the Director.

Major Turner gave Seward a quizzical look, but did as he was ordered.

"The investigation into the leak within the Communications Division was concluded early this morning," said Major Turner. "This diagram represents what I think we all suspected. There is a spy inside the Department."

Gentle fingers of ice crawled up Jamie's spine. "What is it?" he asked. "The diagram?"

"It's a ghost user," replied Turner. "A user on the mainframe that doesn't correspond to an actual Operator, or any of the support staff. It lives inside the code that keeps the systems running. It's been recording every change to any file on the system for at least three months, including the call logs and the security servers. It's been tracking everything."

"How?" asked Jamie, incredulous. "Why didn't we see it until now?"

"Because it's extremely clever," replied Turner. "Whenever a user logs out of the system, it takes their place, appearing in all the logs to still be them. It runs for a minute or so, searching and logging changes. Then it disappears, and waits for another user to log out, and repeats. Over and over. The time difference is so minimal that even if you compare the user logs with the CCTV, you would barely notice the anomaly. It's just been quietly going about its business, recording every single thing that happens on our system, and dumping a report out to a secure drop box every hour."

"Who has access to the drop box?"

"Impossible to know. It's an online file server; no traceable IP addresses, no way to follow who is accessing it. Like I said, very clever."

"Have you killed it?" asked Jamie.

"That's what we're trying to decide," said Admiral Seward. "Obviously, that was our first instinct. But Major Turner has suggested that there might be a way we can use it to find out who is behind it."

"By doing what?" asked Jamie.

"By feeding false data into the system, and seeing who responds to it," said Turner. "We can schedule it so we can eliminate people from suspicion, Operators who are off-base, or who are physically not near a computer. Narrow it down until we find them."

"I think you should kill it," said Jamie, firmly. "It's still going to be recording everything else, along with the false data. That's too dangerous, surely?"

"That's what Major Turner and I have to discuss," said Seward. "But the last time there was a spy in Department 19, three descendants of the founders were killed, including your father. That cannot be allowed to happen again."

Jamie felt the ground move beneath him at the mention of his dad. He tried not to think about him, wherever possible, for very different reasons than before the night his mother had been kidnapped and Frankenstein had rescued him. Then, it had been shame, and hatred; now it was pure grief.

"I would hope," said Major Turner, fixing his glacial stare on Jamie, "that I don't need to tell you that this information cannot leave this room. I would prefer you not to have been told, but Admiral Seward feels that since you were already aware of the possibility of a spy, it was better that you know the facts. Now that you do, I hope you can see that any attempt to uncover the spy will be utterly compromised if word of their existence gets out?"

"I get it," said Jamie. "You can trust me."

"So Henry assures me," said Turner, casting a glance at the Director.

There was a heavy silence for several seconds, as the three men considered the implications of what had been said.

We're tied together, thought Jamie. *The three of us. We're the only ones who know about this.*

Then a chill ran up his spine, and he physically shivered.

What if it's Major Turner? What if he's the spy? He's the Security Officer, just like Thomas Morris was. He'd be under orders to search for himself. He could do whatever he wanted to throw us off the trail.

The thought was nauseating, and Jamie forced it away. The pale, stoical former SAS Sergeant was many things, terrifying not the least of them, but he was as loyal to Blacklight as anyone; he was married to a descendant of the founders, to Henry Seward's sister no less, and his son was a serving Operator.

No way it's him. It just can't be. So who the hell is it?

"There is a second matter I need to raise,' said Seward, and Jamie refocused on the two men in the room with him. "It concerns you both, for different reasons."

The Director picked up the console which controlled the Ops Room's facilities and pressed a series of keys. The giant screen, which covered the majority of the flat wall at one end of the room, burst into life. The Department 19 crest appeared, then the system ran through its series of automatic safety checks.

Not much point in it doing them now, is there? thought Jamie.

The home screen of the Blacklight system appeared: a series of folders and file trees, above a complicated dashboard of controls and programs. Seward clicked more keys, and an audio program loaded, filling the screen with a long waveform track and a series of control buttons.

"This was left on my secure line overnight," said Admiral Seward. "It's from the Field Investigation Team."

He clicked the PLAY button, and a voice boomed out through the Ops Room.

"Operator Ellis, Christian, NS303, 47-J, coding in. Commanding officer, Field Investigation Team 27-R. Twelve-hour status report, submitted at 0055 hours, January 22nd. Report begins. A spectroscopic survey of ninety-five miles of the Northumberland coastline, a value suggested by the atmospheric and oceanic conditions present on the date of the disappearance of Colonel Frankenstein, proved negative. There is no evidence, analytical or anecdotal, to suggest that Colonel Frankenstein returned to the British mainland, either alive or dead. Analysis of the tidal patterns around Lindisfarne on the night in question, along with general oceanic conditions present at the time, confirmed the possibility of Colonel Frankenstein having been washed out to sea, as the currents break around the island of Lindisfarne on a sharp east–west line. Such conditions could have sent the Colonel out to sea, while returning the lycanthrope to land.

As a result of said information, my team were despatched to the main home ports of the fishing fleets of the North Sea, as rescue by a passing boat appeared to be the only likely remaining survival option for Colonel Frankenstein. Negative reports were filed from all the main Belgian and Swedish ports. However, anecdotal evidence provided by the residents of Cuxhaven, in northern Germany, described the appearance of a large figure of unknown origin, who arrived in the town aboard a small fishing boat named the Furchtlos. *The vessel is currently at sea, so questioning her crew has proved impossible thus far. In my opinion, this represents the only viable lead we currently have. I am therefore formally requesting that FTB approval be secured, so that we might officially enter German territory, and continue our search. Report ends."*

*

The array of speakers positioned around the Ops Room fell silent, as the audio file reached its end.

"Have you spoken to the FTB? Are the Germans going to help?" asked Jamie, his voice trembling.

"They have already granted permission for the team to enter their territory," said Seward. "I've transmitted that to Major Ellis. They should be on the ground by now."

Jamie's head spun. His heart had felt as though it might break when the voice had announced that there was nothing to suggest that Frankenstein had ever been returned to the mainland; in his mind, that was the likeliest conclusion, that if they were to find him, they would find him somewhere in northern England, maybe hurt, or incapacitated, or even captured by vampires.

Jamie had not allowed for the possibility that his friend could have been washed the other way, out into the cold vastness of the North Sea. He would not have believed that it would be possible for anyone to survive more than a few minutes in those waters, but then Frankenstein was hardly just anybody; he was ageless, apparently immortal, and if anyone might have survived such an ordeal, Jamie believed it would be him.

But if he was put ashore in Germany, thought Jamie, *if the person the townspeople are talking about really was him, then why hasn't he made contact? Why hasn't he told us to come and get him?*

"Let me go and help them," said Jamie. "I can be there in an hour. Please."

Major Turner rolled his eyes, and Jamie was filled with a sudden compulsion to shove his thumbs against them until they burst like balloons. He fought it back, and looked pleadingly at Admiral Seward.

"No, Jamie," replied the Director, although he had the decency to at least make it appear as though it had been a difficult decision for him to make. "We've been through this. Not while the interrogation is ongoing. You told me you understood that it takes priority; were you lying to me?"

Jamie tried to quell the rage, the familiar, joyous, black-red rage that was threatening to burst from the pit of his stomach and consume him.

"No, sir," he replied, through gritted teeth. "I wasn't lying to you."

"So you do understand that Valentin's interrogation takes priority?"

"Yes, sir."

"And that the Field Investigation Team are perfectly capable of following this lead without your assistance?"

"Yes, sir."

"Good," said Seward, smiling. "Then we are in agreement. I promised you I would keep you up to date with their progress, Jamie. I never told you that you would get to take part. Remember that."

"I will, sir," spat Jamie.

"Fantastic," replied the Director. "In which case, we should be on our way to the detention level. The others will be waiting for us. But before we go, I need to give something to you both."

Jamie glanced over at Paul Turner, whose gaze didn't so much as flicker from his commanding officer's.

"The two of you haven't always seen eye to eye," said Seward. "That's OK. If I wanted robots instead of Operators, I'd have the Science Division working on them now. I haven't always seen eye to eye with either of you myself. But until we find the ghost user, we are going to have to trust each other like never before. After Julian, things got bad, and if this gets out, they could get bad again.

And we have to allow for the possibility that the person we're looking for knows we're looking for them, and may take action against us. With that in mind, I want you both to have these."

Admiral Seward picked up two laminated cards from his desk and handed one to each of the Operators standing before him. Jamie took his, and looked down at it. A ten-digit combination of letters and numbers was printed on the card in plain black text.

"Sir, what is this?" asked Paul Turner.

"It's the Director level override code," replied Seward. "It's the key to the entire Loop. Use it only if you have to."

"This is highly irregular, sir," said Turner, frowning at the card in his hand.

"I know it is, Paul," said Seward. "But the time may come when the situation changes too quickly for you to seek my approval to act. Or something may happen to me which means that you can't. Either way, take them, both of you, and hope you don't need them."

'Yes, sir," said Major Turner, putting the card carefully in his pocket.

Jamie didn't reply; he was still staring at the numbers, a chill climbing up his spine as he thought about the awesome power they represented, and the incredible faith Admiral Seward was showing by giving them to him.

"Jamie," said the Director, sharply, and this time he did look up. "Did you hear me?"

"Yes, sir," Jamie replied. "Loud and clear, sir."

The three men journeyed down to the detention level in silence.

To Jamie, it felt as though the plastic card was about to burn a hole through the pocket of his uniform, presenting itself for all to see, and there was more than a little bit of him that would have loved that to happen. Once they were through the double airlock, they met the rest of the Zero Hour Task Force, who were waiting patiently outside the guard office.

As they approached, Cal Holmwood studied the looks on the faces of the three men, and raised one eyebrow towards Admiral Seward, who gave him the briefest shake of the head, so brief it was almost non-existent.

"Morning," said Jack Williams. The levity in his voice was forced; he could see that there was tension between the late arrivals.

"Morning," said Admiral Seward, sharply. "Let's get on with this, shall we? Paul?"

Major Turner nodded, and led them down the corridor to Valentin Rusmanov's cell.

The ancient vampire was lying on his bed, reading a paperback book, the title of which was in a language that Jamie didn't recognise. Valentin, who Jamie and the rest of the Task Force knew full well could hear their individual heartbeats from the moment they exited the airlock, peered over the top of the book and smiled, as though surprised to see them appear beyond the ultraviolet barrier he had already proven so conclusively was useless.

"Gentlemen," he exclaimed. "What a pleasure. I had forgotten we were continuing our discussion this morning."

There was silence from the line of Operators, and Valentin's grin widened.

"Oh, dear," he said, softly. "I sense tension in the ranks. Did someone forget to lock the doors last night before you went to bed?"

"Valentin Rusmanov," said Major Turner, giving no indication of having heard the vampire's comment. "We are here to continue our interview with you, as agreed. May I enter and speak with you?"

"Of course, my dear Major," said Valentin, sitting up and placing his book aside. "Let's have at it, by all means."

The vampire stood up from his bed, stretched his long, slender arms above his head, then let them drop back down to his sides. He walked quickly across the cell, and sat down in one of the chairs. Major Turner stepped through the barrier, and lowered himself slowly into the other.

"Fire away, Major Turner," said Valentin, smiling broadly.

"Thank you," said Turner, his politeness both impeccable and obviously false. "Mr Rusmanov, your late brother, Alexandru, was responsible for the sequence of events that led to Thomas Morris betraying this Department. To the best of your knowledge, was that an isolated incident, or have vampires attempted to infiltrate Blacklight at other times in the past?"

"That, Major Turner," replied Valentin, "is an excellent question. Excellent."

"Would you care to answer it?" said Turner.

"I'm just considering the best way to do so," replied Valentin. "Your use of the word 'attempted' implies that you are asking about plots to infiltrate your Department that were unsuccessful, and I must confess I don't know about any such plots."

A chill ran up Jamie's spine, and he looked over at Admiral Seward. The Director didn't flinch, didn't so much as move a muscle, but his face had drained of all colour; he looked suddenly like a ghost.

"I'm sorry," said Major Turner. "Are you suggesting that you have knowledge of *successful* attempts to infiltrate us? Beyond the case of Thomas Morris?"

Valentin leant back in his chair, and smiled cruelly.

"My dear Major," he said, softly, "I do not know everything, so

I cannot be sure of every spy that has been placed in your midst. But what I am telling you, what I know for an absolute fact, is that my brother Valeri has had at least one agent inside your Department at all times for the last sixty-five years."

40

VISION QUEST, PART III

The man who was calling himself Robert Smith waited as patiently as he was able for Adam to finish his cigarette. When it was little more than a glowing stub between his fingers, Adam dropped it to the floor, ground it beneath the sole of his shoe and continued his story.

"I never found out what happened to Emily," he said. "Never knew whether she left me, or whether she killed herself. The way she had been talking, the things she said, things that I didn't notice at the time, make me think the latter. She loved me, I know that with all my heart, and I don't believe it was me she was tired of; it was life itself. But to this day, I still don't know. And not knowing has been the worst part.

"When she was gone, I lost myself for a while. I drifted into this circle of vampires in the Tenderloin, savages really, who killed and maimed for sport, not even for sustenance. I trawled the streets of San Francisco with them, and I did things I can never be forgiven for, for which even what was done to me later is not punishment

494

enough. I killed, and tortured, and I drank from humans for the first time in my life.

"And I learnt why most vampires are incapable of stopping themselves from committing the horrors they do: because there is nothing more powerful, more intoxicating, more overwhelming, than running human blood. It made me feel like a god, and I took my anger and my pain out on men and women who didn't deserve it. I'll never forgive myself for the things I did; thankfully, I was stopped before I was able to do more harm."

"What do you mean, stopped?" asked Smith. "Stopped by who?"

"We were living in a tenement building in the Tenderloin. The place had been abandoned for years, and there were about fifty of us in there, like rats. One morning, about ten minutes after the sun had come up, the door was blown off its hinges, and suddenly the building was full of black figures, firing weapons I'd never seen before. Vampires were exploding all around me, bursting into flames, and I was running, trying to get away. Someone was screaming 'NS9! NS9!' over and over again, and then something sharp slammed into my leg, and when I woke up, I was somewhere else."

"Where?"

"I have no idea. I was on the floor of a glass room, a cube really, in a laboratory. There were doctors in white suits and masks staring at me, and then this one doctor, a tall guy with grey hair, even though he couldn't have been more than forty, pressed a button on a handset and the cube was filled with ultraviolet light. Every millimetre of my skin caught fire instantly, and I screamed until my vocal cords were burned away. I fell to the floor as the purple light dissolved me, and the last thing I saw was the grey-haired doctor making notes as he watched me die.

"Then there was a light, and more pain, and I opened my eyes, and I nearly died again from shock. My body was a skeleton, blood was gushing on to me from vents in the ceiling of the cube, and as I watched, my muscles and skin were growing round the bones. The pain was indescribable. I screamed for mercy, screamed for it to be over, and then eventually it was, and I was myself again. Then one of the doctors fired a tranquilliser dart through a hole in the cube, and there was nothing.

"When I woke up the second time, I was chained to the back of a glass cube, which was almost the same as the first one, but had two big differences. This one had no front wall, and it was outside. I was in a desert, a lot like the one we're sat in now, and the sun was minutes away from rising over the mountains in front of me. The doctors were gathered around with their notebooks and their instruments, and the grey-haired man was standing beside the cube, looking at me. I pleaded with him, I begged for mercy, I asked him why he was doing this to me, and do you know what he did?"

"What?" asked Smith, his voice trembling.

"He smiled at me," spat Adam. "Smiled at me, then carried right on making notes. Then he watched as the sun came over the horizon, and the light crept towards the cube, bit by bit. When it reached my feet, they started to burn. By the time it reached my waist my legs were gone below the knees and I was hanging in the manacles around my wrists, my mind completely gone, driven away by the pain. I stayed conscious until it burned through my chest, and then I died. And then they revived me again."

"They collected your ashes," said Smith, quietly. "Didn't they? Soaked them in blood, and brought you back."

Adam nodded.

"Nothing they did ever pierced my heart," he said. "They were very careful not to destroy me. Just kill me."

"Jesus," said Smith. "I've never heard of anything like that. To kill someone twice and bring them back is inhumane."

A look of surprise passed over Adam's face. "I don't think you understand," he said. "They didn't kill me twice. They killed me hundreds and hundreds of times."

Adam rolled another cigarette, and this time Smith asked whether he could have one too. He lit the neat roll-up, took the first mouthful of smoke into his lungs and waited for his host to continue.

"The third time I don't even know what they did to me," said Adam. "They strapped me on to a gurney in the middle of the cube and injected me with something, a syringe of bright blue liquid. Nothing happened for about an hour, but then I started to feel pressure, like I was deep underwater. My limbs started to swell up, and I felt blood start to run from my ears and my nose. I passed out before it got too bad, but the last thing I remember is seeing my fingers burst."

"Jesus Christ," whispered Smith.

"They revived me again, and killed me again. They drowned me, dissolved me in acid, stabbed every part of my body with metal stakes apart from my heart, blew my limbs off with shotguns one at a time, put timed explosives under my skin and blew me to pieces, injected me with hundreds of drugs and chemicals. And every time, they brought me back and did it again. And again. I don't know how many times, I don't how long for. It felt like years, but I don't know if it was. The doctors came and went, new ones appearing, others disappearing, but the one constant was the man with the grey hair. He was there every time I died, and every time I was reborn, watching me, smiling at me, making his damned notes."

Adam spat on the ground, and crushed out his cigarette.

"One day I woke up and I was in the cube in the desert, just before dawn. I don't know how many times they had burned me by then, so I wasn't surprised. I didn't even protest; I knew what was going to happen, and what it was going to feel like, and I could prepare myself for it. It was the new things, the drugs and the chemicals, that scared me. And by then I had realised that begging was useless. So I watched the sun rise over the mountains, I watched it crawl across the floor of the desert and I braced myself as it reached my toes. And nothing happened."

"What?" asked Smith. "Nothing happened? What do you mean, nothing happened?"

"Nothing happened. The sunlight rolled up my legs, and nothing happened. Across my body, and nothing happened. And eventually, across my face, and nothing happened. I hadn't felt the sun on my face for more than twenty years, and I started to weep, and I barely noticed when one of the doctors raised their dart gun, and fired it into my leg.

"I woke up some time later, and I knew immediately that something was different. The surface beneath me wasn't the smooth glass of the cube; it was cracked, and ridged, and uneven. I opened my eyes, to see concrete and spray paint. I was lying in the doorway of an abandoned building. And when I stood up, I saw that it was the building I had been taken from, however many weeks or months earlier."

"They put you back?" asked Smith. "Why would they do that?"

"I don't know," said Adam. "I've asked myself thousands of times. Maybe they were done with me; maybe they couldn't learn anything more. Or maybe they had found what they wanted, and I had just been lucky enough to survive it. I don't know. But they let me go. And I was cured."

Smith sat back against the wall of the cabin, his mind reeling.

There's a cure, he thought. *It exists, it's really real. Somewhere out there, there's a cure.*

"I tried to fly," Adam continued. "But I couldn't. I tried to lift an abandoned car on the street in front of the building, but I couldn't move it. Finally, I tried to lower my fangs, and nothing happened. But to be honest, I knew before I tried anything; I just *felt* different.

"So I ran, again. I grabbed a suitcase worth of my old life from the house I had shared with Emily, mostly photos, and I left San Francisco that day. I headed south, driving my car in the daytime, leaving the windows open all the way, feeling the sun on my skin, until I got to Caliente. I had the keys to this place – they were left to me when my grandfather died – and I moved in. I've been here ever since. And that's my story, Mr Smith. For what it's worth."

The two men sat silently for several long moments, one exhausted by the effort of telling the tale, the other digesting the implications of it. Eventually, it was Smith who spoke first.

"What cured you? Please tell me you know."

"I've no idea," said Adam, shaking his head, sadly. "I don't know what any of the drugs they gave me were, and I don't know which one of them was the cure. I'm sorry."

"Do you know where you were? Do you remember anything that could help me find the place they held you?"

"I don't. The inside was a laboratory, the outside was desert. It could have been anywhere. I'm sorry, I really am."

"Do you know anything that can help me? Anything at all?" Smith's voice was rising, as frustration spilled through him; he was so close, so close to the end of a quest that had taken him more than a year, and to be denied at this last stage was too much.

"I'm afraid not," Adam replied. "I'm sorry, I really am. But if it's any consolation, I still don't believe that's really why you're here."

"So what is?" exploded Smith. "Tell me, please! What the hell am I doing here?"

"You'll see soon enough," replied Adam, an odd smile on his face.

Smith looked at the man, and felt his heart lurch. Adam's outline was shimmering in the heat of the desert, the shape of his body appearing to have become fluid, like the edges of a drop of oil in water. He looked down the canyon, and watched as the vast expanse of the desert began to breathe, slowly, rhythmically, the landscape expanding and contracting, in and out, in and out. Smith looked back at Adam, and realised that the edges of his vision were becoming blurry, shot through with a kaleidoscope of brilliant colours.

Druggggggedd, his mind slurred. *Heee druuggggggged meee.*

"What… did you do… to me?" he managed to ask.

"Nothing bad," replied Adam. "And nothing I didn't do to myself."

Smith looked down at the cup he had placed beside his feet, then the concentrated psilocybin extract that Adam had added to both their coffees overwhelmed his rational mind, and the two men spiralled into their vision.

They wandered across the pulsing desert, holding hands as they walked, their minds' understanding of reality usurped by the psychedelic extract flooding through their brains. They talked, about nothing and everything, conversations that slipped away the moment they were concluded, lost in the wilderness, never to be remembered. They laughed, and on several occasions, they cried. At one point they danced furiously beneath the diffusing, liquid sun, danced as though their lives depended on it, guttural chants spilling from their mouths.

After an unknowable amount of time, they reached a cave.

The opening was low and narrow, little more than a wide crack in a red rock wall at the bottom of a short gulley. They stood in front of it for a long time, until Adam took Smith's hand and led him forward. Smith resisted: he didn't want to go inside. He was incapable of expressing why the dark opening filled him with dread, but it did; his disorientated brain was screaming at him that if he went in there, he would never come out.

"Scared," he managed to slur, when Adam turned back to see why he was resisting.

Then Adam did something that Smith would not have been able to predict, even had his brain been functioning properly. The man stepped forward, and hugged Smith, wrapping his arms tightly round him.

"There's nothing to be scared of," he whispered. "This is why you're here."

Then he took his visitor by the hand, and led him into the cave.

As soon as Smith was inside the cave, a dark crevice of rock no more than five metres deep, his vision intensified. Starved of outside stimulus, his mind roared into overdrive; thick freshets of blood gushed down the cool rock walls of the cave, pooling at the bottom and creeping gradually across the floor to where the two men were standing. The dark black corners of the cave, where the light entirely failed to penetrate, shifted and moved in the corners of his eyes; dark shapes formed and dissolved, lurching towards the light then retreating, tantalisingly out of sight.

Then time seemed to freeze. The blood that was descending the walls stopped, hanging on the smooth surfaces in defiance of gravity, and the dark corners fell still. Smith stood, his hand tightly clenched in Adam's, his heart and mind racing, the darkness surrounding him, and waited.

After what could have been eons or thirty seconds, a shape appeared at the rear of the cave, a pale smudge that slowly coalesced into the form of a teenage boy, who walked slowly forward until he was two metres away from the two visionaries.

The boy was tall and slender, and dressed all in black. One side of his neck was a mess of scar tissue, his face pale and soft-featured, almost feminine.

Smith's heart accelerated until he was sure it would burst in his chest, as his mind teetered on the brink of collapse. He did the only thing he could think of.

"Hello," he said, his words echoing in the tight confines of the cave.

The boy bared his teeth, and then, to Smith's utter horror, his eyes flooded a sickening, glowing red, and two white fangs slid smoothly from behind his upper lip.

"Leave me," the teenager hissed. "You're too late."

Then he backed away, disappearing into the shadows so quickly and completely it was as though he had never been there at all. Smith opened his mouth and screamed, a high, wavering sound tinged with madness, and he didn't stop until Adam dragged him forcibly out of the cave and laid him down on the hot desert sand.

"You're safe," Adam whispered, as Smith's breathing began to slow, and the colour began to creep back into his face.

He had been as white as a ghost when Adam pulled him into the sunlight, and this had scared Adam, who was extremely experienced at handling the psilocybin trip and knew the warning signs to look for, more than the screaming itself. It was the face of

502

a man who had come to believe what he was seeing was real. "You're safe. You're in the Californian desert, just outside of the town of Caliente. You're near my home. You drove here in your own car. I'm with you. You're safe."

When Smith was calm, when the colour had returned to his face and the clarity to his eyes, Adam asked who the boy was, and Smith recoiled in shock, as though he had been slapped.

"You saw him too?" Smith asked, incredulous.

"As clearly as I see you," Adam replied. "Shared visions are rare things. They're usually important. Who was he?"

Smith sat up, and Adam took half a step away; the look of anguish on Smith's face was almost too much for him to bear.

"What was that?" Smith asked, his voice cracked and broken from screaming. "In the cave. Was it real? Tell me."

"I don't know," replied Adam. Fear was creeping through him, the feeling of having unleashed something he should perhaps have left alone. "It might have been, it might not. It could be something that has happened, or something that's going to. Who was he?"

The man who was calling himself Robert Smith took a deep breath.

"His name is Jamie Carpenter," he replied. "He's my son."

41

AND A TORCH TO LIGHT THE WAY

"Say that again," asked Paul Turner.

Valentin smiled. "I have been assured by people I trust that my brother has had informants inside Blacklight for more than half a century, Major Turner. As I said, I cannot speculate about anyone else who might have managed to infiltrate your little organisation."

"You have evidence to back up what you're suggesting?" asked Turner, his voice low.

"This is not a courtroom, Mr Turner," replied Valentin. "You asked me a question, I answered it. Whether you believe me or not is hardly my concern."

Turner stared at the ancient vampire with his glacial grey eyes, a look that would have sent chills running up the spines of most men. But Valentin Rusmanov was not most men; he was, in fact, not a man at all, and so he merely smiled.

"If you're waiting for me to crumble under your fearsome gaze, Mr Turner, I suspect we may be here for some time. I would recommend that you continue with your questions."

Major Turner held the vampire's gaze for a moment longer, then looked away. His pale face remained as unreadable as always.

"Do you know the names of any of the men or women your brother mentioned to you?" he asked.

"I'm afraid not," replied Valentin.

"Ranks? Dates? Anything that would help to identify them?"

"No," replied the vampire. "Sorry."

"Then you will presumably not take offence at my suggestion that this could simply be a move on your part designed to sow fear and doubt within this organisation?"

"I take no offence," said Valentin. "And I will certainly not think any less of you if that is the conclusion you reach. I'm sure investigating what I've told you will involve a large amount of predominantly tedious work, and I will understand if you do not have the appetite for it."

The vampire was now openly goading Major Turner; it was obvious to everyone who was watching, including Jamie.

Keep calm, he thought, staring at the Security Officer. *If you react, you're letting him win. Keep calm.*

"My appetites are my own business, Mr Rusmanov," replied Turner, calmly. "Unlike yours, which you inflict on innocent men and women." A flicker of red crackled in the corners of the vampire's eyes, and Turner continued. "For the sake of clarification, do you possess any information regarding your brother Valeri's claim to have repeatedly infiltrated Blacklight? Beyond mere gossip, that is?"

Valentin narrowed his eyes, and shifted in his chair.

"No," he answered. "I do not."

"Thank you," said Major Turner. "Let's move on, shall we?"

Well done, thought Jamie. *Bloody brilliantly well done.*

A loud beep rang out through the cellblock corridor, and everyone turned to look at the source of the sound. Admiral Seward pulled his console from his pocket, checked the screen and then widened his eyes, fractionally.

"Carry on, please," he said, nodding at Turner. "Lieutenant Carpenter, a word, please."

"Yes, sir," replied Jamie, and followed the Director towards the airlock door. When they were both safely through and standing in the small alcove beside the lift, Seward passed his console to Jamie.

"Read it," he said.

Jamie took it from him, thumbed the control pad and watched the screen power up. He began to read the text that was filling the small rectangle.

FROM: Ellis, Christian (NS303, 47-J)
TO: Seward, Henry (NS303, 27-A)
The trail of the individual suspected of being Colonel Frankenstein remained clear and verifiable as far south as Paris. Witness statements are attached. Last likely sighting was four weeks ago (Christmas Eve) at Notre Dame Cathedral. Investigation suggests that he is, or was, in the company of Jean-Luc Latour (V/A2/87), a Priority Level 2 vampire. Further investigation, including attempts to locate Latour, has proved fruitless. Trail appears to now be cold. Request permission to return to base.

Jamie read the message a second time, so he could be sure that his eyes weren't deceiving him.

"They're coming home?" he asked, incredulous. "That's it? They're giving up?"

"Their investigation is concluded, Jamie," replied Admiral Seward. "I asked them to ascertain whether Colonel Frankenstein was still alive. They have been unable to do so."

506

"It's obvious he's still alive," said Jamie. "Surely it's obvious?"

Seward sighed heavily. "I want him to be alive too, Jamie. I really do. But the Field Investigation Team are coming home. They've done their job, and I've granted their request."

"What about this vampire?" asked Jamie. "Latour?"

Seward took his console back from Jamie, pressed a series of keys, then handed it back. Jamie looked down at the file that had opened on the screen.

Subject name:	LATOUR, JEAN-LUC
Species:	VAMPIRE
Priority level:	A2
Known associates:	VALERIANO, DANTE
	FRANKENSTEIN, VICTOR
Most recent sighting:	18/5/2002
Whereabouts:	PARIS (UNSPECIFIED)

NOTES:
- One of the oldest vampires in Paris, and possibly in all of France.
- Believed to have been turned circa 1900, by an unknown vampire.
- Known to frequent Saint-Germain-des-Prés, the Marais, the Rive Gauche.
- Often sighted in the company of artists, writers and other notable cultural figures.
- Kills to feed and for pleasure, without discrimination.

Jamie made a decision.

It took no thinking whatsoever, and the possible consequences of the decision didn't even occur to him; it was simply one of those rare, liberating moments when you know exactly what you need to do, that there are no other options.

"I'm going to Paris to find him, sir," he said. "I really hope I can go with your permission, but either way, I'm going."

He braced himself for the explosion, but it didn't come. Admiral Seward was staring at him with a look on his face that was full of empathy, and not a little admiration.

"Permission granted," the Director replied.

Jamie fought back the urge to throw himself at Admiral Seward and wrap his arms round the greying, exhausted-looking man.

"Thank you, sir," he said. "Really. Thank you."

Seward nodded. "Assemble a five-man team from the active roster," he said. "Then come back to me for final authorisation. Do not leave without my go, is that understood?"

"Yes, sir," said Jamie. "I'm on it."

"All right then," said Seward. "Go and see to it. Dismissed."

The Director headed back towards the airlock, and stepped through the first door. As it swung slowly shut, he turned to look at Jamie, through the narrowing gap. He looked as though there was something else he wanted to say, the muscles around his mouth twitching as though he was about to speak, but then the door rolled shut with a loud *thunk* and the Director was gone.

Jamie stared after him for a moment, then turned and walked across to the lift. He stepped inside the metal car, pulling his own console from his pocket as he did so. As the lift ascended, taking him up towards Level 0, he quickly typed out and sent a message to every Operator on the active roster.

The lift doors opened, and Jamie strode down the corridor towards the Ops Room, wondering who would be the first to show up.

It turned out to be Angela Darcy, although Jack Williams was less than a minute behind her.

The pretty, deadly former spy strolled into the Ops Room as though she was taking a Sunday morning constitutional, smiled at Jamie and sat down at one of the desks. He nodded in return, about to say hello to her, when the door opened again and Jack Williams bustled through it.

"I came as soon as I got your message," he said, slightly out of breath. "What's going on?"

"Let's wait and see who else turns up," replied Jamie, a broad smile on his face. He was thrilled to see two of the Operators he respected the most in Department 19 answer his call. "I'll tell you all about it then."

"OK," said Jack, and sat down next to Angela. She smiled at her squad leader, and the two of them began to chat, as Jamie watched the door.

Larissa was the next to arrive, floating rapidly through the door. She threw a look of concern towards Jamie, then saw Angela and Jack looking at her, and slid to the ground. She walked over to Jamie, and leant in close to his ear.

"What's the emergency?" she asked, her voice low, her breath hot in his ear. "I came as soon as I could."

"It's Frankenstein," he whispered. "I'm going to find him."

"Then I'm coming with you," she said, firmly.

He smiled at her, a thin curl of his mouth that seemed full of pain, rather than happiness. "We'll see," he said. "Go and sit down. I'm going to give it five more minutes to see if anyone else turns up."

She regarded him with a look of concern, but did as he suggested; she crossed the large semi-circular room and sat down, slightly stiffly, next to Angela and Jack. There was an initial icy moment, but then Angela said hello to her, and she was absorbed into their conversation.

The door opened again, and two Operators he recognised but didn't really know walked through it. The first was a woman in her early twenties called Claire Lock, a former marksman with the Metropolitan Police's elite SO15 unit whom Jamie had chatted to in the mess once or twice. Behind her was a tall, handsome man in his late twenties, who Jamie knew was named Dominique Saint-Jacques.

The quiet, dark-skinned Frenchman had been a legionnaire before Blacklight had recruited him; it had been quite a coup, as the elite soldiers of mainland Europe almost always joined the FTB, the German equivalent of Department 19. But Dominique had an English grandfather, and that had swayed his decision. He had given Blacklight many reasons to be grateful for the quirk of ancestry that had brought him to the Loop; Admiral Seward had once told Jamie that he considered Dominique as fine an Operator as any currently serving in the Department. The fact that he was a native French speaker only made his presence in the Ops Room all the more enticing for Jamie.

That's one, he thought. *Without a doubt. Three more to pick.*

The door opened again, and Kate and Shaun Turner arrived through it at the same time. Kate smiled at Jamie, a look that was not quite convincing, and seemed to him to be shot through with concern. Shaun nodded respectfully at him, and he returned the gesture. They made their way over to the others, sat down and joined in with the low murmur of conversation as Jamie checked his watch.

Ten minutes since I sent out the message, he noted. *Can't wait much longer.*

He managed to force himself to wait five more minutes, before he locked the Ops Room door and addressed the seven Operators who had responded to his call.

"This briefing refers to a Priority Level 1 Operation," he said. "You all know what that means. What I'm about to tell you doesn't leave this room; you can assume that anyone else who needs to know already knows. Clear?"

There were a series of nodded heads and low murmurs of agreement.

"OK," he said, and continued. "Yesterday, Admiral Seward despatched a Field Investigation Team to the north-east coast, with a single objective: to ascertain whether Colonel Frankenstein may still be alive."

Larissa and Kate both gasped, and looked immediately at each other. Jack Williams' eyes widened, as did those of Claire Lock. Dominique Saint-Jacques smiled at Jamie, while Shaun Turner and Angela Darcy remained completely impassive.

"I know what you're thinking," said Jamie. "Why now, right? The team was despatched following the discovery of a body in a cave at the rear of a beach at a place called Bamburgh, in Northumberland. A body that has since been confirmed to be that of a lycanthrope, and which was washed ashore less than ten miles north of Lindisfarne island."

"My God," said Kate, softly. "Is it the—"

"We think so," said Jamie. "For those of you who weren't there,

511

or haven't read the reports, Frankenstein fell to what was assumed to be his death while fighting a werewolf that was a follower of Alexandru Rusmanov, a werewolf that fell with him. The body that was washed ashore had a broken neck, and human fingermarks on its throat; it was killed after it, and Frankenstein, fell over the edge of the cliffs."

"Wait a minute," said Jack Williams. "If Colonel Frankenstein was alive, why wouldn't he have made contact with us?"

"I don't know, Jack," replied Jamie. "And I don't know whether he's alive or not. The Field Investigation Team tracked eyewitness accounts of a man matching his description from a small fishing port in northern Germany, where witnesses claim the man in question came ashore from one of the boats that work the North Sea, as far south as Paris, where the trail ended. The last confirmed sighting of this person, whoever he is, was on Christmas Eve."

"So what's the plan?" asked Angela. Her voice was even, the voice of a professional.

"The Director has authorised me to lead a team to Paris to investigate the whereabouts of this person, to try and locate him. I will be conducting this operation on the assumption that the man we're looking for is Colonel Frankenstein, and that he is in considerable danger from the vampire he was sighted in the company of, a Priority Level 2 vamp called Latour. The primary objective will be to find him and bring him home. All other considerations will be secondary. If that doesn't sit well with any of you, then thanks for listening, and no hard feelings. You know where the door is."

It was a gamble, he knew, exposing his personal interest in the mission, and the conclusion he had already reached, without remotely adequate evidence. He would not be offended if any of the Operators in the room were uneasy at volunteering for what he had essentially just admitted was a personal crusade, but he would also not have any of them risk their lives without being in full possession of the facts.

Nobody moved.

Jamie waited for a long moment, then sighed.

"Thank you," he said, meaning it. "I'm sure I don't need to fill any of you in on my personal history with Colonel Frankenstein, or the circumstances that led to his apparent death. So for me, it's as simple as this: if he's alive, I'm going to find him. I don't care if I have to destroy every vampire in France to do it. Is that clear?"

There was a second chorus of agreement, and Jamie felt his heart lift as he looked at the seven faces staring coolly back at him.

I would walk into the fire with any of them, he thought. *Gladly too.*

"It's a five-man team," said Jamie, and felt a stab of guilt as the seven Operators glanced around at one another. "I'm sorry it has to come to this, but I had no idea how many people might show up, with all the squads so flat out at the moment. There's nothing personal in my decision, I want you all to know that."

He saw smiles break out on the faces of Kate and Larissa, and felt a stab of pain at what he was about to do. As far as they were concerned, it was going to be the two of them, plus two of the others. He didn't blame them for thinking that, but they had no true understanding of the rage that was burning inside his chest when he thought about the possibility of getting Frankenstein back, and he didn't want them around if things in Paris went the way he expected them to.

"Dominique, I'd be grateful if you would be my second on this operation," he said. "How about it?"

He saw Kate and Larissa's smiles falter, just a fraction, as the tall Frenchman eased himself to his feet. He strode over and clasped Jamie's hand.

"I'm in," he said. "Let's bring him home."

"Thank you," said Jamie. "I appreciate it."

Dominique nodded and stood beside Jamie, who looked out at the remaining Operators.

"Are you up for this, Jack?" asked Jamie. "I'd love to have you if you are." His friend leapt to his feet, and Jamie felt a grin threaten to burst across his face. He pushed it back, and gripped Jack's outstretched hand.

"Cheers, Jamie," said Jack, in a low voice, then took his place beside Dominique.

Jamie looked at the five remaining Operators, and felt his face flush with heat. Angela was looking at him with a curious expression on her face, as though she was more interested in what he was doing than whether or not he was going to pick her. Claire Lock was watching him with an even look, in which Jamie believed, or wanted to believe, at least, that he saw encouragement.

Shaun Turner was openly scowling at him, their conversation in the corridor the previous day clearly now long forgotten. And Kate and Larissa were staring at him with the colour draining from their faces, as though they had just entertained for the first time the reality that he might not choose them.

Don't do this to us, their expressions appeared to be saying. *Please don't. Not like this.*

"Claire," Jamie said. "I could really do with your help."

The former marksman shone a quite lovely smile in Jamie's direction, and got to her feet.

"You've got it," she said, shaking his hand briskly before joining the others.

He faced the four men and women who were left; faced three faces full of rapidly rising anger and one of complete detachment.

Do it, he thought. *Get it over with.*

"Angela," he said. He heard a tiny gasp emerge from Larissa, and watched as Kate put her hand over her mouth. The eyes of his two closest friends shone with betrayal; those of Shaun Turner merely blazed with anger. "What do you say?"

"I say yes, sir," she said, and slid slowly to her feet. She walked over to him and leant in beside his ear, so close that he could feel her warm breath against his skin. "You just made your life really, really difficult. You know that, right?"

"I know," replied Jamie, his voice barely audible. "Believe me, I know."

She pulled away, gave him the kind of smile that men spend their whole lives hoping to see a beautiful girl give them, and went and joined the rest of the team that Jamie had selected. He turned to face them, and they stood immediately to attention.

"Weapons and tactics briefing in the hangar in fifteen," he said. "I want wheels up within half an hour. Dismissed."

The four Operators filed quickly past him, and out of the Ops Room. He took a deep breath, and turned to face the three black-clad figures who remained in their seats.

"What the hell was that?" hissed Shaun Turner. "You told me we were cool, that you'd put Wallsend behind you, and you treat me like that?"

"Shaun—"

"I'm the best Operator in this room," spat Shaun, either not noticing or not caring about the look of hurt that appeared on Kate's face. "I'm twice the Operator you are, you spoilt little prick. You think your name gives you licence to behave like this? Well, to hell with that."

Turner bounced up out of his seat, and made as if to launch himself at Jamie.

He never got the chance.

Larissa was out of her seat quicker than any pair of human eyes in the room could follow, and was between the two men before Shaun even had the chance to tense his muscles to leap, her eyes blazing crimson, her fangs bursting into view.

"Don't even think about it, Shaun," she growled. "Just sit down next to Kate, there's a good boy."

Fury, naked and ugly, burst across Shaun's face, but he did as he was told. For all his confidence in his own abilities, confidence that was normally well justified, he knew he was no match for Larissa; the vampire girl could have killed him with one hand tied behind her back, without breaking a sweat. He sat back down heavily in his seat. Kate reached out a hand towards him, and he pushed it angrily away. The look on Kate's face broke Jamie's heart, and he heard Larissa growl again, a clear rumble of warning. Then she spun away from Kate and Shaun, and faced him, her eyes raging with dark red fire.

"After everything we've been through," she growled. "Everything we said to each other, you, me and Kate. You do this. How could you?"

"I'm sorry," said Jamie. "You have to know there's no one I'd rather have on my side than you, than both of you." He leant round Larissa and looked at Kate, who was staring at him with open pain on her face. "You have to believe me when I say that. But I don't want you to come on this mission with me. I meant what I said; if he's still alive, there's nothing living or dead that is going to stop me from bringing him home. I don't want to put the two of you in that position. And if things go bad over there, which I am fully expecting them to, I want to know that the two of you will look after each other. I want to know that you're safe."

Later, when the dust settled, Jamie would have given anything to be able to go back in time, and choose his words differently. But by then it was far too late.

"Shaun, the same goes for you," he continued. "If something happens to me, then I know you'll look after Kate. That's more important to me than whether or not you hate me right now. I'm sorry, but it just is. I don't expect you to understand."

The anger on Turner's face dissipated slightly; the deep red that had risen in his cheeks paled, until it was merely a virulent pink. He got up from his chair, and walked stiffly towards the door; as he passed Jamie, he paused and stared at him with a look that seemed to mostly be full of pity.

"You're making a huge mistake," he said, softly. "I don't think you realise it now, but you will. I promise you that much."

Then he strode across the room, and was gone.

Kate got to her feet, looking frantically between Jamie and the door.

"Go after him," said Jamie. "It's not you he's angry with. And I really am sorry, Kate. I just can't bear the thought of anything happening to you because of me, because of something I have to do. I hope you can forgive me one day."

A look of desperate misery flickered on Kate's face, and then she was moving, across the room and out of the door, leaving Jamie and Larissa alone.

"I know you think you're protecting me," she said, her red eyes looking at him with enormous affection. "But you're not. You're just hurting me. And I think you know that, deep down."

"I'm sorry," he replied. "I really am. I just need to know that you're going to be here when I get back, whatever happens. I need to be able to rely on that."

Larissa sighed, and the red disappeared so quickly from her eyes that it might never have been there.

"I'll be here," she replied, softly. "You know I'll be here. Go do what you have to do."

Jamie leant in and kissed her, hard. For a moment, there was no response from Larissa, but then she gave in; her lips parted, and she kissed him back, fiercely.

"Thank you," said Jamie, breaking the kiss. Three different words had screamed in his mind, but he pushed them away, for now at least.

"So what now?" sighed Larissa. "What happens next?"

"I go to Seward for final authorisation," said Jamie. "Then we fly to Paris, and I start destroying vampires until someone tells me something useful. After that, I don't know."

"All right," replied Larissa. "Go."

Jamie leant in and kissed her again, a hard, fast kiss full of passion. Then he pulled away from her, and strode across the Ops Room. As he put his hand on the handle of the door, Larissa called his name, and he turned back to her.

"Come back to me, Jamie," she said, softly. "OK?"

"I will," he replied. "You can count on it."

42

VISION QUEST, PART IV

LINCOLN COUNTY, NEVADA, USA

Julian Carpenter, the man who had been calling himself Robert Smith, sipped water from the glass the waitress had brought him. His dinner lay untouched in front of him; the burger looked good, but he had realised as soon as it had arrived that he had no appetite. His stomach was squirming at the thought of what he was about to do.

The quest he had embarked on more than a year before, the quest that had occupied his every waking moment since he had slipped unseen on to the Newark docks with a single small bag over his shoulder, had suddenly been rendered unimportant by the vision he had shared in the desert with the man he had crossed the country to find.

His desire to find a cure for vampirism, a cure that could return his wife to normal, that could bring an end to the cursed condition that had destroyed his life, had given him a single-mindedness he had come to rely on; he had allowed nothing else to matter, for what felt like as long as he could remember.

The sporadic information he had been able to gather, from

still-loyal friends in the supernatural Departments around the world, by using old aliases, old dead-drops and long-forgotten back doors, had reassured him that his son was safe, or at least as safe as it was possible to be when you were responsible for the death of the second oldest vampire in the world. But at least he was with Blacklight, and Julian was certain that Henry Seward would be looking after him.

And Marie as well, he thought. *I know he'll have looked after both of them.*

He had been in Savannah when word had reached him of his son's triumph on Lindisfarne. For the first time since the world had believed he had died, Julian Carpenter had got drunk: roaring, falling-down drunk, his heart pounding with pride and relief in equal measure, burning with the desire to break his cover, and go home. He had forced himself not to do so, but it had been touch and go.

He knew that Thomas Morris had been exposed as the true betrayer of Blacklight, and as the man who had framed him for crimes he had never committed. But he had let his friends and his family believe he was dead, and he couldn't predict with enough certainty how the Department would react to his reappearance. He wanted to go home, more than anything, but he could not take the chance that his welcome might be hostile, at least not until he had found what he was searching for.

But he now no longer cared if he exposed himself, or what the consequences of doing so might be. The vision in the cave had shaken him to his very core, and he was now every bit as anxious to make sure Jamie was all right as he was to continue his pursuit of a cure. Mercifully, both roads led to the same place, less than twenty miles from where he found himself.

He was sitting at a table in The Little A'Le'Inn, the modest restaurant and gift shop that accommodated the steady trickle of tourists that ventured to this remote part of the Nevada desert, lured by the small town of Rachel's proximity to the Holy Grail of American ufologists: the classified airbase at the heart of the White Sands test range that was known the world over as Area 51.

The base, built on the vast salt flat of Groom Lake, was where the US Air Force had developed and tested the U2 spy plane, the SR-71 Blackbird, the F-117A stealth fighter and any number of other black projects, projects carried out away from the watchful eyes of the American public, and all but the highest echelons of the American government. It was also, if the conspiracy theorists were to be believed, the place where the remains of an alien spaceship that crashed in Roswell, New Mexico in 1947 had been taken, where the extraterrestrial technology had been studied and incorporated into strange, angular aircraft that could apparently be regularly seen in the night skies around the base.

In the booth behind Julian, two teenagers were expounding on the subject of Area 51, their adolescent voices shot through with posed bravado and hushed caution.

"Groom is for the tourists," said the teenager directly behind Julian, a pale, acne-ridden boy of about seventeen, his long hair jutting out from a woollen beanie and descending over the shoulders of a black T-shirt printed with the slogan of an old TV show. *I Want to Believe* it stated, in urgent fluorescent green letters. "Papoose Lake, that's where the real action is. The S-4 facility. They've got an installation dug into the mountains there, goes a hundred storeys below ground. That's where they keep the greys."

The second teenager, a boy of similar age but hugely increased girth, with a voluminous black hoodie hiding the ripples and folds of his stomach, frowned.

"You saying they've got *live* greys down there?" he asked. "Roswell was sixty-five years ago, dude."

The first teenager rolled his eyes at the stupidity of the question, and sighed. "You're thinking about this all wrong. All wrong. Firstly, you don't know how long the greys live, man. You're thinking they're like us, but they're not. That's the whole point, right? Do you know what the average lifespan is on Zeta Reticuli? I know I don't. No one does. Secondly, you forgot about cryopreservation, dude. The greys that crashed at Roswell, you know some of them were hurt, right?"

"Right."

"Those ones, the injured ones, the government froze them, until it could experiment on the dead ones and the live ones and understand how they worked. *Then* they could thaw out the injured ones and make them better. That's cryopreservation."

"Like what they did to the colonial marines in *Aliens*?"

"Exactly."

"And Fry in *Futurama*?"

"You've got it."

"And Walt Disney?"

"Shut the hell up now, Jonny. Just eat your burger and be quiet."

Julian's face contorted into a sudden mask of misery. Jamie was roughly the same age as the two boys arguing behind him, and Julian wondered whether his son had a friend with whom he argued in such a familiar, friendly way. Two years a lifetime where teenagers were concerned; they regularly appeared to change their personalities completely overnight, and Julian was terrified that when the time came that he saw Jamie again, as it was vital for him to believe he would, he might no longer recognise his son.

He pushed Jamie from his mind. Even though the crazy, dangerous thing he was preparing himself to do he was doing for his son, he couldn't let himself think too hard about him; he needed his mind clear, and his instincts sharp, if he was going to survive the next few hours. So he thought instead about what the teenagers had been saying, and allowed a smile to rise on his face.

They've no idea how right they are, he thought. *They're wrong about what's down there, obviously, but they're right about Papoose Lake. It's where the real action is.*

Julian paid his bill and headed out of the restaurant. It was late afternoon, and the sky to the west was beginning to take on the first hues of evening, fingers of pale red that bled into the sky above the distant mountains. He climbed into his jeep, put it in gear and pulled out of the parking lot, throwing up a cloud of dust that hung in the air behind him. Thirty minutes later he was driving south on Groom Lake Road, towards the end of his long quest.

Julian Carpenter brought the jeep to a halt, in front of the warning signs that marked the entry to the Air Force Flight Test Center (Detachment 3), the strip of runway and collection of small buildings and hangars that the world knew as Area 51.

He had slowly made his way down the dirt road that led to the base, watchful for the cream-coloured pick-up trucks that patrolled the perimeter of the restricted area, waiting for the red and white signs that marked the border between the America that belonged to everyone, and the America that belonged to the government. They stood in front of him now, simple red text on white metal, warning him that going any further was a Federal offence, an act of trespass which the use of deadly force was authorised to prevent.

He scanned the desolate desert to his right and left, noting the black surveillance cameras standing on reinforced metal poles, and the sensors and imaging scanners disguised as trees and rocks. They were invisible, unless you knew what you were looking for, which Julian did.

As he sat in the jeep, collecting himself, one of the cream pick-ups rolled silently into view on the ridge above him. Its occupants, two men in dark sunglasses and desert camouflage, made no move to get out of their vehicle, but Julian knew they were watching him for the first sign of any intention of going further.

Five metres in front of him, the orange poles that marked the perimeter of the base stood at wide intervals, wide enough that many a ufologist had been arrested for trespassing without knowing he had been doing so; the undulations of the desert topography made accurately placing yourself on a map difficult, and GPS was unreliable at best in this empty part of the Nevada wilderness.

This is it. Forty-five seconds. No mistakes. Think about your family.

Julian took a deep breath, then ground his foot hard on to the jeep's accelerator. The little car leapt forward towards the blind curve that protected the rest of the road from prying eyes, accelerating all the time, dust billowing up and around it.

Instantly, the cream pick-up truck's engine roared into life, and it disappeared from view as its driver hurled it down the ridge towards the road. Julian pressed the pedal harder; he knew this was the crucial moment, where the success or failure of his plan would be decided. If the pick-up appeared in front of him on the road, it was over. If it appeared behind him, there was still a chance.

He hauled the jeep's steering wheel to the right, sending it skidding behind the high ridge of rock that blocked the view of the gangs of ufologists who gathered on the safe side of the orange poles, and along a narrow valley. Walls of sloping rock rose on either side of the dirt road, and Julian instantly saw the thick plume of dust rising behind the pick-up truck as it made its way to intercept him.

He gunned the jeep's engine, squeezing every last bit of power from its tired cylinders, and the little car gave him one final effort; it shot forward, devouring the dirt road beneath its tyres, and he gripped the wheel, fighting to keep the car pointing in the right direction. He roared along the valley floor, his eyes flicking from the ground ahead of him to the speeding pick-up, and as he approached the second turn, the turn he knew led to the gatehouse, he realised he was going to beat it to the corner.

Julian let out a primal roar of triumph, his voice deafeningly loud, even above the screaming engine and squealing tyres. Then he was past the pick-up; as he accelerated towards the final turn, at suicidal speed, he saw the large cream-coloured shape crunch down on to the road in his rear-view mirror, where it disappeared into the cloud of dust that was following him.

Suddenly he was at the turn.

Too fast too fast too fast.

Julian crushed the brake pedal, and the jeep's tyres howled with protest as they threw off the speed they had been carrying. He stamped his foot back on the accelerator, felt the back end of the car begin to slide inexorably towards the rocks at the edge of the road, and hung on as he spun the steering wheel to the left. The car teetered at the apex of the corner, its weight shifting radically to the right, and for a moment, Julian was sure it was going to roll, that he was going to be crushed against the side of the road, within sight of his target.

But it didn't roll; with a deafening, high-pitched scream, the tyres dug into the loose surface, found just enough grip, and bit. The jeep exploded around the corner, back on to the straight dirt road, and shot towards the squat structure that rose ahead of it.

The guard post, hidden from all but the most intrepid of public eyes, was a small square building, dug into the desert floor beside a long red and white barrier that covered the entire width of the road. As Julian thundered towards it, the square shape of the pick-up truck still looming in his rear-view mirror, he saw the dark silhouette of a man stand up from a desk, grab something from the wall and run out towards the road. When Julian was twenty metres from the barrier, he slammed on his brakes, and the jeep skidded to a squealing, crunching halt.

Julian shoved the door open, leapt out of the car and immediately threw his hands in the air as the pick-up truck screeched to a halt behind him and a dark shape ran through the dust towards him from the guard post. The dust swirled as he saw two men leap out of the pick-up truck, M16 assault rifles clutched in their hands. They ran towards him, but the guard from the post arrived first, stopping two metres away from Julian, training an enormous M4 carbine on his chest, and shouting at him through the cloud of orange dust.

"Down on the—"

"Code F-357-X!" Julian shouted, and even through the dust he saw the guard's eyes widen. "I need you to take me to General Allen. Right now."

The two men from the pick-up truck arrived at Julian's side, and twisted his arms instantly behind his back. He bent forward as the pressure on his shoulders forced him down, but then the guard shouted for them to release him, and the pressure disappeared. He stood back up straight, and looked at the two men who had chased him along the road. They were standing still, looks of confusion on their faces, their eyes hidden behind reflective sunglasses.

Hired security, Julian thought. *Thank God they recognise the chain of command.*

The guard, who was still pointing his M4 at Julian, wore the dark blue uniform of the United States Air Force with the gold bars on his shoulders that denoted he was a Captain. He looked at the two perimeter guards, then barked at them.

"Get back in your vehicle!" he shouted. "Go back to your station and forget this ever happened! Do you understand?"

The two guards stared at him, then nodded their assent, anger and embarrassment written across their faces. They trudged back to their pick-up, and a moment later they were gone, back the way they had come.

"Thank you," said Julian. "I need—"

"Shut up," ordered the guard, the M4 pointing steadily at Julian's heart. "If you move, I will shoot you. Is that clear?"

Julian nodded, his hands out in front of him, arms wide and submissive.

The guard moved his left hand from the rifle's barrel, and pulled a radio from his belt. The gun didn't so much as tremble as the Captain brought the handset to his ear, thumbed a button and repeated the code that Julian had given him. There was a burst of static and then a voice spoke to the guard, the words unclear to Julian, even with his trained ears. When the voice finished speaking, the Captain confirmed that he understood, then placed the radio back on his belt. He returned his hand to the M4, and looked at Julian with a professionally unreadable stare.

"You're going to be collected," the Captain said. "But make any sudden movement and I will shoot you. I don't care who you are. Is that understood?"

Julian told him that it was. The two men stood, staring at each other, the dust that had clouded the road now swirling lazily round their ankles, and after no more than a couple of minutes, they heard the rumble of an approaching vehicle over the idling motor of Julian's jeep. The vehicle, a sand-brown Humvee, roared round the corner and screeched to a halt.

A man wearing a plain black uniform that reflected no light, even under the blinding desert sun, stepped out, regarded Julian with a look of incredulity, as though he had half-believed that the collection order he had received had been a practical joke, and ordered the guard soldier to stand down. The man did so, shooting Julian an expression of deep distrust as he returned to the guard post.

"Come with me, please," said the black-clad figure, and nodded at the Humvee.

Julian stepped forward without replying, and climbed into the vehicle.

They drove through the guard post and into the barren hills that surrounded the facility. The Humvee's engine roared, a huge cloud of thick dust blowing up from the wide rear tyres as they made their way on to the dry expanse of Groom Lake. Suddenly it lay before them: the sprawling collection of towers, buildings and hangars that comprised the experimental base. They drove past it without stopping, skirting the edge of the enormous runway, and followed the dirt road round the mountains and on to Papoose Lake.

At the base of the hills alongside the lake, a wide opening had been carved into the ancient rock, leading to a cavernous hangar, a gleaming semi-circle of white concrete and silver steel. Beneath this, descending eighteen storeys below the desert floor, lay the facility that the ufologists referred to, in hushed tones, as S-4: the headquarters

528

of National Security Division 9, the American supernatural enforcement Department that had been founded by Bertrand Willis in 1930.

The Humvee stopped inside the hangar, where a tall, powerfully built man in his late fifties was waiting for it. He was wearing the same all-black uniform as the driver, and carried himself with the upright demeanour of a lifelong soldier. He pushed his silver-grey hair back from his temples with one hand as he waited for the passenger to get out of the Humvee. Julian stepped out, smiled at the man and extended his hand. The grey-haired man pushed it aside, and embraced him in a crushing bear hug.

"Hello, Bob," said Julian Carpenter. "It's been a long time."

"That it has," replied General Robert Allen, the Director of NS9. "They told me you died."

"Yes, sir. They thought I did."

"I guess they were wrong then."

"Yes, sir. About a lot of things."

General Allen released his grip on Julian, took a step backwards and regarded him with a look of amazement on his face. "Is it really you?" he asked.

"It's me, Bob," replied Julian. "Really."

"I believe you," said General Allen, a grin on his face. "Come on. Let's get you inside."

He led Julian through the hangar, to the back wall where an enormous American eagle crest was bolted high above the floor, beneath which stood an iris-scanner sealed door. Allen lowered his eye to the scanner, waited for the green authorisation light to blink into life and pushed the heavy door open. They stepped through it and into a long grey corridor with an elevator at the end. As they walked down the corridor, Julian cast his mind back to the last time he had been in the NS9 facility.

God, 1985. That's a lifetime ago.

They stepped into the elevator. General Allen keyed a button, and the car began to descend. The similarities between the NS9 base and the Loop were overwhelming, the result of the fact-finding mission Stephen Holmwood had sent Julian on more than two decades earlier. The Americans had recently finished the purpose-built facility he was now standing in, and Julian had been blown away by the scale and implementation of their vision. He had returned to England with an exhaustive series of recommendations, and the renovations that had turned the Loop into the place it now was had begun the following month.

As the elevator descended, General Allen glanced at Julian twice before he eventually spoke.

"I never believed what they said about you," he said, in a low voice. "About what they said you'd done. I never believed it."

"It's OK," replied Julian, favouring the General with a warm smile. "Tom Morris framed me well. And Blacklight was hurting, after John and George died. I don't blame them for what they did."

The elevator slid to a halt, and the doors opened on a corridor that was an almost exact replica of the cellblock in the bowels of the Loop. Julian rounded on General Allen, his face colouring red with anger.

"What the hell is this, Bob?" he demanded.

"I have to put you in a cell, Julian," replied Allen, gently. His hand moved almost imperceptibly nearer to the butt of the Glock pistol on his hip. "Until we get this all straightened out. You're supposed to be dead and you just walked in out of the desert. What would you do if you were me?"

Julian's anger subsided. "It's OK," he said. "I get it."

The two men walked towards the security airlock that sealed off the twin rows of cells, and the NS9 Director asked the question he really wanted to know the answer to.

"The night you died, Julian. How did you—"

Julian interrupted him as they came to a halt outside a heavy metal door. "That's going to have to wait, Bob. I'm sorry."

General Allen nodded, and told Julian to step into the airlock. Julian did as he was told, felt the familiar moment of claustrophobia as the door sealed itself shut behind him, the rush of the gas as it billowed up from his ankles, and the sensation of relief as the second door opened, and he stepped through it. Thirty seconds later General Allen emerged from the same door, and they began to walk down the corridor.

"I need you to do me one favour, Bob," said Julian. "You can lock me up, I'll go quietly, and I'll tell you everything you want to know. But I need one favour."

"Name it."

"I need you to speak to Henry and ask him to let me see my son. I think he's in danger."

"Jamie?" asked Allen. "Christ, I saw the report on the termination of Alexandru Rusmanov. Absolutely incredible, a kid his age. You must be proud."

A fierce look of love crossed Julian's face. "I am."

General Allen looked at the expression on Julian's face, and his own crumpled with concern. "Oh God," he said. "Julian – do you know—"

"I know what happened to my wife, Bob. She's safe, for now. Jamie might not be."

They reached the end of the corridor, past the long lines of empty-fronted cells with their shimmering UV walls. Allen keyed a code into a door as nondescript as all the others, and pushed it open. Julian stepped through it, and into the cellblock reserved for those prisoners who did not qualify as supernatural. There were no UV barriers here, just thick, sturdy-looking green metal doors set into concrete walls. Allen keyed his code in again, this time on to a pad beside the first of the cells. Its lock disengaged with a series of rumbling clunks and thuds, and it swung open.

"Where the hell have you been, Julian?" Allen asked, staring closely at his old friend. "Why didn't you come in, after Lindisfarne? They cleared you of all charges."

"I wasn't ready to be an Operator again," replied Julian. "And I had something I needed to do."

"What was that?"

Julian took a deep breath. "Find a cure. For Marie, and for everyone else. I've been all over the country, tracking down Adam. You know the legend, right?"

"Sure. The one vampire who was cured."

"That's the one," replied Julian. He paused, for a long moment. "I found him, Bob."

Allen recoiled. "You found him?" he asked, incredulous. "What do you mean you found him? You mean he's real?"

"As real as you and me," replied Julian. "He lives out in the desert in California, miles from anywhere. He doesn't know how he was cured, but he was. And I think I know where, if not how."

"Where?"

"Here," said Julian. "Right here, Bob."

General Allen started, the look on his face one of confusion. "What do you mean here? We've never—"

"This was before you were Director," interrupted Julian. "Probably fifteen years ago. He was taken in San Francisco, and woke up in a high-security lab, somewhere in the desert. Sound familiar?"

General Allen said nothing, so Julian continued. "He remembers a doctor, a scientist, who was running the show. He was youngish, but he had grey hair. Adam never knew his name."

Allen flinched.

"You know who I'm talking about, don't you?" asked Julian, and the General nodded. "Who was he, Bob? And what the hell were you letting him do?"

After a long pause, General Allen looked directly at Julian, and began to talk.

"It was the nineties. The Cold War was over, and the USSR had dissolved. All our missiles, our orbital defence platforms, they all became obsolete overnight. There were a hundred former Soviet factions that sprang up, all over the Caucasus. We were drowning in new intelligence, trying to formulate new strategies and tactics. The world had changed completely; our enemy was gone, and had been replaced by chaos. Then a rumour came out of Polyarny, from an informant in the SPC; a rumour that they were experimenting on vampires, trying to isolate the genetic strand that caused the condition."

"So?" said Julian. "Abraham Van Helsing was working on that over a century ago, trying to find a cure."

"You don't understand," said Allen. "They weren't trying to cure vampirism; they were trying to weaponise it. Preserve the strengths, remove the weaknesses. Create a class of supersoldiers that were invulnerable, immortal."

"So you did the same thing," said Julian. It wasn't a question.

General Allen nodded.

"Did you ever actually ask the SPC what they were doing?" asked Julian.

"No. The Joint Chiefs didn't think we should show our hand."

"That's what happens when you have Joint *Chiefs*. There have always been too many people you have to answer to, Bob."

"Two of the world's largest continents are under our jurisdiction, Julian. You can afford to only have two or three people know about Department 19 because you only cover a little corner of Europe, and let the Germans and the Russians do all the heavy lifting."

Allen smiled at Julian, who broke into a grin. This was an old conversation, so old that it was almost rehearsed by now.

"So this doctor," said Julian. 'Where did he come from?"

"His name was Reynolds," replied Allen. "And I don't know where he came from, I really don't. He arrived from the Pentagon, security-cleared, background-checked, ready to work. The name was an alias of course. One of my staff thought he might have been a genetics professor from Harvard who was supposed to have died a few years earlier, but we didn't know for sure. Orders came down for me to leave him alone, so I did. Was happy to do so, to be honest with you. His lab was... well. You and I have seen things we wish we could forget, right?"

Julian nodded.

"That lab was as bad as anything I've ever seen. It was a hi-tech torture chamber, nothing more. There were gene sequencers, and supercomputers, and teams of biologists and geneticists and doctors and surgeons, but there was no hiding what was going on down there; he was spending a billion dollars of taxpayers' money to cut vampires open and see how they worked."

"Jesus," said Julian, in a low voice.

"Six months in I got a call from Yuri Petrov, highest encryption, asking me why we were trying to make tame vampires. I told him, off the record, that we were responding to what we had been told they were doing. He flatly denied it, and I believed him. So I went to Washington and told the Joint Chiefs and the President that we were acting on false intelligence, that the SPC threat wasn't real. The President, to his credit, ordered me to suspend Reynolds' work, pending an intelligence review. But by the time I got back here, he was gone."

"What do you mean he was gone?"

"I mean he was gone. We chipped him when he arrived, but it had stopped transmitting. His lab was stripped clean – he had run electromagnets over the hard drives – and no one in the whole facility had seen him leave. His staff were all dead from exposure to nerve gas, and all the vampire subjects had been destroyed."

"Didn't you look for him, Bob? Jesus, he could still be out there somewhere."

"I know; he probably is. I ordered his Pentagon records declassified, but they were gone, stripped out by a remotely activated virus. No one knew anything about him, and there was no way to find him."

Julian looked at Allen, a sudden realisation darkening his face. "He faked the intelligence from the SPC, didn't he? So he could get government funding for his work."

"I don't have any proof of that," replied Allen. "But I'm sure he did, yes."

"It worked, though, Bob," said Julian, urgency rising in his voice. "Whatever he was doing down there, it worked. Adam was cured. I saw it for myself with my own eyes. And now you're telling me that the data that led to the most important scientific discovery of all time is gone, taken by some lunatic?"

Allen nodded, slowly. "That's exactly what I'm telling you."

There was silence in the cellblock for a long moment, then General Allen nodded at the open door beside them.

"I'm going to need you to step into the cell, Julian," he said, softly.

Julian nodded. "That's all right, Bob," he said. "I know the position I'm putting you in. Just do me that one favour, OK. Please?"

"I'm going to call Henry right now," said Allen. "I'll send for you as soon as I have an answer."

Julian nodded, and walked slowly into the cell. It was little more than a concrete box, with a narrow bed and a metal sink and toilet. He stood in the middle of the cell and watched General Allen swing the heavy door shut, sealing him in.

The Director of Department 19 was on his way to the Ops Room when his radio buzzed into life, and the Comms Officer told him he had an encrypted personal link from NS9 waiting for him. He thanked the Operator, swore heavily and reversed his direction, heading for his quarters on Level A, anger flooding through him at a distraction he could have done without.

Bloody Americans. Their timing couldn't be worse, as usual.

The mission to rescue Colonel Frankenstein was minutes away from despatch, and the interrogation of Valentin Rusmanov was continuing on the detention level.

This better be important, Bob. It better be bloody vital.

Seward entered the code beside the door to his quarters, pushed it open and strode inside. He stepped round his desk, opened his terminal and hit the button that illuminated the wall screen opposite him. He entered his personal authorisation code, and hit ACCEPT on the MESSAGE WAITING box.

"What is it, Bob?" he asked, before the image had even fully loaded. "It's really not a great time."

The tanned, weathered face of General Allen appeared on the

screen. The NS9 Director was sitting behind his own desk, five thousand miles away, with an expression on his face that Seward instantly didn't like.

This isn't a routine call, he thought, his heart sinking. *Something's wrong.*

"I'm sorry, Henry," Allen replied. "But you're going to want to hear this. You're not going to believe it, but you're going to want to hear."

"What's going on?"

General Allen looked away from the camera for a second, as though he could not believe what he was about to say, then returned his attention to Henry Seward.

"I've just locked Julian Carpenter in one of my cells," he said. "He's alive, Henry. Julian's alive."

Seward's breath froze in his lungs, and he felt a numbing cold spread through his body as he stared at his American counterpart.

Is this a joke? Some kind of stupid, awful joke?

"Say again, Bob?" he managed.

"I got a call from our gatehouse about fifteen minutes ago," said Allen. "They stopped an intruder who made it past the guards and got to the gate. He jumped out of his car, shouting an old clearance code, asking for me. Asking for me by name, Henry."

"Jesus Christ," said Seward, softly. "You're serious, aren't you? This isn't some kind of joke?"

Allen shook his head. "I'm serious. I had him brought in, and went up to see what the hell was happening. And out of the jeep, as casual as you like, steps Julian. He walks over to me, puts out his hand and says hello. It's him, Henry. It really is."

A terrible thought entered Seward's scrambling brain.

"Is he human, Bob?" he asked, urgently. "Have you checked him?"

"He's human," replied Allen. "I took him through two UV grids without him knowing. He's not turned, and he doesn't seem to be anything else. He's just Julian, alive and locked up downstairs."

"How is this possible?" asked Seward, fighting hard to hold on to any sort of equilibrium. "If it's him, where the hell has he been for the last three years?"

"He told me he didn't feel safe to come in," replied Allen. "He's been here in the US, I think. He said he's been looking for a cure."

"A cure for what?"

"For vampirism," said Allen. "I guess it's pretty important to him, what with what happened to Marie."

Seward froze. "He knows about that?" he asked, slowly. "He knows what happened to his wife? How the hell would he know that?"

"I don't know," replied General Allen, shaking his head. "But he does. Knows about Jamie too, about what he did on Lindisfarne. That's partly why I'm calling you, Henry. Julian's worried about Jamie."

"Hold on," barked Seward. "Just hold on a minute. Julian Carpenter is sitting alive and well in one of your cells at Dreamland, we've no idea where he's been for the last three years, but somehow he knows about classified Blacklight Operations, and now he wants information about Jamie? What the hell am I supposed to make of all this?"

"I don't know," said General Allen. "I'll hold him here until you can send a team to debrief him, and I'll make sure no one else but me knows who he is. But he was insistent about being allowed to see Jamie. He says he thinks the boy is in danger."

"Of course he's in danger," snapped Seward. "He's an Operator. He's in danger every day. Now just let me think for a moment."

The Department 19 Director tried to calm his racing mind, and focus on the immediate problem in hand. Julian, if it was indeed him, was secure, which was the first thing. General Allen was right; he would need to send a team to Nevada to find out where Julian had been, and why he had resurfaced, but that would have to wait; there were simply too many demands on the Admiral's attention at the moment for him to begin to address the potential ramifications of what General Allen was telling him.

Who the hell had known Julian was alive, and had been feeding him classified information? How had he faked his death, as surely he must have done? Seward groaned, as the scale of this new revelation began to suggest itself, and turned his attention back to the video screen.

"What did he ask about Jamie, Bob? Precisely."

"He asked me to ask you to let him see his son," replied General Allen. "In those words. I told him I would, and now I have. What do you want to do?"

"I can't allow it," said Seward. "Who knows what Julian's agenda is? He can't just walk in off the street and start acting like an Operator again. Jamie is about to embark on a Priority 1 mission to Paris, and I'm not going to distract him with this, certainly not until Julian has been debriefed and we are in the full possession of the facts. You can tell him that his son is fine, and that's more than I ought to be letting him know. But I'm not going to let him see him, Bob. Not right now. You understand, right?"

"I understand," replied Allen, and gave his old friend a warm smile. "But I'm pretty sure Julian isn't going to."

"Well, he's going to have to," said Seward. "I'll send a team as soon as I can, Bob. In the meantime, if you could please do like you said. Keep him isolated, and keep access to him to zero."

"Done," replied Allen. "Let me know when you're coming to get him. I'm going to be pretty interested to hear what he says to your team."

"Me too, Bob," said Seward, a grim smile on his face. "Me too. Out."

The Department 19 Director cut the connection, and flopped into his chair. A hundred emotions were jostling for space inside his head; largest and most potent was an overwhelming, almost painful hope at the thought that one of his closest friends, a man he had never believed he would see again, and, more importantly, never get the chance to apologise to, could somehow still be alive. But there was confusion as well, over what this would mean for Jamie, and for himself.

And beyond that, a deep sense of being overwhelmed, of one more thing to carry around on his back, of this being almost the final straw, the point where he reached the limit of his ability to cope.

How can he be alive? It makes no sense. I saw his body before they cremated it.

"Admiral?"

The voice came from the door to the Director's quarters, and Seward jumped. He whirled round in his seat, to see Jamie Carpenter standing in the open doorway. He realised he must have forgotten to close it behind him, such was the rush he had been in when the call came through. A flicker of guilt passed momentarily across Seward's face when he saw Julian's son, but if Jamie saw it, he gave no indication.

"What is it, Lieutenant Carpenter?" asked Seward, his equilibrium returning.

"What did the Yanks want, sir?" Jamie asked, his face open and honest.

540

"Routine update. Typically bad timing. Nothing for you to worry about."

Jamie nodded. "We're ready, sir. We're leaving for Paris."

"Understood," said Seward. "Bring him home, son. If he's alive, bring him home."

"I will, sir," replied Jamie, forcefully. "You can count on it."

43

THE TIES THAT BIND

At the western edge of Orly, the second busiest airport in France, lies a sprawl of low metal cabins and a series of wide hangars, the paint flaking from their sides. Away from the terminals where families depart for holidays in the Alps and the Riviera, where couples are reunited under the unforgiving glow of fluorescent lights, where businessmen wait for connections that will take them on to another airport almost identical to the one they are sitting in, the buildings represent the true beating heart of any airport.

Through these offices and the hangars that stand behind them, a timetable of cargo freight every bit as complicated as that maintained by any of the passenger airlines is organised and set in motion; forklift trucks whir incessantly, carrying cases of wine from Bordeaux, of cheese from Rouen and Reims, of machine parts, of cruise missile timing triggers and glow-in-the-dark stuffed animals, all bound for the four corners of the world. Beside the freight offices stand the maintenance hangars, where planes trundle in and out every day of

542

the week, needing new tyres, their carpets steam-cleaning, or their worn, creaking joints oiled.

At Orly, the buildings are older than most, for a very good reason. Until 1967, when the French government withdrew from NATO central command and ordered all non-French forces to leave the country, the sprawling site was a United States Air Force base. The soldiers are long gone, as are the military aircraft, but many of the buildings remain, a crumbling legacy of the airport's former life, of a time when fast jets screamed overhead, and the heavy *thump-thump-thump* of helicopter rotors filled the air. Now all that remains is nondescript industrial sprawl, where nothing much of note ever happens.

Until tonight.

The Blacklight helicopter burst through the clouds that were hanging low over the airport. The sun was drifting lazily towards the horizon in the west, and the squat black shape gleamed in the last of the evening light as it dropped sharply towards the ground.

The Communications Division had made contact with the French Security Services as the chopper made its way across the Channel, and had been granted permission to land on French soil. The agreed site was a helipad in the centre of the industrial complex, a helipad that had once served American helicopters as they ferried senior personnel in and out of the base.

"Thirty seconds," announced the pilot, over the helmet communication system that the five Operators strapped into the chopper's belly were all linked into.

"Roger," said Jamie, over the howl of the rotors and the shriek of the rapidly decelerating engine. "Comms and weapons checks."

The four members of his team, identically clad in their matt-black uniforms, the visors of their helmets pushed up from their faces, quickly ran through the list of final checks, examining their weapons and kit and replacing each item in its proper place on their belts and webbing.

"Check," said Angela Darcy.

"Check," said Jack Williams.

"Check," said Dominique Saint-Jacques.

"Check," said Claire Lock.

"Understood," said Jamie. "Clear in ten seconds, team. I want to be in Paris in thirty minutes. And visors down; no one sees us, clear?"

The four Operators nodded, then pulled their purple visors down over their faces. The flat, featureless screens instantly lent the team an inhuman, unsettling air; it would be difficult for anyone who saw them to believe that there were men and women beneath the plastic façades, and impossible for them to give any clues as to their identities.

The helicopter's engines roared, reaching a volume and pitch that sent bolts of pain through Jamie's ears, despite the protection his earpieces and helmet provided. Then, with a bone-jarring jolt, the heavy wheels of the chopper squealed on to tarmac, and rolled to a halt.

"Move!" shouted Jamie, releasing himself from his safety belt and throwing open the side door of the helicopter. His team leapt out, one after the other, and disappeared from view, as he ordered the pilot to take off as soon as they were clear, and wait at the location the French military had given them, a NATO airbase ninety miles to the east.

"Be ready to come and get us!" he shouted.

"Yes, sir," replied the pilot. "Good luck, sir."

"Thanks!" yelled Jamie, and leapt out of the helicopter.

Dominique and Claire were standing at the rear corners of the vehicle, their MP5s at their shoulders, scanning the area around them. The helipad, cracked and faded by the passage of time, was in the middle of a loose ring of metal huts, rust climbing relentlessly up their sides, their roofs beaten and tarnished by years of neglect. There were no lights on in any of them, or in the first rows of low concrete buildings that stood beyond them, but Jamie was glad to see his team were taking no chances.

The heavy ramp at the back of the helicopter had already been lowered, and as he made his way towards it, he heard the rumble of a powerful engine bursting into life. A second later a jet black SUV rolled down the ramp, and stopped in the empty yard, its headlights blazing, its black windows completely opaque.

As soon as the back wheels hit the tarmac, the ramp rose back into place. The helicopter's engines screamed again, and it hauled itself into the air. The churning rotors whipped the air, and Jamie fought to stay on his feet. Then the helicopter was climbing, and the wind and the noise lessened. Within thirty seconds, all that was left of the huge black chopper was a rapidly diminishing pair of yellow lights, heading east in the gathering gloom.

The passenger side door opened and Angela Darcy stepped out, her pretty face hidden behind the flat purple of her visor.

"Your carriage awaits, sir," she said, motioning towards the rear doors.

Jamie smiled beneath his mask, and ordered everyone into the vehicle. He took the front seat next to Jack Williams, who was sitting comfortably behind the steering wheel, and pushed back his visor. Angela, Claire and Dominique filled the two rows of seats behind them, and did likewise.

"Dominique," said Jamie. "I need to find this Latour, quickly. Where do we start?"

"The Marais," replied Dominique, instantly. "We start in the Marais."

Jack Williams hit the accelerator and the heavy SUV leapt forward. He slid the car carefully between the ageing huts and on to the wide strip of tarmac that served as the industrial area's main thoroughfare. Watery yellow light spilled down from a series of flickering streetlights; the drone of forklift truck engines rumbled in the cool evening air, and the occasional shouted instructions could be heard. Jack turned left, and headed towards where their satellite read-out told him the gate would be.

The black SUV rounded a corner, and passed a small gang of workmen huddled along the long wall of one of the shabby office buildings, sipping coffee from flasks and smoking short white cigarettes. They looked briefly at the car as it passed, then returned to their conversations; the vehicle, and its contents, clearly did not merit a second look.

Two minutes later they were on the motorway, and accelerating north towards Paris.

On the stage of the Fraternité de la Nuit's theatre, Frankenstein heard the door, the door that he had walked through a hundred times in another life, creak open, and used a significant amount of his remaining strength to lift his head.

He had been tied to the wooden pole in the middle of the small stage for more than thirty-six hours, and had long passed through the threshold of what would be conventionally described as agony. His arms and legs, which were pulled back at unnatural angles and tied at the wrists and ankles, had gone from a dull, throbbing ache to white-hot fire to a pain so vast he could not fully comprehend it, a pain that had felt as though every millimetre of the grey-green skin that covered his limbs was being sliced away with razor blades before salt was massaged into the wounds. Now, after a day and a half, they were empty, useless things; he could not feel them at all, and only the ruthless application of logic was able to convince him that they were still there.

He had been given water, sparingly, by Lord Dante's butler, who had refused to speak to him, or even look at him as he delivered it; it felt as though the butler saw this duty as little more than feeding a pet, and not a favoured one at that. There had been no food, and the rumbling and gurgling in his stomach had given way to dull emptiness, a yawning vacuum at the centre of his being. His bodily functions had been taken care of twice, in humiliating fashion. And beneath it all, beneath the pain and the fear and the shame, Frankenstein could feel it coming.

Twice in the past hours he had found himself staring up at the ceiling, at the point where he knew, with absolute certainty, the moon was rising beyond the ornate roof of the theatre. He could feel the grinding sensation in his bones that he had come to dread, feel the prickling of his skin, feel the urge to run and leap and bite.

Now, as he lifted his head, he saw a dark figure standing silently at the rear of the theatre, just inside the door. He watched as the figure slowly walked forward, and emerged into the low lighting that glowed at the edges of the stage, and recognised the pale, narrow face immediately.

"Latour," he breathed. "Are you here to gloat?"

"No, my old friend," replied Latour, floating slowly up on to the stage and landing in front of Frankenstein. "I am not. It causes me great pain to see you like this."

"Then you are the cause of your own suffering," spat Frankenstein.

Latour's eyes flared red, and he closed the gap between the two men in a millisecond.

"You brought this all on yourself," he hissed. "It was you who crippled Lord Dante, and you who returned to the one city in the world where you knew full well there was a generous price on your head. Do not blame me for your own stupidity; had it not been me who found you and delivered you here, it would have been someone else, I can assure you of that."

"Would the someone else you speak of have claimed to be my friend as they handed me over to be murdered?" asked Frankenstein. "Would they have talked of old times as they exchanged my life for nothing more than a pretty young girl, and a pat on the head from their master?"

The fire in Latour's eyes darkened for a moment, then died, as the vampire took a step back and regarded the bound monster.

"No," he said, softly. "It is unlikely that they would."

Frankenstein saw the look on the vampire's face, the pain and sadness that were written clearly upon it, and seized upon what he believed might be his last, and only, chance.

"Let me go, old friend," he said, quietly. "Let me leave this place, this city, and never return. You could come with me."

Latour's eyes widened, and Frankenstein knew that he had never considered the possibility that had just been suggested to him. He pushed ahead.

"If you leave me here, Dante is going to kill me," he said. "For sport. For the entertainment of his friends, of which he counts you among the number. You will have to watch me die, Latour, and know the role you played in it. Can you do that?"

The vampire said nothing; he merely stared at Frankenstein.

"Beyond even that," he continued, "there is something coming, something that I cannot explain to you. But if it is allowed to happen, then I cannot guarantee your safety. Unless you let me down from here, and we leave this place."

Latour recoiled, as if he had been slapped. Then he laughed, shortly.

"Your words are pretty, old friend," he said. "As they always were. But I would not cross Lord Dante for you, or anyone else; I will *not* make the mistake you made. I confess that handing you over to him was hard, far harder than I had imagined it would be, but I do not regret it. My place here is secure, for all eternity. I will watch you die, my friend, and while I will take no pleasure in it, I will shed no tears either. The man I called my friend is gone; all that remains is a monster, whose end is overdue."

Frankenstein's heart sank. He had not believed that he could persuade Latour to free him, not really, but there had been a brief moment when it had appeared that his words were getting through to the vampire. Now that moment had passed, and with it the last of his hope.

"We all have to live with the decisions we make," he said, his voice cracking. "I hope you can live with yours. Truly I do. Goodbye, Latour."

Latour smiled. "There is no need for goodbyes," he said. "I will see you in a matter of hours. See you very clearly, from my seat in the front row."

His smile widened into a grin of pure malice, and then he was gone, disappearing back into the shadows at the rear of the theatre. Frankenstein watched him go, then let his head slump down to his chest.

*

Less than a mile away, Jamie Carpenter raised his pistol for the second time, and then found his arm gripped from behind. He spun round, fury written all over his face, and found Jack Williams staring at him with obvious concern.

"He doesn't know anything, Jamie," said Jack. "He really doesn't."

Jamie wrenched his hand out of his friend's grasp, and turned back to the figure that was cowering on the ground before him.

"*S'il vous plaît*," it whispered, from behind trembling, blood-soaked hands. "*S'il vous plaît, monsieur.*"

Dominique had navigated Jack round the Périphérique and through the maze of one-way systems and side streets until they had arrived at Rue de Bretagne, where Jamie had ordered his team out of the car. The sun was less than forty minutes below the horizon, but the Marais was, as always, full of people; the bars and restaurants heaved with men and women, music and laughter and snatches of conversation filled the air, as street vendors hustled and the earliest casualties of the night's excesses staggered.

It was not, Jamie realised immediately, a place where five figures in black uniforms and purple visors would find it easy to be inconspicuous. On the other hand, the photosensitive filters in their visors made identifying vampires easy, and Jamie found himself, as he often did, torn between caution and recklessness.

He had attempted to compromise, at least initially. His team had stuck to the labyrinthine backstreets and alleys of this old part of Paris, their black forms blending effortlessly into the shadows, and peered out at the passing throngs, looking for the telltale bloom of red that would indicate a vampire.

After fifteen minutes, they had got lucky. A middle-aged vampire was walking briskly down the middle of Rue Debellyme, his hands in the pockets of his coat, his lips pursed together as he whistled a gentle ragtime melody. Angela Darcy had been the first to spot him, and had whispered as much to the rest of the team. Jamie had ordered them to follow him, and they had done so, looping through the dark alleyways that Dominique appeared to know like the back of his hand.

The vampire gave no sign of being aware of their presence; he strolled through the Parisian evening as though he was without a care in the world. At the intersection of Rue de Saintonge and Rue de Turenne, Jamie watched as the man made a left, and saw his chance. As the man passed a dark alleyway, the shadows at the entrance appeared to suddenly come to life, and he found himself pinned against the cold brick wall with stakes pressed against his throat and chest before he had time to even register what was happening.

The vampire, whose name was Alain Devaux, and who had never hurt so much as a fly in the century he had been alive, had been strolling home from a pleasant day in the company of his daughter, Beatrice, who lived on the Rive Gauche in an apartment she had tailored to suit the peculiar needs of her father. The windows were covered in blackout blinds and in the fridge, beside her brie, and her chorizo, and her Pouilly-Fumé, stood a neat row of bottles of blood, procured without any questions asked from her butcher in Saint Germain-des-Prés who, she had come to realise, believed that she made her own black puddings from the thick crimson liquid she ordered so regularly.

Beatrice was Alain's third daughter; he had outlived the first and second, with whom his relationship had ceased at the moment of his turning; he had decided when Beatrice was born that he was not going to make the same mistake again. He was a gentle man, who had spent long years ashamed of what he had become, who had never been able to fully accept that what had been done to him was not his fault.

He kept no company with other vampires, and he had no interest in their affairs; as a result, he was blissfully unaware of the existence of Department 19. So when one of the black figures peered at him from behind a mask of bright purple, fear had overwhelmed him, and he forgot the supernatural strength that lay in his muscles, strength that would have given him a reasonable chance of escape, even against the five shapes that melted out of the shadows.

"Do you know Jean-Luc Latour?" the figure demanded, its voice metallic and emotionless through its helmet filters.

"W-what?" asked Alain, trembling with terror.

The stake at his neck was jabbed hard into his throat, breaking the skin. Alain smelt the rich copper scent of his own blood, and his eyes flared red, involuntarily.

"Eyes!" shouted one of the other figures.

"I can't help it," said Alain, looking pleadingly at the dark shapes. "I can't—"

There was a blur of movement, as the figure that had been peering at him drew a black pistol from its belt. Alain had no time to beg for his life, which he was sure was about to come to an end, before the dark figure raised the gun above its shoulder and brought it crashing down in the centre of his forehead, splitting the skin to the bone.

Blood gushed out, and Alain slid to his knees. His mind was blank, wiped by the enormity of the pain, and his hands gripped involuntarily at the legs of Jamie's uniform, as though he was about to pray to the dark shape in front of him.

"Latour!" bellowed the figure that had hit him. "One of your kind! Jean-Luc Latour!" Alain stared up at him, noticing with absent horror that he could see the steady arc of blood spraying from his forehead and pattering to the cold cobbles of the alleyway. "Don't pretend you don't know who I'm talking about! Have you seen him?"

"*Je ne comprends pas*," whispered Alain. He felt nauseous, and light-headed, as though he was drunk. "*Je suis désolé, je ne comprends pas. Je suis désolé.*"

"Jesus," whispered Claire Lock.

She was watching the awful scene play out from the middle of the alleyway, with the rest of the team; she made no movement to intervene, but the disapproval in her voice was plain to hear, and it served only to enrage Jamie further.

He shoved the vampire, hard, and Alain fell back against the wall, instinctively covering what was left of his face with his pale, shaking hands, as blood pumped out between his fingers and on to his chest, and his wide eyes stared up at Jamie with utter horror.

"Where is Latour?" Jamie roared. "Tell me where he is!"

He raised the gun again, and that was when Jack Williams moved, stepping forward and grabbing his friend's wrist. "He doesn't know anything, Jamie," he said. "He really doesn't."

Jamie wrenched his hand out of Jack's grasp, and turned back to the figure that was cowering on the ground before him.

"*S'il vous plaît,*" it whispered, from behind trembling, blood-soaked hands. "*S'il vous plaît, monsieur.*"

"Fine," said Jamie, his chest heaving with exertion and burning with rage. "Let's find someone who does. Leave him here, and let's move."

"Hold on," said Angela. "He might know where we should go. Let me talk to him."

"Be quick," said Jamie, and stepped back from the bleeding, terrified vampire.

"Yes, sir," Angela replied, watching him move away. Then she walked over, crouched down and raised her visor, so Alain could see her dizzying, dazzling smile.

"*Bonsoir, monsieur,*" she said, gently. "*Vous parlez Anglais, oui?*"

The vampire nodded, slowly.

"OK then," she said. "My name is Angela. What's yours?"

"A-Alain," the vampire replied, hesitantly. "Alain Devaux."

"It's nice to meet you, Alain," said Angela, brightly. "I'm very sorry for what my friend did to you, but it will heal next time you feed. So no harm done, really. Don't you agree?"

Confusion swept across Alain's face, but he nodded again, even more slowly.

"Good," breathed Angela, her voice full of relief. "That's great. Now, Alain, my friend is very worried about a friend of his. That's why he hit you, because he's worried that we might be running out of time, and we need to find him; it's no excuse, mind you, but that's why. I hope you can forgive him, and think about helping me?"

"I don't know about what he asked," said Alain, worry rising in his face once more. "I was telling the truth. I wish I could be more help. I'm sorry."

"I believe you, Alain," said Angela, honestly. "I don't think you know where Latour is. I don't think you'd ever heard of him until a minute ago, had you?"

Alain shook his head eagerly.

"I thought not," she continued. "But we think that somewhere in Paris is someone who does know about him, and knows where he is. So I need you to think, Alain, and tell me anywhere you know where large numbers of vampires gather. Can you do that for me?"

"I do not associate with vampires," said Alain, spitting the last word as though it was poison. "I keep to myself. I never hurt anyone."

"I'm sure you don't," Angela replied, softly. "This doesn't need to be a place that you go to yourself, just anywhere you might have been told about, or heard other vampires discussing. Is there anywhere like that you can think of?"

Alain was silent for a moment, then his brow furrowed, and Angela knew he had an answer for her.

"There is a place," he said, slowly. "I have never been there, but my daughter asks about it. It's for vampires only, down by the river."

"What is it called, Alain?" asked Angela, smiling at the bleeding vampire.

"*Spinal Cord*," read Jamie. "You've got to be kidding me."

The five Operators were standing outside a squat concrete building on Port de la Rapée, having followed the directions that Alain had given to Angela. They had left the frightened, injured vampire in the alleyway; he had watched them depart with a relief on his face so great that it made Jamie feel momentarily ashamed.

Normally, he did not see it as Blacklight's duty to terrorise or destroy every single vampire in the world; one of the first lessons that Frankenstein had taught him were that there were good and bad vampires, just as there were good and bad humans. But the mission they were on was different; nothing could be allowed to derail their chances of finding Frankenstein, not even Jamie's own usually strong moral code.

I told them all before we left, Jamie thought, trying to justify his own behaviour to himself. *Frankenstein is the priority; everything else is secondary. And that's how it stays, until I get him back or someone shows me his body.*

He lowered his visor, and checked the weapons on his belt.

"Follow my lead," he said, and started towards the building.

The door that led into *Spinal Cord* was heavy industrial metal, covered in a layer of flaked and rusting red paint, beneath the neon sign announcing its name. There was a single button set into the alcove wall; Jamie pressed it, and stepped back.

"We're full," said a voice, from behind the door. "Go away."

Jamie pressed the button again, and kept his finger on it. He could hear the bell ringing through the door, and after a few seconds, he heard bolts being withdrawn. He readied himself.

The door was pulled open with a scream of metal on concrete, and a huge vampire loomed out of the darkness within. The doorman was wearing a battered leather vest over a black T-shirt, and black leather trousers. His eyes were glowing red, and he peered out at the five black-clad figures with anger on his face.

"What the hell are you five supposed to be?" he asked. "Some kind of—"

The comparison the vampire was about to make was lost forever, as Jamie pulled the stake from his belt and shoved it into his chest, hard. The vampire's eyes bulged with surprise, and then he burst like a giant balloon, showering Jamie with steaming blood.

Jamie replaced the stake on his belt, and turned to his team.

"Follow me," he said.

Beyond the door lay a concrete passage, plastered on all sides with lurid posters for gigs and club nights. They had been pasted across the floor and ceiling as well as the walls, and Jamie had a strange sensation of dizziness as he led them down the corridor; it

556

was as though he wasn't absolutely sure which way was up. They rounded a corner, and the relentless thud of bass, which had been barely audible as the door opened, intensified. At the end of the corridor before them stood a second door. Jamie didn't even slow down as he approached it; he pushed the rusting sheet of metal with one gloved hand.

It swung open without protest, and suddenly the music was deafening, even through the protection offered by his helmet. The club was a large concrete box, square-sided but with a high ceiling from which sweat was dripping like salty rain; the heat emanating from the room was overpowering. One side of the club was a long bar made from concrete breeze blocks topped with old wooden doors from behind which three bartenders were serving drinks: bottles of beer, shots of whisky and vodka, and glasses full of dark red liquid.

At the rear of the room, a makeshift DJ booth had been erected from three concrete slabs on which a pair of turntables sat precariously; the DJ moved between them faster than the eye could follow, his glowing eyes leaving trails of red light in the neon-soaked darkness of the club.

The rest of the room was dance floor, upon which hundreds of men, women and vampires were grinding and thrusting and groping. Nobody paid the slightest bit of attention to their arrival, so Jamie watched for a few moments; he saw a vampire man sucking hungrily at a wound on the inside of a girl's elbow, saw the pain on her face and the unbridled pleasure on his. He saw a vampire girl lean in and snort a line of red powder from the cleavage of another vampire girl; they looked so similar that they could have been twins.

A thick fug of smoke hung over the dance floor, and Jamie smelt the bitter, telltale scent of Bliss, the vampire drug that he had once helped to make. Strobe lights pounded from the high corners of the room, the music thumped and thudded and thumped again, while sweat and blood and lust mingled in the boiling, smoky air.

Jamie had seen enough. He lifted an ultraviolet grenade from his belt, and nodded to Angela Darcy. She disappeared into the crowd, then appeared seconds later behind the DJ. Jamie watched her press the tip of her T-Bone into the vampire's back, then whisper in his ear. A moment later the deafening music cut out.

The vampires and humans swirling and pounding across the dance floor screeched their displeasure, then spun, as one, in Jamie's direction when he bellowed for their attention. He held the grenade above his head, and smiled at the crowd.

"You all know what this is, right?" he shouted. "Who feels like answering some questions?"

44

BEHIND EVERY GOOD MAN

ONE HOUR LATER

Larissa Kinley stood in the open doors of the Loop's hangar, watching the last of the sunlight crawl across the grass to the west. Once it had climbed over the double fences and rippled away into the thick forest that surrounded the Department 19 base, she stepped out on to the tarmac, and breathed fresh air.

There were many bad things about being a vampire, but the worst of them, the very worst, was the simple fact that for the better part of each day, she could not go outside. Being a Blacklight Operator helped, as the vast majority of their work was done under cover of darkness, and it was not unusual for her to fulfil the oldest vampire cliché, of sleeping all day and emerging after the sun had gone down.

But there were moments, a great many of them in the years since she had been turned, when she longed for the feel of the sun on her skin, for the scents and smells of the day, so different to those of the night, to fill her nostrils and transport her, away from the darkness and the shadows. She had come to terms with the fact that she was never going to experience those things again, but that did not stop her yearning for them.

She had said goodbye to Jamie in the Ops Room almost four hours earlier, and she could still not shake the nagging feeling that their parting had been significant. Partly it was the fact that he had gone to Paris on the most important mission of his life, and decided not to take her with him, but there was more to it than that; he had been on missions without her before, and she without him, and never had she felt the need to so explicitly ask him to come back to her as she had in the Ops Room.

There was no guarantee that Frankenstein was alive, that Jamie and his team would be able to find him if he was, or that there would be any danger attached to doing so; she knew it was extremely likely that he would return home empty-handed, an eventuality she was attempting to prepare herself for. But there was something in the pit of her stomach, something gnawing and clawing, that told her that her boyfriend was in enormous danger.

She would worry about him until he returned; that much she knew. In the meantime, there was someone else who required her attention, someone whom she had seen walking towards the distant perimeter fence half an hour earlier, someone she had been prevented from following by the slow passage of the setting sun. But now the sun was gone.

Larissa soared into the air, feeling with a rush of excitement how effortless it had become for her to do so. She rose slowly towards the hologram that shielded the Loop from view from above, marvelling at the liquid complexity of the image when seen up close.

The field of suspended particles that the image was projected on to was barely a centimetre thick, but the hologrammatic image appeared to rise and fall with the tops of trees and the dark drops of clearings. It was a marvel of technology that Larissa resolved to ask Matt about at some point; she knew he would already have a full understanding of how the effect was achieved, and it would delight him to be able to pass the information on to her.

From her high vantage point, Larissa's razor-sharp eyes picked out the tiny figure of Kate Randall, sitting alone in the rose garden at the far edge of the base.

She swooped through the air, the open sky around her, the soft wind rippling through her hair; it was a sensation of pure joy, and although she would not wish the curse of vampirism on anyone, this was the one aspect of being turned that she would have loved to share with somebody, even just for a few minutes. She banked and spun and looped as she flew across the wide compound, towards the circular garden; her progress was silent, and Kate didn't look up until Larissa dropped soundlessly on to the bench beside her, and said hello.

"Jesus!" shouted Kate, leaping to her feet. "You scared the crap out of me!"

"Sorry," replied Larissa, grinning at her friend. "Completely accidental, I promise."

Kate stared at the vampire girl, trying hard to keep a straight face, and failing miserably. She shook her head in what she hoped was a stern fashion, and smiled back at Larissa.

"So," said Larissa. "I saw you head out here about an hour ago. I'm guessing it didn't go well with Shaun?"

Kate looked exaggeratedly around. "Do you see him here?"

"No," said Larissa.

"Me neither," said Kate. "That's how well it went."

She sat back down on the bench beside her friend and sighed, deeply. "He's blaming me for what happened with the Paris mission," she said. "He thinks Jamie would have taken him if he and I weren't together."

"That's bullshit," said Larissa.

"Is it?" asked Kate. "Jamie said he didn't take him because he wanted to know there'd be someone to look after me if something happens to him in Paris. Maybe he *would* have taken Shaun if we weren't seeing each other."

"You can't know that, though," said Larissa. "Jamie and Shaun haven't exactly seen eye to eye. He still might have left him behind."

"Might," replied Kate. "Might not. Like you say, we don't know. So I can't tell Shaun that his being with me didn't hurt his chances, because I don't know that's true."

"So what's he going to do?"

"I don't know," said Kate, softly. "He said he needs time to think about things. One of my two closest friends in the world is out there on some crazy redemption crusade, but *he* needs time to think about things. Ridiculous."

She saw the look on Larissa's face change as she mentioned Jamie's mission, saw the worry that she was barely managing to conceal burst to the surface, and felt a stab of pain in her chest. "Jesus, I'm sorry," she said. "I'm sure Jamie's fine, Larissa. I'm certain of it. He was born to do this; you know how good an Operator he is."

"I know," said Larissa, fiercely. "I'm so proud of him, even though I hate his stupid guts right now for not letting me go with him and look after him. And I know how important Frankenstein was to him; I totally get it. I just wish he'd let me help."

"They're just boys," said Kate. "Him and Shaun both. They don't know how to let anyone help them, much less ask for it."

The two girls sat in silence for a moment, looking at the roses in the fading light of the evening. Eventually, Kate spoke again.

"Do you believe him?" she asked.

"Believe who?" replied Larissa.

"Jamie," said Kate. "Do you think he was really trying to protect us, or do you think he just didn't want to take us with him?"

"I have to believe that what he told us was the truth," replied Larissa. "The alternative is just too awful. You know?"

Kate nodded her head.

"Do you believe him?" asked Larissa. "Do you think he meant what he said?"

"I do," Kate replied, firmly. "I think it was stupid, and arrogant, but I think he meant it."

"Do you think they'll find him?" asked Larissa. "Frankenstein, I mean."

"I don't think there's anything to find," replied Kate. "I would never tell Jamie this, because I know how desperately he wants to believe, but I think he's dead. I think he's been dead for three months."

"Me too," sighed Larissa. "It means so much to Jamie; he sees it as this miraculous chance to make up for what happened, and I'm scared it's just going to crush him all over again. But I guess we'll know when they get back, one way or the other."

"Let's hope so," said Kate, then smiled at Larissa. "I'm hungry," she said. "Do you want to get something to eat? It might take our minds off all this doom and gloom."

"Sounds like a plan," replied Larissa, standing up.

Kate did the same, and the two girls walked slowly down the wooden path that ran through the heart of the memorial garden. As they passed through the gate, Kate did something that surprised herself; she reached out and took Larissa's hand. She had never done so before; she had held hands with her girlfriends on

Lindisfarne all the time, thinking less than nothing of it, but never with Larissa.

The muscles in the vampire girl's neck and shoulders twitched, and for a second, her hand lay limply in Kate's grasp. Then she slowly laced her fingers with her friend's, as they walked towards the low rise of the Loop's central dome.

They were three-quarters of the way across the wide grass field when Larissa smelt something on the still evening air. It didn't smell bad, not exactly; it smelt *huge*, as though she was only able to perceive a small corner of some gigantic whole. Her eyes flickered red, involuntarily; Kate saw them, and stopped.

"What is it?" she asked. There was concern in her voice; she knew that Larissa's senses were many times more acute than her own, and knew that her life had been saved, on more than one occasion, by taking the vampire's instincts seriously.

"I don't know," said Larissa, pulling free from Kate's hand. "Something big. It's coming, though, whatever it is. Coming fast."

A sound became audible behind them, a fluttering sound like the wings of a thousand birds. As the two girls looked at each other, their eyes widening with fear, a ragged shadow crept across them, plunging them into darkness. They turned and looked in the direction it was coming from, and Kate made a small involuntary sound deep in her throat, a tiny gasp of utterly unbridled fear.

"Run," growled Larissa, her eyes bursting into deep, swirling crimson. "Sound the alarm."

"What about you?" cried Kate. "I can't leave you here."

"There's no time," said Larissa. "Run, Kate. Go now!"

Kate turned and sprinted for the open doors of the hangar, shouting at the top of her lungs as she went. The shadow rolled across the grass, keeping pace with her; it was ragged, and shifting, and impossibly wide.

Larissa stood alone in the middle of the grass, her eyes fixed on what was approaching. Her eyes burned in the darkness as she pulled the radio from her belt, typed four numbers on its small keypad and pressed it to her ear.

45

CURTAIN CALL

SPINAL CORD NIGHTCLUB
PARIS, FRANCE

With rising snarls of anger, the vampire crowd threw themselves towards the tight huddle of Department 19 Operators. Jamie didn't move; he stood absolutely still, the grenade resting loosely in his hand, a narrow smile on his face, as his team went to work around him.

Jack Williams raised his T-Bone to his shoulder and pulled the trigger. The metal stake erupted from the end of the wide barrel and screamed through the hot, sticky air. It crunched through the chest of an approaching vampire wearing a fluorescent green T-shirt and shot into the mass of vampires who hadn't moved. It tore the nose off a girl in a pink minidress, who screamed and clasped her hands to her face.

The vampire in the green T-shirt was still moving, his teeth grinding through the Bliss high that was coursing through him, the thick metal wire twanging through the hole in his body. His face was contorted with pain and adrenaline, his eyes blazing; he was less than a metre away from Jack when his body finally realised what had been done to it, and he exploded into a pillar of steaming blood.

Screams echoed through the crowd, and several of the vampires ran to the far corners of the nightclub, desperately searching for a way out. A vampire wearing head-to-toe black leapt for Jamie, her hands twisted into claws, her eyes wide and fixed on the grenade in his hand. Claire Lock stepped sharply forward and plunged her stake into the airborne woman's heart; she splashed to the concrete floor as a dark smear of blood.

The ring of vampires who had approached the Operators paused. The expressions on their faces, which had been anger mingled with bloodlust, now slid slowly to fear. The communal will to attack left them, and they scuttled back into the crowd, staring at the dark huddle of figures, waiting to see what they would do next.

"It's very simple, ladies and gentlemen," said Jamie, smiling at the swaying, trembling crowd. "If one of you tells me where I can find Jean-Luc Latour, then I walk out of here with this grenade in my hand, and you all get to live. If no one tells me what I want to know, then I press the trigger."

He stood waiting, the UV grenade resting in his hand.

"No takers?" he asked, his voice light and friendly. "Well, that's disappointing. But I suppose I have to respect your decision."

Jamie twisted the grenade, and it sprang open, exposing the purple bulb at its core. He raised it into the air, let his thumb rest over its trigger, and was about to press it when a voice emerged from the crowd.

"Don't," it said. "I'll tell you."

Jamie removed his thumb from the trigger, but did not close the grenade.

"Tell me what?" he asked. "What are you going to tell me?"

"Latour. He's at his club, not far from here."

"Tell me where," said Jamie, sharply.

"On Rue de Sévigné. It's a building with no windows."

"Why is he there?" demanded Jamie. "Who lives in the building?"

"The king of Paris lives there."

"I know where that is," said Dominique Saint-Jacques. "We can be there in ten minutes. Let's go."

"OK," agreed Jamie. "Destroy them all, and let's get out of here."

There was a chorus of screams and terrified moans from the crowd. Jamie placed his thumb back on the grenade's trigger and was about to press it when he felt hands grip his shoulders, and then he was spun round towards his team.

The four Operators of his team surrounded him, their visors raised, expressions of hostility on their faces.

"Don't, Jamie," said Claire Lock. "I won't be part of this."

Jamie stared at her, incredulous. "Part of what?" he barked. "Part of destroying a room full of vampires?"

"That's not what this is," said Angela. "This is murder, pure and simple. Trust me, I know the difference."

"She's right, Jamie," said Jack Williams. "This isn't what we do. And it's not what Colonel Frankenstein would want."

Jamie stared at his friend. "Don't bring him into this, Jack," he warned. "You didn't know him. Don't tell me what he would want."

"You're right," said Jack. "I didn't know him. None of us did apart from you. But I *knew* him, Jamie. He was a legend in Blacklight before any of us were even born; my grandfather has been telling me stories about him since the day I turned twenty-one. And I won't stand by and let you dishonour his name by committing murder in the supposed service of it."

Jamie felt something give inside him, and lowered the grenade.

Shame, hot and sharp, spilled through him, as he pictured the look on the monster's face if he could see what he had been about to do. Frankenstein detested vampires, he felt they were unnatural, but he believed that they were not inherently evil; he would not have stood idly by and let Jamie murder a roomful of them for no other reason than because he was angry.

"You're right," he said, his voice low. "I'm sorry. I just can't explain to you..." He stopped, and tried again. "I need to get him back," he said, simply. "I have to. Will you help me?"

"We're here, aren't we?" asked Angela, smiling at him.

Jamie smiled back. "Jack," he said, "I think you should assume command of this mission. I'm too close to this."

"No way," replied Jack, instantly. "This is your Operation, Jamie, and I've got nothing but faith in you. Just calm down, and stop pushing so hard. We're nearly there."

"What about the rest of you?" Jamie asked.

"No, sir," said Claire. "We're with you."

"Agreed," said Angela.

"Me too," said Dominique.

Jamie grinned. "Thank you," he said, his voice cracking slightly. "Really. Let's go and find him."

Frankenstein watched with morbid curiosity as the audience for his death filed into the theatre of the Fraternité de la Nuit.

The pain in his arms and legs had become so constant that he no longer even felt it, which was the smallest of mercies. It had enabled him to raise his head as the first chattering voices became audible through the door at the back of the theatre, and watch as a vampire couple, dressed in beautiful evening wear, had floated through the door and down to a pair of seats in the second row.

Every one of the red velvet seats in the theatre was topped with a small RESERVATION card, with names written on them in flamboyant handwriting; Lord Dante was clearly expecting a full house.

The couple watched him intently, and whispered to each other as they made their way down the central aisle, their red eyes burning with curiosity; their expressions were similar to those of children in a zoo, children who found themselves facing a wild animal and were unable to fully convince themselves that they were safe. He stared back at them, until they took their seats and returned their attention to each other.

Frankenstein no longer felt any fear. He was exhausted, and miserable, and if this was to be his moment to die, then he was ready to embrace it. But he had no intention of dying without a fight, and he had an ace up his sleeve that no one else knew about; he knew what his body was readying itself to do, could feel his bones creaking, hear his flesh screaming for transformation.

Please, he thought. *Please let it come before he kills me.*

More vampires filed into the theatre in ones and twos, holding champagne flutes or heavy crystal-bottomed glasses in their pale fingers. All were dressed immaculately, and all peered up at him with expressions of naked surprise on their faces, as though they could not believe what their eyes were seeing. Several shouted greetings at him, and he supposed that these were men and women, like Latour, who he had once socialised with, most likely in this very building. Not for the first time, Frankenstein was glad that he could remember nothing of the life he had lived.

When every seat was taken, when every name card had been removed and stowed away in pockets and purses as keepsakes, the house lights suddenly dimmed, and an expectant hush fell over the audience.

570

Silently, the door to Lord Dante's dining room slid open. Frankenstein saw it happen, but the audience's gaze was focused on the stage, and on him. The vampire king floated silently out of his dining room, and along the rear of the curved theatre; when he reached the back of the central aisle, a spotlight burst into life, illuminating him. Lord Dante was resplendent in a gleaming black tuxedo that all but hid the bulging line of metal on his chest. His skin was lush and vibrant, his hair glossy and slicked back with oil, and his face wore an expression of utter delight, as though he had been waiting his entire life for this moment.

I suppose he has, thought Frankenstein. *Almost a century of it anyway.*

Lord Dante floated silently down the aisle of the theatre as his audience erupted with applause around him. Several vampire women threw themselves prostrate before him, clawing at his feet. He swept past without so much as a glance in their direction; his eyes, his burning, smouldering, crimson eyes, were locked on Frankenstein.

As he reached the stage, he pirouetted gracefully in the air and faced his audience, raising his arms wide. The applause grew to a standing ovation, a deafening chorus of cheers and shouts of "Bravo" filling the small space. The vampire king basked in his own glory, reborn by the adulation of his subjects, and by the realisation of a quest for revenge that was almost a hundred years old.

"Thank you," he said, and the cheers intensified anew. "Thank you, my loyal friends. Thank you."

He lowered his arms, and the noise began to subside. When it was quiet once more, Lord Dante floated up on to the stage, and faced his adoring public.

"This is an auspicious night," he said. "A night that I had begun to doubt I would ever see. But here it is, delivered to me by one of your number. Take a bow, my most faithful friend."

Latour rose from his seat in the front row to a fresh outpouring of applause. Frankenstein watched as the vampire's face broke into a huge smile of pure pleasure, and realised that there had never been any chance of persuading Latour to change his mind. Nothing would have robbed the old vampire of this moment of superiority, of praise from lesser beings.

"Thank you," said Lord Dante, favouring Latour with a beaming smile of approval. "Your actions will not be forgotten, not by anyone in this Fraternité. And most certainly not by me."

Latour sat back down in his seat. Frankenstein watched as a number of the tuxedo-clad vampires reached over and thumped him on the back, or offered their hands to be shaken, and felt his stomach twist. Then, suddenly, he felt a burning sensation along the length of his spine, as though white-hot needles were being pushed into his back.

The change was coming and, for the first time, Frankenstein relished the prospect.

Soon, he thought, through the pain. *So soon. Please be soon enough.*

"This creature you see before you," continued Lord Dante, casting a vengeful glance in Frankenstein's direction, "was the perpetrator of a great wrong, done to me a long time ago. For almost a century he has avoided being held to account for his actions, but no more. Now he will learn, as will you all, what it is to cross the vampire king of Paris."

Lord Dante's butler floated silently on stage from the wings. In his hands he held a simple wooden table, and a large roll of black cloth. He placed the table beside his master, set the cloth on its surface and departed as silently as he had arrived.

"Thank you," said the vampire king. He took the roll of cloth carefully in his pale hands, and gripped one end. Then he lifted it sharply into the air, allowing it to roll theatrically open. There was a murmur of excitement from the crowd, and the number of pairs of glowing red eyes increased dramatically. Frankenstein was pleased he couldn't see what they were looking at, but Lord Dante had no intention of sparing him the knowledge of what was coming; he turned in the air, holding the cloth at his side like a bullfighter, and showed his prisoner the contents.

The cloth was full of knives.

In dozens of loops and pockets, gleaming in the spotlight that still engulfed Lord Dante, lay blades of every shape and size: heavy, dull-looking hatchets and saws, long triangular carving knives and daggers, curved filleting blades and hunting weapons, tiny wicked-looking scalpels and stilettos. They tinkled gently as the cloth moved in the air, their reflections swimming against the domed ceiling of the theatre.

Frankenstein felt an icicle of fear stab at him as he looked more closely and saw the items that were at the very bottom of the cloth, almost appearing as an afterthought. There was a jar of white powder, which he knew for certain would be salt, and five small vials of clear liquid, about which he had no desire to speculate. Finally, and most appallingly, a small plastic tub sat in the very corner of the cloth. It was full of maggots, fat and yellow and writhing softly in the heat of the theatre.

The cloth was a sadist's dream come true; a collection of items that had no purpose other than to torture, to maim and, eventually, to kill.

"I considered adding other entertainment to this evening's bill," said Lord Dante, grinning wickedly. "Aperitifs, if you will, to warm your palates for the main course. But I reconsidered; after all, we know what we're here to see."

The vampire king laid the cloth gently on the table and leant over it, studying the blades carefully. After a few seconds, he plucked a shiny silver scalpel from its loop and held it up to the light. It flickered and gleamed, reflecting both the white light of the spotlight and the red glow of the ancient vampire's eyes.

"Let us begin," he said, softly, and turned towards Frankenstein.

"Where are we?" demanded Jamie, as Jack Williams pointed their black vehicle between rows of parked cars, gunning the engine as he did so. "Where the hell is this place?"

"This is Rue de Sévigné," replied Dominique Saint-Jacques. "It should be right here."

"I see it!" shouted Claire Lock from the back seat, where she was peering out of her window. "Back up!"

Jack hit the brakes, throwing his four passengers forward in their seats. He shoved the car into reverse, and accelerated backwards.

"Tell me where!" he shouted, peering over his shoulder and out through the rear window.

"Right here!" shouted Claire.

Jack pumped the brakes, and the five members of Jamie's team piled out of the car. In front of them, just as Claire had said, was a beautiful grey stone building, identical to its neighbours to the left and right in every way but one.

Where the windows should have been were slabs of grey stone.

"This is it," breathed Jamie. "This is where he meant."

They stepped up on to the kerb, and examined the building. It had only a single door, a large, imposing block of old, varnished wood that stood in the precise centre of the building. Between it and them was a high metal fence, beautifully ornate but also clearly difficult to scale. In the middle of the fence, directly in front of the door, was an equally elegant gate, with a large, rectangular lock, and a single keyhole.

"Open it," said Jamie.

Dominique Saint-Jacques stepped forward, pulling a thin metal barrel from his belt. He inserted it into the lock, and hit a button on the side. Fluid carbon flowed into the lock, pushing the tumblers into place. A second press of the button sent an electrical pulse through the material, hardening it instantly. Dominique turned the barrel, and the lock, which was designed to deter casual visitors and petty criminals, slid easily open. Dominique pushed open the gate, and withdrew his device.

Jamie walked up to the door, waited until the rest of his team were arrayed behind him, then raised the heavy knocker and let it fall back against its brass plate. There was a high, ringing thud, and almost immediately, the door slid open to reveal an elderly vampire in an immaculate white tie.

"You're late," he said. His voice was full of professional disappointment. "The evening's entertainment is already—" He paused, appearing to notice the five Operators for the first time. His eyes flooded red, but he had no time to say anything more.

There was a thunderclap of noise, and a deafening rush of air, and then a metal stake flew past Jamie's head; it was moving so fast it was merely a blur, and it missed him by no more than a few centimetres, but he didn't so much as flinch.

The stake burst through the vampire's chest, exiting out through a hole in his back the size of a dinner plate. There was a moment's silence, in which the butler had just enough time to cast his eyes down at his ruined chest, before he erupted in a steaming explosion of gore, splattering Jamie's uniform with warm, dripping blood. He turned his head ever so slightly to see who had fired the shot, and saw Angela Darcy smiling at him, her T-Bone locked against her shoulder.

"Good shot," he said, calmly.

"Thanks, sir," she replied.

He nodded, and strode quickly up the stairs into the building, his team following behind him. They found themselves standing in a small lobby the colour of blood; Jamie was taking in the red velvet carpet and walls, the dark crimson of the ceiling, when a roar of pain so loud that it shook the floor beneath them thundered through the building.

Jamie froze.

He knew that voice; it was the one he had spent the last three months believing he was never going to hear again. It was mangled by pain, but it was unmistakable.

"Oh my God," he whispered. "It's him. It's really him."

He turned to the four members of his team, his eyes wide.

"Whatever it takes," he said. "Whatever the cost. We bring him home. Clear?"

"Yes, sir," said the four Operators, in unison.

"OK then," said Jamie, lowering his visor, watching as his team did likewise. "This ends here."

Frankenstein roared with pain as the scalpel dug into his stomach.

He didn't want to give Lord Dante the pleasure of hearing him scream, but he failed. There was a palpable gasp of enjoyment from the crowd as he howled; the vampires were staring up at him, transfixed, their faces contorted into grimaces of sadistic lust. Several of the audience were furtively groping the people in the seats next to them, their hands disappearing beneath skirts and dresses, and below belts. Their almost boundless depravity sickened him and the roar, when it came, was as full of fury and disgust as it was of pain.

Blood was running freely down his chest, where Lord Dante had sliced away the shirt he had been wearing. The vampire king's touch on his skin had been gentle, almost comforting, until he had drawn the scalpel down the centre of his mottled grey-green torso, cutting him open from chest to stomach button. His flesh had slid apart like butter, and blood had welled instantly in a straight, neat line.

The cut wasn't deep, the pain manageable, but Frankenstein knew it was only the beginning. Lord Dante quickly drew the blade across his skin again, eight short horizontal lines crossing the long vertical one. It was a neat pattern, one that immediately began to bleed, and it made Frankenstein grit his teeth.

Lord Dante looked at him enquiringly, as if wondering when he was going to stop pretending that what was happening didn't hurt, but Frankenstein simply stared back at him, his jaw clenched. The vampire king nodded slightly, as though in admiration, then shoved the scalpel into the monster's stomach and twisted it.

The pain that flared from Frankenstein's midsection was huge and hot, and he screamed, a vast roar of damnation.

Too late, he thought, resignation spreading through him. *Too late. I'm going to die in this theatre, with this void inside my head.*

But then his body began to tremble, and savage elation burst through him. Pain exploded through every particle of his being, but he welcomed it, drawing back his lips into a snarling grin that made Lord Dante widen his eyes with surprise. As he felt himself begin to slip, as he felt the change begin, at last, to overwhelm him, the

577

last thing he saw before his eyes turned yellow and everything faded to black and white, were five dark figures emerging into the rear of the theatre.

Jamie slipped silently through the door at the rear of the lobby. He found himself in sudden darkness, and stepped to the right as his eyes adjusted to the gloom. The rest of his team filed in and took positions beside him, their backs against a curving, red velvet wall.

They were standing at the back of a theatre with its house lights lowered, and Jamie's eyes were immediately drawn to the dark red glow emanating from the sixty or so seats that faced the stage.

Vampires, he realised. *Lots and lots of vampires.*

Then he followed their gaze, and forgot all about the creatures in the audience.

In the middle of the stage, bound to a thick wooden pole, was Frankenstein's monster. His head was back, the tendons in his neck standing out, his teeth clenched against whatever had caused him to issue the deafening scream. There was a dark figure leaning in close to the monster's chest, but Jamie barely saw him; his mind was temporarily overwhelmed.

He's alive. I didn't want to let myself believe it. But he's really alive.

The figure on the stage stepped aside and Jamie felt a surge of almost uncontrollable rage burst through him as he saw the tattered remains of his friend's chest. Blood was running from what looked like a hundred cuts, pooling at his waist and dripping steadily to the wooden floor. He felt words starting to form in his throat; he didn't know what they were going to be, he only knew that he was going to scream them as loudly as his vocal cords would allow, and used every ounce of his strength to push them back down.

578

Giving yourself away won't help him, he told himself. *You need a distraction.*

Jamie felt something press against his gloved hand, and looked round. Jack Williams was holding an ultraviolet light grenade, and was nodding pointedly at the aisle that ran the length of the theatre; it began less than two metres from where Jamie was standing. Jamie grinned behind his visor, then nodded.

Jack stepped silently round Jamie, and slid sideways along the wall until he was facing down the aisle. The matt-black of his uniform made him invisible in the shadows, and the material that clung to his body prevented any scent escaping that might have attracted the attention of the vampire audience. It didn't matter, though, as none of the vampires were looking anywhere other than at the stage; they were absolutely focused on the bleeding, howling monster.

Jack twisted the grenade open, crouched and rolled it slowly down the aisle, a remote trigger resting in his hand.

"This is it," whispered Jamie over the comms link in his helmet. "Ready One when Jack pulls the trigger."

He heard the faintest rustling as his team unsheathed their T-Bones and MP5s. Jamie left his where they were; he was watching Jack.

The grenade rolled silently down the aisle, between the throngs of watching vampires. As it reached the halfway point, a woman in a dark green dress turned to look at it, a curious expression on her face. She opened her mouth to say something, but at that moment, Jack Williams pressed his trigger, and before she got the chance her mouth was full of flames.

The UV grenade burst into life without the slightest noise; one second there was only the darkened throng of vampires, the next the theatre was full of blinding purple light. A millisecond later the screaming began.

579

Jamie, whose attention had returned to the stage, saw something strange in the split second before the grenade pulsed into life. He saw what was left of Frankenstein's shirt ripple, as though something was running under the grey-green skin beneath it. Then the grenade exploded, and all he saw was fire.

There was a sudden, enormous bloom of heat, as half the vampires in the audience burst into flames. They leapt into the air, screaming, beating at their clothes and skin, trying to extinguish the purple fire. On the stage, Lord Dante recoiled in horror, more at the usurping of his moment of triumph than out of any genuine concern for his burning guests.

The vampires at the edges of the crowd, who had been shielded from the ultraviolet light by their wives and husbands, their friends and lovers, jumped up from their seats, their eyes blazing red, searching for the source of the carnage.

Screams filled the theatre, as the most badly burned vampires fell from the air and crashed down on to the seats. Jamie pulled the T-Bone from his belt, set it against his shoulder, sighted down the barrel and pulled the trigger. His stake rocketed across the auditorium, smashing clean through the chest of a vampire in a dark grey suit, who was desperately attempting to beat out the flames that were consuming a vampire woman in a cocktail dress. He was driven backwards half a step, then burst like a balloon, coating the burning woman in gore.

The stake whistled back into the barrel of Jamie's weapon, as he heard a series of loud bangs from his right and left. Stakes flew through the air, their metal wires trailing behind them, and four more vampires erupted in columns of steaming blood. Finally, eventually, the vampires at the edges of the crowd, the ones whose burns were minimal, followed the flight of the weapons, and saw the five figures lurking in the shadows.

580

There was a deafening howl of rage from one of them, who pointed with a skeletal finger. The vampires who were still able to stand, perhaps thirty of them, turned en masse, and regarded the dark shapes. Then, with a chorus of snarls and howls, they leapt towards the intruders.

Frankenstein's body shook as though an electric current was being passed through it.

He could see the flames that were sweeping through the theatre, the burning seats, the screaming, roasting vampires, but what was far, far worse, was that he could smell them. His nostrils flared as the scents, complicated, swirling things, almost physical objects, floated through the air; he could smell fear, and pain, and the anger of the panicking vampires, could smell charring bones and cooking flesh, could smell, with enormous satisfaction, the fury rising from Lord Dante, who was staring out over his audience with a look of helpless rage on his face. Then the change began in earnest, and all he was aware of was his own agony.

His legs snapped back on themselves, the bones splintering and knitting back together in a completely different shape. He felt thick hair burst from every pore on his body, felt his arms crack, bend and eventually break. The pain was so huge he couldn't even scream; he had known what was coming, had been through it twice before, but there was simply no way to prepare for the feeling of your body being broken and rebuilt.

Frankenstein felt the ropes that had bound him tightly to the post give way as his limbs changed shape beneath them, and then his mind, what little of it remained in his possession, slipped away, as the animal overcame him.

*

"Spread!" yelled Jamie, as the vampires came for him and his team. "Move!"

He threw himself to the ground, beneath the flying lunge of a vampire who had to have been in at least his sixties. The man crashed into the wall where Jamie had been standing against it, and crumpled to the floor. Jamie leapt forward, as quick as a striking cobra, and buried his stake in the vampire's chest.

He didn't wait for the explosion of blood that he knew would follow; he was moving before it came, crouched low, running along the wall towards the corner of the stage. He threw one backward glance as he did so, and felt a surge of pride as he saw his team fan out through the theatre, Claire and Dominique heading to the right, Jack and Angela moving down the aisle, into the heart of the vampire audience.

As he ran, Jamie pulled his MP5 from his belt, and flicked the safety off. When he reached the corner of the theatre, from where he knew he could not be ambushed from the rear, he dropped to one knee and aimed into the burning hell of the theatre. Angela and Jack had cut a swathe through the flaming, screaming vampires, staking them as they moved forward; blood boomed into the air in a series of thunderclaps left in the wake of the two Operators.

Five or six vampires had floated up to the highest point of the ceiling, either to avoid the carnage beneath them or to get a better vantage point from which to attack. Jamie didn't wait to find out which; he pointed his MP5 into the group of dark, floating figures, and pulled the trigger. The submachine gun was deafeningly loud in the small theatre, and Jamie saw a number of vampires howl, and cover their ears.

Must be so painful with their super-hearing, he thought, and smiled grimly behind his visor. *Good.*

The stream of bullets tore through the floating vampires, and they tumbled back down to the seats like falling leaves. A fresh bout of screaming erupted, before Angela and Jack were on top of them, their stakes flashing up and down in the purple light of the fire.

Jamie felt motion to his right, and spun round; a door was opening, a door that he had not noticed as he made his way along the curved wall. He fumbled for his T-Bone, and had it to his shoulder just before a vampire in a spotless tuxedo emerged, his red eyes blazing. Jamie pulled the trigger; the shot was high, as he had been forced to rush, but it made no difference. The stake tore the vampire's head clean away from his shoulders, and carried it on its flight.

The headless torso staggered, its hands groping at its neck, before Jamie's weapon reached the end of its wire, and began to rewind. The stake jerked to a halt, and the head was thrown clear; as it bounced and rolled away into the shadows, Jamie saw a look of outrage on what remained of its face. He ran forward, plunged his stake into the headless body's heart, and returned to his position.

He watched Claire and Dominique T-Bone two vampires that were attempting to flank them, watched Angela fire her Glock 17 empty, the bullets thudding unerringly into the heads of a dozen smouldering vampires, and then he saw movement in the corner of his eye, and turned to look up at the stage.

What he saw stopped his heart cold.

Oh God, no, he thought. *Oh Jesus, no. Why didn't I think of this? Why didn't I realise?*

On the stage, the vampire who had been torturing Frankenstein was standing motionless with his back to Jamie. Beyond him, where Jamie's friend had been bound to the post, was something from the deepest circles of hell, a mewling, howling monstrosity.

Frankenstein's face was still recognisable, atop the grey body of a swollen, grotesquely misshapen wolf. Its legs kicked savagely against the post that it was still loosely tied to, and as Jamie watched, the heavy wood shattered under the impact. The wolf fell forward, landing heavily on three of its legs; it shook the fourth one until the last of the ropes that had held it were gone, and stood shakily on all fours. Jamie saw the last of his friend's humanity ebb away, saw his face twist and lengthen, saw the jaw break and reset in less than a second. Then Frankenstein was gone, and the enormous wolf that had replaced him threw back its giant head and howled.

The noise was otherworldly, so huge and so full of dancing, running misery that every living thing in the theatre stopped and turned towards the stage. Angela Darcy, ever the professional, took the chance to survey the situation.

"Fourteen vamps still alive, Jamie," she said.

"We've got a bigger problem," replied Jamie, his voice low and full of shock. "Much, much bigger."

"Why didn't we see this coming?" asked Jack Williams. "Why didn't Intelligence flag this up?"

"There was no time for an Intelligence evaluation," said Jamie, distantly. "I was told to get wheels up ASAP. I never thought... I never..."

"What do we do about it?" demanded Angela. "We can worry about who should have seen it coming later. Bringing him home just got a hell of a lot more difficult."

The wolf was peering around the theatre, its breath blasting out of its nostrils, its tongue hanging from its vast mouth; it appeared to be trying to make sense of its surroundings. The huge head swung slowly to the left, and then to the right, where its yellow eyes landed on the vampire who had been torturing it. With a deafening snarl, it hurled itself towards him.

Lord Dante flung himself up and back, evading the crunching jaws by mere millimetres.

This can't be happening, he thought. *This is not fair.*

The vampire king swooped up to the ceiling of his theatre, desperately trying to think of a way to salvage the situation or, if that proved impossible, to guarantee that he made it out of the building with his life. The wolf was back on its feet below him, howling up at him, but he knew he was beyond its reach. He looked down at the five black-clad figures as they began to move again, plunging their stakes into the burning bodies of his audience.

You'll pay for this, whoever you are, he thought. *You will rue the day you crossed Lord Dante, the vampire king of Paris.*

Jamie backed away from the wolf, his heart screaming with pain as he saw what had become of his friend. It was almost too much for him to bear. He had no idea what to do now; in none of the scenarios he had run in his head on the flight across the Channel had he even allowed for the possibility that was now unfolding before him.

He was furious with himself for not having made the connection; he had seen the rising full moon from the helicopter as they made their way to Paris, and he had seen Alexandru's werewolf close its mouth over Frankenstein's hand before the two of them fell over the cliffs. He had replayed that memory, one of the most painful he possessed, a thousand times since it had happened, but his focus had always been on the terrible final moment when his friend disappeared from view; the injury done to him before he fell had seemed irrelevant, in light of what had followed. Now his mind was racing as he tried to think of a way, any way, that he could still save his friend.

He circled round to the back of the theatre, away from the wolf, which was staring up at the vampire floating high above, its jaws hanging open, its yellow eyes narrow.

"Regroup!" he shouted, and watched as his team peeled away from the remaining vampires and backed quickly towards him. They met at the top of the aisle; below them the theatre burned, the purple ultraviolet flames that had burst from the vampires' bodies now replaced with flickering yellow and orange as the seats and the carpets were engulfed.

The remaining vampires, twelve by Jamie's count, not including the one floating above them, were huddled together in the middle of the theatre. They looked lost, and disoriented, as though they were unable to believe what was happening. One woman was holding the charred body of a man in her arms, and appeared to be whispering softly to it, her face close to the smouldering ruin.

"Let's end this," said Jamie, softly, and led his team down the aisle.

Destroying the last twelve vampires was the work of less than a minute; none of them put up any resistance at all, and the looks on their faces, as they stared around at the rivers of spilled blood, at the roaring flames that licked round their ankles, suggested that many considered their destruction to be a kindness.

"You devils!" bellowed the vampire who was floating near the ceiling. "How dare you? Don't you know who I am?"

Angela drew her T-Bone to her shoulder and fired. She was so quick that Jamie gasped, but the floating vampire knocked the projectile aside with a derisory sneer.

"I am Lord Dante!" it screamed. "The vampire king of Paris. This is my home!"

At the sound of the vampire's voice, the enormous wolf howled anew, shaking the theatre. Then the howl was cut short, replaced by a low, guttural growl. Jamie turned to see what had prompted it, and saw a lone vampire had floated up on to the stage and was slowly approaching the wolf, his hands out before him in a gesture of placation.

"What the hell is this?" asked Dominique.

"I've no idea," replied Jamie.

The vampire stopped a couple of metres away from the wolf, which had lowered its head towards the ground, its weight back on its rear legs. It was still growling, and from this side view Jamie saw with horror the metal bolts sticking out of the thick grey fur at its neck.

"Henry," said the vampire, slowly. "That's your name. Henry. Don't you recognise me? It's me, Latour. What has become of—"

He got no further.

At the mention of the vampire's name, the wolf's growl exploded into a snarl of rage. In one huge, lightning-fast step it closed the distance between them, and clamped its huge jaws round the vampire's head, cutting off his words. The vampire began to scream from inside the giant maw, his fists thumping uselessly against the wolf's snout. Then, with a terrible crunching sound that would haunt Jamie for the rest of his life, the wolf closed its jaws. Blood squirted out between its yellow teeth and splattered to the floor, before the wolf tore Latour's head from his body with a shake of its giant snout that seemed almost casual, and swallowed it whole.

There was a scream of rage from the ceiling, and Jamie looked up at the vampire who called himself the king of Paris. His hands were clawing at his face, his eyes wide and blazing.

"You foul monster!" he shrieked. "I will hunt you to the ends of the earth! I will pursue you with every breath I have left! You will die a thousand deaths for what you have done!"

"T-Bones," said Jamie, suddenly, looking up at the raving vampire. "Everyone. Right now."

He raised his weapon to his shoulder, waited a split second for the rest of his team to do the same, then fired. The combined bang of exploding gas was incredibly loud, and Lord Dante, whose attention had been focused entirely on Frankenstein, looked round in time to see the projectiles coming, but not in time to avoid them.

The five metal stakes tore through his body from all sides. Two crunched through his thighs before burying themselves in his stomach, one ploughed through his armpit before crashing into the red plaster of the ceiling, one thudded deep into the heavy bone at his shoulder and the last one tore through his throat, obliterating it.

A huge spray of blood burst from Lord Dante's neck, and fell the long distance to the floor of the theatre. For a moment, the vampire king twisted in the air, as the heavy metal wires hung from his body; he seemed to be trying to speak, but all that emerged from his gaping mouth was a series of bloody gurgles.

Then the winches of the five T-Bones fired, and he was pulled to pieces.

The five stakes whirred back into the barrels of the weapons with heavy *thunks*. A second later the vampire king of Paris fell into the aisle of his theatre, landing with a series of wet thuds. His legs were severed, as was one of his arms; they landed on the sloping floor, and rolled away towards the stage. His midsection was ruined, but his chest and his head were intact; blood was still gushing from his throat, and as Jamie watched, his bile rising despite the things he had seen in the last three months, the vampire began to age.

His hair turned bright white, and great tufts of it fell to the red carpet. His skin greyed, and wrinkled, and suddenly his face was that of an old man. His chest rose and fell so slightly it was barely noticeable. His eyes stared up at Jamie's visor, a look of desperate pain etched into them.

Jamie was about to give the order for the vampire king to be staked, when a shadow fell across him, and he felt a blast of hot air on the back of his neck. He turned his head, ever so slowly, and found himself staring into the huge yellow eyes of the wolf that had been his friend. The blood-soaked snout was only centimetres away from his visor.

More slowly than he had ever moved in his life, Jamie twisted his body round so that he was crouching in front of the huge animal. It tilted its head to one side as he did so, its eyes never leaving his purple visor, its mouth hanging open. He backed away, lifting his feet and placing them down as carefully as he could; he did not want to make a sound, or a sudden movement.

The gap between himself and the wolf slowly increased, and then he was at the top of the aisle, standing with the rest of his team. They stared as the wolf padded forward, and stood over what remained of Lord Dante.

The vampire king's mouth worked silently as the great wolf's breath blasted against his face, blowing the long strands of white hair back against the blood-soaked floor. With great effort, Lord Dante lifted his one remaining hand, and placed it gently against the thick fur of the wolf's snout. The wolf closed its huge yellow eyes for a moment, seeming to enjoy the vampire's touch. Then it lowered its head, and began to eat the vampire king's chest.

Lord Dante didn't scream, but Jamie was sure that was only because he was incapable of doing so. His eyes stared up at the ceiling, his hand gripping the wolf's fur, his mouth forming a perfect circle, as the thick, razor-sharp yellow teeth chewed through his flesh; he was still alive as Frankenstein broke through his ribcage, and tore his beating heart from his body. The wolf mashed it between his teeth, growling with pleasure, then swallowed the raw meat.

As the remains of Lord Dante exploded around it, showering its grey fur with crimson, it threw back its head and howled a deafening roar of unmistakable triumph.

46

THE TWIST OF THE KNIFE

"What now?" breathed Jack Williams, asking the question that all five members of the Blacklight team were thinking. "What the hell do we do now?"

The wolf was standing in the aisle before them, less than three metres away, licking Lord Dante's blood from the soaked, steaming carpet. It appeared to have no interest in them, but it had growled, without looking up, when Jack had stepped alongside Jamie. The inference seemed to be clear; that it had not yet decided what to do with them, and would prefer it if they stayed still while it did.

"Dominique," said Jamie, softly. "You have tranquilliser darts, right?"

"Not darts," replied Dominique Saint-Jacques. "I have tranquillisers, but they're hypodermics. You can't fire them."

"Then what the hell use are they?" hissed Jamie.

"They're for human witnesses," said Dominique, sharply. "Not for werewolves."

Jamie sighed. "Give them to me," he said.

"How many?"

"All of them."

Dominique lifted three hypodermic needles from a metal container on his belt, and passed them down the line to Jamie. He flipped the plastic caps off, and looked at the tiny needles.

"Will these put him down?" he asked.

"I don't have the slightest idea," said Dominique. "I hope so, for all our sakes, but I don't know. That's the truth."

"Great," said Jamie. "Well, I guess we're going to find out."

Jamie lifted his visor, blinking as his eyes adjusted to the gloom. The fires were burning themselves out, the chairs and small patches of carpet that had been aflame now merely smouldering. There was blood everywhere, and Jamie took a moment to appreciate the work his team had done.

Sixty vampires, give or take. No injuries, no casualties. Not bad at all.

He smiled again.

No injuries yet anyway. That might be about to change.

He took a slow, deliberate step into the aisle. The wolf growled again, a little louder than the last time, and then Angela's voice rang in his ears.

"What the hell do you think you're doing?" she asked.

"What does it look like?" he replied.

"It looks like you're trying to commit suicide by werewolf."

"I assure you I'm not," he said. He was staring at the enormous animal as it lapped blood from the floor, and was, frankly, terrified. But he knew what he had to do. "I'm not leaving without him. He's why we came."

"He?" demanded Angela. "It's not *he* any more, can't you see that? Are you going to take a werewolf back to the Loop with us?"

"That's the plan," Jamie replied, taking a second step forward.

The wolf growled again, more urgently, and Jamie felt his legs begin to shake.

"What are you going to tell Admiral Seward?" demanded Angela.

"Don't worry, he's still my friend for twenty-nine days of the month? What do you think he's going to say to that?"

"I'm hoping he's going to say congratulations on a successful mission," said Jamie. "Now shut the hell up and let me do this."

He took a third step, bringing him within two metres of the animal, and then suddenly the wolf's head was up, quicker than Jamie's eyes could follow, its mouth wide and coated red, its nostrils flared, a sawing growl of warning emanating from its throat as its misshapen yellow eyes locked on Jamie's own.

Jamie stopped dead. He didn't know how he knew, but he was absolutely sure that if he dropped his gaze, the animal would tear his throat out. So he stared back at the wolf, and saw something remarkable happen.

The huge eyes, sunflower yellow with pupils as black as night, suddenly narrowed, in an unmistakably human gesture of recognition.

"That's right," said Jamie, softly. "You know me. Don't you?"

He took another step forward. The wolf reared up, but it didn't step back, or leap forward and kill him.

"Don't you?" he repeated. "What's my name? You know it. What's my name?"

He was within a metre of the animal now. The wolf looked confused, and suddenly miserable, as though the elation of victory had been replaced by deep anguish. It moved its head quickly from side to side, its growl lowering in volume and rising in pitch, until it sounded almost questioning.

"What's my name?" Jamie asked, stepping forward again.

He was directly under the enormous snout; he could have reached out and touched the slick-red grey fur.

"Tell me," he whispered. "What's my name?"

The wolf's mouth opened, and it looked down at him with an

expression of abject suffering. Jamie braced himself for the sensation of teeth closing round his head, but he did not shut his eyes.

"*Jaaaaaaaaaaaaaaamieeeeeeeeeeeeee,*" howled the wolf.

Jamie threw himself against the enormous snout and wrapped his arms round the animal's head, his mind empty of everything but the knowledge that he had found his friend, and saved him, as Frankenstein had once saved him.

The wolf's enormous tongue flicked out of its mouth and licked Jamie's face. The huge animal was still growling, but the tone of the rumbling noise had changed. It no longer sounded like a warning; now it sounded oddly like the purring of a cat. Jamie felt the rough texture of the tongue on the side of his face, and fought back tears. The wolf lowered its head, and nuzzled against him, its yellow eyes closed. Jamie saw his chance and, with guilt stabbing at his heart, plunged the three hypodermic needles into the thick fur at the animal's neck.

The yellow eyes flew open, but the wolf didn't pull away from him. It regarded him with a look in its eyes that Jamie initially took for sadness, for disappointment, but realised almost instantly was trust, was faith, in him. The eyes closed again, as the huge animal slumped to the floor, its grey flank settling on the blood-soaked carpet. Its chest rose and fell steadily, as its tongue rolled out between its teeth and hung limply towards the ground.

Jamie sighed, a deep, rattling release of everything that had built up inside him over the past three months. He felt elation, and pride, and fear, and guilt, all mingled together in a cloud of emotion that threatened to overwhelm him. He pulled the needles out of the wolf's neck, and took a faltering step back.

"Holy shit," whispered Jack Williams. "You did it, Jamie. You did it."

Jamie was turning to his friend, a smile spreading on his face, when the radio on his belt suddenly buzzed into life. He lifted it from his belt, keyed the RECEIVE button and held it to his ear.

"Jamie, it's me," said the voice on the other end of the line.

"Larissa!" exclaimed Jamie. "Larissa, we got him! We were almost too late, but we found this—"

"Jamie, listen to me," interrupted Larissa. "I called to tell you that I love you. OK? I don't want to never have said it."

"What are you talking about?" Jamie asked. "We'll be home in forty-five minutes."

"I'm sorry," said Larissa. "You're going to be too late."

47

NOWHERE TO RUN, NOWHERE TO HIDE

Kate Randall sprinted into the vast hangar and skidded to a halt in front of the control panel that stood beside the wide-open doors. She thumped the flat red button in the centre, and instantly the deafening klaxon of the general alarm screamed through the Loop.

The Duty Officer came flying out of his office on the other side of the door, shouting at her as he ran.

"Hey!" he yelled. "What the hell do you think you're doing?"

Kate turned to face him, and her expression stopped him dead in his tracks.

"Open the armoury!" she shouted. "Open everything we've got, and get everyone up here now."

"What the hell is…"

The Operator's voice trailed off as something caught his eye beyond the open hangar doors, and he turned his head towards it. His mouth fell open momentarily, then snapped shut. He turned away from her without another word, and sprinted towards the side of the hangar. Kate watched him work a series of controls, then saw two wide panels of the side walls slide back, revealing long racks of T-Bones, Russian Daybreakers and countless other weapons. She watched him lift a T-Bone from a rack, then turned and sprinted back out of the hangar.

"Wait!" bellowed the Duty Officer, and she turned back to face him. "Where are you going?"

"My friend is out there!" she yelled, and ran towards the runway.

Larissa replaced the radio on her belt. She could hear Jamie's voice shouting her name as she did so, but there was nothing more to say. She flexed the muscle in her jaw that few people possessed; her fangs slid smoothly down from her gums, and her eyes blazed a deep, swirling crimson. She stood in the vast shadow as it swept towards the Loop, her feet set, her shoulders back, her hands dangling at her sides, her gaze locked on what was coming.

Valeri Rusmanov floated above the grass, at the head of an army of vampires.

They numbered more than two hundred; they flew at his back, their combined shadow sweeping before them. They were not hurrying; their progress was steady, and ominously silent. Valeri had sent word throughout Europe, and the men and women who followed him now were the ones who had answered the call. They had arrived at the chateau in ones and twos; some he knew, or knew of, many he had never met before in his life.

He didn't care. His master had given him an order, and he needed soldiers to help him carry it out. They had flown to England the previous night, and lain low in the stately home of a loyal follower of Valeri's late brother, Alexandru, an elderly vampire whose excitement at hosting the oldest Rusmanov brother, even for as little as twelve hours, had bordered on the pitiful.

He had given two orders before they departed, as simple as any he had ever given in his former life as a General of the Wallachian Army: Henry Seward was to be captured alive; everyone else was to be killed. His new army had hungrily agreed, excited at the prospect of unrestrained violence against the men and women of Blacklight. Everyone who had answered Valeri's call knew someone who had been destroyed by the infernal black soldiers; it was the reason the vast majority of them were there.

The others, the small number who had come for the sport, for the opportunity to maim and murder, were the ones that Valeri knew he had to keep an eye on. They would be useful, he knew, but they might also be difficult to control. For their benefit, he had a large printout of the photo from Henry Seward's ID, and had explained in intricate biological detail the punishment that would befall anyone who failed to obey the order to bring him back alive.

They had made their way carefully through the woods that surrounded the Department 19 base; Valeri had been prepared to alter his plan if they were detected, but the information his informant had supplied was accurate. The long column of vampires had snaked through the trees, keeping beyond the range of the motion sensors, floating over the pressure pads that littered the forest floor.

When they had reached the fence that marked the perimeter of the compound, Valeri had taken a deep breath; this was a moment he had often dreamt of, although he had never foreseen a time that it could be put into action. Dracula's order had changed that; it no longer mattered if a frontal assault on Blacklight was foolhardy, or suicidal. He had been ordered to do it, and he was nothing if not a loyal soldier.

He had barked a simple command at his assembled army, and as one, they had leapt into the air, over the high fence, over the ultraviolet no-man's-land, over the laser array, and had flown steadily towards the distant dome of the Department 19 headquarters. As they crossed the runway that bisected the circular base, Valeri's superhuman eyes picked out two figures on the grass below; as he watched, one turned and ran for the open side of the dome, from which yellow light blazed in the gathering gloom.

"She's going to raise the alarm," hissed the vampire at his side, a Ukrainian he had once hunted with on the Russian steppes, whose name was Alexey Grigoriev.

"Let her raise it," said Valeri. "It will do no good now."

The second figure turned to face them, and Valeri saw twin points of red light blazing from the place where it stood.

The traitor, realised Valeri, with a rush of pleasure. *The vampire girl who helped them to kill Alexandru. How fitting that she will be the first to die.*

Kate screeched to a halt beside Larissa, and grabbed at the vampire girl's arm. Her friend turned on her, her eyes blazing.

"Come on!" Kate yelled. "You can't stay here!"

"Go back to the hangar, Kate," said Larissa. "Before it's too late."

"It's already too late!" Kate screamed. "And I'm not going without you. So come with me. Now, Larissa!"

Larissa looked at her friend; her face was full of worry, but there was no fear to be seen. The vampire's heart was suddenly full of love for Kate; she was so brave, so determined that she would not leave her friend behind.

She smiled at Kate, then grabbed her effortlessly round the waist and rocketed into the air. Larissa flew through the air like a missile, barely two metres above the ground, and slid easily on to the concrete floor of the hangar. She released her grip on Kate, who stared at her with disbelief.

"When did you get so fast?" asked Kate, breathlessly.

"Later," said Larissa. "If there is one."

There was a thundering noise behind them, audible even above the howl of the general alarm, and then the doors at the rear of the hangar burst open, and black shapes poured into the wide-open space. An intense din of shouted orders and the metallic hammering of loading weapons filled the air, and then Admiral Seward was beside the two girls, staring out at the oncoming vampires, a look of utter horror on his face.

"Report!" he yelled. "Where the hell did they come from?"

"Out of the trees, sir!" shouted Kate. "On the far side of the Loop."

Paul Turner skidded to a halt beside his Director, a Russian Daybreaker in his hands. "Why didn't Surveillance pick them up?" he demanded. "How did they get so close without us knowing?"

"They must have come in below the radar," replied Seward. "Stayed on the ground until they got to the fence."

"The sensor arrays," said Turner, his voice as blank as always. "In the woods. There's no way through them unless—"

"Unless you know the way," finished Seward, his eyes never leaving the slowly approaching army. "Unless someone gives you the maps."

There was a moment of silence, as they all considered the implications of Admiral Seward's words. Then a voice bellowed from behind them, and they turned towards it.

It was Cal Holmwood who had shouted. He was standing to attention, his jaw set, a look of formidable determination on his face. To his left and right, stretching to the very edges of the hangar,

600

stood the entire roster of Department 19: almost two hundred black-clad figures, bristling with as much weaponry as they could carry. Every one of them was staring at their Director, who felt his heart surge with pride as he saw the absence of fear on their faces.

"Weapons free," Seward barked. "No quarter, no mercy. We fight to the last. Understood?"

"Yes, sir," boomed the Operators, with one voice.

Seward turned back to the open hangar, and watched the vampires slide gently to the ground, two hundred metres away.

Valeri Rusmanov looked at the assembled ranks of Blacklight, and stifled a laugh.

"We outnumber them," he said, softly. "This will be the work of minutes."

He felt an incredible sense of nostalgia sweep through him. This was how battles had been fought in his day, before laser-guided cruise missiles, before remote Predator drones and pinhole satellites; two lines of soldiers on the opposite sides of a field, until death or surrender.

It was almost always death.

But because he lacked the sadism of his late brother, or the appetite for chaos of his master, Valeri would at least offer them the alternative.

"Henry Seward!" he shouted, his voice rumbling and echoing across the open space between the two armies. "You know me, and who I stand for. Submit both yourself and my brother to me, willingly, and I will make the deaths of your men quick. This is the only offer I will make."

Kate gripped her Director's arm, tightly. Admiral Seward looked down at it, a look of surprise on his face, then smiled at her. He turned back towards the vampires, opened his mouth to reply, but was beaten to it.

"We reject your offer, Valeri!" shouted Paul Turner, his usually expressionless face raging with pure anger. "It is as worthless as you and your master."

"So be it!" shouted Valeri. "By all means, have it your way."

"When they come," said Seward, loudly, "move out to meet them. We'll engage them in the open."

"Inside the hangar their speed will not help them as much," said Turner, in a low voice. "We should let them come."

Seward looked at his Security Officer. "It will not be enough," he said, softly. "Our only chance lies out there."

"With what, sir?" asked Turner.

Seward didn't respond; instead, he pulled a small metal screen from his belt, and placed his thumb in the middle of a black panel. The panel powered up, and a ten-digit number display appeared. Seward quickly typed in a long series of numbers, and waited; after a long moment, the panel turned red, and the word ARMING appeared in the middle. Beneath it, a counter began to run down from four minutes, the seconds and milliseconds rolling back in a red blur.

Then Valeri's vampire army burst forward, a pulsating mass of red eyes and violent lust, and the time for talking was over.

"Go," bellowed Admiral Seward, and the Operators of Department 19 sprinted forward. There was no cheer, no battle cry, just the drumming of boots on concrete, and the flat crackle of gunfire.

Paul Turner led the charge; he sprinted out on to the black tarmac of the landing area that lay before the hangar, and lifted his Daybreaker to his shoulder. The heavy Russian weapon was not standard issue for Blacklight Operators; it had been deemed by the

Chief of the General Staff to be nothing more than a portable war crime, and too unsafe for general use. It was, however, remarkably effective.

Turner rapid-fired the weapon, rolling with the recoil that forced his shoulder back each time he pulled the trigger. The sticky charges whined through the air and attached themselves to six of the oncoming vampires; the Security Officer's aim was unerring. With a series of revolting crunches, the pneumatic charges on the rounds fired, and the vampires screamed in pain as the explosive cores punched through their flesh and into their bodies. A second later the charges fired, and the six vampires exploded like fireworks, huge sprays of blood thumping into the night sky and falling to the ground like rain.

Turner didn't even wait to see the results of his shots; he trusted his own abilities completely, and by the time the explosives had detonated he had pulled the T-Bone from his belt and sent its metal stake whistling through the heart of an onrushing vampire woman. She burst with an audible pop, spraying her contents across the tarmac. As the stake wound itself back into the T-Bone's barrel, Turner drew his MP5 and fired it into the tight mass of vampires, sending blood spilling into the air as he ran to his left, seeking the flank of the vampire army.

Kate Randall paused for a moment, despite herself, and watched the former SAS Sergeant go to work. Paul Turner was a legend in Blacklight, but she had never seen him fight. His role as the Security Officer kept him almost permanently at the Loop, and seeing him unleashed was a sight to behold; he was nothing less than a killing machine, a calm, precise instrument of death. She watched him run to the far end of the landing area, then returned her attention to the battle.

The vampire army cannoned into the Operators like a tsunami, spilling them left and right, splintering their line almost instantly. They descended on them like birds of prey, dropping from the air to rend flesh and spill blood. Kate was suddenly inside the chaos; around her black figures fired weapons, and blurred shapes swooped and dived.

She ducked her head and ran forward, her T-Bone in her hands. Ahead of her, a vampire man in his early twenties hauled an Operator she recognised from the dining hall into the air, then sent him crashing back down to the tarmac. She heard the dry snap of breaking bones, and sprinted forward as the vampire leant over the stricken man, his mouth wide open, his eyes glowing red.

She raised her T-Bone as she ran, and pulled the trigger when she was within range. The stake whistled through the cool evening air, and crunched through the vampire's armpit. He threw back his head and howled in pain, before the injured Operator raised his remaining working arm and hammered his stake into its heart. It erupted in a column of foul-smelling blood as the metal stake thumped back into the barrel of Kate's weapon, and she skidded to the floor beside the wounded man.

His right arm and leg were broken, she saw instantly; open fractures had sent jagged splinters of bone through his skin and out through the material of his uniform. She was about to tell him he was going to be all right when he suddenly slid away across the tarmac, screaming in pain as his broken limbs thudded against the ground.

Kate jumped to her feet, and saw a vampire woman dragging the Operator away by his ankles. Kate screamed for her to stop, and raised her T-Bone to her shoulder, but before she could pull the trigger, the vampire pirouetted off the ground, holding the screaming Operator like a rag doll, spun in a full circle and hurled the flailing man into the air. He disappeared into the twilight, and out of sight.

Kate fired her weapon, but the vampire skipped out of the way, and grinned at her. She felt for her stake, but the vampire turned and disappeared towards the hangar, leaving her on the edge of the battle. Then she heard a distant thud, and nausea swept through her as she realised what had made it. She swallowed it down, and threw herself back into the fight.

Larissa leapt into the air as soon as the vampires moved, and shot forward to meet them. She felt an anger burning inside her that was stronger than she had ever felt before; she was outraged at the sheer brazenness of Valeri's attack, and she was beyond furious that he would dare to endanger her friends.

She cut through the first wave of vampires like a knife through butter, her arms wide, her razor-sharp fingernails slicing through flesh and sending blood splashing to the tarmac below. A vampire man in his fifties growled, and changed his course towards her; she waited until he was about to grab for her throat with his gnarled hands, then at the last possible second she flipped up and over him, moving through the air as though she was weightless.

The vampire's hands grabbed at nothing, and then Larissa was behind him, one hand tearing out his throat in a shocking explosion of scarlet arterial blood, the other punching through his ribs from the rear and destroying his beating heart. The vampire barely had time to realise what had happened before he exploded, splattering to the ground in a splash of crimson.

Larissa easily ducked beneath the outstretched arms of a vampire who had thrown himself towards her from behind, and drew her T-Bone almost lazily. She fired it from her hip, and watched with satisfaction as it thudded through the vampire's solar plexus, destroying him instantly. She spun in the air, surveying the battle, and then swooped down to join it.

Admiral Henry Seward looked around with rising horror at what was unfolding on the wide landing area which had become a battlefield. His Operators were fighting with all the skill and bravery he expected, but there were simply too many vampires for them to deal with.

The tarmac was strewn with the bodies of his friends and colleagues. He lifted his T-Bone and punctured the chest of a vampire who dropped from the sky in front of him, and felt savage enjoyment at the look of enormous surprise on its face as it burst into a shower of gore. He pulled the small metal panel from his belt, and checked its read-out.

2:36...

2:35...

2:34...

Not fast enough, he thought. *Nowhere near fast enough.*

He replaced the panel in its pouch on his belt, and ran forward through the chaos, looking for Valeri Rusmanov.

Shaun Turner saw Kate through a momentary gap in the carnage, and ran to her side. He grabbed her arm, and she spun round, raising her metal stake in her hand. He caught it before she had time to plant it in his chest, and pulled her towards the runway.

"This way!" he yelled. "We have to spread out."

She nodded, then ran with him, ducking and weaving between snarling vampires and black-clad Operators. Around them the battle raged; the rattle of gunfire and the deafening bangs of T-Bones and

Daybreakers merged with screams of pain, and roars of guttural lust as the vampires attacked, again and again. Something thudded to the ground to her left, and she glanced at it as they ran. She immediately wished she hadn't; lying on the tarmac was the ruined torso of an Operator, her arms and legs missing, her face a frozen mask of unutterable pain.

They hit the edge of the runway, and Shaun threw her one of the two Daybreakers he was carrying. She had never fired the heavy weapon before, but that didn't worry her; what worried her was what was being done to her fellow Operators. At the runway's edge, removed from the epicentre of the battle, she and Shaun dropped to one knee, and began to fire round after round into the swirling, swooping mass of vampires.

Valeri hung in the air above the carnage his army was inflicting, and waited for his victory.

Although the resistance from the Blacklight men and women had been far fiercer than he had expected, causing him to have already lost a greater number of his soldiers than he had allowed for, it was still only a matter of time. For every vampire the black figures destroyed, they lost at least one of their own number. Already the Blacklight force had been reduced by a quarter, possibly more; within minutes, sheer weight of numbers would overwhelm them, and then Valeri's mission would be accomplished.

He was floating lazily back and forth above the battle, searching for his prize; he saw no need to involve himself in the fighting, and instead was devoting himself to the capture of Admiral Seward. It was difficult; the plain black uniforms made every Operator look alike, preventing Valeri from getting an accurate lock on his quarry. He rotated slowly, and then stopped; there was still no sign of

Admiral Seward, but his sharp eyes picked out something else that interested him. He began to descend, slowly, towards his unsuspecting target.

Larissa sprinted across the tarmac, faster than human eyes could see, and with a single swipe of her hand, tore off the head of a teenage vampire boy who was about to sink his fangs into Cal Holmwood's neck. She had seen the vampire creep up behind the Colonel, who had just staked an enormously obese vampire woman; she had burst into what seemed like enough blood to fill a swimming pool. He had been distracted, for the briefest of moments, by the eruption of gore in front of him, and the teenage vampire had seen his chance.

But Larissa, who could now move with a speed that frightened even her, had been too quick for him; his head was still bouncing away along the runway when she plunged her stake into his headless body, destroying him. Colonel Holmwood didn't even thank her; he just nodded briefly, and ran back into the battle. Larissa watched him go, and then something crashed into the back of her neck so hard that she cracked the tarmac of the runway as she hit it, face down.

For a second, she lay still, unable to move.

The impact felt like someone had dropped a car on the back of her head; she had never felt anything like it, not even during the beating she had suffered at the hands of Alexandru, the beating that had almost killed her. She heard an involuntary groan emerge from her mouth, and she slowly rolled over on to her back.

Standing over her, his face completely expressionless, was Valeri Rusmanov.

The second oldest vampire in the world was huge, almost as

broad as he was tall, his enormous frame hidden beneath a thick grey greatcoat. He peered down at her, his face wrinkled with distaste.

"You are the traitor they speak about," he said. It was not a question. "You are the one they are scared of, the one who helped to kill my brother. And yet you lie before me after a single blow. How disappointing."

He leant down, and then his fist hammered towards her face, as quick as a lightning bolt. Larissa flung herself to the side, and heard the crunch of rubble as the runway exploded under the impact. She forced herself to her feet, trying not to show him how much the blow to the back of her neck had taken out of her.

"Better," he grunted. "Dying on your back is for old men; dying on your feet is for soldiers."

He lunged forward, swinging one of his tree-trunk arms; she ducked underneath it, and circled to her right. He laughed, a loud grunt that sounded more animal than human, and came for her again. She skipped out of his reach, and lunged, thrusting her fingers towards his eyes, hoping to blind him; he moved his head impossibly quickly for a creature of his size, then almost casually curled his hand round her wrist, and snapped it.

A thunderclap of pain shot up Larissa's arm, and she cried out, her head thrown back. Valeri swung his other fist with the slow inevitability of a wrecking ball, and crunched it into her stomach. Every single molecule of air was driven out of her lungs by the punch, and her eyes widened as she realised she couldn't breathe.

Valeri drew her close, and looked carefully at her, like a scientist examining an interesting specimen. With a gargantuan effort, she forced her screaming lungs to inhale, and pulled sickly sweet air in through her nose and mouth. The pain in her wrist was still huge, bright red and throbbing, and as she struggled weakly in his grip, she watched his fangs slide slowly down from above his upper lip.

He smiled narrowly at her, then suddenly dipped her at the waist, like a ballroom dancer finishing a routine. She hung in his grasp, powerless to resist; as he slowly lowered his huge fangs towards her throat, Larissa turned her face away from the burning coals of the ancient vampire's eyes, and waited for the inevitable.

"Valeri!"

The single word boomed out across the wide-open space of the Loop, and Larissa jerked her head back around. At the sound of his name, Valeri looked up, and Larissa watched his face contort into the purest depiction of hatred she had ever seen on the face of a living creature; she twisted in his grip, craning her neck towards the source of his venom.

Valentin Rusmanov strode across the tarmac towards them, his face twisted into a smile of pure violence. As he walked, he shrugged his suit jacket from his shoulders, letting it fall to the ground, and rolled his sleeves past his elbows. Around him, the fighting ceased; everyone, human or vampire, stopped to watch the third oldest vampire in the world make his entrance.

"Why don't you pick on someone your own age, brother?" he snarled.

Valeri's answering growl shook the ground beneath Larissa's feet, and then he dropped her, as though she was nothing. She hit the ground hard, and scrambled backwards away from him, her wrist flaring with pain every time it touched the cool tarmac of the runway.

Valentin strode towards his brother, four hundred years of hatred burning in his heart. A vampire woman in her twenties ran at him as he walked through the bloody carnage of the battlefield, her teeth bared, her arms outstretched. Without even a glance in her direction,

Valentin swung his right arm, so fast that it was nothing more than a blur, and connected with the vampire woman's head. It disintegrated into a fine spray of blood and bone, leaving the body to take several faltering steps before it crashed to the ground.

Paul Turner, who like everyone else had stopped when Valentin had bellowed his brother's name, took advantage of the momentary confusion, and fired Daybreaker rounds into the spines of four vampires who had been distracted by the impending collision of the two remaining Rusmanov brothers. Their screams, and the explosions of blood that followed them, broke the truce that had settled temporarily over the landing area, and vampires and Operators threw themselves back into the fight.

Valentin and Valeri faced each other on the dark tarmac of the runway, their eyes glowing molten red so dark it was almost black. At the edge of the long strip of tarmac, Larissa lay on the grass and watched, her heart pounding.

"You have always been a stain on our family's name, brother," spat Valeri. "But I would have thought that this betrayal was beneath even you."

"You know nothing about me, *brother*," replied Valentin, smiling. "You have no idea what I'm capable of."

"You are a traitor," said Valeri, simply. "I know that much. And you will die."

He moved, so fast that even Larissa could barely see him, and swung his fist towards Valentin. The power in the punch was devastating; it would have smashed his brother's head to pulp had it connected.

But it didn't.

Valentin moved in a blur, sliding away and down from where

the punch was aimed. He appeared behind his brother like a jack-in-the-box, and brought both his fists down on the back of the ancient vampire's neck. Valeri crashed to the ground, blood exploding from his face where it was driven into the tarmac. But he was moving before the crimson liquid even began to run, leaping back to his feet and expanding the distance between himself and his brother.

"You're faster than I remember," grunted Valeri, grudgingly.

"And you are as slow and predictable as always," replied Valentin, then looked over at Larissa. "Are you hurt?" he asked.

Larissa shook her head, bewildered.

"I would have helped sooner," continued Valentin, his attention returned to his brother, who was circling him slowly. "But no one thought to come and let me know I was needed. I was forced to make my own way out, to get away from that infernal alarm, if nothing else. Just in time too, it would appear."

Larissa opened her mouth to shout a warning, but there was no time. Valeri shot forward like a bullet out of a gun, his arms wide, intending to grab his brother round the waist and drag him to the ground, but Valentin needed no warning. He stepped effortlessly into the air, and brought his foot down on the back of his brother's head, stamping it into the tarmac with a revolting crunch as Valeri's nose and jaw broke. This time Valeri was still for a moment, as pain exploded through his head.

This cannot be, he thought, as he tasted his own blood in his mouth. *This is impossible.*

Valentin leapt away, and regarded the prone figure.

"So strong, brother," he said, softly. "So powerful but so slow, as you always have been. You never understood that there was more to battle than brute strength. Hopefully, you're realising it now?"

With a roar that shook the ground, Valeri pushed himself to his feet, and stared at Valentin, his expression clouded with raging, all-consuming hatred. His face was squashed flat, the nose broken in at least two places, the jaw crooked and lumpen, and blood was running freely from a dozen cuts. Valeri shook his head quickly, as if to clear it, then came for his brother again.

Henry Seward ducked under the outstretched arms of a vampire woman, and plunged his stake into her chest. He was running again before she exploded, hauling the small panel from his belt and checking the timer, willing the numbers to be low.

0:58...

0:57...

0:56...

Come on, he screamed to himself. *Come on goddamn you. Another minute, just one more tiny little minute.*

Then something barrelled into him from the side, below the waist, and he heard his leg break as he was driven to the ground. The pain was enormous, but bigger, and sharper, was the despair that flooded through him as he thudded to the cool tarmac. He gritted his teeth, and rolled on to his back. Anderson was standing over him, his child's face alive with excitement. He reached down and picked Seward up by the collar of his uniform, and waved him enthusiastically back and forth, like a child who has won a prize at a funfair.

"Got him!" he bellowed. "Valeri! I've got him!"

Shaun Turner looked over from his vantage point at the edge of the runway, and saw the swollen, misshapen vampire holding the Director of Department 19 aloft like a rag doll. Without hesitating, he leapt to his feet and sprinted back into the battle. Kate was on her feet less than a second later and sprinting after him, calling his name.

Valeri and Valentin looked around at the sound of Anderson's voice, then returned their attention to each other. Valentin saw his brother's eyes flick towards the captive Seward, and he circled so that he was between his brother and the stricken Director.

"Forget it, brother," he said.

Valeri shifted his gaze to Anderson, then back to his brother, and then to the ground beneath his feet. He was standing where the tarmac of the runway ended, and the grass began. A light suddenly came on inside Valeri's head; he turned away from his brother to where Larissa lay on the grass.

Valentin realised what his brother was going to do a matter of milliseconds too late to prevent it. He screamed a warning at Larissa as he leapt forward, but he was too late. Valeri raced across the grass, covering the gap between himself and Larissa in less than a heartbeat. Without slowing, he reached down with one ancient hand, and pulled her throat out with one quick flick of his wrist.

Larissa felt no pain, just a terrible sensation of being pulled *open*, and then she slid on to her back as blood gushed out into the air above her. Less than a second later Valentin was kneeling at her side, his crimson eyes burning in the darkness. He glanced up and saw Valeri sprinting towards Anderson and Admiral Seward, and then looked down at Larissa. Blood was spraying out of her neck in staggering quantities, and she was already turning pale. He looked again at the fleeing Valeri, felt the rage burning in his chest at the mere thought of letting his brother escape, then made his decision.

614

Valentin reached into Larissa's throat with his long, elegant fingers, pinched shut her carotid artery and her jugular vein, and then thrust his other forearm into her mouth. Larissa bit down on pure reflex, and Valentin gave out a gasp that was as full of pleasure as it was of pain. His blood began to run into the girl's mouth, and he felt the delicate tissue in her neck begin to grow back. He craned his head around as Larissa drank from him, and watched his brother arrive at Anderson's side.

Valeri screeched to a halt beside Anderson, lifting Henry Seward out of his grip. The Director of Department 19 kicked with his one good leg, and beat at the vampire's arm, but it was futile.

"I got him," said Anderson, happily. "I did. Me."

"Shut up," snarled Valeri, looking around at the raging battle. "Shut up and let me think."

The fighting ranging across the landing area was furious, and brutal. There were no elegantly choreographed duels, or miraculous rescues or escapes; the men and women of Blacklight were fighting for their lives, and were fighting hard. Valeri surveyed the scene, saw his brother crouched next to the bleeding vampire girl and made the only decision he could make.

"Home," he barked at Anderson. "Tell my master I'm bringing him his prize."

Anderson didn't reply; instead, he stepped into the air, and disappeared over the thick forest to the east.

Valeri took a last look around at the scene, a final check as to whether it was possible to achieve both the objectives his master had given him. But he saw no way to do so; his men would kill the rest of the Blacklight soldiers, but Valentin was stronger than he remembered, and faster, and the tiny, frightening thought occurred to him at the very back of his mind that it was possible that he could no longer defeat his younger brother. And Seward was the priority, he reasoned; he was about to step into the air, to leave the remnants of his army to fend for themselves, when he sensed movement behind him.

Shaun Turner drew his stake as he closed on Valeri Rusmanov. Admiral Seward was dangling from the second oldest vampire in the world's grasp, and the monster himself appeared to be deep in thought. Shaun focused on the spot on Valeri's wide back, just to the left of the spinal column, where he would plant his stake less than a second from now.

Then Valeri moved.

Shaun tried to stop, but his momentum carried him forward, directly into the arm that Valeri swung with all the power of a tornado. The vampire's closed fist caught Shaun on the side of his jaw, lifting him off the ground. Kate, who was less than two metres behind her boyfriend, yelling for him to stop, heard the terrible crunch as Shaun's neck broke under the impact of Valeri's haymaker swing. He fell to the ground completely limp, his legs and arms tangled over themselves. She slid to the ground beside him, and heard someone screaming; several seconds passed before she realised it was her.

Standing over her, Valeri grunted with satisfaction, then floated easily into the air.

Paul Turner heard Kate scream, and began to run. The pitch of the scream, the absolute horror contained in the long syllable, told him something was wrong, more wrong than everything else that was happening around him. He saw Valeri rising gently into the air, saw Kate on her knees on the tarmac, and saw—

616

An awful sensation of cold spilled through his body.

He knew he was still running, because he could hear the sound of his feet hitting the tarmac, but the sound seemed to be coming from somewhere else; it was low, and muffled, and unreal.

His mind yawed wildly as the world began to grey at the corners. Then he was stationary, without any memory of having slowed or stopped, and he was looking down at the broken body of his son.

Cal Holmwood saw Valeri rise into the air, and ran towards the fleeing monster. He saw one Operator, he thought it might be Kate Randall, kneeling beside another, but he ignored them. Admiral Seward hung helplessly in Valeri's huge, ancient hand, and that was all Cal could think about.

He drew his T-Bone as he sprinted across the tarmac, noticing that Paul Turner was running in the same direction as he was.

Of course he is, he thought, full of admiration for his colleague. *No surprise there.*

Cal fired his T-Bone as he ran, and watched the stake whistle past Valeri's torso. Holmwood engaged the winch immediately, winding the stake back towards the barrel without breaking his stride. He looked over at Turner as he approached, and saw that the Security Officer was standing still, almost directly beneath the rising Valeri.

"Shoot!" he bellowed, as he ran. "For God's sake, Paul, shoot!"

Henry Seward watched the ground retreating below him, and scrabbled for the metal panel on his belt. His fingers slipped across its smooth surface, then caught one of the corners, and pulled it free. He twisted it in his hand, looked down at the small screen, and felt a surge of savage elation. The screen contained three words.

FIRE?
YES/NO

He felt a grim smile on his face as he pressed his thumb against the word **YES**.

Nothing happened.

He raised the panel again, and felt his heart sink as he read the words on the screen.

RANGE EXCEEDED

Beneath him, he saw Paul Turner standing motionless, his eyes cast towards the ground, and saw Cal Holmwood arriving beneath him at a flat sprint. He flicked his wrist, and sent the metal panel spinning down towards him.

Cal Holmwood felt the thud of the stake returning to the barrel of his T-Bone, and was about to raise it to his shoulder again when something landed at his feet with a metallic *thunk*; he looked down, and saw a small square of metal lying on the tarmac in front of him. His gaze flicked up to the shrinking figure of Admiral Seward, who was rising steadily in Valeri's grip. They were almost out of reach; if he was going to shoot, it had to be now. But the square of metal on the ground could only have come from Seward, and if he had had the presence of mind to throw it down as he was carried to his likely death, then Holmwood reasoned it must be pretty important.

Swearing heartily, he threw his T-Bone to the ground, darted forward and picked up the metal rectangle. He turned it over, and saw three words of red text glowing on the black screen.

618

Fire? Fire what?

He pressed his thumb against the **YES**, and the screen changed. A small series of dots lit up and then winked out, over and over again. Cal Holmwood stared at them, wondering what they meant, then suddenly realised that the ground beneath him was rumbling.

Around the perimeter of the Loop, just inside the interior fence, along the length of the long runway, and at wide intervals across the grounds between, circular sections of the ground were opening. Grass, tarmac, concrete; four-metre-wide circles lowered into the ground, then slid aside, revealing dark holes in the surface of the earth. Operators and vampires scattered out of the way of the holes that opened on the landing area where the battle was being fought, and ceased fighting; humans and vampires alike stared, and wondered what was happening.

An almighty thud rattled the entire base, as the lids that had covered the hidden holes reached the end of their tracks, and stopped. Then the rumbling began anew, and shapes began to rise from the dark openings.

Huge circular balls of glass emerged from the holes, glittering in the light spilling from the open hangar doors and the red laser array beyond the fence. The balls were at least three metres in diameter, and resting on thick metal poles. The glass had a purple tint, and Cal Holmwood, with a flash of clarity, realised what they were.

Oh my God, he had time to think.

"Visors!" he bellowed over the Operational channel. "Everybody, right now!"

He reached up and pulled his own down over his face, as a high-pitched whine suddenly stabbed into his ears. He felt the hair on his body begin to stand up, even through the material of his uniform; it was as though the air itself was suddenly full of electricity. Around him, Operators retreated from the vampires they were engaging, pulling their visors down over their faces. The whine became a scream, so loud and high that Cal thought his eardrums must be about to burst. Then his visor suddenly turned jet black, completely shutting out the world beyond it.

As a result, he didn't see the world explode into blinding, brilliant ultraviolet light.

48

SOME WOUNDS NEVER HEAL

At a distance of 22,245 miles above the surface of the earth, Skynet 6-1 cruised in geostationary orbit.

Its vast solar panel wings, the same width as those of a commercial airliner, reflected the sun's rays in a glittering kaleidoscope of colours, twinkling and shimmering in the freezing air of the troposphere. They hummed as they gathered solar energy and converted it into the electricity that would fuel the satellite for the duration of its twenty-year lifespan.

Skynet 6-1 was the first of its class, a highly classified Ministry of Defence black project that was a secret to even Britain's closest allies, equipped with photographic and thermographic capabilities far beyond those known to the public. It was capable of pinpointing a section of the earth's surface as small as a matchbox, of monitoring and assessing every civilian and encrypted communication frequency currently in use, of detecting heat blooms from further beneath the surface of the earth than the deepest missile silo, or the very limits of the vertical ranges of the latest submarines.

On the underside of the square, gold-coloured body of the satellite, a two-metre-diameter lens pointed towards the distant blue planet. The laser that could be fired from the lens was capable of striking a single human being, or heating a nuclear reactor to the point of meltdown in less than thirty seconds. The satellite represented the absolute front line of Britain's national security; it floated silently, watching and listening, far above the men and women it was designed to protect, men and women who were completely oblivious to its existence.

Its hundreds of regular systems and routines were cycling when a tiny corner of the British countryside suddenly erupted into blinding purple light.

There was a conversation taking place in Kabul that had triggered a number of the deep Echelon code words, and the satellite's processor, a remarkably advanced series of microchips that represented a quantum leap towards the realisation of artificial intelligence, was assessing whether to bring the discussion to the attention of the Security Services. In the Sudan, there was sporadic radio contact between two factions of rebel guerrillas, who were exploring the possibility of a combined assault on a Russian-owned oil refinery in the deep jungles near the ocean. In Washington, a Congressman was confessing to his brother that he had cheated on his wife, and that there were pictures to prove it.

Skynet 6-1 recorded them all, and hundreds more, stacking and analysing and prioritising them, before transmitting a report to the GCHQ in southern England. It sent its reports every fifteen minutes, every day of the year, and would continue to do so until it reached its planned obsolescence, at which point its orbit would gradually begin to degrade, until eventually it tumbled into the earth's atmosphere, disintegrating entirely in the searing heat below.

The huge bloom of purple light lasted for less than five seconds, but in that time the satellite's sensors reacted and assessed the situation. Thermodynamic imaging was instantly used to assess the likely nature of the event, and returned negative results. It was not an explosion; there had been a sharp spike in the ground temperature, but it was already receding. There were a number of tiny fires burning in the area beneath the burst of light, but they were not assessed to be a significant threat to the surrounding area.

The footage of the event, the results of the initial scans, and thermographic and high-definition photographs of the before and after were parcelled together to be sent as an immediate report, as was the protocol for anomalous events. The satellite's geo-positioning sensors determined the location of the event, and a tiny subroutine, buried deep within the code that powered the satellite's computer brain, was activated. It triggered a protocol that changed the destination of the report the satellite had prepared, and as soon as the report had been encrypted and despatched, it deleted all trace of the event ever having taken place.

Skynet 6-1 returned to its normal operating mode, all proof that it had witnessed the burst of purple light completely exorcised from its memory banks. But more than 22,000 miles below, only 390 miles above the surface of the earth, RapidEye 4, a commercial imaging satellite, cruised slowly over eastern England, its high-definition cameras silently recording everything below it.

Cal Holmwood's visor returned to normal, and he found himself looking at a vision of hell.

Purple fire was streaming from what seemed like at least a hundred burning vampires; thick black smoke billowed into the air, as the screaming, pleading vampires stumbled, and crawled, and lay still, their bodies burning. The smell was terrible, a thick fog of roasting meat and boiling blood, and Holmwood gagged.

In among the fires, the surviving Operators were standing around, dazed expressions on their faces, their weapons hanging limply at their sides. Several of them were staggering, holding their faces, and Cal realised with rising horror that they were not wearing their helmets. He ran to the nearest such man, an Operator he knew was named Potts, and grabbed him by his shoulders.

"I can't see," screamed the Operator. "Oh God, I can't see anything."

"Let me see," said Holmwood, gently taking hold of the man's gloved hands.

Blood was running thickly from the man's ears, but he responded to the sound of Cal's voice.

"Colonel Holmwood?" asked Potts, his voice thick with pain.

"That's right, son," said Cal. "Let me see now. Move your hands."

Potts lifted his trembling hands slowly away from his face. Holmwood looked at the young Operator, and forced himself not to cry out.

The skin on his face was a red so dark it was almost black; in several places it had already cracked, and blood was oozing slowly down towards his neck. His eyes were bleeding at the corners; the white sclera had been burned a bright orange, and his blue irises were a virulent purple. The Operator's pupils had constricted to such a tiny diameter that Holmwood could barely see them; they were little more than tiny black pinpricks in the middle of the young man's ruined eyes. The corneas, the transparent film that covered the visible part of the eye, were dried out and shredded; it looked like Potts was wearing contact lenses that had been attacked with a razor blade.

"You're going to be all right," Cal said, firmly. "You hear me, son? You're going to be fine."

"I can't see anything, sir," said Potts. The fear in his voice was urgent.

"I know you can't," replied Cal. "I have to go and get you some help, so I want you to sit down right here and not move. OK?"

Potts nodded, an expression of misery on his shattered face.

"OK," said Holmwood. "I'll be back for you. I promise."

He helped the Operator lower himself to the ground, then ran towards the hangar, stepping between the burning vampires that littered the wide stretch of tarmac.

"All medical staff to Landing Area 1," he shouted over his helmet's comms link. "All staff right now."

He ran through the wide door of the hangar, his mind racing as he headed towards the row of emergency medical kits that hung on the armoury wall.

What the hell just happened out there? What were those things that came out of the ground? They were like ultraviolet bombs. Who the hell knew about them?

Holmwood hauled four green cases down off the wall, tucked them under his arms, then ran back towards the burning carnage of the landing area. A small group of Operators were waiting for him as he emerged, their faces pale at the scale of the destruction that had taken place around them, their eyes wide with horror and confusion.

"Colonel Holmwood," said one, as he approached. "What the hell was—"

"No time," snapped Cal. "We've got wounded out there. Take these and start isolating the injured."

He dropped the green cases to the ground, and ran back into the hangar for the rest. Behind him he heard the running thuds of footsteps as the Operators did as he had ordered. He skidded to a halt in front of the two medical kits that were still hanging on the wall, then noticed the white door next to them. A red refrigeration triangle was printed on it, and something suddenly clicked in his mind.

"Oh Jesus," he whispered, and hauled open the white door. Inside it stood twelve plastic litre bottles of O negative blood. He ran across the room, grabbed a black holdall from one of the racks, ran back and threw the bottles into it. Cal swung the bag over his shoulder, and sprinted for the exit.

"Larissa!" he bellowed, surveying the smouldering remnants of Valeri's vampire army. "Operator Kinley! Where are you?"

Nothing moved.

The purple flames that had leapt so violently from the bodies of the vampires were starting to subside, leaving behind the crackling of burning skin and the groans and growls of the few vampires who were still able to make sound. Around him, he saw Operators kneeling beside their colleagues, applying gauze and bandages to wounds, whispering reassuringly to their injured friends. Kate Randall was still kneeling over Shaun Turner, as his father stood motionless beside them.

Can't think about that now, thought Holmwood. *Can't think about that.*

There was a rush of noise and activity behind him, and he heard shouts and exclamations of surprise as the Loop's medical staff poured out on to the tarmac, carrying trauma kits and wheeling stretchers between them. The white-coated doctors and nurses immediately took charge of the situation, barking orders and shouting for the uninjured Operators to clear the way. Holmwood left them behind, running through the human and vampire wreckage, shouting Larissa's name as he did so.

He reached the edge of the runway, looking frantically across the blood-soaked tarmac and burning concrete.

"Larissa!" he bellowed, and then the tiniest flicker of movement caught the corner of his eye. He turned, seeing a thin column of smoke rising from the grass at the edge of the runway. He ran towards it, praying he was not too late, and slid to a halt beside a twisted pile of charred flesh and bone.

Larissa was lying on her back, her skin as black as the night sky, her arms and legs burned down to the bone. Her face was destroyed; her eyes and ears were gone, and her lips had burned away to reveal her teeth, giving her an awful skeletal look. In her mouth was the charred remains of an arm, the bones and tendons of which were still clearly visible. Holmwood followed the arm to where it met the white nub of a shoulder bone, and then on to the body of a second vampire. Cal could see the flapping remnants of a white shirt, and clarity burst through him.

It's Valentin, he realised. *Why the hell is his arm in her mouth?*

He looked more closely at Larissa, and saw empty space where her throat should have been; even with the terrible damage the flames had done to her, it was still obvious. The muscles and tendons that had been laid open to the evening sky by the punishing purple fire were torn and ripped, in a single direction.

He fed her his own blood, Cal realised. *She was hurt, and he fed her. Dear Jesus.*

He looked down at the two smouldering bodies for a long moment, then made a decision. Cal shrugged the holdall off his shoulder, and tore it open. He lifted the first bottle of blood out, twisted the top off and tipped it directly into Larissa's mouth. The effect was instantaneous; small sections of her flesh immediately turned red, then pink, then white, knitting back together as they did so.

When the first bottle was empty, he threw it aside, and tore open

627

the second. As it glugged down her savaged throat, her eyes swam back up into their sockets, and her tongue grew back into place. She groaned in agony, and swivelled her eyes to look at him.

The third bottle saw her begin to move, ever so slightly, as she began to resemble the Larissa he knew, and when it was empty, she was able to lift one trembling hand, and push the burnt remnant of Valentin's arm out of her mouth. She groped for the fourth bottle as he opened it, and he placed it gently in her hand; she raised it to her mouth, and drank, slowly. Holmwood watched until he was sure she could feed herself, then grabbed four of the bottles and leant down next to Valentin.

He paused as he twisted the first one open and lowered it towards the vampire's mouth.

Valentin Rusmanov had killed and tortured for more than four centuries, and nobody could have blamed Cal if he had sunk his stake into the ancient vampire's heart, ending him forever. But they had made a deal with him, a deal that it appeared Valentin, when presented with the opportunity to renege, had honoured. Cal had seen him fight Valeri with his own eyes, and it was clear that he had given up his own blood to help Larissa.

Cal Holmwood tipped the bottle, and poured sweet, reviving blood into the mouth of the third oldest vampire in the world, a creature that represented everything that Department 19 stood against. He watched as the vampire's body responded to the blood, and began the torturous, agonising process of rebuilding itself. There was a long, rattling gasp from beside him, as Larissa pushed herself up into a seated position, and looked at him, gratitude burning in her eyes.

"Thank you," she croaked, then looked down at Valentin. "He didn't leave me," she said, in a voice that was little more than a whisper. "He was beating his brother, but when Valeri attacked me, he stayed, and gave me his arm. He could have let me bleed out."

"I know," replied Cal. "That's why I'm doing this."

Holmwood threw the first bottle aside and opened the second. He was tipping it towards Valentin's mouth when two beams of yellow light burst over the trees at the edge of the Loop, and the steady thump of a helicopter engine thundered through the night air.

"Five minutes," yelled the pilot.

Jamie Carpenter checked his watch, and swore. Thirty-one minutes had passed since he and his team had emerged from the smouldering darkness of La Fraternité de la Nuit, carrying the unconscious grey wolf between them. Their chopper was idling in the middle of Rue de Sévigné, its side doors standing open.

Jamie knew it was a violation of operational protocol to bring the helicopter down in the middle of the Marais, but there was no other option that he could see. The pilot had expressed surprise when he heard Jamie's order, but he had not objected; by the time the team emerged from the building he had set the chopper down in the centre of the wide boulevard, and loaded the black SUV into its hold.

Carrying Frankenstein in his wolf form took all five of the team; the animal was incredibly heavy, and his fur slid through their gloved fingers like spiders' webs. The pilot saw them emerge, ran over and shoved the gate open. They hauled the wolf through the narrow gap, and, with a huge effort, loaded it into the helicopter. The pilot leapt inside and began strapping the animal down with restraining belts, as Jamie's team removed their helmets and took their seats.

Jamie climbed in last, his eyes on the many windows that overlooked their extraction; there were lights on in several of them, and he thought he saw a number of curtains twitch, but he saw no one. He took a quick last look at the grey windowless building, then turned and leapt up into the helicopter.

"Go!" he yelled, and strapped himself into his seat as the engine noise rose to a piercing scream, and the squat helicopter lumbered into the air.

Too late, thought Jamie. *She said I was going to be too late. Too late for what?*

"I've got a General Alarm at the Loop!" yelled the pilot, above the howl of the engines. "It was sounded two minutes ago, sir."

"Get us there as quickly as you can!" shouted Jamie.

The helicopter tore across western France, and boomed out over the English Channel, heading north-west. There was silence in the back of the helicopter; Jamie had told the rest of the team Larissa's message, and all five of them were wondering what was happening at the base they all thought of as home.

"Five minutes," repeated the pilot. "We're coming in—"

The pilot's voice died out as the interior of the helicopter suddenly blazed purple. The team threw their hands over their eyes, as the light pierced every corner of the helicopter's cabin. Then, just as suddenly as it had arrived, the light was gone.

"Report!" yelled Jamie. "What the hell was that?"

"I don't know, sir," said the pilot. His voice was low, and full of shock. "Whatever it was, it came from the Loop. It looked like a million UV grenades went off at once, sir."

Jamie looked around at the worried faces of his team.

"Fly faster," he said.

Cal Holmwood watched the helicopter roar overhead, descending rapidly towards the landing area. Beside him, Larissa tried to get to her feet, and fell back on the grass. She swore, and grabbed another bottle of blood out of the holdall. She tipped it into her mouth, her eyes fixed on the helicopter as it touched down outside the hangar, its tyres screeching on the burning tarmac.

As soon as the huge vehicle came to a stop, Jamie hauled the door open and leapt out. For a moment, he merely stood, staring; fires were burning from the doors of the hangar to the edges of the long runway, and the ground was scattered with dark, motionless figures, and splashes of drying blood.

My God, he thought. *This can't be real.*

Then he saw Kate, kneeling on the ground, and ran towards her.

"Kate!" he shouted, his feet thudding across the tarmac. "Kate! Where's Larissa? Are you—"

She turned to look at him, and he skidded to a halt, three metres away from her. Her face was a mask of agony, and his heart lurched with fear.

It's Larissa. Something's happened to Larissa.

Then he noticed Paul Turner standing beside her, as still as a statue. He walked forward on trembling legs, and saw what his friend was kneeling beside.

Shaun Turner lay on the cold tarmac of the landing area, his eyes wide, staring up at nothing. His neck was bent horribly to one side; a ridge of bone, cracked almost in half, was visible beneath the skin. His chest was still, and his hands lay limply at his sides. Kate was cradling his head, her hands buried in his hair. She was not crying; the word did not do justice to the guttural, primal sounds of grief that were emerging from her throat.

Jamie tried to make his body respond; he wanted to run to Kate and wrap his arms round her, wanted to pull her away from the

631

terrible lifeless thing that had been her boyfriend, but he could not make himself move. He stared dumbly as he watched his friend suffering through a nightmare he knew all too well.

Slowly, like a statue coming haltingly to life, Paul Turner stepped forward. Jamie watched, his eyes wide, his mind unable to begin to comprehend what the Security Officer must be seeing with his glacial grey eyes, his heart breaking for a man who had generally treated him with a respect he had not always deserved. Turner took two robotic steps, and then knelt beside Kate, looking down at his son.

"Let him go," he said, his voice soft. Kate looked round at him, her face streaked with tears. "Please," said Turner. "Please let him go."

Kate stared at him for a long moment, and Jamie felt a terrible bond of grief crystallise between them. It was palpable, even from where he was standing. Then she gently slid her hands out from under Shaun's head. Turner replaced them with his own, and Kate stumbled to her feet, backing away, towards Jamie. She stood beside him, her eyes locked on Shaun's father as he entered the worst nightmare of every parent.

Jamie looked at her, trying desperately to think of something to say, but everything his mind could come up with sounded pitifully inadequate. Then a small noise floated through the night air, a hitching, rattling sound that seemed to be full of all the grief in the world. He looked on, utterly helpless, as one of the most desperate, stomach-churning moments of his life played out.

He watched as Paul Turner began to weep over the body of his son.

Jamie reached out and touched Kate's shoulder. She flinched, then turned to face him, the expression on her face appearing to teeter on the brink of catatonia. Her eyes were wide and staring, her mouth hung open, as though her internal processes had been shut down.

He looked at her, completely unable to think of anything to say; instead, he fumbled for her shoulders, and pulled her tightly against him. She came willingly, burying her head against his chest, and beginning to tremble as the first of a series of terrible, racking sobs escaped her. He held her as tight as he dared, as if trying to shut out everything that had happened around her, as if he could make it better by preventing her from seeing it. He lowered his head so his mouth was beside her ear, and started to whisper to her.

"I'm sorry," he said. "I'm sorry. I'm sorry. I'm sorry."

She didn't respond; he held her as she shook and shivered in his arms.

They stayed that way for a long time, as the Operators who had survived whatever had happened while Jamie and his team were in Paris began to gather round Paul Turner, their heads lowered in respect for his loss.

Doctors in white coats ran between injured men and women, and a steady stream of stretchers rolled in and out of the hangar. Three Operators were making their way across the landing area, systematically staking the smouldering remains of the vampires; they exploded with small claps of air, the blood in their veins boiled dry by the searing ultraviolet fire.

Jamie stared desperately around; he couldn't see Larissa, or Admiral Seward, and he could feel panic rising in his chest, even as he tried to comfort Kate. He saw Jack Williams talking to his brother Patrick, and when Patrick walked away, Jamie called Jack's name. He made his way over to Jamie, as Angela Darcy appeared at his side, her eyes wide with distress.

"What happened?" he asked, quietly. "What the hell happened, Jack?"

His friend's face was a ghostly mask as he replied. "Valeri attacked us," he said, softly. "Brought an army, at least two hundred of them, and attacked the Loop."

"Let me take her," said Angela, nodding towards Kate. "You two need to talk."

For a second, Jamie resisted; he didn't want to let go of his friend. But Angela was right; even in the midst of all the horror surrounding them, there were things that needed to be said, and done. He gently eased Kate away from his chest, and let Angela slip her arms round her; she went unprotestingly, and as Angela began to stroke her hair, Jamie led Jack out of earshot.

"Why wasn't there a warning?" he asked, looking around at the carnage that had taken place on the very doorstep of the Blacklight base. "How did they get so close before we fought back?"

"Someone gave them a route through the sensors," said Jack. "Or that's what people are saying anyway. I'm not sure anyone really knows."

"Where's Admiral Seward? He'll know."

Jack looked at his friend, and pain broke across his face.

"Jamie…"

Oh no, thought Jamie, cold running up his spine. *Oh, please no. Not him too.*

"Don't tell me he's dead, Jack," warned Jamie, tears welling in the corners of his eyes. "Don't tell me that, OK? Please?"

"He's not dead," said Jack. "At least, as far as we know. Valeri took him. Alive."

"Took him where?" asked Jamie. "Have they run his chip?"

The locator chip that was embedded in the arm of every Operator

634

could mark their position anywhere in the world, to within less than a metre. Each one had a unique frequency, and a battery that would last a century. Jamie had been implanted with one when he was young, so young he didn't remember it happening; his father had done it as a way of protecting him, and it had worked; it had been what led Frankenstein to him, the night his mother was taken.

"It stopped transmitting halfway across the North Sea," said Jack. "It's gone."

Jamie stared at Jack, horrified. The chips were located beneath the muscle of the forearm; a surgical procedure would be required to remove it, and that didn't even allow for the fact that the locator chips' very existence was one of Blacklight's most closely guarded secrets. The implications of the Director's chip ceasing to transmit were unavoidable, and deeply unsettling.

"Have you seen Larissa?" asked Jamie, his voice thick with emotion.

Admiral Seward was in the hands of a monster, and his closest friend, his girlfriend, was nowhere to be seen; he felt as though he was standing on quicksand.

"I haven't, Jamie," said Jack, softly.

Jamie's stomach lurched. Larissa was a vampire, with superhuman strength and healing, so her being injured was, unfortunately, the least likely outcome. If he couldn't find her, if she was nowhere to be seen, it was far more likely that she was dead, especially as whatever had happened before they landed had decimated what he assumed had once been Valeri's army; he couldn't see a living vampire anywhere.

At the edge of the long runway that split the middle of the Loop's grounds, where the tarmac gave way to the wide expanse of grass, three figures climbed slowly to their feet, and began to walk towards the burning landing area.

Cal Holmwood walked in the middle, ready to offer support to either of the two vampires that walked at his sides. Valentin Rusmanov walked with slow determination; the blood that Holmwood had fed him, tipping it into his mouth like a mother feeding a newborn baby, had revived his body, but he was still far from fully recovered. He was bleeding from a number of places: from his ears, from beneath his fingernails and from the back of his throat. Every few paces he spat a thick wad of dark blood on to the ground. His body was screaming with pain, but it was holding together, and that was enough, for now at least.

His memory of what had happened ended only seconds after the ultraviolet bombs had detonated. He had been feeding Larissa, his mind screaming at him to chase his brother, to put an end to Valeri once and for all, but he had found himself unable to leave the wounded vampire girl. His blood had been flowing into her mouth when the ground began to shake.

Valentin had watched as a wide hole opened in the ground, less than twenty metres from where he was kneeling beside Larissa, and a huge transparent ball had risen from the darkness. Then a high-pitched whine, louder and more painful than any sound he had ever heard, had split his head open, and the world had turned purple. He had remained conscious just long enough to realise that the foul smell permeating his nostrils was his own burning flesh, and then there had been nothing but deep, empty darkness.

Larissa remembered even less; she had not seen the huge bombs emerge from beneath the grounds of the Loop, had not seen the flash that had burned her eyes from their sockets. She remembered the terrible feeling of Valeri laying her throat open to the cool evening air, and the soothing feeling of Valentin's arm beneath her fangs, and then there was nothing.

She was in less pain than the ancient vampire; Holmwood had given more of his supply of blood to her than to Valentin, but every step still sent rivers of agony coursing up her spine. The skin at her throat was pink, and tender, and she knew she was still weak; she had tried to fly, tried to step into the air and go looking for Jamie, but had folded back to the ground, bleeding from her eyes and ears.

After she had told Cal Holmwood to help Valentin, after she had told him that the vampire had tried to help her, Jamie's name had been the first word she uttered when the Colonel returned to her side.

Holmwood had told her that his helicopter had returned, had landed only minutes earlier, and that was what had prompted her ill-fated attempt to fly, an attempt that had seen Holmwood bellow angrily at her, telling her to take it easy. She had acquiesced, forcing herself to remain still as he finished tending to Valentin; but now she was on her feet, and they were making their way back towards the survivors of Valeri's attack, and Jamie was all she could think about.

"What happened?" asked Larissa, as they crossed the runway and walked on to the landing area. Patches of fire still burned where the vampires of Valeri's army had fallen, even though almost all the bodies had now been staked. Three Operators were diligently destroying the last of them, a small cluster who had burned together by the entrance to the hangar. "What did this?"

"Bombs," said Valentin, shakily. "Ultraviolet bombs. They came up out of the ground."

"Did you know about them?" asked Larissa, looking over at Cal Holmwood, who shook his head.

"No," he said. "I don't think anyone did, apart from the Director. He threw me the trigger as Valeri took him."

There was a long moment of silence.

"*You* fired them?" asked Larissa, stopping in her tracks. "When you knew we were out here too?"

"What did you want me to do?" asked Holmwood, fiercely. "Operators were dying all around me; we were on the verge of being overrun. I didn't know what was going to happen, didn't know what the trigger was for. Admiral Seward threw it to me, the last thing he did before that monster carried him away, so I pressed it. He would have, if he'd had the chance, and that was good enough for me."

"Promise me you didn't know what the weapon was," said Larissa. "Promise me."

Holmwood sighed. "I promise," he said. "I can't promise you that if I *had* known, I would have done anything differently. But I didn't know; you have my word."

Larissa opened her mouth to reply, completely unsure of what she was going to say, when she saw something that stopped the words in her throat.

Running across the dark grass towards her was Jamie Carpenter.

She shrugged Cal Holmwood's arm away, and stumbled towards him. Her supernaturally sharp eyes, which worked every bit as well in the dark as in the daylight, saw his eyes widen as they settled on her, and he accelerated into a flat sprint. She braced herself, her eyes flaring red with overwhelming joy, and a second later he crashed into her, driving her backwards, his arms, wrapped tightly round her, the only things that stopped her falling to the ground.

She clamped her arms round him, and felt his face bury itself in her neck, felt the heat from his skin and the damp that was

638

gathering around his eyes, and felt her heart swell with happiness and relief.

"You're alive," Jamie whispered. "Oh, thank God, you're alive."

"So are you," she said, then laughed, despite herself.

"Are you OK?" he asked, pulling back and looking closely at her.

"I've been better," she replied. "But I'm all right. What about you? What happened in Paris?"

"We found him," said Jamie. "We brought him home, but..."

His voice trailed away.

"What's wrong?" asked Larissa.

"It doesn't matter," said Jamie. "I'll tell you later. Where's Matt? Have you seen him?"

"I haven't," said Larissa, her brow furrowing. "I haven't seen Kate either. Not since all this started."

"I saw her," said Jamie, and Larissa felt relief flood through her. "She's on the landing area. She's not hurt."

"Is she OK?"

"No," said Jamie, and dropped his eyes to the ground. "Not even close. But she's safe."

"What happened to her?"

"We have to find Matt," said Jamie, as though he either hadn't heard her, or couldn't bear to answer her. "He might be hurt."

"Matt?" asked a voice from beside them. "The civilian boy? Is that who you're looking for?"

Jamie and Larissa turned to see a doctor in a white coat standing next to them. The front of the coat was smeared with blood, and his face was pale.

"Have you seen him?" asked Jamie.

The doctor nodded. "About twenty minutes ago," he said.

"Downstairs. He was with Professor Talbot, heading towards the lift."

"While the base was being attacked?" asked Jack.

The doctor nodded.

Larissa looked at Jamie, whose brow had furrowed into a frown. *Why wouldn't Talbot have tried to help up here?* he thought. *If the base fell, then it would have been the end of the Lazarus Project. Why didn't he come and fight?*

"Let's go," said Larissa, and stepped in the air. She hung there for a second, then slumped back to the ground, her arms wrapped round herself. The doctor stepped forward, concern on his face, but she pushed him away. "I'm all right," she said, angrily. "Jamie, go and find him. I'll come after you as soon as I can."

"Are you sure you're OK?" asked Jamie.

"Just go," said Larissa. "Right now."

Jamie looked at her, his face full of open, obvious love. She held his gaze for a long, pregnant moment, then he turned away and sprinted towards the open doors of the hangar. He was accelerating across the tarmac, when he heard a voice say his name, a voice he knew better than any in the world. He skidded to a halt, his heart lurching in his chest, and turned towards it.

Standing in front of him, her hands clasped tightly together in front of her chest, was Marie Carpenter. She was wearing a T-shirt and a pair of pyjama bottoms, both of which were splattered with blood, and she was looking at her son with an expression of utter wonder on her face.

"Mum?" said Jamie, his voice choking in his throat. "Mum, what are you—"

He didn't get the chance to finish the question. His mother closed the gap between them in a millisecond, and lifted him off the ground in a crushing hug. He wrapped his arms round her, felt her lower her face against his shoulder. He could barely breathe, so tightly was she holding him, but he managed to force himself to speak.

"Are you OK?" he gasped. "Mum, are you hurt?"

"I'm OK," she replied, without lifting her head. "I'm OK. Oh, Jamie, I was so worried about you. Are you all right?"

"I'm all right," he managed. "Mum, you're crushing me; you have to put me down."

Marie loosened her grip, and lowered him back to the tarmac. Her eyes were wide and brimming with tears, but he didn't notice; he was staring at the thick splashes of crimson on his mother's torso and legs.

"Mum," he said. "You're bleeding, Mum. We have to get you to the infirmary."

"It's not mine," said Marie, her voice trembling. "The blood. It's not mine."

Jamie raised his head and stared incredulously at his mother.

"What do you mean?" he asked. "Mum, what are you doing out here?"

Marie looked at her son. She had clasped her hands back together and was wringing them nervously, without realising it.

"The vampire in the cells," she said. "Valentin. He told me what was happening up here, and I told him I wanted to help, and he took me out of my cell and brought me with him. I was looking for you, Jamie, looking for you and Kate, and I couldn't find you, and then I saw vampires hurting your friends, and I…"

Her voice trailed off. She suddenly looked profoundly miserable, and Jamie felt his heart break. He reached out and took her gently by the shoulders.

"Did you fight them?" he asked, softly. "Did you fight the vampires, Mum?"

Marie nodded, slowly. Jamie felt tears rise in the corners of his eyes, and he stepped forward and hugged his mother tightly. Slowly, she raised her arms and placed them round him, as though she hadn't been sure how he might respond.

"People are saying that bombs went off," she said, her voice shaking. "I was in one of the corridors when it happened. I think I was lucky."

That's an understatement, thought Jamie.

"I love you, Mum," he whispered, fiercely. "Thank you."

Jamie gently pulled away from her, and after a moment's resistance, she let him go. He looked at her with fiery pride burning on his face.

"I have to go and find my friends," he said. "They might be in trouble. But I'll come and find you as soon as I'm done. OK?"

"OK," said Marie, a smile creeping on to her face. "Do you want me to come with you?"

Jamie shook his head.

"I have to do this myself," he said.

49

THROUGH THE LOOKING GLASS

Jamie ran through the grey corridors of the Loop, his heart pounding with adrenaline. The enormity of what had happened on the wide-open grounds of the base above him kept threatening to burst into his mind, but he pushed it away each time.

Can't think about that now. Too big. Just find Matt, and then you can worry about everything else.

He pressed the CALL button on the wall beside the lift, and kept pressing it until he heard the whirring of metal cables. The doors slid open and he stepped into the lift, pressed the button marked F and tried to catch his breath as he descended into the depths of the base.

The lift slid smoothly to a halt, and he was moving before the doors had even fully opened, sliding out between the narrow gap, and sprinting along the corridor. Around him, the alarms continued to scream, but he barely heard them. His feet pounded the concrete floor as he approached the door that led into the Lazarus Project.

Jamie skidded to a halt in front of it, and gripped the keypad on the wall.

I hope this works, he thought, then keyed in Admiral Seward's override code. For a long second nothing happened, and his heart sank. Then the red light on the panel turned green, and he heard the heavy locks begin to disengage.

Come on. Come on.

The door clunked open, and he shoved it aside and stepped into the wide room; he took one look around, and his heart froze in his chest.

Scattered around the white floor, or slumped at their desks and counters, were the men and women of the Lazarus Project.

They were all dead.

Their eyes bulged from their heads, staring up at the ceiling with fear and terrible surprise. The stench in the room was appalling, from where the men and women's bodies had betrayed them at the last; blood and body fluids ran across the floor, bright against the uniform white of the Lazarus Project nerve centre.

On the table in the middle of the room, beside the hologram of the double helix which was still revolving slowly in the midst of the foulness that had erupted all around it, was a square metal box that was folded open. Inside it stood an aerosol canister, stamped with black lettering. Jamie stood, staring at the carnage that had befallen the doctors and scientists that had called this room home, and then panic burst through him, and he fumbled the gas mask from its pouch on his belt and fastened it over his nose and mouth.

Too late, he thought, wildly. *It's too late if it hasn't dispersed, whatever it is.*

Then a second thought occurred to him.

If it killed them all this quickly, you're going to know in the next minute or so.

The realisation broke the paralysis that gripped him, and he ran to the centre of the room. With his gloved hands, he lifted the canister out of the box and read the lettering on the side.

$$\text{SARIN } (CH_3)_2CHO]CH_3P(O)F$$

Nerve gas. Jesus, what happened down here?

Jamie took a deep breath, and waited to see if he was going to die.

If there were Sarin residue in the room, if he had ingested it, he would know when his nose began to run. After that, his chest would tighten, his pupils would constrict and he would begin to drool, before he lost control of his body, began to spasm and suffocated. The upside was that at high concentrations, such as would be caused by releasing it in an enclosed room, the whole process would take less than a minute. The downside was that, by all accounts, it was a horrendous, agonising way to die.

He breathed slowly, in and out, in and out, his eyes glued to the digital watch on his wrist. The seconds ticked past sadistically slowly – 46, 47, 48, 49 – and Jamie held his breath as they crept towards one minute.

...57, 58, 59, 60, 61, 62.

Breath burst out of Jamie in a rush, and relief flooded through him.

Thank God. Oh, thank God.

He reached for the gas mask and was about to pull it free, then thought again, and left it in place.

Christ only knows what else they had down here. Take no chances.

Jamie pulled the MP5 from his belt, and crossed the wide room towards the computer banks. They were all dead; their screens were blank, and pressing the buttons on the keyboards provoked no response. He moved on to the gene sequencers, and found the same thing. The shelves on the opposite wall, which had been full of files and folders, were bare; Jamie glanced at them, then ran across the room to the decontamination portal.

The heavy airlock door hissed open. Jamie pushed through it, ignoring the NBC suits hanging on the wall and the door that led to the sterilising showers, and waited impatiently at the second door. The first locked back into place, and he threw the gas mask aside as the light above the second door turned green. The robotic female voice warned him that he had not completed the decontamination procedure, but he ignored her; he keyed the Director's code into the internal door, pushed it open and stepped into the inner sanctum of the Lazarus Project.

He had never been through the double airlock that protected the secrets of Professor Talbot's team. He glanced around as he stepped through the airlock, and felt horror rise in his chest as he fought back the urge to vomit.

The second room of the Lazarus Project was nothing more than a cutting-edge torture chamber.

In the middle of the long rectangular room stood a row of operating tables: silver frames, and thin white mattresses. Computers and medical monitoring equipment stood beside each bed, as did sleek silver video cameras on heavy tripods. The circular lenses were pointing at the beds, and Jamie felt a horror so huge it was almost physical as his brain contemplated, involuntarily, the possible contents of the cameras' memory cards.

Large circular drains sat in the floor beneath each of the operating stations; the drain covers, the floors, and in several cases the distant walls, were splattered with blood. A white curtain on a portable metal rail surrounded the last operating bed, the one furthest away from where Jamie was standing. He stared at it, unable to pretend that he couldn't see the pale silhouette behind the white material.

He walked slowly down the room, passing the operating beds one after the other. Out of the corners of his eyes, they teased him with their horrors.

Jamie found his eye drawn to a silver tray as he passed the second bed; resting in the tray, in about a centimetre of thick, jellied blood, were a series of crimson-streaked implements, that only the most deranged of doctors would have believed belonged anywhere near a medical facility. A hacksaw gleamed under the fluorescent lights, its teeth coated in gore and tiny chips of white bone. Beside it lay a circular power saw, its cable running away to a socket on the trolley that held the monitoring equipment; it seemed to exude overkill, to exude viciousness.

Jamie couldn't help himself; he stopped and regarded the rest of the tray. Three scalpels, one of them bent almost to forty-five degrees, by what force Jamie attempted not to speculate about. A long-handled pair of separators, the kind that he had seen used on television to pry ribcages open. Clamps and pins, discarded towels and sheets of gauze, soaked through with blood.

Jamie stared, frozen, unable to stop his imagination doing its worst. Then his paralysis broke; he turned away, gripped his knees and vomited into the drain beneath the bed.

What the hell have they been doing down here? he thought, his mind racing as his stomach lurched and spasmed. Then cold, creeping horror spilled through him. *Oh God, what happened to all the vampires I sent here? The ones I told were going to be safe?*

Jamie forced himself upright, and gripped the edge of the operating trolley to steady himself. When he pulled his hands away, thick smears of blood covered his skin, making his head swim. He

647

rubbed his palms furiously on his black uniform, and breathed deeply, trying to prevent his teetering system from collapsing completely. As his vision slowly cleared, he brought his hands up before his face. The worst of the blood was gone.

Unsteadily, he turned back towards the far end of the room, and began to slowly make his way towards the last trolley, the one wrapped in the sheet, the one with the shape lying on it.

His heart was pounding in his chest as he approached the operating station. The curtain surrounding it was white, suspended from a metal frame and reaching down to the slick, gore-streaked floor. On the trolley beside it, a monitor beeped steadily, a green line peaking rhythmically as it made its way across the screen. The silhouette beyond the curtain was still: a long, dark shape lying on top of the bed.

Jamie reached out a trembling hand, gripped the material of the curtain, took a deep breath, and pulled it open. He looked down at the bed, and felt the air freeze in his lungs.

Lying on the operating table, his skin the colour of ash, his body open and empty, was Ted Ellison.

The elderly man, who had held Kate's hand as they walked out of the Twilight Care Home, had been butchered. His torso was open to the cool air of the laboratory; it had been sliced from throat to groin and across the width of his ribcage. The four resulting flaps of skin and muscle had been folded back and clamped open. Where Ted's major organs should have been, there was little more than a crimson cavern; Jamie could see the white pillar of the old man's spine, and the slowly beating fist of his heart. Everything else had been removed.

Jamie felt pressure rising in his chest, and forced himself to breathe. His eyes were drawn to a long silver tray beside the table, on which the contents of Ted Ellison's torso had been carefully laid out. His liver, kidneys, lungs, pancreas, bowels, the long purple ropes of his intestines – all were lying on the tray, ghoulishly colourful against the metal.

A loud hiss made Jamie jump, and he turned towards the source of it. A bag of bright blue liquid hung on a drip stand beside the table, a pump attached above it. The compression of the pump was what had made the noise. He followed the tube down from the drip to where it disappeared into Ted's throat.

As he looked at the stricken face of the old man, who had had such horrendous torture inflicted upon him, he saw the eyes flicker behind their lids, then saw the man's mouth move as his fangs slid down from his gums. The compressor hissed again, pushing the bright blue liquid down the tube. It disappeared into Ted's neck and immediately the fangs withdrew, rising back out of sight.

I don't understand, thought Jamie, his eyes welling up with tears. *Why would anyone do this? Never mind why, how could anyone do this to someone?*

Then another thought struck him.

Oh God. I brought children here. I brought a man and his daughter, only a few days ago. What were their names? Patrick? And the girl, Maggie. Patrick and Maggie Connors.

A little girl, in this place.

He tried to push the thought from his mind, to let the instincts that had served him so well over the previous months take over, to focus on the task at hand; the Lazarus Project staff were all dead, what was being done down here was far, far worse than anyone could have imagined and Professor Talbot was nowhere to be seen.

Nor was Matt.

But if he was here – if Maggie Connors was here – Jamie was going to find them.

He pulled his MP5 from his belt, and set it against his shoulder.

The door at the end of the room was shut as he approached it, and seemed to exude menace. He didn't dare imagine what might be beyond it, imagine just how far this chamber of horrors might go, but he was certain of one thing. Whatever was through the door, he would be ready for it.

The white door swung open silently on its hinges, and Jamie stepped inside. Instantly, he felt the tension gripping his chest relax, ever so slightly; the third room of the Lazarus Project contained none of the stomach-churning horror of the second. It was long and narrow; the two walls were separated into rows of small rooms, the fronts of which were covered by thick plastic. A narrow slot stood in the middle of the clear wall, through which Jamie presumed blood was passed.

He stepped into the room, his MP5 at his shoulder, peered into the cell nearest to him and saw a familiar face staring wildly back. It was Patrick Connors; he was shouting something that Jamie couldn't hear, and was pointing frantically back towards one of the cells on the opposite side of the room.

Jamie followed the direction of his finger, and crossed the wide, cavernous room. The first cell on the other wall was unoccupied, but had clearly only become so recently; a vast spray of blood and meat was dripping thickly down the three white walls and the clear plastic front. A crumbling hole had been punched into the rear wall, a size and shape Jamie recognised well.

T-Bone shot, he thought. *Point blank through the food slot. No chance for whoever was in there.*

He moved on to the second cell and found the same thing, a recent eruption of blood filling the small cell. The third was the same, but the blood was still steaming in the chilly air of the laboratory; it had clearly been spilled only minutes earlier. Jamie felt

650

his head swim as he moved across towards the fourth cell; what had been done to the helpless, captive vampires that had clearly occupied these cells until extremely recently was exactly what Angela Darcy had warned him about in Paris.

It was not destruction, or self-defence. It was murder, pure and simple.

Jamie reached the fourth cell, and felt his heart lurch. Backed as far as was possible into the corner at the back of the cell was Maggie Connors, the little girl he had promised would be safe with the Lazarus Project, whom he had persuaded to go with Dr Yen willingly. Her eyes were wide and full of panic, and she was twisting against the wall, as if she hoped she might be able to burrow an escape hole in the flat white surface.

Oh, thank God, she's alive. But she would have been next, he thought, wildly. *If I hadn't come down here, it would have been—*

"Not another step, Mr Carpenter."

The voice was pleasant, and familiar, and it stopped Jamie dead in his tracks.

He turned slowly towards the source of the voice; standing calmly by the airlock door, with a gun pointing steadily at Matt Browning's head, was Professor Talbot.

"Shoot him, Jamie," cried Matt. "Shoot him before—"

Talbot's arm flashed out, and the barrel of the gun crashed into the back of Matt's head with a sickening crunch. The teenager folded to his knees, a bright jet of blood erupting from his head, then he slumped to the floor, his eyes rolling back in his head. Talbot swung his arm and levelled the pistol at Jamie's chest before he had the chance to take more than a single step towards the old man.

Jamie stared at him, incredulous, his MP5 trembling against his shoulder.

Professor Talbot was holding the gun steadily in one hand; in the other he was gripping a portable hard drive. He had a T-Bone slung over his shoulder, obviously the weapon he had been using to execute the captive vampires. His face wore a gentle smile, and a slightly sheepish expression, like that of a child who had been caught doing something he shouldn't.

"What are you doing?" asked Jamie, slowly. His voice was full of disbelief; he simply could not comprehend what he was seeing, could not believe this was happening again.

I can't trust anyone, he thought, and felt his heart throb with pain. *No one.*

"Tidying up," replied Professor Talbot, briskly. "I do hate to leave a mess behind me when I leave. Nothing worse than loose ends."

Jamie's eyes flicked down to Matt, who was lying motionless on the white laboratory floor. Blood was streaming out of his head, but his chest was steadily rising and falling.

"Who are you?" asked Jamie. "Really, I mean."

"Names aren't important, Jamie," said Talbot, smiling at the teenager. "Actions are what matter. I can see you're bursting to know what this is all about, and since I'm going to kill you before I leave, I don't mind telling you. Everything you've seen down here, everything I've shown you—"

The barrel of Jamie's MP5 twitched fractionally upwards, and he pulled the trigger. The report was deafening in the enclosed space, and a neat black hole appeared in the centre of Professor Talbot's forehead. A bright spray of red blood and oatmeal-coloured brain splashed against the airlock door. Talbot fell backwards, a look of complete surprise on his face. He hit the ground hard, the pistol spilling from his hand and sliding across the floor.

Jamie sighed, a deep exhalation of throbbing pain and razor-sharp betrayal, and walked across the lab. He stood over the Professor, and looked down at him; the old man's eyes were wide, staring lifelessly with a look of profound outrage.

"I don't care," said Jamie. "I don't want to hear your story. I just don't care."

He heard a muffled banging to his left, and slowly turned his head. Patrick Connors was leaping up and down in his cell, his eyes blazing red; he was beating the thick plastic wall of his cell, a look of unbridled joy on his face. Jamie nodded at him, softly, then walked over to where Matt was lying.

He crouched down beside his friend, and wiped the blood from his hair. The cut beneath was not as bad as Jamie had feared, despite the spray of blood that had burst from it; it was little more than a deep graze. He pulled the field medical kit from his belt, and plastered a thick wad of adhesive bandage over the cut. As he pressed the dressing down at the edges, Matt began to groan, softly.

"Hey," said Jamie, gently. "You OK?"

Matt's eyelids flickered, and then slowly opened. The eyes beneath them were dazed, and unfocused, then he blinked, as they cleared. He looked up at Jamie, smiled and then suddenly his eyes widened with panic, and he lurched upright. He groaned, and grabbed his head.

"Take it easy," said Jamie, slipping an arm round his friend. "Easy. Can you sit up?"

Matt screwed up his face with concentration, and pushed himself upright. The exertion clearly caused him pain, but he pursed his lips, and didn't cry out. He breathed out, deeply, then caught sight of Professor Talbot's body, and gasped.

"Is he…"

"He's dead," said Jamie. "I shot him."

Matt's face curdled into a savage grin. "Good," he spat. "He killed Dr Yen, Jamie, and all the others. He was going to kill me too."

"I know," said Jamie. "And me. But he's not going to be able to now."

Matt looked at the body, and then reached over and grabbed something out of the dead man's hand. He showed it to Jamie; it was the black portable hard drive.

"He wiped all the machines," said Matt. "After... when the others were dead. Destroyed all the data, everything they'd been working on."

"Why?" asked Jamie. "Do you know?"

"He said he was finished," replied Matt. "He copied everything on to this, and said he had to leave. He came in here to destroy all the vampires; he said it was the last thing left to do."

"You can understand what's on that drive," said Jamie, softly. "Can't you? You can find out what he was really doing down here."

"I don't know," said Matt. "I can try." He looked at his friend, and then his face crumpled, tears rising in the corners of his eyes. "Who was he, Jamie? I was so scared."

"It's all right," replied Jamie. "You did brilliantly."

Matt smiled, and tried to clamber to his feet.

"Easy," said Jamie, quickly. "Just stay where you are, OK?"

"OK," replied Matt. The trust on his friend's face sent a lump hurtling into Jamie's throat, and he turned away before he lost what was left of his composure.

He crossed the room to the first cell on the right-hand wall. Patrick Connors appeared to calm as he approached; he stopped leaping around the small room, and his eyes flared a deep, uncertain crimson as Jamie stopped before him. His face still blazed with euphoria, presumably at the death of Professor Talbot, but it was also lined with fear, and worry, and Jamie realised he couldn't allow himself to consider the reality of what the vampire had been through in his time down here in the basement of the Loop.

He searched for something to say, something that would have any meaning for the imprisoned man, that could even begin to apologise for having sentenced him to this nightmarish fate.

The teenage boy and the middle-aged vampire looked at each other for a long moment, separated by the few centimetres of unbreakable plastic standing between them. Then Jamie reached out and typed Admiral Seward's override code into the panel beside the door to the cell. There was a release of gears, and the plastic wall rose silently into the ceiling.

If he attacks me, I'm dead, thought Jamie, as the last of the wall disappeared.

For several seconds, Connors didn't move. Then he stepped forward and did the last thing that Jamie was expecting. He wrapped his arms round the teenager and pulled him into a chest-crushing hug.

"Thank you," whispered Connors, tears streaming from his eyes. "Thank you."

Jamie hung in the vampire's grip, his arms at his sides. He had no idea how to respond to this display of generosity, generosity that he felt utterly undeserving of.

"You're... welcome..." he managed.

Connors released his crushing embrace, and held Jamie by his shoulders at arm's length. Tears were cascading down the vampire's face, but there was the beginning of a smile there too, a hard, narrow smile that was more victory than it was happiness, a smile born out of nothing less than survival. Then suddenly Connors was moving. He let go of Jamie and ran across the wide white room, skidding to halt in front of the cell that contained Maggie.

Jamie watched as father and daughter pressed themselves against the opposite sides of the plastic wall, both crying, both whispering words of relief, their hands grasping futilely for each other.

He walked slowly across the room, and stopped beside the panel on the wall outside the cell. He entered the Director's code again, and both vampires cried out as the plastic wall between them abruptly began to rise. It had barely reached waist-height when Maggie ducked beneath it and hurled herself against her father; he bore her to his knees and wrapped her in his arms, her head pressed against his chest, his eyes closed and streaming with tears as he felt her breathe against him.

Jamie watched them, his own eyes welling up, then became aware that Matt had arrived beside him. He turned to his friend, who was standing unsteadily, his face pale, his attention locked firmly on the crying vampires.

"Jesus Christ, Jamie," he whispered, never taking his eyes off the Connors family. "What the hell was this place? What were they doing down here?"

"I don't know," replied Jamie. "Terrible things, by the look of it. Really, really terrible." He gave Matt as encouraging a look as he was able, then crouched down beside the vampires. "Mr Connors," he said, his voice threatening to break with every word. "I didn't know. When I sent you both down here, I didn't know what they were doing. You have to believe me. I'm so sorry, I didn't know. I'm sorry."

Patrick Connors turned his head, slowly, and looked at Jamie. His eyes had reverted to their usual pale blue, and he kept his daughter's head pressed firmly against him.

"I believe you," he said, softly. "I do. But that's not going to bring back the men and women who died down here, or undo the things that monster did to them." His eyes flicked to Talbot's corpse as he said the word 'monster', a ripple of fear spreading across his face as he did so, as if he was suddenly worried the Professor might not be dead. Jamie looked around, saw the pool of blood expanding beneath Talbot's head, and turned back.

"He's gone," he said. "He's dead. He's not going to hurt anyone else."

Patrick Connors nodded. He held Jamie's gaze for a moment, a moment in which the vampire didn't say any of the things he might have said, then turned back to his daughter.

Jamie pushed himself back to his feet, and felt a hand land gently on his shoulder. He turned to look at Matt, whose expression was full of worry.

"What about Kate and Larissa?" he asked. "Are they OK?"

"They're alive," replied Jamie. "Beyond that, I really don't know. But they're alive."

50

REDUCED TO ASH

Larissa Kinley, Valentin Rusmanov and Cal Holmwood reached the edge of the shuffling, wandering mass of survivors, and moved among them. Several of them nodded in their direction as they walked, one or two said hello, or offered half-hearted hugs and handshakes.

God, there are so few of them, thought Larissa. *How badly did Valeri hurt us?*

Then she saw Kate, clinging hopelessly to Angela Darcy, and she ran towards her friend. She swept Kate out of Angela's arms and held her tight.

"Oh God, you're all right," she whispered. "I'm so pleased to see you. Are you hurt?"

Kate didn't respond, and Larissa set her down and looked at her. Her blonde hair was matted and dirty, and her eyes were wide; Larissa took in the entirety of her friend's face and demeanour, and felt panic rumble in the pit of her stomach.

"What's wrong?" she asked. "Kate? What is it?"

Kate's mouth curled down at the edges, and her shoulders heaved.

"Is it Shaun?" asked Larissa. "Did something happen to Shaun?"

Kate looked at her friend, nodded and burst into a fresh bout of tears. Larissa wrapped her arms round her again, and looked over her shuddering shoulders towards Angela, who was watching the scene with obvious distress on her face. Larissa grimaced and caught Angela's attention; she raised her eyebrows in a silent enquiry, and felt her heart sink as Angela just slowly shook her head.

Please no. Oh, please no.

She felt a hand land on her back, and she craned her neck round to see who it belonged to. Jack Williams was standing behind her, looking at her with an expression of enormous relief.

"Thank God," he said, and wrapped his arms round the two girls. "Oh, thank God you're all right."

"You too," said Larissa. She hugged him back, tightly, although her attention was not really focused on Jamie's friend. Her eyes were fixed on Kate. "How's your brother, Jack? Is he OK?"

"Patrick's fine," said Jack, releasing his grip. A brief smile crossed his face. "He's helping down in the infirmary. He's OK."

"That's good," said Larissa. "That's really good."

"Have you seen Jamie?" asked Jack. "He was looking for you. Did he find you?"

"I saw him," nodded Larissa. "He's gone to look for Matt. I need to go and help him."

"OK," said Jack. "Do you want me to come with you?"

Larissa shook her head. "I've got it," she said. "But I need to go now."

She turned away from Jack and put her hand on her friend's shoulder.

"Kate," she said, softly. "Can you hear me?"

"I'm not deaf, Larissa," replied Kate, her voice torn and broken from crying. She took Larissa's hand and squeezed it, and Larissa smiled at her friend's resilience.

"I have to go and look for Jamie and Matt," she said. "Are you going to be all right if I go and do that?"

"I'll be all right," replied Kate, but Larissa felt her friend's grip tighten round her fingers. It was only for a moment, less than a second, but it had been there; Larissa had felt it. "Go," said Kate, letting go and stepping back. "Go and find them. I can't lose anyone else today."

Her face threatened to collapse again, and Larissa took a step towards her. Kate backed away, her hands up before her chest.

"Go," she said. "Really."

"I love you, Kate," said Larissa, suddenly. She had had no idea she was going to say it, but she was instantly glad that she had. Kate smiled at her, a smile so small and weak that it almost broke the vampire girl's heart. "I love you too," replied Kate. "I'll be here when you get back. When all three of you get back."

Larissa smiled at her friend, then turned and ran towards the hangar and the medical containers of blood that would restore her to her full strength.

Jamie let the door of the infirmary hiss shut, his face pale at what was inside.

He had walked Matt slowly up out of the bowels of the Loop, and into the wide, usually spotless white room that housed the medical department of Department 19. Jamie had pushed open the door and been assaulted by a cacophony of noise, and a vision of something that resembled the First World War hospitals he had seen in the old films he had watched with his dad when he was young.

Every bed, and every spare centimetre of floor was covered in bleeding Blacklight Operators. A flurry of doctors and nurses, their white coats long since soaked red, ran among them, dispensing pain relief, applying bandages and gauze, and in several horrible, desperate instances, administering CPR.

An Operator Jamie had once been on a mission to the Welsh valleys with, a man who was barely five years older than him, lay in the bed nearest the door, blood pumping out of his throat. A doctor was leaning over him, his hand inside the wound up to the wrist, and was futilely trying to pinch the arteries and veins closed with latex-covered fingers.

Jamie watched from just inside the door, Matt leaning against his shoulder, as the Operator's heartbeat, weakly flickering on the monitor that stood beside the bed, collapsed into a flat, endless line, and a screaming beep from the machines he was attached to. The doctor pulled his fingers out of the man's neck, and immediately began chest compression, alternating every five presses with a deep breath of oxygen into the stricken Operator's mouth.

But it did no good. After several agonising minutes, a nurse put her hand on the doctor's shoulder.

"He's gone," she said, softly.

The doctor stepped back and staggered, as though his legs would no longer hold him up. Then he set his jaw in a firm line, and moved on to the next wounded man who needed attention.

Jamie was horrified. He had seen men and women die in battle, had seen innocent victims murdered by vampires, but he had never seen anything as desperately sad as the last minutes of the young Operator's life, had never seen someone's body simply unable to cope with the damage that had been done to it, even as the finest doctors in the country fought to keep him alive.

"My God," whispered Matt. "Jamie, there's so many of them."

"I know," replied Jamie. "It's really bad."

Blood was running freely across the white floor of the infirmary, and the air, made hot and sweaty by the presence of so many men and women, was punctured every few seconds by screams and deep groans of pain.

In a bed to the right of the two boys, an Operator stared at the ceiling, grinding his teeth together with a noise like chalk on a blackboard as he tried not to scream. His left arm was gone, pulled clean out at the shoulder. A nurse was cleaning and sterilising the wound; when she slid a large hypodermic needle into the ragged centre of the hole, the Operator lost his battle, and screamed at the ceiling, a howl of pain and anguish.

Black uniforms filled the room; a group of Operators were standing in one corner, staring around at their stricken friends and colleagues with looks of open disbelief on their faces. They were clutching broken arms and wrists, holding wads of bandage over cuts and gouges; they were clearly the Operators who had escaped with minor injuries, and Jamie told Matt to go and stand with them.

"Aren't you staying with me?" asked Matt, panic in his voice.

"I have to go and help," Jamie replied, softly. "You understand that, right?"

Matt looked at his friend, then pushed out his chin, his jaw set in a firm, straight line.

"Of course I do," he said. "I'll be fine down here. Go and do what you can."

Jamie hauled his friend into a rough bear hug, then released him.

"Thank you," he said. "I'll come and check on you as soon as I can. I promise."

"I know you will," said Matt. "Just go, all right?"

Jamie nodded, and pushed open the infirmary door. He ran along the grey corridor, and rattled the CALL button beside the lift. It seemed to take an eternity to arrive, and Jamie had to stop himself hopping from one foot to the other with impatience. Then he heard the lift car slow to a halt, and watched the doors slide open in front of him.

Larissa was standing in the lift.

Her eyes were blazing red, and she had her Glock 17 in her hand; her shoulders were tensed, and she was floating a few centimetres off the ground. It was a look Jamie had seen before, on countless missions, but it had never made him as happy to see it as it did right now.

Larissa's eyes flared as she saw him. She opened her mouth to say something, but Jamie didn't give her the chance; he hurtled into the lift and wrapped his arms round her, and held on to her as though his life depended on it.

Sleep, when it eventually came to the Loop, and the survivors of Valeri's attack, did not come easily. Exhaustion, both physical and mental, finally drove the Operators who had either been uninjured, or had been discharged from the infirmary, to their quarters and into their beds, where nightmares awaited them.

The Loop was alive with rumours of the worst kind; no one knew how many Operators had died in the attack, how many were wounded, or turned. Everyone knew that Admiral Seward had been taken by Valeri Rusmanov, and everyone knew that Jamie and his team had brought Frankenstein home; this was news that on any other day would have been cause for celebration, but the Colonel's condition had merely added to the sense of fear and desperation that permeated the Department 19 base.

There was one question being asked more than any other, throughout the wide, shockingly quiet corridors of the Loop, a question that everyone who had survived agreed needed answering quickly, and well: who was going to lead them with Henry Seward gone?

Jamie and Larissa slept curled up against each other in Jamie's narrow bed. It was a violation of Blacklight protocol, and their own rules, but neither of them cared; they had been apart as the world had descended into chaos, each of them fearing they would never see the other again, and they had no intention of being parted again so soon.

Matt slept next door, his head swathed in bandages. He had waited patiently in the infirmary until the early hours, until the doctors had tended to the critically and seriously injured Operators, of which there were a frighteningly large number.

Kate lay awake in her bed, far from the sweet void of sleep, her mind racing with images of Shaun, a cruel slideshow she appeared powerless to stop. She had watched, feeling utterly useless, as Paul Turner had carried his son into the Loop, with Cal Holmwood at his side. She had wanted to offer to help, to offer to share the Security Officer's grief, but she had not been able to make herself do so; instead, she had merely watched.

Colonel Holmwood sat at the desk in his quarters, working. He had finished video calls with the Chief of the General Staff and the Prime Minister, bringing them up to date on what had happened, and answering their panicked questions as honestly as he was able. He had set a watch on the grounds of the Loop, had scrambled the sensor arrays and kept the entire Department at Ready One. Now he was trying to make sense of what had happened, of how things had fallen apart so completely.

Frankenstein slept heavily in a cell on Level H of the huge base; the heavy sedative that Jamie had injected into his throat had still not worn off, and he had shifted back to his human form without waking, sparing him the agony of transformation. He slept curled in the corner of the heavily locked and guarded room, his grey-green chest rising and falling slowly, his face twisted with the pain of bad dreams.

Out on the grounds of the base, two-man patrols walked slowly round the long perimeter, T-Bones at their shoulders. The men were exhausted, to the point of collapse, but they did not complain. Their thoughts were with their friends, their colleagues, lying injured in the infirmary or cold in the morgue, and they would not let them down by dropping their guard.

Eventually, with incredible, painstaking slowness, the watery yellow sun hauled itself into the sky to the east, and the Loop let out a collective sigh of relief.

The long, seemingly endless night was over.

Now would come the morning after.

86 DAYS TILL
ZERO HOUR

51

A COUNCIL OF WAR

Jamie woke to the sound of both his and Larissa's consoles beeping into life.

He groaned, and fumbled across the top of his bedside table, trying to locate it. Beside him, Larissa stirred, stretching her arms above her head.

"What time is it?" she asked, sleepily.

"I've no idea," replied Jamie. His fingers closed round his console, and he held it up in front of his half-open eyes.

ALL/COMPULSORY_LIVE_BRIEFING/OR/0900

As he read the message, Jamie felt for his watch, and held it up beside the console. The digital screen told him that it was 8:35am. He groaned, deeply.

"It's eight thirty-five," he said. "There's a briefing at nine. Compulsory."

"For who?" asked Larissa, sitting up and rubbing her eyes.

"Everyone," replied Jamie, and swung his legs out of bed. Larissa's hand fell on his shoulder; he paused, and turned to look at her. Her black hair was spread out across the thin pillow, and fell carelessly over one of her eyes. She looked, in Jamie's deeply biased opinion, as beautiful as she had ever done.

"Last night really happened," she said, softly. "Didn't it?"

He nodded, slowly. "It happened," he said. "The question is, what happens now?"

Twenty minutes later Jamie and Larissa stepped out of the lift on Level 0, and found themselves in the middle of a crowd of Operators. Men and women in black uniforms were milling about in the corridor outside the door to the Ops Room, their conversations exclusively concerned with what had befallen Department 19 the previous night.

Information still appeared to be scarce; Jamie heard a number of what he hoped were wild pieces of speculation as he and Larissa picked their way through the crowd towards the door. There were rumours that they had lost half of the Department's Operators in the attack, that a second vampire assault was going to take place as soon as the sun set, that there had been, or possibly still were, as many as twenty-five Operators loyal to Valeri Rusmanov, who had helped him decimate their ranks. He felt Larissa's hand flutter briefly across his lower back as they made their way through, a sure sign that she had heard the same things as him.

At the door to the Ops Room they found Jack and Patrick Williams leaning against the wall. The two brothers were pale, and wore expressions of tight concern on their faces, but both smiled as Jamie and Larissa approached.

"All right?" asked Patrick.

"All right," agreed Jamie. "Under the circumstances."

"Jack told me about what you did," said Patrick. "In Paris. Well done, mate. Bloody well done."

"We did it," said Jamie, looking squarely at Jack, who grinned.

"Have you told everyone?" asked Patrick.

Jamie shook his head. "I didn't know who to tell, to be honest with you," he said. There was a moment of tangible sadness, as the four Operators' minds turned to Admiral Seward. "I haven't even thought about writing a report. But I had the Security Division put him in one of the non-supernatural cells on H, so I'm pretty sure word's got around by now, though."

"How's he doing?" asked Jack.

"No idea," said Jamie, softly. "He was still transformed when they took him down, and still tranquillised. I'm going to go and check on him as soon as this is over, whatever it is."

"A werewolf," said Patrick, in a low voice. "That's unbelievable."

"I should have thought," said Jamie. "I saw him get bitten, the night he fell. I just didn't think about it, until it was too late."

"Hey," said Larissa, sharply. "It wasn't too late. You found him and you brought him home. Don't be so hard on yourself."

"She's right, Jamie," said Jack. "He's still alive, thanks to you. If we'd got there half an hour later, he wouldn't be. That's the thing to focus on."

Jamie nodded, then peered through the window in the Ops Room door. He could see Cal Holmwood beneath the wall screen with Admiral Seward's assistant; Marlow was typing furiously into a keypad, opening window after window on the huge screen.

"What's going on in there?" he asked "Why aren't they letting us—"

The words died in his throat as a second Operator walked across the Ops Room and stood next to Cal Holmwood. The face was even paler than usual, but the robotic stillness, and the piercing grey eyes were unmistakable.

It was Major Paul Turner.

"Jesus," said Jamie, his voice low. "What the hell is he doing in there?"

Larissa and the Williams brothers turned to see what he was looking at. He heard Larissa gasp, as they saw what he saw.

"The man's a machine," said Patrick, his voice little more than a whisper.

"His son's body is barely cold," said Larissa. "You'd think he might take a morning off."

"Why?" asked Jack, his voice solemn. "How would that help Shaun?"

The question hung in the air as the four of them watched Turner and Holmwood confer with each other, while Marlow waited for further instructions. Cal Holmwood suddenly turned towards the door, looking directly at them. They froze, caught, but Holmwood merely rolled his eyes and beckoned them into the Ops Room.

Jack pushed open the door, and they filed in, taking seats at the desks nearest the front. Behind them, the clamour of conversation dwindled as the throng of Operators followed suit. Holmwood and Turner stood beneath the huge screen, waiting for them to settle. Once every Operator was seated, Jamie noticing painfully as they did so that there were a large number of ominously empty seats left over, Marlow clicked a series of commands on his console, and ten windows opened on the giant screen, containing the pale, tightly drawn faces of the ten Directors of the world's supernatural protection Departments. White text sat at the bottom of each window, announcing the country that the person in the window represented: America, Russia, Germany, China, Japan, Canada, India, Egypt, South Africa and Brazil.

"Can you all hear me?" asked Cal Holmwood. The ten

Directors affirmed that they could, and he continued. "As Deputy Director of Department 19, it falls to me to lead this briefing. It is not a job I relish, nor one I have ever sought. I have been proud to serve one of the greatest men in the history of this organisation, who was taken from us last night. Admiral Henry Seward."

There was a murmur from the assembled Operators, and from the ten men on the screen.

"The situation is still unfolding," said Holmwood. "And details remain sketchy. But this is what we know so far. Last night, a vampire army led by Valeri Rusmanov attacked us; the specific purpose of the attack is not yet clear, although the capture of Director Seward can be assumed to have been at least one of its objectives. In the course of repelling the attack, sixty-eight Operators of this Department lost their lives, and a further fifty-three were injured. This, as you all know, accounts for more than half of the Blacklight roster."

There were audible gasps, both from the black figures inside the Ops Room and the foreign Directors on the wall screen.

Sixty-eight, thought Jamie, his mind swimming. *I never could have believed it would be so many.*

Larissa squeezed his hand, as Holmwood continued.

"The attack was successfully halted only by the deployment of a last-resort weapons system that was unknown to anyone in this Department beyond the Director himself. I am now given to understand that his fellow Directors were aware of its existence?"

"That's correct," said General Robert Allen, the Director of the American NS9. "It was a Director-only protocol. As you said, it was last resort only."

"Thank you," replied Holmwood. "We are still assessing the

damage that deploying the weapon may have caused, particularly as regards to the ongoing security of the Loop, and possible public relations risks. But it worked; for that much we are to be grateful."

He's furious, Jamie suddenly realised, as he looked at Cal Holmwood. *He's absolutely furious that only Admiral Seward knew about the weapon.*

"We have come to the conclusion that Valeri's attack was facilitated by the man we knew as Professor Richard Talbot, the former Director of Department 19's Lazarus Project."

Marlow punched a series of keys, and a photo of Talbot appeared on the screen, filling Jamie's stomach with revulsion. "I know him," said General Allen immediately, his voice low. "That's Christopher Reynolds. He worked for us, a long time ago."

"I'm sorry?" said Cal Holmwood. "He worked for you in what capacity?"

Allen looked uneasily into the camera. "He ran a special weapons division here in the desert," he said. "Then he disappeared."

"Disappeared?" asked Colonel Ovechkin, the Director of the Russian SPC. "How do you mean disappeared?"

"I mean disappeared," replied Allen. "Emptied his labs, destroyed all his work, murdered his entire staff and disappeared. We've been looking for him for ten years."

"And you never told us this?" asked Ovechkin.

"It was classified," said Allen. "At the highest level."

"That's a shame," said Cal Holmwood, tightly. "Because all twenty-three scientists of the Lazarus Project died last night, at this man's hand. All the information was gone, and his work destroyed; only the actions of one of our Operators stopped him escaping again."

"I've never seen the words Lazarus Project on any update," said

Allen. "You can't blame me for you not telling me what you were doing over there."

"You're right," said Holmwood. "Although I am not the Director, and the decision was not mine to make, this illustrates the central problem that has plagued our Departments since the beginning. We simply do not trust each other. Am I wrong?"

The ten foreign Directors stared at him, Ovechkin and Allen with faces like thunder.

"If we did," continued Holmwood, "then perhaps this man could have been prevented from killing twenty-three innocent men and women last night, or from helping Valeri Rusmanov to cause the deaths of sixty-eight more." His voice was rising, as he struggled to contain the rage that was building inside him. "So I'm going to ask you all a simple question, gentlemen. Are we on the same side, or aren't we?"

There was complete silence in the Ops Room, as the Blacklight Operators hung on Cal Holmwood's every word. On the screen, the ten Directors looked down from their offices, in every corner of the world, their expressions full of concern.

"I spoke this morning to my superiors in London," said Holmwood. "They have authorised me to declare war on Valeri Rusmanov, and on his master, Count Dracula. From this point forward, this Department's first priority is the recovery of Henry Seward from wherever Valeri Rusmanov has taken him. Its second is the destruction of both Valeri, and Dracula."

He turned back to the screen. "From you gentlemen, many of whom I have fought beside over the years, I will expect nothing less than your complete support and assistance as we work towards these goals. If you do not feel able, or willing, to provide us with that, then tell me now, and relations between us will be terminated.

There is no more room for secrecy, or political manoeuvring, or distrust; we face a common enemy, and we will stand together, or we will fall alone."

He fell silent, and stared up at the screen. The ten Directors looked at each other, their faces wide with shock. It had never occurred to any of them, as they received Holmwood's request for an emergency conference, that he would present them with such an ultimatum, and it had left them reeling.

Colonel Ovechkin was the first to regain his composure.

"I do not appreciate your tone," he said, slowly. "But I believe that you are right, that the time for rivalry has passed. You should consider the resources of the SPC at your disposal, Cal."

Thank you, Aleksandr, thought Holmwood, relief bursting through him. The stoical, hugely experienced Russian Colonel had been the man whose cooperation he wanted more than any of the others, even more so than General Allen's. *The rest will follow now, just you watch.*

He was right.

One by one, the other Directors offered their cooperation, and their support. Cal Holmwood thanked them all, in turn, and told them he would speak to them when he had an implementable strategy for the recovery of Admiral Seward. Then he instructed Marlow to sever the conference link, and turned back to face the men and women of Blacklight.

Somewhere to Jamie's left, an Operator began to applaud. It was a lone sound for several seconds, before it was joined by a second pair of hands, and then another, and another, until the room was full of deafening acclamation for Cal Holmwood.

"Thank you," he said, waving his hands in an attempt to quieten them. "Thank you." Eventually, the applause subsided, and he

676

regarded them solemnly. "The operating protocols of this Department state that I, as Deputy Director, assume the post of Interim Director in circumstances such as these," he said. "I assure you, I take no pleasure from this temporary promotion. The protocols also state that any member of the Department may challenge this, and suggest an alternative candidate. Anyone who wishes to do so, please speak now."

The silence in the Ops Room was deafening.

"I appreciate you placing your trust in me," said Holmwood, the tiniest suggestion of a smile flickering at the corners of his mouth. "I will not let you down." He stared out at the rows of black-clad figures, and felt his heart swell with pride at the sight of them.

"Operators," he continued, his voice firm. "We are facing the greatest challenge that humanity has ever faced, and as always, we must carry the burden so the public doesn't have to. If Dracula is allowed to rise, if he is allowed to regain his full strength, then life as we know it on this planet will cease to exist. There will be dark times ahead; I would not lie to you and tell you otherwise. But I am proud to fight alongside each and every one of you, and face what is to come.

"I have never been more proud to be a member of this Department than I am this morning, and I tell you this now: we will stand and face Valeri, and Dracula, and we will prevail. We will push back the darkness, as we always have, and we will emerge from the shadows triumphant, or we will die in the attempt. Each of you will have a part to play in what is to come; individual and squad briefings will begin this afternoon. Until then, you are all dismissed."

The Operators rose as one, and applauded their Interim Director.

Cal Holmwood stood where he was, a quiet, determined smile on his face, as the first of the black figures made their way through the door, and out into the Loop.

52

ONLY FORWARD

ONE HOUR LATER

Jamie, Larissa, Kate and Matt stood outside Interim Director Holmwood's quarters, waiting to be called inside.

They had gathered in Jamie's room after the briefing had ended, their excitement at Cal Holmwood's words tempered by Kate's grief over the death of Shaun Turner. She had sat on Jamie's bed, able to talk, and even laugh with the rest of them, but there was something unmistakably different about her, something altered from the girl she had been the previous day.

Jamie, Larissa and Matt all knew loss; they had left behind friends and loved ones as their lives had taken the twists and turns that had led them to where they found themselves, some of which had been voluntary, some of which had been thrust upon them, without warning.

But only Jamie was intimately acquainted with what Kate was going through; in the days after his father had been killed, he had found himself entirely at the mercy of his own unpredictable, unreliable emotions. One minute he had been his usual self, able to talk coherently to his equally devastated mother, the next he found himself in a fit of absolutely uncontrollable sobbing, which was far beyond his power to stop.

What was worse, though, was the way his own brain, conditioned by the social protocols of death, and grief, had responded to his emotions; when he was able to function, his brain had chastised him for being able to do so, accusing him of not having loved his father, because any son whose father died shouldn't be able to talk to their neighbour about the weather, or the Arsenal result. But when his emotions overcame him, when he cried, and sobbed, and wailed, sometimes for hours on end, his brain told him to stop being pathetic, that he was embarrassing his dad, who would never have wanted to see his son like this. It was an uncertain torment, and the only thing that fixed it was the passage of time.

Jamie looked at Kate, and knew there was nothing he could really say to her that would make any difference; all he, and Larissa, and Matt, could do was be there for her when she needed them, and wait for time to heal her wounds.

The four of them had discussed the implications of Cal Holmwood's speech; it had been less a briefing and more a call to arms, a declaration of war on Valeri and on Dracula, and the four young Operators were ready to lead the charge if asked, which they hoped they would be. Larissa and Kate had told Jamie and Matt about the attack on the Loop, Larissa steering the tale away from what had happened to Shaun; there was no need for Kate to actively relive that terrible moment, even though the vampire girl was sure it was playing incessantly inside her friend's head.

Larissa described the fight between Valeri and Valentin, trying to articulate the sheer power that had been on display, the ancient, unstoppable power; she had felt like an insect as she watched them, like a Greek hero standing beneath two warring gods. She explained how Valentin had tried to help her, had fed her his blood, noticing the colour rise in Jamie's cheeks as she did so. Then Jamie had told the other three what had happened in Paris.

He had considered leaving out certain parts of the story; he was extremely aware, in the cold light of day, that some of his behaviour had been at best reckless, at worst unacceptable. But in the end, he told them the whole story. When he was finished, he asked them if they wanted to come with him to check on Frankenstein, but before they got the chance to reply, their consoles burst into life, summoning them to Cal Holmwood's quarters.

"You can go in," said the Operator stationed outside the Interim Director's room.

Jamie nodded, and pushed the door open. The room beyond was far smaller than Admiral Seward's quarters; it was, in truth, barely bigger than his own. Cal Holmwood sat behind his desk, a vast mountain of files, boxes and reports teetering on its wooden surface. He looked up as they entered.

"Come in," he said, then leant back in his chair and looked at them as they arranged themselves in a line before his desk. "Kate," he said, softly. "I'm very sorry about Shaun Turner. I know the two of you were friends."

It was clear from the Interim Director's face that he knew they had been more than that, but also that he had no intention of embarrassing Kate by letting her know she had been breaking one of Blacklight's fundamental rules. Jamie felt a rush of gratitude towards the man behind the desk.

"Thank you, sir," replied Kate. Her face crumpled momentarily, but she held it together, and Holmwood nodded.

"Until yesterday," he continued, "there were almost two hundred

Operators on the roster of this Department. All of them highly skilled, experienced men and women, the very best of the very best. And yet, it always seems to be the three of you at the centre of everything. The *four* of you, in fact, given the events of last night. I wonder why that is?"

"Bad luck, sir?" suggested Jamie.

Holmwood grinned at him. "Perhaps, Mr Carpenter. Perhaps. For whatever reason, the four of you were intimately involved in everything that happened last night, both here, and in Paris. For that reason, I'm going to tell you certain things that I'm not telling the majority of your colleagues. I'm hoping I'm right to trust you?"

Jamie, Larissa and Kate exchanged a quick glance, a half-smile that contained a thousand unsaid words.

"Yes, sir," replied Jamie. "I think I speak for all of us, sir."

"Good," replied the Interim Director. "The first thing I should tell you is that as a result of my own observations, and a series of recommendations that have been made to me this morning, I am proposing all four of you for the Order of Gallantry, Second Class. In different ways, your behaviour and conduct last night was in keeping with the very highest standards of this Department, and did not go unnoticed. There will be a ceremony in due course, but I thought you should know now."

Jamie felt himself sway on his feet; he looked at his three friends, and felt a surge of love for the boy and the two girls standing beside him.

"Thank you, sir," said Larissa, proudly.

"Thank you, sir," said Kate, her eyes shining fiercely.

"Thank you, sir," said Jamie.

"But..." said Matt. "I didn't do anything, sir. Jamie almost got killed coming to find me. I don't deserve a medal."

"Mr Browning," said Holmwood, kindly. "The CCTV logs showed me what you said to Lieutenant Carpenter when he entered the Lazarus Project laboratory, when you had Professor Talbot's gun to your head. Not 'Help me' or 'Run', but 'Shoot him'. Your concern for your own safety was secondary to your desire to see an enemy of this Department apprehended. You should be very proud of yourself today, Mr Browning."

Matt blushed, and looked studiously at the ground.

"On that subject," continued the Interim Director, "we have begun analysis of the hard drive that was recovered from the late Professor Talbot. Mr Browning, I understand you will be joining the combined Intelligence and Science Division analysis team later on today, is that correct?"

"I think so, sir," said Matt. Excitement suddenly bloomed on his face, as he thought about the prospect of getting his hands on the data contained on the hard drive.

"Good," said Holmwood. "You are very probably the only currently serving member of this Department who is able to understand the recovered data. But the provisional analysis does support a preliminary conclusion – the motive behind Professor Talbot's work."

Jamie felt cold spill through him.

"He wasn't working on a cure," he said, softly, "was he?"

"He was," said Holmwood. "But not a cure for vampirism. A cure *for* vampires."

"What do you mean, sir?" asked Larissa, instantly.

"A cure to be used by vampires," explained the Interim Director. "A genetic fix for their weaknesses: vulnerability to sunlight, susceptibility to the hunger. Everything. He was trying to perfect the vampire condition, not cure it."

"But why didn't Dr Yen or anyone else stop him?" asked Matt.

"The research required was the same," said Holmwood. "The mapping of the vampire genome, the understanding of the viral patterns, the ability to interrupt and overwrite the vampire DNA – everything he would need to search for a cure. He just had no intention of using it for that purpose. There was no way the Lazarus staff could have known what he was planning."

"Those poor people," said Matt, softly, his voice choked with emotion. "They thought they were helping make the world better."

"They were," said Holmwood. "Their work will be invaluable as we take the project forward. Everything they did has brought us closer to a cure than we've ever been. Their deaths need not have been in vain; we have their work, thanks to you and Lieutenant Carpenter."

Jamie smiled and glanced at his friend; Matt returned his smile with one so full of emotion that Jamie had to look away, before the lump that had appeared in his chest was able to climb into his throat.

"We are not yet able to conclusively prove," said Holmwood, "that Professor Talbot provided the information that allowed Valeri to launch his surprise attack on the Loop. But we expect to have that proof soon, together with proof that he has been working for Valeri Rusmanov his entire life. We have documents coming in from NS9 and the SPC that should conclusively prove it."

"It's a shame we didn't have those documents already," said Kate, her voice low. "We might have been able to stop this before it happened."

"Miss Randall," said Holmwood, solemnly, "I could not agree with you more. There is a huge amount we need to learn from what has happened, as you heard me say this morning; not least of which is that the Departments of the world need to begin to trust one another in deeds, not just in words. If we had shared information freely, it's possible we could have prevented any of this from happening; that cannot ever be allowed to happen again."

"That's not going to bring Major Turner his son back, though, is it, sir?"

"No," replied Holmwood. "I'm afraid it is not."

There was a moment's silence, then the Interim Director continued.

"Mr Browning, we are also expecting, once a thorough forensic analysis of the Blacklight mainframe is complete, to be able to prove that Professor Talbot alerted Valeri or one of his subordinates when you made the emergency call that attracted our attention. It seems one of his responsibilities was alerting his master to anything that might have exposed vampires to public attention. This is useful information, as it suggests that Valeri has an interest in keeping the existence of his kind a secret, at least for now. A small mercy, I know."

Matt nodded his head. There was a tight expression on his pale face; for a brief moment, he had been back in the darkly lit park, watching the smiling vampires approach him, and the memory had turned his insides to water.

"Mr Carpenter," said Holmwood. "The whole of Department 19 owes you a debt of gratitude for the return of Colonel Frankenstein. I shall await your report with great interest."

"It wasn't just me," protested Jamie, immediately. "It was Jack, and Angela, and Claire and Dominique as well, sir. They were incredible."

"I'm sure they were," replied Holmwood. "Nonetheless, it was your mission, that you petitioned Admiral Seward for permission to run, and which you led. So take a little credit, son, especially when it's deserved."

The Interim Director smiled at Jamie, who felt heat rise in his cheeks.

"There is more to be said," continued Holmwood. "And there will be time to say it later. But what barely needs saying is that we were hurt last night, ladies and gentlemen, hurt badly. And before we can even think about engaging Valeri Rusmanov and his master, or trying to rescue Henry Seward, I need to get this Department back on its feet, starting immediately. So I have news for all four of you, both good and bad."

Jamie looked along the line of his friends; he had a sudden urge to take Larissa's hand, and tell her to take Matt's, and tell him to take Kate's, but he resisted.

"Mr Browning," said Cal Holmwood. "You are hereby placed in interim charge of the Lazarus Project." A gasp emerged from Matt's throat, and his face flushed a deep crimson. "You are to liaise with the Intelligence and Science Divisions to restaff and resupply the Project, and you are to get it up and running again as soon as possible. At that point, you will hand the Project over to a suitably experienced successor to Professor Talbot. Do you understand?"

"I can't do that," spluttered Matt. "I wouldn't know where to start."

"If I thought that was true," said Holmwood, "I would not have suggested you do it. You understand the science, and you are, as of this moment, a full member of this Department. You are the only choice; Lazarus is too important to be allowed to fail."

"You can do this," said Jamie, looking calmly at his friend, who was staring wildly around the room, looking anywhere but at Cal Holmwood's face. "You know you can."

"I *don't* know that," said Matt.

"Then you do your best," said Larissa. "For me, and for Jamie's mum, and for every other vampire who wishes they weren't. OK?"

Matt swallowed hard, and nodded.

"Good," said Holmwood. "There are copies of the recovered hard drive waiting in your quarters; I will expect your preliminary recommendations, staff numbers, equipment requirements, that sort of thing, first thing tomorrow. Clear?"

"Yes, sir," said Matt, his eyes widening.

"Miss Kinley, Miss Randall," said Holmwood. "You are hereby both promoted to Lieutenant, and your security clearances are upgraded to Noble, the same as my own, or Director Seward's. Mr Carpenter, the same clearance upgrade applies to you. Congratulations to you all."

There was silence for a long moment; the three Operators were quite literally speechless. Jamie's mind was racing with incomprehension, even as he felt a smile begin to creep involuntarily on to his face. He turned his head, incredibly slowly, and looked at Kate and Larissa. Kate's mouth had popped open into a perfect little circle, and Jamie had to fight back laughter when he saw it. Larissa was staring at the Interim Director, as though she didn't quite believe what she had heard him say.

Cal Holmwood looked at their faces, and laughed. "You can thank me later," he said. "And I'm afraid that constitutes the good news. The bad news is that I am disbanding Operational Squad G-17, and assigning each of you as squad leader to a new squad. You will no longer be working together in the field."

Larissa was the first to respond. "Why, sir?" she asked. "How can you recommend us for honours and punish us at the same time?"

"Miss Kinley, this is not punishment," replied Holmwood, gently.

"I have no wish to break up squads unnecessarily, especially one with as high an Operational success rating as yours. But after the events of last night, the three of you are now senior Operators in this Department, with significant Operational experience. We are going to need to recruit heavily in the coming months, and new Operators need experienced Operators to be their squad leaders; it's necessary for the continuation of the Department. I hope you can understand."

The room lapsed back into silence.

He's right, thought Jamie. *I know he's right. But that isn't going to make it any easier when I head out on a mission and Larissa and Kate aren't with me. No easier at all.*

He thought of all the places they had been together, all the things they had seen, and done, and he was suddenly overcome with an enormous sense of change, a feeling that things were never going to be the same as they had been. He looked at the two girls, in whose hands he had willingly placed his life, time and again, and wondered if they were feeling the same thing.

A small alarm buzzed once on Interim Director Holmwood's desk, and he reached over and turned it off.

"You will have questions," he said. "Many of them, I'm sure, in the coming days and weeks. When they occur to you, I'll be here. But for now, I'm afraid I must say dismissed."

Jamie looked at the Interim Director, his mind brimming with things he wanted to say, but held his tongue. Instead, he walked across the small room, and pulled open the door. He stepped out into the grey corridor, his friends following behind him.

The four Operators walked silently back to Jamie's quarters, aware even as they did so that something had changed between them; that their futures no longer lay on a single path.

They sat on the chair and on his bed, and they tried to discuss the implications of what Cal Holmwood had told them, but they got nowhere; it was all too big, too profound, and all four of them needed time to process what they had heard.

Kate was the first to leave, telling them she would see them at dinner; she had agreed to visit Major Turner in his quarters. This raised the eyebrows of both Jamie and Larissa, but they said nothing; instead, they let her go without a word.

Matt went next, saying that he had better get a start on the data from the recovered hard drive if he was going to be able to say anything coherent the following morning. He too promised to see them at dinner, but Jamie wasn't quite sure he believed his friend; again, though, he said nothing, and neither did Larissa, even after Matt shut the door and left them alone.

Jamie and Larissa lay on his bed in silence for a long time, their minds racing with thoughts they were not ready, or not willing, to express to each other. Eventually, Larissa's hand crept across the gap between them and curled gently round Jamie's own; he held it tightly, holding on to the one thing in his life that still felt the same.

After a period of time that neither Jamie nor Larissa could have accurately estimated, Jamie asked her if she wanted to come and see Frankenstein with him. She smiled, but told him she thought he should go on his own. Then she released his hand, and floated up into the air. She paused when she reached the door, and smiled at him, a wide, warm smile, full of love.

"I'll see you later," she said.

Then she was gone.

Jamie watched the space where she had been floating for a long moment, then hauled himself off his bed. He had no idea what to do about her, or Kate, or Matt; perhaps there was nothing to be done, or nothing that needed doing. He had felt the shift that occurred as Colonel Holmwood spoke, however, as though the world had suddenly tilted a degree or two on its axis. Not enough to cause disaster, but enough to shake foundations.

He walked slowly out of his quarters, and to the lift at the end of the corridor. Inside the car, he pressed the button marked G, and realised, quite suddenly, that he was about to see Frankenstein again, about to see the man he had believed was dead. A smile crept on to his face, widened into a big grin; when the lift doors slid open, Jamie took off down the corridor at a flat sprint.

The non-supernatural cells were located on Level H, but were only accessible via a secure lift from Level G. Jamie entered the Director override code into the panel beside the door that sealed the corridor that led to the lift, a corridor that was restricted under normal circumstances to Operators from the Security Division. The door slid open, and Jamie ran down the long curved corridor to the secure lift. He pressed the CALL button, stepped in between the opening doors and waited impatiently for it to take him down.

On Level H, Jamie signed in with the Duty Operator. Then he was past the small guard desk, and on to the block itself. It was a much smaller version of the supernatural containment block, just four cells on either side of a white corridor, with heavy metal doors instead of ultraviolet walls. Seven of the doors were standing open; the eighth, the last one on the right, was not. He stopped in front of it, and shouted to the Operator. The guard keyed a code into a pad on his desk, and the heavy door unlocked with a series of rumbling clicks and thuds, and the heavy tone of a buzzer. Jamie stood stock still, and watched it swing open.

Inside the cell, sitting on the floor opposite a narrow bed that could never have possibly held his huge, mangled frame, was Frankenstein's monster. He looked up as the door opened, his great grey-green head swivelling in Jamie's direction, where it stopped.

Jamie stared at his friend, unable to breathe. Then he took a tentative step into the room. Frankenstein lumbered to his feet, his head scraping the ceiling of the cell, and peered at Jamie with wonder on his face.

"I remember you," he said, softly. "I know your name. It's Jamie, isn't it?"

Jamie felt tears spill down his cheeks, and then he was running into the cell, and hurling himself against the monster's broad, uneven chest. He wrapped his arms round the monster's back, as far as he was able to reach, then felt Frankenstein slowly envelop him in his huge arms. He laid his head on the monster's chest, and closed his eyes, and they stayed like that for a long time.

"I forgot myself," said Frankenstein. He was sitting on the floor again, while Jamie perched on the narrow bed. "I couldn't remember anything. Who I was, where I'd been. Nothing."

"Do you remember what happened after Lindisfarne?" asked Jamie, gently. "After you fell?"

Frankenstein shook his head. "I remember falling," he said. "Then I remember waking up aboard a fishing boat. What happened in between is lost to me."

"We wondered why you hadn't contacted us," said Jamie. "It was the main reason no one believed you had survived. It makes sense now."

There was silence for a moment.

"You saved me," said Frankenstein. "Like your grandfather did. Saved me from my own past. From myself."

"We don't have to talk about this now," said Jamie. "You need to rest."

"How did you find me?" asked Frankenstein, his voice trembling. "How did you come to be there last night?"

"That's a long story," said Jamie, smiling at his friend.

Frankenstein looked round at his cell. "I don't think I'm going anywhere," he said.

Jamie smiled, and sat down on the floor beside the monster. "I almost don't know where to start," he said.

"At the beginning is traditional," replied Frankenstein, the corners of his mouth curling into the faintest of smiles.

FIRST EPILOGUE:
IN THE FLESH

Deep, empty darkness gave way to a midnight purple shot through with scarlet ribbons of pain. Henry Seward forced his eyes open, and stifled a scream.

He couldn't see anything. His field of vision was nothing more than a sheet of inky blackness.

The Director of Department 19 grabbed for his face, his hands clutching upwards from where they had been dangling at his sides, and he felt soft material covering his skin. The relief that flooded through him was so sweet it made him gasp, but was short-lived. Claustrophobia burst through Seward, and he clawed at the material. It came free easily, sliding up and clear, until light streamed into the Director's eyes, and he hauled in a deep, aching breath as he waited for them to adjust.

Not blind. Thank God. Oh, thank God.

Slowly, the bright motes of light before him began to shrink, and solidify. He breathed deeply, in and out, and watched a large, wood-panelled room take shape before his eyes.

He was sitting in a chair in the middle of the floor, a worn, comfortable armchair made of green leather. In front of him was a huge, imposing desk, its brown leather surface empty. Beyond it, the wall was wood, stained dark with ancient varnish. Pictures hung on it, oil paintings of ancient-looking battles and medieval encampments. To his right, a large window looked out over dark forest, and he realised he could faintly hear the rustling of the trees.

Henry Seward gripped the arms of the chair, intending to push himself up on to his feet, and felt pain flare from his right forearm. He looked down at the limb, and saw a neat square of white bandage halfway between his wrist and his elbow. He looked at it, nonplussed, then sank back into his seat as memory and realisation flooded into him.

He had fought and struggled against Valeri Rusmanov's grip, every second of the way, but the ancient vampire had not so much as flinched.

They had already reached the Lincolnshire coast when the silent explosion of purple light had filled the sky behind him. Seward, who had been marvelling, even through his panic, at the awesome speed of the old monster, let out an involuntary roar of triumph, a roar that was cut off as he was jerked through the air and lifted to face Valeri.

"What was that?" growled the vampire. "What did you do?"

Seward smiled, then spat in the oldest Rusmanov brother's face.

Valeri recoiled, raised his hand towards his face to wipe the saliva away, then thought better of it. Faster than Seward could follow, he reversed the course of the hand, and crunched it into the Director's stomach. A noise like a bursting balloon exploded from his mouth, and he felt his eyes bulge in their sockets as the weight of the impact shuddered through his body. He opened his mouth to gasp in fresh oxygen, but nothing happened; his body was spasming, jerking and flailing in Valeri's grip.

As he fought to stay calm, as he tried desperately to open his airways and pull in the cold night air, he felt a hot spike of pain in his forearm. He looked down, panic gathering at the edges of his mind, and saw Valeri had sliced his flesh open with one of his long, pointed fingernails. The old vampire dug his fingers into the wound, sending blood pouring out in thick, dark rivers and fresh agony pulsed through Seward's reeling system. The vampire's fingers stopped moving, then pulled sharply at something.

The Blacklight Director tried to scream as his locator chip was torn from the thick muscle of his forearm, dragging ragged strips of dark red matter with it. Valeri crushed it in his hand, let the pieces fall to the dark waters below, then regarded his captive.

"You are lucky," the vampire breathed. "If my master did not want you alive, I would make you watch while I flayed the skin from your bones. Now breathe, damn it."

Valeri's other hand sliced through the air and thumped Seward's back. The paralysis in his lungs and throat was broken, and with a great quavering shriek, he dragged air back into his lungs. He breathed out, in, then out again, before the damage to his system overwhelmed him, and he sank into unconsciousness.

Henry Seward let the terror that the memory induced fill him, then took a deep breath and pushed it aside. There was no time for him to be scared; he knew who had him, why he had been taken.

Then he froze.

There had been no sound, but something was suddenly obvious to Henry Seward. It was a change in pressure, the softest shift in the still air of the room.

There was somebody standing behind him.

Slowly, he pushed himself up to his feet, waiting for a blow to land from behind. When no such assault came, he gritted his teeth, and turned to face whoever was in the room with him, his face set with determination. But when he saw the figure standing less than a metre before him, it took every ounce of his resilience not to cry out.

Standing in front of him, a warm, welcoming smile on his thin mouth, his eyes shimmering the colour of infected blood, was Count Dracula.

Seward stumbled backwards, his mind reeling at the reality before him. The world's first vampire made no move to pursue him; he remained where he was, standing easily, his arms behind his back, his pale face alive with excitement.

The Director felt the small of his back thud against the edge of the desk, and realised he had nowhere to go. He stared at the original vampire, fighting for control of himself.

This is where it ends, he thought. *At the hands of this monster, far from home. Dear God, I didn't even tell Jamie his father was alive.*

Dracula stepped lightly round the chair in which Seward had awoken, and crossed the space between them. Seward braced himself for the worst, determined that he would not give this creature the satisfaction of breaking him, that he would die as well as his friend Yuri Petrov, the former General of the SPC, had done, with honour.

The reborn vampire stopped less than a metre away from the Director. Seward found his gaze drawn to the swirling insanity of the monster's eyes, and forced himself to look away.

"Admiral Henry Seward," said the vampire. "I am Vlad Dracula. It's a pleasure to make your acquaintance."

SECOND EPILOGUE:
THREE FATHERS

Thousands of miles apart, three men who had never met found themselves in three very similar prisons.

In the town of Staveley, Greg Browning strode down the hallway of his small house, stepped round his wife's trembling figure and marched up the stairs. He threw open the door to his son's room, which was exactly how he had left it, right down to the socks on the floor and the half-finished coffee on the desk.

Mould was sprouting above the rim of the mug, but Matt's mother had refused to move it. It was as if she believed that touching anything, tidying anything, in any way accepting that life was continuing to move forward, meant admitting that her son was not coming back. He had been returned to her once, and she still believed, in some deep, hopeful part of herself, that if everything stayed exactly as it was, then he would come home to her again.

When she heard the door open above her, she uttered a plaintive wail and ran up the stairs after her husband. She reached the open doorway, saw him digging through the chest of drawers next to Matt's bed and shrieked.

"What are you doing, Greg?"

He rounded on her, his eyes blazing.

"I'm doing what we should have done the minute we knew he was gone!" he bellowed. "I'm looking for what made him do it! There has to be something here, Lynne. He was God knows where for more than three months, then he's home for two and he disappears again? Are you bloody stupid? He didn't just go for no reason, Lynne. It has something to do with where he was all that time!"

Across the hallway, Matt's sister woke in her cot and began to cry.

"Don't, Greg!" begged Lynne. "Oh, please don't!"

"Go and see to the baby," Greg said, shoving the drawers closed and sitting down heavily at Matt's desk. He flicked his son's computer on and watched the monitor flare into life. He looked round and saw his wife standing in the doorway to the bedroom, staring at him with something that was close to hate.

"Go and see to the baby!" he roared.

Lynne recoiled, then fled across the landing. Greg double-clicked on the Internet Explorer icon as he heard his daughter's cries start to lessen, and opened the browser's history.

What the hell was going on with you? There had to be something.

The screen filled with a list of websites, and a sudden tightness gripped his chest.

Vampires Among Us. The Crimson Coven. Garlic and Crosses. LifeBlood. They Walk At Night. The Undead Resource. Vampires: The Last Free Spirits.

Without warning, images flashed into Greg's mind, images he had worked so hard to suppress.

The girl in the garden. Matt's neck, his poor neck. Blood.

Fear crawled over his skin, and he shook his head, hoping to clear it. The images receded, but they refused to leave entirely; they crowded at the back of his head, just out of reach, whispering darkly. Greg covered his face with his hands and leant back in his son's chair, away from the screen, away from the list of names and what they meant. He sat that way for a long time, trying to find the courage to face what had happened that night, to truly face it, not just pretend it no longer mattered once his son had come home.

Eventually, he lowered his hands, and lifted himself up from the chair. He left the computer on; he didn't want to touch it, or have to look at the screen again. He flicked the light off in Matt's room and was about to pull the door closed behind him, when a single beep sounded in the darkened bedroom.

Greg Browning turned back, and saw an instant message flashing in the corner of his son's monitor. He walked back to the desk, and opened it.

In his empty house on Lindisfarne, Pete Randall sat waiting for the phone to ring.

He had been waiting for it to ring for almost three months, since the police had made their way over from the mainland to tell him that although they were still officially listing his daughter as missing, he should start to come to terms with the fact that she wasn't coming back, and try to move on with his life.

"What life?" he had asked, before telling them to leave.

He was sitting in the tattered armchair by the living room window. On the window sill beside him, a mug of tea had gone cold, and developed a film. Mrs McGarry from three doors down had made it for him, when she had stopped by earlier to see how he was doing. She had started doing this most days, even though his answer, a broken, desultory 'Fine' was always the same, even though they invariably sat in silence for the duration of her visits. She came anyway, though, most days. Her husband had been lost on the night Lindisfarne had died, and she was coping with the hole that been opened up in her world by keeping relentlessly, almost manically busy.

Pete, on the other hand, was not coping.

Not in the slightest.

If they had found Kate's body, he would have killed himself; he knew it with absolute certainty. It would have been a simple decision, a logical equation based on what remained in his life that was worth living for. If Kate's body had been found, there would be nothing, and he would have gone gladly into the dark.

But her body had not been found, not by the armies of police divers who had dredged every millimetre of the island's small coastline, not by the dogs and forensic scientists who had combed through the woods and meadows, millimetre by painstaking millimetre. And that meant he had hope; not much, little more than a pitifully flickering ember, but enough. Enough to keep him breathing in and out, and enough to keep him staring at the phone, waiting for the call that would tell him she had been found, alive and well, and asking for him.

Today, he thought to himself. *Today will be the day she calls. Today she will come home.*

Far beneath the burning Nevada desert, Julian Carpenter lay on the bed in his cell on National Security Division 9's detention level.

In one hand he held a small rectangle of paper that had been hidden in his wallet behind one of his many driving licences, this one in the name of John Sullivan of Great Falls, Michigan.

The rectangle was a photograph.

It was creased and torn, battered by time. But the lines and small tears did nothing to diminish the power of the image, power that he sought to draw on yet again, power that had sustained him as he made his long journey through the dark heart of America.

Marie Carpenter sat easily on the stone wall at the bottom of the garden of their old house in Brenchley, Jamie standing beside her. Julian's wife looked as happy as he could remember seeing her; her face was lit by the bright sunlight that had been shining down when the photo was taken, but also by a wide, beaming smile that filled him with equal amounts of love and pain when he looked at it.

Jamie looked embarrassed, in the way of teenagers everywhere when they are forced to pose for a family photo, but his eyes were bright and clear, and his arm was draped casually round his mother. He was half-smiling at the camera, at his father behind it, his brown hair blowing in the summer breeze.

Julian Carpenter gripped the photo in his hand. Bob Allen had come down personally to give him Henry Seward's response to his request; he had told Julian he owed him that much at least. When Bob had explained to him that Seward was refusing to let him see his son, he had not screamed, or yelled, or attacked the NS9 Director. He had merely thanked him, and lain back down on his bed.

He had known there was a chance that Admiral Seward would say no, but he had not quite, in the deepest depths of his heart, been able to believe that Henry would stand between him and his family.

He knew that his reappearance would cause shock inside Blacklight, and he knew that they would have every reason to be suspicious of it, suspicious of him; he didn't begrudge Henry that, not in the slightest. But he had hoped that surrendering himself to

NS9 custody would have given his old friend some confidence that his motives were pure, that all he wanted was what he had asked for, the chance to make sure his only son was all right.

It's not Henry's fault, he thought. *There wasn't anything else he could do, you old fool. Jamie's an Operator now: no one is even supposed to know he exists, let alone just turn up out of the blue and ask to speak to him. Stupid. Now you're stuck in here, no use to Jamie, no use to Marie, no use to anyone. Just a stupid, useless old man in a cell under the ground.*

Tears began to flood down his cheeks, and patter softly on to the narrow mattress, but he made no effort to brush them away; his gaze remained fixed on the only two things in the world he still cared about.

Eventually, long hours later, he fell asleep, and dreamt of his family.

85 DAYS TILL
ZERO HOUR

ACKNOWLEDGEMENTS

My endless thanks and gratitude go, first and foremost, to my agent Charlie Campbell and my editor Nick Lake. *The Rising* is a long novel, and was a long process from first draft to finished book, and their support, creativity and endless patience helped get me through it.

My friend Katherine Wheatley saved my skin by introducing me to Dr Lewis Dartnell of University College London when I was fast approaching the point of scientific despair. Lewis is the reason that the genetic explanation for vampirism makes as much sense as it hopefully does; he answered my (extremely basic) questions about DNA and gene therapy with admirable patience, and very kindly managed not to laugh while doing so. Where the science is accurate it's thanks to him; where it isn't it's unsurprisingly down to me.

My friend Matt Powell and I spent five weeks driving seven thousand miles across the USA, in which time much of the climax of *The Rising* was researched and plotted. For the endless coffees and racks of ribs, for his truly expert map reading and patient willingness to discuss the finer points of how someone would attempt to sneak into Area 51, and above all for *Mysterons*, my love and thanks go to him.

My girlfriend Sarah coped admirably with the mood swings and bouts of manic hyperactivity that characterised the final months of the writing of *The Rising*, my petulant sulking whenever she refused to immediately put down what she was doing and read a new, slightly altered version of a chapter, and my turning our living room into an Armageddon of printouts, spider diagrams and post-it notes. Thanks for always being on my side.

Love and thanks, as always, go to my friends and family – Mum, Peter, Sue, Ken, Joe, Mick, Adam, Paul, Iso, Rich, Clemmie – and the fabulous teams at HarperCollins and Razorbill – Laura, Tom, Alison, Ben, Rebecca, Rosi, Lily, Tom, Sarah, Rachel, Tom, Kate, Geraldine, Mary, Tiffany, Sam, JP, James.

Lastly, my heartfelt thanks to everyone who read *Department 19*. As a debut author, my fingers were crossed that a few people might read the book, and hopefully like it – as a result I've been completely overwhelmed by the number of people who have taken the time to send me tweets, Facebook messages, letters, drawings and emails telling me they enjoyed *Department 19* and expressing their excitement about *The Rising*. I hope it lived up to your expectations.

Will Hill
London, January 2012